PAN

NEW TALES
OF THE VAMPIRES

THE VAMPIRE ARMAND

THE VAMPIRE CHRONICLES

Anne Rice

arrow books

Published in the United Kingdom in 2006 by
Arrow Books

10

Pandora first published in the United Kingdom in 1998 by
Chatto & Windus
The Vampire Armand first published in the United Kingdom in
1998 by Chatto & Windus

Arrow Books Limited
Random House UK Ltd
20 Vauxhall Bridge Road, London, SW1V 2SA

Random House Australia (Pty) Limited
20 Alfred Street, Milsons Point, Sydney,
New South Wales 2061, Australia

Random House New Zealand Limited
18 Poland Road, Glenfield, Auckland 10, New Zealand

Random House South Africa (Pty) Limited
Endulini, 5a Jubilee Road, Parktown, 2193, South Africa

Random House UK Limited Reg. No. 954009

A CIP catalogue record for this book is available
from the British Library

Papers used by Random House UK Limited are natural,
recyclable products made from wood grown in sustainable
forests. The manufacturing processes conform to the
environmental regulations of the country of origin

Typeset by SX Composing DTP, Rayleigh, Essex
Printed and bound in Great Britain by
Cox & Wyman Ltd, Reading, Berkshire.

ISBN 0091915414

PANDORA

NEW TALES
OF THE VAMPIRES

DEDICATED

TO

STAN, CHRISTOPHER AND MICHELE RICE

TO

SUZANNE SCOTT QUIROZ

AND

VICTORIA WILSON

TO THE MEMORY OF

JOHN PRESTON

TO

THE IRISH OF NEW ORLEANS

WHO, IN THE 1850S,

BUILT ON CONSTANCE STREET

THE GREAT CHURCH OF ST. ALPHONSUS,

WHILE PASSING ON TO US

THROUGH FAITH, ARCHITECTURE AND ART

A SPLENDID MONUMENT

TO

'THE GLORY THAT WAS GREECE

AND

THE GRANDEUR THAT WAS ROME'

Of Mrs. Moore and the echo
in the Marabar Caves:

. . . but the echo began in some indescribable way to undermine her hold on life. Coming at a moment when she chanced to be fatigued, it had managed to murmur 'Pathos, piety courage – they exist, but are identical, and so is filth. Everything exists, nothing has value.'

E. M. FORSTER
A Passage to India

Thou believest that there is one God; thou doest well: the devils also believe, and tremble.

The General Epistle of James
2:19

How ridiculous and what a stranger he is who is surprised at anything which happens in life.

MARCUS AURELIUS
Meditations

Another part of our same belief is that many creatures will be damned; for example the angels who fell from heaven through pride, and are now fiends; and those men on earth who die apart from the Faith of Holy Church, namely, the heathen; and those, too, who are christened but live unchristian lives, and so die out of love – all these shall be condemned to hell everlastingly as Holy Church teaches me to believe. This being so I thought it quite impossible that everything should turn out well, as our Lord was now showing me. But I had no answer to this revelation save this: 'What is impossible to you is not impossible to me. I shall honour my word in every respect, and I will make everything turn out for the best.' Thus was I taught by God's grace. . . .

JULIAN OF NORWICH
Revelations of Divine Love

Not twenty minutes has passed since you left me here in the café, since I said No to your request, that I would never write out for you the story of my mortal life, how I became a vampire – how I came upon Marius only years after he had lost his human life.

Now here I am with your notebook open, using one of the sharp pointed eternal ink pens you left me, delighted at the sensuous press of the black ink into the expensive and flawless white paper.

Naturally, David, you would leave me something elegant, an inviting page. This notebook bound in dark varnished leather, is it not, tooled with a design of rich roses, thornless, yet leafy, a design that means only Design in the final analysis but bespeaks an authority. What is written beneath this heavy and handsome book cover will count, sayeth this cover.

The thick pages are ruled in light blue – you are practical, so thoughtful, and you probably know I almost never put pen to paper to write anything at all.

Even the sound of the pen has its allure, the sharp scratch rather like the finest quills in ancient Rome when I would put them to parchment to write my letters to my Father, when I would write in a diary my own laments . . . ah, that sound. The only thing missing here is the smell of ink, but we have the fine plastic pen which will not run out for volumes, making as fine and deep a black mark as I choose to make.

I am thinking about your request in writing. You see you will get something from me. I find myself yielding to it, almost as one of our human victims yields to us, discovering perhaps as the rain continues to fall outside, as the café continues with its noisy chatter, to think that this might not be the agony I presumed – reaching back over the two thousand years – but almost a pleasure, like the act of drinking blood itself.

I reach now for a victim who is not easy for me to overcome: my own past. Perhaps this victim will flee from me with a speed that equals my own. Whatever, I seek now a victim that I have never faced. And there is the thrill of the hunt in it, what the modern world calls investigation.

Why else would I see those times so vividly now? You had no magic potion to give me to loosen my thoughts. There is but one potion for us and it is blood.

You said at one point as we walked towards the café, 'You will remember everything.'

You, who are so young amongst us yet were so old as a mortal, and such a scholar as a mortal. Perhaps it is natural that you so boldly attempt to collect our stories.

But why seek to explain here such curiosity as yours, such bravery in face of blood-drenched truth?

How could you have kindled in me this longing to go back, two thousand years, almost exactly – to tell of my mortal days on Earth in Rome, and how I joined Marius, and what little chance he had against Fate.

How could origins so deeply buried and so long denied suddenly beckon to me. A door snaps open. A light shines. Come in.

I sit back now in the café.

I write, but I pause and look around me at the people of this Paris café. I see the drab unisex fabrics of this age, the fresh American girl in her olive green military clothes, all of her

3

possessions slung over her shoulder in a back-pack; I see the old Frenchman who has come here for decades merely to look at the bare legs and arms of the young, to feed on the gestures as if he were a vampire, to wait for some exotic jewel of a moment when a woman sits back laughing, cigarette in hand, and the cloth of her synthetic blouse becomes tight over her breasts and there the nipples are visible.

Ah, old man. He is gray-haired and wears an expensive coat. He is no menace to anyone. He lives entirely in vision. Tonight he will go back to a modest but elegant apartment which he has maintained since the last Great World War, and he will watch films of the young beauty Brigitte Bardot. He lives in his eyes. He has not touched a woman in ten years.

I don't drift, David. I drop anchor here. For I will not have my story pour forth as from a drunken oracle.

I see these mortals in a more attentive light. They are so fresh, so exotic and yet so luscious to me, these mortals; they look like tropical birds must have looked when I was a child; so full of fluttering, rebellious life, I wanted to clutch them to have it, to make their wings flap in my hands, to capture flight and own it and partake of it. Ah, that terrible moment in childhood when one accidentally crushes the life from a bright-red bird.

Yet they are sinister in their darker vestments, some of these mortals: the inevitable cocaine dealer – and they are everywhere, our finest prey – who waits for his contact in the far corner, his long leather coat styled by a noted Italian designer, his hair shaved close on the side and left bushy on the top to make him look distinctive, which it does, though there is no need when one considers his huge black eyes, and the hardness of what nature intended to be a generous mouth. He makes those quick impatient gestures with his cigarette lighter on the small marble table, the mark of the addicted; he twists, he turns, he cannot be comfortable. He doesn't know that he will never be comfortable in life again. He wants to leave to snort the cocaine for which he burns and yet he must wait for the contact. His shoes are too shiny and his long thin hands will never grow old.

I think he will die tonight, this man. I feel a slow gathering desire to kill him myself. He has fed so much poison to so many. Tracking him, wrapping him in my arms, I would not even have to wreathe him with visions. I would let him know that death has come in the form of a woman too white to be human, too smoothed by the centuries to be anything but a statue come to life. But those for whom he waits plot to kill him. And why should I intervene?

What do I look like to these people? A woman with long wavy clean brown hair that covers me much like a nun's mantle, a face so white it appears cosmetically created, and eyes, abnormally brilliant, even from behind golden glasses.

Ah, we have a lot to be grateful for in the many styles of eyeglasses in this age – for if I were to take these off, I should have to keep my head bowed, not to startle people with the mere play of yellow and brown and gold in my eyes, that have grown ever more jewel-like over the centuries, so that I seem a blind woman set with topaz for her pupils, or rather carefully formed orbs of topaz, sapphire, even aquamarine.

Look, I have filled so many pages, and all I am saying is Yes, I will tell you how it began for me.

Yes, I will tell you the story of my mortal life in ancient Rome, how I came to love Marius and how we came to be together and then to part.

What a transformation in me, this resolution.

How powerful I feel as I hold this pen, and how eager to put us in sharp and clear perspective before I begin fulfilling your request.

This is Paris, in a time of peace. There is rain. High regal gray buildings with their double windows and iron balconies line this boulevard. Loud, tiny, dangerous automobiles race in the streets. Cafés, such as this, are overflowing with international tourists. Ancient churches are crowded here by tenements, palaces turned to museums, in whose rooms I linger for hours gazing at objects from Egypt or Sumer which are even older than me. Roman architecture is everywhere, absolute replicas of Temples of my time now serve as banks. The words of my native Latin suffuse the English language. Ovid, my beloved Ovid, the poet who predicted his poetry would outlast the Roman Empire, has been proved true.

Walk into any bookstore and you find him in neat, small paperbacks, designed to appeal to students.

Roman influence seeds itself, sprouting mighty oaks right through the modern forest of computers, digital disks, microviruses and space satellites.

It is easy here – as always – to find an embraceable evil, a despair worth tender fulfillment.

And with me there must always be some love

of the victim, some mercy, some self-delusion that the death I bring does not mar the great shroud of inevitability, woven of trees and earth and stars, and human events, which hovers forever around us ready to close on all that is created, all that we know.

Last night, when you found me, how did it seem to you? I was alone on the bridge over the Seine, walking in the last dangerous darkness before dawn.

You saw me before I knew you were there. My hood was down and I let my eyes in the dim light of the bridge have their little moment of glory. My victim stood at the railing, no more than a child, but bruised and robbed by a hundred men. She wanted to die in the water. I don't know if the Seine is deep enough for one to drown there. So near the Ile St.-Louis. So near Notre Dame. Perhaps it is, if one can resist a last struggle for life.

But I felt this victim's soul like ashes, as though her spirit had been cremated and only the body remained, a worn, disease-ridden shell. I put my arm around her, and when I saw the fear in her small black eyes, when I saw the question coming, I wreathed her with images. The soot that covered my skin was not enough to keep me from looking like the Virgin Mary,

8

and she sank into hymns and devotion, she even saw my veils in the colors she had known in churches of childhood, as she yielded to me, and I – knowing that I needn't drink, but thirsting for her, thirsting for the anguish she could give forth in her final moment, thirsting for the tasty red blood that would fill my mouth and make me feel human for one instant in my very monstrosity – I gave in to her visions, bent her neck, ran my fingers over her sore tender skin, and then it was, when I sank my teeth into her, when I drank from her – it was then that I knew you were there. You watched.

I knew it, and I felt it, and I saw the image of us in your eye, distractingly, as the pleasure nevertheless flushed through me, making me believe I was alive, somehow connected to fields of clover or trees with roots deeper in the earth than the branches they raise to the welkin above.

At first I hated you. You saw me as I feasted. You saw me as I gave in. You knew nothing of my months of starvation, restraint, wandering. You saw only the sudden release of my unclean desire to suck her very soul from her, to make her heart rise in the flesh inside her, to drag from her veins every precious particle of her that still wanted to survive.

And she did want to survive. Wrapped in

saints, and dreaming suddenly of the breasts that nursed her, her young body fought, pumping and pumping against me, she so soft, and my own form hard as a statue, my milkless nipples enshrined in marble, no comfort. Let her see her mother, dead, gone and now waiting. Let me glimpse through her dying eyes the light through which she sped towards this certain salvation.

Then I forgot about you. I would not be robbed. I slowed the drinking, I let her sigh, I let her lungs fill with the cold river air, her mother drawing closer and closer so that death now was as safe for her as the womb. I took every drop from her that she could give.

She hung dead against me, as one I'd rescued, one I would help from the bridge, some weakened, sickened, drunken girl. I slid my hand into her body, breaking the flesh so easily even with these delicate fingers, and I closed my fingers around her heart and brought it to my lips and sucked it, my head tucked down by her face, sucked the heart like fruit, until no blood was left in any fiber or chamber, and then slowly – perhaps for your benefit –I lifted her and let her fall down into the water she had so desired.

Now there would be no struggle as her lungs filled with the river. Now there would be no last desperate thrashing. I fed from the heart one last time, to take even the color of blood out of it, and then sent it after her – crushed grapes – poor child, child of a hundred men.

Then I faced you, let you know that I knew you watched from the quay. I think I tried to frighten you. In rage I let you know how weak you were, that all the blood given to you by Lestat would make you no match should I choose to dismember you, pitch a fatal heat into you and immolate you, or only punish you with penetrating scar – simply for having spied upon me.

Actually I have never done such a thing to a younger one. I feel sorry for them when they see us, the ancient ones, and quake in terror. But I should, by all the knowledge of myself I possess, have retreated so quickly that you could not follow me in the night.

Something in your demeanor charmed me, the manner in which you approached me on the bridge, your young Anglo-Indian brown-skinned body gifted by your true mortal age with such seductive grace. Your very posture seemed to ask of me, without humiliation:

'Pandora, may we speak?'

My mind wandered. Perhaps you knew it. I don't remember whether I shut you out of my thoughts, and I know that your telepathic abilities are not really very strong. My mind wandered suddenly, perhaps of itself, perhaps at your prodding. I thought of all the things I could tell you, which were so different from the tales of Lestat, and those of Marius through Lestat, and I wanted to warn you, warn you of the ancient vampires of the Far East who would kill you if you went into their territory, simply because you were there.

I wanted to make certain you understood what we all had to accept – the Fount of our immortal vampiric hunger did reside in two beings – Mekare and Maharet – so ancient they are now both horrible to look upon, more than beautiful. And if they destroy themselves we will all die with them.

I wanted to tell you of others who have never known us as a tribe or known our history, who survived the terrible fire brought down on her children by our Mother Akasha. I wanted to tell you that there were things walking the Earth that look like us but are not of our breed any more than they are human. And I wanted suddenly to take you under my wing.

It must have been your prodding. You stood there, the English gentleman, wearing your decorum more lightly and naturally than any man I'd ever seen. I marveled at your fine clothes, that you'd indulged yourself in a light black cloak of worsted wool, that you had even given yourself the luxury of a gleaming red silk scarf – so unlike you when you were newly made.

Understand, I was not aware the night that Lestat transformed you into a vampire. I didn't feel that moment.

All the preternatural world shimmered weeks earlier, however, with the knowledge that a mortal had jumped into the body of another mortal; we know these things, as if the stars tell us. One preternatural mind picks up the ripples of this sharp cut in the fabric of the ordinary, then another mind receives the image, and on and on it goes.

David Talbot, the name we all knew from the venerable order of psychic detectives, the Talamasca, had managed to move his entire soul and etheric body – into that of another man. That body itself was in the possession of a body thief whom you forced from it. And once anchored in the young body, you, with all your scruples and values, all your knowledge of seventy-four years, remained anchored in the young cells.

And so it was David the Reborn, David with

the high-gloss India beauty and raw well-nourished strength of British lineage, that Lestat had made into a vampire, bringing over both body and soul, compounding miracle with the Dark Trick, achieving once more a sin that should stun his contemporaries and his elders.

And this, this was done to you by your best friend!

Welcome to the darkness, David. Welcome to the domain of Shakespeare's 'inconstant moon.'

Bravely you came up the bridge towards me.

'Forgive me, Pandora,' you said so quietly. Flawless British upper-class accent, and the usual beguiling British rhythm that is so seductive it seems to say that 'we will all save the world.'

You kept a polite distance between us, as if I were a virgin girl of the last century and you didn't want to alarm me and my tender sensibilities. I smiled.

I indulged myself then. I took your full measure, this fledgling that Lestat – against Marius's injunction – had dared to make. I saw the components of you as a man: an immense human soul, fearless, yet half in love with despair, and a body which Lestat had almost injured himself to render powerful. He had

14

given you more blood than he could easily give in your transformation. He had tried to give you his courage, his cleverness, his cunning; he had tried to transport an armory for you through the blood.

He had done well. Your strength was complex and obvious. Our Queen Mother Akasha's blood was mixed with that of Lestat. Marius, my ancient lover, had given him blood as well. Lestat, ah, now what do they say, they say that he may even have drunk the blood of the Christ.

It was this first issue I took up with you, my curiosity overwhelming me, for to scan the world for knowledge is often to rake in such tragedy that I abhor it.

'Tell me the truth of it,' I said. 'This story *Memnoch the Devil*. Lestat claimed he went to Heaven and to Hell. He brought back a veil from St. Veronica. The face of Christ was on it! It converted thousands to Christianity, it cured alienation and succored bitterness. It drove other Children of Darkness to throw up their arms to the deadly morning light, as if the sun were in fact the fire of God.'

'Yes, it's all happened, as I described it,' you said, lowering your head with a polite but unexaggerated modesty. 'And you know a few ... of *us* perished in this fervor, whilst newspapers and scientists collected our ashes for examination.'

I marveled at your calm attitude. A Twentieth-Century sensibility A mind dominated by an incalculable wealth of information, and quick of tongue with an intellect devoted to swiftness, synthesis, probabilities, and all this against the backdrop of horrid experiences, wars, massacres, the worst perhaps the world has ever seen.

'It all happened,' you said. 'And I did meet with Mekare and Maharet, the ancient ones, and you needn't fear for me that I don't know how fragile is the root. It was kind of you to think so protectively of me.'

I was quietly charmed.

'What did you think of this Holy Veil yourself?' I asked.

'Our Lady of Fatima,' you said softly. 'The Shroud of Turin, a cripple rising from the Miraculous Waters of Lourdes! What a consolation it must be to accept such a thing so easily.'

'And you did not?'

You shook your head. 'And neither did Lestat, really. It was the mortal girl, Dora, snatching the Veil from him, who took it out into the world. But it was a most singular and meticulously made thing, I'll tell you that, more worthy of the word 'relic' perhaps than any other I've ever seen.'

You sounded dejected suddenly.

'Some immense intent went into its making,' you said.

'And the vampire Armand, the delicate boy-like Armand, he believed it?' I asked. 'Armand looked at it and saw the face of Christ,' I said, seeking your confirmation.

'Enough to die for it,' you said solemnly. 'Enough to open his arms to the morning sun.'

You looked away, and you closed your eyes. This was a simple unadorned plea to me not to make you speak of Armand and how he had gone into the morning fire.

I gave a sigh – surprised and gently fasci-nated to find you so articulate, skeptical, yet so sharply and frankly connected to the others.

You said in a shaken voice, 'Armand.' And still looking away from me. 'What a Requiem. And does he know now if Memnoch was real, if God Incarnate who tempted Lestat was in fact the Son of the God Almighty? Does anyone?'

I was taken with your earnestness, your pas-sion. You were not jaded or cynical. There was an immediacy to your feelings for these happen-ings, these creatures, these questions you posed.

'They locked up the Veil, you know,' you

17

said. 'It's in the Vatican. There were two weeks of frenzy on Fifth Avenue in St. Patrick's Cathedral in which people came to look into the eyes of The Lord, and then they had it, gone, taken to their vaults. I doubt there is a nation on the Earth with the power to gain even a glimpse of it now.'

'And Lestat,' I said. 'Where is he now?'

'Paralyzed, silent,' you said. 'Lestat lies on the floor of a chapel in New Orleans. He doesn't move. He says nothing. His Mother has come to him. You knew her, Gabrielle, he made a vampire of her.'

'Yes, I remember her.'

'Even she draws no response from him. Whatever he saw, in his journey to Heaven and Hell, he doesn't know the truth of it one way or the other – he tried to tell this to Dora! And eventually, after I'd written down the whole story for him, he passed within a few nights into this state.

'His eyes are fixed and his body pliant. They made a curious Pietà, he and Gabrielle, in this abandoned convent and its chapel. His mind is closed, or worse – it's empty'

I found I liked very much your manner of speaking. In fact, I was taken off guard.

'I left Lestat because he was beyond my help

18

and my reach,' you said. 'And I must know if
there are old ones who want to put an end to me;
I must make my pilgrimages and my progresses
to know the dangers of this world to which I've
been admitted.'

'You're so forthright. You have no cunning.'

'On the contrary. I conceal my keenest assets
from you.' You gave me a slow, polite smile.
'Your beauty rather confuses me. Are you used
to this?'

'Quite,' I said. 'And weary of it. Come
beyond it. Let me just warn, there are old ones,
ones no one knows or can explain. It's rumored
you've been with Maharet and Mekare, who are
now the Eldest and the Fount from which we all
spring. Obviously they've drawn back from us,
from all the world, into some secret place, and
have no taste for authority.'

'You're so very correct,' you said, 'and my
audience with them was beautiful but brief.
They don't want to rule over anyone, nor will
Maharet, as long as the history of the world and
her own physical descendants are in it – her
own thousands of human descendants from a
time so ancient there is no date for it – Maharet
will never destroy herself and her sister, thereby
destroying all of us.'

'Yes,' I said, 'in that she believes, the Great

19

Family, the generations she has traced for thousands of years. I saw her when we all gathered. She doesn't see us as evil – you, or me, or Lestat – she thinks that we're natural, rather like volcanoes or fires that rage through forests, or bolts of lightning that strike a man dead.'

'Precisely' you said. 'There is no Queen of the Damned now. I fear only one other immortal, and that's your lover, Marius. Because it was Marius who laid down the strict rule before he left the others that no more blood drinkers could be made. I'm base-born in the mind of Marius. That is, were he an Englishman, those would be his words.'

I shook my head. 'I can't believe he would harm you. Hasn't he come to Lestat? Did he not come to see the Veil with his own eyes?'

You said No to both questions.

'Heed this advice: whenever you sense his presence, talk to him. Talk to him as you have to me. Begin a conversation which he won't have the confidence to bring to a close.'

You smiled again. 'That's such a clever way of putting it,' you said.

'But I don't think you have to fear him. If he wanted you gone off the Earth, you'd be gone. What we have to fear is the same things humans fear – that there are others of our same species, of varying power and belief, and we are never entirely sure where they are or what they do. That's my advice to you.'

'You are so kind to take your time with me,' you said.

I could have wept. 'On the contrary. You don't know the silence and solitude in which I wander, and pray, you never know it, and here you've given me heat without death, you've given me nourishment without blood. I'm glad you've come.'

I saw you look up at the sky, the habit of the young ones.

'I know, we have to part now.'

You turned to me suddenly 'Meet me tomorrow night,' you said imploringly. 'Let this exchange continue! I'll come to you in the café where you sit every night musing. I'll find you. Let us talk to each other.'

'So you've seen me there.'

'Oh, often,' you said. 'Yes.' You looked away again. I saw it was to conceal feeling. Then your dark eyes turned back to me.

'Pandora, we have the world, don't we?' you whispered.

'I don't know, David. But I'll meet you tomorrow night. Why haven't you come to me there? Where it was warm and lighted?'

21

'It seemed a far more outrageous intrusion, to move in on you in the sanctified privacy of a crowded café. People go to such places to be alone, don't they? This seemed somehow more proper. And I did not mean to be the voyeur. Like many fledglings, I have to feed every night. It was an accident that we saw each other at that moment.'

'That is charming, David,' I said. 'It is a long time since anyone has charmed me. I'll meet you there . . . tomorrow night.'

And then a wickedness possessed me. I came towards you and embraced you, knowing that the hardness and coldness of my ancient body would strike the deepest chord of terror in you, newborn as you were, passing so easily for mortal.

But you didn't draw back. And when I kissed your cheek, you kissed mine.

I wonder now, as I sit here in the café, writing . . . trying to give you more with these words perhaps than you ask for . . . what I would have done had you not kissed me, had you shrunk back with the fear that is so common in the young.

David, you are indeed a puzzle.

You see that I have begun to chronicle not my life here, but what has passed these two nights between you and me.

Allow this, David. Allow that I speak of you and me, and then perhaps I can retrieve my lost life.

When you came into the café tonight, I thought nothing much about the notebooks. You had two. They were thick.

The leather of the notebooks smelled good and old, and when you set them down on the table, only then did I detect a glimmer from your disciplined and restrained mind that they had to do with me.

I had chosen this table in the crowded center of the room, as though I wanted to be in the middle of the whirlpool of mortal scent and activity. You seemed pleased, unafraid, utterly at home.

You wore another stunning suit of modern cut with a full cape of worsted wool, very tasteful, yet Old World, and with your golden skin and radiant eyes, you turned the head of every woman in the place and you turned the heads of some of the men.

You smiled. I must have seemed a snail to you beneath my cloak and hood, gold glasses covering well over half my face, and a trace of commercial lipstick on my lips, a soft purple pink that had made me think of bruises. It had seemed very enticing in the mirror at the store, and I liked that my mouth was something I didn't have to hide. My lips are now almost colorless. With this lipstick I could smile.

I wore these gloves of mine, black lace, with their sheared-off tips so that my fingers can feel, and I had sooted my nails so they would not sparkle like crystal in the café. And I reached out my hand to you and you kissed it.

There was your same boldness and decorum. And then the warmest smile from you, a smile in which I think your former physiology must have dominated because you looked far too wise for one so young and strong of build. I marveled at the perfect picture you had made of yourself.

'You don't know what a joy it is to me,' you said, 'that you've come, that you've let me join you here at this table.'

'You have made me want this,' I said, raising my hands, and seeing that your eyes were dazzled by my crystalline fingernails, in spite of the soot.

I reached towards you, expecting you to pull back, but you entrusted to my cold white fingers your warm dark hand.

'You find in me a living being?' I asked you.

'Oh, yes, most definitely, most radiantly and perfectly a living being.'

We ordered our coffee, as mortals expect us to do, deriving more pleasure from the heat and aroma than they could ever imagine, even stirring our little cups with our spoons. I had before me a red dessert. The dessert is still here of course. I ordered it simply because it was red – strawberries covered in syrup – with a strong sweet smell that bees would like.

I smiled at your blandishments. I liked them.

Playfully, I mocked them. I let my hood slip down and I shook out my hair so that its fullness and dark brown color could shimmer in the light.

Of course it's no signal to mortals, as is Marius's blond hair or that of Lestat. But I love my own hair, I love the veil of it when it is down over my shoulders, and I loved what I saw in your eyes.

'Somewhere deep inside me there is a woman,' I said.

To write it now – in this notebook as I sit here alone – it gives architecture to a trivial moment, and seems so dire a confession.

David, the more I write, the more the concept of narrative excites me, the more I believe in the weight of a coherence which is possible on the page though not in life.

But again, I didn't know I meant to pick up

this pen of yours at all. We were talking:

'Pandora, if anyone does not know you're a woman, then he is a fool,' you said.

'How angry Marius would be with me for being pleased by that,' I said. 'Oh, no. Rather he would seize it as a strong point in favor of his position. I left him, left him without a word, the last time we were together – that was before Lestat went on his little escapade of running around in a human body, and long before he encountered Memnoch the Devil – I left Marius, and suddenly I wish I could reach him! I wish I could talk with him as you and I are talking now.'

You looked so troubled for me, and with reason. On some level, you must have known that I had not evinced this much enthusiasm over anything in many a dreary year.

'Would you write your story for me, Pandora?' you asked suddenly.

I was totally surprised.

'Write it in these notebooks?' you pressed.

'Write about the time when you were alive, the time when you and Marius came together, write what you will of Marius. But it's your story that I most want.'

I was stunned.

'Why in the world would you want this of me?'

You didn't answer.

'David, surely you've not returned to that order of human beings, the Talamasca, they know too much –'

You put up your hand.

'No, and I will never; and if there was ever any doubt of it, I learnt it once and for all in the archives kept by Maharet.'

'She allowed you to see her archives, the books she's saved over the course of time?'

'Yes, it was remarkable, you know . . . a storehouse of tablets, scrolls, parchments – books and poems from cultures of which the world knows nothing, I think. Books lost from time. Of course she forbade me to reveal anything I found or speak in detail of our meeting. She said it was too rash tampering with things, and she confirmed your fear that I might go to the Talamasca – my old mortal psychic friends. I have not. I will not. But it is a very easy vow to keep.'

'Why so?'

'Pandora, when I saw all those old writings – I knew I was no longer human. I knew that the history lying there to be collected was no longer mine! I am not one of these!' Your eyes swept the room. 'Of course you must have heard this a thousand times from fledgling vampires! But

27

you see, I had a fervent faith that philosophy and reason would make a bridge for me by which I could go and come in both worlds. Well, there is no bridge. It's gone.'

Your sadness shimmered about you, flashing in your young eyes and in the softness of your new flesh.

'So you know that,' I said. I didn't plan the words. But out they came. 'You know.' I gave a soft bitter laugh.

'Indeed I do. I knew when I held documents from your time, so many from your time, Imperial Rome, and other crumbling bits of inscribed rock I couldn't even hope to place. I knew. I didn't care about them, Pandora! I care about what we are, what we are now.'

'How remarkable,' I said. 'You don't know how much I admire you, or how attractive is your disposition to me.'

'I am happy to hear this,' you said. Then you leaned forward towards me: 'I don't say we do not carry our human souls with us, our history; of course we do.

'I remember once a long time ago, Armand told me that he asked Lestat, 'How will I ever understand the human race?' Lestat said, 'Read or see all the plays of Shakespeare and you will know all you ever need to know about the human race.' Armand did it. He devoured the poems, he sat through the plays, he watched the brilliant new films with Laurence Fishburne and Kenneth Branagh and Leonardo DiCaprio. And when Armand and I last spoke together, this is what he said of his education:

"'Lestat was right. He gave me not books but a passage into understanding. This man Shakespeare writes," – and I quote both Armand and Shakespeare now as Armand spoke it, as I will to you – as if it came from my heart:

Tomorrow, and tomorrow, and tomorrow,
Creeps in this petty pace from day to day,
To the last syllable of recorded time;
And all our yesterdays have lighted fools
The way to dusty death. Out, out brief candle.
Life's but a walking shadow; a poor player,
That struts and frets his hour upon the stage,
And then is heard no more; it is a tale
Told by an idiot, full of sound and fury,
Signifying nothing.

"'This man writes this," said Armand to me, "and we all know that it is absolutely the truth and every revelation has sooner or later fallen before it, and yet we want to love the way he has said it, we want to hear it again! We want to remember it! We want to never forget a single word."'

We were both silent for a moment. You looked down, you rested your chin on your knuckles. I knew the whole weight of Armand's going into the sun was on you, and I had so loved your recitation of the words, and the words themselves.

Finally, I said, 'And this gives me pleasure. Think of it, pleasure. That you recite these words to me now.'

You smiled.

'I want to know now what we can learn,' you said. 'I want to know what we can see! So I come to you, a Child of the Millennia, a vampire who drank from the Queen Akasha herself, one who has survived two thousand years. And I ask you, Pandora, please will you write for me, write your story, write what you will.'

For a long moment I gave you no answer.

Then I said sharply that I could not. But something had stirred in me. I saw and heard arguments and tirades of centuries ago, I saw the poet's lifted light shine on eras I had known intimately out of love. Other eras I had never known, wandering, ignorant, a wraith.

Yes, there was a tale to be written. There was. But at the moment I could not admit it.

You were in misery, having thought of Armand, having remembered his walking into the morning sun. You mourned for Armand.

'Was there any bond between you?' you asked. 'Forgive me my boldness, but I mean was there any bond between you and Armand when you met, because Marius had given you both the Dark Gift? I know no jealousy exists, that I can feel. I wouldn't bring up the very name Armand if I detected a hurt in you, but all else is an absence, a silence. Was there no bond?'

'The bond is only grief. He went into the sun. And grief is absolutely the easiest and safest of bonds.'

You laughed under your breath.

'What can I do to make you consider my request? Have pity on me, Gracious Lady, entrust to me your song.'

I smiled indulgently, but it was impossible, I thought.

'It's far too dissonant, my dear,' I said. 'It's far too –'

I shut my eyes.

I had wanted to say that my song was far too painful to sing.

Suddenly your eyes moved upwards. Your expression changed. It was almost as if you

31

were deliberately trying to appear to enter a trance. Slowly you turned your head. You pointed, with your hand close to the table, then let your hand go lax.

'What is it, David?' I said. 'What are you seeing?'

'Spirits, Pandora, ghosts.'

You shuddered as if to clear your head.

'But that's unheard of,' I said. Yet I knew that he was telling the truth. 'The Dark Gift takes away that power. Even the ancient witches, Maharet and Mekare, told us this, that once Akasha's blood entered them, and they became vampires, they never heard or saw the spirits again. You've recently been with them. Did you tell them of this power?'

He nodded. Obviously some loyalty bound him not to say that they did not have it. But I knew they did not. I saw it in his mind, and I had known it myself when I had encountered the ancient twins, the twins who had struck down the Queen of the Damned.

'I can see spirits, Pandora,' you said with the most troubled expression. 'I can see them any-where if I try, and in some very specific places when they choose. Lestat saw the ghost of Roger, his victim in *Memnoch the Devil*.'

'But that was an exception, a surge of love in

the man's soul that somehow defied death, or delayed the soul's termination – something we can't understand.'

'I see spirits, but I haven't come to burden you with this or frighten you.'

'You must tell me more about this,' I said. 'What did you see right now?'

'A weak spirit. It couldn't harm anyone. It's one of those sad sad humans who does not know he's dead. They *are* an atmosphere around the planet. The "earthbound" is the name for them. But Pandora, I have more than that in myself to explore.'

You continued:

'Apparently each century yields a new kind of vampire, or let us say that our course of growth was not set in the beginning any more than the course of human beings. Some night perhaps I will tell you everything I see – these spirits who were never clear to me when I was mortal – I'll tell you about something Armand confided to me, about the colors he saw when he took life, how the soul left body in waves of radiating color!'

'I've never heard of such a thing!'

'I too see this,' you said.

I could see it hurt you almost too much to speak of Armand.

'But whatever possessed Armand to believe in the Veil?' I asked, suddenly amazed at my own passion. 'Why did he go into the sun? How could such a thing kill Lestat's reason and will? Veronica. Did they know the very name means *Vera Ikon,* that there was never any such person, that she could not be found by one drawn back to ancient Jerusalem on the day Christ carried his cross; she was a concoction of Priests. Didn't they know?'

I think I had taken the two notebooks in hand, for I looked down and I saw that I did indeed hold them. In fact, I clutched both of them to my breast and examined one of the pens.

'Reason,' I whispered. 'Oh, precious reason! And consciousness within a void.' I shook my head, smiling kindly at you. 'And vampires who speak now with spirits! Humans who can travel from body to body.'

I went on with a wholly unfamiliar energy.

'A lively fashionable modern cult of angels, devotion thriving everywhere. And people rising from operating tables to speak of life after death, a tunnel, an embracing love! Oh, you have been created perhaps in an auspicious time! I don't know what to make of it.'

You were obviously quite impressed by these words, or rather the way that my perspective had been drawn from me. So was I.

'I've only started,' you said, 'and will keep company alike with brilliant Children of the Millennia and street-corner fortune tellers who deal out the cards of the Tarot. I'm eager to gaze into crystal balls and darkened mirrors. I'll search now among those whom others dismiss as mad, or among *us* – among those like you, who have looked on something that they do not believe they should share! That's it, isn't it? But I ask you to share it. I'm finished with the ordinary human soul. I am finished with science and psychology, with microscopes and perhaps even with the telescopes aimed at the stars.'

I was quite enthralled. How strongly you meant it. I could feel my face so warm with feeling for you as I looked at you. I think my mouth was slack with wonder.

'I am a miracle unto myself,' you said. 'I am immortal, and I want to learn about us! You have a tale to tell, you are ancient, and deeply broken. I feel love for you and cherish that it is what it is and nothing more.'

'What a strange thing to say!'

'Love.' You shrugged your shoulders. You looked up and then back at me for emphasis. 'And it rained and it rained for millions of years, and the volcanoes boiled and the oceans

35

cooled, and then there was love?' You shrugged to make a mock of the absurdity.

I couldn't help but laugh at your little gest. Too perfect, I thought. But I was suddenly so torn.

'This is very unexpected,' I said. 'Because if I do have a story, a very small story –'

'Yes?'

'Well, my story – if I have one – is very much to the point. It's linked to the very points you've made.'

Suddenly something came over me. I laughed again softly.

'I understand you!' I said. 'Oh, not that you can see spirits, for that is a great subject unto itself.

'But I see now the source of your strength. You have lived an entire human life. Unlike Marius, unlike me, you weren't taken in your prime. You were taken near the moment of your natural death, and you will not settle for the adventures and faults of the earthbound! You are determined to forge ahead with the courage of one who has died of old age and then finds himself risen from the grave. You've kicked aside the funeral wreaths. You are ready for Mount Olympus, aren't you?'

'Or for Osiris in the depths of the darkness,'

you said. 'Or for the shades in Hades. Certainly I am ready for the spirits, for the vampires, for those who see the future and claim to know past lives, for you who have a stunning intellect encased beautifully, to endure for so many years, an intellect which has perhaps all but destroyed your heart.'

I gasped.

'Forgive me. That was not proper of me,' you said.

'No, explain your meaning.'

'You always take the hearts from the victims, isn't it so? You want the heart.'

'Perhaps. Don't expect wisdom from me as it might come from Marius, or the ancient twins.'

'You draw me to you,' you said.

'Why?'

'Because you do have a story inside you; it lies articulate and waiting to be written – behind your silence and your suffering.'

'You are too romantic, friend,' I said.

You waited patiently. I think you could feel the tumult in me, the shivering of my soul in the face of so much new emotion.

'It's such a small story,' I said. I saw images, memories, moments, the stuff that can incite souls to action and creation. I saw the very faintest possibility of faith.

I think you already knew the answer.

You knew what I would do when I did not.

You smiled discreetly, but you were eager and waiting.

I looked at you and thought of trying to write it, write it all out . . .

'You want me to leave now, don't you?' you said. You rose, collected your rain-spattered coat and bent over gracefully to kiss my hand.

My hands were clutching the notebooks.

'No,' I said, 'I can't do it.'

You made no immediate judgment.

'Come back in two nights,' I said. 'I promise you I will have your two notebooks for you, even if they are completely empty or only contain a better explanation of why I can't retrieve my lost life. I won't disappoint you. But expect nothing, except that I will come and I will put these books in your hands.'

'Two nights,' you said, 'and we meet here again.'

In silence I watched you leave the café.

And now you see it has begun, David.

And now you see, David, I have made our meeting the introduction to the story you asked me to tell.

2

PANDORA'S STORY

I was born in Rome, during the reign of
Augustus Caesar, in the year that you now
reckon to have been 15 B.C., or fifteen years
'before Christ.'

All the Roman history and Roman names I
give here are accurate; I have not falsified them
or made up stories or created false political
events. Everything bears upon my ultimate fate
and the fate of Marius. Nothing is included for
love of the past.

I have omitted my family name. I did this
because my family has a history, and I cannot
bring myself to connect their ancient reputa-
tions, deeds, epitaphs to this tale. Also Marius,
when he confided in Lestat, did not give the full
name of his Roman family. And I respect this
and that also is not revealed.

Augustus had been Emperor for over ten

years, and it was a marvelous time to be an educated woman in Rome, women had immense freedom, and I had a rich Senator for a father, five prosperous brothers, and grew up Motherless but cherished by teams of Greek tutors and nurses who gave me everything I wanted.

Now, if I really wanted to make this difficult for you, David, I'd write it in classical Latin. But I won't. And I must tell you that, unlike you, I came by my education in English haphazardly, and certainly I never learnt it from Shakespeare's plays.

Indeed I have passed through many stages of the English language in my wanderings and in my reading, but the great majority of my true acquaintance with it has been in this century and I am writing for you in colloquial English.

There's another reason for this, which I'm sure you'll understand if you've read the modern translation of Petronius's *Satyricon* or Juvenal's satires. Very modern English is a really true equivalent to the Latin of my time.

The formal letters of Imperial Rome won't tell you this. But the graffiti scratched on the walls of Pompeii will make it obvious. We had a sophisticated tongue, countless clever verbal shortcuts and common expressions.

I'm going to write, therefore, in the English

which feels equivalent and natural to me.

Let me say here quickly – while the action is at a halt – that I was never, as Marius said, a Greek Courtesan. I was living with such a pretense when Marius gave me the Dark Gift, and perhaps out of consideration for old mortal secrets he so described me. Or maybe it was contemptuous of him to style me this way. I don't know.

But Marius knew all about my Roman family, that it was a Senatorial family, as purely aristocratic and privileged as his own mortal family, and that my people dated back to the time of Romulus and Remus, the same as Marius's mortal line. Marius did not succumb to me because I had 'beautiful arms', as he indicated to Lestat. This trivialization was perhaps provocative.

I don't hold anything against either of them, Marius or Lestat. I don't know who got what wrong.

My feeling for my Father is so great to this very night, as I sit in the café, writing for you, David, that I am astonished at the power of writing – of putting words to paper and bringing back so vividly to myself my Father's loving face.

My Father was to meet a terrible end. He did

not deserve what happened to him. But some of our kinsmen survived and re-established our family in later times.

My Father was rich, one of the true millionaires of that age, and his capital was invested widely. He was a soldier more often than required of him, a Senator, a thoughtful and quiet man by disposition. And after the terrors of the Civil War, he was a great supporter of Caesar Augustus and very much in the Emperor's good graces.

Of course he dreamed that the Roman Republic would come back; we all did. But Augustus had brought unity and peace to the Empire.

I met Augustus many times in my youth, and it was always at some crowded social function and of no consequence. He looked like his portraits; a lean man with a long thin nose, short hair, average face; he was rather rational and pragmatic by nature and not invested with any abnormal cruelty. He had no personal vanity.

The poor man was really blessed that he couldn't see into the future – that he had no inkling of all the horrors and madness that would begin with Tiberius, his successor, and go on for so long under other members of his family.

Only in later times did I understand the full singularity and accomplishment of Augustus's long reign. Was it forty-four years of peace throughout the cities of the Empire?

Alas, to be born during this time was to be born during a time of creativity and prosperity, when Rome was *caput mundi,* or capital of the world. And when I look back on it, I realize what a powerful combination it was to have both tradition and vast sums of money; to have old values and new power.

Our family life was conservative, strict, even a little dusty. And yet we had every luxury. My Father grew more quiet and conservative over the years. He enjoyed his grandchildren, who were born while he was still vigorous and active.

Though he had fought principally in the Northern campaigns along the Rhine, he had been stationed in Syria for a while. He had studied in Athens. He had served so much and so well that he was being allowed an early retirement in the years during which I grew up, an early withdrawal from the social life that whirled around the Imperial Palace, though I did not realize this at the time.

My five brothers came before me. So there was no 'ritual Roman mourning' when I was born, as you hear tell of in Roman families when a girl comes into the world. Far from it.

Five times my Father had stood in the atrium – the main enclosed courtyard, or peristyle, of our house with its pillars and stairs and grand marble-work – five times he had stood there before the assembled family and held in his hands a newborn son, inspected it and then pronounced it perfect and fit to be reared as his own, as was his prerogative. Now, you know he had the power of life and death over his sons from that moment on.

If my Father hadn't wanted these boys for any reason, he would have 'exposed' them to die of starvation. It was against the law to steal such a child and make it a slave.

Having five boys already, my Father was expected by some to get rid of me immediately. Who needs a girl? But my Father never exposed or rejected any of my Mother's children.

And by the time I arrived, I'm told, he cried for joy

'Thank the gods! A little darling.' I heard the story ad nauseam from my brothers, who, every time I acted up – did something unseemly, frisky, and wild – said sneeringly, 'Thank the gods, a little darling!' It became a charming goad.

My Mother died when I was two, and all I recall of her are gentleness and sweetness. She'd lost as many children as she had birthed, and early death was typical enough. Her Epitaph was beautifully written by my Father, and her memory honored throughout my life. My Father never took another woman into the house. He slept with a few of the female slaves, but this was nothing unusual. My brothers did the same thing. This was common in a Roman household. My Father brought no new woman from another family to rule over me.

There is no grief in me for my Mother because I was simply too young for it, and if I cried when my Mother did not come back, I don't remember it.

What I remember is having the run of a big old rectangular palatial Roman house, with many rectangular rooms built onto the main rectangle, one off another, the whole nestled in a huge garden high on the Palatine Hill. It was a house of marble floors and richly painted walls, the garden meandering and surrounding every room of it.

I was the true jewel of my Father's eye, and I remember having a marvelous time watching my brothers practice outside with their short broadswords, or listening as their tutors instructed them, and then having fine teachers of my own who taught me how to read the entire *Aeneid* of Virgil before I was five years old.

I loved words. I love to sing them and speak them and even now, I must admit, I have fallen into the joy of writing them. I couldn't have told you that nights ago, David. You've brought back something to me and I must make the admission. And I must not write too fast in this mortal café, lest human beings notice!

Ah, so we continue.

My Father thought it was hysterical that I could recite verses from Virgil at so young an age and he liked nothing better than to show me off at banquets at which he entertained his conservative and somewhat old-fashioned Senatorial friends, and sometimes Caesar Augustus himself. Caesar Augustus was an agreeable man. I don't think my Father ever really wanted him at our house, however. But now and then, I suppose, the Emperor had to be wined and dined.

I'd rush in with my nurse, give a rousing recital and then be whisked away to where I could not see the proud Senators of Rome glutting themselves on peacock brains and *garum* – surely you know what *garum* is. It's the horrible sauce the Romans put on everything, rather like today's ketchup. Definitely it defeated the purpose of having eels and squids on your plate, or ostrich brains or unborn lamb or whatever other absurd delicacies were being brought by the platterful.

The point is, as you know, the Romans seemed to have a special place in their hearts for genuine gluttony, and the banquets inevitably became a disgrace. The guests would go off to the vomitorium of the house to heave up the first five courses of the meal so that they could then swallow the others. And I would lie upstairs, giggling in my bed, listening to all this laughter and vomiting.

Then the rape of the entire catering staff of slaves would follow, whether they were boys or girls or a mixture of both.

Family meals were an entirely different affair. Then we were old Romans. Everyone sat at the table; my Father was undisputed Master of his house, and would tolerate no criticism of Caesar Augustus, who, as you know, was Julius Caesar's nephew, and did not really rule as Emperor by law.

'When the time is right, he will step down,' said my Father. 'He knows he can't do it now. He is more weary and wise than ever he was ambitious. Who wants another Civil War?'

The times were actually too prosperous for men of stature to make a revolt.

Augustus kept the peace. He had profound respect for the Roman Senate. He rebuilt old Temples because he thought people needed the piety they had known under the Republic.

He gave free corn from Egypt to the poor. Nobody starved in Rome. He maintained a dizzying amount of old festivals, games and spectacles – enough to sicken one actually. But often as patriotic Romans we had to be there.

Of course there was great cruelty in the arena. There were cruel executions. There was the ever present cruelty of slavery.

But what is not understood by those today is that there coexisted with all this a sense of individual freedom on the part of even the poorest man.

The courts took time over their decisions. They consulted the past laws. They followed logic and code. People could speak their minds fairly openly.

I note this because it is key to this story: that Marius and I both were born in a time when Roman law was, as Marius would say, based on reason, as opposed to divine revelation.

We are totally unlike those blood drinkers

brought to Darkness in lands of Magic and Mystery.

Not only did we trust Augustus when we were alive, we also believed in the tangible power of the Roman Senate. We believed in public virtue and character; we held to a way of life which did not involve rituals, prayers, magic, except superficially. Virtue was embedded in character. That was the inheritance of the Roman Republic, which Marius and I shared.

Of course, our house was overcrowded with slaves. There were brilliant Greeks and grunting laborers and a fleet of women to rush about polishing busts and vases, and the city itself was choked with manumitted slaves – freedmen – some of whom were very rich.

They were all our people, our slaves.

My Father and I sat up all night when my old Greek teacher was dying. We held his hands until the body was cold. Nobody was flogged on our estate in Rome unless my Father himself gave the order. Our country slaves loafed under the fruit trees. Our stewards were rich, and showed off their wealth in their clothes.

I remember a time when there were so many old Greek slaves in the garden that I could sit day after day and listen to them argue. They had nothing else to do. I learned much from this.

I grew up more than happy. If you think I exaggerate the extent of my education, consult the letters of Pliny or other actual memoirs and correspondence of the times. Highborn young girls were well educated; modern Roman women went about unhampered for the most part by male interference. We partook of life as did men.

For example, I was scarcely eight years old when I was first taken to the arena with several of my brothers' wives, to have the dubious pleasure of seeing exotic creatures, such as giraffes, tear madly around before being shot to death with arrows, this display then followed by a small group of gladiators who would hack other gladiators to death, and then after that came the flock of criminals to be fed to the hungry lions.

David, I can hear the sound of those lions as if it were now. There's nothing between me and the moment that I sat in the wooden benches, perhaps two rows up – the premium seats – and I watched these beasts devour living beings, as I was supposed to do, with a pleasure meant to demonstrate a strength of heart, a fearlessness in the face of death, rather than simple and utter monstrousness.

The audience screamed and laughed as men and women ran from the beasts. Some victims would give the crowd no such satisfaction.

They merely stood there as the hungry lion attacked; those who were being devoured alive almost invariably lay in a stupor as though their souls had already taken flight, though the lion had not reached the throat.

I remember the smell of it. But more than anything, I remember the noise of the crowd.

I passed the test of character, I could look at all of it. I could watch the champion gladiator finally meet his end, lying there bloody in the sand, as the sword went through his chest.

But I can certainly remember my Father declaring under his breath that the whole affair was disgusting. In fact, everybody I knew thought it was all disgusting. My Father believed, as did others, that the common man needed all this blood. We, the highborn, had to preside over it for the common man. It had a religious quality to it, all this spectacular viciousness.

The making of these appalling spectacles was considered something of a social responsibility.

Also Roman life was a life of being outdoors, involved in things, attending ceremonies and spectacles, being seen, taking an interest, coming together with others.

You came together with all the other highborn and lowborn of the city and you joined in

51

one mass to witness a triumphant procession, a great offering at the altar of Augustus, an ancient ceremony, a game, a chariot race.

Now in the Twentieth Century, when I watch the endless intrigue and slaughter in motion pictures and on television throughout our Western world, I wonder if people do not need it, do not need to see murder, slaughter, death in all forms. Television at times seems an unbroken series of gladiatorial fights or massacres. And look at the traffic now in video recordings of actual war.

Records of war have become art and entertainment.

The narrator speaks softly as the camera passes over the heap of bodies, or the skeletal children sobbing with their starving mothers. But it is gripping. One can wallow, shaking one's head, in all this death. Nights of television are devoted to old footage of men dying with guns in their hands.

I think we look because we are afraid. But in Rome, you had to look so that you would be hard, and that applied to women as well as men.

But the overall point is – I was not closeted away as a Greek woman might have been in some old Hellenistic household. I did not suffer under the earlier customs of the Roman Republic.

I vividly remember the absolute beauty of that time, and my Father's heartfelt avowal that Augustus was a god, and that Rome had never been more pleasing to her deities.

Now I want to give you one very important recollection. Let me set the scene. First, let's take up the question of Virgil, and the poem he wrote, the *Aeneid,* greatly amplifying and glorifying the adventures of the hero Aeneas, a Trojan fleeing the horrors of defeat by the Greeks who came out of the famous Trojan horse to massacre Helen's city of Troy.

It's a charming story. I always loved it. Aeneas leaves dying Troy, valiantly journeys all the way to beautiful Italy and there founds our nation.

But the point is that Augustus loved and supported Virgil all of Virgil's life, and Virgil was a respected poet, a poet fine and decent to quote, an approved and patriotic poet. It was perfectly fine to like Virgil.

Virgil died before I was born. But by ten I'd read everything he'd written, and had read Horace as well, and Lucretius, much of Cicero, and all the Greek manuscripts we possessed, and there were plenty.

My Father didn't erect his library for show. It was a place where members of the family spent hours. It was also where he sat to write his letters – which he seemed endlessly to be doing – letters on behalf of the Senate, the Emperor, the courts, his friends, etc.

Back to Virgil. I had also read another Roman poet, who was alive still, and deeply and dangerously out of favor with Augustus, the god. This was the poet Ovid, the author of the *Metamorphoses,* and dozens of other earthy, hilarious and bawdy works.

Now, when I was too young to remember, Augustus turned on Ovid, whom Augustus had also loved, and Augustus banished Ovid to some horrible place on the Black Sea. Maybe it wasn't so horrible. But it was the sort of place cultured city Romans expect to be horrible – very far away from the capital and full of barbarians.

Ovid lived there a long time, and his books were banned all over Rome. You couldn't find them in the bookshops or the public libraries. Or at the book stands all over the marketplace.

You know this was a hot time for popular reading; books were everywhere – both in scroll form and in codex, that is, with bound pages – and many booksellers had teams of Greek slaves spending all day copying books for public consumption.

To continue, Ovid had fallen out of favor with Augustus, and he had been banned, but men like my Father were not about to burn their copies of the *Metamorphoses,* or any other of Ovid's work, and the only reason they didn't plead for Ovid's pardon was fear.

The whole scandal had something to do with Augustus's daughter, Julia, who was a notorious slut by anyone's standards. How Ovid became involved in Julia's love affairs I don't know. Perhaps his sensuous early poetry, the *Amores,* was considered to be a bad influence. There was also a lot of 'reform' in the air during the reign of Augustus, a lot of talk of old values.

I don't think anyone knows what really happened between Caesar Augustus and Ovid, but Ovid was banished for the rest of his life from Imperial Rome.

But I had read the *Amores* and the *Metamorphoses* in well-worn copies by the time of this incident which I want to recount. And many of my Father's friends were always worried about Ovid.

Now to the specific recollection. I was ten years old, I came in from playing, covered with dust from head to foot, my hair loose, my dress torn, and breezed into my Father's large receiving room – and I plopped down at the foot of his couch to listen to what was being said, as he lounged there with all appropriate Roman dignity, chatting with several other lounging men who had come to visit.

I knew all of the men but one, and this one was fair-haired and blue-eyed, and very tall, and he turned, during the conversation – which was all whispers and nods – and winked at me.

This was Marius, with skin slightly tanned from his travels and a flashing beauty in his eyes. He had three names like everyone else. But again, I will not disclose the name of his family. But I knew it. I knew he was sort of the 'bad boy' in an intellectual way, the 'poet' and the 'loafer.' What nobody had told me was that he was beautiful.

Now, on this day, this was Marius when he was alive, about fifteen years before he was to be made a vampire. I can calculate that he was only twenty-five. But I'm not certain.

To continue, the men paid no attention to me, and it became plain to my ever curious little mind that they were giving my Father news of Ovid, that the tall blond one with the remarkable blue eyes, the one called Marius, had just returned from the Baltic Coast, and he had given my Father several presents, which were in fact good copies of Ovid's work, both past and current.

The men assured my Father that it was still far too dangerous to go crying to Caesar Augustus over Ovid, and my Father accepted this. But if I'm not mistaken, he entrusted some money for Ovid to Marius, the blond one.

When the gentlemen were all leaving, I saw Marius in the atrium, got a measure of his full height, which was quite unusual for a Roman, and let out a girlish gasp and then a streak of laughter. He winked at me again.

Marius had his hair short then, clipped military-Roman-style with a few modest curls on his forehead; his hair was long when he was later made a vampire, and he wears it long now, but then it was the typical boring Roman military cut. But it was blond and full of sunlight in the atrium, and he seemed the brightest and most impressive man I'd ever laid eyes upon. He was full of kindness when he looked at me.

'Why are you so tall?' I asked him. My Father thought this was amusing, of course, and he did not care what anyone else thought of his dusty little daughter, hanging onto his arms and speaking to his honored company.

'My precious one,' Marius said, 'I'm tall because I'm a barbarian!' He laughed and was flirtatious when he laughed, with a deference to me as a little lady, which was rather rare.

Suddenly he made his hands into claws and ran at me like a bear.

I loved him instantly!

'No, truly!' I said. 'You can't be a barbarian. I know your Father and all your sisters; they live just down the hill. The family is always talking about you at the table, saying only nice things, of course.'

'Of that I'm sure,' he said, breaking into laughter.

I knew my Father was getting anxious.

What I didn't know was that a ten-year-old girl could be betrothed.

Marius drew himself up and said in his gentle very fine voice, trained for public rhetoric as well as words of love, 'I am descended through my mother from the Keltoi, little beauty, little muse. I come from the tall blond people of the North, the people of Gaul. My mother was a princess there, or so I am told. Do you know who they are?'

I said of course I knew and began to recite verbatim from Julius Caesar's account of conquering Gaul, or the land of the Keltoi: 'All

Gaul is made up of three parts . . .'

Marius was quite genuinely impressed. So was everybody. So I went on and on, 'The Keltoi are separated from the Aquitani by the river Garonne, and the tribe of the Belgae by the rivers Marne and Seine –'

My Father, being slightly embarrassed by this time, with his daughter glorying in attention, spoke up to gently assure everyone that I was his precious joy, and I was let to run wild, and please make nothing of it.

And I said, being bold, and a born trouble-maker, 'Give my love to the great Ovid! Because I too wish he would come home to Rome.'

I then rattled off several steamy lines of the *Amores*:

> *She laughed and gave her best, whole hearted*
>   *kisses,*
> *They'd shake the three pronged bolt from*
>   *Jove's hand.*
> *Torture to think that fellow got such good*
>   *ones!*
> *I wish they hadn't been of the same brand!*

All laughed, except my Father, and Marius went wild with delight, clapping his hands. That was all the encouragement I needed to rush at him now like a bear, as he had rushed at me, and to continue singing out Ovid's hot words:

What's more these kisses were better than I'd
taught her,
She seemed possessed of knowledge that was
new.
They pleased too well – bad sign! Her tongue
was in them,
And my tongue was kissing too.

My Father grabbed me by the small of my upper arm, and said, 'That's it, Lydia, wrap it up!'

And the men laughed all the harder, commiserating with him, and embracing him, and then laughing again.

But I had to have one final victory over this team of adults.

'Pray Father,' I said, 'let me finish with some wise and patriotic words which Ovid said:

' "I congratulate myself on not having arrived into the world until the present time. This age suits my taste." '

This seemed to astonish Marius more than to amuse him. But my Father gathered me close and said very clearly:

'Lydia, Ovid wouldn't say that now, and now you, for being such a . . . a scholar and philosopher in one, should assure your Father's dearest friends that you know full well Ovid was banished from Rome by Augustus for good reason and that he can never return home.'

In other words, he was saying 'Shut up about Ovid.'

But Marius, undeterred, dropped on his knees before me, lean and handsome with mesmeric blue eyes, and he took my hand and kissed it and said, 'I will give Ovid your love, little Lydia. But your Father is right. We must all agree with the Emperor's censure. After all, we are Romans.' He then did the very strange thing of speaking to me purely as if I were an adult. 'Augustus Caesar has given far more to Rome, I think, than anyone ever hoped. And he too is a poet. He wrote a poem called "Ajax" and burnt it up himself because he said it wasn't good.'

I was having the time of my life. I would have run off with Marius then and there!

But all I could do was dance around him as he went out of the vestibule and out the gate.

I waved to him.

He lingered. 'Goodbye, little Lydia,' he said. He then spoke under his breath to my Father, and I heard my Father say:

'You are out of your mind!'

My Father turned his back on Marius, who gave me a sad smile and disappeared.

'What did he mean? What happened?' I asked my Father. 'What's the matter?'

'Listen, Lydia,' said my Father. 'Have you in all your readings come across the word "betrothed"?'

'Yes, Father, of course.'

'Well, that sort of wanderer and dreamer likes nothing better than to betroth himself to a young girl of ten because it means she is not old enough to marry and he has years of freedom, without the censure of the Emperor. They do it all the time.'

'No, no, Father,' I said. 'I shall never forget him.'

I think I forgot him the next day.

I didn't see Marius again for five years.

I remember because I was fifteen, and should have been married and didn't want to be married at all. I had wriggled out of it year after year, feigning illness, madness, total uncontrollable fits. But time was running out on me. In fact I'd been eligible for marriage since I was twelve.

At this time, we were all standing together at the foot of the Palatine Hill, watching a most sacrosanct ceremony – the Lupercalia – just one of so many festivals that were integral in Roman life.

Now the Lupercalia was very important to us, though there's no way to relate its significance to a Christian's concept of religion. It was pious to enjoy such a festival, to participate as a citizen and as a virtuous Roman.

And besides it was a great pleasure.

So I was there, not so far from the cave of the Lupercal, watching with other young women, as the two chosen men of that year were smeared with blood from a sacrifice of goats and then draped in the bleeding skins of the sacrificed animals. I couldn't see all of this very well, but I had seen it many times, and when years before two of my brothers had run in this festival, I had pushed to the front to get a good look at it.

On this occasion, I did have a fairly good view when each of the two young men took his own company and began his run around the base of the Palatine Hill. I moved forward because I was supposed to do it. The young men were hitting lightly on the arm of every young woman with a strip of goatskin, which was supposed to purify us. Render us fertile.

I stepped forward and received the

ceremonial blow, and then stepped back again, wishing I was a man and could run around the hill with the other men, not an unusual thought for me at any time in my mortal life.

I had some sarcastic inner thoughts about 'being purified,' but by this age I behaved in public and would not on any account have humiliated my Father or my brothers.

These strips of goatskin, as you know, David, are called *Februa,* and February comes from that word. So much for language and all the magic it unwittingly carries with it. Surely the Lupercalia had something to do with Romulus and Remus; perhaps it even echoed some ancient human sacrifice. After all, the young men's heads were smeared with goat blood. It gives me shivers, because in Etruscan times, long before I was born, this might have been a far more cruel ceremony.

Perhaps this was the occasion that Marius saw my arms. Because I was exposing them to this ceremonial lash, and was already, as you can see, much of a show-off in general, laughing with the others as the company of men continued their run.

In the crowd, I saw Marius. He looked at me, then back to his book. So strange. I saw him standing against a tree trunk and writing. No one did this – stand against a tree, hold a book in one hand and write with the other. The slave stood beside him with a bottle of ink.

Marius's hair was long and most beautiful. Quite wild.

I said to my Father, 'Look, there's our barbarian friend Marius, the tall one, and he's writing.'

My Father smiled and said, 'Marius is always writing. Marius is good for writing, if for nothing else. Turn around, Lydia. Be still.'

'But he looked at me, Father. I want to talk to him.'

'You will not, Lydia! You will not grace him with one small smile!'

On the way home, I asked my Father, 'If you're going to marry me to someone – if there's no way short of suicide that I can avoid this disgusting development – why don't you marry me to Marius? I don't understand it. I'm rich. He's rich. I know his Mother was a wild Keltoi princess, but his Father has adopted him.'

My Father said witheringly, 'Where have you learned all this?' He stopped in his tracks, always an ominous sign. The crowd broke and streamed around.

'I don't know; it's common knowledge.' I

turned. There was Marius hovering about, glancing at me. 'Father,' I said, 'please let me speak to him!'

My Father knelt down. Most of the crowd had gone on. 'Lydia, I know this is dreadful for you. I have caved to every objection you have raised to your suitors. But believe you me, the Emperor himself would not approve of you marrying such a mad wandering historian as Marius! He has never served in the military, he cannot enter the Senate, it is quite impossible. When you marry, you will marry well.'

As we walked away, I turned again, thinking only to pick Marius out from the others, but to my surprise he was stark still, looking at me. With his flowing hair, he much resembled the Vampire Lestat. He is taller than Lestat, but he has the same lithe build, the same very blue eyes and a muscular strength to him, and a squareness of face which is almost pretty.

I pulled away from my Father and ran up to him.

'Well, I wanted to marry you,' I said, 'but my Father has said no.'

I'll never forget the expression on his face. But before he could speak, my Father had gathered me up and gone into obliterating respectable conversation:

'How now, Marius, how goes it with your brother in the Army. And how is it with your history. I hear you have written thirteen volumes.'

My Father backed up, virtually carrying me away.

Marius did not move or answer. Soon we were with others hurrying up the hill.

All the course of our lives was changed at that moment. But there was no conceivable way Marius or I could have known it.

Twenty years would pass before we would meet again.

I was thirty-five, then. I can say that we met in a realm of darkness in more respects than one.

For now, let me fill up the gap.

I was married twice, due to pressure from the Imperial House. Augustus wanted us all to have children. I had none. My husbands seeded plenty, however, with slave girls. So I was legally divorced and freed twice over, and determined then to retire from social life, just so the Emperor Tiberius, who had come to the Imperial throne at the age of fifty, would not meddle with me, for he was more a public puritan and domestic dictator than Augustus. If I kept to the house, if I didn't go abroad to banquets and parties and hang around with the Empress Livia, Augustus's wife and mother of Tiberius, perhaps I wouldn't be pushed into becoming a stepmother! I'd stay home. I had to care for my Father. He deserved it. Even though he was perfectly healthy, he was still old!

With all due respect for the husbands I have mentioned, whose names are more than footnotes in common Roman histories, I was a wretched wife.

I had plenty of my own money from my Father, I listened to nothing, and yielded to the act of love only on my own terms, which I always obtained, being gifted with enough beauty to make men really suffer.

I became a member of the Cult of Isis just to spite these husbands and get away from them, so that I could hang around at the Temple of Isis, where I spent an enormous amount of time with other interesting women, some far more adventurous and unconventional than I dared to be. I was attracted to whores. I saw the brilliant, loose women as having conquered a barrier which I, the loving daughter of my Father, would never conquer.

I became a regular at the Temple. I was initiated at last in a secret ceremony, and I walked in every procession of Isis in Rome.

My husbands loathed this. Maybe that's why after I came home to my Father I gave up the worship. Whatever, it was a good thing perhaps that I had. But fortune could not be so easily shaped by any decision of mine.

Now Isis was an imported goddess, from Egypt, of course, and the old Romans were as suspicious of her as they were of the terrible Cybele, the Great Mother from the Far East, who led her male devotees to castrate themselves. The whole city was filled with these 'Eastern cults,' and the conservative population thought them dreadful.

These cults weren't rational; they were ecstatic or euphoric. They offered a complete rebirth through understanding.

The typical conservative Roman was far too practical for that. If you didn't know by age five that the gods were made-up creatures and the myths invented stories, then you were a fool.

But Isis had a curious distinction – something that set her far apart from the cruel Cybele. Isis was a loving mother and goddess. Isis forgave her worshipers anything. Isis had come before all Creation. Isis was patient and wise.

That's why the most degraded woman could pray at the Temple. That's why none were ever turned away.

Like the Blessed Virgin Mary, who is so well known today throughout the East and West, the Queen Isis had conceived her divine child by divine means. From the dead and castrated Osiris, she had drawn the living seed by her own power. And many a time she was pictured or sculpted holding her divine son, Horus, on her knee. Her breast was bare in all innocence to feed the young god.

And Osiris ruled in the land of the dead, his phallus lost forever in the waters of the Nile, where an endless semen flowed from it, fertilizing the remarkable fields of Egypt every year when the River overflowed its banks.

The music of our Temple was divine. We used the sistrum, a small rigid metal lyre of sorts, and flutes and timbrels. We danced, and we sang together. The poetry of Isis's litanies was fine and rapturous.

Isis was the Queen of Navigation, much like the Blessed Virgin Mary would be called later, 'Our Lady Star of the Sea.'

When her statue was carried to the shore each year, the procession was so splendid that all Rome turned out to see the Egyptian gods with their animal heads, the huge abundance of flowers and the statue of the Queen Mother herself. The air rang with hymns. Her Priests and

Priestesses walked in white linen robes. She herself, made of marble, and carried high, holding her sacred sistrum, dressed regally in a Grecian gown with Grecian hair.

That was my Isis. I fell away from her after my last divorce. My Father didn't like the worship, and I myself had enjoyed it long enough. As a free woman, I wasn't infatuated with prostitutes. I had it infinitely better. I kept my Father's house and he was just old enough, in spite of his black hair and his remarkably sharp vision, that the Emperor left me alone.

I can't say I remembered or thought of Marius. No one had mentioned Marius for years. He had disappeared out of my mind after the Lupercalia. There was no force on Earth that could come between me and my Father.

My brothers all had good luck. They married well, had children and came home from the hard wars in which they fought, keeping the boundaries of the Empire.

My youngest brother, Lucius, I did not like much, but he was always a little anxious and given to drinking and apparently also to gambling, which very much annoyed his wife.

She I loved, as I did all my sisters-in-law and my nieces and nephews. I loved it when they descended upon the house, these flocks of children, squealing and running rampant with 'Aunt Lydia's blessing,' as they were never allowed to do at home.

The eldest of my brothers, Antony, was in potential a great man. Fate robbed him of greatness. But he had been most ready for it, well schooled, trained and most wise.

The only foolish thing I ever knew Antony to do was say to me very distinctly once that Livia, Augustus's wife, had poisoned him so that her son, Tiberius, would rise. My Father, the only other occupant of the room, told him sternly:

'Antony, never speak of that again! Not here, not anywhere!' My Father stood up, and without planning it, put in perspective the style of life which he and I lived. 'Stay away from the Imperial Palace, stay away from the Imperial families, be in the front ranks of the games and always in the Senate, but don't get into their quarrels and their intrigues!'

Antony was very angry but the anger had nothing to do with my Father. 'I said it only to those two to whom I can say it, you and Lydia. I detest eating dinner with a woman who poisoned her husband! Augustus should have re-established the Republic. He knew when death was coming.'

'Yes, and he knew that he could not restore

the Republic. It was simply impossible. The Empire had grown to Britannia in the North, beyond Parthia in the East; it covers Northern Africa. If you want to be a good Roman, Antony, then stand up and speak your conscience in the Senate. Tiberius invites this.'

'Oh, Father, you are much deceived,' said Antony.

My Father put an end to this argument.

But he and I did live exactly the life he had described.

Tiberius was immediately unpopular with the noisy Roman crowds. He was too old, too dry, too humorless, too puritanical and tyrannical at the same time.

But he had one saving grace. Other than his extensive love and knowledge of philosophy, he had been a very good soldier. And that was the most important characteristic the Emperor had to possess.

The troops honored him.

He strengthened the Praetorian Guard around the Palace, hired a man named Sejanus to run things for him. But he didn't bring legions into Rome, and he spoke a damned good line about personal rights and freedom, that is, if you could stay awake to listen. I thought him a brooder.

The Senate went mad with impatience when he refused to make decisions. They didn't want to make the decisions! But all this seemed relatively safe.

Then a horrible incident occurred which made me positively detest the Emperor wholeheartedly and lose all my faith in the man and his ability to govern.

This incident involved the Temple of Isis. Some clever evil man, claiming to be the Egyptian god Anubis, had enticed a highborn devotee of Isis to the Temple and gone to bed with her, fooling her completely, though how on Earth he did it I can't imagine.

I remember her to this day as the stupidest woman in Rome. But there's probably more to it.

Anyway, it had all happened at the Temple.

And then this man, this fake Anubis, went before the highborn virtuous woman and told her in the plainest terms that he had had her! She went screaming to her husband. It was a scandal of extraordinary flair.

It had been years since I had been at the Temple, and I was glad of it.

But what followed from the Emperor was more dreadful than I ever dreamed.

The entire Temple was razed to the very

ground. All the worshipers were banished from Rome, and some of them executed. And our Priests and Priestesses were crucified, their bodies hung on the tree, as the old Roman expression goes, to die slowly and to rot, for all to see.

My Father came into my bedroom. He went to the small shrine of Isis. He took the statue and smashed it on the marble floor. Then he picked up the larger pieces and smashed each of them. He made dust of her.

I nodded.

I expected him to condemn me for my old habits. I was overcome with sadness and shock at what had happened. Other Eastern cults were being persecuted. The Emperor was moving to take away the right of Sanctuary from various Temples throughout the Empire.

'The man doesn't want to be Emperor of Rome,' said my Father. 'He's been bent by cruelty and losses. He's stiff, boring and completely in terror for his life! A man who would not be Emperor cannot be Emperor. Not now.'

'Maybe he'll step down,' I said sadly. 'He has adopted the young General Germanicus Julius Caesar. This means Germanicus is to be his heir, does it not?'

'What good did it do to the earlier heirs of

Augustus when they were adopted?' my Father asked.

'What do you mean?' I asked.

'Use your head,' said my Father. 'We cannot continue pretending we are a Republic. We must define the office of this Emperor and the limits of his power! We must outline a form of succession other than murder!'

I tried to calm him.

'Father, let's leave Rome. Let's go to our house in Tuscany. It's always beautiful there, Father.'

'That's just it, we can't, Lydia,' he said. 'I have to remain here. I have to be loyal to my Emperor. I must do so for all my family. I must stand in the Senate.'

Within months, Tiberius sent off his young and handsome nephew Germanicus Julius Caesar to the East, just to get him away from the adulation of the Roman public. As I said, people spoke their minds.

Germanicus was supposed to be Tiberius's heir! But Tiberius was too jealous to listen to the crowds screaming praise of Germanicus for his victories in battle. He wanted the man far from Rome.

And so this rather charming and seductive young general went to the East, to Syria; he vanished from the loving eyes of the Roman people, from the core of the Empire where a city crowd could determine the fate of the world.

Sooner or later there would be another campaign in the North, we all figured. Germanicus had hit hard at the German tribes in his last campaign.

My brothers vividly described it to me over the dinner table.

They told how they had gone back to avenge the hideous massacre of General Varus and his troops in the Teutoburg Forest. They could finish the job, if called up again, and my brothers would go. They were exactly the kind of old-fashioned patricians who would go!

Meantime there were rumors that the *Delatores,* the notorious spies of the Praetorian Guard, pocketed one-third of the estate of those against whom they informed. I found it horrible. My Father shook his head, and said, 'That started under Augustus.'

'Yes, Father,' I said, 'but then treason was considered a matter of what one did, not what one said.'

'Which is all the more reason to say nothing.' He sat back wearily. 'Lydia, sing to me. Get your lyre. Make up one of your comic epics. It's been a long time.'

'I'm too old for that,' I said, thinking of the silly, bawdy satires on Homer which I used to make up so quickly and freely that everyone marveled. But I jumped at that idea. I remember that night so palpably that I cannot tear myself loose now from the writing of this story, even though I know what pain I must confess and explore.

What does it mean to write? David, you'll see this question repeated, because with each page I understand more and more – I see the patterns that have before eluded me, and driven me to dream rather than live.

That night I did make a very funny epic. My Father laughed. He fell asleep on his couch. And then, as if from a trance state, he spoke, 'Lydia, don't live out your life alone on account of me. Marry for love! You must not give up!'

By the time I turned around, he was breathing deeply again.

Two weeks later, or maybe it was a month, our life came abruptly to an end.

I came home one day, found the house completely empty except for two terrified old slave men – men who actually belonged to the household of my brother Antony – who let me in and bolted the door ferociously.

I walked through the huge vestibule and then

into the peristyle and into the dining room. I beheld an amazing sight.

My Father was in full battle dress, armed with sword and dagger, lacking only his shield. He even wore his red cloak. His breastplate was polished and gleaming.

He stared at the floor and with reason. It had been dug up. The old Hearth from generations ago had been dug up. This had been the first room of this house in the very ancient days of Rome, and it was around this Hearth that the family gathered, worshiped, dined.

I had never even seen it. We had our household Shrines, but this, this giant circle of burnt stones! There were actually ashes there, uncovered. How ominous and sacred it appeared.

'What in the name of the gods is going on?' I asked. 'Where is everybody?'

'They are gone,' he said. 'I have freed the slaves, sent them packing. I've been waiting for you. You have to leave here now!'

'Not without you!'

'You will not disobey me, Lydia!' I had never seen such an imploring yet dignified expression in his face. 'There's a wagon out back, ready to take you to the coast, and a Jewish merchant who is my most trusted friend who will take you by ship out of Italy! I want you to go! Your money's been loaded on board the ship. Your clothing. Everything. These are men I trust. Nevertheless take this dagger.'

He picked up a dagger from the nearby table and gave it to me. 'You've watched your brothers enough to know how to use it,' he said, 'and this.' He reached for a sack. 'This is gold, the currency that all the world accepts. Take it and go.'

I always carried a dagger, and it was in the sling on my forearm but I could not shock him with this just now, so I put the dagger in my girdle and took the purse.

'Father, I'm not afraid to stand by you! Who's turned on us? Father, you are Senator of Rome. Accused of any crime, you are entitled to a trial before the Senate.'

'Oh, my precious quick-witted daughter! You think that evil Sejanus and his *Delatores* bring charges out in the open? His *Speculatores* have already surprised your brothers and their wives and children. These are Antony's slaves. He sent them to warn me as he fought, as he died. He saw his son dashed against the wall. Lydia, go.'

Of course I knew this was a Roman custom — to murder the entire family, to wipe out the spouse and offspring of the condemned. It was even the law. And in matters such as this, when word got out that the Emperor had turned his back on a man, any of his enemies could precede the assassins.

'You come with me,' I said. 'Why do you stay here?'

'I will die a Roman in my house,' he said. 'Now go if you love me, my poet, my singer, my thinker. My Lydia. Go! I will not be disobeyed. I have spent the last hour of my life arranging for your salvation! Kiss me and obey me.'

I ran to him, kissed him on the lips and at once the slaves led me through the garden.

I knew my Father. I could not revolt against him in this final wish. I knew that, in old-fashioned Roman style, he would probably take his life before the *Speculatores* broke down the front door.

When I reached the gate, when I saw the Hebrew merchants and their wagon, I couldn't go.

This is what I saw.

My Father had cut both his wrists and was walking around the household hearth in a circle, letting the blood flow right down onto the floor. He had really given his wrists the slash. He was turning white as he walked. In his eyes there was an expression I would only come to understand later.

There came a loud crash. The front door was being bashed in. My Father stopped quite still. And two of the Praetorian Guard came at him, one making sneering remarks, 'Why don't you finish yourself off, Maximus, and save us the trouble. Go on.'

'Are you proud of yourselves!' my Father said. 'Cowards. You like killing whole families? How much money do you get? Did you ever fight in a true battle. Come on, die with me!'

Turning his back on them, he whipped around with sword and dagger, and brought down both of them, as they came at him, with unanticipated thrusts. He stabbed them repeatedly.

My Father wobbled as if he would faint. He was white. The blood flowed and flowed from his wrists. His eyes rolled up into his head.

Mad schemes came to me. We must get him into the wagon. But a Roman like my Father would never have cooperated.

Suddenly the Hebrews, one young and one elderly, had me by the arms and were carrying me out of the house.

'I vowed I would save you,' said the old man.

'And you will not make a liar of me to my old friend.'

'Let go of me!' I whispered. 'I will see him through it!'

Throwing them off in their polite timidity I turned and saw from a great distance my Father's body by the hearth. He had finished himself with his own dagger.

I was thrown into the wagon, my eyes closed, my hands over my mouth. I fell among soft pillows, bolts of fabric, tumbling as the wagon began to roll very slowly down the winding road of the Palatine Hill.

Soldiers shouted at us to get the hell out of the way.

The elderly Hebrew said, 'I am nearly deaf, sir, what did you say?'

It worked perfectly. They rode past us.

The Hebrew knew exactly what he was doing. As crowds rushed past us he kept to his slow pace.

The one young one came into the back of the wagon. 'My name is Jacob,' he said. 'Here, put on all these white mantles. You look now like an Eastern woman. If questioned at the gate, hold up your veil and pretend you do not understand.'

We went through the Gates of Rome with

amazing ease. It was 'Hail David and Jacob, has it been a good trip?'

I was helped aboard a large merchant vessel, with galley slaves and sails, nothing unusual at all, and then into a small barren wooden room.

'This is all we have for you,' said Jacob. 'But we are sailing now.' He had long wavy brown hair and a beard. He wore striped robes to the ground.

'In the dark?' I asked. 'Sailing in the dark?'

This was not usual.

But as we moved out, as the oars began to dip, and the ship found its proper distance and began to move South, I saw what we were doing.

All the beautiful Southwestern coast of Italy was well lighted by her hundreds and hundreds of palatial villas. Lighthouses stood on the rocks.

'We will never see the Republic again,' said Jacob wearily, as though he were a Roman citizen, which I think in fact he was. 'But your Father's last wish is fulfilled. We are safe now.'

The old man stepped up to me. He told me that his name was David.

The old man apologized profusely that there were no female attendants for me. I was the only woman on board.

'Oh, please, banish any such thoughts from your mind! Why have you taken these risks?'

'For years we have done business with your Father,' said David. 'Years ago, when pirates sank our ships, your Father carried the debt. He trusted us again, and we repaid him fivefold. He has laid up riches for you. They are all stowed, among cargo we carried, as if they were nothing.'

I went into the cabin and collapsed on the small bed. The old man, averting his eyes, brought a cover for me.

Slowly I realized something. I had fully expected them to betray me.

I had no words. I had no gestures or sentiments inside me. I turned my head to the wall. 'Sleep, lady,' he said.

A nightmare came to me, a dream such as I have never had in my life. I was near a river. I wanted to drink blood. I waited in high grass to catch one of the villagers, and when I had this poor man, I took him by his shoulders, and I sank two fang teeth into his neck. My mouth filled with delicious blood. It was too sweet and too potent to be described, and even in the dream I knew it. But I had to move on. The man was nearly dead. I let him fall. Others who were more dangerous were after me. And there was another terrible threat to my life.

I came to the ruins of a Temple, far from the marsh. Here it was desert – just with the snap of the fingers, from wetland to sand. I was afraid. Morning was coming. I had to hide. Besides, I was also being hunted. I digested this delicious blood, and I entered the Temple. No place to hide! I laid my whole body on the cold walls! They were graven with pictures. But there was no small room, no hiding place for me.

I had to make it to the hills before sunrise, but that wasn't possible. I was moving right towards the sun!

Suddenly, there came above the hills a great fatal light. My eyes hurt unbearably. They were on fire. 'My eyes,' I cried and reached to cover them. Fire covered me. I screamed. 'Amon Ra, I curse you!' I cried another name. I knew it meant Isis, but it was not that name, it was another title for her that flew from my lips.

I woke up. I sat bolt upright, shivering.

The dream had been as sharply defined as a vision. It had a deep resonance in me of memory. Had I lived before?

I went out on the deck of the ship. All was well enough. We could see the coastline clearly still, and the lighthouses, and the ship moved on. I stared at the sea, and I wanted blood.

'This is not possible. This is some evil omen, some twisted grief,' I said. I felt the fire. I could not shut out the taste of the blood, how natural it had seemed, how good, how perfect for my thirst. I saw the twisted body of the villager again in the marshes.

This was a horror; it was no escape from what I had just witnessed. I was incensed, and feverish.

Jacob, the tall young one, came to me. He had with him a young Roman. The young man had shaved his first beard, but otherwise he seemed a flushed and glistening child.

I wondered wearily if I were so old at thirty-five that everyone young looked beautiful to me.

He cried, 'My family, too, has been betrayed. My Mother made me leave!'

'To whom do we owe this shared catastrophe?' I asked. I put my hands on his wet cheeks. He had a baby's mouth, but the shaven beard was rough. He had broad strong shoulders, and wore only a light, simple tunic. Why wasn't he cold out here on the water? Perhaps he was.

He shook his head. He was pretty still and would be handsome later. He had a nice curl to his dark hair. He didn't fear his tears, or apologize for them.

'My Mother stayed alive to tell me. She lay gasping until I came. When the *Delatores* had told my Father that he plotted against the Emperor, my Father had laughed. He had actually laughed. They had accused him of plotting with Germanicus! My Mother wouldn't die until she'd told me. She said that all my Father was accused of doing was talking with other men about how he would serve under Germanicus again if they were sent North.'

I nodded wearily. 'I see. My brothers probably said the same thing. And Germanicus is the Emperor's heir and *Imperium Maius* of the East. Yet this is treason, to speak of serving Rome under a pretty general.'

I turned to go. To understand gave no consolation.

'We are taking you to different cities,' said Jacob, 'to different friends. Better that we not say.'

'Don't leave me,' said the boy. 'Not tonight.'

'All right,' I said. I took him into the cabin and closed the door, with a polite nod to Jacob, who was watching all with a guardian's conscience.

'What do you want?' I asked.

The boy stared at me. He shook his head. He flung his hands out. He turned and drew close to me and kissed me. We went into a rampage of kisses.

I took off my shift and sank into the bed with him. He was a man all right, tender face or no.

And when I came to the moment of ecstasy, which was quite easy, given his phenomenal stamina, I tasted blood. I was the blood drinker in the dream. I went limp, but it didn't matter. He had all he needed to finish the rites to his satisfaction.

He rose up. 'You're a goddess,' he said.

'No,' I whispered. The dream was rising. I heard the wind on the sand. I smelled the river. 'I am a god . . . a god who drinks blood.'

We did the rites of love until we could do them no more.

'Be circumspect and very proper with our Hebrew hosts,' I said. 'They will never understand this sort of thing.'

He nodded. 'I adore you.'

'Not necessary. What is your name?'

'Marcellus.'

'Fine, Marcellus, go to sleep.'

Marcellus and I made a night of every night after that until we finally saw the famous lighthouse of Pharos and knew we had come to Egypt.

It was perfectly obvious that Marcellus was

being left in Alexandria. He explained to me that his maternal grandmother was still alive, a Greek, and indeed her whole clan.

'Don't tell me so much, just go,' I said. 'And be wise and safe.'

He begged me to come with him. He said he had fallen in love with me. He would marry me. He didn't care if I bore no children. He didn't care that I was thirty-five. I laughed softly, mercifully.

Jacob noted all this with lowered eyes. And David looked away.

Quite a few trunks followed Marcellus into Alexandria.

'Now,' I said to Jacob, 'will you tell me where I'm being taken? I might have some thoughts on the matter, though I doubt I could improve on my Father's plan.'

I still wondered. Would they deal honestly with me? What about now that they had seen me play the whore with the boy? They were such religious men.

'You're headed to a great city,' Jacob said. 'It couldn't be a better place. Your Father has Greek friends there!'

'How could it be better than Alexandria?' I said.

'Oh, it is far and away better,' Jacob said.

'Let me talk to my Father before I talk to you further.'

We had put out to sea. The land was going away. Egypt. It was growing dark.

'Don't be afraid,' Jacob said. 'You look as though you are terrified.'

'I'm not afraid,' I said. 'It's only that I have to lie in my bed and think and remember and dream.' I looked at him, as he shyly looked away. 'I held the boy like a Mother, against me, night after night.'

This was about the biggest lie I've told in my life.

'He was a child in my arms.' Some child! 'And now I fear nightmares. You must tell me – what is our destination? What is our fate?'

3

'Antioch,' said Jacob, 'Antioch on the Orontes.
Greek friends of your Father await you. And
they are friends with Germanicus. Perhaps in
time . . . but they will be loyal to you. You are
to be married to a Greek of breeding and
means.'

Married! To a Greek, a provincial Greek? A
Greek in Asia! I stifled my laughter and my
tears. That was not going to happen to me. Poor
man! If he really was a provincial Greek, he was
going to have to experience the conquest of
Rome all over again.

We sailed on, from port to port. I mulled all
this over.

It was nauseating trivia like this which of
course protected me from my full and inevitable
grief and shock over what happened. Worry
about whether your dress is properly girdled.

Don't see your Father lying dead with his own dagger in his chest.

As for Antioch, I had been far too embroiled in the life of Rome to know or hear much about this city. If Tiberius had stationed his 'heir,' Germanicus, there to get him away from Roman popularity, then I thought: Antioch must be the end of the civilized world.

Why in the name of the gods had I not run away in Alexandria, I thought? Alexandria was the greatest city in the Empire, next to Rome. It was a young city, built by Alexander, for whom it was named, but it was a marvelous port. No one would ever dare raze the Temple of Isis in Alexandria. Isis was an Egyptian goddess, wife of the powerful Osiris.

But what had that to do with things? I must have been plotting in the back of my mind already, but I didn't allow any conscious plot to surface and blemish my highborn Roman moral character.

I quietly thanked my Hebrew guardians for this intelligence, for keeping it even from the young Roman Marcellus, the other man they had rescued from the Emperor's assassins, and I asked for frank answers to my questions regarding my brothers.

'All taken by surprise,' said Jacob. 'The

Delatores, those spies of the Praetorian Guard, are so swift. And your Father had so many sons. It was your eldest brother's slaves who jumped the wall at their Master's command and ran to warn your Father.'

Antony. I hope you shed their blood. I know you fought with your last breath. And my niece, my little niece Flora, had she run screaming from them, or did they do it with mercy? The Praetorian Guard doing anything with mercy! Stupid to even think so.

I didn't say anything aloud. Just sighed.

After all, when they looked at me, these two Jewish merchants beheld the body and face of a woman; naturally my protectors should think a woman was inside of me. The disparity between outward appearances and inner disposition had disturbed me all my life. Why disturb Jacob and David? On to Antioch.

But I had no intention of living in any old-fashioned Greek family, if such still existed in the Greek city of Antioch, a family in which women lived apart from the men, and wove wool all day, never going out, having no part in the life of the world whatsoever.

I'd been taught all the virtuous female arts by my nurses and I could indeed do anything with yarn or thread or loom that any other woman could do, but I knew well what the 'Old Greek Ways' had been, and I remembered vaguely my Father's Mother, who had died when I was very young – a virtuous Roman matron who was always making wool. So they had said of her in her Epitaph, and in fact, they had said in my Mother's Epitaph: 'She kept the House. She made wool.'

And so they had said of my Mother! The very same tiresome words.

Well, no one was going to say that on mine. (How humorous to reflect on the fact now, thousands of years later, that I have no Epitaph!)

What I failed to realize in my overall dejection was that the Roman world was enormous, and the Eastern portion of it differed dramatically from the Northern barbarian lands, where my brothers had fought.

The entire of Asia Minor, towards which we sailed, had been conquered by Alexander of Macedon hundreds of years before. As you know, Alexander had been the pupil of Aristotle. Alexander had wanted to spread Greek culture everywhere. And in Asia Minor Greek ideas and styles found not mere country towns or farmers, but ancient cultures, like the Empire of Syria, willing to receive the new ideas, the grace and beauty of the Greek enlightenment, and willing to bring in tune with it their own centuries-old literature, religion, styles of life and dress.

Antioch had been built by a general of Alexander the Great who sought to rival the beauty of other Hellenistic cities, with splendid Temples, administrative buildings and libraries of books in the Greek language, its schools where Greek philosophy was taught. A Hellenistic government was established – quite enlightened compared to ancient Eastern despotism, and yet there lay beneath all this the knowledge and customs and possibly the wisdom of the mysterious East.

The Romans had conquered Antioch early on because it was a huge trade center. It was unique in this way, as Jacob showed to me, drawing a crude map with his wet finger on the wooden table. Antioch was a port of the great Mediterranean because she was only twenty miles up the Orontes River.

Yet on the Eastern side she was open to the desert: all the old caravan routes came to Antioch, the camel merchants who brought fantastic wares from fabled lands – lands we know now to have been India and China – silk, carpet and jewels which never reached the markets of Rome.

Countless other traders came and went to Antioch. Fine roads connected it in the East with the Euphrates River and the Parthian Empire beyond, and to the South you could go to Damascas and Judea, and to the North, of course, lay all the cities made by Alexander, which had flowered under Roman rule.

Roman soldiers loved it there. It was an easy and interesting life. And Antioch loved the Romans because the Romans protected the trade routes, and the caravans, and kept peace in the port.

'You will find open places, arcades, Temples, all that you seek and such markets you would not believe. There are Romans everywhere. I hope to One Most High that you are not recognized by someone from your own background! That is one danger of which your Father had no time to plan.'

I waved it away.

'Does it have teachers now, and markets of books?'

'From everywhere. You will find books which no one can read. And Greek is spoken by everyone. You have to go out in the country to find some poor farmer who does not understand Greek. Latin has now become common.

'The philosophers never stop; they speak of

Plato and Pythagoras, names that don't mean much to me; they talk about Chaldean magic from Babylon. Of course there are Temples to every imaginable god.'

He went on, reflecting as he spoke:

'The Hebrews? I think personally they are too worldly – they want to hang around in short tunics with the Greeks and go to the public baths. They are too interested in the Greek philosophy. It invades everything, all this thinking that Greeks did. Not good. But a Greek city is an inviting world.'

He glanced up. His Father was watching over us, and we were too close together, at this table on the deck.

He hastily filled me in on other facts:

Germanicus Julius Caesar, heir to the Imperial throne, the official adopted son of Tiberius, had been granted the *Imperium Maius* in Antioch. That is, he controlled all of this territory. And Gnaeus Calpurnius Piso was the governor of Syria.

I assured him that they would know nothing of me or my old-fashioned family or our quiet, old house on the Palatine Hill, squeezed between so many other extravagant new mansions.

'It's all Roman-style,' Jacob protested. 'You'll see. And you come with money! And forgive me, but you are still beautiful at your age; you have fresh skin and you move your limbs like a girl.'

I sighed and gave Jacob thanks. Time for him to break away unless we wanted his Father coming down upon us.

I watched the ever rolling blue waves.

I was thankful in secret that our family had withdrawn from the parties and banquets at the Imperial Palace, but then I blamed myself for such thankfulness, knowing that our reclusiveness must have paved the way for our downfall.

I'd seen Germanicus on his triumphal procession through Rome, a gorgeous young man, much as Alexander had been, and I knew from my Father and my brothers that Tiberius, fearing the popularity of his appointed heir, had sent him off to the East to get him away from the Roman crowds.

The Governor Piso? I had never laid eyes on him. The gossip was that he was sent East to devil Germanicus. Oh, such a waste of talent and thought.

Jacob returned to me.

'Well, you go nameless and unknown into this vast city,' said Jacob. 'And you have protectors of high character who are beloved of Germanicus. He's young and sets a tone of vitality and gaiety in the city.'

'And Piso?' I asked.

'Everyone hates him. Especially the soldiers, and you know what that means in a Roman province.'

You can look at the crashing, undulating sea from the railing of a deck forever, or just for so long.

That night I had my second blood dream. It was keenly similar to the first. I was thirsty for blood. And enemies were after me, enemies that knew I was a demon and must be destroyed. I was running. My own kind had forsaken me, thrust me out unprotected to the superstitions of the people. Then I saw the desert and knew I would die; I awoke, sitting up and crying out, but covering my mouth quickly so no one heard it.

What disturbed me so terribly was the thirst for blood. I could not imagine such a thing when I was awake, but in these dreams I was the monster that Romans called the Lamia. Or so it seemed. Blood was sweet, blood was all. Was the old Greek Pythagoras right? Souls do migrate from body to body? But my soul in this past life had been that of a monster.

During the day, I closed my eyes now and then and found myself dangerously on the edge of the dream, as if it were a trap in my mind, waiting to engulf my consciousness. But at night, that is when they came most strongly. *You have served me before!* What could this mean? *Come to me.*

Blood thirst. I closed my eyes, curled up in bed and prayed, 'Mother Isis, Cleanse my Mind of this Blood madness.'

Then I resorted to plain old ordinary eroticism. Get Jacob into bed! No such luck. Little did I know that Hebrews had been, and would be forever, the most difficult of men to seduce!

It was all made clear with great grace and tact.

I considered all the slaves. Out of the question. First off were the galley slaves, among whom no great 'Ben Hur' was chained, waiting for me to rescue him. They were just the dregs of the criminal poor, fastened Roman-style, so they would drown if the ship went down, and they were dying, as all galley slaves do from the monotony and the whip. It wasn't a pleasant sight to go down into the hold of a galley ship and see those men bending their backs.

But my eyes were as cold as those of an American watching color television pictures of the starving babies of Africa, little black skeletons with big heads screaming for water. News Break, Commercial Break, Sound Bite, CNN now switches to Palestine: rock throwing, rubber bullets. Television blood.

The rest on board were boring sailors, and two old pious merchant Hebrews who stared at me as if I were a whore, or worse, and turned their heads whenever I came out on deck in my long tunic with my long hair swinging free.

Such a disgrace I must have seemed! But what a fool I was then, really, living in numbness, and how pleasant that voyage – all because true grief and rage had not yet taken hold of me. Things had happened too fast.

I gloated over my last glimpse of my Father dispatching those soldiers of Tiberius, those cheap assassins sent by a cowardly, indecisive Emperor. And the rest – I banished it from my mind, affecting the attitude of the hardened Roman man or woman.

A modern Irish poet, Yeats, best characterizes the official Roman attitude towards failure and tragedy.

Cast a cold eye on life, on death.
Horseman, pass by!

There was never a Roman born who would not have agreed with that.

That was my stance – sole survivor of a great

house, commanded by her Father to 'live.' I didn't dare to dwell on the fate of my brothers, their lovely wives, their little children. I couldn't envision the slaughter of the children – little boys being run through by broadswords, or babies bashed against the wall. Oh, Rome, you and your bloody old wisdom. Be sure to kill the offspring. Kill the whole family!

Lying alone at night, I found myself amid more horrid blood dreams. They seemed fragments of a lost life, a lost land. Deep echoing vibrant tones of music dominated the dreams, as though someone were striking a gong, and others beside him beat solemnly on deep drums with soft coverings. I saw in a haze a world of stiff and flat alien paintings on the walls. Painted eyes around me. I drank blood! I drank it from a small shuddering human being, who knelt before me as if I were Mother Isis.

I woke to take the big jug of water by my bed and drink all of it down. I drank water to defy and satisfy this dream thirst. I was almost sick from drinking water.

I racked my mind. Had I ever had such dreams as a child?

No. And now these dreams had the heat of recollection! Of initiation into the doomed Temple of Isis, when it had been still the fashion. I had been intoxicated, and drenched in the blood of a bull, and dancing wildly in circles. My head was filled with the litanies of Isis. We were promised rebirth! 'Never tell, never tell, never tell . . .' How could an initiate tell anything of the rites, when you were so drunk you could hardly remember them?

Isis brought me memories now of lovely music of lyres, flutes, timbrels, of the high magical sound of the metal strings of the sistrum, which the Mother Herself held in her hand. There were only fleeting recollections of that naked blood dance, that night of rising into the stars, of seeing the scope of life in its cycles, of accepting perfectly just for a little while that the moon would always be changing, and the sun would set as it always rose. Embraces of other women. Soft cheeks and kissing and bodies rocking in unison. 'Life, death, rebirth, it's no series of miracles,' said the Priestess. 'To understand it and accept it, that is the miracle. Make the miracle within your own breast.'

Surely we had not drunk blood! And the bull – it was a sacrifice only for the initiation. We did not bring helpless animals to her flower-laden altars, no, our Blessed Mother did not ask that of us.

Now, at sea, alone, I lay awake to avoid

these blood dreams.

When exhaustion won out, a dream came with sleep as if it had been waiting for my eyes to close.

I lay in a gold chamber. I was drinking blood, blood from the throat of a god, or so it seemed, and choruses were singing or chanting – it was a dull, repetitive sound not quite worthy of being called music, and when I had had my fill of blood, this god or whoever this was, this silken-skinned proud thing, lifted me and placed me on an altar.

Vividly, I could feel the cold marble beneath me. I realized I wore no clothes. I felt no modesty. Somewhere far off, echoing through these great halls, came the weeping of a woman. I was full of blood. Those who chanted approached with little clay oil lamps. Faces around me were dark, dark enough to be from far faraway Ethiopia or India. Or Egypt. Look. Painted eyes! I looked at my hands and arms. They were dark. But I was this person who lay on the altar, and I say person now because it had come clear to me with no disturbance during the dream itself that I was a man lying there. Pain tore at me. The god said, 'This is merely the passage. You will now drink from each of us, only a little blood.'

Only when I woke did the brief transition in

the masculine gender leave me as puzzled as everything else. I was drenched with a sense of Egyptian art, Egyptian mystery – as I'd seen it in golden statues for sale in the marketplace, or when the Egyptian dancers performed at a banquet, like walking sculptures with their black-lined eyes, and black plaited wigs, whispering in that mysterious tongue. What had they thought of our Isis in Roman dress?

A mystery taunted me; something attacked my reason. The very thing the Roman Emperors had so feared in Egyptian cults and Oriental cults swept over me: mystery and emotion which claim a superiority to reason and law.

My Isis had been a Roman goddess, really, a universal goddess, the Mother of us all, her worship spreading out in a Greek and Roman world long before it had come into Rome itself. Our Priests were Greeks and Roman, poor men. We the congregation were all Greeks and Romans.

Something scratched at the back of my mind. It said, 'Remember.' It was a tiny desperate voice within my own brain that urged me to 'remember' for my own sake.

But remembering only led to confused and jumbled thoughts. Suddenly a veil would fall between the reality of my cabin on the ship, and the tumbling of the sea – between that and some dim and frightening world, of Temples covered in words that made magic! Long narrow beautifully bronzed faces. A voice whispered, 'Beware the Priests of Ra; they lie!'

I shivered. I closed my eyes. The Queen Mother was bound and chained to her throne! She wept! It had been her crying. Unspeakable. 'But you see, she has forgotten how to rule. Do as we say.'

I shook myself awake. I wanted to know and I did not want to know. The Queen wept beneath her monstrous fetters. I couldn't see her clearly. It was all in progress. It was busy. 'The King is with Osiris, you see. You see how he stares; each one whose blood you drink, you give to Osiris; each one becomes Osiris.'

'But why did the Queen scream?'

No, this was madness. I couldn't let this confusion overcome me. I couldn't deliberately slip from reason into these fantasies or recollections supposing they had a true root.

They had to be nonsense, twisted images of grief and guilt, guilt that I had not rushed to the hearth and driven the dagger into my breast.

I tried to remember the calming voice of my Father, explaining once how the blood of the gladiators satisfied the thirst of the dead, the *Manes*.

107

'Now, some say that the Dead drink blood,' spoke my Father from some long ago dinner talk. 'That's why we are so fearful on all these unlucky days, when the Dead are supposed to be able to walk the Earth. I personally think this is nonsense. We should revere our ancestors . . .'

'Where are the Dead, Father?' my brother Lucius asked.

Who had piped up from the other side of the table, to quote Lucretius in a sad little female voice that nevertheless commanded silence of all these men? Lydia:

Of earth return to earth, but any part
Sent down from heaven, must ascend again
Recalled to the high temples of the sky
And death does not destroy the elements
Of matter, only breaks the combinations.

'No,' my Father had replied to me quite gently. 'Rather quote Ovid: "The ghosts ask for but little; they value piety more than a costly gift."' He drank his wine. 'The ghosts are in the Underworld where they can't harm us.'

My eldest brother Antony had said, 'The Dead are nowhere and are nothing.'

My Father had raised his cup. 'To Rome,' he said, and it was he this time who had quoted

Lucretius: ' "Too many times, religion mothers crimes and wickedness." '

Shrugs and sighs all around. The Roman attitude. Even the Priests and Priestesses of Isis would have joined Lucretius when he wrote:

Our terrors and our darknesses of mind
Must be dispelled, then, not by sunshine's
rays,
Not by those shining arrows of light,
But by insight into nature, and a scheme
Of systematic contemplation.

Drunk? Drugged? Bull's blood? Systematic? Well, it all came down to the same thing. Know! Twist the poetry as you will. And the phallus of Osiris lives forever in the Nile, and the water of the Nile inseminates the Mother Egypt eternally, death giving birth to life with the blessing of Mother Isis. Merely a particular scheme and a sort of systematic form of contemplation.

The ship sailed on.

I languished some eight more days in this torment, often lying awake in the dark, and sleeping only in the day to avoid the dreams.

Suddenly, in the early morning, Jacob pounded my door.

We were midway up the Orontes to the city.

Twenty miles now from Antioch. I did up my hair as best I could (I'd never done it without a slave) into a chignon on the back of my head, then covered my Roman gowns with a great black cloak and prepared to disembark – an Eastern woman, her face draped, protected by Hebrews.

When the city came into view – when the immense harbor greeted us and then embraced us with all its masts and racket and odors and cries, I ran to the deck of the ship and looked out at this city. It was splendid.

'You see,' Jacob said.

Taken from the ship by litter I found myself carried rapidly through vast waterfront markets, and then into a great open square, crowded with people. I saw everywhere the Temples, porticoes, booksellers, even the high walls of an amphitheater – all that I could have expected in Rome. No, this was no town.

The young men were crowded about the barbershops ready to have their obligatory shave and the inevitable fancy curls on their foreheads, which Tiberius with his own hairstyle had made fashionable. There were wine shops all over. The slave markets were jammed. I glimpsed the entrances to the streets devoted to crafts – the street of the tentmakers, the street of the silversmiths.

And there in all its glory, in the very center of Antioch, stood the Temple of Isis!

My goddess, Isis, with her worshipers coming and going, undisturbed, and in huge numbers. A few very proper-looking linen-clad Priests stood at the doors! The Temple was aswarm.

I thought, I can run away from any husband in this place!

Gradually I realized a great commotion had come upon the Forum, the center of the city. I heard Jacob ordering the men to hurry out of the broad market street and into the back streets. My bearers were running. The curtains were brought shut by Jacob's hand so I couldn't see out.

News was being shouted out in Latin, in Greek, in Chaldean: Murder, Murder, Poison, Treachery.

I peeped out of the curtain.

People were weeping and cursing the Roman Gnaeus Calpurnius Piso, cursing him and his wife, Placina. Why? I didn't much like either one of them, but what was all this?

Jacob shouted again at my bearer to hurry.

We were rushed through the gates and into the vestibule of a sizable house no different in design or color than my own in Rome, only much smaller. I could see the same refinements, the distant peristyle, clusters of weeping slaves.

The litter was promptly set down and I stepped out, deeply concerned that they had not stopped me at the doors to wash my feet, as was proper. And my hair, it had all fallen down in waves.

But no one noticed me. I turned round and round, amazed at the Oriental curtains and tassels that hung over the doorways, the caged birds everywhere singing in their little prisons. The woven carpets lying all over the floor, one heaped upon another.

Two obvious ladies of the house came towards me.

'What's the matter!' I asked.

They were as fashionable as any rich woman in Rome, drenched in bracelets and wearing gold-trimmed gowns.

'I implore you,' said one of the women, 'for your own sake, go! Get back into the litter!'

They tried to push me inside the curtained cell of the litter. I wouldn't go. I became furious.

'I don't know where I am,' I said. 'And I don't know who you are! Now, stop pushing me!'

The Master of the House, or someone who certainly appeared to be such, came dashing towards me, with tears streaming down his cheeks and his short tousled gray hair a mess – torn as if in mourning. He'd ripped his long tunic. He'd smeared dirt on his face! He was old with a bent back and a massive head, loaded with skin and wrinkles.

'Your Father was my young colleague,' he said to me in Latin. He grabbed me by the arms. 'I dined in your house when you were a baby. I saw you when you crawled on all fours.'

'Tender,' I said quickly.

'Your Father and I studied in Athens, slept under the same roof.'

The women stood panic-stricken with their hands over their mouths.

'Your Father and I fought with Tiberius on his first campaign. We fought those lurid barbarians.'

'Very brave,' I said.

My black outer cloak fell down, revealing my unkempt wild long hair and plain dress. Nobody cared.

'Germanicus dined in this house because your Father spoke of me!'

'Oh dear, I see,' I said.

One of the women motioned for me to get in the litter. Where was Jacob? The old man wouldn't let me go.

113

'I stood with your Father and with Augustus when news came to us of the massacre of our troops in the Teutoburg Forest, that General Varus and all his men were slain. My sons fought with your brothers in the legions of Germanicus when he punished those Northern tribes! Oh, God!'

'Yes, very marvelous, indeed,' I said gravely.

'Get back in the litter and get out,' said one of the women.

The old man clutched me.

'We fought the madman, King Arminius!' said the old man. 'We could have won! Your brother Antony wasn't for giving up and coming back, was he?'

'I . . . no . . .'

'Get her out of here!' screamed a young patrician man, who had also been weeping. He came forward and shoved me towards the litter.

'Stand back, you imbecile!' I said to him. I slapped his face.

All this while, Jacob had been talking to the slaves, getting the scoop.

Jacob appeared beside me, as the gray-haired Greek sobbed and kissed my cheeks.

Jacob took over, guiding me into the litter.

'Germanicus has just been murdered,' Jacob said in my ear. 'Everybody loyal to him is convinced that the Emperor Tiberius put the Roman Governor Piso up to the murder. It was done with poison. Word is spreading through the city like fire.'

'Tiberius, you idiot!' I whispered, rolling my eyes. 'One cowardly step after another!'

I sank back into the darkness. The litter was being lifted.

Jacob went right on: 'Gnaeus Calpurnius Piso has allies here, naturally. Everybody's fighting everybody else. Settling scores. Mayhem. This Greek family traveled with Germanicus to Egypt. There are riots already. We go!'

'Farewell, friend,' I cried to the old Greek, as I was carried from the house. But I don't think he heard me. He had gone down on his knees. He cursed Tiberius. He screamed of suicide and begged for the dagger.

We were outside once more, hurrying through the street.

I lay askew in the litter, thinking dully in the darkness. Germanicus dead. Poisoned by Tiberius!

I knew that this recent trip of Germanicus to Egypt had made Tiberius very angry. Egypt was like no other Roman province. Rome was so dependent upon it for grain that Senators could not go there. But Germanicus had gone, 'just to see the ancient relics,' his friends had said in the streets of Rome.

'A mere excuse!' I thought in desperation. 'Where was the trial? The sentence? Poison!'

My bearers were running. People were screaming and sobbing around us. 'Germanicus, Germanicus! Give us back our beautiful Germanicus!'

Antioch had gone mad.

At last, we were obviously in a small narrow street that was little more than an alleyway – you know the kind, for a grid of them was uncovered in the ruins of Pompeii in Italy. You could smell the male urine collected in the jugs on the corner. You could smell food cooking from high chimneys. My bearers were running and stumbling over rough cobblestones.

Once we were all thrown to the side as a chariot came crashing through the narrow place, its wheels no doubt finding the ruts in the stone intended for it.

My head had hit the wall. I was furious and frightened. But Jacob said, 'Lydia, we are with you.'

I covered up all over with the cloak, so that only one eye allowed me to see the seams of light between the curtains on either side of me. I had my hand on my dagger.

116

The litter was set down. It was a cool indoor place. I heard Jacob's father, David, arguing. I knew no Hebrew. And I wasn't even sure that he was speaking in Hebrew.

Finally, Jacob took over in Greek, and I realized that they were purchasing outright a proper house for me which came with all fine appointments, including much fine furniture, left recently by a rich widow who had lived there alone, but alas, the slaves had been sold off. No slaves. This was a quick cash deal.

Finally, I heard Jacob say in Greek:

'You damn well better be telling me the truth.'

As the litter was lifted I beckoned to him. 'I owe you my life twice over now. That Greek family who was to shelter me? They are truly in danger?'

'Of course,' he said. 'When a riot starts, who cares? They went with Germanicus to Egypt! Piso's men know that! Anybody with the slightest excuse will attack, murder and plunder someone else. Look, fire.' He told the men to hurry.

'All right,' I said. 'Never say my real name again. From now on say this name: My name is Pandora. I am a Greek from Rome. I paid you to bring me here.'

117

'You have it, my dear Pandora,' he replied. 'You are some strong woman. The Deed to your new house is made up in a fake name with less charm. But the Deed verifies you are widowed, emancipated and a Roman Citizen. We'll get the Deed when we pay up the gold, which we won't do until we are in the house. And if the man does not give me that Deed with everything written out in full to protect you, I'll strangle him!'

'You're very clever, Jacob,' I said wearily.

On and on went this dark bouncing journey in the litter until at last it came to a halt. I could hear the metal key turning in the lock of the gate, and then we were brought into the large vestibule of the house itself.

I should have waited out of consideration for my guardians, but frantically I climbed out of this miserable little black veiled prison, throwing off the cloak and taking a deep breath.

We were in the broad vestibule of a fine house, with great charm to it and much ingenuity in its decoration.

Even now, my thoughts scattered, I saw the lion-head fountain right near the gate through which we'd just come, and I washed my feet in the cool of the water.

The receiving room, or atrium, was huge, and

beyond it I saw the rich couches of the dining room on the far side of a rather large enclosed garden – the peristyle.

It was not my massive ancient opulent old home on the Palatine Hill, which had grown new corridors and rooms over many generations, penetrating its broad gardens.

It was a bit too glossy. But it was grand. All the walls were freshly painted with a more Oriental bent, I think – more swirls and serpentine lines. How could I judge? I could have fainted from relief. Would people really leave me alone here?

There sat the desk in the atrium, and near it books! Along the porticoes flanking the garden, I saw the many doors; I looked up and saw the second-story windows closed on the porches. Splendor. Safety.

The mosaic floors were old; I knew the style, the festive figures of the Saturnalia on parade. They had to have been brought here from Italy.

Little real marble, plastered columns, but so many well-executed murals full of the requisite happy nymphs.

I went out into the soft wet grass of the peristyle and looked up at the blue sky.

I wanted only to breathe, but now came the moment of truth regarding my belongings. I was too dazed to ask about what was mine. And as it turned out, no such thing was necessary.

Jacob and David first did an entire inventory of the household furnishings they were purchasing for me, as I stood there staring at them in near disbelief at their patience with detail.

And when they'd found every room quite fine, and a bedchamber down the hall to the right, and a small open garden somewhere to the left, beyond the kitchen, they went upstairs, found things proper and then unloaded my possessions. Trunk followed trunk.

Then to my utter shock, Jacob's father, David, drew out a scroll and actually started taking a full inventory of everything that belonged to me, from hairpins to ink and gold.

Jacob was meantime sent on an errand!

I could see the hasty writing of my Father on this inventory that David read under his breath.

'Personal toilet articles,' David said in final summation of one portion of this examination. 'Clothes, one, two, three trunks – to the largest bedroom, go! Household plate to the kitchen. Books here?'

'Yes, please.' I was too shocked at his honesty and meticulousness to speak.

'Ah, so many books!'

'Fine, don't count them!' I said.

'I cannot, you see, these fragile . . .'

'Yes, I know. Carry on.'

'You want your ivory and ebony shelves assembled here in the front room?'

'Magnificent.'

I slumped down on the floor, only to be lifted at once by two helpful Asian slaves and settled in an amazingly soft cross-legged Roman chair. I was given a cup of fresh clean-smelling water. I drank it down, thought of blood. Closed my eyes.

'Ink, writing materials on the desk?' asked the old man.

'If you will,' I sighed.

'Now, everybody out,' said the old man, dispensing coins quickly and generously to these Asian slaves, who bowed from the waist and backed out of the room, nearly stumbling over each other.

I was about to try to form some sensible words of gratitude when a fresh brace of slaves rushed in – nearly colliding with the departing crew – carrying baskets of everything edible that a marketplace could yield, including at least nine kinds of bread, jugs of oil, melons, green vegetables and much smoked food that would last for days – fish, beef and exotic sea creatures dried out to look like parchment.

At once to the kitchen, save for a plate of olives and cheese and bread at once for the lady on that table to her left. Fetch the lady's wine, which her Father has sent.

Oh, how incredible. My Father's wine.

Then everyone was ordered out again with lots of coins freely given and the old man at once returned to his inventory.

'Jacob, come here, count for me this gold as I read off the list to you! Plate, coin, more coin, jewels of exceptional value? Coin, bars of gold. Yes . . .'

On and on they went, rushing at it.

Where had my Father hidden all this gold? I couldn't imagine it.

What was I going to do with it? Were they really going to let me keep this? They were honest men but this was such a fortune.

'You must wait until everyone is gone,' said David, 'and then hide this gold yourself in various places about the house. You will find such places. We cannot do that for you, for then we would know where it was. Your jewels? Some I leave here to be hidden for they are much too valuable to be flashed abroad among the populace in your first days.' He opened a casket of gems. 'See this ruby? It is superb. Look at the size of it. This can feed you for the rest of your life if sold to a honest man for half of its worth. Every jewel in this box is exceptional. I know jewels. These are hand-picked from the finest. See these pearls? Perfection.' He returned the ruby and the pearls to the casket and shut the lid.

'Yes,' I said weakly.

'Pearls, more gold, silver, plate . . .' he muttered. 'It's all here! We should take more care but . . .'

'Oh, no, you have done wonders,' I declared.

I stared at the bread and the wine in the cup. My Father's wine bottle. My Father's amphorae around the room.

'Pandora,' said Jacob, addressing me most seriously. 'Here in my hand is the Deed to this house. And another paper which describes your official entry into the port under your new made-up name, Julia, La, La, La and so forth. Pandora, we have to leave you.'

The old man shook his head and bit his lip.

'We have to sail for Ephesus, child,' he said. 'I am ashamed that I must leave you, but the harbor will soon be blocked!'

'There are ships on fire already in the harbor,' said Jacob under his breath. 'They've pulled down the statue of Tiberius in the Forum.'

'The transaction is closed,' said the old man

to me. 'The man who sold the house has never laid eyes on you and does not know your real name, and there is no evidence of it remaining here. Those were not his slaves who brought you here.'

'You've done miracles for me,' I said.

'You are on your own, my beautiful Roman princess,' Jacob said. 'It hurts my soul to leave you like this.'

'We must,' said the old man.

'Don't go out for three days,' said Jacob, coming near to me, about as near as he could, as if he even meant to break all the rules and kiss my cheek. 'There are enough legions here to quell this riot, but they will let it burn itself out, rather than slaughter Roman citizens. And forget those Greek friends. Their house is already an inferno.'

They turned to leave!

'Were you well paid for all this?' I asked. 'If not, take from my gold now, freely. I insist!'

'Don't even think of such things,' said the old man. 'But for your peace of mind, know this: your Father staked me twice after my ships were captured by pirates in the Adriatic. Your Father put his money in with mine and I made profits for both of us. The Greek owed your Father money. Worry about those matters no more. But we must go!'

'God be with you, Pandora,' said Jacob.

Jewels. Where were the jewels? I leapt up and opened the casket. There were hundreds of them, flawless, dazzlingly clear and exquisitely polished. I saw their value, their clarity and the care of the polishing. I took the big egg-shaped ruby David had shown to me and then another just like it and thrust them at the two men.

They put up their hands to say No.

'Oh, but you must,' I said. 'Give me this respect. Confirm for me that I am a free Roman woman and that I shall live as my Father told me to do! It will give me courage! Take this from me.'

David shook his head sternly, but Jacob took the ruby.

'Pandora, here, the keys. Follow us and lock the gate at the street and then the doors to the vestibule. Don't fear. There are lamps everywhere. Plenty of oil –'

'Go!' I said as they passed over the threshold. I locked the gate and held to the bars, staring at them. 'If you can't get out, if you need me, come back here,' I said.

'We have our own people here,' Jacob said soothingly. 'Thank you from my heart for the beautiful ruby, Pandora. You will survive. Go back in, bolt the doors.'

I made it to the chair but I did not sit in it. Rather I collapsed and prayed, '*Lares familiares* . . . spirits of the house, I should find your altar. Welcome me, please, I bring no ill will to anyone. I will heap your altar with flowers and light your fire. Give me patience. Let me . . . rest.'

Yet I did nothing but sit in shock on the floor, my hands limp, for hours as the daylight waned. As the strange little house grew dark.

A blood dream began, but I wouldn't have it. Not that alien Temple. Not the altar, no! Not the blood. I banished it and imagined I was home.

I was a little girl. Dream of that, I told myself, of listening to my eldest brother, Antony, talk of war in the North, driving the mad Germans back to the sea! He had so loved Germanicus. So had my other brothers. Lucius, the young one, he was so weak by nature. It broke my heart to think of him crying out for mercy as soldiers cut him down.

The Empire was the world. All that lay beyond was chaos and misery and struggle and strife. I was a soldier. I could fight. I dreamt I was putting on my armor. My brother said, 'I am so relieved to discover you are a man, I always thought so.'

I didn't waken till the following morning.

And then it was that grief and pain made

themselves known to me as never before.

Note this. Because I knew the full absurdity of Fate and Fortune and Nature more truly than a human can bear to know it. And perhaps the description of this, brief as it is, may give consolation to another. The worst takes its time to come, and then to pass.

The truth is, you cannot prepare anyone for this, nor conv an understanding of it through language. It must be known. And this I would wish on no one in the world.

I was alone. I went from room to room of this small house, banging upon the walls with my fists and crying with my teeth clenched, and whirling. There was no Mother Isis.

There were no gods. Philosophers were fools! Poets sang lies.

I sobbed and tore at my hair; I tore at my dress as naturally as if it had been a newborn custom. I knocked over chairs and tables.

At times I felt a huge exhilaration, a freedom from all falsehoods and conventions, all means by which a soul or body can be held hostage!

And then the awesome nature of this freedom spread itself out around me as if the house did not exist, as if the darkness knew no walls.

Three nights and days I spent in this agony.

I forgot to eat food. I forgot to drink water.

I never lighted a lamp. The moon nearing her fullness gave enough light to this meaningless labyrinth of little painted chambers.

Sleep was gone from me forever.

My heart beat fast. My limbs clenched, then slackened, only to clench again.

At times, I lay on the moist good Earth of the courtyard, for my Father, because no one had laid his body on the moist good Earth, as it should have been done, right after his death and before any funeral.

I knew suddenly why this disgrace was so important, his body rent with wounds and not placed on the Earth. I knew the gravity of this omission as few have ever known the meaning of anything. It was of the utmost importance because it did not matter at all!

Live, Lydia.

I looked at the small leafy trees of the garden. I felt a strange gratitude that I had opened human eyes in this darkness on Earth long enough to see such things.

I quoted Lucretius:

'That which comes from Heaven ascends to Heaven'?

Madness!

Alas, as I said, I wandered, crawled, wept and cried for three nights and days.

4

Finally, one morning, when the sun came spilling down through the open roof, I looked at the objects in the room and I realized I didn't know what they were, or what they'd been made for. I didn't know their common names. I was removed from their definitions. I didn't even know this place.

I sat up and realized I was looking at the Lararium, the shrine of the household gods.

This was the dining room of course, and those were the couches, and there the glorious conjugal bed!

The Lararium was a high three-sided shrine, a little temple with three pediments, and inside stood figures of old household gods. No one in this profane city had even taken them away with the dead woman.

The flowers were dead. The fire had simply

gone out. No one had quenched it with wine, as should have been done.

On hands and knees I crawled in my torn dress around the garden of the peristyle, gathering flowers for these gods. I found the wood and made their sacred fire.

I stared at them. I stared for hours. It seemed I would never move again.

Night fell. 'Don't sleep,' I whispered. 'Keep watch with the night! They wait for you by dark, those Egyptians! The moon, look, it's almost full, only a night or so from being full.'

But the worst of my agony had passed and I was exhausted, and sleep rose to embrace me. Sleep rose as if to say 'Care no more.'

The dream came.

I saw men in gilded robes. 'You will be taken now in the sanctum.' But what's there? I didn't want to see. 'Our Mother, our beloved Mother of Sorrows,' said the Priest. The paintings on the walls were rows upon rows of Egyptians in profile, and words made of pictures. Myrrh burned in this place.

'Come,' said those who held me. 'All the impurities have gone from you now, and you will partake of the sacred Fount.'

I could hear a woman crying and moaning. I peeped into the great room before I entered it.

There they were, the King and the Queen on their thrones, the King still and staring as in the last dream, and the Queen struggling against her golden fetters. She wore the crown of Upper and Lower Egypt. And pleated linen. Her hair was not a wig but real plaits. She cried and her white cheeks were stained in red. Red stained her necklace and her breasts. She looked soiled and ignominious.

'My Mother, my goddess,' I said. 'But this is an abomination.'

I forced myself to wake.

I sat up and I laid my hand on the Lararium, and looked at the spiderwebs in the trees of the garden, made visible by the climbing sun.

I thought I heard people whispering in the ancient Egyptian tongue.

I was not going to allow this! I would not go mad.

Enough! The only man I had ever loved, my Father, said, 'Live.'

It was time for action. To get up and get going. I was suddenly all strength and purpose.

My long nights of mourning and weeping had been equivalent to the initiation in the Temple; death had been the intoxicant; comprehension had been the transformation.

It was over now, and the meaningless world

was tolerable and need not be explained. And never would it be, and how foolish I had ever been to think so.

The facts of my predicament warranted action.

I poured out a cup of wine, and took it with me to the front gate.

The city seemed quiet. People walked to and fro, casting their eyes away from a half-dressed, ragged woman in her vestibule.

At last a workman trudging under his burden of bricks.

I thrust forth the wine. 'I have been ill for three days,' I said. 'What of the death of Germanicus? How goes it in the city?'

The man was so grateful for the wine. Labor had made him old. His arms were thin. His hands shook.

'Madam, thank you,' he said. He drained the cup, as if he could not stop himself. 'Our Germanicus was laid out in the public square for all to see. How beautiful he was. Some compared him to the great Alexander. People could not determine. Had he been poisoned or not? Some said Yes, some said No.

'His soldiers loved him. Governor Piso, thank the gods, is not here and dares not come back. Germanicus's wife, the gracious

Agrippina, has the ashes of Germanicus in an urn she carries next to her breast. She sails for Rome, seeking justice for Tiberius.'

He handed me the cup. 'I humbly thank you.'

'The city is as usual again.'

'Oh, yes, what could stop this glorified marketplace?' he declared. 'Business goes on as always. The loyal soldiers of Germanicus keep the peace, waiting for justice. They will not let the murderous Piso return, and Sentius gathers to himself here all who served under Germanicus. The city is happy. The flame burns for Germanicus. If there is war, it won't be here. Don't worry.'

'Thank you, you have helped me marvelously much.'

I took the cup, locked the gate, shut the door and went into action.

Nibbling on enough bread to give me strength, and murmuring aloud the common sense of Lucretius, I surveyed the house. It had a large luxurious bath on the right side of the courtyard. Full of light. Water flowed steadily from the seashells of the nymphs into the plastered basin, and the water was fine. There was no need to light a fire for it.

In the bedchamber were my clothes.

Roman dresses were simple, as you know,

just long shifts or tunics, and we wore two or three of them, plus an outdoor cover-up tunic, the stola, and finally the palla, or mantle, which hung to the ankles and belted below the breasts.

I chose the finest tunics, composing three layers of gossamer silk, and then a brilliant red palla that covered me from head to toe.

In all my life, I had never had to put on my own sandals. This was hysterically funny and annoying!

All my toilet articles had been laid out on tables which held burnished mirrors. What a mess!

I sat down in one of the many gilded chairs, pushed the burnished metal mirror close, and tried to work with the paints as my slaves had always done.

I managed to darken my eyebrows, but my horror of the painted Egyptian eyes stopped me. I rouged my lips, put some white powder on my face, but that was it. I couldn't attempt powdering my arms, as would have been done for me in Rome.

I don't know what I looked like. Now I had to braid this damned hair, and I managed it, and fixed the braids in a big coil on the back of my head. I used enough pins for twenty women. Dragging down the loose curls around my face, on my forehead and cheeks, I saw in the mirror a Roman woman, modest and acceptable, I thought, her brown hair parted in the middle, her eyebrows black and her lips rosy red.

Gathering up all this drapery was the biggest nuisance. I attempted to match length with length. I tried to get the silk stola straight and then belt it tightly beneath my breasts. I mean, all this folding, all this drapery and fastening. I'd always had slave girls around me. Finally with two undertunics and a long, fine red stola, I snatched up a silk palla, a very large one, fringed and decorated all over with gold.

I put on rings, bracelets. But I intended to hide under this mantle as much as possible. I could remember my Father cursing every day of his life that he had to wear the toga, the official outer garment of the highborn Roman male. Well, only prostitutes wore togas. At least I didn't have to cope with that.

I headed straight for the slave markets.

Jacob was right about the population here. The city was filled with men and women of all nations. Many women walked in pairs, arm in arm.

Loose Greek cloaks were entirely acceptable here, and so were long exotic Phoenician or Babylonian gowns, both for men and women.

Long hair among the men was common, as were heavy beards. Some women went about in tunics no longer than a man's. Others were completely veiled, revealing only the eyes, as they walked, accompanied by guards and servants.

The streets were cleaner than they might have been in Rome, the sewage flowing to wider gutters in the center and more swiftly to its destination.

Long before I reached the Forum, or the central plaza, I had passed three different doors in which rich courtesans stood arguing sarcastically over price with wealthy young Greeks and Romans.

One said, as I passed, to a handsome young man, 'You want me in bed? You're dreaming. Any of the girls you can have, as I told you. If you want me, go home and sell everything you own!'

Rich Romans in their full togas stood at the corner wine shops, and respected my quick glance away with a simple nod as I passed.

Pray none of them would recognize me! It was not a likely thing, by any means, and we were so far from Rome, and I had lived so long in my Father's house, happily reprieved by him from banquets and suppers, and even ceremonial gatherings.

The Forum was far larger than I had remembered from my brief glimpse. When I came to the edge of it and beheld the huge square flooded with sun, flanked on all sides with porticoes or Temples or Imperial buildings, I was amazed.

In the canopied markets, everything was for sale, silversmiths grouped together, the weavers in their own place, the silk merchants in a row, and I could see down the side street that came in to my right that it was dedicated to the sale of slaves – the better slaves, who might never have to go to an auction block.

Far away I saw the high masts of the ships. I could smell the river. There stood the Temple of Augustus, its fires burning, its uniformed Legionnaires in lazy readiness.

I was hot and anxious, because my mantle kept slipping, in fact, all this silk seemed to slip and to slide, and there were many open wine gardens where women gathered in groups, chatting. I could have found a place near enough to someone to have a drink.

But I had to have a household. I had to have loyal slaves.

Now, in Rome, of course I had never gone to a slave market. I would never have had to do such a thing. Besides, we had so many families of slaves on our land in Tuscany and in Rome that we seldom if ever bought a new slave. On the contrary, my Father had a habit of inheriting the decrepit and wise from his friends, and we had often teased my Father about the Academy, which did nothing in the slaves' garden but argue about history.

But now I had to act the shrewd woman of the world. I inspected every quality household slave on display, quickly settled upon a pair of sisters, very young and very frightened that they were going to be auctioned at noon and go to a brothel. I sent for stools and we sat together.

We talked.

They came from a small fine family household in Tyre; they'd been born slaves. They knew Greek and Latin well. They spoke Aramaic. They were angelic in their sweetness.

They had immaculate hands. They demonstrated every skill I required. They knew how to dress hair, paint a face, cook food. They rattled off recipes for Eastern dishes of which I'd never heard; they named different pomades, rouges. One of them flushed with fear, and then said, 'Madam, I can paint your face for you, and very quickly and perfectly!'

I knew this meant I had made a mess of the job.

I also knew that, coming from a small household, they were far more versatile than our slaves at home.

I bought them both, the answer to their prayers; I demanded clean tunics of modest length for both of them, got the tunics, made of blue linen, though they weren't very fine, then found a roaming merchant with an armful of pallae. I brought each sister a blue mantle. They were in such happiness. They were reticent and wanted their heads covered.

I had no doubt of them. They would have died for me.

It didn't occur to me that they were starving until, while searching for other slaves, I heard a nasty slave dealer remind an impudent educated Greek that he would get no food until he was sold.

'Horrors,' I said. 'You girls, you're probably hungry. Go to the cookshop in the Forum. Look down the street. See there, the scattering of benches and tables.'

'Alone?' they said in dismay.

'Listen, girls. I have no time to feed you like birds from my hand. Don't look any man in the eye; eat and drink what you want.' I gave them a seemingly shocking amount of money. 'And don't leave the cookshop till I come for you. If a man comes to you, pretend to be in terror, bow your heads and protest as best you can that you don't speak his language. If worst comes to worst, go to the Temple of Isis.'

They ran together down the narrow street towards the distant banquet, their mantles such a beautiful blue as they ballooned in the breeze that I can see it even now, the color of the sky streaking through the tight sweaty crowds beneath the jumble of canopies. Mia and Lia. Not hard to remember, but I could not tell them apart.

A low derisive laughter surprised me. It was the Greek slave who had just been threatened with starvation by his Master.

He said to his Master:

'All right, starve me. And then what will you have to sell? A sickened and dying man, instead of an unusual and great scholar.'

Unusual and great scholar!

I turned and looked at the man. He sat on a stool and did not rise for me. He wore nothing but a filthy loincloth, which was plain stupidity on the part of the merchant, but this neglect certainly revealed that this slave was one very handsome man, beautiful in face, with soft brown hair and long almond-shaped green eyes, and a sarcastic expression to his pretty mouth. He was maybe thirty years old, perhaps a little younger. He was fit for his age, as Greeks like to be, having a sound musculature.

His brown hair was filthy, had been hacked off, and around his neck by a rope was the most wretched small board I ever beheld, crowded with tiny cramped letters in Latin.

Pulling up the mantle again, I stepped up very close to his gorgeous naked chest, a little amused by his audacious stare, and tried to read all this.

It seemed he could have taught all philosophy, all languages, all mathematics, could sing everything, knew every poet, could prepare whole banquets, was patient with children, had known military service with his Roman Master in the Balkans, could perform as an armed guard, was obedient and virtuous and had lived all his life in Athens in one house.

I read this a bit scornfully. He glared at me impertinently when he saw this scorn. Impudently, he folded his arms just below this little plaque. He leaned back against the wall.

Suddenly I saw why the merchant, hovering near, had not made the Greek rise. The Greek had only one good leg. The left leg below the knee was made of well-carved ivory, complete with carefully engraved foot and sandal. Perfect toes. Of course it had been pieced together, this

fine ivory leg and foot, but in three proportion-
ate sections, each girded with decorative work,
and separate parts for the feet, nails defined and
sandal straps exquisitely carved.

I had never seen such a false limb, such a surrender to artifice rather than a meager attempt to
imitate nature.

'How did you lose your leg?' I asked him in
Greek. No answer. I pointed to the leg. No
answer.

I asked again in Latin. Still no answer.

The slave trader was rising on his toes in his
anxiety and wringing his hands.

'Mistress, he can keep records, run any business; he writes in perfect hand, keeps honest
numbers.'

Hmmm. So no mention of tutoring children?
I did not look like a wife and mother. Not
good.

The Greek sneered and looked away. He said
softly under his breath in piercing Latin that if I
did spend money for him, I was spending it for
a dead man. His voice was soft and beautiful,
though weary and full of contempt, his enunci-
ation unaffected and refined.

I threw off all patience. I spoke quickly in
Greek.

'Learn from me, you arrogant Athenian

idiot!' I said, red in the face, and furious to be so misjudged both by a slave and a slave dealer. 'If you can write Greek and Latin at all, if you have in fact studied Aristotle and Euclid, whose name you misspelled, by the way, if you have been schooled in Athens and have seen battle in the Balkans, if even half of this great epic is true, why wouldn't you want to belong to one of the most keenly intelligent women you'll ever meet, who'll treat you with dignity and respect in exchange for your loyalty? What do you know of Aristotle and Plato that I don't? I've never struck a slave in my life. You pass up the one mistress to whom your loyalty might earn you any reward of which you could dream. That tablet is a pack of lies, isn't it?'

The slave was stunned, but not angered. He sat forward, trying to appraise me further, without being obvious. The merchant gestured furiously for the slave to rise to his feet, which the slave did, giving him an admirable height over me. His legs were sound and strong up to the ivory limb.

'What about telling me the real truth as to what you can do?' I said, switching to Latin.

I turned to the slave dealer. 'Get me a pen to correct this, the spelling of these names. If this man has any chance of becoming a teacher, these misspellings destroy it. He looks like a fool for writing such.'

'I didn't have space enough to write!' declared the slave suddenly, whispering in perfect Latin fury. He bent towards me, as if I should understand.

'Look at this little tablet, if you're so keenly intelligent! Do you realize the ignorance of this dealer here. He has not sense enough to know he has an emerald, and thinks it a piece of green glass! This is wretched. I crammed here what generalities I could.'

I laughed. I was seduced and thrilled. I couldn't stop laughing. This was too funny! The slave merchant was confused. Chastise the slave and lower his value? Or let the two of us work this out?

'What was I to do,' he demanded in the same confidential whisper, only this time in Greek, 'shout to every man passing, "Here sits a great teacher, here sits a philosopher!"?' He grew a little calm, having thus released this rage. 'The names of my grandfathers are carved on the Acropolis at Athens,' he said.

The merchant was mystified.

But I was so obviously delighted and interested.

My mantle slipped again and I gave it a hard

jerk. These clothes. Had no one ever told me silk slides on silk?

'And what about Ovid?' I said, taking a deep breath. I almost laughed myself into tears. 'You wrote Ovid's name here. Ovid. Is Ovid popular here? Nobody would dare write that on your card in Rome, I can tell you. You know, I don't even know if Ovid is still alive, and it's a shame. Ovid taught me to kiss when I was ten years old, when I read the *Amores*. You ever read the *Amores?*'

His entire demeanor altered. He softened and I could see he was just on the verge of hope, hope that I might be a good mistress for him. But he couldn't let himself believe it.

The merchant was waiting for the slightest signal as to what he might do. Clearly he could follow our exchanges.

'Look, you insolent one-legged slave,' I said. 'If I thought you could even read Ovid to me in the evenings, I'd buy you in a moment. But this tablet here makes you a glorified Socrates and Alexander the Great smashed in one. In what war in the Balkans did you carry arms? Why are you dumped in the hands of this lowly merchant rather than taken at once to some fine house? How could anyone believe all this? If blind Homer had sung such a preposterous tale, people would have gotten up and left the tavern.'

He grew angry, frustrated.

The merchant put out his hand in warning, as if to control the man.

'What the hell happened to your leg?' I asked. 'How did you lose it? Who made you this glorious replacement?'

Lowering his voice to an angry yet eloquent whisper, the slave declared slowly and patiently:

'I lost it in a boar hunt, with my Roman Master. He saved my life. We hunted often. It was on Pentelikon, the mountain . . .'

'I know where Pentelikon is, thank you,' I said.

His facial expressions were elegant. He was utterly confused. He licked his parched lips and said:

'Just make this merchant fetch the parchment and the ink.' He spoke his Latin with such beauty, the beauty of an actor or rhetorician, yet with no effort. 'I'll write the *Amores* of Ovid from memory for you,' he said, gently pleading through clenched teeth, which is no mean feat. 'And then I'll copy out all of Xenophon's history of the Persians for you, if you have the time, in Greek, of course! My Master treated me like a son; I fought with him, studied with him, learned with him. I wrote his letters for him. His education I made my education because he wanted it so.'

'Ah,' I said in proud relief.

He looked the full gentleman now, angered, caught in impossible circumstance yet dignified, and reasoning with just enough spirit to strengthen his own soul.

'And in bed? Can you do it in bed?' I asked. I can't say what rage or desperation prompted this question.

He was genuinely shocked. Good sign. His eyes really widened. He furrowed his brow.

Meantime the slave trader emerged with the table, stool, parchment, ink, and set it all down on the hot cobblestones.

'Here, write,' he said to the slave. 'Make letters for this woman. Add sums. Or I'll kill you and sell your leg.'

I broke again into helpless laughing. I looked at the slave, who still stood dazed. He broke away from my gaze to cast a disdainful look on the merchant.

'Are you safe around the slave girls?' I said patronizingly 'Are you a lover of boys?'

'I am completely trustworthy!' the slave said. 'I am not capable of crimes for any Master.'

'And what if I desire you in my bed? I'm the

Mistress of the house, twice widowed and on my own, and I am Roman.'

His face darkened. I couldn't name the emotions that seemed to pass over his expression, the sadness, indecision, confusion and ultimate perplexity that transformed him.

'Well?' I asked.

'Let's put it this way, Madam. You would be much more pleased with my recitation of Ovid than with any attempted enactment of his verses by me.'

'You like boys,' I said with a nod.

'I was born a slave, Madam. I made do with boys. I know nothing else. And I need neither.' His face was crimson now, and he had lowered his eyes.

Lovely Athenian modesty.

I gestured for him to sit down.

This he did with amazing simplicity and grace, considering the circumstances: the heat, the dirt, crowds, the fragile stool and the wobbling table.

He picked up the pen and quickly wrote in flawless Greek, 'Have I foolishly offended this great lady of learning and exceptional patience? Have I brought about, through rashness, my own doom?' He wrote on in Latin, 'Does Lucretius tell us the truth when he says that

148

death is nothing to fear?' He thought for a moment, and then he wrote in Greek again, 'Are Virgil and Horace really equal to our great poets? Do the Romans truly believe this, or only hope it is true, knowing their achievements shine in other arts?'

I read this all very thoughtfully, smiling most agreeably. I had fallen in love with him. I looked at his thin nose, his cleft chin, and I looked into the green eyes that looked up at me.

'How did you come to this?' I asked. 'A slave shop in Antioch? You're Athenian-bred, just as you say.'

He tried to stand to answer. I pushed him to sit down.

'I can tell you nothing of that,' he said. 'Only that I was much beloved by my Master, that my Master died in his bed with his family around him. And that here I am.'

'Why didn't he set you free in his will?'

'He did, Madam, and with means.'

'What happened?'

'I can tell you no more.'

'Why not? Who sold you, why?'

'Madam,' he said, 'please place a value upon my loyalty to a house in which I served all my life. I cannot speak more. If I become your servant, you will have the same loyalty from me.

Your house will become my house, and sacred to me. What happens within your walls will remain within your walls. I speak of virtue and kindness in my Master because this is proper to say. Let me say no more.'

Sublime old-Greek morality.

'Write more, hurry!' said the slave merchant.

'Be quiet,' I told him. 'He's written quite enough.'

The handsome brown-haired slave, this enticingly beautiful one-legged man, had fallen into some deep pit of woe and looked towards the distant Forum, flash of figures back and forth over the mouth of the street.

'What would I do as a free man?' he said to me, looking up at me from a position of utter careless loneliness. 'Copy all day for a pittance at the booksellers? Write letters for coins? My Master risked his own life to save me from that boar. In battle I served under Tiberius in Illyricum, where with some fifteen legions he put down all revolts. I chopped the head off a man to save my Master. What am I now?'

I was filled with pain.

'What am I now?' he repeated the question.

'If I were free, I would live hand to mouth, and when I slept in some filthy tenement, my ivory leg would be severed and stolen!'

I gasped and put my hand to my lips.

His eyes filled with tears as he looked at me, and his voice became all the more softer, yet sharply articulate:

'Oh, I could teach philosophy beneath the arches out there, you know, prattle on about Diogenes, and pretend that I liked wearing rags, as do his followers these days. What a circus out there, have you seen it? I have never seen so many philosophers in my life as in this city! Take a look when you go back. You know what it takes to teach philosophy here? You have to lie. You have to fling meaningless words as fast as you can at young people, and brood when you can't answer, and make up nonsense and ascribe it to the old Stoics.'

He broke off, and tried to gain command of himself.

I was almost in tears as I looked down at him.

'But you see, I have no skill at lying,' he said. 'That has been my undoing with you, Great Lady.'

I was shattered inside, my wounds silently opened. The nerve which had carried me out of confinement was ebbing away But surely he saw my tears.

He looked towards the Forum again.

'I dream of an honorable Master or Mistress,

a house with honor. Can a slave through the contemplation of honor thereby have honor? The law says not. So any slave called to testify in a court trial must be tortured, for he has no honor! But reason says otherwise. I have learned and I can teach both bravery and honor. And yes, all of this tablet is true. I didn't have time or opportunity to temper its boastful style.'

He bowed his head and looked again towards the Forum, as though towards the lost world. He drew himself up in the chair, for bravery's sake. Again, he tried to stand.

'No, sit,' I said.

'Madam,' he said, 'if you seek my services for a house of ill repute, let me tell you now . . . if it is to torture and force young girls such as those you just purchased, if you order me to advertise their charms abroad, I won't do it. It is as dishonorable to me as to steal or to lie. Why do you want me?'

The tears were halted, merely resting between him and his vision of the world around him. His face was serene.

'Do I look as if I am a whore?' I asked him with shock. 'Yea gods, I wore all my best clothes. I'm doing my best to look revoltingly respectable in all these fancy silks! Do you see cruelty in my eyes? Can't you believe that it is perhaps the tempered soul that survives grief? One need not fight on a battlefield to have courage.'

'No, Madam, no!' he said. He was so very sorry.

'Then why fling these insults at me now?' I said, full of hurt. 'And no, I agree with you, what you've written there, our Roman poets are not the equals of the Greeks. I don't know our destiny as an Empire and this weighs as heavily on me as it ever did on my Father and his Father! Why? I don't know!' I turned as if to go, but I had really no intention of going! His insults had simply gone too far.

He bent towards me over the writing table.

'Madam,' he said whispering even lower and with greater solicitude. 'Forgive me my rash words. You are absolutely a paradox. Your face is eccentrically painted, and I think the lip rouge is not properly set. You have rouge on your teeth. You have no powder on your arms. You wear three dresses of silk and I can see through all of them! Your hair is in two barbarian-style braids lying on your shoulders, and you are raining little silver and gold pins galore. Look at these little pins falling. Madam, you will be hurt by these pins. Your mantle, more appropriate for evening, has fallen on the ground. Your hems drag in the dirt.'

Not missing a beat of his speech, he reached down deftly and picked up the palla, standing at once to offer it to me, coming round the table with a heavy shift of his leg, to lay the palla on my shoulders.

'You speak with miraculous speed, and stunning gibes,' he went on, 'yet you carry a huge dagger in your girdle. It should be hidden on your forearm under your mantle. And your purse. You take gold out of it to pay the girls. It's huge, carelessly visible. And your hands, your hands are beautiful, fine as your Latin and your Greek, but they are deeply creased with dirt as though you have been digging in the Earth itself.'

I smiled. I had stopped my tears.

'You are very observant,' I said cheerfully. I was charmed. 'Why did I have to cut you so deeply to find your soul? Why can't we simply reveal ourselves to one another? I need a strong steward, a guardian who can bear arms, run my house and protect it because I am alone. Can you really see through all this silk?'

He nodded. 'Well, now that the mantle is over your shoulders and hiding the . . . the dagger and the girdle –' He blushed. Then as I smiled at him, trying to regain my calm, trying to fight back the engulfing darkness that would take away all confidence from me, all faith in any task, he spoke on.

'Madam, we learn to hide our souls because we are betrayed by others. But I would entrust to you my soul! I know it, if you would reconsider your judgment! I can protect you, I can run your house. I will not molest your little girls. But mark, for all my time fighting in Illyricum I have one leg. I came home from three years of bloody constant battle to lose it to a boar because a spear, poorly tempered and made, broke as I thrust it into the boar.'

'What's your name?' I asked.

'Flavius,' he answered. This was a Roman name.

'Flavius,' I said.

'Madam, the palla is slipping again from your head. And these little pins, they are sharp, they are everywhere, they'll hurt you.'

'Never mind that,' I said, though I let him drape me again properly as if he were Pygmalion, and I his Galatea. He used the tips of his fingers. But the mantle was already soiled.

'Those girls,' I said, 'whom you glimpsed. They are my household, as of the past half-hour. You have to be their loving master. But if you lie in any woman's bed under my roof, the bed had better be mine. I am flesh and blood!'

He nodded, at a total loss for words.

I pulled open my purse and took out what I thought to pay, a reasonable price in Rome, I thought, where slaves were always bragging about how much they had cost. I laid down the gold, oblivious to the imprint of the coin, only gauging the value.

The slave stared at me with ever increasing fascination, then his eyes whipped the merchant.

The slimy, merciless, weasling slave trader puffed up like a toad and told me this priceless Greek scholar was to be auctioned for a high price. Several rich men had expressed interest. An entire school class was to question him within the hour. Roman officers had sent their stewards to inspect him.

'I have no more stamina for it,' I said, and reached in my purse again.

At once, my new slave Flavius put his hand out gently to prevent me.

He glared at the merchant with great authority and fearless contempt.

'For a man with one leg!' said Flavius between his teeth. 'You thief! You charge my Mistress that, here in Antioch, where slaves are so plentiful the ships take them on to Rome, for it's the only way to cut their losses!'

I was quite impressed. All had gone so well. The darkness flowed back away from me, and there seemed for the moment a divine meaning in the warmth of the sun.

'You cheat my Mistress and you know it! You're the scum of the Earth!' he went on. 'Madam, do we ever purchase from this scoundrel again? I advise never!'

The slave trader broke into an inane smile, a hideous grimace of cowardice and stupidity, bowed and gave me back a third of what I'd given him.

I could hardly keep from another burst of laughing. I had to fetch the mantle from the ground again. Flavius did it. This time, I knotted it properly in front.

I looked at the gold which had been returned, scooped it up, entrusted it to Flavius and off we went.

When we had plunged into the thick crowd in the center of the Forum I did laugh and laugh at the whole affair.

'Well, Flavius, you're protecting me already, saving me money, giving me excellent advice. If there were more men like you in Rome, the world might be better for it.'

He was choked up. He couldn't talk. It was an effort to whisper:

'Lady, you have on trust my body and soul forever.'

I went up on tiptoe and kissed his cheek. I realized that his nakedness, the filth of the loin-cloth, all this was a disgrace he bore without a sign of protest.

'Here,' I said, giving him some money. 'Take the girls home, put them to work, then you go to the baths. Get clean. Get Roman clean. Have a boy if you want. Have two. Then buy fine clothes for yourself, not slave clothes, mind you, but clothes that you would buy for a rich young Roman Master!'

'Madam, please hide that purse!' he said as he took the coins. 'And what is my Mistress's name? To whom shall I say I belong, if asked.'

'To Pandora of Athens,' I said. 'Though you shall have to fill me in on the current state of my birthplace, because I have never actually been there. But a Greek name serves me well. Now go. See, the girls watch!'

Lots of people were watching. Oh, this red silk! And Flavius was such a splendid figure of a male.

I kissed him again, and whispered in his ear, calculatingly, devil that I am, 'I need you, Flavius.'

He looked down at me, awestruck. 'I am

yours forever, Madam,' he whispered.

'Are you sure you can't do with me in bed!'

'Oh, believe me, I have tried!' he confessed, flushing again.

I made my hand into a fist and punched his muscular arm.

'Very well,' I said.

The damsels had already risen, at my gesture. They knew I sent him to them.

I gave him my key, the directions to my house, described the particularities of its gate, and the old bronze lion fountain right inside the gate.

'And you, Madam?' he asked. 'You're going in the crowd unaccompanied? Madam, the purse is huge! It's full of gold.'

'Wait till you see the gold in the house,' I said. 'Appoint yourself the only one who can open chests, and then hide them in obvious places. Replace all the furniture I've smashed in my . . . my solitude. There are many pieces stored in rooms above.'

'Gold in the house!' He was alarmed. 'Chests of gold!'

'Now, don't worry about me,' I said, 'I know where to seek help now. And if you betray me, if you steal my legacy and I find my house ruined when I return, I suppose I shall have deserved it. Cover up the chests of gold with carpets. The place has heaps of little Persian carpets. Look upstairs. And tend to the Shrine!'

'I shall do everything you ask and more.'

'So I thought. A man who cannot lie cannot steal. Now the sun is intolerable here. Go to the girls. They wait.'

I turned.

He caught me by coming round in front of me.

'Madam, there is something I must tell you.'

'What!' I said with an ominous face. 'Not that you're a eunuch,' I said. 'Eunuchs don't grow muscles in their arms and legs like that.'

'No,' he said. Then he took on a sudden gravity. 'Ovid, you spoke of Ovid. Ovid is dead. Ovid died two years ago in the wretched town of Tomis on the upper rim of the Black Sea. It was a miserable choice of exile, a barbarian outpost.'

'No one told me this. What a revolting silence.' I threw up my hands over my face. The mantle fell. He retrieved it. I scarce noticed. 'I had so prayed that Tiberius would let Ovid come back to Rome!' I told myself I had no time to stop for this. 'Ovid. No time to weep for him now . . .'

'His books are no doubt plentiful here,'

Flavius said. 'They are very easily found in Athens.'

'Good, perhaps you will have time to find some for me. Now, I'm off; pins or tumbled braids or sliding mantle, I do not care. And don't look so worried. When you leave the house, just lock up the girls and the gold.'

When I finally turned around he was making his way rather gracefully towards the girls. The sun rippled prettily on his well-muscled back. His hair was curly and brown, rather like my own. He stopped for one moment when a vendor attacked him with an armful of cheaply made tunics, cloaks and whatnot, more than likely stolen goods, full of dye that would run in the first rain, but who knows? He bought a tunic hastily and slipped it over his head, and purchasing a red sash, tied it around his waist.

Such a transformation. The tunic went halfway to his knees. That must have been a great relief to him, to have on something clean. I should have thought of this before I left him. Stupid.

I admired him. Naked or clothed, you can't carry such beauty and dignity unless you have been cherished. He wore the raiment of the affection bestowed on him and inscribed in the art of his ivory leg.

161

In our brief encounter, a bond had been forged forever.

He greeted the girls. With his arms around them, he guided them out of the crowd.

I went straight to the Temple of Isis, and thereby, unwittingly, took the first firm step towards a larcenous immortality, an inglorious and unearned supernature, a never ending and utterly useless doom.

5

As soon as I entered the Temple Compound I was received by several rich Roman women, who welcomed me generously. They were all properly painted with white on their arms and their faces, well-drawn eyebrows, lip color – all the details of which I'd made a hash that morning.

I explained that though I had means, I was on my own. They were for helping me in every way. When they heard I had been actually initiated in Rome, they were in awe.

'Thank Mother Isis they didn't discover you and execute you,' said one of the Roman women.

'Go in and see the Priestess,' they said. Many of them had not yet undergone the secret ceremonies and were waiting to be called by the goddess for this momentous event.

There were many other women here, some

Egyptian, some Babylonian perhaps. I could only guess. Jewels and silks were the order of the day. Fancy painted gold borders lined their mantles; some wore simple dresses.

But it seemed to me that all of them spoke Greek.

I couldn't bring myself to enter the Temple. I looked up and saw in my mind our crucified Priests in Rome.

'Thank God you were not identified,' said one.

'Quite a few people fled to Alexandria,' said another.

'I raised no protest,' I said dismally.

There came a chorus of sympathy. 'How could you, under Tiberius? Believe me, every one who could escaped.'

'Don't be laden with misery,' said a young blue-eyed Greek woman, very properly dressed.

'I'd fallen away from the worship,' I said.

Again came a comforting round of soft voices.

'Go in now,' said one woman, 'and ask to pray in the very sanctuary of Our Mother. You are an initiate. Most of us here are not.'

I nodded.

I went up the steps of the Temple and entered inside it.

I paused to shake from my mantle the mundane, that is, all the trivia I had discussed. My mind was focused upon the goddess, and desperate to believe in her. I loathed my hypocrisy, that I used this Temple and this worship, but then it didn't seem significant. My despair of the three nights had penetrated too deep.

What a shock awaited me as I found myself inside.

The Temple was far more ancient than our Temple in Rome, and Egyptian paintings covered its walls. A shiver at once went through me. The columns were in the Egyptian style, not fluted but smoothly round, and brightly painted in orange, and rising to giant lotus leaves at the capitals. The smell of the incense was overpowering and I could hear music emanating from the Sanctuary. I could hear the thin notes of the lyre, and of the wires of the sistrum being plucked, and I could hear a litany being chanted.

But this was a thoroughly Egyptian place, which enveloped me as firmly as my blood dreams. I almost fainted.

The dreams came back – the deep paralytic sense of being in some secret Sanctuary in Egypt, my soul swallowed within another body!

The Priestess came to me. This too was a shock.

In Rome, her dress would have been purely Roman, and she might have worn a small exotic headdress, a little cap to her shoulders, perhaps.

But this woman wore Egyptian clothes of pleated linen, in the old style, and she wore a magnificent Egyptian headdress and wig, the broad mass of long black braids falling down stiffly over her shoulders. She looked as extravagant perhaps as Cleopatra had ever looked, for all I knew.

I had only heard stories of Julius Caesar's love of Cleopatra, then her affair with Mark Antony and Cleopatra's death. All that was before my birth.

But I knew that Cleopatra's fabulous entrance into Rome had much affrighted the old Roman sense of morality. I had always known the old Roman families feared Egyptian magic. In the recent punitive Roman massacre, which I've described, there was a lot of shouting about license and lust; but beneath it, there had been an unspoken fear of the mystery and the power hidden behind the Temple doors.

And now as I gazed at this Priestess, at her painted eyes, I felt in my soul this fear. I knew it. Of course this woman seemed to have stepped from the dreams, but it was not that which struck me so much, for after all, what are dreams? This was an Egyptian woman – wholly alien and inscrutable to me.

My Isis had been Greco-Roman. Even her statue in the Roman Sanctuary had been clothed in a gorgeously draped Greek dress and her hair had been done softly in the old Greek style, with waves around her face. She had held her sistrum and an urn. She had been a Romanized goddess.

Perhaps the same had happened with the goddess Cybele in Rome. Rome swallowed things and made them Roman.

In a very few centuries, though I had no thought of it then – how could I – Rome would swallow and shape the followers of Jesus of Nazareth, and make of his Christians the Roman Catholic church.

I suppose you are familiar with the modern expression, 'When in Rome, do as the Romans do.'

But here, in this reddish gloom, among flickering lights and a deeper muskier incense than I had ever smelled, I resented my timidity in silence. Then the dreams did descend, like so many veils lowered one by one to enclose me. In a flash I saw the beautiful Queen weeping. No. She screamed. Cried for help.

'Get away from me,' I whispered to the air around me. 'Fly from me, all things that are impure and evil. Get away from me as I enter the house of my Blessed Mother.'

The Priestess took me in hand. I heard voices from my dream in violent argument. I strained to clear my vision, to see the worshipers coming and going towards the Sanctuary to meditate or to make sacrifice, to ask for some favor. I tried to realize it was a big busy crowd, very little different from Rome.

But the touch of the Priestess enfeebled me. Her painted eyes struck terror. Her broad necklace caused me to blink my eyes. Row upon row of flat stones.

I was taken into a private apartment of the Temple by her, offered a sumptuous couch. I lay back exhausted. 'Fly from me, all things evil,' I whispered. 'Including dreams.'

The Priestess sat beside me and enfolded me in her silken arms. I looked up into a mask!

'Talk to me, suffering one,' she said in Latin with a thick accent. 'Speak all that must come forth.'

Suddenly – uncontrollably – I poured out my whole family story, the annihilation of my family, my guilt, my travails.

'What if I was the cause of my family's downfall – my worship at the Temple of Isis? What if Tiberius had remembered it? What have I done? The Priests were crucified and I did nothing. What does Mother Isis want of me? I want to die.'

'That she does *not* want of you,' said the Priestess, staring at me. Her eyes were huge, or was it the paint? No, I could see the whites of her eyes, so glistening and pure. Her painted mouth let loose words like a tiny breeze in a monotone.

I was fast becoming delirious and totally unreasonable. I murmured what I could about my initiation, what details I could tell a Priestess, for all these things were highly secret, you know, but I confirmed for her that I had been reborn in the rites.

All the stored-up weakness in me was cut loose in a flood.

Then I laid down my guilt. I confessed that I had, early on, left the Cult of Isis, that in recent years, I had walked only in the public processions to the sea, when the goddess was carried to the shore to bless the ships. Isis, the goddess of Navigation. I had not lived a life of devotion.

I had done nothing when the Priests of Isis were crucified, except speak out with many others behind the Emperor's back. There had been a solidarity between me and those Romans who thought Tiberius was a monster, but we had not raised our voices in defense of Isis. My

Father had told me to remain silent. So I had. This was the same Father who had told me to live.

I turned over and slipped down off this couch and I lay on the tiled floor. I don't know why. I pressed my cheek to the cold tile. I liked the coldness against my face. I was in a state of madness, but not an uncontrollable state. I lay staring.

I knew one thing. I wanted to get out of this Temple! I didn't like it. No, this had been a very bad idea.

I hated myself suddenly for having become so vulnerable to this woman, whatever sort she was, and the atmosphere of the blood dreams beckoned to me.

I opened my eyes. The Priestess bent over me. I saw the weeping Queen of my nightmares. I turned away and shut my eyes.

'Be at peace,' she said in her calculated and perfected voice. 'You did nothing wrong,' said the Priestess.

It seemed preposterous that such a voice should issue from such a painted face and form, but the voice was definite.

'First,' the Priestess said, 'you must understand that Mother Isis forgives anything. She is the Mother of Mercy.' Then she said, 'You have been more fully initiated by your description than most here or anywhere. You made a long fast. You bathed in the sacred blood of the bull. You must have drunk the potion. You dreamed and saw yourself reborn.'

'Yes,' I said, trying to revive the old ecstasy, the priceless gift of belief in something. 'Yes. I saw the stars and great fields of flowers, such fields . . .'

It was no good. I was scared of this woman and I wanted to get out of there. I'd go home and confess all this to Flavius and make him let me weep on his shoulder.

'I am not pious by nature,' I confessed. 'I was young. I loved the free women who went there, the women who slept with whom they chose, the whores of Rome, the keepers of the houses of pleasure, I liked women who thought for themselves, and followed the goings-on of the Empire.'

'You can enjoy such company here as well,' said the Priestess, without batting an eye. 'And don't fear that your old ties to the Temple caused your downfall in Rome. We have plenty of news to confirm that the highborn were not persecuted by Tiberius when he destroyed the Temple. It is always the poor who suffer: the street whore and the simple weaver, the hairdresser, the bricklayer. No noble family was persecuted in the name of Isis. You know that. Some women fled to Alexandria because they would not give up the worship, but they were never in danger.'

The dreams approached. 'Oh, Mother of God,' I whispered.

The Priestess went on talking.

'You, like Mother Isis, have been the victim of tragedy. And you, like Mother Isis, must take strength and walk alone, as Isis did when her husband, Osiris, was slain. Who helped her when she searched all over Egypt for the body of her murdered husband, Osiris? She walked alone. She is the greatest of the goddesses. When she recovered the body of her husband, Osiris, and could find no organ of generation for him with which she might be impregnated, she drew the semen right from his spirit. Thus, the god Horus was born of a woman and a god. It was the power of Isis who drew the spirit from the dead man. It is Isis who tricked the god Ra into revealing his name.'

That was the old tale all right.

I looked away from the Priestess. I was unable to look at her decorated face! Surely she felt my revulsion. I must not hurt her. She meant well. It wasn't her fault that she looked to me like a monster. Why in hell had I come here!

I lay dazed. The room had a soft golden light coming mainly through its three doors, and they were cut Egyptian-style, these doors, wider at the base than at the top, and I let this light make a blur of my vision. I asked the light to do this.

I felt the Priestess's hand. Such silken warmth. So lovely, her touch, her sweetness.

'Do you believe all of it!' I suddenly whispered.

She completely ignored this question. Her painted mask gave forth the creed.

'You must be like Mother Isis. Depend on no one. You don't have the burden of recovering a lost husband or father. You are free. Receive into your house men with love as you choose. You belong to no one but Mother Isis. Remember, Isis is the goddess who loves, the goddess who forgives, the goddess of infinite understanding because she herself has suffered!'

'Suffered!' I gasped. I moaned, a very uncommon sound for me, most of my life. But I saw the weeping Queen of my nightmares, bound to her throne.

'Listen to this,' I said, 'the dreams I will now recount, and then tell me why it is happening.' I knew my voice sounded angry. I was sorry for it. 'These dreams don't come from wine or

potions, or after long periods of wakefulness
that twist the mind.'

Then I launched into another totally
unplanned confession.

I told this woman of the blood dreams, the
dreams of ancient Egypt in which I had drunk
blood – the altar, the Temple, the desert, the sun
rising.

'Amon Ra!' I said. This was the Egyptian
name for the sun god, but I had never spoken it
to my knowledge. I said it now. 'Yes, Isis
tricked him into revealing his name, but he
killed me and I was her blood drinker, do you
hear me, a thirsty god!'

'No!' said the Priestess. She sat motionless.

She thought for a long while. I had scared her
and now this scared me all the more.

'Can you read the ancient picture writing of
Egypt?' she asked.

'No,' I said.

Then she said, in a more relaxed and vulnerable tone:

'You speak of very old legends, legends
buried in the history of our worship of Isis and
Osiris; that they once did indeed take the blood
of their victims as sacrifice. There are scrolls
here that tell of this. But nobody can really deci-
pher them, except for one . . .'

174

Her voice trailed off.

'Who is the one?' I asked. I sat up on my elbows. I realized the plaits of my hair had come undone. Good. It felt good because it was free now and clean. I raked my hair with both hands.

What did it feel like to be entombed in paint and wig like this Priestess?

'Tell me,' I said, 'who is the one who can read these legends. Tell me!'

'These are evil tales,' she said, 'that Isis herself and Osiris live on, somewhere, in material form, taking blood even now.' She made an expression of denial and disgust. 'But this is not our worship! We sacrifice no humans here! Egypt was old and wise before Rome was born!'

Who was she trying to convince? Me?

'I've never had such dreams, in a string like this, with the same theme.'

She became very worked up with her declarations.

'Our Mother Isis has no taste for blood. She has conquered death and set her husband Osiris as King of the Dead, but for us, she is life itself. She didn't send you these dreams.'

'Probably not! I agree with you. But then who did? Where do they come from? Why did they pursue me at sea? Who is this one who can read the old writing?'

She was shaken. She had let go of me and she stared off, her eyes taking on a deceptive ferocity due to the black lining.

'Perhaps somewhere in childhood you heard an old tale, maybe an old Egyptian Priest told it to you. You forgot it, and now it flames in your tortured mind. It feeds on fires to which it has no right – your Father's death.'

'Yes, well, I certainly hope so, but I've never known an old Egyptian. At the Temple, the Priests were Roman. Besides, if we take the dreams and lay them out, what is the pattern there? Why is the Queen weeping? Why does the sun kill me? The Queen is in fetters. The Queen is a prisoner. The Queen is in agony!'

'Stop.' The Priestess shuddered. Then she put her arms around me, as if it was she who needed me. I felt her stiff linen and the thick hair of her wig, and beneath it the hurried pounding of her heart. 'No,' she said. 'You're possessed of a demon, and we can drive this demon out of you! Maybe the way was opened for this wretched demon when your Father was attacked at his own Hearth.'

'You really believe it's possible?' I asked.

'Listen,' she said as casually now as one of the women outside. 'I want you to be bathed, to have fresh garments. This money, what portion can you give me? If none, we will provide all for you. We are rich here.'

'Here's plenty. I don't care.' I pulled the purse loose from my girdle.

'I will have everything done for you. Fresh clothes. This silk is too fragile.'

'You are telling me!' I said.

'This mantle is torn. Your hair is uncombed.'

I spilled out a dozen or so gold coins, more than I had paid for Flavius.

It shocked her, but she covered up the shock very quickly. Suddenly she stared at me, and her painted mask managed to make a flexible expression, a frown. I thought it might crack.

I thought she might weep. I was becoming a regular expert in making people weep. Mia and Lia had wept. Flavius had wept. Now she was going to cry. The Queen in the dream was crying!

I laughed in madness, throwing back my head, but then I saw the Queen! I saw her in distant wavery recollection, and I felt such sorrow that I too could have cried. My mockery was blasphemy. It was a lie unto myself.

'Take the gold for the Temple,' I said. 'Take it for new clothes, for all I need. But my offering to the goddess, I want it to be flowers, and bread, warm from the oven, a small loaf.'

'Very good,' she said with an eager nod.

'That is what Isis wants. She wants no blood. No! No blood!'

She started to help me up.

I paused. 'In the dream, you understand that she weeps. She is not happy with these blood drinkers, she protests, she objects. She herself is not the one who drinks blood.'

The Priestess was confounded, and then she nodded. 'Yes, that is obvious, is it not?'

'I too protest and suffer,' I said.

'Yes, come,' she said leading me through a thick tall door. She left me in the hands of the Temple slaves. I was relieved. I was weary.

I was taken into the ceremonial bath, cleansed by Temple maidens and re-dressed carefully by Temple maidens.

What a pleasure to have it all done right.

For a little while I wondered helplessly if they would frame me in white pleats and black plaits but they used the Roman style.

My hair was properly done by these girls in a correct circlet that would hold, leaving a generous frame of ringlets around the face.

The clothes given me were new and made of fine linen. Flowers had been stitched along the borders. This finery, so precise, so minute, seemed more valuable than gold.

It certainly gave more joy to me than gold.

I felt so tired! I was so grateful.

The girls then made up my face more artfully than I could have done it, and more in the Egyptian style, and I flinched when I saw myself in the mirror. Flinched. It wasn't the full paint of the Priestess, but my eyes were rimmed with black.

'How dare I complain?' I whispered.

I put down the mirror. One doesn't have to see oneself, fortunately.

I emerged into the great hall of the Temple, a proper Roman woman, with the extravagant face paint of the East. A common sight in Antioch.

I found the Priestess with two others, as formally dressed as she, and a Priest who wore the same old-fashioned Egyptian headdress, only he wore no wig, just a striped hood. His tunic was short, pleated. He turned and glared at me as I came forward.

Fear. Crushing fear. Flee this place! Forget about the offering, or have them make it for you. Go home. Flavius is waiting. Get out!

I was struck dumb. I let the Priest draw me aside.

'Pay attention,' he said to me gently. 'I will take you now into the holy place. I will let you talk to the Mother. But when you come out, you must come to me! Don't leave without coming to me. You must promise me, you will return each day, and if you have more of these dreams, you will lay them before us. There is one to whom they should be told, that is, unless the goddess drives them from your mind.'

'Of course I will tell anyone who can help,' I said. 'I hate these dreams. But why are you so anxious? Are you afraid of me?'

He shook his head. 'I don't fear you, but there is something I must confide to you. I must talk to you either today or tomorrow. I must speak with you. Go now to the Mother, then come to me.'

The others led me to the chamber of the Sanctuary; there were white linen curtains before the shrine. I saw my sacrifice lying there, a great garland of sweet-smelling white flowers, and the warm loaf of bread. I knelt. The curtains were pulled back by unseen hands and I found myself alone in the chamber kneeling before the *Regina Caeli*, the Queen of Heaven.

Another shock.

This was an ancient Egyptian statue of our Isis, carved from dark basalt. Her headdress was long, narrow, pushed behind her ears. On her head she wore a great disk between horns. Her breasts were bare. On her lap sat the adult

Pharaoh, her son Horus. She held her left breast to offer him her milk.

I was struck with despair! This image meant nothing to me! I groped for the essence of Isis in this image.

'Did you send me the dreams, Mother!' I whispered.

I laid out the flowers. I broke the bread.

I heard nothing in the silence from the serene and ancient statue.

I prostrated myself on the floor, stretching out my arms. And from the depths of my soul, I struggled to say, I accept, I believe, I am yours, I need you, I need you!

But I wept. All was lost to me. Not merely Rome and my family, but even my Isis. This goddess was the embodiment of the faith of another nation, another people.

Very slowly a calm settled over me.

Is it so, I thought. The Cult of my Mother is in all places, North and South and East and West. It is the spirit of this Cult which gives it power. I need not literally kiss the feet of this effigy. That is not the point.

I raised my head slowly, then sat back on my heels. A real revelation came upon me. I cannot fully record it. I knew it, fully, in an instant.

I knew that all things were symbols of other

things! I knew that all rituals were enactments of other happenings! I knew that out of our practical human minds we devised these things with an immensity of soul that would not allow the world to be devoid of meaning.

And this statue represented love. Love above cruelty. Love above injustice. Love above loneliness and condemnation.

That was what mattered, that single thing. I stared up at the face of the goddess and I knew her! I stared at the little Pharaoh, the proffered breast.

'I am yours!' I said coldly.

Her stark primitive Egyptian features were no obstacle to my heart; I looked at the right hand which held her breast.

Love. This requires strength from us; this requires endurance; this requires an acceptance of all that is unknown.

'Take the dreams away from me, Heavenly Mother,' I said. 'Or reveal their purpose. And the path I must follow. Please.'

Then in Latin I said an old litany:

You are she who has separated the Heavens
   and the Earth.
You are she who rises in the Dog Star.
You are she who makes strong the right.

*You are she who makes the children to love
their parents.*

*You are she who decreed mercy for all who
ask for it.*

I believed these words, but in a wholly profane way. I believed them because I saw her
worship as having collected together from the
minds of men and women the best ideas of
which men and women were capable. That
was the function for which a goddess existed;
that was the spirit from which she drew her
vitality.

The lost phallus of Osiris exists in the Nile.
And the Nile inseminates the fields. Oh, it was
so lovely.

The trick was not to reject it, as Lucretius
might have suggested, but to realize what her
image meant. To extract from that image the
best in my own soul.

And when I looked down at the beautiful
white flowers, I thought, 'It is your wisdom,
Mother, that these bloom.' And I meant by that
only that the world itself was filled with so
much to be cherished, preserved, honored, that
pleasure itself was resplendent – and she, Isis,
embodied these concepts that were too deep to
be called ideas.

I loved her – this expression of goodness which was Isis.

The longer I looked at her stone face, the more it seemed she saw me. An old trick. The more I knelt there, the more it seemed she spoke to me. I allowed this to happen, fully aware that it meant nothing. The dreams were remote. They seemed a puzzle which would find its idiot resolution.

Then with true fervor, I crawled towards her and kissed her feet.

My worship was over.

I went out refreshed, jubilant.

I wasn't going to have those dreams anymore. There was still daylight. I was happy.

I found many friends in the courtyard of the Temple, and sitting down with them under the olive trees, I drew out of them all the information I needed for practical life, how to get caterers, hairdressers, all that. Where to buy this thing and the other.

In other words, I was armed by my rich friends with full equipment to run a fine house without actually cluttering it up with slaves I didn't want. I could stick with Flavius and the two girls. Excellent. Anything else could be hired or bought.

Finally, very tired, with my head full of

names to remember and directions to recall, and very amused by the jokes and stories of these women, delighted with their ease in speaking Greek – which I had always loved – I sat back and thought, I can go home now.

I can begin.

The Temple was still very busy. I looked at the doors. Where was the Priest? Well, I would come back tomorrow. I didn't want to revive those dreams now, that was certain. Many people were coming and going with flowers and bread and some with birds to be set free for the goddess, birds that would take wing out of the high window of her Sanctuary.

How warm it was here. What a blaze of flowers covered the wall! I had never thought there could be a place as beautiful as Tuscany, but maybe this place was beautiful too.

I went out of the courtyard, before the steps, and into the Forum.

I approached a man under the arches who was teaching a group of young boys all of what Diogenes has espoused, that we give up the flesh and all its pleasures, that we live pure lives in denial of the senses.

It was so much as Flavius had described it. But the man meant his words, and was well versed. He spoke of a liberating resignation. He caught my fancy. For this is what I thought had come to me in the Temple, a liberating resignation.

The boys who listened were too young to know this. But I knew it. I liked him. He had gray hair and wore a simple long tunic. He was not ostentatiously in rags.

I at once interrupted. With a humble smile I offered the counsel of Epicurus, that the senses wouldn't have been given us were they not good. Wasn't this so? 'Must we deny ourselves? Look, back at the courtyard of the Temple of Isis, look at the flowers covering the top of the wall! Is this not something to savor? Look at the roaring red of those flowers! Those flowers are in themselves enough to lift a person out of sorrow. Who is to say that eyes are wiser than hands or lips?'

The young men turned to me. I fell into discussions with several of them. How fresh and pretty they were. There were long-haired men from Babylon and even highborn Hebrews here, all with very hairy arms and chests, and many colonial Romans who were dazzled by the points I made, that in the flesh and in the wine, we find the truth of life.

'The flowers, the stars, the wine, the kisses of one's lover, all is part of Nature, surely,' I said. I was of course on fire, having just come from the Temple, having just unburdened all fears and having resolved all doubts. I was for the moment invincible. The world was new.

The Teacher, whose name was Marcellus, came from under the arch to greet me.

'Ah, Gracious Lady, you amaze me,' he said. 'But from whom did you really learn what you believe? Was it from Lucretius? Or was it from experience? You realize that we must not ever encourage people to abandon themselves to the senses!'

'Have I said anything about abandon?' I asked. 'To yield is not to abandon. It is to honor. I speak of a prudent life; I speak of listening to the wisdom of our bodies. I speak of the ultimate intelligence of kindness, and enjoyment. And if you will know, Lucretius didn't teach me as much as one might think. He was always too dry for me, you know. I learned to embrace the glory of life from poets like Ovid.'

The crowd of boys cheered.

'I learnt from Ovid,' came shout after shout.

'Well, that's fine, but remember your manners as well as your lessons,' I said firmly.

More cheering. Then the young men began tossing out verses from Ovid's *Metamorphoses*.

'That's splendid,' I declared. 'How many here? Fifteen. Why don't you come to my house for a supper?' I asked. 'Five nights from now, all of you. I need the time to prepare. I have many books I want to show you. I promise you, I will show you what a delicious feast can do for the soul!'

My invitation was accepted with amusement and laughter. I disclosed the location of my house.

'I am a widow. My name is Pandora. I invite you with all propriety, and the feast awaits you. Don't expect dancing boys and girls, for you will not find them under my roof. Expect delicious food. Expect poetry. Which of you can sing the verses of Homer? Truly sing them? Which of you sings them now from memory for pleasure!'

Laughter, conviviality. Victory. It seemed everybody could do this, and welcomed the opportunity. Someone made a soft mention of another Roman woman who would be most jealous when she discovered she had competition in Antioch.

'Nonsense,' said another, 'her table is overcrowded. Lady, may I kiss your hand?'

'You must tell me who she is,' I said. 'I'll welcome her. I want to know her, and what I can learn from her.'

The Teacher was smiling. I slipped him some money.

It was getting dusk. I sighed. Look. The rising stars of the tinted evening that precedes blackness.

I received the boys' chaste kisses and confirmed our feast.

But something had changed. It was as quick as the opening of one's eyes. Ah, painted eyes, no.

Perhaps it was only the awful pall of twilight.

I felt a shudder. *It is I who summoned you.* Who spoke those words? *Beware, for you would be stolen from me now and I will not have it.*

I was dumbstruck. I held the Teacher's hand warmly. He talked about moderation in living. 'Look at my plain tunic,' he said. 'These boys have so much money, they can destroy themselves.'

The boys protested.

But this was dim to me. I tried to listen. My eyes roved. Whence came that voice! Who spoke those words! Who summoned me and who would attempt the theft?

Then to my silent astonishment I saw a man, his head covered by his toga, watching me. I knew him immediately, by his forehead and his eyes. I recognized his walk now as he moved steadily away.

This was my brother, the youngest, Lucius, the one I despised. It had to be him. And behold the sly manner in which he fled from notice into the shadows.

I knew the whole person. Lucius. He waited at the end of the long portico.

I couldn't move, and it was getting dark. All the merchants who are open only in the day were gone. The taverns were putting out their lanterns or torches. One bookseller remained open, with great displays of books under the lamps above.

Lucius – my much detested youngest brother – not coming to welcome me with tears but gliding in the shadows of the portico. Why?

I feared I knew.

Meantime, the boys were begging me to go to the nearby wine garden with them, a lovely place. They were fighting over who would pay for my supper there.

Think, Pandora. This sweet little invitation is some keen test of the degree of my daring and freedom. And I should not go to a common tavern with the boys! But within moments I would be alone.

The Forum grew quiet. The fires blazed before the Temples. But there were great spaces of darkness. The man in the toga waited.

'No, I must be off now,' I said. Desperately I thought, what I shall I do for a torchbearer? Dare I ask these youths to see me home? I could see their slaves waiting about, some already lighting their torches or lanterns.

Singing came from the Temple of Isis.

It was I who summoned you. Beware . . . for me and my purpose!

'This is madness,' I muttered, waving goodnight to those who left in pairs or trios. I forced smiles and kind words.

I glared at the distant figure of Lucius, who now slouched at the end of the portico in front of doors closed for the night. His very posture was furtive and cowardly.

Quite suddenly, I felt a hand on my shoulder. I brushed it off immediately, wishing to lay down limits to such familiarity, and then I realized a man was whispering in my ear:

'The Priest at the Temple begs for you to come back, Madam. He needs to talk with you. He did not mean for you to leave without talking.'

I turned to see a Priest there beside me, in full Egyptian headdress and impeccable white linen and wearing a medallion of the goddess around his neck.

Oh, thank Heaven.

But before I could recover myself or answer,

another man had stepped up boldly, heaving forward his ivory leg and foot. Two torch-bearers accompanied him. We were embraced by a warm light.

'Does my Mistress wish to talk to this Priest?' he asked.

It was Flavius. He had followed my commands. He was wonderfully dressed as a Roman gentleman in the long tunic and a loose cloak. As a slave, he couldn't wear a toga. His hair was neat and trimmed and looked as impressive as any free man's. He was shining clean and appeared completely confident.

Marcellus, the Philosopher-Teacher, lingered. 'Lady Pandora, you are most gracious, and let me assure you that the tavern these boys frequent may give rise to another Aristotle or Plato but it is not a fit place for you.'

'I know that,' I said. 'Don't worry.'

The Teacher looked warily at the Priest and at the handsome Flavius. I slipped my arm about Flavius's waist. 'This is my steward, who will welcome you the night you come to me. Thank you for letting me disrupt your teaching. You're a kind man.'

The Teacher's face stiffened. Then he leaned closer. 'There's a man under the portico; don't look at him now, but you need more slaves to protect you. This city is divided, dangerous.'

'Yes, so you see him too,' I said. 'And his glorious toga, the mark of his genteel birth!'

'It's getting dark,' Flavius said. 'I'll hire more torchbearers now and a litter. Right over there.'

He thanked the Teacher, who reluctantly slipped away.

The Priest. He was still waiting. Flavius gestured for two more torchbearers and they came trotting to join us. We now had a plenitude of light.

I turned to the Priest. 'I will come to the Temple directly, but I must first talk with that man over there! The man in the shadows?' I pointed quite visibly. I stood in a flood of light. I might as well have been on a stage.

I saw the distant figure cringe and try to fade into the wall.

'Why?' Flavius asked with about as much humility as a Roman Senator. 'Something is very wrong about that man. He's hovering. The Teacher was right.'

'I know,' I answered. I heard the dim, echoing laughter of a woman! Yea gods, I had to stay sane long enough to get home! I looked at Flavius. He had not heard the laughter.

There was one sure way to do this. 'You

torchbearers, all of you, come with me,' I said to the four of them. 'Flavius, you stand here with the Priest and watch as I greet this man. I know him. Come only if I call.'

'Oh, I don't like it,' said Flavius.

'Neither do I,' said the Priest. 'They want you in the Temple, Madam, and we have many guards to escort you home.'

'I won't disappoint you,' I said, but I walked straight towards the toga-clad figure, crossing yard after yard of paved squares, the torches flaring around me.

The toga-clad man gave a violent start, with his whole body, and then he took a few steps away from the wall.

I stopped, still out in the square.

He had to come closer. I wasn't going to move. The four torches gasped and blew in the breeze. Anybody anywhere near could see us. We were the brightest thing in the Forum.

The man approached. He walked slow, then fast. The light struck his face. He was consumed with rage.

'Lucius,' I whispered. 'I see you, but I can't believe what I see.'

'Nor can I,' he said. 'What the hell are you doing here?' he said to me.

'What?' I was too baffled to answer.

'Our family is in disgrace in Rome and you're making a spectacle of yourself in the middle of Antioch! Look at you! Painted and perfumed and your hair full of ointment! You are a whore.'

'Lucius!' I cried. 'What in the name of the gods are you thinking? Our Father is dead! Your own brothers may be dead. How did you escape? Why aren't you glad to see me? Why don't you take me to your house?'

'Glad to see you!' he hissed. 'We are in hiding here, you bitch!'

'How many of you? Who? What about Antony? What happened to Flora?'

He sneered with exasperation.

'They are murdered, Lydia, and if you do not get yourself to some safe corner where no roaming citizen of Rome can find you, you are dead too. Oh, that you would turn up here, spouting philosophy! Everybody in the taverns was talking about you! And that slave with the leg made of ivory! I saw you at noon, you wretched and infernal nuisance. Damn you, Lydia!'

This was pure unadulterated hate.

Again, came that distinct echoing laughter. Of course he did not hear it. Only I could hear it.

'Your wife, where is she. I want to see her! You *will* take me in!'

'I will not.'

'Lucius, I am your sister. I want to see your wife. You're right. I've been foolish. I didn't think things through very well. There are so many miles of sea between here in Rome. It never occurred to me –'

'That's just it, Lydia, you never really think of anything sensible or practical. You never did. You're an uncompromising dreamer, and stupid on top of it.'

'Lucius, what can I do?'

He turned from right to left, sizing up the torchbearers.

He narrowed his eyes. I could feel his hatred. Oh, Father, do not see this from Heaven or the Underworld. My brother wants me dead!

'Yes,' I said, 'four torchbearers and we are in the middle of the Forum. And don't forget about the man with the ivory leg over there and the Priest,' I said softly, 'And do regard the soldiers outside the Emperor's Temple. Take note. How goes it with your wife? I must see her. I'll come in secret. She'll be happy that I am alive, surely, for I love her like a sister. I will never connect myself with you in public. I've made a grevious error.'

'Oh, knock it off,' he said. 'Sisters! She's dead!' He looked from right to left again. 'They were all massacred. Don't you understand? Get away from me.' He took a few steps back but I moved forward, drawing the light around him again.

'But who is with you, then? Who escaped with you? Who else is alive?'

'Priscilla,' he said, 'and we were damned lucky to get away when we did.'

'What? Your mistress? You came here with your mistress? The children, they are all dead?'

'Yes, of course, they must be. How could they have escaped? Look, Lydia, I give you one night to get out of this city and away from me. I am lodged here comfortably and will not tolerate you. Get out of Antioch. Go by sea or land, I don't care, but go!'

'You left your wife and children to die? And came here with Priscilla?'

'How the hell did you get away, you stinking bitch in heat, answer me that! Of course you had no children, the great famous barren womb of our family!' He looked at the torchbearers. 'Get away from here!' he shouted.

'Stay right where you are.'

I put my hand on my dagger. I moved the mantle so that he could see the flash of the metal.

He looked genuinely surprised and then gave a ghastly false smile. Oh, revolting!

'Lydia, I wouldn't hurt you for the world!' he said as if insulted. 'I am only worried for us all. Word came from the house. Everyone had been killed. What was I to do, go back and die for nothing?'

'You're lying. And don't you call me a bitch in heat again unless you want to become a gelding. I know you lie. Somebody tipped you off, and you got out! Or it was you who betrayed us all.'

Ah, how sad for him that he was not more clever, more quick. He did not take umbrage at these loathsome charges as he should have. He just tilted his head and said:

'No, that's not true. Look, come with me now. Send these men away, get rid of that slave, and I will help you. Priscilla adores you.'

'She's a liar and slut! And how calm you have become in the face of my suspicions. Nothing as steamed as when you saw me! I just accused you of betraying our family to the *Delatores*. I accused you of abandoning your wife and children to the Praetorian Guard. Can you hear these words?'

'It's utter stupidity, I would never do such a thing.'

'You reek of guilt. Look at you. I should kill you now!'

He backed up. 'Get out of Antioch!' he said. 'I don't care how you judge me or what I had to do to save myself and Priscilla. Get out of Antioch!'

There were no words for my judgment. It was harsher than my soul could hold.

He backed away, and then walked fast into the darkness, disappearing before he reached the portico. I listened to his steps as they echoed down the street.

'Dear Heaven!' I whispered. I was about to cry. My hand was still on the dagger, however.

I turned around. The Priest and Flavius stood much closer than ordered. I was frankly utterly baffled, stopped.

I didn't know what to do.

'Come to the Temple at once,' said the Priest.

'All right,' I said. 'Flavius, you come with me, stand watch with the four torchmen, I want you right by the Temple guards, and keep an eye out for that man.'

'Who is he, Madam,' Flavius whispered as I strode towards the Temple, leading them both.

How regal he looked. He had the presence of a free man. And his tunic was beautiful thin wool, striped in gold, belted in gold, well fitted across his chest. Even his ivory leg had been polished. I was more than pleased. But was he armed?

Beneath his quiet demeanor, he was deeply protective of me.

In my misery, I couldn't form words to answer him.

Several litters were now crisscrossing the square, carried on the shoulders of hurrying slaves, and other slaves carried the torches beside them. A kind of soft glow rose from the commotion. People were on their way to dinners or private ceremonies. Something was happening in the Temple.

I turned to the Priest. 'You will guard my slave and my torchbearers?'

'Yes, Madam,' he said.

It was full night. The breeze was sweet. A few lanterns had been lighted under the long porticoes. We drew near to the braziers of the goddess.

'Now I must leave you,' I said. 'You have my permission to protect my property, as you so eloquently put it earlier, unto death. Don't move from these doors. I won't leave here without you. I won't stay long. I don't want to. But have you a knife?'

'Yes, Madam, but it's untried. It was among your possessions, and when you did not come home and it grew dark . . .'

'Don't recount the history of the world,' I

said. 'You did the right thing. You probably will always do the right thing.'

I turned my back to the square and said, 'Let me see it. I'll know if it's decorative or sharp.'

When he drew it from the forearm sling, I touched it with my finger and blood came from the cut. I returned it. This had belonged to my Father. So my Father had filled my trunk with his weapons as well as his wealth, so that I might live!

Flavius and I exchanged one last slow glance.

The Priest grew very anxious. 'Madam, please come inside,' he said.

I found myself ushered right through the tall doors into the Temple, and with the Priestesses and the Priest of that earlier afternoon.

'You want something of me?' I asked. I was out of breath. I was faint. 'I have much on my mind, things that must be done. Can this wait?'

'No, Lady, it cannot!' said the Priest.

I felt a shudder in my limbs as if I were being watched by someone. The tall shadows of the Temple were too concealing.

'All right,' I said. 'It's about those awful dreams, isn't it?'

'Yes,' said the Priest. 'And more than that.'

6

We were taken into another chamber, and this one had only one dim light.

I couldn't see well in the flickering of the flame and I realized I could not make out the faces of the other Priest and Priestess. An Oriental screen, a screen of worked ebony partitioned off the end of this room, and I felt certain someone was behind it.

But I felt nothing but gentleness emanating from all of these gathered here. I looked around. I was so miserable over my brother, and so impatient that I couldn't find polite words.

'Please, you must forgive me,' I said. 'A dire matter requires me to hurry.' I was becoming afraid for Flavius's safety. 'Do send guards to flank my slave outside, now.'

'Done, Lady,' said the Priest, the one I knew. 'I beg you to stay and recount your story again.'

'Who is there!' I pointed. 'Behind that screen. Why is this person concealed?' This was very rude and irreverent, but I was in a full state of alarm.

'That is one of our most devoted supporters,' said the Priest who had escorted me to the shrine of Isis earlier. 'This one often comes by night to pray at the shrine and has given much money to the Temple. He only wants to hear what we have to say.'

'Well, I'm not so sure of that. Tell him to come out!' I said. 'Besides, what is it we're supposed to say?'

I was infuriated suddenly that they might have betrayed my confidences. I hadn't told them my true Roman name, only of my tragedy, but the Temple was sacred.

They became all flustered in their gentleness.

The figure, draped in the toga, much taller than my brother, in fact, remarkably tall, stepped out from behind the screen. The toga was dark, but nevertheless the classical garment. His face was hidden by the toga. I could only see his lips.

He whispered:

'Don't be afraid. You told the Priest and Priestesses this afternoon of blood dreams.'

'This was in confidence!' I said indignantly.

I was completely suspicious, for I had told a good deal more than blood dreams to these people.

I tried better to see the figure. There was something distinctly familiar about the figure – the voice, even in a whisper . . . something else.

'Lady Pandora,' said the Priestess who had so consoled me earlier. 'You talked to me of an old legendary worship, worship which we oppose and condemn. A worship of our Beloved Mother which once involved human sacrifice. I told you that we abhor such things. And we do.'

'However,' said the Priest, 'there is someone afoot in the city of Antioch who does drink blood from humans, draining them until they are dead. Then he flings the bodies before dawn on our steps. The very steps of our Temple.' He sighed. 'Lady Pandora, I am entrusting you with a powerful confidence.'

All thought of my evil brother left me. The hound of the dreams bore down upon me with its evil breath. I tried to gather my wits. I thought again of the voice I'd heard in my head: *It is I who summoned you.* The feminine laughter.

'No, it was a woman's laughter,' I murmured.

'Lady Pandora?'

'You tell me there is someone afoot in Antioch who drinks blood.'

'By night. He cannot walk in the day,' said the Priest.

I saw the dream, the rising sun, knowing I the blood drinker would die in the rays of the sun.

'You're telling me that these blood drinkers I saw in my dream exist?' I asked. 'That one of them is here.'

'Someone wants us to believe this,' said the Priest, 'that the old legends have truth, but we don't know who it is. And we are leery of the Roman authorities. You know what happened in Rome. You came speaking of dreams in which the sun killed you, in which you were a blood drinker. Lady, I'm not betraying your confidences here. This one –' He gestured to the tall man. 'This is the one who reads the ancient writing. He's read the legends. Your dreams echo the legends.'

'I am sick,' I said. 'I need a chair. I have enemies to worry about.'

'I'll protect you from your enemies,' said the mysterious tall man in the toga.

'How can you? You don't even know who they are.'

There came a silent voice from the tall man in the toga:

205

Your brother Lucius betrayed the entire family. He did it out of jealousy of your brother Antony. He sold out everybody to the Delatores for a guaranteed one-third of the family's wealth and left before the killing began. He had the cooperation of the Sejanus of the Praetorian Guard. He wants to kill you.

I was shocked but also not about to let this person overwhelm me.

You speak just like the woman, I said silently. *You speak right to my thoughts. You speak like the woman who said to me in my head, 'It is I who summoned you.'*

I could feel his shock at this. But I too slumped as if dealt a mortal blow. So this creature knew all about my brothers, and Lucius had betrayed us. And this creature knew.

What are you? I fired off to the mind speaker, the tall one. *Are you a magician?*

No answer.

The Priest and Priestess, unable to hear this silent exchange, pursued their course.

'This blood drinker, Lady Pandora, he leaves human victims on the steps of the Temple before dawn. He writes an old name in Egyptian on his victims with their blood. Should the government discover this, our Temple might be held accountable. This is not our worship.

'Will you recount again for us – for our friend here – your dreams? We must protect the worship of Isis. We did not believe in these old legends . . . until this creature appeared and began his killing, then comes out of the sea a beautiful Roman woman who speaks of similar beings who are in her dreams.'

'What name does he write on his victims?' I asked. 'This blood drinker. Is it Isis?'

'It's meaningless, it's forbidden, it's old Egyptian. It is one of the names by which Isis was once called, but never by us.'

'What is it?'

None of them, including the silent one, answered me.

In the silence, I thought of Lucius and I almost wept. Then hatred came over me, deep hatred, as it had in the Forum when I spoke with him, saw his cowardly rage. Betrayed the entire family. To be weak is a dangerous thing. Antony and my Father had been such strong men.

'Lady Pandora,' said the Priest. 'Tell us what you might know of this creature in Antioch. Have you dreamed of him?'

I thought of the dreams. I tried to respond in depth to what these people in this Temple were telling me.

The tall distant Roman spoke:

'Lady Pandora knows nothing about this blood drinker. She is telling you the truth. She knows only the dreams and there have been no names spoken in her dreams. In her dreams she sees an earlier time of Egypt.'

'Well, thank you, Gracious Lord!' I said furiously. 'And just how have you arrived at that conclusion?'

'By reading your thoughts!' the Roman said, quite unruffled. 'The same as I have regarding those who would put you in danger here. I'll protect you from your brother.'

'Indeed. You had better leave that to me. It is I who will settle that score with him. Now, let us leave the question of my personal misfortune. And you explain to me, most clever one, why I am having these dreams! Fork up some useful magic from your mind reading. You know, a man with your gifts should post yourself at the courthouse, and determine cases for the judges if you can read minds. Why don't you go to Rome and become the advisor to the Emperor Tiberius?'

I could feel, positively feel, the little tumult in the heart of the distant concealed Roman. Again, there came that sense of something familiar about this creature. Of course I was no stranger to necromancers, astrologists or oracles. But this man had mentioned specific names – Antony, Lucius. He was an astounder.

'Tell me, oh, mysterious one,' I said. 'How close do my dreams come to what you've read in the old writing? And this blood drinker, the one that's roaming Antioch, is he a mortal man?'

Silence.

I strained to see the Roman more clearly but couldn't. He had in fact receded somewhat into the darkness. My nerves were on the breaking point. I wanted to kill Lucius; in fact, I had no choice.

The Roman said softly, 'She knows nothing of this blood drinker in Antioch. Tell her what you know of him – for it may be he, this blood drinker, who is sending her the dreams.'

I was confused. The woman's voice had been so clear in my head earlier, *It is I who summoned you.*

This was causing confusion in the Roman; I could feel it like a little turbulence in the air.

'We've seen him,' said the Priest. 'Indeed, we watch, in order to collect these poor drained corpses before anyone finds them and blames the deed on us. He is burned, burned all over his body, blackened. He cannot be a man. He is an

209

old god, burnt black as if in an inferno.'

'Amon Ra,' I said. 'But why didn't he die? In the dreams, I die.'

'Oh, it is a horror to behold,' said the Priestess suddenly, as if she could contain herself no longer. 'This thing cannot be human. Its bones show through its blackened skin. But it is weak and its victims are weak. It barely staggers, yet it can drain the blood from the poor maimed souls upon whom it feeds. It crawls away in the morning as if it hasn't the strength to walk.'

The Priest seemed impatient.

'But he's alive,' said the Priest. 'Alive, god or demon or man, he lives. And each time he drinks blood from one of these weaklings, he grows a little stronger. And he is straight from the old legends, and you have dreamed of them. He wears his hair long in the old Egyptian style. He is in agony from his burns. He spits curses at the Temple.'

'What kind of curses?'

The Priestess interjected at once. 'He seems to think that Queen Isis has betrayed him. He speaks in old Egyptian. We barely understand him. Our Roman friend here, our benefactor, has translated the words for us.'

'Stop!' I demanded. 'My head is reeling.

Don't say any more. The man over there has told the truth. I know nothing of this bloody burnt creature. I don't know why I have the dreams. I think a woman is sending the dreams to me. It may be the Queen I described to you, the Queen on the throne, in fetters, who weeps, I don't know why!'

'You have never seen this man?' asked the Priest.

The Roman answered for me. 'She has not.'

'Oh, your marvelous talents as spokesman again!' I said to the Roman. 'I am so delighted! Why are you hiding behind your toga? Why do you stand over there, so far away that I can't see you? Have you seen this blood drinker?'

'Be patient with me,' he said. It was spoken with such charm that I couldn't bring myself to say more to him. I turned on the Priest and the Priestess.

'Why don't you lie in wait for this black burnt thing,' I said, 'this weakling? I am hearing voices in my head. But it's the words of a woman that come to me, warning me of danger. It's a woman laughing. I want to leave now. I want to go home. I have something that must be done, and must be done cleverly. I need to go.'

'I will protect you from your enemy,' said the Roman.

'That's charming,' I answered. 'If you can protect me, if you know who my enemy is, then why can't you lie in wait for this blood drinker? Catch him in a gladiator's net. Sink five tridents into him. Five of you can hold him. All you have to do is hold him till the sun rises, the rays of Amon Ra will kill him. It may take two days, even three, but they'll kill him. He'll burn like I did in the dream. And you, mind reader, why don't you help?'

I broke off, shocked and disoriented. Why was I so certain of this. Why was I using the name Amon Ra so casually, as if I believed in the god? I scarcely knew his fables.

'The creature knows when we are lying in wait,' said the Priest and Priestess. 'He knows when the tall friend is here, and does not come. We are vigilant, we are patient, we think we will see no more of him, and then he comes. And now you have come with the dreams.'

A vivid garish flash of the dream returned. I was a man. I argued and cursed. I refused to do something which I had been ordered to do. A woman was weeping. I fought off those who tried to stop me. But I had not foreseen that I would, as I ran away, come to a desert place where I could find no shelter.

If the others spoke, I took no note of it. I

heard the woman of the dream crying, the fettered Queen, and the woman was a blood drinker too. 'You must drink from the Fount,' said the man in my dream. And he wasn't a man. I wasn't a man. We were gods. We were blood drinkers. That's why the sun destroyed me. It was the force of a more powerful god. Layers upon layers of the dream lay below this polished bit of remembrance.

I came to my senses, or back to an awareness of the others, when someone placed a cup of wine in my hands. I drank it. It was excellent wine, from Italy, and I felt refreshed, though at once tired. It would make the walk home much too tiring if I drank any more. I needed my strength.

'Take this away,' I said. I looked at the Priestess. 'In the dream, I told you, I was one of them. They wanted me to drink from the Queen. They called her 'the Fount.' They said she did not know how to rule. I told you.'

The Priestess burst into tears and turned her back, hunching up her narrow shoulders.

'I was one of the blood drinkers,' I said. 'I was thirsty for blood. Listen, I am no lover of blood sacrifice. What do you know here? Does Queen Isis exist somewhere, within this Temple, bound in fetters –'

'No!' cried the Priest. The Priestess turned around, echoing the same horrified denial.

'All right, then, but you said there were legends that she did exist somewhere in material form. Now, what do you think is happening? She has summoned me here to assist this one, this burnt-up weakling? Why me? How can I do it? I'm a mortal woman. Remembering dreams of a past life does not enhance my power. Listen! It was a woman's voice, I told you, which spoke in my head to me, not an hour ago out there in the Forum, and she said 'It is I who summoned you,' I heard this, and she swore she would not have me stolen from her. Then up comes this mortal man who's more of a threat to me than anything in my head. The voice in my head had warned me of him! I don't want any of your mysterious Egyptian religion. I refuse to go mad. It is you, all of you – especially the talented mind reader – who must find this thing before he makes any more trouble. Allow me to go on.'

I stood up and began to walk out of the chamber.

The Roman spoke behind me, most gently, 'Are you really going out into the night alone, knowing full well what awaits you – that you have an enemy who wants to kill you, and that you have in your dreams knowledge that may draw this blood drinker to you?'

This was such a change of pace for the lofty mind reader, such a slip into semi-sarcastic vernacular, that I almost laughed.

'I'm going home now!' I said firmly.

They all pleaded, in different modes and tones. 'Stay in the Temple.'

'Absolutely not,' I said. 'If the dreams return I'll write them down for you.'

'How can you be so foolish!' said the Roman with genteel impatience. You would have thought *he* was my brother!

'That is an unforgivable impertinence,' I said. 'Are not magicians and mind readers bound by manners?' I looked to the Priest and Priestess. 'Who is this man?'

I went out and they followed me. I hurried to the door.

In the light I saw the Priestess's face. 'We know only that he's our friend. Please listen to his advice. He has never done anything but good for the Temple. He comes to read the Egyptian books we have here. He buys them up from the shops as soon as the sea brings them to us. He is wise. He can read minds, as you see.'

'You promised an escort of guards,' I said.

And I will be with you. The voice came from

the Roman, though I did not know where he was now at all. He was not in the great hall.

'Come, live within the Temple of Isis, and nothing can harm you,' said the Priest.

'I'm not quite the woman for living in the Temple Compound,' I said, trying to sound as humble and grateful as I could. 'I'd drive you mad in a week. Please open the door.'

I slipped out. I felt I had escaped from a dark corridor of spiderwebs, back into the Roman night, among Roman columns and Roman temples.

I discovered Flavius pressed against the column beside me, staring down into the stairs. Our four torchbearers were gathered next to us, very much alarmed.

There were men who were obviously Temple guards, but they stood cleaving to the doors, as did Flavius.

'Madam, go back in!' whispered Flavius.

At the foot of the stairs stood a group of helmeted Roman soldiers in full military dress with polished muscled breastplates and short red cloaks and tunics. They carried their deadly swords as if they were in battle. Their bronze helmets shone in the light of the Temple braziers.

Battle dress within the city. Everything but

shields. And who was the leader?

Lucius, my brother, stood beside the leader. Lucius wore his battle tunic of red, but no breastplate or sword. His toga was doubled and redoubled over his left arm. He was clean, with shining hair, exuding money. A jeweled dagger was on his forearm; another dagger was in his belt.

Trembling, he pointed at me.

'There she is,' said Lucius. 'Of the entire family, she escaped the order of Sejanus. It was a plot to kill Tiberius and somehow she bribed her way out of Rome!'

I quickly sized up the soldiers. There were two young Asiatics but the others were *old* and *Roman;* six in number. Yea gods, they must have thought I was Circe!

'Go back in,' said my beloved and loyal Flavius, 'seek sanctuary.'

'Be still,' I said. 'There's always time for that.'

The leader, he was the key, and I saw that he was an older man, older than my brother Antony, yet not as old as my Father. He had thick gray eyebrows and was impeccably clean shaven.

He wore battle scars proudly, one on his cheek, another on his thigh. He was exhausted.

His eyes were red and he shook his head as if to clear his vision.

This man's arms were very tanned, yet he was well muscled. This meant war – lots and lots of war.

Lucius declared, 'The entire family stands condemned. She should be executed on the spot!'

I decided my strategy as if I were Caesar himself. I spoke up at once, proceeding two steps down:

'You are the Legate, are you not? How tired you must be!' I took his hand in both of mine. 'Were you under the command of Germanicus?'

He nodded.

First blow struck!

'My brothers fought with Germanicus in the North,' I said. 'And Antony, the eldest, after the Triumphal March in Rome, lived long enough to tell us of the bones found in the Teutoburg Forest.'

'Ah, Madam, to see that field of bones, an entire army ambushed and the bodies left to rot!'

'Two of my brothers died in the battle. It was in a storm, in the North Sea.'

'Madam, you never saw such a disaster, but do you think the Barbarian God, Thor, could frighten our Germanicus?'

'Never. And you came here with the General?'

'Went everywhere with him, from the banks of the Elbe in the North to the South end of the River Nile.'

'How marvelous, and you are so tired, Tribune, look at you, you need sleep. Where is the famous Governor Gnaeus Calpurnius Piso? Why did it take him so long to quiet the city?'

'Because he's not here, Madam, and he doesn't dare to come back. Some say he makes a mutiny in Greece, others that he flees for his life.'

'Stop listening to her!' shouted Lucius.

'He was never much loved in Rome, either,' I said. 'It was Germanicus whom my brothers loved and my Father praised.'

'Indeed, and if we had been given one more year – one more year, Madam – we could have extinguished the fire of that bloody upstart King Arminius forever! We didn't even need that long! You spoke of the North Sea. We fought on all terrain.'

'Oh, yes, in the thick of the forest, and tell me this, were you there, Sir, when they found the lost standard of General Varus's legions? Is the story true!'

'Ah, Madam, when that golden eagle was

raised, you never heard such cries as from the soldiers.'

'This woman is a liar and a traitor,' shouted Lucius.

I turned on him. 'Don't push me too far! You're past all patience now. Do you even know the numbers of the Legions of General Varus who were ambushed in the Teutoburg Forest? I thought not! They were the Seventh, the Eighth and the Ninth.'

'Right, correct,' said the Legate. 'And we could have wiped out those tribes completely. The Empire would reach to the Elbe! But for some reason, and mine is not the place to question, our Emperor Tiberius called us back.'

'Hmmm, and then condemns your beloved leader for going to Egypt.'

'Madam, it was no trip to seize power, Germanicus's trip to Egypt. It was because of a famine.'

'Yes, and Germanicus had been declared *Imperium Maius* of all the Eastern provinces,' I said.

'And there was so much trouble!' said the Legate. 'You can not imagine the morale, the habits of the soldiers here, but our General never slept! He went directly when he heard of the famine.'

'And you with him?'

'All of us, his cohorts. In Egypt he delighted in seeing the old monuments. So did I.'

'Ah, how marvelous for him. You must tell me about Egypt! You know that I, as a Senator's daughter, cannot go to Egypt any more than can a Senator. I would so love –'

'Why is that, Madam?' asked the Legate.

'She's lying to you!' roared Lucius. 'Her whole family was murdered.'

'Very simple reason, Tribune,' I said to the Legate. 'It's no state secret. Rome is so dependent upon Egypt for corn that the Emperor wants to prevent the country from ever falling under the control of a powerful traitor. Surely you grew up as I did in dread of another Civil War.'

'I put my faith in our Generals,' said the Legate.

'You are right to do so. And you saw nothing from Germanicus but loyalty is that not so?'

'It is absolutely so. Ah, Egypt. We saw such Temples and statues!'

'The singing statues,' I asked, 'did you see them, the colossal man and woman who wail in the rising of the sun?'

'Yes, I heard it, Madam,' he said, nodding furiously. 'I heard the sound! It is magical. Egypt is full of magic!'

'Hmmm.' A tremor ran through me. I banished it. In a flash I saw two images mixed: that of the tall Roman in his toga, and that of a burnt and cunning creature! Think straight, Pandora!

'And in the Temple of Ramses the Great,' said the Legate, 'one of the Priests read the writing on the walls. All about victory? All about battle? We laughed because nothing really changes, Madam.'

'And Governor Piso, do you believe these rumors? Can we not speak safely of them, of rumors as if rumors were not things?'

'Everyone here despises him!' said the Legate. 'He was a bad soldier, plain and simple! And Agrippina the Elder, Germanicus's beloved wife, is on her way to Rome now with the General's ashes. She will officially accuse the Governor before the Senate!'

'Yes, how courageous of her, and that is how it should be done. If families are judged without trial, then we have fallen into tyranny, haven't we? Here, our friendly lunatic, don't you agree to that?'

Lucius was speechless. He turned red.

'And in the Teutoburg Forest,' I said tenderly, 'that gloomy arena for our doom, did you see all the bones of our lost legions, scattered about?'

'Buried them, Madam, with these hands!' The Legate held up his weathered callused palms. 'For who could tell what bones were ours and what bones were theirs? And Madam, the platform of that cowardly, sneaking King was still standing, from which the loathsome long-haired slob had ordered the sacrifice to his pagan gods of our men.'

Nods and noble mumbles came from the other soldiers.

'I was but a small child,' I said, 'when word came of the ambush of General Varus. But I remember our Divine Emperor Augustus – how he let his hair grow long in mourning and how he would pound his head on the walls, crying, "Varus, bring me back my legions."'

'You actually saw him this way?'

'Oh, many a time, and was present one night when he discussed his often mentioned thoughts – that the Empire must not try to push further. Rather it should police the states which it now contains.'

'Then Caesar Augustus did say this!' said the Legate in fascination.

'He cared about you,' I said to the Legate. 'How many years have you been in the field? Do you have a wife?'

'Oh, how I long to go home,' said the Legate.

'And now that my General has fallen. My wife is gray-haired as I am. I see her when we go to Rome for parades.'

'Yes, and compulsory service was only six years under the Republic, but now, you must fight for what? Twelve? Twenty? But who am I to criticize Augustus, whom I loved as I loved my Father and all my dead brothers?'

Lucius could see what was happening. He sputtered when he spoke:

'Tribune, read my Safe Conduct! Read it!'

The Legate looked truly annoyed.

My brother marshaled what he could of his rhetoric, which wasn't much. 'She lies. She is condemned. Her family is dead. I was compelled to bear witness to Sejanus because they sought to kill Tiberius himself!'

'You turned on your own family?' asked the soldier.

'Oh, don't wear yourself out with this,' I said. 'The man has harried me all day. He has discovered that I am a woman alone, an heiress, and thinks that this is some uncivilized outpost of the Empire where he can bring a charge against a Senator's daughter with no proof. Dear lunatic, do pay attention. Julius Caesar gave Antioch its municipal standing less than one hundred years ago. There are legions stationed here, are there not?'

I looked at the Legate.

The Legate turned and glowered at my trembling brother.

'What is this Safe Conduct?' I asked. 'This bears the name Tiberius.'

The Legate snatched it from Lucius before Lucius could respond and handed the scroll to me. I had to take my hand off my dagger to unroll the paper.

'Ah, Sejanus of the Praetorian Guard! I knew it. And the Emperor probably knows nothing of it. Tribune, do you know those palace guards make one and one half times what a Legionnaire makes? And now they have these *Delatores,* given incentive to charge others with crimes for one-third of the condemned man's property!'

The Legate was now sizing up my brother and every flaw in Lucius shone in the light; his cowardly posture, his trembling hands, his shifty eyes, his growing desperation in the pursing of his lips.

I turned to Lucius.

'Do you realize, you madman, whoever you are, what you are asking of this seasoned and wise Roman officer? What if he should believe your insane lies? What will become of him when the letter arrives from Rome inquiring into my whereabouts and the disposition of my fortune!'

'Sir, this woman is a traitor!' shouted Lucius. 'On my honor I swear –'

'What honor is that?' asked the soldier under his breath. His eyes fixed on Lucius.

'If Rome were such,' I said, 'that families as old as mine could be so easily dispatched as this man asks you now to do with me, then why would the widow of Germanicus dare to go before the Senate for a trial?'

'They are all executed,' said my brother, who was at his worst and most solemn, and seemed to have lost all touch with the effect of his words, 'every one of them, because they were in a plot to kill Tiberius and I was given Safe Conduct and passage out for reporting them, as was my duty, to the *Delatores,* and to Sejanus, with whom I spoke myself!'

The possibilities were making themselves known slowly to the Legate.

'Sir,' I said to Lucius, 'have you anything else on your person that identifies you?'

'I don't need anything else!' said Lucius. 'Your fate is death.'

'Same as it was for your Father?' asked the Legate, 'and your wife? Had you children?'

'Throw her into prison tonight, and write to Rome!' declared Lucius. 'You'll see that I speak the truth!'

'And where will you be, whoever you are, while I am in prison? Looting my house?'

'You slut!' shouted Lucius. 'Don't you see this is all feminine wiles and lurid distraction!'

There was shock among the soldiers, revulsion in the face of the Legate. Flavius moved next to me.

'Officer,' asked Flavius with tempered dignity, 'what am I allowed to do on behalf of my Mistress against this madman?'

'You use such words again, Sir,' I said firmly to Lucius, 'and I'll lose my patience.'

The Legate took Lucius's arm. Lucius's right hand went to his dagger.

'Just who are you?' the Legate demanded. 'Are you one of the *Delatores*? You tell me you turned on your whole family?'

'Tribune,' I said, laying the gentlest touch yet on his arm. 'My Father's roots went back to the time of Romulus and Remus. We know no origins other than those in Rome. It was the same with my Mother, who was herself the daughter of a Senator. This man is saying rather . . . horrible things.'

'So it seems,' said the Legate, narrowing his

gaze, as he inspected Lucius. 'Where are your friends here, your companions; where do you live?'

'You can't do anything to me!' said Lucius.

The Legate glared at Lucius's hand on the dagger.

'You prepare to draw that against me!' asked the Legate.

Lucius clearly was at a loss.

'Why did you come to Antioch?' I demanded of Lucius. 'Were you the bearer of the poison that killed Germanicus?'

'Arrest her!' shouted Lucius.

'No, I don't believe my own accusation. Not even Sejanus would put such treachery in the hands of a petty scoundrel like you! Come now, what else do you have on your person to connect you with this family, this Safe Conduct which you say came from the pen of Sejanus?'

Lucius was utterly baffled.

'I certainly have nothing belonging to me to connect me to your wild and bloody sagas and tales,' I said.

The Legate interrupted me. 'Nothing to connect you to this name?' He took the Safe Conduct from my hand.

'Absolutely nothing,' I said, 'nothing but this madman here who is spouting horrors, and would lead the world to believe that our Emperor has lost his wits. Only he connects me with his bloody plot without witness or verification, and hurls insults at me.'

The Legate rolled up the Safe Conduct. 'And your purpose here, Madam?' he asked in a whisper.

'To live in peace and quiet,' I said softly. 'To live in safety and under the true shelter of Roman rule.'

Now I knew the battle had been won. But something else was required to seal the victory. I took another gamble.

Slowly I reached for my dagger and slowly I brought it out of its sling.

Lucius leapt back at once. He drew his dagger and lunged at me. He was immediately stabbed by the Legate and at least two of the soldiers.

He hung there bleeding on their weapons, staring from right to left and then he spoke, but his mouth was too full of blood. His eyes widened; it seemed again he would speak. Then, as the soldiers withdrew their daggers, his body folded up on the cobblestones at the foot of the stairs.

My brother Lucius was quite mercifully dead.

I looked at him and shook my head.

The Legate looked at me. This was a significant moment, and I knew it.

'What is it, Tribune,' I asked, 'that separates us from the long-haired barbarians of the North? Is it not law? Written law? Traditional law? Is it not justice? That men and women are called to account for what they do?'

'Yes, Madam,' he said.

'You know,' I went on in a reverent voice, staring at this heap of blood and clothes and flesh that lay on the stones, 'I saw our great Emperor Caesar Augustus on the day of his death.'

'You saw him? You did?'

I nodded. 'When they were certain he was to die, we were rushed to him with a few other close friends. It was his hope to put down rumors in the capital that might lead to unrest. He had sent for a mirror and combed his hair. He was primly propped up. And he asked us as we entered the room: Didn't we think he'd played his part well in the comedy of life?

'I thought, what courage! And then he made some further joke, the old theatrical line they say after plays:

If I have made you happy, kindly let me know your appreciation with a warm goodbye.

*

'I could tell you more, but –'

'Oh, please do,' said the Legate.

'Well, why not?' I asked. 'It was told to me that the Emperor said of Tiberius, his chosen successor, 'Poor Rome, to be chewed slowly by those sluggish jaws!'

The Legate smiled. 'But there wasn't anyone else,' he said under his breath.

'Thank you, Tribune, for all your assistance. Would you allow me to take from my purse sufficient funds to treat you and your soldiers to a fine dinner –'

'No, Madam, I wouldn't have it be said I or any man here was bribed. Now this dead man. Do you know anything more of him?'

'Only this, Officer, that his body probably belongs in the river.'

The soldiers all laughed among themselves.

'Good night, Gracious Lady,' said the soldier.

And off I went, striding across the blackness of the Forum, with my beloved one-legged Flavius at my side and the torchbearers round us.

Only now did I shake all over. Only now did the sweat cover my whole body.

When we had plunged deeply into the unbroken darkness of a small alleyway, I said,

'Flavius, let these torchbearers go. There is no reason for them to know where we are headed.'

'Madam, I don't have any lantern.'

'The night's full of stars and has a near full moon. Look! Besides, there are others from the Temple who are following us.'

'There are?' he asked. He paid off the torch-bearers and they ran back towards the mouth of the street.

'Yes. There is one watching. And besides, we can see well enough by the lighted windows and Heaven's light, don't you think? I am tired, so tired.'

I walked on, reminding myself again and again that Flavius could not keep up. I began to weep.

'Tell me something with your great philo-sophical knowledge,' I said as I walked on, determined to make the tears stop. 'Tell me why evil people are so stupid? Why are so many of them just plain stupid?'

'Madam, I think there are quite a few evil people who are quite clever,' he said. 'But never have I seen such skilled rhetoric on the part of anyone, either bad or good, as your talents revealed just now.'

'I'm delighted that you know that that is all it was,' I said. 'Rhetoric. And to think he had the same teachers as I, the same library, the same Father –' My voice broke.

He put his arm gingerly about my shoulder and this time I didn't tell him to move away. I let him steady me. We walked faster as a pair.

'No,' I said, 'Flavius, the majority of the evil are just plain dumb, I've seen it all my life. The true crafty evil person is rare. It's bumbling that causes most of the misery of the world, utter stupid bumbling. It's underestimation of one's fellow man! You watch what happens with Tiberius. Tiberius Caesar and the Guard. Watch what happens to that damned Sejanus. You can sow the seeds of distrust everywhere, and lose yourself in an overgrown field.'

'We are home, Madam,' he said.

'Oh, thank God, you know it. I could never have told you this was the house.'

Within moments, he stopped and turned the key in a lock. The smell of urine was everywhere overpowering, as it always was in the back streets of ancient cities. A lantern threw a dim light on our wooden door. The light danced in the jet of water which fell from the lion's mouth in the fountain.

Flavius gave a series of knocks. It sounded to me as if the women answering the inner door were crying.

'Oh, Lord, now what?' I said. 'I am too sleepy. Whatever it is, tend to it.'

I went inside.

'Madam,' squealed one of the girls. I couldn't remember her name. 'I didn't let him in. I swear I never unbolted the door. I have no key to the gate. We had this house, all this, ready for you!' She sobbed.

'What on Earth are you talking about?' I asked.

But I knew. I'd seen in the corner of my eye. I knew. I turned and saw a very tall Roman sitting in my newly refurbished living room. He sat relaxed with ankle on knee in a gilded wooden chair.

'It's all right, Flavius,' I said. 'I know him.'

And I did. Because it was Marius. Marius the tall Keltoi. Marius, who had charmed me in childhood. Marius, whom I had almost identified in the shadows of the Temple.

He rose at once.

He came towards me, where I stood in the darkness on the edges of the atrium, and he whispered, 'My beautiful Pandora!'

He stopped just short of touching me.

'Oh, do, please,' I said. I moved to kiss him, but he moved away. The room had scattered lamps. He played the shadows.

'Marius, of course, Marius! And you look not one day older than when I saw you in my girl-hood. Your face is radiant, and your eyes, how beautiful are your eyes. I would sing these praises to the accompaniment of a lyre if I could.'

Flavius had slowly withdrawn, taking the distressed girls with him. He made not a sound.

'Pandora,' Marius said, 'I wish I could take you in my arms, but there are reasons why I can-not, and you mustn't touch me, not because I want it so much, but because I'm not what you think. You don't see the evidence of youth in me; it is something so far afield of the promises

235

of youth that I've only just begun to understand its agonies.'

Suddenly he looked off. He raised his hand for my silence and patience.

'That thing is abroad,' I said. 'The burnt blood drinker.'

'Don't think on your dreams just now,' he said to me directly. 'Think on our youth. I loved you when you were a girl of ten. When you were fifteen I begged your Father for your hand.'

'You did? He never told me this.'

He looked away again. Then he shook his head.

'The burnt one,' I said.

'I feared this,' he cursed himself. 'He followed you from the Temple! Oh, Marius! You are fool. You have played into his hands. But he is not as clever as he thinks.'

'Marius, was it you who sent me the dreams!'

'No, never! I would do anything in my power to protect you from myself.'

'And from the old legends?'

'Don't be quick of wit, Pandora. I know your immense cleverness served you well back there with your loathsome brother Lucius and the gentleman Legate. But don't think too much about . . . dreams. Dreams are nothing, and dreams will pass.'

'Then the dreams came from him, this hideous burnt killer?'

'I can't figure it!' he said. 'But don't think on the images. Don't feed him now with your mind.'

'He reads minds,' I said, 'just as you do.'

'Yes. But you can cloak your thoughts. It's a mental trick. You can learn it. You can walk with your soul locked up in a little metal box in your head.'

I realized he was in much pain. An immense sadness came from him. 'This cannot be allowed to happen!' he insisted.

'What is that, Marius? You speak about the woman's voice, you –'

'No, be quiet.'

'I will not! I will get to the bottom of this!'

'You must take my instructions!' He stepped forward and again he reached to touch me, to take me by the arms, as my Father might have done, but then he did not.

'No, it is you who must tell me everything,' I said.

I was amazed at the whiteness of his skin, its utter blemishless perfection. And once again the radiance of his eyes seemed almost impossible. Inhuman.

Only now did I see the full glory of his long

hair. He did look like the Keltoi, who had been his ancestors. His hair touched his shoulders. It was a gleaming gold, overly bright, yellow as corn and full of soft curls.

'Look at you!' I whispered. 'You're not alive!'

'No, take your last look, for you are leaving here!'

'What?' I said. 'Last look?' I repeated his words. 'What are you talking about! I've only arrived, laid my plans, rid myself of my brother! I am not leaving here. Do you mean to say you are leaving me?'

There was a terrible anguish in his face, a courageous appeal that I had never seen in any man, not even in my Father, who had worked swiftly in those last fatal moments at home, as if he were merely intent on sending me on an important appointment.

Marius's eyes were filmed with blood. He was crying, and his eyes were sore with the tears! No! These were tears like the tears of the magnificent Queen in the dream, who, bound to her throne, wept and stained her cheeks and her throat and her linen.

He wanted to deny it. He shook his head, but he knew I was quite convinced.

'Pandora, when I saw it was you,' he said,

'when you came into the Temple and I saw it was you who had had these blood dreams, I was beside myself. I must get you far from this, far from all danger.'

I separated myself from his spell, from the aura of his beauty. I beheld him with a cold eye, and I listened as he went on, noting all about him, from the glitter of his eyes to the way that he gestured.

'You have to leave Antioch at once,' he said. 'I will stay here the night with you. Then in the day, you pick up your faithful Flavius and your two girls, they are honest, and you take them with you. You put miles between you and this place by day, and this thing can't follow you! Don't tell me now where you mean to go. You can discuss all this at the docks in the morning. You have plenty of money.'

'You are the one who is dreaming now, Marius; I am not going. Who is it precisely that you want me to flee? The weeping Queen on her throne? Or the prowling, burnt one? The former reaches me over miles and miles of sea with her summons. She warns me against my evil brother. The other I can easily dispatch. I have no fear of him. I know what he is from the dreams, and I know how the sun has hurt him, and I will myself pin him to the wall in the sun.'

He was silent, biting his lip.

'I will do that for her, for the Queen in the dreams, to avenge her.'

'Pandora, I am begging you.'

'In vain,' I said. 'Do you think I have come so far only to run again? And the woman's voice –'

'How do you know it was this Queen of whom you dreamt? There could be other blood drinkers in this city. Men, women. They all want the same thing.'

'And you fear them?'

'Loathe them! And I must keep clear of them, not give them what they want! Never give them what they want.'

'Ah, I see it all,' I said.

'You do not!' he said, scowling down at me. So fierce, so perfect.

'You are one of them, Marius. You are whole. You are unburnt. They want your blood to heal themselves.'

'How could you think of such a thing?'

'In my dreams, they called the Queen "the Fount."'

I flew at him and imprisoned him in my arms! He was powerfully strong, solid as a tree! I never felt such hardness of muscle in a man. I lay my head on his shoulder, and his cheek against the top of my head was cold!

But he enfolded me gently with both arms, stroking my hair, pulling it down out of all the pins and letting it flow down my back. I felt a rich tingling all over the surface of my skin.

Hard, so hard, yet with no pulse of life. No warmth of human blood in his gentle, sweet gestures.

'My darling,' he said, 'I don't know the source of your dreams, but I know this. You will be protected from me and from them. You will never become part of this old tale that goes on verse by verse no matter how the world changes! I won't allow it.'

'Explain these things to me. I will not cooperate with you until you explain everything. Do you know the anguish of the Queen of the dream? Her tears are like yours. Look. Blood. You stain your tunic! Is she here, this Queen; has she summoned me?'

'And what if she has and she wants to punish you for this former life you dreamt in which the evil gods kept her fettered. What if that is so!'

'No,' I said. 'That is not her intention. Besides, I wouldn't do what the dark gods of the dream said. I wouldn't drink from "the Fount." I ran and that's why I died in the desert.'

'Ah!' He threw up his hands! And walked

away. He stared out into the dark peristyle. Only the stars lighted the trees there. I saw a faint glow coming from the far dining room on the other side of the house.

I looked at him, at his great height and the straightness of his back, and the way his feet were so firmly fixed on the mosaic floor. The lamps made his blond hair glorious.

I heard him, though he whispered with his back to me.

'How could this stupid thing have happened!'

'What stupid thing!' I demanded. I came to his side. 'You mean that I am here, in Antioch. I'll tell you how. My Father arranged my escape, that's how . . .'

'No, no, I don't mean that. I want you to be safe, alive, out of all danger, protected, so that you flower as you are meant to do. Your petals aren't even bruised at the edges, look at you, and your boldness heats your beauty! Your brother had no chance against your learning or your rhetoric. And yet you charmed the soldiers and made slaves of them with your superiority, never once rousing their resentment. You have years of life in you! But I must think of some way to make you safe. Look. This is the heart of it. You have to leave Antioch during the day.'

'"Friend of the Temple," that's what the

Priest and Priestess called you. They said you could read the old script. They said you bought up all the Egyptian books when they came into the port. Why? If you seek her, the Queen, then seek her through me, because it is she who said that she had summoned me.'

'She didn't speak in the dreams! You don't know who spoke the words! What if the dreams do have their root in your migrant soul? What if you have lived before? And now you come to the Temple and there is one of these loathed ancient gods on the prowl and you are in danger. You must get away, from here, from me, from this wounded hunter, whom I will find.'

'You're not telling me all you know! What happened to you, Marius! What happened! Who did this to you, this miracle of your radiance. This is no cloak; the light comes from within!'

'Damn it, Pandora, do you think I wanted my life foreshortened and my destiny extended forever!' He was suffering. He looked at me, unwilling to speak, and I felt such pain coming from him, such loneliness, that for a moment it was unbearable.

I felt a wave of my own anguish of the long night before, when the utter vacuity of all religions and creeds had struck me hard and the sheer effort of a good life seemed a fool's trap, and nothing more.

He suddenly closed his arms around me, surprising me, holding me firmly and rubbing his cheek gently against my hair, and kissing my head. Silken, polished, gentle beyond words. 'Pandora, Pandora, Pandora,' he said. 'The beautiful little girl grown into the marvelous woman.'

I held this hard effigy of the most spectacular and singular man I had ever known or seen: I held it and this time heard the beating of his heart, the distinct rhythm of it. I laid my ear on his chest.

'Oh, Marius, if only I could lay my head to rest next to yours. If I could only yield to your protection. But you are driving me away! You don't promise guardianship, you ordain flight for me, wandering and more nightmares, and mystery, and despair. No. I can't.'

I turned away from his caresses. I could feel his kisses on my hair.

'Don't tell me that I'll never see you again. Don't think I can bear that along with everything else that's happened. I have no one here, and then who comes but one who left such a stamp on my girlish heart that the details are as deep as the finest coin. And you say you will never see me again, that I must go.'

I turned around.

It was lust shining in his eyes. Yet he checked it. In a soft voice, he confessed with a little smile:

'Oh, how I admired your work with the Legate. I thought the two of you would plan out the whole conquest of the Germanic tribes on your own.' He sighed. 'You must find a good life, a rich life, a life where your soul and body are fed.' The color flared in his face. He looked at me, at my breasts, at my hips and then at my face. Ashamed and trying to conceal it. Lust.

'Are you a man still?' I asked.

He didn't answer me. But his expression grew chilly.

'You will never know the full extent of what I am!' he said.

'Ah, but not a man!' I said. 'Am I right? Not a man.'

'Pandora, you are deliberately taunting me. Why? Why do this?'

'This transformation, this induction into the blood drinkers; it's added no inches to your height. Did it add any inches anywhere else?'

'Please stop this,' he said.

'Want me, Marius. Say that you do. I see it. Confirm it in words. What does that cost you?'

'You are infuriating!' he said. His face colored

deeply with his rage, and pressed his lips together so hard that they went white. 'Thank the gods that I don't want you! Not enough to betray love for brief and bloody ecstasy.'

'The Temple people, they don't really know what you are, do they?'

'No!' he said.

'And you will not lay open your heart to me.'

'Never. You will forget me and these dreams will fade. I wager I can make them fade, myself, through prayer for you. I will do it.'

'That's a pious tack,' I said. 'What grants you such favor with the ancient Isis, who drank blood and was the Fount?'

'Don't say those words; it's all lies, all of it. You do not know that this Queen you saw was Isis. What did you learn in these nightmares? Think. You learned that this Queen was the prisoner of those who drank blood and she condemned them! They were evil. Think. Go back into the dream. Think. You thought them evil, evil then, and you think them evil now. In the Temple, you caught the scent of evil. I know you did. I watched you.'

'Yes. But you're not evil, Marius, you can't convince me of this! You have a body like marble, you're a blood drinker, but like a god, but not evil!'

He was about to protest when he stopped again. He looked out of the corner of his eye. And then slowly turned his head and let his gaze drift up through the roof of the peristyle.

'Is it the dawn coming,' I asked, 'the rays of Amon Ra?'

'You are the most maddening human being I've ever known!' he said. 'If I had married you, you would have put me in an early grave. I would have been spared all of this!'

'All of what?'

He called out for Flavius, who had been close all the while, listening to everything.

'Flavius, I'm leaving now,' he said. 'I must. But guard her. When night falls, I'll be here again, as quickly as I can. Should anything precede me, any badly scarred and frightening assailant, go for its head with your sword. The head, remember? And of course your Mistress here will no doubt be quite able to lend a hand in defending herself.'

'Yes, sir. Must we leave Antioch?'

'Watch your words, my faithful Greek,' I said. 'I am Mistress here. We are not leaving Antioch.'

'Try to persuade her to prepare,' said Marius. He looked at me.

A long silence fell between us. I knew he read my thoughts. Then a shudder of the blood

247

dreams passed over me. I saw his eyes brighten. Something quickened in his expression. I shook off the dream, filled with terror. I am no hostess to terror.

'It's all interwound,' I murmured, 'the dreams, the Temple, you being there, their calling on you for help. What are you, some white god put on Earth to hunt the dark blood drinkers? Does the Queen live?'

'Oh, I wish I were such a god!' he said. 'I would be if I could be! That no more blood drinkers will ever be made, of that I am certain. Let them lay flowers on an altar before a statue of basalt!'

I felt such love for him and rushed to him suddenly. 'Take me with you now, wherever you are going.'

'I can't!' he said. He blinked as though something hurt his eyes. He couldn't fully lift his head.

'It's the coming light, isn't it? You are one of them.'

'Pandora, when I come to you, be ready to leave this place!' he said.

And he vanished.

Like that, he vanished. Like that, he was gone from my arms and from my living room and from my house.

I turned away and walked slowly about the shadowy living room. I looked at the murals on the walls; the happy dancing figures with their laurels and their crowns of leaves – Bacchus and his nymphs, so modestly covered for such a riotous crew!

Flavius spoke. 'Madam, a sword which I found among your possessions, may I have it in readiness?'

'Yes, and daggers galore, and fire, do not forget fire. It will run from fire.' I sighed. How did I know this? I did. So much for it. 'But Flavius.' I turned around. 'It won't come until dark. There is only a small margin of the night left. We can both sleep as soon as we see the sky turn purple.' I lifted my hand to my forehead. 'I am trying to remember . . .'

'What, Madam?' Flavius said. He looked no less splendid after the spectacle of Marius, simply a man of different proportion but equally fine, and with warm human skin.

'Whether the dreams ever came by day. Was it always night? Oh, I am sleepy and they summon me. Flavius, put a light in my bath. But I'm going to bed. I am drowsy. Can you watch?'

'Yes, Madam.'

'Look, the stars have all but faded. What is it like to be one of them, Flavius, to be admired only in the darkness, when men and women live with candles and lamps. To be known and described, only in the heaviness of night, when all the business of day has ended!'

'You are truly the most resourceful woman I've ever known,' he said. 'How you brought justice to the man who accused you.' He took my arm, and we moved towards the bedchamber where I had dressed that morning.

I loved him. An entire lifetime of crises could not have made it stronger.

'You will not sleep in the great bed of the house, in the dining room?'

'No,' I said. 'That is for the display of marriage, and I will never know marriage again. I want to bathe, but I'm so sleepy.'

'I can wake the girls.'

'No, to the bed. You have a chamber proper?'

'Yes,' he led the way. It was still quite dark. I thought I heard a rustling noise. Realized it was nothing.

And there lay the bed with its small lamp, and on the bed so many pillows in the Oriental style, a soft soft nest into which I fell, like a Persian.

At once, the dream:

We blood drinkers stood in a vast Temple. It was meant to be dark. We could see this dark, as certain animals must see in the dark. We were all bronze-skinned, or tanned, or golden. We were all men.

On the floor lay the Queen screaming. Her skin was white. Pure white. Her long hair was black. Her crown bore the horns and the sun! The crown of Isis. She was the goddess! It took five blood drinkers on either side to hold her down. She thrashed her head from side to side, her eyes seeming to crackle with Divine Light.

'I am your Queen! You cannot do this to me!' How purely white she was, and her screams grew ever more desperate and imploring. 'Great Osiris, save me from this! Save me from these blasphemers! Save me from the profane!'

The Priest beside me sneered at her.

The King sat motionless on the throne. But it was not to this King that she prayed. She prayed to an Osiris beyond.

'Hold her more tightly.'

Two more came to secure her ankles.

'Drink!' said the Priest to me. 'Kneel down and drink from her blood. Her blood is more powerful than any blood that exists in the world. Drink.'

She cried softly.

'Monsters, demon children!' she sobbed.

'I won't do it,' I said.

'Do it! You must have her blood!'

'No, not against her will. Not like this! She's our Mother Isis!'

'She is our Fount and our prisoner.'

'No,' I said.

The Priest shoved me forward. I knocked him down to the floor. I looked at her.

She looked at me as indiscriminately as she looked at the others. Her face was delicate and exquisitely painted. Her rage did not distort her features. Her voice was low and full of hatred.

'I will destroy you all,' she said. 'Some morning, I will escape and walk into the sun's light and all of you will burn! All of you will burn! As I burn! Because I am the Fount! And the evil in me will be burnt and extinguished in all of you forever. Come, you miserable fledgling,' she said to me. 'Do as they say. Drink, and wait my vengeance.

'The god Amon Ra will rise in the East and I will walk towards him, and his deadly rays will kill me. I shall be a sacrifice of fire to destroy every one of you who has been born of me, transformed by my blood! You greedy wanton gods who would use the power we possess for gain!'

Then a hideous transformation befell the entire dream. She rose to her feet. She was pristine and freshly adorned. Torches burst into flame around her, one and two and three and then many and more, flaring as if they'd just been ignited, till she was surrounded by flame. The gods were gone. She smiled and beckoned to me. She lowered her head; the white beneath her eyes shone as she looked up at me. She smiled. She was cunning.

I woke up screaming.

I was in my bed. Antioch. The lamp burned. Flavius held me. I saw the light shine on his ivory leg as it was stretched out. I saw the light shine on the carved toes.

'Hold onto me, hold me!' I said. 'Mother Isis! Hold me.'

'How long have I been asleep?'

'Only moments,' he said.

'No.'

'The sun has just risen. Do you want to go out, lie in the warm sun perhaps?'

'No!' I screamed.

He tightened his warm, desperate comforting grip. 'It was only a bad dream, my beautiful lady,' he said. 'Close your eyes. I'll sleep by your side, with my dagger here.'

'Oh, yes, please, please, Flavius. Don't let me go. Hold me,' I cried.

I lay down and he snuggled next to me, his knees behind mine, his arm over me.

My eyes opened. I heard Marius's voice again:

253

'Thank the gods that I don't want you! Not enough to betray love for brief and bloody ecstasy.'

'Oh, Flavius,' I said. 'My skin! Is my skin burning!' I started to rise. 'Put out the light. Put out the sun!'

'No, Madam, your skin is as beautiful as it always was. Lie down. Let me sing to you.'

'Yes, sing . . .' I said.

I followed his song, it was Homer, it was Achilles and Hector, and I loved the way he sang it, the pauses he made, I pictured those heroes, and the high walls of doomed Troy, and my eyes grew heavy. I drifted. I rested.

He placed his hand over my head, as if to keep the dreams out, as if to be a human dream catcher. And I sighed as he smoothed my hair.

I pictured Marius, the sheen of his skin. It had been so like that of the Queen, and the dazzle of his eyes, so truly like that of the Queen, and I heard him say, 'Damn it, Pandora, do you think I wanted my life foreshortened and my destiny extended forever!'

And there followed, before unconsciousness, the utter despair, the sense of worthlessness of all striving. Better that we be no more than beasts, like the lions in the arena.

8

I awoke. I could hear the birds. I wasn't sure. I calculated that it was still morning, midmorning.

I walked barefoot into the next room, and through it into the peristyle. I walked on the tiled edge of the Earth and looked up at the blue sky. The sun had not yet risen high enough to be seen directly above.

I unbolted the door and went barefoot to the gate. To the first man I saw, a man of the desert, wearing a long head veil, I said:

'What time is it? Noon?'

'Oh, no, Madam,' he said. 'Not by half. Have you overslept? How lucky for you.' He nodded and went on.

A lamp burned in the living room. I walked into the living room and saw that the lamp stood on the desk which my servants had prepared for me.

The ink was there and so were the pens, and so were sheets of clean parchment.

I sat down and I wrote down everything that I could remember of the dreams, my eyes straining to see by the miserable little lamp in the shadows, too far from the light that filled the fresh green garden of the peristyle.

My arm hurt finally from the speed with which I scratched at the parchment. In detail I described the last dream, the torches, the Queen's smile, her beckoning to me.

It was done. All the while, I had set aside the pages to dry all about me on the floor. There was no breeze or wind to threaten them. I gathered them up.

I went to the edge of the garden deliberately to look at the blue sky, this sheaf of papers close to my breast. Blue and clear.

'And you cover this world,' I said. 'And you are changeless, save for one light that rises and sets,' I said to the sky. 'Then comes the night with deceptive and seductive patterns!'

'Madam!' It was Flavius behind me, and very sleepy. 'You've scarcely slept at all. You need rest. Go back to bed.'

'Go get my sandals now, hurry,' I said.

And as he disappeared, so did I – out the front gate of the house, walking as fast as I could.

I was halfway to the Temple of Isis when I realized the discomfort of confronting this filthy street in bare feet. I realized I wore the rumpled linen dresses in which I'd slept. My hair streamed. I didn't slow my pace.

I was elated. I was not helpless as when I had fled my Father's house. I was not edgy and in deep danger as when Lucius had pointed me out to the Roman soldiers last night.

I was not gripped in fear as I had been when the Queen smiled to me in the dream. Nor shivering as I had been upon waking.

I walked on and on. I was in the grip of an immense drama. I would see it through to the last act.

People passed – laborers of the morning, an old man with a crooked stick. I barely saw these people.

I took a cold small delight in the fact that they noticed my loose, free hair and my wrinkled gowns. I wondered what it must be like to separate oneself from all civilization and never worry again about the position of a fastening or a pin, to sleep on grass, to fear nothing!

Fear nothing! Ah, that was so beautiful to me.

I came to the Forum. The markets were busy; the beggars were out in full force. Curtained litters were being carried every which way The philosophers were teaching under the porticoes. I could hear those huge strange noises that always come from a harbor – of the cargo being dropped, perhaps, I didn't know. I smelled the Orontes. I hoped Lucius's body was floating in it.

I went up the steps and right into the Temple of Isis.

'The High Priest and Priestess,' I said. 'I must see them.' I walked past a confused and distinctly virginal-looking young woman and went into the side chamber where they had first spoken to me. No table. Only the couch. I went into another apartment of the Temple. A table. Scrolls.

I heard feet rushing. The Priestess came to me. She was already painted for the day and her wig and ornaments were in place. I felt no shock as I looked at her.

'Look,' I said. 'I had another dream.' I pointed to the sheets which I had piled neatly on the table. 'I've written down everything for you.'

The Priest arrived. He approached the table and stared at the sheets.

'Read it all, every word. Read it now. Bear witness lest something happens to me!'

The Priest and Priestess stood on opposite sides of me, the Priest carefully lifting the pages

258

to study each one, while not actually turning over the stack.

'I am a migrant soul,' I said. 'She wants some reckoning or favor of me, I don't know which, but she lives! She is no mere statue.'

They stared at me.

'Well? Speak up? Everyone comes to you for guidance.'

'But Madam,' said the Priest, 'we can't read any of this.'

'What?'

'It's written in the most ancient and ornate form of the old picture writing.'

'What!'

I stared down at the pages. I saw only my own words as they had flowed in a cadence from my mind, through my hand, through my pen. I couldn't make my eyes fix upon the form of the letters.

I lifted the last page and read aloud, 'Her smile was cunning. It filled me with fear.' I held out the page.

They shook their heads in firm denial.

Suddenly there was a little ruckus and Flavius, much out of breath and red in the face, was admitted to the room. He had my sandals. He took one look at me and rested back against the wall in great and obvious relief.

'Come here,' I said.

He obeyed.

'Now look at these pages, read them, are they not in Latin?'

Two slaves came timidly, hastily washing my feet and fastening on my sandals. Above me Flavius looked at the pages.

'This is ancient Egyptian writing,' Flavius said. 'The oldest form I've ever seen. This would fetch a fortune in Athens!'

'I just wrote it!' I said. I looked at the Priest, then the Priestess. 'Summon your tall blond-haired friend,' I said. 'Get him here. The mind reader, the one who can read the old script.'

'We can't, Madam.' The Priest looked helplessly at the Priestess.

'Why not? Where is he? He only comes after dark, doesn't he?' I asked.

They both nodded.

'And when he shops for books, all the books on Egypt, he does this by the light of lamps too?' I asked. I already knew the answer.

They looked at one another helplessly.

'Where does he live?'

'Madam, we do not know. Please don't try to find him. He will be here as soon as the light fades. He cautioned us last night that you were most precious to him.'

'You don't know where he lives.'

I stood up.

'All right,' I said, I picked up the sheaf of my pages, my spectacular ancient writing.

'Your burnt one,' I said, as I walked out of the room, 'your murdering blood drinker. Did he come last night? Did he leave you an offering?'

'Yes,' said the Priest. He looked humiliated. 'Lady Pandora, rest and take some food.'

'Yes,' said my loyal Flavius, 'you must.'

'Not a chance,' I said. Clutching the pages, I walked across the great hall to the front doors. They pleaded with me. I ignored them.

I went out into the heat of the day. Flavius followed. The Priest and Priestess pleaded with us to remain.

I scanned the enormous marketplace. The good booksellers were all grouped at the far left end of the Forum. I walked across the square.

Flavius struggled to keep up. 'Madam, please, what are you going to do? You've lost your mind.'

'I have not and you know it,' I said. 'You saw him last night!'

'Madam, wait for him at the Temple, as he asked,' Flavius said.

'Why? Why should I do that?' I asked.

The bookshops were numerous, containing manuscripts in all languages. 'Egypt, Egypt!' I cried out, both in Latin and Greek. There was lots of noise, many buyers and sellers. Plato was everywhere, and Aristotle. There was a whole stack of the book of his life by Caesar Augustus, which he had completed in the years before his death.

'Egypt!' I cried out. Merchants pointed to old scrolls. Fragments.

The canopies flapped in the breeze. I looked into one room after another, at rows of slaves busily copying, slaves dipping their pens, who did not dare to look up from their work.

There were slaves outside, in the shade, writing letters dictated by humble men and women. It was all very busy.

Trunks were being brought into one shop. The owner, an elderly man, came forward.

'Marius,' I said. 'I come from Marius, the tall blond one who comes to your shop only by night.'

The man said nothing.

I went into the next shop. Everything was Egyptian, not merely the scrolls rolled out for display but the fragments of painting on the walls, the chunks of plaster holding still the profile of a King or Queen, rows of little jars, figures from some long-defiled tomb. How the Egyptians loved to make those tiny wooden figures.

And there I beheld just the sort of man I sought, the true antiquarian. Only reluctantly did he look up from his book, a gray-haired man, the book a codex in modern Egyptian.

'Nothing that would interest Marius?' I asked, walking into the shop. Trunks and boxes blocked me at each turn. 'You know, the tall Roman, Marius, who studies the ancient manuscripts, buys the most prized of them? You know the man I mean. Very blue eyes. Blond hair. He comes by night; you stay open for him.'

The man nodded. He glanced at Flavius and said with a lift of his eyebrows. 'Quite an ivory leg there.' Cultured Greek. Excellent. 'Grecian, Oriental and perfectly pale.'

'I come on Marius's behalf,' I said.

'I save everything for him, as he asks,' said the man with a little shrug. 'I sell nothing that isn't offered first to Marius.'

'I'm sure you do. I come on his behalf.' I looked around. 'May I sit down?'

'Oh, please do, forgive me,' said the man. He gestured to a sturdy trunk. Flavius stood perplexed. The man sat back down at his cluttered table.

'I wish I had a proper table. Where is my slave? I know I have some wine around here. I just . . . I was reading in this text the most amazing story!'

'Really,' I said. 'Well, take a look at this!' I thrust the pages into his hand.

'My god, but this is beautiful copying,' he said, 'and so fresh!' He whispered under his breath. He could make out many of the words. 'Marius will be very interested in this. This is about the legends of Isis, this is what Marius studies.'

I drew back the papers gently. 'I've written this for him!'

'You wrote it?'

'Yes, but you see, I want to surprise him with something, a gift! Something newly arrived, something he hasn't seen yet.'

'Well, there's quite a lot.'

'Flavius, money.'

'Madam, I don't have any'

'That's not true, Flavius; you wouldn't leave the house without the keys and some money. Hand it over.'

'Oh, I'll take it on credit if it's for Marius,' said the old man. 'Hmmm, you know, several things came onto the market this very week. It's because of the famine in Egypt. People were forced to sell, I suppose. You never know where an Egyptian manuscript comes from. But here –' He reached up and took a fragile papyrus from its niche in the dusty crisscross of wooden shelves.

He laid it down reverently and most cautiously opened it. The papyrus had been well preserved, but it was flaking at the edges. The thing would disintegrate if not handled with care.

I stood to look at it over his shoulder. A dizziness overcame me. I saw the desert and a town of huts with roofs of palm branches. I strained to open my eyes.

'This is,' said the old man, 'positively the oldest manuscript in Egyptian which I have ever seen! Here, steady yourself, my dear. Lean upon my shoulder. Let me give you my stool.'

'No, not necessary,' I said gazing at the letters. I read aloud, 'To my Lord, Narmer, King of Upper and Lower Egypt, who are these enemies of me that say I do not walk in righteousness? When has Your Majesty ever known me not to be righteous? Indeed I seek to do always more than what is asked of me or expected. When have I not heard every word of the accused so that he may be judged in fairness, as would Your Majesty? . . .'

I broke off. My head swam. Some brief recollection. I was a child and we were all going up into the mountains over the desert to ask the god Osiris, the blood god, to look into the heart of the evildoer. 'Look,' said those around me. The god was a man of perfection, bronze of skin and under the moon; he took the condemned and slowly drew out his blood. Beside me a woman whispered that the god had made his judgment and rendered punishment and the evil blood would go back now to be cleansed and reborn in another in which it would do no harm.

I tried to banish this vision, this sense of enclosing remembrance. Flavius was greatly concerned and held me by the shoulders.

I stood suspended in two worlds. I gazed out at the bright sun striking the stones of the Forum, and I lived somewhere else, a young man running up a mountain, declaring my innocence. 'Summon the old blood god! He will look into my husband's heart and see that the man lies. I never lay with another.' Oh, sweet darkness, come, I needed it to shroud the mountains because the blood god slept by day hidden, lest Ra, the sun god, find him and destroy him out of jealousy.

'Because she had conquered them all,' I whispered. I meant Queen Isis. 'Flavius, hold me.'

'I have you, Madam.'

'There,' said the old man, who had risen and pushed me down on his stool.

The night over Egypt filled with stars. I saw it as distinctly as I saw this shop around me in Antioch at midday. I saw the stars and knew I had won. The god would rule. 'Oh, come forth, please, from this mountain, our beloved Osiris, and look into my husband's heart and my heart, and if you find me in the wrong, then my blood is yours, I pledge it.' He was coming! There he was, as I had seen him in childhood before the Priests of Ra had forbidden the old worship. 'Righteousness, righteousness, righteousness!' the crowd chanted. The man who was my husband cowered as the god pointed his finger in judgment at him. 'Give me this evil blood and I shall devour it,' said the god. 'Then bring back my offerings. Do not be cowards in the face of a rich priesthood. You stand before a god.' He pointed at each of the villagers and pronounced his or her name. He knew trades. He could read their minds! He drew back his lips and showed his fangs. The vision dissolved. I stared at common objects as though they had life and venom.

'Oh, ye gods,' I said in genuine distress. 'I must reach Marius. I must reach him now!' When he heard these things, Marius would draw me into the truth with him. He had to do it.

'Hire a litter for your Mistress,' said the old bookseller to Flavius. 'She is overtired, and it's too long a walk up that hill!'

'Hill?' I perked up. This man knew where Marius lived! I quickly went faint again, bowing my head, and with a weary gesture said, 'Please, old gentleman, tell my steward precisely how to reach the house.'

'Of course. I know two short cuts, one slightly more difficult than another. We deliver books to Marius all the time.'

Flavius was staring aghast.

I tried to suppress my smile. This was going much better than I had ever hoped. But I was torn and bruised from the visions of Egypt. I hated the look of the desert, the mountains, the thought of blood gods.

I rose to go.

'It's a pink villa on the very edge of the city,' said the old man. 'It's just within the walls, overlooking the river, the last house. Once it was a country house outside the walls. It is on a mountain of stones. But no one will answer Marius's gate by day. All know how he wants to sleep all day and study all night, as is his custom. We leave our books with the boys.'

'He'll welcome me,' I said.

'If you wrote that, most likely he will,' said the old man.

Then we were off. The sun had fully risen. The square was filled with shoppers. Women carried baskets on their heads. The Temples were thriving. It was a game, darting through the crowd, one way and then another.

'Come on, Flavius,' I said.

It was a torture keeping to Flavius's slow pace as we mounted the hill, turn by turn, drawing ever closer.

'You know this is madness!' said Flavius. 'He can't be awake during the light of day; you've proven this to me and to yourself! I, the incredulous Athenian, and you the cynical Roman. What are we doing?'

Up and up we climbed, passing one sumptuous house after another. Locked gates. The bark of guard dogs.

'Hurry up. Must I listen to this lecture forever? Ah, there, look, my beloved Flavius. The pink house, the last house. Marius lives in style. Look at the walls and the gates.'

At last I had my hands on the iron bars. Flavius collapsed on the grass across the small road. He was spent.

I pulled on the bell rope.

Trees laid down heavy limbs over the top of

the walls. Through the mesh of leaf, I could make out a figure that came out on the high porch of the second floor.

'No admittance!' he cried out.

'I have to see Marius,' I said. 'He's expecting me!' I cupped my hands and shouted. 'He wants me to come. He told me to come.'

Flavius said a quick prayer under his breath. 'Oh, Mistress, I hope you know this man better than you knew your own brother.'

I laughed. 'There is no comparison,' I said. 'Stop complaining.'

The figure had disappeared. I heard running feet.

Finally two dark-headed young boys appeared before me, little more than children, beardless, with long black curls, and beautifully dressed in gold-trimmed tunics. They looked Chaldean.

'Open the gate, hurry!' I said.

'Madam, I can't admit you,' said the speaker of the two. 'I cannot admit anyone to this house until Marius himself comes. Those are his orders.'

'Comes from where?' I asked.

'Madam, he appears when he wishes, then he receives who he will. Madam, please, tell me your name and I will tell him that you have called.'

'You either open the gate or I will climb over the wall,' I said.

The boys were horrified. 'No, Madam, you can't do that!'

'Well? Aren't you going to shout for help?' I asked.

The two slaves stared amazed. They were so pretty. One was slightly taller than the other. Both wore exquisite bracelets.

'Just as I thought,' I said. 'There's no one else here but you.' I turned and tested the thick snaggle of vine that rose over the plastered brick. I leapt up and planted my right foot as high as I could in the thick mesh and rose in one leap to throw my arms over the top of the wall.

Flavius had risen from the grass and rushed to me.

'Madam, I beg you not to do this,' said Flavius. 'Madam, this is bad, bad, bad! You can't just climb this man's wall.'

The servants within were chattering frantically with one another. I think it was in Chaldean.

'Madam, I fear for you!' cried Flavius. 'How can I protect you from such a man as this Marius? Madam, the man will be angry with you!'

I lay on the top of the wall, on my stomach,

catching my breath. The garden inside was vast and lovely. Ah, what marble fountains. The two slaves had backed up and were staring at me as if I were a powerful monster.

'Please, please!' both boys pleaded with me at once. 'He'll exact a terrible vengeance! You don't know him. Please, Madam, wait!'

'Hand me the sheets of paper, Flavius, hurry. I have no time for disobedience!'

Flavius complied. 'Oh, this is wrong, wrong, wrong!' he said. 'Nothing can come of this but the most fearful misunderstandings.'

Then I slid down the inside of the wall, tickled all over by the thick overlay of bristling and brilliant leaves, and I laid my head in the matted tendrils and blossoms. I didn't fear the bees. I never have. I rested. I held tight to my written pages. Then moved to the gate so I could see Flavius.

'You let me handle Marius,' I said. 'Now, you didn't come out without your dagger.'

'No, I did not,' he said, lifting his cloak to reveal it, 'and with your permission I would like to plunge it through my heart now so that I will be most assuredly stone-cold dead before the Master of this house arrives home to find you running rampant in his garden!'

'Permission denied,' I said. 'Don't you dare.

Haven't you heard all that has been said? You are on guard not against Marius but against a shriveled limping demon of burnt flesh. He'll come at dark! What if he reaches here before Marius?'

'Oh, yea gods, help me!' His hands flew to his face.

'Flavius, straighten up. You are a man! Do I have to remind you of this perpetually? You are watching for this dreaded burnt bag of bones, and he is weak. Remember what Marius said. Go for his head. Stab him in the eyes, just cut him and cut him and shout for me, and I will come. Now go to sleep until dark. He can't come till then, if he even knows to come here! Besides, I think Marius will arrive first.'

I turned and walked towards the open doors of the villa. The beautiful long-haired boys were in tears.

For a moment the tranquillity and moist cool air of the garden lulled all fear in me, and I seemed safe, among patterns I understood, far far from dark Temples, safe in Tuscany in our own family gardens there, which had been so rich like this.

'Let me beg you one last time to come back out of this man's garden!' Flavius shouted.

I ignored him.

All the doors of this lovely plastered villa stood open to the porches above or the outdoors below. Listen to the trickling of the fountains. There were lemon trees, and many a marble statue of a lazy sensuous god or goddess, round which flowers grew in rich purple or blue. Diana, the huntress, rose from a bed of orange blossoms, the marble old and pitted. And there, a lazy Ganymede, half-covered in green moss, marked some path that had been overgrown. Far off, I could see the naked bending Venus at her bath on the edge of a pool. Water flowed into the pool. I glimpsed fountains all around me.

The small common white lilies had gone wild, and there stood old olive trees with marvelously twisted trunks, so wondrous to climb in childhood.

A pastoral sweetness hung over all, yet nature had been kept at bay The stucco of the walls was freshly painted, and so were the wooden shutters, opened wide.

The two boys were crying. 'Madam, he'll be so angry.'

'Well, not with you,' I said, as I entered the house. I had come across the grass and left scarcely any footprint on the marble floor.

'Boys, do stop sobbing! You don't even have to plead with him to believe you. Isn't that true?

274

He'll read the truth in your thoughts?'

This startled each in his own way. They looked at me warily.

I stopped just past the threshold. Something emanated from the house, not loud enough to be called a sound, but very like the rhythmic precursor of a sound. I had heard this very soundless rhythm before. When was it? In the Temple? When first I entered the room where Marius had hidden behind the screen?

I walked on marble floors from room to room. Breezes everywhere played with the hanging lamps. There were many lamps. And the candles. How many candles. And lamps on stands. Why, when this place was lighted up, it must have been bright as day!

And gradually I realized the entire lower floor was a library, except for the inevitable sumptuous Roman bath, and an enormous wardrobe of clothes.

Every other room was filled with books. Nothing but books. Of course there were couches for lying and reading, and desks for writing, but every wall had its prodigious stack of scrolls or shelves of bound books.

Also there were strange doors. They appeared to open onto concealed stairwells. But they had no locks and seemed to be made of polished granite. I found at least two of these! And one chamber of the first floor was totally enclosed in stone and locked in the same way, by impenetrable doors.

As the slaves trembled and sobbed I went outside and up the stairs to the second floor. Empty. Every room simply empty, except the room that obviously belonged to the boys! There were their beds, and their little Persian altars and gods, and rich rugs and tasseled pillows and the usual Oriental swirl of design.

I came down.

The boys sat at the main door, as if positioned like marble statues, each with his knees up, head down, weeping softly, perhaps getting a bit worn out.

'Where are the bedrooms of this house? Where is Marius's bedroom? Where is the kitchen? Where is the household shrine?'

One of them let out a soft choking cry. 'There are no bedrooms.'

'Of course not,' I said.

'Our food is brought to us,' wailed the other. 'Cooked and most delicious. But I fear that, unwittingly, we have enjoyed our last meal.'

'Oh, do take it easy. How can he blame you for what I've done? You're merely children and he's a gentle being, is he not? Here, put these

pages on his desk, and weight them down so
that they don't fly away.'

'Yes, he is most gentle,' said the boy. 'But
most set in his ways.'

I closed my eyes. I sensed the sound again,
the emanating encroaching sound. Did it want
to be heard? I couldn't tell. It seemed imper-
sonal, like the beat of a sleeping heart or the
flow of the water in the fountains.

I walked over to a large beautiful couch,
draped in fine silk with Persian designs. It was
very wide and seemed to bear, despite much
straightening, the imprint of a man's form.
There was the pillow there, all fluffed and fresh,
yet still I could see the indentation of the head,
where the man had lain.

'Does he lie here?'

The boys leapt to their feet, curls flying.

'Yes, Madam, that is his couch,' said the
speaker of the two. 'Please, please, don't touch
it. He lies there for hours and reads. Madam,
please! He is most particular that we do not lie
on it playfully in his absence, though he gives
us free rein in every other regard.'

'He'll know if you even touch it!' said the
other boy, speaking up for the first time.

'I'm going to sleep on it,' I said. I lay down
and closed my eyes. I rolled over and brought

up my knees. 'I am tired. I want only sleep. I feel safe for the first time in so long.'

'You do?' asked one of the boys.

'Oh, come here and lie by me. Bring pillows for your heads, so that he will see me before he sees you. He knows me well. The pages I have brought, where are they, yes, on the desk, well, they will make it clear why I have come in. It's all changed now. Something is wanted from me. I have no choice. There is no road home. Marius will understand. I've come as close to him as possible for my protection.'

I lay back right in the hollow of the pillow where he lay. I took a long deep breath. 'The breeze is like music here,' I whispered, 'do you hear it?'

I slept the deep exhausted sleep which I had held off now for so many hours of both night and day.

Hours must have passed.

I woke with a start. The sky was purple. The slaves were curled up next to the couch, just beneath me, like terrified little animals.

I heard the noise again, the sound, distinct, a pulse. I thought oddly of something I used to like to do as a child. It was this: I would put my ear to my Father's chest. And when I heard his heart, then I would kiss it. It had always made him happy.

I rose, realizing that I was not fully awake but certain this was no dream. I was in the beautiful villa of Marius in Antioch. The marble rooms opened one upon another.

I went to the last room, the room enclosed in stone. The doors were impossibly heavy. But suddenly, silently, they opened as if pushed from within.

I entered a massive chamber. Another pair of doors lay ahead of me. They too were made of stone. They had to lead to a stairwell, for the house ended just beyond.

These doors too suddenly opened, as if released by a spring!

Light from below.

A stairway went down from the threshold of the door. It was white marble, and newly made, with no wear of feet on it. So smooth, each slab, so clean.

A soft series of flames burned below, sending their antic shadows up the stairwell.

The sound now seemed louder. I closed my eyes. Oh, that all the world were these polished chambers and all that exists could be explained within.

Suddenly, I heard a loud cry.

'Lady Pandora!'

I spun around.

'Pandora, he is over the wall!'

The boys came screaming through the house, echoing Flavius's cry, 'Lady Pandora!'

A great darkness gathered itself right before my eyes and then descended on me, throwing the helpless, beseeching boys to the side. I was almost pitched down the stairwell.

Then I realized I was in the grasp of the burnt thing. I looked down to see the black wrinkled arm, like old leather, that held me. Strong spices filled my nostrils. Fresh clothing covered the hideously thin leg I saw, the dried-up foot.

'Boys, get the lamps, set it on fire!' I shouted. I fought desperately, driving us both back from the stairwell, but I couldn't get loose from the creature. 'Boys, the lamps downstairs!'

The boys clung to each other.

'I have you!' this creature said tenderly in my ear.

'No, you don't!' I said, and gave him one fine blow with my right elbow. It drove him off balance. He nearly toppled. But he didn't let me go. The whiteness of his tunic glowed in the shadows as he once more enclosed my arms, and rendered me almost helpless.

'Boys, downstairs, lamps full of oil!' I said. 'Flavius!'

The creature hugged me as if he were a giant snake. I could scarce breathe.

'We can't go downstairs!' one of the boys cried.

'We're not allowed,' said the other.

The creature laughed in my ear, a rich deep laugh. 'Not everyone is so bound to rebellion as you are, beautiful woman, outwitting your brother at the foot of the Temple steps.'

It was shocking to hear this clear articulate voice coming from a body which seemed burnt beyond all hope of life. I watched the blackened fingers moving over my own. I felt the touch of something cold on my neck. Then I felt the punctures. His fangs.

'No!' I cried. I thrashed back and forth in his grip, then threw all of my weight against him so that he almost toppled again but didn't fall.

'Stop it, bitch, or I'll kill you now.'

'Why don't you?' I demanded.

I twisted to see his face. It was like that of a long-dead corpse dried in the desert, burnt black with a spine of a nose, and arched lips that seemed quite unable to close over white teeth and the two fangs he bared now as he looked at me.

His eyes were full of blood, as Marius's eyes had been. His hair was a fine black mop, very thick, fresh and clean, as though it had sprung from his body, renewing itself like magic.

'Yes,' he said confidently. 'That is just what happened. And very soon I will have the blood I need to renew all of me! I won't be this hideous monster you see. I'll be what I was before those Egyptian fools put her in the sun!'

'Hmmm, so she kept her promise,' I said. 'She walked into the rays of Amon Ra so you would all burn up.'

'What do you know of it? She hasn't moved or spoken in a thousand years. I was that old when they removed the stones that enclosed her. She couldn't have walked into the sun. She is a great sacred vial of blood, an enthroned source of power, that's all, and I will have that blood, which your Marius has stolen out of Egypt.'

I pondered, searching desperately for a means to free myself.

'You came to me as a gift,' said the burnt one. 'You were all I needed to take on Marius! He wears his affections and weakness for you like bright silk garments for me to see!'

'I see,' I said.

'No, you don't!' he said. My head was pulled back by my hair. I screamed in annoyance.

His sharp teeth went into my neck. A series of heated wires threaded me through and through.

I swooned. An ecstasy rendered me motionless. I tried to resist, but I saw visions. I saw him in his glory, a golden man of an Eastern land, in a Temple of skulls. He was dressed in bright green silk breeches with an ornamented band around his forehead. Face delicate of nose and mouth. Then I saw him, without explanation, burst into flames that sent his slaves screaming. He twisted and turned in these flames, not dying but suffering exquisitely.

My head was swimming, and I was weakening. My blood flowed from all parts of my body into his wretched form. I thought of my Father, of my Father saying, 'Live, Lydia!' I wrenched my neck away from him and turned, poking him hard with my shoulder, and then pushed him with two hands so that he slid backwards on the floor. I brought my knee up against him. Nothing could get him off me!

I tried to reach for my dagger, but I was too dizzy, and besides, I didn't have my dagger. My only chance lay with the burning oil in the lamps at the foot of the stairs. I turned, reeling, and the monster caught me again with both hands by my long hair. He yanked me back.

'You demon!' I said. His strength had worn me out. He tightened his grip slowly. I knew that soon my arms would break.

'Ah,' he said, twisting free of me, and holding tight as ever. 'My purpose is served.'

A brighter light suddenly filled up the stairway.

A torch was placed at the foot of the steps. Then Marius stepped into view.

He appeared utterly calm and he appeared to be looking past me into the eyes of my captor.

'And what will you do now, Akbar?' Marius asked. 'Hurt her, violate her but one more time, and I shall kill you. Kill her, and you will die in agony. Let her go and you can run.'

He mounted the steps one by one.

'You underestimate me,' said the burnt thing, 'you arrogant Roman bumbler, you think I don't know you keep the Queen and the King, that you stole them out of Egypt? It is known. The word is spread through the world, through the Northern woods, through the wild lands, through the lands of which you know nothing. You killed the Elder who guarded the King and the Queen and stole them! The King and Queen have not moved or spoken in a thousand years. You took our Queen from Egypt. You think you are a Roman Emperor? You think she is a Queen you can take captive, like Cleopatra! Cleopatra was a Greek whore. This is our Isis, our Akasha! You blaspheming fool. Now let me into Akasha's presence. Stand against me, and this woman, the only mortal whom you truly love, dies.'

Marius came up step by step towards us.

'Akbar, did your informants tell you that it was the Elder in Egypt, her long keeper himself who left the Royal Pair to stand in the sun?' asked Marius. He took another step upward. 'Did they tell you that it was the Elder that caused the sun to strike them, the fire which destroyed hundreds of us, and spared the oldest only so they could live in agony as you do?'

Marius made a quick gesture. I felt the fangs deep in my neck. I couldn't get away. Again, I saw this creature in his former splendor, taunting me with his beauty, his jeweled feet as he danced, surrounded by painted women.

I heard Marius right beside me, but I couldn't make out the words.

The folly of it all went through my mind. I had led this creature to Marius, but was that what the Mother wanted? Akasha, that was the ancient name written on the bodies dumped on the steps of the Temple. I knew her name. I knew it in the dreams. I was losing consciousness. 'Marius,' I called out with all my strength.

My head fell forward, free of the fangs. I fought this total captivating weakness. I deliberately pictured the Emperor Augustus receiving us on his deathbed. 'I shall not see the end of this comedy,' I whispered.

'Oh, yes, you shall.' It was Marius's calm voice right near us. I opened my eyes. 'Akbar, don't risk it again, you've shown your determination.'

'Don't reach for me again, Marius,' said the burnt creature. 'My teeth caress her neck. But one more drop and her heart is silent.'

The rich dark of night brightened the torch below. That was all I could see. The torch. 'Akasha,' I whispered.

The burnt thing took a deep breath, his chest heaving against me. 'Her blood is beautiful,' he said. He kissed my cheek with the parched burnt lips. I closed my eyes. It was becoming harder and harder for me to breathe. I couldn't open my eyes.

He went on talking.

'You see, I have no fear to take her into death with me, Marius, for if I must die by your hand, why not with her as my consort?'

These words were distant, echoing.

'Pick her up in your arms,' said Marius. He was very close to us. 'And carry her gently, as if she were your only beloved child, and come down with me into the Shrine. Come and see the

Mother. Kneel before Akasha and see what she will allow!'

I swooned again, but I heard the creature laugh. He did lift me now, under the knees, and my head fell back. We went down the steps.

'Marius,' I said, 'he's weak. You can kill him.' My face fell against the chest of the burnt one as we descended. I could feel the bones of his chest. 'Really, very weak,' I said, scarcely able to remain conscious. Akasha, yes, her true name.

'Carefully, my friend,' said Marius. 'She dies and I destroy you. You've almost overplayed your hand. She narrows your chances with every labored breath. Pandora, be silent, please. Akbar is a great blood drinker, a great god.'

I felt a cold firm hand clasp mine.

We had reached the lower floor. I tried to lift my head. I saw rows of lamps, splendid wall paintings hammered with gold, a ceiling veiled in gold.

Two great stone doors were opened. A chapel lay within, a chapel full of dense fluttering devotional light and the overpowering scent of lilies.

The blood drinker who held me let out a cry. 'Mother Isis,' he said piteously. 'Oh, Akasha!'

He released me, setting me down on my feet, as Marius at once took hold of me, and the blistered and damaged one rushed towards the altar.

I stared, amazed. But I was dying. I couldn't breathe. I was falling to the floor. I tried to swallow air but I could not. I could not stand without Marius.

But oh, to leave the Earth and all its miseries with such a vision:

There they sat, The Great Goddess Isis and the King Osiris, or so it seemed, bronzed in skin, not white like the poor captive Queen in my dreams, but perfectly arrayed in garments of spun gold pleated and sewn in the fixed Egyptian style. Their black hair was long, plaited, real. The paint on their faces was fresh, the dark eyelining and mascara, the reddened lips.

She wore no crown of the horns and sun disk. Her collar of gold and jewels was superb, shimmering and alive in my eyes.

'I must get the crown, restore the crown!' I said aloud, hearing this voice come from me as if it had been born elsewhere to instruct me. My eyes closed.

The black thing knelt before the Queen.

I couldn't see clearly. I felt Marius's arms, and then a gush of hot blood come into my mouth. 'No, Marius, protect her!' I tried to speak. My words were washed away in this infusion of blood. 'Protect the Mother!' Again it came filling my mouth so that I had to swallow. Immediately I felt the strength, the power of this blood, infinitely stronger than the pull of Akbar. The blood rushed like so many rivers to the sea, through my body. It would not be stopped. Another gush followed, as if a giant storm had driven the river even faster into its delta, its broken and random streams seeking every morsel of flesh.

A wide and wondrous world opened and would have welcomed me, sunlight in the deep forest, but I wouldn't see it. I broke free. 'The Queen, save her from him!' I whispered. Did the blood drip from my lips? No, it was gone inside me.

Marius wouldn't listen to me. Again a bloody wound was pressed to my mouth, and the blood was driven ever faster. I felt the air fill my lungs. I could feel the length of my own body, sturdy, standing on its own. The blood brightened inside me like light, as though it had enflamed my heart. I opened my eyes. I was a pillar. I saw Marius's face, his golden eyelashes, his deep blue eyes. His long hair parted in the middle fell to his shoulders. He was ageless, a god.

'Protect her!' I cried. I turned and pointed.

A veil was lifted that had all my life hung between me and all things; now in their true color and shape, they gave forth their deliberate purpose: the Queen stared forward, immobile as the King. Life could not have imitated such serenity, such utter paralysis. I heard water dropping from the flowers. Tiny drops striking the marble floor, the fall of a single leaf. I turned and saw it, curled and rocking on the stones, this tiny leaf. I heard the breeze move under the golden canopied ceiling. And the lamps had tongues of flame to sing.

The world was a woven song, a tapestry of song. The multicolored Mosaics gleamed, then lost all form, then even pattern. The walls dissolved into clouds of colored mist which welcomed us, through which we could roam forever.

And there she sat, The Queen of Heaven, reigning over all in supreme and unperturbed stillness.

All the yearning of my childish heart was fulfilled. 'She lives, she is real, she reigns over Earth and Heaven.'

The King and the Queen. They didn't stir. Their eyes beheld nothing. They did not look at us. They did not look at the burnt thing as he drew closer and closer to their throne.

The arms of the Royal Pair were covered in many inscribed and intricate bracelets. Their hands rested on their thighs. It was the manner of many an Egyptian statue. But there never has been a statue to equal either of them.

'The crown, she would have her crown,' I said. With astonishing vigor I walked forward towards her.

Marius took my hand. Keenly, he watched the progress of the burnt one.

'She was before all such crowns,' Marius said, 'they do not mean anything to her.'

The thought itself burst with the sweetness of a grape on my tongue. Of course she was there before. In my dreams, she had had no crown. She was safe. Marius kept her safe.

'My Queen,' said Marius from behind me. 'You have a supplicant. It is Akbar from the East. He would drink the royal blood. What is your will, Mother?'

His voice was so tranquil! He had no fears.

'Mother Isis, let me drink!' cried this burnt creature. He stood up, threw up his arms and created another dancing vision of his former self. He wore human skulls hanging from his belt. He wore a necklace of blackened human fingers! Another of blackened human ears! It was grisly and revolting, yet he seemed to think it seductive and overpowering. At once the image left him. The god from the faraway land was on his knees.

'I am your servant and always was! I slew only the evildoer, as you commanded. I never abandoned your true worship.'

How fragile and insignificant seemed this pleading one, so revolting, so easy to clear away now from her presence. I looked at the King Osiris, as remote and indifferent as the Queen.

'Marius,' I said, 'the corn for Osiris; doesn't he want the corn? He's the god of the corn.' I was filled with visions of our processions in Rome, of people singing and bearing the offerings.

'No, he doesn't want the corn,' said Marius. He laid his hand on my shoulder.

'They are true, they are real!' I cried out. 'It is all real. Everything is changed. Everything is redeemed.'

The burnt thing turned and glared at me. But I was quite beyond all reason. He turned back to the Queen and reached out for her foot.

How her toenails flashed in the light with the golden flesh beneath them. But she was stone-still, as was the crownless King, without seeming judgment or power.

The creature suddenly sprang up and tried to seize the Queen by the neck!

I screamed.

'Shameless, despicable.'

Swiftly the frozen right arm of the Queen rose, her hand surrounding the burnt thing's skull and crushing it, the blood gushing down her as the monster gave his last fractured cry for mercy. She caught his body as it dropped over her waist. She hurled it in the air, and all its limbs broke loose from it, crashing to the floor like so much timber.

A gusting wind caught each remnant and gathered them all in one as a lamp fell from its three-legged stand to spill its burning oil on the remains.

'The heart, look,' I said. 'I can see its heart. The heart beats.'

But the fire quickly consumed the heart, consumed the flexing fingers and the writhing toes. There was a great stirring, a dance in the fire of bones, bones whirling in the flames, and then the bones blackened, thinned, snapped to pieces, became fragments; all of this thing was reduced at last to smoking cinders, crisping and skittering on the floor.

Then came the breeze again, full of the breath of the garden, lifting these cinders and carrying them away, like so many fragile tiny black insects, into the shadows of the antechamber.

I was spellbound.

The Queen was as before, her hand in its old place. She and the King stared at nothing, as if nothing had taken place. Only the wretched stain on her gown bore witness.

Their eyes took no heed of Marius or of me.

Then there was only quiet in the chapel. Only sweet perfumed quiet. Golden light. I breathed deeply. I could hear the oil in the lamps turned to flame. The Mosiacs were peopled with finely made worshipers. I could see the slow minute beginnings of decay of the various flowers, and it seemed but another strain of the same song that expressed their growth, their browning edges but another color in no contradiction to their brilliant colors.

'Forgive me, Akasha,' Marius said softly, 'that I let him come so close. I was not wise.'

I cried. Great gushing tears came from me.

'You summoned me,' I said to the Queen through my tears. 'You called me here! I will do all you want of me.'

Slowly her right arm rose; it rose from her thigh and extended itself and her hand very gently curved in the beckoning gesture of the dream, but there was no smile, no change in her frozen face.

I felt something invisible and irresistible

wrap itself around me. It came from her out-stretching welcoming arm. It was sweet and soft and caressing. It made a flush of pleasure through all my limbs and my face.

I moved forward, wound up in its will.

'I beg you, Akasha!' Marius said softly. 'I beg you under the name of Inanna, under the name of Isis, under the name of all goddesses, don't hurt her!'

Marius simply didn't understand! Marius had never known her worship! I knew. I knew that her blood drinker children had meant to be judges of the evildoer, and drink only from the condemned, according to her laws. I saw the god of the dark cave, whom I'd seen in my vision. I understood all.

I wanted to tell Marius. But I couldn't. Not now. The world was reborn, all systems built upon skepticism or selfishness were as fragile as spiderwebs and meant to be swept away. My own moments of despair had been nothing more than detours into an unholy and self-centered blackness.

'The Queen of Heaven,' I whispered. I knew I was speaking in the ancient tongue. A prayer came to my lips.

'And Amon Ra, the Sun God, for all his power, shall never conquer the King of the

Dead or his bride, for she is the ruler of the starry heavens, of the moon, of those who would bring the sacrifice of the evildoer. Cursed be those who misuse this magic. Cursed be those who seek to steal it!'

I felt myself, a human, held together by the intricate threads of blood which Marius had given me. I felt the design of its support. It had no weight, my body.

I was lifted towards her. Her arm came around me and pulled my hair back from my face. I put out my arms to embrace her neck because I could do nothing else. We were too close for any other possible sign of love.

I felt the soft silk of her real plaited hair, and the coldness and firmness of her shoulders, her arm. Yet she did not look at me. She was a pet-rified thing. Could she look at me? Did she choose to remain silent, staring forward? Did some evil spell hold her helpless, a spell from which a thousand hymns might waken her?

In my delirium I saw the words engraved in gold pieces among the jewels of her collar: 'Bring to me the evildoer and I shall drink his blood.'

It seemed I was in the desert and the necklace was tumbling over and over in the sand, in the wind, rather like the body of the burnt one had tumbled. Fallen, lost, to be remade.

I felt my head drawn to her neck. She had opened her fingers over my hair. She directed it, that my lips should feel this skin.

'It's what you want, isn't it?' I asked. But my words seemed remote from me, a pathetic expression of the fullness of my soul. 'That I am to be your daughter!'

She tipped her head slightly, away from me, so that I saw her neck. I saw the vein displayed, the vein from which she wanted me to drink.

Her finger rose gently through my hair, never pulling it or hurting it, merely embracing my head, sending rampant ecstasy through me, and urging my head gently down so that my lips could no longer avoid her shimmering skin.

'Oh, my adored Queen,' I whispered. I had never known such certainty, such ecstasy without limits or mundane cause. I had never known such bursting, triumphant faith as my faith in her.

I opened my mouth. Nothing human could bite through this hard flesh! Yet it gave, as though it were thin, and the blood pumped into me, 'the Fount.' I heard her heart driving it, a deafening force that vibrated in the drums of my ears. This was not blood. This was nectar. This was all that any created being could ever desire.

9

With the nectar flowing into me, there came another realm. Her ringing laughter filled the corridor; she ran ahead of me, girlish, feline, unencumbered by grandeur. She beckoned for me to follow. Out under the stars, Marius sat alone in his soft shapeless garden. She pointed to him. I saw Marius rise and take me in his arms. His long hair was such a fine adornment. I saw what she wanted. It was Marius I kissed in this vision as I drank from her; it was Marius with whom I danced.

A shower of flower petals descended upon us as upon a bridal couple in Rome, and Marius held my arm as though we had just been wed, and all around us people sang. There was a flawless happiness, a happiness so keen that perhaps there are those born who never even have the capacity for it.

She stood atop a broad black altar of diorite.

It was night. This was an enclosed place, filled with people, but it was dark and cool with the sandy wind off the valley floor, and she looked down at the one they offered up to her. He was a man, his eyes closed, his hands were bound. He didn't struggle.

She showed her teeth; a gasp rose from the worshipers who filled the place, and then she took the man by the throat and drank his blood. When she had finished, she let him fall and she held up her arms.

'All things are cleansed in me!' she cried out. Once again the petals fell, petals of all colors, and peacock feathers waved about us, and branches of palm, and there was singing in great lusty bursts, and the sound of a riotious drum, and she smiled looking down from where she stood, her face remarkably flushed and mobile and human, her black-painted eyes sweeping over her worshipers.

All began to dance, save she, who watched, and then her eyes rose slowly and she looked over their heads, out the high rectangular windows of this place, at the twinkling firmament. Pipes played. The dance had become a frenzy.

A weary and secretive darkness crept into her face, a distraction, as though her soul had traveled out of doors towards Heaven, and then she looked sadly down. She looked lost. Anger overcame her.

Then she cried out in a deafening voice, 'The rogue blood drinker!' The crowd fell silent. 'Bring him to me.'

The crowd parted to let this struggling furious god be forced to her altar.

'You dare judge me!' he cried. He was Babylonian, with full long curly locks and beard and mustache. It took ten mortals to hold him.

'Into the burning place, in the mountains, in the sun, in the strongest fetters!' she cried. He was dragged away.

Once again she looked up. The stars grew big and age-old patterns were clear. We floated under the stars.

A boy in a delicate gilded chair argued with those around him. The men were old, half-invisible in the darkness. The lamp shone on the boy's face. We stood in the door. The boy was frail, his little limbs like sticks.

'And you say,' said the incredulous boy, 'that these blood drinkers are worshiped in the hills!'

I knew he was the Pharaoh by the sacred lock of hair that grew from his bald head, by the manner in which the others waited upon him. He looked up in horror as she approached. His guardians fled.

'Yes,' she said, 'and you will do nothing to stop it!'

She lifted him, this small fragile boy, and tore at his throat as an animal might do it, letting the blood flood from the fatal wound. 'Little King,' she said. 'Little Kingdom.'

The vision ended.

Her cold white skin was closed beneath my lips. I kissed her now. I no longer drank.

I felt my own form, felt myself fall back over her arm, felt myself slipping out of her embrace.

In the dim radiance, her profile remained as it had before, silent and without feeling. Stark, a face without a blemish or a line. I sank back into Marius's arms. Her arm and hand returned to their former rigid position.

Everything was brilliantly clear, the motionless King and Queen, the artful figures fixed in lapis lazuli in the gold mosaics.

I felt a sharp pain in me, in the heart, in the womb, as if someone had stabbed me. 'Marius!' I cried out.

He picked me up and carried me from the chamber.

'No, I want to kneel at her feet,' I said. The pain took the breath out of me. I tried not to scream from this pain. Oh, the world had just been reborn. And now this agony.

He set me down on the high grass, letting it be crushed under me. A flood of sour human fluid came out of my womb, even out of my mouth. I saw flowers right near me. I saw the friendly Heavens, vivid as in my vision. The pain was unspeakable.

I knew now why he had removed me from the Shrine.

I wiped at my cheek. I couldn't bear this filth. The pain devoured me. I struggled to see again what she had revealed to me, remember what she said, but there was too much obstruction in this pain.

'Marius!' I cried.

He covered me and kissed my cheek. 'Drink from me,' he said, 'drink until the pain goes away. It's only the body dying, drink. Pandora, you are immortal.'

'Fill me, take me,' I said. I reached down between his legs.

'It doesn't matter now.'

But it was hard, this organ I sought, the organ forever lost to the god Osiris. I guided it, hard and cold as it was, into my body. Then I drank and drank, and when I felt his teeth again on my neck, when he began to draw from me the new mixture that filled my veins, it was sweet suckling, and I knew him and loved him and knew all his secrets in one flash which meant nothing.

He was right. The lower organs meant nothing. He fed on me. I fed on him. This was our marriage. All around us, the grass was waving softly in the breeze, a majestic conjugal bed, and the smell of the green flooded me.

The pain was gone. I flung out my arm and felt the softness of flowers.

He tore off my fouled dress and lifted me. He carried me into the pool where the marble Venus stood forever with back bent, and one foot raised above the cool water.

'Pandora!' he whispered.

The boys stood at his side, offering him pitchers.

He dipped a pitcher and poured the water over me. I felt beneath my feet the tile at the bottom of the pool as the water ran down my skin. I had never known such sensation! Another pitcherful washed over me, deliciously. I feared for one instant the pain would return, but no, it was gone.

'I love you with all my heart,' I said. 'All my love belongs to them and to you, Marius. Marius, I can see in the darkness, I can see in the deep dark beneath the trees.'

Marius held me. The boys slowly bathed us both, dipping their pitchers and pouring the silvery water over us.

'Oh, to have you with me,' Marius said, 'to have you here; not to be alone, but to be with you, my beauty, you of all souls! You.' He stood back, and I gloried in him, drenched as I was, reached to touch his long wild foreign hair. He sparkled all over with droplets.

'Yes,' I said. 'It was exactly what she wanted.'

His face stiffened. He scowled. He stared at me. Something had changed altogether, and for the worse. I could feel it.

'What?' he asked.

'It is what she wanted. She made it plain to me in the visions. She wanted me to be with you, so you wouldn't be alone.'

He stood back. Was this anger?

'Marius, what is the matter with you? Can't you see what she's done?'

He stepped back again, away from me.

'You didn't realize that's what was happening?' I asked.

The boys thrust forth towels. Marius took one and wiped his face and his hair.

I did the same.

He was furious. He shook with anger.

This was a moment of mingled and inexplicable beauty and horror – his white body there, the shimmering pool, the lights falling gracefully from the open doors of the house, and above, the stars, her stars. And Marius angry and bristling, his eyes full of outrage.

I looked at him.

'I am her Priestess now,' I said. 'I'm to restore her worship. That's what she wants. But she brought me also for you, because you were alone,' I said. 'Marius, I saw all this. I saw our own wedding in Rome, as if it were the old days and our families were with us. I saw her worshipers.'

He was plainly horrified.

I didn't want to see this. Surely I was misunderstanding him.

I stepped up on the grass. I let the boys dry my body. I looked up at the stars. The house with all its warm lamps seemed crude and fragile, a bumbled attempt to make an order of things, which could not compare to the making of one complete flower.

'Oh, how spectacular is the simple night,' I said. 'It seems an insult to the night to speak of purpose and intent, when this common moment is so brimming full of blessed design and tranquillity All things follow their course.'

I stood back and spun around, letting the water fly from me. I was so strong. No dizziness overcame when I stopped. I had a sense of infinite power.

One of the boys held out a tunic for me. It was a man's, but as I've said so often here, Roman clothes are very simple. It was just a short tunic. I put it on and let him tie the sash around my waist. I smiled at him. He trembled and stepped back from me.

'Dry my hair,' I told him. Ah, such sensations.

Slowly I looked up. Marius too was dried and dressed. He was still looking at me with violent protest, and downright indignation.

'Someone has to go in,' I said, 'to change her golden gown. That blasphemer, he left her bloody.'

'I will do that!' Marius said in plain anger.

'Oh, so it comes to this,' I said. I looked around me, seduced by beauty to forget his altogether, to come back to him at some later hour after I had roamed beneath the olive trees and consorted with the constellations.

But his anger hurt me. The hurt was strange, and deep, without the various stages mortal flesh and mind command of pain.

'Oh, isn't it splendid!' I said. 'I learn that the goddess reigns, that she is real, that she has made all things! That the world is not just a giant graveyard! But I learn this as I find myself in an arranged marriage! And behold the groom! How he nurses his own temper.'

He sighed and bowed his head. Was I to see him cry again, this flawless familiar and beloved god among crushed flowers?

He looked up. 'Pandora,' he said. 'She's not a goddess. She didn't make the world.'

'How dare you say this!'

'I have to say it! I would have died for the truth when I was alive and will die for it now. But she will not let this happen. She needs me and she needs you to make me happy!'

'So very well!' I threw my hands. 'I am happy to do it. And we will restore her worship.'

'We will not!' he said. 'How can you even think of such a thing.'

'Marius, I want to sing it from the tops of mountains; I want to tell the world that this miracle exists. I want to run through the streets singing. We are to restore her to her throne in a great Temple in the very middle of Antioch!'

'You're talking madness!' he shouted.

The boys had run away.

'Marius, have you stopped up your ears to her commands? We are to hunt down and kill her renegade gods and see that new gods are born from her, gods who look into souls, gods who seek justice, not lies, gods who are not fantastical, lustful idiots or the drunken whimsical creatures of the Northern sky who hurl thunderbolts. Her worship is founded in the good, in the pure!'

'No, no, no,' he said. He stepped back as if that would make it all the more emphatic. 'You're talking rot!' he said. 'Stupidity, rank superstition!'

'I don't believe you said those words!' I cried. 'You are a monster!' I said. 'She deserves her throne! So does the King, who sits beside her. They deserve their worshipers bringing flowers to them. Did you think you had the power to read minds for no good reason!' I came forward. 'Do you remember when I first mocked you in the Temple? When I said you ought to station yourself at the courts and look into the minds of the accused? I had hit the mark in my ridicule!'

'No!' he roared. 'This is absolutely not true,' he said.

He turned his back on me, rushing into the house.

I followed him.

He rushed down the stairway and into her sanctum, stopping short before her. She and her King sat as before. Not an eyelash moved. Only the flowers clung to life in the perfumed air.

I looked down at my hands, so white! Could I die now? Would I live centuries like the burnt one?

I studied their seemingly divine faces. They did not smile. They did not dream. They looked, and nothing more.

I fell down on my knees.

'Akasha,' I whispered. 'May I call you this name? Tell me what you want.'

There was no change in her. None whatsoever.

'Well, speak, Mother!' declared Marius, his voice thick with sadness. 'Speak! Is it what you've always wanted?'

Suddenly he dashed forward, mounted the two steps of her dais and pounded on her breasts with his fists.

I was horrified.

She didn't move, she didn't blink. His fist struck a hardness he could not budge. Only her hair, struck by his arm, gave a little sway.

I ran to him and tried to pull him away.

'Stop it, Marius, she'll destroy you!'

I was amazed at my strength. Surely it equalled his. But he allowed me to pull him back, his face flooded with tears.

'Oh, what have I done!' he said staring at her. 'Oh, Pandora, Pandora! What have I done! I've made another blood drinker when I swore that there would never, never be another made, not so long as I survived!'

'Come upstairs,' I said calmly. I glanced at

309

the King and Queen. No sign of response or recognition. 'It isn't proper, Marius, that we argue here in the Shrine. Come upstairs.'

He nodded.

He let me lead him slowly out of the room. His head was bowed.

'Your long barbarian hair is most becoming,' I said. 'And I have eyes now to see you as never before. Our blood is intertwined as it might be in a child born to us.'

He wiped at his nose, and didn't look at me.

We walked into the large library.

'Marius, is there nothing in me that fills your eye, nothing you find beautiful?'

'Oh, yes, my dear, there is everything!' he said. 'But for the love of Heaven, bring your wits with you into this! Don't you see! Your life's been stolen not for a sacred truth but for a degraded mystery! Reading minds doesn't make me any wiser than the next man! I kill to live! As she once did, thousands and thousands of years ago. Oh, and she knew she had to do this. She knew the time had come.'

'What time? What did she know?'

I stared at him. I was gradually realizing that I could no longer read his thoughts, and surely he couldn't read mine. But the hovering boys, they were just open books in their fear, thinking themselves the servants of kindhearted but very loud-voiced demons.

Marius sighed. 'She did it because I had almost gained the courage to do what I had to do! To place them both and myself in the sun and finish forever what the Egyptian Elder had sought to do – rid the world of the King and Queen and all the fanged men and women who glut themselves on death! Oh, she is too clever.'

'You really planned to do that?' I asked. 'To immolate them and yourself?'

He made a small sarcastic sound. 'Yes, of course, I planned it. Next week, next month, next year, next decade, after another hundred years, maybe in two hundred, maybe after I'd read all the books in the world and seen all the places, maybe in five hundred years, maybe . . . maybe soon in my loneliness.'

I was at first too stunned to speak

He smiled at me wisely and sadly. 'Oh, but I cry like a child,' he said softly.

'Where comes the confidence,' I asked, 'to put an end so swiftly to such bold and complex evidence of divine magic!'

'Magic!' he cursed.

'I'd rather if you did not do this,' I said. 'I don't mean the crying, I mean burning up the Mother and Father and . . .'

'I'm sure you would!' he answered. 'And do you think I could bear to do it against your will, subject you to the fire? You innocent desperate idiot of a woman! Restore her altars! Oh! Restore her worship! Oh! You are out of your mind!'

'Idiot! You dare sling your insults at me! You think you've brought a slave into your household? You haven't even brought a wife.'

Yes. Our minds were locked now to each other, and later I would find out that it was because of our heavy exchange of blood. But all I knew then was that we had to content ourselves with words like mortal men and women.

'I did not mean to use petty insults!' he said. He was stung.

'Well, then sharpen your great male reason and your lofty elegant patrician mode of expression!' I said.

We glowered at each other.

'Yes!' he said. 'Reason,' he said. He held up his finger. 'You are the most clever woman I've ever known. And you listen to reason. I will explain and you will see. That is what must be done.'

'Yes, and you are hotheaded and sentimental and give way to tears again and again – and you pound upon the Queen herself like a child throwing a tantrum!'

His face went red with immediate anger. It sealed his lips against his words.

He turned and went away.

'Do you cast me out?' I said. 'Do you want me gone!' I shouted. 'This is your house. Tell me now if you want me gone. I'll go now!'

He stopped. 'No,' he said.

He turned around and looked at me, shaken, and caught off guard. In a raw voice, he said, 'Don't go, Pandora!' He blinked as if to clear his vision. 'Don't go. Please, don't.' And then he let fall a final whisper. 'We have each other.'

'And where do you go now, to get away from me?'

'Only to change her dress,' he said with a sad bitter smile. 'To clean and recostume "such bold evidence of complex and divine magic."'

He disappeared.

I turned to the violet outdoors. To the clouds stirred in a cauldron by the moon, to defy the darkness. To the big old trees that said, Mount our limbs, we will embrace you! To the scattered flowers everywhere that said, We are your bed. Lie down with us.

And so the two-hundred-year brawl began.

And it never really ended.

10

With my eyes still closed, I heard voices of the city, voices from nearby houses; I heard men talking as they passed on the road outside. I heard music coming from somewhere, and the laughter of women and children. When I concentrated I could understand what they said. I chose not to do this, and their voices melded with the breeze.

Suddenly, the state seemed unbearable. There seemed nothing to do but rush back to the chapel and kneel there and worship! These senses I had been given seemed fit for nothing else. If this was my destiny, then what was to become of me?

Through it all, I heard a soul weeping in agony; it was an echo of my own, a soul broken from a course of great hope, who could scarce believe that such fine beginnings

314

should end in terror!

It was Flavius.

I leapt into the old gnarled olive tree. It was as simple as taking a step. I stood among the branches, and then leapt to the next, and then to the top of the wall, encrusted with vine. I walked along the wall towards the gate.

There he stood, his forehead pressed to the bars, both hands clutching at the iron. He bled from several slash marks on his cheek. He gnashed his teeth.

'Flavius!' I said.

He looked up with a start. 'Lady Pandora!'

Surely by the light of the moon, he saw the miracle wrought in me, whatever its cause. For I saw the mortality in him, the deep wrinkles of his skin, the painful flutter of his gaze, a thin layer of soil clinging to him all over in the natural moisture of his mortal skin.

'You must go home,' I said, climbing to sit on the wall, with legs on the outside. I bent down so he could hear me. He didn't back away but his eyes were huge with fascination. 'Go see to the girls, and sleep, and get those marks attended to. The demon's dead, you needn't worry anymore about him. Come back here tomorrow night at sundown.'

He shook his head. He tried to speak but he

couldn't. He tried to gesture but he couldn't. His heart thundered in his chest. He glanced back down the road to the small far-flung lights of Antioch. He looked at me. I heard his heart galloping. I felt his shock, and his fear, and it was fear for me, not him. Fear that some awful fate had befallen me. He reached for the gate and clung to the bars, right arm hooked around and left hand clasping it as if he wouldn't be moved.

I saw myself as he saw me in his mind – in a boy's sashed tunic, my hair wildly free, sitting atop the wall, as if my body were young and pliant. All lines of age had gone from me. He saw a face on me no one could have ever painted.

But the point was this. The man had reached his limit. He could go no further. And I knew most fully how I loved him.

'All right,' I said. I stood up and leaned over with both my hands. 'Come on, I'll lift you over the wall if I can.'

He raised his arms, doubtful, eyes still drinking up every detail of my transformation.

He weighed nothing. I lifted him up and deposited him on his feet within the gate. I dropped down on the grass beside him and put my arm around him. How hot was his alarm. How strong his courage.

316

'Still your heart,' I said. I led him towards the house, as he looked down at me, his chest heaving as though he were out of breath, but it was mere shock. 'I'll take care of you.'

'I had the thing,' he said, 'I had it by its arm!' How opaque his voice sounded, how filled with living fluid and effort. 'I sank my dagger into it over and over, but it just slashed at my face and it was gone over the wall like a swarm of gnats, just darkness, immaterial darkness!'

'Flavius, it's dead, burnt to cinders!'

'Had I not heard your voice, oh, I was going mad! I heard the boys crying. I couldn't climb the wall with this damned leg. Then I heard your voice, and I knew, knew you were alive!' He was filled with happiness. 'You were with your Marius.' The ease with which I could feel his love was sweet, and awe inspiring.

A sudden sense of the Shrine came back to me, of the Queen's nectar and the shower of flower petals. But I had to maintain my equilibrium in this new state. Flavius was also profoundly baffled.

I kissed him on the lips, warm, mortal lips, and then quickly like an artful cat I licked all the blood from the slash marks on his cheeks, feeling a shiver run through me.

I took him into the library, which in this house

was the main room. The boys hovered somewhere about. They had been lighting lamps
everywhere, and now they cowered. I could
smell their blood and their young human flesh.

'You'll stay with me, Flavius. Boys, can you
make a bedroom for my steward on this floor?
You have fruit and bread, don't you? I can smell
it. Have you enough furniture to make him a
comfortable place to the far right, where he is
out of the way?'

They came rushing out of their respective
hiding places, and they too struck me as vividly
human. I was distracted. The smallest natural
things about them seemed precious, their thick
black eyebrows, their round little mouths, their
smooth cheeks.

'Yes, Madam, yes!' they said almost in one
voice. They hurried forward.

'This is Flavius, my steward. He will stay
with us. For now, take him to the bath, heat the
water and attend to him. Get him some wine.'

They took Flavius in hand at once. But he
paused.

'Don't abandon me, Madam,' he said suddenly with the most serious and thoughtful
expression. 'I am loyal in all respects.'

'I know,' I said. 'Oh, how clearly I understand. You cannot imagine.'

Then it was off to the bath with the Babylonian boys, who seemed delighted to have something to do.

I found Marius's huge closets. He had enough clothes for the Kings of Parthia, Armenia, the Emperor's Mother, Livia, the dead Cleopatra, and an ostentatious patrician who paid no attention to Tiberius's stupid sumptuary laws.

I put on a much finer, long tunic, woven of silk and linen, and I chose a gold girdle. And with Marius's combs and brushes, I made a clean free mantle of my hair, free of all tangles, rippled and soft as it had been when I was a girl.

He had many mirrors, which, as you know, in those days were only polished metal. And I was rendered somber and mystified by the single fact that I was young again; my nipples were pink, as I had said; the lines of age no longer interrupted the intended endowments of my face or arms. Perhaps it is most accurate to say that I was timeless. Timeless in adulthood. And every solid object seemed there to serve in me my new strength.

I looked down at the blocks of marble tile which made up the floor and saw in them a depth, a proof of process wondrous and barely understood.

I wanted to go out again, speak to the flowers, pick them up in handfuls. I wanted to talk urgently with the stars. I dared not seek the Shrine for fear of Marius, but if he had not been around I would have gone there and knelt at the Mother and merely looked at her, looked at her in silent contemplation, listening for the slightest articulation, though I knew, quite certainly after watching Marius's behavior, that there would be none.

She had moved her right arm without the seeming knowledge of the rest of her body. She had moved it to kill, and then to invite.

I went into the library, sat down at the desk, where lay all my pages, and I waited.

Finally, when Marius came, he too was freshly dressed, his hair parted in the middle and combed to his shoulders. He took a chair near me. It was ebony and curved and inlaid with gold, and I looked at him, realizing how very like the chair he was – a great preserved extension of all the raw materials which had gone into it. Nature did the carving and inlay and then the whole had been lacquered.

I wanted to cry in his arms, but I swallowed my loneliness. The night would never desert me, and it was faithful in every open door with its intruding grass, and the veined olive branches rising to catch the light of the moon.

'Blessed is she who is made a blood drinker,' I said, 'when the moon is full, and the clouds are rising like mountains in the transparent night.'

'Probably so,' he said.

He moved the lamp that stood on the desk between us, so that it didn't flicker in my eyes.

'I made my steward at home here,' I said. 'I offered him bath, bed and clothes. Do you forgive me? I love him and will not lose him. It's too late now for him to go back into the world.'

'He's an extraordinary man,' Marius said, 'and most welcome here. Tomorrow perhaps he can bring your girls. Then the boys will have company and there will be some discipline by day. Flavius knows books, among other things.'

'You're most gracious. I was afraid you would be angry. Why do you suffer so? I cannot read your mind; I did not obtain that gift.' No, this wasn't correct. I could read Flavius's mind. I knew the boys at this very moment were very relieved by Flavius's presence as they helped him dress for bed.

'We are too closely linked by blood,' he said. 'I can never read your thoughts again either. We are thrown back on words like mortals, only our senses are infinitely keener, and the detachment we know at some times will be as cold as the ice in the North; and at other times feelings will enflame us, carry us on waves of burning sea.'

'Hmmm,' I said.

'You despise me,' he said softly, contritely, 'because I quenched your ecstasy, I took from you your joy, your convictions.' He looked quite genuinely miserable. 'I did this to you right at the happiest moment of your conversion.'

'Don't be so sure you quenched it. I might still make her Temples, preach her worship. I'm an initiate. I have only begun.'

'You will not revive her worship!' he said. 'Of that I assure you! You will tell no one about her or what she is or where she is kept, and you will never make another blood drinker.'

'My, if only Tiberius had such authority when he addressed the Senate!' I said.

'All Tiberius ever wanted was to study at the gymnasium at Rhodes, to go every day in a Greek cloak and sandals and talk philosophy. And so the propensity for action flowers in men of lesser mettle, who use him in his loveless loneliness.'

'Is this a lecture for my improvement? Do you think I don't know this? What you don't know is that the Senate won't help Tiberius govern. Rome wants an Emperor now to worship and to like. It was your generation, under

Augustus, which accustomed us to forty years of autocratic rule. Don't talk to me of politics as though I were a fool.'

'I should have realized that you understood it all,' he said. 'I remember you in your girlhood. Nobody could match your brilliance. Your fidelity to Ovid and his erotic writings was a rare sophistication, an understanding of satire and irony. A well-nourished Roman frame of mind.'

I looked at him. His face too had been wiped clean of discernible age. I had time now to relish it, the squareness of his shoulders, the straightness and firmness of his neck, the distinct expression of his eyes and well-placed eyebrows. We had been made over into portraits of ourselves in marble by a master sculptor.

'You know,' I said, 'even under this crushing and annoying barrage of definition and declaration which you make to me, as if I were weeping for your ratification, I feel love for you, and know full well that we are alone in this, and married to one another, and I am not unhappy.'

He appeared surprised, but said nothing.

'I am exalted, bruised in the heart,' I said, 'a hardened pilgrim. But I do wish you would not speak to me as if my full indoctrination and education were your primary concern!'

'I have to speak this way!' he said gently. His voice was all kindness in its heat. 'It *is* my primary concern,' he said. 'If you can understand what happened with the end of the Roman Republic, if you can understand Lucretius and the Stoics, whole, then you can understand what we are. You have to do this!'

'I'll let that insult pass,' I answered. 'I'm not in the mood for listing for you every philosopher or poet I have read. Nor for recounting the level of talk around our nighttime table.'

'Pandora, I don't mean any offense! But Akasha is not a goddess! Remember your dreams. She is a vial of precious strength. Your dreams told you she could be used, that any unscrupulous blood drinker could pass on the blood to another, that she is a form of demon, host to the power we share.'

'She can hear you!' I whispered, outraged.

'Of course, she can. For fifteen years I've been her guardian. I've fought off those renegades from the East. And other connivers from the African hinterlands. She knows what she is.'

No one could have guessed his age, save from the seriousness of his expression. A man in perfect form, that was what he seemed. I tried not to be dazzled by him, by the pulsing night behind him, and yet I wanted so to drift. 'Some wedding feast,' I said. 'I have things to say to the trees.'

'They will be there tomorrow night,' he said.

The last image I had of her passed before my eyes, colored in ecstasy; she took the young Pharaoh from his chair and broke him into sticks. I saw her before that revelation, at the beginning of the swoon, running down the corridor laughing.

A slow fear crept over me.

'What is it?' Marius asked. 'Confide in me.'

'When I drank from her, I saw her like a girl, laughing.' I recounted then the marriage, the flood of rose petals, and then her strange Egyptian Temple full of frenzied worshipers. At last I told him how she had entered the chamber of the little King, whose advisors warned him of her gods.

'She broke him up as if he were a boy of wood. She said, 'Little King, little Kingdom.'

I picked up my pages, which earlier I had placed on this desk. I described the last dream I had had of her, when she threatened, screaming, to walk into the sun and destroy her disobedient children. I described all the things I had seen – the many migrations of my soul.

My heart hurt so much. Even as I explained,

I saw her vulnerability, the danger that was embodied in her. I explained finally how I had written all this in Egyptian.

I was weary and wished truly that I had never opened eyes on this life! I feel the keen and total despair again of those nights of weeping in my little house in Antioch when I had pounded on walls, and driven my dagger into the dirt. If she had not run, laughing down that corridor! What did the image mean? And the little boy King, broken so helplessly?

I made a sum of it easily enough. I waited for Marius's belittling remarks. I hadn't much patience for him now.

'How do you interpret it?' he asked gently. He tried to take my hand but I withdrew it.

'It's bits and pieces of her recollection,' I said. I was heartbroken. 'It's what she remembers. There is but one suggestion of a future in it all,' I said. 'There is only one comprehensible image of a wish: our wedding, that we be together.' My voice was full of sadness, yet I asked him.

'Why do you weep again, Marius?' I asked. 'She must gather recollections like flowers picked at random from the garden of the world, like leaves falling into her hands, and from these recollections she fastened for me a garland! A wedding garland! A trap. I have no migrant soul. I think not. If I did have a migrant soul, then why would she alone, one so archaic, helpless, irrelevant to the world itself, so out of fashion and out of power, be the one to know this? To make it known to me? The only one to know?'

I looked at him. He was engaged yet crying. He showed no shame in it, and would obviously render no apology.

'What was it you said before?' I asked. '"That I can read minds makes me no wiser than the next man?"' I smiled. 'That is the key. How she laughed as she led me to you. How she wanted me to behold you in your loneliness.'

He only nodded.

'I wonder how she knew to cast her net so far,' I said, 'to find me across the rolling sea.'

'Lucius, that's how she knew. She hears voices from many lands. She sees what she wants to see. One night here I badly startled a Roman, who appeared to recognize me and then slunk away as if I were a danger to him. I went after him, thinking vaguely that there was something to this, his excessive fear.

'I soon realized a great weight distorted his conscience and twisted his every thought and movement. He was terrified to be recognized by someone from the capital. He wanted to leave.

'He went to the house of a Greek merchant, pounding on the door late, by torchlight, and demanded the payment of a debt owed to your Father. The Greek told him what he had told him before, that the money would be repaid only to your Father himself.

'The next night I sought Lucius out again. This time the Greek had a surprise for him. A letter had just come from your Father by military ship. This was perhaps four days before your own arrival. The letter plainly stated that a favor was being asked of the Greek by your Father in the name of Hospitality and Honor. If the favor was granted, all debts were canceled. Everything would be explained by a letter accompanying a cargo destined for Antioch. The cargo would take some time, as the ship had many stops to make. The favor was of crucial importance.

'When your brother saw the date of this letter, he was stricken. The Greek, who was thoroughly sick of Lucius by this time, slammed the door in his face.

'I accosted Lucius only steps away. Of course he remembered me, the eccentric Marius of long ago. I pretended surprise to see him here and asked after you. He was in a panic and made up some story about your being married and living in Tuscany, and said that he was on his way out of town. He hurried off. But the moment's contact had been enough to see the testimony he'd given the Praetorian Guard against his family – all lies – and to imagine the deeds that had resulted from it.

'The next time, on waking, I couldn't find him. I kept watch on the house of the Greeks. I weighed in my mind a visit to the old man, the Greek merchant, some way to lay down a friendship with him. I thought of you. I pictured you. I remembered you. I made up poems in my head about you. I didn't hear or see anything of your brother. I presumed he'd left Antioch.

'Then one night I awoke and came upstairs and looked out to see the city full of random fires.

'Germanicus had died, never retracting his accusations that Piso had poisoned him.

'When I reached the house of the Greek merchant, it was nothing but burnt timbers. I caught no sight or sound of your brother anywhere. For all I knew they were all dead, your brother, and the Greek merchant family.

'All through the nights after, I searched for sight or sound of Lucius. I had no idea you were here, only an obsessive longing for you. I tried to remind myself that if I mourned for every mortal tie I had had when alive, I would go mad long before I had learnt anything about my gifts from our King and Queen.

'Then, I was in the bookseller's and it was early evening and the Priest slipped up to me. He pointed to you. There you stood in the Forum, and the philosopher and students were bidding you farewell. I was so close!

'I was so overcome with love I didn't even listen to the Priest until I realized he was speaking of strange dreams as he pointed to you. He was saying that only I could put it all together. It had to do with the blood drinker who had recently been in Antioch, not an uncommon occurrence. I have slain other blood drinkers before. I've vowed to catch this one.

'Then I saw Lucius. I saw you come together. His anger and guilt were nearly blinding to me with this blood drinker's vision. I heard your words effortlessly from a great distance, but would not move until you were safely away from him.

'I wanted to kill him then, but the wiser course seemed to stay right with you, to enter the Temple and stay by your side. I was not certain of my right to kill your brother for you, that it was what you wanted. I didn't know that until

330

I'd told you of his guilt. Then I knew how much you wanted it done.

'Of course I had no idea how clever you had become, that all the talent for reason and words I'd loved in you when you were a girl was still there. Suddenly you were in the Temple, thinking three times faster than the other mortals present, weighing every aspect of what faced you, outwitting everyone. And then came the spectacular confrontation with your brother in which you caught him in the most clever net of truths, and thereby dispatched him, without ever touching him, but instead drawing three military witnesses into complicity with his death.'

He broke off, then said, 'In Rome, years ago, I followed you. You were sixteen. I remember your first marriage. Your Father took me aside, he was so gentle. "Marius, you're destined to be a roaming historian," he said. I didn't dare tell him my true estimation of your husband.

'And now you come to Antioch, and I think, in my self-centered manner, as you will promptly note – if ever a woman was created for me, it is this woman. And I know as soon as I leave you in the morning, that I must somehow get the Mother and Father out of Antioch, get them away, but then this blood drinker has to be

331

destroyed, and then and only then can you be safely left.'

'Safely abandoned,' I said.

'Do you blame me?' he asked.

The question caught me off guard. I looked at him for a seemingly endless moment, allowing his beauty to fill my eyes, and sensing with intolerable keenness his sadness and desperation. Oh, how he needed me! How desperately he needed not just any mortal soul in which to confide, but me.

'You really did want to protect me, didn't you?' I asked. 'And your explanation of all points is so completely rational; it has the elegance of mathematics. There is no need for reincarnation, or destiny, or any miraculous allowance for any part of what's happened.'

'It's what I believe,' he said sharply. His face grew blank, then stern. 'I would never give you anything short of truth. Are you a woman who wants to be humored?'

'Don't be fanatical in your dedication to reason,' I said.

These words both shocked and offended him.

'Don't cling to reason so desperately in a world of so many horrid contradictions!'

He was silenced.

'If you so cling to reason,' I said, 'then in the

passage of time reason may fail you, and when it does you may find yourself taking refuge in madness.'

'What on Earth do you mean?'

'You're made of reason and logic religion. It's obviously the only way you can endure what's happened to you, that you're a blood drinker and custodian, apparently, of these displaced and forgotten dieties.'

'They aren't dieties!' He grew angry. 'Thousands of years ago, they were made, through some mingling of spirit and flesh that rendered them immortal. They find their refuge obviously in oblivion. In your kindness you characterize it as a garden from which the Mother gathered flowers and leaves to make a garland for you, a trap, as you said. But this is your sweet girlish poetry. We do not know that they string very many words together.'

'I am no sweet girl,' I said. 'Poetry belongs to everyone. Speak to me!' I said. 'And put aside these words, "girl" and "woman." Don't be so frightened of me.'

'I am not,' he said angrily.

'You are! Even as this new blood races through me still, eats at me and transforms me, I cling to neither reason nor superstition for my safety. I can walk through a myth and out of it!

333

You fear me, because you don't know what I am. I look like a woman, I sound like a man, and your reason tells you the sum total is impossible!'

He rose from the table. His face took on a sheen like sweat but far more radiant.

'Let me tell you what happened to me!' he said resolutely.

'Good, do tell me,' I said. 'In straightforward manner.'

He let this go by. I spoke against my heart. I wanted only to love him. I knew his cautions. But for all his wisdom, he displayed an enormous will, a man's will, and I had to know the source of it. I concealed my love.

'How did they lure you?'

'They didn't,' he said calmly. 'I was captured by the Keltoi in Gaul, in the city of Massilia. I was brought North, my hair allowed to grow long, then shut up amid barbarians in a great hollow tree in Gaul. A burnt blood drinker made me into a "new god" and told me to escape the local Priests, go South to Egypt and find out why all the blood drinkers had been burnt, the young ones dying, the old one suffering. I went for my own reasons! I wanted to know what I was!'

'I can well understand,' I said.

'But not before I saw blood worship at its

most grisly and unspeakable – I was the god, mind you, Marius, who followed you adoringly all over Rome – and it was to me that these men were offered.'

'I've read it in Caesar's history.'

'You've read it but you haven't seen it. How dare you throw at me such a trivial boast!'

'Forgive me, I forgot your childish temper.'

He sighed. 'Forgive me, I forgot your practical and naturally impatient intellect.'

'I'm sorry. I regret my words. I had to witness executions of Rome. It was my duty. And that was in the name of law. Who suffers more or less? Victims of sacrifice or the law?'

'Very well. I escaped these Keltoi and went to Egypt, and there I found the Elder, who was the keeper of the Mother and the Father, the Queen and the King, the first blood drinkers of all time, from which this enhancement of our blood flows. This Elder told me stories that were vague but compelling. The Royal Pair had once been human, no more. A spirit or demon had possessed one or both, lodging itself so firmly that no exorcism could oust it. The Royal Pair could transform others by giving the blood. They sought to make a religion. It was overthrown. Again and again it was overthrown. Anyone who possesses the blood can make another! Of course this Elder claimed ignorance of why so many had been burnt. But it was he who had dragged his sacred and royal charges into the sun after centuries of meaningless guardianship! Egypt was dead, he said to me. 'The granary of Rome,' he called it. He said the Royal Pair had not moved in a millennium.'

This filled me with the most remarkable and poetic sense of horror.

'Well, one day's hot light was not enough anymore to destroy the ancient parents, but all over the world the children suffered. And this cowardly Elder, given only pain for his reward, a burned skin, lost the courage required to continue the exposure of the Royal Pair. He had no cause, one or another.

'Akasha spoke to me. She spoke as best she could. In images, pictures of what had happened since the beginning, how this tribe of gods and goddesses had sprung from her, and rebellions had occurred, and how much history was lost, and purpose was lost, and when it came to the forming of words, Akasha could make but only a few silent sentences: "Marius, take us out of Egypt!"' He paused. '"Take us out of Egypt, Marius. The Elder means to destroy us. Guard us or we perish here."'

He took a breath; he was calmer now, not so

angry, but very much shattered, and in my ever increasing vampiric vision, I knew more about him, how very courageous he was, how very determined to hold to principles in which he believed, in spite of the magic that had swallowed him whole before he had had time even to question it. His was an attempt at a noble life, in spite of all.

'My fate,' he said, 'was directly connected to hers, to them! If I left them, the Elder would sooner or later put them in the sun again, and I, lacking the blood of centuries, would burn up like wax! My life, already altered, would have been ended. But the Elder did not ask me to install a new priesthood. Akasha did not ask me to install a new religion! She did not speak of altars or worship. Only the old burnt-out god in the Northern grove among the barbarians had asked me to do such a thing when he sent me to the South, to Egypt, the motherland of all mysteries.'

'How long have you kept them?'

'Over fifteen years. I lose count. They never move or speak. The wounded ones, those burnt so badly that time will take centuries to heal them, they learn that I am here. They come. I try to extinguish them before their minds can give forth a flash of a confirming image to other distant minds. She doesn't guide these burnt children to where she is, as she once guided me! If I am tricked or overwhelmed, she moves only as you saw, to crush the blood drinker. But she has called you, Pandora, reached out for you. And we know now to what exact purpose. And I've been cruel to you. Clumsy.'

He turned to me. His voice grew tender. 'Tell me, Pandora,' he asked. 'In the vision you saw, when we were married, were we young or old? Were you the girl of fifteen I sought too early perhaps, or the mature full blossom of a creature you are now? Are the families happy? Are we comely?'

I was hotly embraced by the sincerity of his words. The anguish and the pleading that lay behind them.

'We were as we are now,' I said, cautiously answering his smile with my own. 'You were a man fixed in the prime of life forever, and I? As I am at this hour.'

'Believe me,' he said with sweetness in his voice, 'I would not have spoken so harshly on this of all nights, but you have now so many other nights to come. Nothing can kill you now, but the sun or fire. Nothing in you will deteriorate. You have a thousand experiences to discover.'

Anne Rice

'And what of the ecstasy when I drank from her?' I asked. 'What of her own beginnings and her suffering? Does she in no way connect herself to the sacred?'

'What is sacred?' he asked, shrugging his shoulder. 'Tell me. What is sacred? Was it sanctity you saw in her dreams?'

I bowed my head. I couldn't answer.

'Certainly not the Roman Empire,' he said, 'Certainly not the temples of Augustus Caesar. Certainly not the worship of Cybele! Certainly not the cult of those who worship fire in Persia. Is the name Isis sacred anymore, or was it ever? The Elder in Egypt, my first and only instructor in all this, said that Akasha invented the stories of Isis and Osiris to suit her purposes, to give a poetry to her worship. I think rather she grafted herself upon old stories. The demon in those two grows with each new blood drinker made. It must.'

'But to no purpose?'

'That it may know more?' he said. 'That it may see more, feel more, through each of us which carries its blood? Perhaps it is such a creature as that and each of us is but a tiny part of it, carrying all its senses and capacities and returning our experiences to it. It reaches out through us to know the world!

339

'I can tell you this,' he said. He paused and put his hands on the desk. 'What burns in me does not care if the victim is innocent or guilty of any crime. It thirsts. Not every night, but often! It says nothing! It does not talk of altars to me in my heart! It drives me as though I were the battle steed and it the mounted General! It is Marius who weeds the good from the bad, according to the old custom, for reasons you can well understand, but not this ravening thirst; this thirst knows nature but no morality.'

'I love you, Marius,' I said. 'You and my Father are the only men I've ever really loved. But I must go out alone now.'

'What did you say!' He was amazed. 'It's just past midnight.'

'You've been very patient, but I have to walk alone now.'

'I'll come with you.'

'You will not,' I said.

'But you can't simply roam around Antioch on your own, alone.'

'Why not? I can hear mortal thoughts now if I want to. A litter just passed. The slaves are so drunk it's a wonder they don't drop the thing and heave the Master into the road, and he himself is fast asleep. I want to walk alone, out there, in the city in the dark places and the dangerous places and the evil places and the places where even . . . where even a god would not go.'

'This is your vengeance on me,' he said. I walked towards the gate and he followed. 'Pandora, not alone.'

'Marius, my love,' I said, turning, taking his hand. 'It is not vengeance. The words you spoke earlier, "girl" and "woman," they have always circumscribed my life. I want only now to walk fearlessly with my arms bare and my hair down my back, into any cavern of danger I choose. I am drunk still from her blood, from yours! Things shimmer and flicker that should shine. I must be alone to ponder all you've said.'

'But you have to be back before dawn, well before. You have to be with me in the crypt below. You can't merely lie in some room somewhere. The deadly light will penetrate–'

He was so protective, so lustrous, so infuriated.

'I will be back,' I said, 'and well before dawn, and for now, my heart will break if we are not, as of this moment, bound together.'

'We are bound,' he said. 'Pandora, you could drive me mad.'

He stopped at the bars of the gate.

'Don't come any farther,' I said as I left.

I walked down towards Antioch. My legs had

such strength and spring, and the dust and pebbles of the road were nothing to my feet, and my eyes penetrated the night to see the full conspiracy of owls and little rodents that hovered in the trees, eyeing me, then fleeing as if their natural senses warned them against me.

Soon I came into the city proper. I think the resolution with which I moved from little street to little street was enough to frighten anyone who would have contemplated molesting me. I heard only cowardice and erotic curses from the dark, those tangled ugly curses men heap on women they desire – half threat, half dismissal.

I could sense the people in their houses fast asleep, and hear the guards on watch, talking in their barracks behind the Forum.

I did all the things the new blood drinkers always do. I touched the surfaces of walls and stared, enchanted at a common torch and the moths that gave themselves up to it. I felt against my naked arms and fragile tunic the dreams of all Antioch surrounding me.

Rats fled up and down the gutters and the streets. The river gave off its own sound, and there came a hollow echoing from the ships at anchor, even from the faintest stirring of the water.

The Forum, resplendent with its ever burning

lights, caught the moon as if it were a great human trap for it, the very reverse of an earthy crater, a man-made design that could be seen and blessed by the intransigent heavens.

When I came to my own house, I found I could climb to the very top easily, and there I sat on the tiled roof, so relaxed and secure and free, looking down into the courtyard, into the peristyle, where I had really learned – alone on those three nights – the truths that had prepared me for Akasha's blood.

In calmness and without pain, I thought it through again – as if I owed this reconsideration to the woman I had been, the initiate, the woman who had sought refuge in the Temple. Marius was right. The Queen and King were possessed of some demon which spread through the blood, feeding upon it and growing, as I could feel it doing in me now.

The King and Queen did not invent justice! The Queen, who broke the little Pharaoh into sticks, did not invent law or righteousness!

And the Roman courts, bumbling awkwardly towards each decision, weighing all sides, refusing any magical or religious device, they did even in these terrible times strive for justice. It was a system based not upon the revelation of the gods, but upon reason.

343

But I could not regret the moment of intoxication when I'd drunk her blood and believed in her, and seen the flowers come down upon us. I could not regret that any mind could conceive of such perfect transcendence.

She had been my Mother, my Queen, my goddess, my all. I had known it as we were meant to know it when we drink the potions in the Temple, when we sing, when we are rocking in delirious song. And in her arms I had known it. In Marius's arms I'd known it as well, and in a safer measure, and I wanted only to be with him now.

How ghastly her worship seemed. Flawed and ignorant, being elevated to such power! And how revealing suddenly that at the core of mysteries there should lie such degrading explanations. Blood spilt on her golden gown!

All images and meaningful glimpses do but teach you deeper things. I thought again, as I had in the Temple, when I had settled for the consolation of a basalt statue.

It is I, and I alone, who must make of my new life a heroic tale.

I was very happy for Marius that he had such comfort in reason. But reason was only a created thing, imposed with faith upon the world, and the stars promise nothing to no one.

I had seen something deeper in those dark nights of hiding in this house in Antioch, in mourning for my Father. I had seen that at the very heart of Creation there very well might lie something as uncontrollable and incomprehensible as a raging volcano.

Its lava would destroy trees and poets alike.

So take this gift, Pandora, I told myself. Go home, thankful that you are again wed, for you have never made a better match or seen a more tantalizing future.

When I returned, and my return was very rapid, full of new lessons in how I might pass quickly over rooftops, scarce touching them, and over walls – when I returned, I found him as I had left him, only much sadder. He sat in the garden, just as he had in the vision shown to me by Akasha.

It must have been a place he loved, behind the villa with its many doors, a bench facing a thicket and a natural stream bubbling up and over the rocks and spilling down into a current through high grass.

He rose at once.

I took him in my arms.

'Marius, forgive me,' I said.

'Don't say such a thing, I'm to blame for it all. And I didn't protect you from it.'

345

We were in each other's arms. I wanted to press my teeth into him, drink his blood, and then I did, and felt him taking the blood from me. This was a union more powerful than any I had ever known in a marriage bed, and I yielded to it as I never yielded in life to anyone.

I felt an exhaustion sweep me suddenly. I withdrew my kiss with its teeth.

'Come on, now,' he said. 'Your slave is asleep. And during the day, while we must sleep, he will bring all your possessions here, and those girls of yours, should you want to keep them.'

We walked down the stairs, we entered another room. It took all Marius's strength to pull back the door, which meant simply that no mortal man could do it.

There lay a sarcophagus, plain, of granite.

'Can you lift the lid of the sarcophagus?' Marius asked.

'I am feeling weak!'

'It's the sun rising, try to lift the lid. Slide it to one side.'

I did, and inside I found a bed of crushed lilies and rose petals, of silken pillows, and bits of dried flower kept for scent.

I stepped in, turned around, sat and stretched out in this stone prison. At once he took his place in the tomb beside me, and pushed the lid back to its place, and all the world's light in any form was shut out, as if the dead would have it so.

'I'm drowsy. I can hardly form words.'

'What a blessing,' he said.

'There is no need for such an insult,' I murmured. 'But I forgive you.'

'Pandora, I love you!' he said helplessly.

'Put it inside me,' I said, reaching between his legs. 'Fill me and hold me.'

'This is stupid and superstitious!'

'It is neither,' I said. 'It is symbolic and comforting.'

He obeyed. Our bodies were one, connected by this sterile organ which was no more to him now than his arm, but how I loved the arm he threw over me and the lips he pressed to my forehead.

'I love you, Marius, my strange, tall and beautiful Marius.'

'I don't believe you,' he said, his voice barely a whisper.

'What do you mean?'

'You'll despise me soon enough for what I've done to you.'

'Not so, oh, rational one. I am not as eager to grow old, wither and die, as you might think. I should like a chance to know more, to see more . . .'

I felt his lips against my forehead.

'Did you really try to marry me when I was fifteen?'

'Oh, agonizing memories! Your Father's insults still sting my ears! He had me all but thrown out of your house!'

'I love you with my whole heart,' I whispered. 'And you have won. You have me now as your wife.'

'I have you as something, but I do not think that "wife" is the word for it. I wonder that you've already forgotten your earlier strenuous objection to the term.'

'Together,' I said, scarce able to talk on account of his kisses. I was drowsy and loved the feel of his lips, their sudden eagerness for pure affection. 'We'll think of another word more exalted than "wife".'

Suddenly I moved back. I could not see him in the dark.

'Are you kissing me so that I will not talk?'

'Yes, that's exactly what I was doing,' he said.

I turned away from him.

'Turn back, please,' he said.

'No,' I said.

I lay still, realizing dimly that his body felt quite normal to me now, because mine was as hard as his was, as strong perhaps. What a sublime advantage. Oh, but I loved him. I loved him! So let him kiss the back of the neck! He could not force me to turn towards him!

The sun must have risen.

For a silence fell on me which was as if the universe with all its volcanoes and raging tides – and all its Emperors, Kings, judges, Senators, philosophers and Priests – had been erased from existence.

11

Well, David, there you have it.

I could continue the Plautus-Terence style comedy for pages. I could vie with Shakespeare's *Much Ado About Nothing*.

But that is the basic story. That is what lies behind the flippant capsule version in *The Vampire Lestat*, fashioned into its final trivial form by Marius or Lestat, who knows.

Let me lead you through those points which are sacred and burn still in my heart, no matter how easily they have been dismissed by another.

And the tale of our parting is not mere dissonance but may contain some lesson.

Marius taught me to hunt, to catch the evil-doer only, and to kill without pain, enwrapping the soul of my victim in sweet visions or allowing the soul to illuminate its own death with a cascade of fantasies which I must not judge, but merely devour, like the blood. All that does not require detailed documentation.

We were matched in strength. When some burnt and ruthlessly ambitious blood drinker did find his way to Antioch, which happened only a few times and then not at all, we executed the supplicant together. These were monstrous mentalities, forged in ages we could hardly understand, and they sought the Queen like jackals seek the bodies of the human dead.

There was no argument between us over any of them.

We often read aloud to each other, and we laughed together at Petronius's *Satyricon,* and we shared both tears and laughter later as we read the bitter satires of Juvenal. There was no end of new satire and history coming from Rome and from Alexandria.

But something forever divided Marius from me.

Love grew but so did constant argument, and argument became more and more the dangerous cement of the bond.

Over the years, Marius guarded his delicate rationality as a Vestal Virgin guards a sacred flame. If ever any ecstatic emotion took hold of me, he was there to grab me by the shoulders and tell me in no uncertain terms that it was irrational. Irrational, irrational, irrational!

When the terrible earthquake of the second century struck Antioch, and we were unharmed, I dared speak of it as a Divine Blessing. This set Marius into a rage, and he was quick to point that the same Divine Intervention had also protected the Roman Emperor Trajan, who was in the city at the time. What was I to make of that?

For the record, Antioch quickly rebuilt itself, the markets flourished, more slaves poured in, nothing stopped the caravans headed for the ships, and the ships headed for the caravans.

But long before that earthquake we had all but come to blows night after night.

If I lingered for hours in the room of the Mother and the Father, Marius invariably came to collect me and bring me back to my senses. He could not read in peace with me in such a state, he declared. He could not think because he knew I was downstairs deliberately inviting madness.

Why, I demanded, must his domination extend to every corner of our entire house and garden? And how was it that I was his match in strength when an old burnt blood drinker found his way to Antioch and we picked up the word of his killing and had to do away with him?

'We are not matched in minds?' I demanded.

'Only you could ask that question!' came his reply.

Of course the Mother and Father never moved or spoke again. No blood dreams, no divine directive ever reached me. Only now and then did Marius remind me of this. And after a long while, he allowed me to tend the Shrine with him, to see full well the extent of their silent and seemingly mindless compliance. They appeared utterly beyond reach; their cooperation was sluggish and frightening to witness.

When Flavius fell ill in his fortieth year, Marius and I had the first of our truly terrible battles. This came early on, well before the earthquake.

It was, by the way, a wondrous time because the wicked old Tiberius was filling Antioch with new and wonderful buildings. She was the rival of Rome. But Flavius was ill.

Marius could scarce bear it. He had become more than fond of Flavius – they talked about Aristotle all the time, and Flavius proved one of those men who can do anything for you, from managing a household to copying the most esoteric and crumbling text with complete accuracy.

Flavius had never put a single question to us

as to what we were. In his mind, I found, devotion and acceptance far superseded curiosity or fear.

We hoped Flavius had only a minor illness. But finally, as Flavius's fever grew worse, Flavius turned his head away from Marius whenever Marius came to him. But he held on to my hand always when I offered it. Frequently I lay beside him for hours, as he had once lain beside me.

Then one night Marius took me to the gate and said, 'He'll be dead by the time I come back. Can you bear this alone?'

'Do you run from it?' I asked.

'No,' he said. 'But he doesn't want me to see him die; he doesn't want me to see him groan in pain.'

I nodded.

Marius left.

Marius had long ago laid down the rule that no other blood drinker was ever to be made. I didn't bother to question him on this.

As soon as he was gone, I made Flavius into a vampire. I did it just the way the burnt one, Marius and Akasha had done it to me, for Marius and I had long discussed the methods – withdraw as much blood as you can, then give it back until you are near to fainting.

I did faint and wake to see this splendid Greek standing over me, smiling faintly, all disease gone from him. He reached down to take my hand and help me to my feet.

Marius walked in, stared at the reborn Flavius in amazement and said, 'Get out, out of this house, out of this city, out of this province, out of this Empire.'

Flavius's last words to me were:

'Thank you for this Dark Gift.' That is the first I ever heard that particular phrase, which appears so often in Lestat's writings. How well this learned Athenian understood it.

For hours I avoided Marius. I would never be forgiven! Then I went out into the garden. I discovered Marius was grieving, and when he looked up, I realized that he had been utterly convinced that I meant to go off with Flavius. When I saw this, I took him in my arms. He was full of quiet relief and love; he forgave me at once for my 'absolute rashness.'

'Don't you see,' I said, taking him in hand, 'that I adore you? But you cannot rule over me! Can you not consider in your reasonable fashion that the greatest part of our gift eludes you – it's the freedom from the confines of male, female!'

'You can't convince me,' he said, 'for one

moment that you don't feel, reason and act in the manner of a woman. We both loved Flavius. But why another blood drinker?'

'I don't know except that Flavius wanted it, Flavius knew all about our secrets, there was a ... an understanding between me and Flavius! He had been loyal in the darkest hours of my mortal life. Oh, I can't explain it.'

'A woman's sentiments, exactly. And you have launched this creature into eternity.'

'He joins our search,' I replied.

About the middle of the century, when the city was very rich and the Empire was about as peaceful as it was ever going to be for the next two hundred years, the Christian Paul came to Antioch.

I went to hear him speak one night and came home, saying casually that the man could convert the very stones to this faith, such was his personal power.

'How can you spend your time on such things!' Marius demanded. 'Christians. They aren't even a cult! Some worship John, some worship Jesus. They fight amongst one another! Don't you see what this man Paul has done?'

'No, what?' I said. 'I didn't say I was going to join the sect. I only said I stopped to hear him. Who is hurt by that?'

'You, your mind, your equilibrium, your common sense. It's compromised by the foolish things in which you take an interest, and frankly the principle of truth is hurt!' He had only just begun.

'Let me tell you about this man Paul,' Marius said. 'He never knew either the Baptizer John or the Galilean Jesus. The Hebrews have thrown him out of the group. Jesus and John were both Hebrews! And so Paul has now turned to everyone. Jew and Christian alike, and Roman and Greek, and said, "You needn't follow the Hebrew observance. Forget the Feasts in Jerusalem. Forget Circumcision. Become a Christian."'

'Yes, that is true,' I said with a sigh.

'It's a very easy religion to take up,' he said. 'It's nothing. You have to believe that this man rose from the Dead. And by the way, I've combed the available texts which are floating all over the marketplaces. Have you?'

'No. I'm surprised you've found this search worthy of your time.'

'I don't see anywhere in the writings of those who knew John and Jesus where these two are quoted as saying either one of them will rise from the Dead, or that all who believe in them will have life after death. Paul added all that.

What an enticing promise! And you should hear your friend, Paul, on the subject of Hell! What a cruel vision – that flawed mortals could sin in this life so grievously that they would burn for all eternity.'

'He's not my friend. You make so much of my passing remarks. Why do you feel so strongly?'

'I told you, I care about what is true, what is reasonable!'

'Well, there's something you're missing about this group of Christians, some way in which when they come together they share a euphoric love and they believe in great generosity –'

'Oh, not again! And are you to tell me this is good?'

I didn't answer.

He was returning to his work when I spoke.

'You fear me,' I said to him. 'You fear that I'll be swept off my feet by somebody of belief and abandon you. No. No, that's not right. You fear that you will be swept up. That the world will somehow entice you back into it, so that you won't live here with me, the superior Roman observer recluse, anymore, but go back, seeking mortal comforts of companionship and proximity to others, friendship with mortals, their recognition of you as one of them when you are not one of them!'

'Pandora, you talk gibberish.'

'Keep your proud secrets,' I said. 'But I do fear for you, that I will admit.'

'Fear for me? And why?' he demanded.

'Because you don't realize everything perishes, everything is artifice! That even logic and mathematics and justice have no ultimate meaning!'

'That's not true,' he said.

'Oh, yes it is. Some night will come when you will see what I saw, when I first came to Antioch, before you'd found me, before this transformation which should have swept away everything in its path.

'You will see a darkness,' I went on, 'a darkness so total that Nature never knows it anywhere on Earth at any time, in any place! Only the human soul can know it. And it goes on forever. And I pray that when you finally can no longer escape from it, when you realize it is all around you, that your logic and your reason give you some strength against it.'

He gave me the most respectful look. But he didn't speak. I continued:

'Resignation will do you no good,' I said, 'when such a time comes. Resignation requires will, and will requires decision, and decision requires belief, and belief requires that there is something to believe in! And all action or acceptance requires a concept of a witness! Well, there is nothing, and there are no witnesses! You don't know that yet, but I do. I hope, when you find it out, someone can comfort you as you dress and groom those monstrous relics below the stairs! As you bring their flowers!' I was so angry, I went on:

'Look back on me when this moment comes – if not for forgiveness, look back on me as a model. For I have seen this, and I have survived. And it matters not that I stopped to listen to Paul preach of Christ, or that I weave flowers into crowns for the Queen, or that I dance like a fool under the moon in the garden before dawn, or that I . . . that I love you. It matters not. Because there is nothing. And no one to see. No one!' I sighed. It was time to finish.

'Go back to your history, this stack of lies that tries to link event to event with cause and effect, this preposterous faith that postulates that one thing follows from another. I tell you, it's not so. But it is very Roman of you to think so.'

He sat silent looking up at me. I couldn't tell what his thoughts were or what his heart felt. Then he asked:

'What would you have me do?' He had never looked more innocent.

Bitterly, I laughed. Did we not speak the same language? He heard not one word I had uttered. Yet he presented me not with a reply, but only with this simple question.

'All right,' I said. 'I'll tell you what I want. Love me, Marius, love me, but leave me alone!' I cried out. I had not even thought. The words just came. 'Leave me alone, so that I may seek my own comforts, my own means to remain alive, no matter how foolish or pointless these comforts appear to you. Leave me alone!'

He was wounded, so uncomprehending, looking so innocent still.

We had many similar arguments as the decades passed.

Sometimes he would come to me after; he would fall into long thoughtful talks about what he felt was happening with the Empire, how the Emperors were going mad and the Senate had no power, how the very progress of man was unique in Nature and something to be watched. How he would crave life, he thought, until there was no more life.

'Even if there is nothing left but desert waste,' he said, 'I should want to be there, to see dune folding upon dune,' he went on. 'If there was but one lamp left in all the world, I'd want to watch its flame. And so would you.'

But the terms of the battle, and its heat, never really changed.

At heart he thought I hated him for having been so unkind on the night I was given the Dark Blood. I told him this was childish. I could not convince him that my soul and my intelligence were infinitely too large for such a simple grudge, and that I owed him no explanation for my thoughts, words and deeds.

For two hundred years, we lived and loved together. He became ever more beautiful to me.

As more and more barbarians from the North and from the East poured into the city, he felt no necessity to dress like a Roman anymore, and frequently wore the jeweled clothes of the Easterners. His hair seemed to be growing finer, lighter. He seldom cut it, which of course he would have had to do every night had he wanted it short. It was a splendor on his shoulders.

As his face grew ever more smooth, away went the few lines that could so easily design anger in his expression. As I've told you before, he greatly resembles Lestat. Only he is more compact of build, and jaw and chin had hardened just a little more with age before the Dark

Gift. But the unwanted folds were receding from his eyes.

Sometimes for nights on end, in fear of a fight, we didn't speak. There was between us always a continuous physical affection – embraces, kisses, sometimes the mere silent lock of our hands.

But we knew we had now lived far beyond a normal human life span.

You need from me no detailed history of that remarkable time. It is too well known. Only let me place here a few reminders. Only let me describe for you my perspective on the changes happening all over the Empire.

Antioch as a thriving city proved indestructible. The Emperors began to favor it and visit it. More Temples went up to the Eastern cults. And then Christians of all kinds poured into Antioch.

Indeed, the Christians of Antioch comprised at last an immense and fascinating bunch of people arguing with one another.

Rome went to war on the Jews, crushing Jerusalem completely and destroying the sacred Hebrew Temple. Many brilliant Jewish thinkers came to Antioch as well as Alexandria.

Twice or perhaps even three times, Roman legions pushed past us, North of us, into

Parthia; once we even had a little rebellion of our own, but Rome always resecured the city of Antioch. So the market closed for a day! On went the trade, the great lust of the caravans for the ships, and of the ships for the caravans, and Antioch was the bed in which they must wed each other.

There was little new poetry. Satire. Satire seemed the only safe or honest expression of the Roman mind now, and so we had the riotously funny story *The Golden Ass,* by Apuleius, which seemed to make fun of every religion. But there was a bitterness to the poet Martial. And those letters of Pliny which reached me were full of dire judgments on the moral chaos of Rome.

I began as a vampire to feed exclusively on soldiers. I liked them, their look, their strength. I fed so much so on them, that in my carelessness, I became a legend amongst them, 'The Greek Lady Death,' this on account of my clothes which to them appeared archaic. I struck at random in the dark streets. There wasn't a chance of their ever surrounding me or stopping me, so great was my skill, my strength and my thirst.

But I saw things in their rebellious deaths, the blaze of a pitched battle in a march, a hand-to-hand struggle on a steep mountain. I took them down gently into the finish, filling myself to the brim with their blood, and sometimes, through a veil it seemed, I saw the souls of those whom they themselves had slain.

When I told Marius this, he said it was just the kind of mystical nonsense he would expect of me.

I didn't press the point.

He watched with keen interest the developments of Rome. To me they seemed merely surprising.

He pored over the histories of Dio Cassius and Plutarch and Tacitus, and pounded his fist when he heard of the endless skirmishes on the Rhine River, and the push Northward into Britannia and the building of Hadrian's wall to forever keep away the Scots, who like the Germans would yield to no one.

'They are not patrolling, preserving, containing an Empire any longer,' he said. 'Conserving a way of life! It's just war, and trade!'

I couldn't disagree.

It was really even worse than he knew. If he had gone as often as I did to listen to the philosophers he would have been appalled.

Magicians were appearing everywhere, claiming to be able to fly, to see visions, to heal

with the laying on of hands! They got into battles with the Christians and the Jews. I don't
think the Roman army paid them any attention.

Medicine as I had known it in my mortal life
had been flooded with a river of Eastern secret
formulae, amulets, rituals, and little statues to
clutch.

Well over half the Senate was no longer
Italian by birth. This meant that our Rome was
no longer our Rome. And the title of Emperor
had become a joke. There were so many assas-
sinations, plots, squabbles, false emperors and
palace coups that it soon became perfectly clear
that the Army ruled. The Army chose the
Emperor. The Army sustained him.

The Christians were divided into warring
sects. It was positively astonishing. The religion didn't burn itself out in dispute. It gained
strength in division. Occasional furious perse-
cutions – in which people were executed for not
worshiping at Roman altars – only seemed to
deepen the sympathy of the populace with this
new cult.

And the new cult was rampant with debate on
every principle with regard to the Jews, God
and Jesus.

The most amazing thing had happened to this
religion. Spreading wildly on fast ships, good

roads and well-maintained trade routes, it suddenly found itself in a peculiar position. The world had not come to an end, as Jesus and Paul had predicted.

And everybody who had ever known or seen Jesus was dead. Finally everyone who had ever known Paul was dead.

Christian philosophers arose, picking and choosing from old Greek ideas and old Hebrew traditions.

Justin of Athens wrote that Christ was the Logos; you could be an atheist and still be saved in Christ if you upheld reason.

I had to tell this to Marius.

I thought sure it would set him off, and the night was dull, but he merely countered with more outlandish talk of the Gnostics.

'A man named Saturninus popped up in the Forum today,' he said. 'Perhaps you heard talk of him. He preaches a wild variant of this Christian creed you find so amusing, in which the God of the Hebrews is actually the Devil and Jesus the new God. This was not the man's first appearance. He and his followers, thanks to the local Christian Bishop Ignatius, are headed for Alexandria.'

'There are books with those ideas already here,' I said, 'having come from Alexandria.

They are impenetrable to me. Perhaps not to you. They speak of Sophia, a female principle of Wisdom, which preceded the Creation. Jews and Christians alike want somehow to include this concept of Sophia in their faith. It so reminds me of our beloved Isis.'

'Your beloved Isis!' he said.

'It seems that there are minds who would weave it all together, every myth, or its essence, to make a glorious tapestry.'

'Pandora, you are making me ill again,' he warned. 'Let me tell you what your Christians are doing. They are tightly organizing. This Bishop Ignatius will be followed by another, and the Bishops want to lay down now that the age of private revelation had ended; they want to weed through all the mad scrolls on the market and make a canon which all Christians believe.'

'I never thought such could happen,' I said. 'I agreed with you more than you knew when you condemned them.'

'They are succeeding because they are moving away from emotional morality,' he said. 'They are organizing like Romans. This Bishop Ignatius is very strict. He delegates power. He pronounced on the accuracy of manuscripts. Notice the prophets are getting thrown out of Antioch.'

'Yes, you're right,' I said. 'What do you think? Is it good or bad?'

'I want the world to be better,' he said. 'Better for men and women. Better. Only one thing is clear: the old blood drinkers have by now died out, and there is nothing you or I, or the Queen and the King can do to interfere in the flow of human events. I believe men and women must try harder. I try to understand evil ever more deeply with any victim I take.

'Any religion that makes fanatical claims and demands on the basis of a god's will frightens me.'

'You are a true Augustan,' I said. 'I agree with you, but it is fun to read these mad Gnostics. This Marcion and this Valentinus.'

'Fun for you perhaps. I see danger everywhere. This new Christianity, it isn't merely spreading, it's changing in each place as it spreads; it's like an animal which devours the local flora and fauna and then takes on some specific power from the food.'

I didn't argue with him.

By the end of the second century, Antioch was a heavily Christian city. And it seemed to me as I read the works of new Bishops and philosophers that worse things than Christianity could come upon us.

Realize, however, David, that Antioch did not lie under a cloud of decay; there was no sense in the air of the end of the Empire. If anything there was bustling energy everywhere. Commerce gives one this feel, that false sense that there is growth and creativity, perhaps, when there is none. Things are exchanged, not necessarily improved.

Then came the dark time for us. Two forces came together which bore down on Marius, straining all his courage. Antioch was more interesting than it had ever been.

The Mother and the Father had never stirred since the first night of my coming!

Let me describe the first disaster, because for me it was not so hard to bear, and I had only sympathy for Marius.

As I've told you, the question of who was Emperor had become a joke. But it really became a howl with the events of the early 200s.

The Emperor of the moment was Caracalla, a regular murderer. On a pilgrimage to Alexandria to see the remains of Alexander the Great, he had – for reasons no one knows even now – rounded up thousands of young Alexandrians and slaughtered them. Alexandria had never seen such a massacre.

Marius was distraught. All the world was distraught.

Marius spoke of leaving Antioch, of getting far far away from the ruin of the Empire. I began to agree with him.

Then this revolting Emperor Caracalla marched in our direction, intending to make a war on the Parthians North of us and to the East of us. Nothing out of the ordinary for Antioch!

His Mother – and you need not remember these names – Julia Domna, took up residence in Antioch. She was dying from cancer of her breast. And let me add here that this woman had, with her son Caracalla, helped murder her other son, Geta, because the two brothers had been sharing Imperial power and threatening to make a Civil War.

Let me continue, and again you need not remember the names.

Troops were massed for this Eastern war against two Kings to the East, Vologases the Fifth and Artabanus the Fifth. Caracalla did make war, achieve victory and return in triumph. Then, only miles from Antioch, he was assassinated by his own soldiers while trying to relieve himself!

All this cast Marius in a hopeless frame of mind. For hours he sat in the Shrine staring at the Mother and the Father. I felt I knew what he was thinking, that we should immolate ourselves and them, but I couldn't bear the thought of it. I didn't want to die. I didn't want to lose life. I didn't want to lose Marius.

I did not care so much about the fate of Rome. Life still stretched before me, extending the promise of wonders.

Back to the Comedy. The Army promptly made an Emperor out of a man from the Provinces named Macrinus, who was a Moor and wore an earring in his ear.

He at once had a fight with the dead Emperor's Mother, Julia Domna, because he wouldn't allow her to leave Antioch to die elsewhere. She starved herself to death.

This was all too close to home! These lunatics were in our city, not far away in a capital which we mourned.

Then war broke out again, because the Eastern Kings, who were caught off guard before by Caracalla, were now ready, and Macrinus had to lead the Legions into battle.

As I told you, the Legions now controlled everything. Somebody should have told Macrinus. Instead of fighting he bought off the enemy. The troops were hardly proud of this. And then he cracked down on them, taking away some of their benefits.

He didn't seem to grasp that he had to maintain their approval to survive. Though of course what good had this done for Caracalla, whom they loved?

Whatever, the sister of Julia Domna, named Julia Maesa, who was a Syrian and of a family dedicated to the Syrian sun god, seized this dreary moment in the lift of the lusty legions to put her grandson, born of Julia Soemis, in power as Emperor! It was an outrageous plan actually, for any number of reasons. First and foremost, all three Julias were Syrian. The boy himself was fourteen years old, and also he was a hereditary Priest of the Syrian sun god.

But somehow or other Julia Maesa and her daughter's lover, Gannys, managed to convince a bunch of soldiers in a tent that this fourteen-year-old Syrian boy should become the Emperor of Rome.

The Army deserted the Imperial Macrinus, and he and his son were hunted down and murdered.

So, high on the shoulders of proud soldiers rode this fourteen-year-old boy! But he didn't want to be called by his Roman name. He wanted to be called by the name of the god he worshiped in Syria, Elagabalus. The very presence of him in Antioch shook the nerves of all citizens. At last, he and three remaining Julias – his aunt, his Mother and his grandmother, all of them Syrian Priestesses – left Antioch.

In Nicomedia, which was very near to us, Elagabalus murdered his Mother's lover. So who was left? He also picked up an enormous sacred black stone and brought it back to Rome, saying that this stone was sacred to the Syrian sun god, whom all must now worship.

He was gone, across the sea, but it took sometimes no more than eleven days for a letter to reach Antioch from Rome, and soon there were rampant rumors. Who will ever know the truth about him?

Elagabalus. He built a Temple for the stone on the Palatine Hill. He made Romans stand around in Phoenician gowns while he slaughtered cattle and sheep in sacrifice.

He begged the physicians to try to transform him into a woman by creating a proper opening between his legs. Romans were horrified by this. At night he dressed as a woman, complete with a wig, and went prowling taverns.

All over the Empire the soldiers started to riot.

Even the three Julias, grandmother Julia Maesa, his aunt Julia Domna, and his own

Mother, Julia Soemis, started to get sick of him. After four years, four years, mind you, of this maniac's rule, the soldiers killed him and threw his body in the Tiber.

It did not seem to Marius that there was anything left of the world we had once called Rome. And he was thoroughly sick of all the Christians in Antioch, their fights over doctrine. He found all mystery religions dangerous now. He served up this lunatic Emperor as a perfect example of the fanaticism gaining ground in the times.

And he was right. He was right.

It was all I could do to keep him from despair. In truth he had not yet confronted that terrible darkness I had once spoken of; he was far too agitated, far too irritated and quarrelsome. But I was very frightened for him, and hurt for him, and didn't want him to see more darkly, as I did, to be more aloof, expecting nothing and almost smiling at the collapse of our Empire.

Then the very worst thing happened, something we had both feared in one form or another. But it came upon us in the worst possible form.

One night there appeared at our eternally open doors five blood drinkers.

Neither of us had caught the sound of their approach. Lounging about with our books, we looked up to see these five, three women and a man and a boy, and to realize that all wore black garments. They were dressed like Christian hermits and ascetics who deny the flesh and starve themselves. Antioch had a whole passel of these men in the desert roundabouts.

But these were blood drinkers.

Dark of hair and eye, and dark of skin, they stood before us, their arms folded.

Dark of skin, I thought quickly. They are young. They were made after the great burning. So what if there are five?

They had in general rather attractive faces, well-shaped features and groomed eyebrows, and deep dark eyes, and all over them I saw the marks of their living bodies – tiny wrinkles next to their eyes, wrinkled around their knuckles.

They seemed as shocked to see us as we were to see them. They stared at the brightly lighted library; they stared at our finery, which was in such contrast to their ascetic robes.

'Well,' said Marius, 'who are you?'

Cloaking my thoughts, I tried to probe theirs. Their minds were locked. They were dedicated to something. It had the very scent of fanaticism. I felt a horrid foreboding.

They started timidly to enter the open door.

'No, stop, please,' said Marius in Greek.

'This is my house. Tell me who you are, and then I perhaps shall invite you over my threshold.'

'You're Christians, aren't you?' I said. 'You have the zeal.'

'We are!' said one in Greek. It was the man. 'We are the scourge of humanity in the name of God and his son, Christ. We are the Children of Darkness.'

'Who made you?' asked Marius.

'We were made in a sacred cave and in our Temple,' said another, a woman, speaking in Greek also. 'We know the truth of the Serpent, and his fangs are our fangs.'

I climbed to my feet and moved towards Marius.

'We thought you would be in Rome,' said the young man. He had short black hair, and very round innocent eyes. 'Because the Christian Bishop of Rome is now supreme among Christians and the theology of Antioch is no longer of great matter.'

'Why would we be in Rome?' asked Marius. 'What is the Roman Bishop to us?'

The woman took the fore. Her hair was severely parted in the middle but her face was very regal and regular. She had in particular beautifully defined lips.

377

'Why do you hide from us? We have heard of you for years! We know that you know things – about us and where the Dark Gift came from, that you know how God put it into the world, and that you saved our kind from extinction.'

Marius was plainly horrified, but gave little sign of it.

'I have nothing to tell you,' he said, perhaps too hastily. 'Except I do not believe in your God or your Christ and I do not believe God put the Dark Gift, as you call it, into the world. You have made a terrible mistake.'

They were highly skeptical and utterly dedicated.

'You have almost reached salvation,' said another, the boy at the far end of the line, whose hair was unshorn and hung to his shoulders. He had a manly voice, but his limbs were small. 'You have almost reached the point where you are so strong and white and pure that you need not drink!'

'Would that that were true, it's not,' said Marius.

'Why don't you welcome us?' asked the boy. 'Why don't you guide us and teach us that we may better spread the Dark Blood, and punish mortals for their sins! We are pure of heart. We were chosen. Each of us went into the cave bravely and there the dying devil, a crushed creature of blood and bone, cast out Heaven in a blaze of fire, passed on to us his teachings.'

'Which were what?' asked Marius.

'Make them suffer,' the woman said. 'Bring death. Eschew all things of the world, as do the Stoics and the hermits of Egypt, but bring death. Punish them.'

The woman had become hostile. 'This man won't help us,' she said under her breath. 'This man is profane. This man is a heretic.'

'But you must receive us,' said the young man who had spoken first. 'We have searched so long and so far, and we come to you in humility. If you wish to live in a palace, then perhaps that is your right, you have earned it, but we have not. We live in darkness, we enjoy no pleasure but the blood, we feast on the weak and the diseased and the innocent alike. We do the will of Christ as the Serpent did the will of God in Eden when he tempted Eve.'

'Come to our Temple,' said one of the others, 'and see the tree of life with the sacred Serpent wound around it. We have his fangs. We have his power. God made him, just as God made Judas Iscariot, or Cain, or the evil Emperors of Rome.'

'Ah,' I said, 'I see. Before you happened on the god in the cave, you were worshipers of the snake. You're Ophites, Sethians, Nassenians.'

'That was our first calling,' said the boy. 'But now we are of the Children of Darkness, committed to sacrifice and killing, dedicated to inflicting suffering.'

'Oh, Marcion and Valentinus,' Marius whispered. 'You don't know the names, do you? They're the poetic Gnostics who invented the morass of your philosophy a hundred years ago. Duality – that, in a Christian world, evil could be as powerful as good.'

'Yes, we know this.' Several spoke at once. 'We don't know those profane names. But we know the Serpent and what God wants of us.'

'Moses lifted the Serpent in the desert, up over his head,' said the boy. 'Even the Queen of Egypt knew the Serpent and wore him in her crown.'

'The story of the great Leviathan has been eradicated in Rome,' said the woman. 'They took it out of the sacred books. But we know it!'

'So you learned all this from Armenian Christians,' said Marius. 'Or was it Syrians.'

A man, short of stature, with gray eyes, had not spoken all this while, but he stepped forward now and addressed Marius with considerable authority.

'You hold ancient truths,' he said, 'and you

use them profanely. All know of you. The blond Children of Darkness in the Northern woods know of you, and that you stole some important secret out of Egypt before the Birth of Christ. Many have come here, glimpsed you and the woman, and gone away in fear.'

'Very wise,' said Marius.

'What did you find in Egypt?' asked the woman. 'Christian monks live now in those old rooms that once belonged to a race of blood drinkers. The monks don't know about us, but we know all about them and you. There was writing there, there were secrets, there was something that by Divine Will belongs now in our hands.'

'No, there was nothing,' said Marius.

The woman spoke up again, 'When the Hebrews left Egypt, when Moses parted the Red Sea, did the Hebrews leave something behind? Why did Moses raise the snake in the desert? Do you know how many we are? Nearly a hundred. We travel to the far North, to the South, and even to the East to lands you would not believe.'

I could see Marius was distraught.

'Very well,' I said, 'we understand what you want and why you have been led to believe that we can satisfy you. I ask you, please, to go out in the Garden and let us speak. Respect our house. Don't harm our slaves.'

'We wouldn't dream of it.'

'And we'll be back shortly.'

I snatched Marius's hand and pulled him down the stairs.

'Where are you going?' he whispered. 'Block all images from your mind! They must glimpse nothing.'

'They won't glimpse,' I said, 'and from where I will stand as I talk to you, they won't hear either.'

He seemed to catch my meaning. I led him into the sanctuary of the unchanged Mother and Father, closing the stone doors behind me.

I drew Marius behind the seated King and Queen.

'They can probably hear the hearts of the Pair,' I whispered in the softest manner audible. 'But maybe they won't hear us over that sound. Now, we have to kill them, destroy them completely.'

Marius was amazed.

'Look, you know we have to do this!' I said. 'You have to kill them and anybody like them who ever comes near us. Why are you so shocked? Get ready. The simplest way is cut them to pieces first, and then burn them.'

'Oh, Pandora,' he sighed.

'Marius, why do you cringe?'

'I don't cringe, Pandora,' he said. 'I see myself irrevocably changed by such an act. To kill when I thirst, to keep to myself and keep these here who must be kept by somebody, that I have done for so long. But to become an executioner? To become like the Emperors burning Christians! To commence a war against this race, this order, this cult, whatever it is, to take such a stand.'

'No choice, come on. There are many decorative swords in the room where we sleep. We should take the big curved swords. And the torch. We should go to them and tell them how sorry we are for what we must impart to them, then do it!'

He didn't answer.

'Marius, are you going to let them go so that others will come after us? The only security lies in destroying every blood drinker who ever discovers us and the King and Queen.'

He walked away from me and stood before the Mother. He looked into her eyes. I knew that he was silently talking to her. And I knew that she was not answering.

'There is one other possibility,' I said, 'and it's quite real.' I beckoned for him to come back, behind them, where I felt safest to plot.

'What is it?' he asked.

'Give the King and the Queen over to them. And you and I are free. They will care for the King and Queen with religious fervor! Maybe the King and Queen will even allow them to drink –'

'That's unspeakable!' he said.

'Exactly my feelings. We shall never know if we are safe. And they shall run rampant through the world like supernatural rodents. So do you have a third plan?'

'No, but I'm ready. We use the fire and the swords together. Can you tell the lies that will charm them as we approach, armed and carrying torches?'

'Oh, yes, of course,' I said.

We went into the chamber and took up the big curved swords that were keenly sharp and came from the desert world of the Arabs. We lighted another torch from that at the foot of the stairs and we went up together.

'Come to me, Children,' I said as I entered the room, loudly, 'come, for what I have to reveal requires the light of this torch, and you will soon know the sacred purpose of this sword. How devout you are.'

We stood before them.

'How young you are!' I said.

Suddenly, the panic swept them together. They made it so simple for us by clustering in this manner that we had the task done in moments, lighting their garments, hacking their limbs, ignoring their piteous cries.

Never had I used my full strength and speed, never my full will, as I did against them. It was exhilarating to slash them, to force the torch upon them, to slash them until they fell, until they lost all life. Also, I did not want them to suffer.

Because they were so young, so very young as blood drinkers, it took quite some time to burn the bones, to see that all was ashes.

But it was finally done, and we stood together – Marius and I – in the garden, our garments smeared with soot, staring down at blowing grass, making certain with our eyes that the ashes were blown in all directions.

Marius turned suddenly and walked fast away from me, and down the stairs and into the Mother's Sanctuary.

I rushed after him in panic. He stood holding the torch and the bloody sword – oh, how they had bled – and he looked into Akasha's eyes.

'Oh, loveless Mother!' he whispered. His face was soiled with blood and grime. He looked at the flaming torch and looked up at the Queen.

Akasha and Enkil showed no sign of any knowledge of the massacre above. They showed neither approval, nor gratitude, nor any form of consciousness. They showed no awareness of the torch in his hand, or his thoughts, whatever they might be.

It was a finish for Marius, a finish to the Marius I had known and loved at that time.

He chose not to leave Antioch. I was for getting away and taking them away, for wild adventures, and seeing the wonders of the world.

But he said no. He had but one obligation. And that was to lay in wait for others until he had killed every one of them.

For weeks he wouldn't speak or move, unless I shook him and then he pleaded with me to leave him alone. He rose from the grave only to sit with the sword and the torch waiting.

It became unbearable to me. Months passed. I said, 'You are going mad. We should take them away!'

Then one night, very angry and alone, I cried out foolishly, 'I would I were free of them and you!' And leaving the house, I did not return for three nights.

I slept in dark safe places I made for myself with ease. Every time I thought of him, I thought of his sitting motionless there, so very like them, and I was afraid.

If only he did know true despair; if only he had confronted what we now call 'the absurd.' If only he had faced the nothingness! Then this massacre would not have demoralized him.

Finally one morning just before sunrise, when I was safely hidden, a strange silence fell over Antioch. A rhythm I had heard there all my days was gone. I was trying to think, What could this mean? But there was time to find out.

I had made a fatal miscalculation. The villa was empty. He had arranged for the transport by day. I had no clue as to where he had gone! Everything belonging to him had been taken, and all that I possessed scrupulously left behind.

I had failed him when he most needed me. I walked in circles around the empty Shrine. I screamed and let the cry echo off the walls.

He never returned to Antioch. No letter ever came.

After six months or more, I gave up and left.

Of course you know the dedicated, religious Christian vampires never died out, not until Lestat came dressed in red velvet and fur to dazzle them and make a mockery of their beliefs. That was in the Age of Reason. That is when Marius received Lestat. Who knows what other vampire cults exist?

As for me, I had lost Marius again by then.

I had seen him for only a single precious night one hundred years earlier, and of course thousands of years after the collapse of what we call 'the ancient world.'

I saw him! It was in the fancy fragile times of Louis XIV, the Sun King. We were at a court ball in Dresden. Music played – the tentative blend of clavichord, lute, violin – making the artful dances which seemed no more than bows and circles.

Across a room, I suddenly saw Marius!

He had been looking at me for a great while, and gave me now the most tragic and loving smile. He wore a big full-bottomed curly wig, dyed to the very color of his true hair, and a flared velvet coat, and layers of lace, so favored by the French. His skin was golden. That meant fire. I knew suddenly he had suffered something terrible. A jubilant love filled his blue eyes, and without forsaking his casual posture – he was leaning his elbow on the edge of the clavichord – he blew a kiss to me with his fingers.

I truly could not trust my eyes. Was he really there? Was I, myself, sitting here, in boned and low-necked bodice, and these huge skirts, one pulled back in artful folds to reveal the other? My skin in this age seemed an artificial contrivance. My hair had been professionally gathered and lifted into an ornate shape.

I had paid no mind to the mortal hands which had so bound me. During this age I let myself be led through the world by a fierce Asian vampire, about whom I cared nothing. I had fallen into an ever existing trap for a woman: I had become the noncommittal and ostentatious ornament of a male personality who for all his tiresome verbal cruelty possessed sufficient force to carry us both through time.

The Asian was off slowly taking his carefully chosen victim in a bedroom above.

Marius came towards me and kissed me and took me in his arms. I shut my eyes. 'This is Marius!' I whispered. 'Truly Marius.'

'Pandora!' he said, drawing back to look at me. 'My Pandora!'

His skin had been burned. Faint scars. But it was almost healed.

He led me out on the dance floor! He was the perfect impersonation of a human being. He guided me in the steps of the dance. I could scarce breathe. Following his lead, shocked at each new artful turn by the rapture of his face, I could not measure centuries or even millennia. I wanted suddenly to know everything – where he had been, what had befallen him. Pride and shame in me held no sway. Could he see that I was no more than a ghost of the woman he'd known? 'You are the hope of my soul!' I whispered.

Quickly he took me away. We went in a carriage to his palace. He deluged me with kisses. I clung to him.

'You,' he said, 'my dream, a treasure so foolishly thrown away, you are here, you have persevered.'

'Because you see me, I am here,' I said bitterly. 'Because you lift the candle, I can almost see my strength in the looking glass.'

Suddenly I heard a sound, an ancient and terrible sound. It was the heartbeat of Akasha, the heartbeat of Enkil.

The carriage had come to a halt. Iron gates. Servants.

The palace was spacious, fancy, the ostentatious residence of a rich noble.

'They are in there, the Mother and the Father?' I asked.

'Oh, yes, unchanged. Utterly reliable in their eternal silence.' His voice seemed to defy the horror of it.

I couldn't bear it. I had to escape the sound of her heart. An image of the petrified King and

Queen rose before my eyes.

'No! Get me away from here. I can't go in. Marius, I cannot look on them!'

'Pandora, they are hidden below the palace. There is no need to look on them. They won't know. Pandora, they are the same.'

Ah! The same! My mind sped back, over perilous terrain, to my very first nights, alone and mortal, in Antioch, to the later victories and defeats of that time. Ah! Akasha was the same! I feared I would begin to scream and be unable to control it.

'Very well,' said Marius, 'we'll go where you want.'

I gave the coachman the location of my hiding place.

I couldn't look at Marius. Valiantly, he kept the pretense of happy reunion. He talked of science and literature, Shakespeare, Dryden, the New World full of jungles and rivers. But behind his voice I heard the joy drained from him.

I buried my face against him. When the carriage stopped I leapt out and fled to the door of my little house. I looked back. He stood in the street.

He was sad and weary, and slowly he nodded and made a gesture of acceptance. 'May I wait it out?' he asked. 'Is there hope you'll change your mind? I'll wait here forever!'

'It's not my mind!' I said. 'I leave this city tonight. Forget me. Forget you ever saw me!'

'My love,' he said softly. 'My only love.'

I ran inside, shutting the door. I heard the carriage pull away. I went wild, as I had not since mortal life, beating the walls with my fists, trying to restrain my immense strength and trying not to let loose the howls and cries that wanted to break from me.

Finally I looked at the clock. Three hours left until dawn.

I sat down at the desk and wrote to him:

Marius,
At dawn we will be taken to Moscow. The very coffin in which I rest is to carry me many miles the first day. Marius, I am dazed. I can't seek shelter in your house, beneath the same roof as the ancient ones. Please, Marius, come to Moscow. Help me to free myself of this predicament. Later you can judge me and condemn me. I need you. Marius, I shall haunt the vicinity of the Czar's palace and the Great Cathedral until you come. Marius, I know I ask of you that *you* make a great journey, but

please come. I am a slave to this blood drinker's will.

> I love you,
> Pandora

Running back out in the street, I hurried in the direction of his house, trying to retrace the path which I had so stupidly ignored.

But what about the heartbeat? I would hear it, that ghastly sound! I had to run past it, run through it, long enough to give Marius this letter, perhaps to let him grasp me by the wrist and force me to some safe place, and drive away before dawn the Asian vampire who kept me.

Then the very carriage appeared, carrying in it my fellow blood drinker from the ball.

He stopped for me at once.

I took the driver aside. 'The man who brought me home,' I said. 'We went to his house, a huge palace.'

'Yes, Count Marius,' said the driver. 'I just took him back to his own home.'

'You must take this letter to him. Hurry! You must go to his house and put it in his hands! Tell him I had no money to give you, that he must pay you, I demand that you tell him. He will pay you. Tell him the letter is from Pandora. You must find him!'

'Who are you speaking of?' demanded my Asian companion.

I motioned to the driver to leave! 'Go!' Of course my consort was outraged. But the carriage was already on its way.

Two hundred years passed before I learned the very simple truth: Marius never received that letter!

He had gone back to his house, packed up his belongings and, the following night, left Dresden in sorrow, only finding the letter long after, as he related it to the Vampire Lestat, 'a fragile piece of writing,' as he called it, 'that had fallen to the bottom of a cluttered traveling case.'

When did I see him again?

In this modern world. When the ancient Queen rose from her throne and demonstrated the limits of her wisdom, her will and her power.

Two thousands years after, in our Twentieth Century still full of Roman columns and statues and pediments and peristyles, buzzing with computers and warmth-giving television, with Cicero and Ovid in every public library, our Queen, Akasha, was wakened by the image of Lestat on a television screen, in the most modern and secure of shrines, and sought to reign as a goddess, not only over us, but over humankind.

In the most dangerous hour, when she threatened to destroy us all if we did not follow her lead – and she had already slaughtered many – it was Marius with his reasoning, his optimism, his philosophy who talked to her, tried to calm her and divert her, who stalled her destructive intent until an ancient enemy came to fulfill an ancient curse, and struck her down with ancient simplicity.

David, what have you done to me in prodding me to write this narrative?

You have made me ashamed of the wasted years. You have made me acknowledge that no darkness has been ever deep enough to extinguish my personal knowledge of love, love from mortals who brought me into the world, love for goddesses of stone, love for Marius.

Above all, I cannot deny the resurgence of this love for Marius.

And all around me in this world I see evidence of love. Behind the image of the Blessed Virgin and her Infant Jesus, behind the image of the Crucified Christ, behind the remembered basalt image of Isis. I see love. I see it in the human struggle. I see its undeniable penetration in all that humans have accomplished in their poetry, their painting, their music, their love of one another and refusal to accept suffering as their lot.

Above all, however, I see it in the very fashioning of the world which outshines all art, and cannot by sheer randomness have accumulated such beauty.

Love. But whence comes this love? Why it is so secretive about its source, this love that makes rain and trees and has scattered the stars over us as the gods and goddesses once claimed to do?

So Lestat, the brat Prince, woke the Queen; and we survived her destruction. So Lestat, the brat Prince, had gone to Heaven and Hell and brought back disbelief, horror and the Veil of Veronica! Veronica, an invented Christian name which means *vera ikon,* or true icon. He found himself plunged into Palestine during the very years that I lived, and there saw something that has shattered the faculties in humans which we cherish so much: faith, reason.

I have to go to Lestat, look into his eyes. I have to see what he saw!

Let the young sing songs of death. They are stupid.

The finest thing under the sun and the moon is the human soul. I marvel at the small miracles of kindness that pass between humans, I marvel at the growth of conscience, at the persistence of reason in the face of all superstition or despair. I marvel at human endurance.

I have one more story to tell you. I don't know why I want to record it here. But I do. Perhaps it's because I feel you – a vampire who sees spirits – will understand this, and understand perhaps why I remained so unmoved by it.

Once in the Sixth Century – that is, five hundred years after the birth of Christ and three hundred years since I had left Marius – I went wandering in barbarian Italy. The Ostrogoths had long ago overrun the peninsula.

Then other tribes swept down on them, looting, burning, carrying off stones from old Temples.

It was like walking on burning coals for me to go there.

But Rome did struggle with some conception of itself, its principles, trying to blend the pagan with the Christian, and find some respite from the barbarian raids.

The Roman Senate still existed. Of all institutions it had survived.

And a scholar, sprung from the same stock as myself, Boethius, a very learned man who studied the ancients and the saints, had recently been put to death, but not before he had given us a great book. You can find it in any library today. It is, of course, *The Consolation of Philosophy*.

I had to see the ruined Forum for myself, the burnt and barren hills of Rome, the pigs and goats roaming where once Cicero had spoken to the crowds. I had to see the forsaken poor living desperately along the banks of the Tiber.

I had to see the fallen classical world. I had to see the Christian churches and shrines.

I had to see one scholar in particular. Like Boethius he had come from old Roman stock, and like Boethius he had read the classics and the saints. He was a man who wrote letters that went all over the world, even as far as to the scholar Bede in England.

And he had built a monastery there, some great flare of creativity and optimism, in spite of ruin and war.

This man was of course the scholar Cassiodorus, and his monastery lay at the very tip of the boot of Italy, in the paradisal land of green Calabria.

I came upon it in early evening, as I planned, when it looked like a great and splendid lighted little city.

Its monks were copying away ferociously in the Scriptorium.

And there in his cell, wide open to the night, sat Cassiodorus himself, at his writing, a man past ninety years of age.

He had survived the barbarian politics that doomed his friend Boethius, having served the Aryan Ostrogoth Emperor Theodoric, having lived to retire from Civil Service – he had survived to build this monastery, his dream, and to write to monks all over the world, to share what he knew with them of the ancients, to conserve the wisdom of the Greeks and the Romans.

Was he truly the last man of the ancient world, as some have said? The last man who could read both Latin and Greek? The last man who could treasure both Aristotle and the dogma of the Roman Pope? Plato and Saint Paul?

I didn't know then that he would be so well remembered. And I didn't know how soon he'd be forgotten!

Vivarium, on its mountains slopes, was an architectural triumph. It had its sparkling ponds to catch and hold fish – the characteristic which gave it its name. It had its Christian church with the inevitable cross, its dormitories, its rooms for the weary guest traveler. Its library was rich in the classics of my time, as well as gospels which have now been lost. The monastery was rich in all the fruits of the field, all crops needed for food, trees laden with fruit, fields of wheat.

The monks cared for all of this, and they dedicated themselves to copying books day and night in their long Scriptorium.

There were beehives there, on this gentle moonlighted coast, hundreds of beehives from which the monks harvested honey to eat, and wax for sacred candles, and royal jelly for an ointment. The beehives covered a hill as big as the orchard or the farmland of Vivarium.

I spied on Cassiodorus. I walked among the beehives, and marveled as I always do at the inexplicable organization of bees, for the mysteries of the bees and their dance and their hunting for pollen and their breeding was all known to my eye long before it was understood by the human world.

As I left the hives, as I moved away towards the distant beacon of Cassiodorus's lamp, I looked back. I beheld something.

Something collected itself from the hives, something immense and invisible and forceful that I could both feel and hear. I was not gripped by fear, merely sparked by a temporary hope that some New Thing had come into the world. For I am not a seer of ghosts and never was.

This force rose out of the very bees themselves, out of their intricate knowledge and their countless sublime patterns, as though they had somehow accidentally evolved it, or empowered it with consciousness through the means of their endless creativity, meticulousness and endurance.

It was like an old Roman woodland spirit of the forest.

I saw this force fly loosely over the fields. I saw it enter the body of a straw man who stood in the fields, a scarecrow which the monks had made with a fine round wooden head, painted eyes, crude nose and smiling mouth – a creature whole and entire who could be moved from time to time, intact in his monk's hood and robe.

I saw this scarecrow, this man of straw and wood hurry whirling and dancing through the fields and the vineyards until he had reached Cassiodorus's cell.

I followed!

Then I heard a silent wail rise from the being. I heard it and I saw the scarecrow in a bending, bowing dance of sorrow, its bundled straw hands over ears it didn't have. It writhed with grief.

Cassiodorus was dead. He had died quietly within his lamp-lighted cell, his door open, at his writing table. He lay, gray-haired, ancient, quiet against his manuscript. He had lived over ninety years. And he was dead.

This creature, this scarecrow, was wild with suffering and grief, rocking and moaning, though it was a sound no human could have heard.

I who have never seen spirits stared at it in wonder. Then it perceived that I was there. It turned. He – for so it seemed in this ragged attire and body of straw – reached out to me. He flung out his straw arms. The straw fell from his sleeves. His wooden head wobbled on the pole that was his spine. He – It – implored me: he begged me for the answer to the greatest questions humans and immortal have ever posed. He looked to me for answers!

Then glancing back again at the dead Cassiodorus, he ran to me, across the sloping grass, and the need came out of him, poured from him, his arms out as it beheld me. Could I not explain? Could I not contain in some Divine Design the mystery of the loss of Cassiodorus! Cassiodorus who had with his Vivarium rivaled the hive of bees in elegance and glory! It was Vivarium which had drawn this consciousness together from the hives! Could I not ease this creature's pain!

'There are horrors in this world,' I whispered. 'It is made up of mystery and dependent upon mystery. If you would have peace, go back to the hives; lose your human shape, and descend again, fragmented into the mindless life of the contented bees from which you rose.'

He was fixed, and he listened to me.

'If you would have fleshly life, human life, hard life which can move through time and space, then fight for it. If you would have human philosophy then struggle and make yourself wise, so that nothing can hurt you ever. Wisdom is strength. Collect yourself, whatever you are, into something with a purpose.

'But know this. All is speculation under the sky. All myth, all religion, all philosophy, all history – is lies.'

The thing, whether it be male or female, drew up its bundled straw hands, as if to cover its mouth. I turned my back on it.

I walked away silently through the vineyards. In a little while the monks would discover that their Father Superior, their genius, their saint, had died at his work.

I looked back in amazement to discover that the figure of straw remained, organized, assuming the posture of an upright being, watching me.

'I will not believe in you!' I shouted back to this man of straw. 'I will not search with you for any answer! But know this: if you would become an organized being as you see in me, love all mankind and womankind and all their

children. Do not take your strength from blood!
Do not feed on suffering. Do not rise like a god
above crowds chanting in adoration. Do not
lie!'

It listened. It heard. It remained still.

I ran. I ran and ran up the rocky slopes and
through the forests of Calabria until I was far far
away from it. Under the moon, I saw the
sprawling majesty of Vivarium with its cloisters
and sloped roofs as it surrounded the shores of
its shimmering inlet from the sea.

I never saw the straw creature again. I don't
know what it was. I don't want you to ask me
any question about it.

You tell me spirits and ghosts walk. We
know such beings exist. But that was the last I
saw of that being.

And when next I drifted through Italy,
Vivarium had been long destroyed. The earth-
quakes had shaken loose the last of its walls.
Had it been sacked first by the next wave of
ignorant tall men of Northern Europe, the
Vandals? Was it an earthquake that brought
about its ruin?

No one knows. What survives of it are the letters that Cassiodorus sent to others.

Soon the classics were declared profane. Pope
Gregory wrote tales of magic and miracles,

because it was the only way to convert thousands of superstitious uncatechized Northern tribes to Christianity in great en masse baptisms.

He conquered the warriors Rome could never conquer.

The history of Italy for one hundred years falls into absolute darkness after Cassiodorus. How do the books put it? For a century, nothing is heard from Italy.

Ah, what a silence!

Now David, as you come to these final pages, I must confess, I have left you. The smiles with which I gave you these notebooks were deceptive. Feminine wiles, Marius would call them. My promise to meet with you tomorrow night here in Paris was a lie. I will have left Paris by the time you come to these lines. I go to New Orleans.

It's your doing, David. You have transformed me. You have given me a desperate faith that in narrative there is a shadow of meaning. I now know a new strident energy. You have trained me through your demand upon my language and my memory to live again, to believe again that some good exists in this world.

I want to find Marius. Thoughts of other immortals fill the air. Cries, pleas, strange messages . . .

One who was believed gone from us is now apparently known to have survived.

I have strong reason to believe that Marius has gone to New Orleans, and I must be reunited with him. I must seek out Lestat, to see this fallen brat Prince lying on the chapel floor unable to speak or move.

Come join me, David. Don't fear Marius! I know he will come to help Lestat. I do the same.

Come back to New Orleans.

Even if Marius is not there, I want to see Lestat. I want to see the others again. What have you done, David? I now contain – with this new curiosity, with this flaming capacity to care once more, with reborn capacity to sing – I now contain the awful capacity to want and to love.

For that, if for nothing else, and there is indeed much more, I shall always thank you. No matter what suffering is to come, you have quickened me. And nothing you do or say will ever cause the death of my love for you.

THE END

Final: July 5, 1997

THE VAMPIRE ARMAND

THE VAMPIRE CHRONICLES

For
Brandy Edwards,
Brian Robertson
and
Christopher and Michele Rice

Jesus, speaking to Mary Magdalene:

Jesus saith unto her, Touch me not;
for I am not yet ascended to my Father:
but go to my brethren, and say unto them,
I ascend unto my Father; and your Father;
and to my God, and your God.

THE GOSPEL ACCORDING TO ST. JOHN 20:17

PART I

BODY and BLOOD

1

They said a child had died in the attic. Her clothes had been discovered in the wall.

I wanted to go up there, and to lie down near the wall, and be alone.

They'd seen her ghost now and then, the child. But none of these vampires could see spirits, really, at least not the way that I could see them. No matter. It wasn't the company of the child I wanted. It was to be in that place.

Nothing more could be gained from lingering near Lestat. I'd come. I'd fulfilled my purpose. I couldn't help him.

The sight of his sharply focused and unchanging eyes unnerved me, and I was quiet inside and full of love for those nearest me – my human children, my dark-haired little Benji and my tender willowy Sybelle – but I was not strong enough just yet to take them away.

I left the chapel.

I didn't even take note of who was there. The whole convent was now the dwelling place of vampires. It was not an unruly place, or a neglected place, but I didn't notice who remained in the chapel when I left.

Lestat lay as he had all along, on the marble floor of the chapel in front of the huge crucifix, on his side, his hands slack, the left hand just below the right hand, its fingers touching the marble lightly, as if with a purpose, when there was no purpose at all. The fingers of his right hand curled, making a little hollow in the palm where the light fell, and that too seemed to have a meaning, but there was no meaning.

This was simply the preternatural body lying there without will or animation, no more purposeful than the face, its expression almost defiantly intelligent, given that months had passed in which Lestat had not moved.

The high stained-glass windows were dutifully draped for him before sunrise. At night, they shone with all the wondrous candles scattered about the fine statues and relics which filled this once sanctified and holy place. Little mortal children had heard Mass under this high coved roof; a priest had sung out the Latin words from an altar.

It was ours now. It belonged to him – Lestat, the man who lay motionless on the marble floor.

Man. Vampire. Immortal. Child of Darkness. Any and all are excellent words for him.

Looking over my shoulder at him, I never felt so much like a child.

That's what I am. I fill out the definition, as if it were encoded in me perfectly, and there had never been any other genetic design.

I was perhaps seventeen years old when Marius made me into a vampire. I had stopped growing by that time. For a year, I'd been five feet six inches. My hands are as delicate as those of a young woman, and I was beardless, as we used to say in that time, the years of the sixteenth century. Not a eunuch, no, not that, most certainly, but a boy.

It was fashionable then for boys to be as beautiful as girls. Only now does it seem something worthwhile, and that's because I love the others – my own: Sybelle with her woman's breasts and long girlish limbs, and Benji with his round intense little Arab face.

I stood at the foot of the stairs. No mirrors here, only the high brick walls stripped of their plaster, walls that were old only for America, darkened by the damp even

4

inside the convent, all textures and elements here softened by the simmering summers of New Orleans and her clammy crawling winters, green winters I call them because the trees here are almost never bare.

I was born in a place of eternal winter when one compares it to this place. No wonder in sunny Italy I forgot the beginnings altogether, and fashioned my life out of the present of my years with Marius. 'I don't remember.' It was a condition of loving so much vice, of being so addicted to Italian wine and sumptuous meals, and even the feel of the warm marble under my bare feet when the rooms of the palazzo were sinfully, wickedly heated by Marius's exorbitant fires.

His mortal friends . . . human beings like me at that time . . . scolded constantly about these expenditures: firewood, oil, candles. And for Marius only the finest candles of beeswax were acceptable. Every fragrance was significant.

Stop these thoughts. Memories can't hurt you now. You came here for a reason and now you have finished, and you must find those you love, your young mortals, Benji and Sybelle, and you must go on.

Life was no longer a theatrical stage where Banquo's ghost came again and again to seat himself at the grim table.

My soul hurt.

Up the stairs. Lie for a little while in this brick convent where the child's clothes were found. Lie with the child, murdered here in this convent, so say the rumormongers, the vampires who haunt these halls now, who have come to see the great Vampire Lestat in his Endymion-like sleep.

I felt no murder here, only the tender voices of nuns.

I went up the staircase, letting my body find its human weight and human tread.

After five hundred years, I know such tricks. I could frighten all the young ones – the hangers-on and the gawkers – just as surely as the other ancient ones did it, even the most modest, uttering words to evince their telepathy, or vanishing when they chose to leave, or now and then even making the building tremble with their power – an interesting accomplishment even with these walls eighteen inches thick with cypress sills that will never rot.

He must like the fragrances here, I thought. Marius, where is he? Before I had visited Lestat, I had not wanted to talk very much to Marius, and had spoken only a few civil words when I left my treasures in his charge.

After all, I had brought my children into a menagerie of the Undead. Who better to safeguard them than my beloved Marius, so powerful that none here dared question his smallest request.

There is no telepathic link between us naturally – Marius made me, I am forever his fledgling – but as soon as this occurred to me, I realized without the aid of this telepathic link that I could not feel the presence of Marius in the building. I didn't know what had happened in that brief interval when I knelt down to look at Lestat. I didn't know where Marius was. I couldn't catch the familiar human scents of Benji or Sybelle. A little stab of panic paralyzed me.

I stood on the second story of the building. I leaned against the wall, my eyes settling with determined calm on the deeply varnished heart pine floor. The light made pools of yellow on the boards.

Where were they, Benji and Sybelle? What had I done in bringing them here, two ripe and glorious humans? Benji was a spirited boy of twelve, Sybelle, a womanling of twenty-five. What if Marius, so generous in his own soul, had carelessly let them out of his sight?

'I'm here, young one.' The voice was abrupt, soft, welcome.

My Maker stood on the landing just below me, having come up the steps behind me, or more truly, with his powers, having placed himself there, covering the preceding distance with silent and invisible speed.

'Master,' I said with a little trace of a smile. 'I was afraid for them for a moment.' It was an apology. 'This place makes me sad.'

He nodded. 'I have them, Armand,' he said. 'The city seethes with mortals. There's food enough for all the vagabonds wandering here. No one will hurt them. Even if I weren't here to say so, no one would dare.'

It was I who nodded now. I wasn't so sure, really. Vampires are by their very nature perverse and do wicked and terrible things simply for the sport of it. To kill another's mortal pet would be a worthy entertainment for some grim and alien creature, skirting the fringes here, drawn by remarkable events.

'You're a wonder, young one,' he said to me smiling. Young one! Who else would call me this but Marius, my Maker, and what is five hundred years to him? 'You went into the sun, child,' he continued with the same legible concern written on his kind face. 'And you lived to tell the tale.'

'Into the sun, Master?' I questioned his words. But I myself did not want to reveal any more. I did not want to talk yet, to tell of what had happened, the legend of Veronica's Veil and the Face of Our Lord emblazoned upon it, and the morning when I had given up my soul with such perfect happiness. What a fable it was.

He came up the steps to be near me, but kept a polite distance. He has always been the gentleman, even

7

before there was such a word. In ancient Rome, they must have had a term for such a person, infallibly good mannered, and considerate as a point of honor, and wholly successful at common courtesy to rich and poor alike. This was Marius, and it had always been Marius, insofar as I could know.

He let his snow-white hand rest on the dull satiny banister. He wore a long shapeless cloak of gray velvet, once perfectly extravagant, now downplayed with wear and rain, and his yellow hair was long like Lestat's hair, full of random light and unruly in the damp, and even studded with drops of dew from outside, the same dew clinging to his golden eyebrows and darkening his long curling eyelashes around his large cobalt-blue eyes.

There was something altogether more Nordic and icy about him than there was about Lestat, whose hair tended more to golden, for all its luminous highlights, and whose eyes were forever prismatic, drinking up the colors around him, becoming even a gorgeous violet with the slightest provocation from the worshipful outside world.

In Marius, I saw the sunny skies of the northern wilderness, eyes of steady radiance which rejected any outside color, perfect portals to his own most constant soul.

'Armand,' he said. 'I want you to come with me.'

'Where is that, Master, come where?' I asked. I too wanted to be civil. He had always, even after a struggle of wits, brought such finer instincts out of me.

'To my house, Armand, where they are now, Sybelle and Benji. Oh, don't fear for them for a second. Pandora's with them. They are rather astonishing mortals, brilliant, remarkably different, yet alike. They love you, and they know so much and have come with you rather a long way.'

8

I flushed with blood and color; the warmth was stinging and unpleasant, and then as the blood danced back away from the surface of my face, I felt cooler and strangely enervated that I felt any sensations at all.

It was a shock being here and I wanted it to be over.

'Master, I don't know who I am in this new life,' I said gratefully. 'Reborn? Confused?' I hesitated, but there was no use stopping it. 'Don't ask me to stay here just now. Maybe some time when Lestat is himself again, maybe when enough time has passed –. I don't know for certain, only that I can't accept your kind invitation now.'

He gave me a brief accepting nod. With his hand he made a little acquiescent gesture. His old gray cloak had slipped off one shoulder. He seemed not to care about it. His thin black wool clothes were neglected, lapels and pockets trimmed in a careless gray dust. That was not right for him.

He had a big shock of white silk at his throat that made his pale face seem more colored and human than it otherwise would. But the silk was torn as if by brambles. In sum, he haunted the world in these clothes, rather than was dressed in them. They were for a stumbler, not my old Master.

I think he knew I was at a loss. I was looking up at the gloom above me. I wanted to reach the attic of this place, the half-concealed clothing of the dead child. I wondered at this story of the dead child. I had the impertinence to let my mind drift, though he was waiting.

He brought me back with his gentle words:

'Sybelle and Benji will be with me when you want them,' he said. 'You can find us. We aren't far. You'll hear the *Appassionata* when you want to hear it.' He smiled.

9

'You've given her a piano,' I said. I spoke of golden Sybelle. I had shut out the world from my preternatural hearing, and I didn't want just yet to unstop my ears even for the lovely sound of her playing, which I already missed overly much.

As soon as we'd entered the convent, Sybelle had seen a piano and asked in a whisper at my ear if she could play it. It was not in the chapel where Lestat lay, but off in another long empty room. I had told her it wasn't quite proper, that it might disturb Lestat as he lay there, and we couldn't know what he thought, or what he felt, or if he was anguished and trapped in his own dreams.

'Perhaps when you come, you'll stay for a while,' Marius said. 'You'll like the sound of her playing my piano, and maybe then we'll talk together, and you can rest with us, and we can share the house for as long as you like.'

I didn't answer.

'It's palatial in a New World sort of way,' he said with a little mockery in his smile. 'It's not far at all. I have the most spacious gardens and old oaks, oaks far older than those even out there on the Avenue, and all the windows are doors. You know how I like it that way. It's the Roman style. The house is open to the spring rain, and the spring rain here is like a dream.'

'Yes, I know,' I whispered. 'I think it's falling now, isn't it?' I smiled.

'Well, I'm rather spattered with it, yes,' he said almost gaily. 'You come when you want to. If not tonight, then tomorrow . . .'

'Oh, I'll be there tonight,' I said. I didn't want to offend him, not in the slightest, but Benji and Sybelle had seen enough of white-faced monsters with velvet voices. It was time to be off.

I looked at him rather boldly, enjoying it for a moment, overcoming a shyness that had been our curse in this modern world. In Venice of old, he had gloried in his clothes as men did then, always so sharp and splendidly embellished, the glass of fashion, to use the old graceful phrase. When he crossed the Piazza San Marco in the soft purple of evening, all turned to watch him pass. Red had been his badge of pride, red velvet – a flowing cape, and magnificently embroidered doublet, and beneath it a tunic of gold silk tissue, so very popular in those times.

He'd had the hair of a young Lorenzo de' Medici, right from the painted wall.

'Master, I love you, but now I must be alone,' I said. 'You don't need me now, do you, Sir? How can you? You never really did.' Instantly I regretted it. The words, not the tone, were impudent. And our minds being so divided by intimate blood, I was afraid he'd misunderstand.

'Cherub, I want you,' he said forgivingly. 'But I can wait. Seems not long ago I spoke these same words when we were together, and so I say them again.'

I couldn't bring myself to tell him it was my season for mortal company, how I longed just to be talking away the night with little Benji, who was such a sage, or listening to my beloved Sybelle play her sonata over and over again. It seemed beside the point to explain any further. And the sadness came over me again, heavily and undeniably, of having come to this forlorn and empty convent where Lestat lay, unable or unwilling to move or speak, none of us knew.

'Nothing will come of my company just now, Master,' I said. 'But you will grant me some key to finding you, surely, so that when this time passes . . .' I let my words die.

11

'I fear for you!' he whispered suddenly, with great warmth.

'Any more than ever before, Sir?' I asked.

He thought for a moment. Then he said, 'Yes. You love two mortal children. They are your moon and stars. Come stay with me if only for a little while. Tell me what you think of our Lestat and what's happened. Tell me perhaps, if I promise to remain very quiet and not to press you, tell me your opinion of all you've so recently seen.'

'You touch on it delicately, Sir, I admire you. You mean why did I believe Lestat when he said he had been to Heaven and Hell, you mean what did I see when I looked at the relic he brought back with him, Veronica's Veil.'

'If you want to tell me. But more truly, I wish you would come and rest.'

I put my hand on top of his, marveling that in spite of all I'd endured, my skin was almost as white as his.

'You will be patient with my children till I come, won't you?' I asked. 'They imagine themselves so intrepidly wicked, coming here to be with me, whistling nonchalantly in the crucible of the Undead, so to speak.'

'Undead,' he said, smiling reprovingly. 'Such language, and in my presence. You know I hate it.'

He planted a kiss quickly on my cheek. It startled me, and then I realized that he was gone.

'Old tricks!' I said aloud, wondering if he were still near enough to hear me, or whether he had shut up his ears to me as fiercely as I shut mine to the outside world.

I looked off, wanting the quiet, dreaming of bowers suddenly, not in words but in images, the way my old mind would do it, wanting to lie down in garden beds among growing flowers, wanting to press my face to earth and sing softly to myself.

12

The spring outside, the warmth, the hovering mist that would be rain. All this I wanted. I wanted the swampy forests beyond, but I wanted Sybelle and Benji, too, and to be gone, and to have some will to carry on.

Ah, Armand, you always lack this very thing, the will. Don't let the old story repeat itself now. Arm yourself with all that's happened.

Another was nearby.

It seemed so awful to me suddenly, that some immortal whom I didn't know should intrude here on my random private thoughts, perhaps to make a selfish approximation of what I felt.

It was only David Talbot.

He came from the chapel wing, through the bridge rooms of the convent that connect it to the main building where I stood at the top of the staircase to the second floor.

I saw him come into the hallway. Behind him was the glass of the door that led to the gallery, and beyond that the soft mingled gold and white light of the courtyard below.

'It's quiet now,' he said. 'And the attic's empty and you know that you can go there, of course.'

'Go away,' I said. I felt no anger, only the honest wish to have my thoughts unread and my emotions left alone.

With remarkable self-possession he ignored me, then said:

'Yes, I am afraid of you, a little, but then terribly curious too.'

'Oh, I see, so that excuses it, that you followed me here?'

'I didn't follow you, Armand,' he said. 'I live here.'

'Ah, I'm sorry then,' I admitted. 'I hadn't known. I suppose I'm glad of it. You guard him. He's never alone.' I meant Lestat of course.

'Everyone's afraid of you,' he said calmly. He had taken up a position only a few feet away, casually folding his arms. 'You know, it's quite a study, the lore and habits of the vampires.'

'Not to me,' I said.

'Yes, I realize that,' he said. 'I was only musing, and I hope you'll forgive me. It was about the child in the attic, the child they said was murdered. It's a tall story, about a very small little person. Maybe if your luck is better than that of everyone else, you'll see the ghost of the child whose clothes were shut up in the wall.'

'Do you mind if I look at you?' I said. 'I mean if you're going to dip your beak into my mind with such abandon? We met some time ago before all this happened – Lestat, the Heavenly Journey, this place. I never really took stock of you. I was indifferent, or too polite, I don't know which.'

I was surprised to hear such heat in my voice. I was volatile, and it wasn't David Talbot's fault.

'I'm thinking of the conventional knowledge about you,' I said. 'That you weren't born in this body, that you were an elderly man when Lestat knew you, that this body you inhabit now belonged to a clever soul who could hop from living being to living being, and there set up shop with his own trespassing soul.'

He gave me a rather disarming smile.

'So Lestat said,' he answered. 'So Lestat wrote. It's true, of course. You know it is. You've known since you saw me before.'

'Three nights we spent together,' I said. 'And I never really questioned you. I mean I never really even looked directly into your eyes.'

'We were thinking of Lestat then.'

'Aren't we now?'

'I don't know,' he said.

14

'David Talbot,' I said, measuring him coldly with my eyes, 'David Talbot, Superior General of the Order of Psychic Detectives known as the Talamasca, had been catapulted into the body in which he now walks.' I didn't know whether I paraphrased or made it up as I went along. 'He'd been entrenched or chained inside it, made a prisoner by so many ropey veins, and then tricked into a vampire as a fiery unstanchable blood invaded his lucky anatomy, sealing his soul up in it as it transformed him into an immortal – a man of dark bronzed skin and dry, lustrous and thick black hair.'

'I think you have it right,' he said with indulgent politeness.

'A handsome gent,' I went on, 'the color of caramel, moving with such catlike ease and gilded glances that he makes me think of all things once delectable, and now a potpourri of scent: cinnamon, clove, mild peppers and other spices golden, brown or red, whose fragrances can spike my brain and plunge me into erotic yearnings that live now, more than ever, to play themselves out. His skin must smell like cashew nuts and thick almond creams. It does.'

He laughed. 'I get your point.'

I had shocked myself. I was wretched for a moment. 'I'm not sure I get myself,' I said apologetically.

'I think it's plain,' he said. 'You want me to leave you alone.'

I saw the preposterous contradictions in all this at once.

'Look,' I whispered quickly. 'I'm deranged,' I whispered. 'My senses cross, like so many threads to make a knot: taste, see, smell, feel. I'm rampant.'

I wondered idly and viciously if I could attack him, take him, bring him down under my greater craft and cunning and taste his blood without his consent.

15

'I'm much too far along the road for that,' he said, 'and why would you chance such a thing?'

What self-possession. The older man in him did indeed command the sturdier younger flesh, the wise mortal with an iron authority over all things eternal and supernaturally powerful. What a blend of energies! Nice to drink his blood, to take him against his will. There is no such fun on Earth like the raping of an equal.

'I don't know,' I said, ashamed. Rape is unmanly. 'I don't know why I insult you. You know, I wanted to leave quickly. I mean I wanted to visit the attic, and then be out of here. I wanted to avoid this sort of infatuation. You are a wonder, and you think me a wonder, and it's rich.'

I let my eyes pass over him. I'd been blind to him when we met last, that was most true.

He dressed to kill. With the cleverness of olden times, when men could preen like peacocks, he'd chosen golden sepia and umber colors for his clothes. He was smart and clean and fretted all over with careful bits of pure gold, in a wristband timepiece and buttons and a slender pin for his modern tie, that tailored spill of color men wear in this age, as if to let us grab them all the more easily by its noose. Stupid ornament. Even his shirt of polished cotton was tawny and full of something of the sun and the warmed earth. Even his shoes were brown, glossy as beetles' backs.

He came towards me.

'You know what I'm going to ask,' he said. 'Don't wrestle with these unarticulated thoughts, these new experiences, all this overwhelming understanding. Make a book out of it for me.'

I couldn't have predicted that this would be his question. I was surprised, sweetly so, but nevertheless taken off guard.

'Make a book? I? Armand?'

I went towards him, turned sharply and fled up the steps to the attic, skirting the third floor and then entering the fourth.

The air was thick and warm here. It was a place daily baked by the sun. All was dry and sweet, the wood like incense and the floors splintery.

'Little girl, where are you?' I asked.

'Child, you mean,' he said.

He had come up behind me, taking a bit of time for courtesy's sake.

He added, 'She was never here.'

'How do you know?'

'If she were a ghost, I could call her,' he said.

I looked over my shoulder. 'You have that power? Or is this just what you want to say to me right now? Before you venture further, let me warn you that we almost never have the power to see spirits.'

'I'm altogether new,' David said. 'I'm unlike any others. I've come into the Dark World with different faculties. Dare I say, we, our species, vampires, have evolved?'

'The conventional word is stupid,' I said. I moved further into the attic. I spied a small chamber with plaster and peeling roses, big floppy prettily drawn Victorian roses with pale fuzzy green leaves. I went into the chamber. Light came from a high window out of which a child could not have seen. Merciless, I thought.

'Who said that a child died here?' I said. All was clean beneath the soil of years. There was no presence. It seemed perfect and just, no ghost to comfort me. Why should a ghost come from some savory rest for my sake?

So I could cuddle up perhaps to the memory of her, her tender legend. How are children murdered in orphanages where only nuns attend? I never thought of

17

women as so cruel. Dried up, without imagination perhaps, but not aggressive as we are, to kill.

I turned round and round. Wooden lockers lined one wall, and one locker stood open, and there the tumbled shoes were, little brown Oxfords, as they called them, with black strings, and now I beheld, where it had been behind me, the broken and frayed hole from which they'd ripped her clothes. All fallen there, moldy and wrinkled they lay, her clothes.

A stillness settled on me as if the dust of this place were a fine ice, coming down from the high peaks of haughty and monstrously selfish mountains to freeze all living things, this ice, to close up and stop forever all that breathed or felt or dreamed or lived.

He spoke in poetry:

'"Fear no more the heat of the sun,"' he whispered. '"Nor the furious winter's rages. Fear no more . . ."'

I winced with pleasure. I knew the verses. I loved them.

I genuflected, as if before the Sacrament, and touched her clothes. 'And she was little, no more than five, and she didn't die here at all. No one killed her. Nothing so special for her.'

'How your words belie your thoughts,' he said.

'Not so, I think of two things simultaneously. There's a distinction in being murdered. I was murdered. Oh, not by Marius, as you might think, but by others.'

I knew I spoke soft and in an assuming way, because this wasn't meant for pure drama.

'I'm trimmed in memories as if in old furs. I lift my arm and the sleeve of memory covers it. I look around and see other times. But you know what frightens me the most – it is that this state, like so many others with me, will prove the verge of nothing but extend itself over centuries.'

18

'What do you really fear? What did you want from Lestat when you came here?'

'David, I came to see him. I came to find out how it was with him, and why he lies there, unmoving. I came –.' I wasn't going to say any more.

His glossy nails made his hands look ornamental and special, caressive, comely and lovely with which to be touched. He picked up a small dress, torn, gray, spotted with bits of mean lace. Everything dressed in flesh can yield a dizzying beauty if you concentrate on it long enough, and his beauty leapt out without apology.

'Just clothes.' Flowered cotton, a bit of velvet with a puffed sleeve no bigger than an apple for the century of bare arms by day and night. 'No violence at all sur-rounding her,' he said as if it were a pity. 'Just a poor child, don't you think, and sad by nature as well as circumstance.'

'And why were they walled up, tell me that! What sin did these little dresses commit?' I sighed. 'Good God, David Talbot, why don't we let the little girl have her romance, her fame? You make me angry. You say you can see ghosts. You find them pleasant? You like to talk with them. I could tell you about a ghost –.'

'When will you tell me? Look, don't you see the trick of a book?' He stood up, and dusted off his knee with his right hand. In his left was her gathered dress. Something about the whole configuration bothered me, a tall creature holding a little girl's crumpled dress.

'You know, when you think of it,' I said, turning away, so I wouldn't see the dress in his hand, 'there's no good reason under God for little girls and little boys. Think of it, the other tender issue of mammals. Among puppies or kitten or colts, does one find gender? It's never an issue. The half-grown fragile thing is sexless. There is no determination. There is nothing as splendid

19

to look at as a little boy or girl. My head is so full of notions. I rather think I'll explode if I don't do something, and you say make a book for you. You think it's possible, you think . . .'

'What I think is that when you make a book, you tell the tale as you would like to know it!'

'I see no great wisdom in that.'

'Well, then think, for most speech is a mere issue of our feelings, a mere explosion. Listen, note the way that you make these outbursts.'

'I don't want to.'

'But you do, but they are not the words you want to read. When you write, something different happens. You make a tale, no matter how fragmented or experimental or how disregarding of all conventional and helpful forms. Try this for me. No, no, I have a better idea.'

'What?'

'Come down with me into my rooms. I live here now, I told you. Through my windows you can see the trees. I don't live like our friend Louis, wandering from dusty corner to dusty corner, and then back to his flat in the Rue Royale when he's convinced himself once more and for the thousandth time that no one can harm Lestat. I have warm rooms. I use candles for old light. Come down and let me write it, your story. Talk to me. Pace, and rant if you will, or rail, yes, rail, and let me write it, and even so, the very fact that I write, this in itself will make you make a form out of it. You'll begin to . . .'

'What?'

'To tell me what happened. How you died and how you lived.'

'Expect no miracles, perplexing scholar. I didn't die in New York that morning. I almost died.'

20

He had me faintly curious, but I could never do what he wanted. Nevertheless he was honest, amazingly so, as far as I could measure, and therefore sincere.

'Ah, so, I didn't mean literally. I meant that you should tell me what it was like to climb so high into the sun, and suffer so much, and, as you said, to discover in your pain all these memories, these connecting links. Tell me! Tell me.'

'Not if you mean to make it coherent,' I said crossly. I gauged his reaction. I wasn't bothering him. He wanted to talk more.

'Make it coherent? Armand, I'll simply write down what you say.' He made his words simple yet curiously passionate.

'Promise?'

I flashed on him a playful look. Me! To do that.

He smiled. He wadded up the little dress and then dropped it carefully so it might fall in the middle of the pile of her old clothes.

'I'll not alter one syllable,' he said. 'Come be with me, and talk to me, and be my love.' Again, he smiled.

Suddenly he came towards me, much in the aggressive manner in which I'd thought earlier to approach him. He slipped his hands under my hair, and felt of my face, and then he gathered up the hair and he put his face down into my curls, and he laughed. He kissed my cheek.

'Your hair's like something spun from amber, as if the amber would melt and could be drawn from candle flames in long fine airy threads and let to dry that way to make all these shining tresses. You're sweet, boylike and pretty as a girl. I wish I had one glimpse of you in antique velvet the way you were for him, for Marius. I wish I could see for one moment how it was when you dressed in stockings and wore a belted doublet sewn

21

with rubies. Look at you, the frosty child. My love doesn't even touch you.'

This wasn't true.

His lips were hot, and I could feel the fangs under them, feel the urgency suddenly in his fingers pressing against my scalp. It sent the shivers through me, and my body tensed and then shuddered, and it was sweet beyond prediction. I resented this lonely intimacy, resented it enough to transform it, or rid myself of it utterly. I'd rather die or be away, in the dark, simple and lonely with common tears.

From the look in his eyes, I thought he could love without giving anything. Not a connoisseur, just a blood drinker.

'You make me hungry,' I whispered. 'Not for you but for one who is doomed and yet alive. I want to hunt. Stop it. Why do you touch me? Why be so gentle?'

'Everyone wants you,' he said.

'Oh, I know. Everyone would ravage a guilty cunning child! Everyone would have a laughing boy who knows his way around the block. Kids make better food than women, and girls are all too much like women, but young boys? They're not like men, are they?'

'Don't mock me. I meant I wanted only to touch you, to feel how soft you are, how eternally young.'

'Oh, that's me, eternally young,' I said. 'You speak nonsense words for one so pretty yourself. I'm going out. I have to feed. And when I've finished with that, when I'm full and hot, then I'll come and I'll talk to you and tell you anything you want.' I stepped back just a little from him, feeling the quivers through me as his fingers released my hair. I looked at the empty white window, peering too high for the trees.

'They could see nothing green here, and it's spring outside, southern spring. I can smell it through the walls.

22

I want to look just for a moment on flowers. To kill, to drink blood and to have flowers.'

'Not good enough. Want to make the book,' he said. 'Want to make it now and want you to come with me. I won't hang around forever.'

'Oh, nonsense, of course you will. You think I'm a doll, don't you? You think I'm cute and made of poured wax, and you'll stay as long as I stay.'

'You're a bit mean, Armand. You look like an angel, and talk like a common thug.'

'Such arrogance! I thought you wanted me.'

'Only on certain terms.'

'You lie, David Talbot,' I said.

I headed past him for the stairs. Cicadas sang in the night as they often do, to no clock, in New Orleans.

Through the nine-pane windows of the stairwell, I glimpsed the flowering trees of spring, a bit of vine curling on a porch top.

He followed. Down and down we went, walking like regular men, down to the first floor, and out the sparkling glass doors and into the broad lighted space of Napoleon Avenue with its damp, sweet park of green down the middle, a park thick with carefully planted flowers and old gnarled and humble, bending trees.

The whole picture moved with the subtle river winds, and wet mist swirled but would not fall into rain itself, and tiny green leaves drifted down like wilting ashes to the ground. Soft soft southern spring. Even the sky seemed pregnant with the season, lowering yet blushing with reflected light, giving birth to the mist from all its pores.

Strident perfume rose from the gardens right and left, from purple Four O'Clocks, as mortals call them here, a rampant flower like unto weed, but infinitely sweet, and the wild irises stabbing upwards like blades out of the

23

black mud, throaty petals monstrously big, battering themselves on old walls and concrete steps, and then as always there were roses, roses of old women and roses of the young, roses too whole for the tropical night, roses coated with poison.

There had been streetcars here once on this center strip of grass. I knew it, that the tracks had run along this wide deep green space where I walked ahead of him, slumward, riverward, deathward, bloodward. He came after me. I could close my eyes as I walked, never losing a step, and see the streetcars.

'Come on, follow me,' I said, describing what he did, not inviting him.

Blocks and blocks within seconds. He kept up. Very strong. The blood of an entire Royal Vampire court was inside him, no doubt of it. Count on Lestat to make the most lethal of monsters, that is, after his initial seductive blunders – Nicolas, Louis, Claudia – not a single one of the three able to take care of themselves alone, and two perished, and one lingering and perhaps the weakest vampire yet walking in the great world.

I looked back. His tight, polished brown face startled me. He looked lacquered all over, waxed, buffed, and once again I thought of spicy things, of the meat of candied nuts, and delicious aromas, of chocolates sweet with sugar and dark rich butterscotch, and it seemed a good thing suddenly to maybe grab a hold of him.

But this was no substitute for one rotten, cheap, ripe and odoriferous mortal. And guess what? I pointed. 'Over there.'

He looked as I directed him. He saw the sagging line of old buildings. Mortals everywhere lurked, slept, sat, dined, wandered, amid tiny narrow stairs, behind peeling walls and under cracked ceilings.

I had found one, most perfect in his wickedness, a

24

great flurry of hateful embers, of malice and greed and contempt smoldering as he waited for me.

We'd come to Magazine Street and passed it, but we were not at the river, only almost, and this was a street I had no recollection of, or knowledge of, in my wanderings of this city – their city, Louis's and Lestat's – just a narrow street with these houses the color of driftwood under the moon and windows hung with makeshift coverings, and inside there was this one slouching, arrogant, vicious mortal fixed to a television set and guzzling malt from a brown bottle, ignoring the roaches and the pulsing heat that pressed in from the open window, this ugly, sweating, filthy and irresistible thing, this flesh and blood for me.

The house was so alive with vermin and tiny despicable things that it seemed no more than a shell surrounding him, crackling and friable and the same color in all its shadows as a forest. No antiseptic modern standards here. Even the furniture rotted in the trashy clutter and damp. Mildew covered the grinding white refrigerator.

Only the reeky personal bed and rags gave off the clue to reigning domesticity.

It was a proper nest in which to find this fowl, this ugly bird, thick rich pluckable, devourable sack of bones and blood and shabby plumage.

I pushed the door to one side, the human stench rising like a swirl of gnats, and thereby put it off its hinges, but not with much sound.

I walked on newspapers strewn on painted wood. Orange peels turned to brownish leather. Roaches running. He didn't even look up. His swollen drunken face was blue and eerie, black eyebrows thick and unkempt, and yet he looked quite possibly a bit angelic, due to the light from the tube.

He flicked the magic plastic twanger in his hand to make the channels change, and the light flared and flickered soundlessly, and then he let the song rise, a band playing, a travesty, people clapping.

Trashy noises, trashy images, like the trash all around him. All right, I want you. No one else does.

He looked up at me, a boy invader, David too far off for him to see, waiting.

I pushed the television set to the side. It teetered, then fell onto the floor, its parts breaking, like so many jars of energy were inside, and now splinters of glass.

A momentary fury overcame him, charging his face with sluggish recognition.

He rose up, arms out, and came at me.

Before I sank my teeth, I noticed that he had long tangled black hair. Dirty but rich. He wore it back by means of a knotted bit of rag at the base of his neck and then straggling down his checkered shirt in a thick tail.

Meantime, he had enough syrupy and beer-besotted blood in him for two vampires, delicious, ugly, and a raging fighting heart, and so much bulk it was like riding a bull to be on him.

In the midst of the feed, all odors rise to sweetness, even the most rancid. I thought I would quietly die of joy, as always.

I sucked hard enough to fill my mouth, letting the blood roll over my tongue, and then to fill my stomach, if I have one, but above all just to stanch this greedy dirty thirst, but not hard enough to slow him down.

He swooned and fought, and did the stupid thing of tearing at my fingers, and then the most dangerous and clumsy thing of trying to find my eyes. I shut them tight and let him press with his greasy thumbs. It did him no good. I am an impregnable little boy. You can not blind the blind. I was too full of blood to care. Besides it felt

26

good. Those weak things that would scratch you do only stroke you.

His life went by as if everyone he ever loved were riding a roller coaster under snazzy stars. Worse than a Van Gogh painting. You never know the palette of the one you kill until the mind disgorges its finest colors.

Soon enough he sank down. I went with him. I had my left arm all the way around him now, and I lay childlike against his big muscular belly, and I drew the blood out now in the blindest gushes, pressing everything he thought and saw and felt down into only color, just give me color, pure orange, and just for a second, as he died – as the death passed me by, like a big rolling ball of black strength which turns out to be nothing actually, nothing but smoke or something even less than that – as this death came into me and went out again like the wind, I thought, Do I by crushing everything that he is deprive him of a final knowing?

Nonsense, Armand. You know what the spirits know, what the angels know. The bastard is going home! To Heaven. To Heaven that would not have you, and might never.

In death, he looked most excellent.

I sat beside him. I wiped my mouth, not that there was a drop to wipe. Vampires slobber blood only in motion pictures. Even the most mundane immortal is far too skilled to spill a drop. I wiped my mouth because his sweat was on my lips and on my face, and I wanted it to go away.

I admired him, however, that he was big and wondrously hard for all his seeming roundness. I admired the black hair clinging to his wet chest where the shirt had been so inevitably torn away.

His black hair was something to behold. I ripped the

27

knotted cloth that tied it. It was as full and thick as a woman's hair.

Making sure he was dead, I wrapped its length around my left hand and purposed to pull the whole mass from his scalp.

David gasped. 'Must you do this?' he asked me.

'No,' I said. Even then a few thousand strands had ripped loose from the scalp, each with only its tiny blooded root winking in the air like a tiny firefly. I held the mop for a moment and then let it slip out of my fingers and fall down behind his turned head.

Those unanchored hairs fell sloppily over his coarse cheek. His eyes were wet and wakeful-seeming, dying jelly.

David turned and went out into the little street. Cars roared and clattered by. A ship on the river sang with a steam calliope.

I came up behind him. I wiped the dust off me. One blow and I could have set the whole house to falling down, just caving in on the putrid filth within, dying softly amid other houses so no one indoors here would even know, all this moist wood merely caving.

I could not get the taste and smell of this sweat gone.

'Why did you so object to my pulling out his hair?' I asked. 'I only wanted to have it, and he's dead and beyond caring and no one else will miss his black hair.'

He turned with a sly smile and took my measure.

'You frighten me, the way you look,' I said. 'Have I so carelessly revealed myself to be a monster? You know, my blessed mortal Sybelle, when she is not playing the Sonata by Beethoven called the *Appassionata*, watches me feed all the time. Do you want me to tell my story now?'

I glanced back at the dead man on his side, his shoulder sagging. On the windowsill beyond and above him stood a blue glass bottle and in it was an orange flower. Isn't that the damnedest thing?

'Yes, I do want your story,' David said. 'Come, let's go back together. I only asked you not to take his hair for one reason.'

'Yes?' I asked. I looked at him. Rather genuine curiosity. 'What was the reason then? I was only going to pull out all his hair and throw it away.'

'Like pulling off the wings of a fly,' he offered seemingly without judgment.

'A dead fly,' I said. I deliberately smiled. 'Come now, why the fuss?'

'I wanted to see if you'd listen to me,' he said. 'That's all. Because if you did then it might be all right between us. And you stopped. And it is.' He turned around and took my arm.

'I don't like you!' I said.

'Oh, yes, you do, Armand,' he answered. 'Let me write it. Pace and rail and rant. You're very high and mighty right now because you have those two splendid little mortals hanging on your every gesture, and they're like acolytes to a god. But you want to tell me the story, you know you do. Come on!'

I couldn't stop myself from laughing. 'Have these tactics worked for you in the past?'

Now it was his turn to laugh and he did, good-naturedly. 'No, I suppose not,' he said. 'But let me put it to you this way, write it for them.'

'For whom?'

'For Benji and Sybelle.' He shrugged. 'No?'

I didn't answer.

Write the story for Benji and Sybelle. My mind raced forwards, to some cheerful and wholesome room, where we three would be gathered years hence – I, Armand, unchanged, boy teacher – and Benji and Sybelle in their mortal prime, Benji grown into a sleek tall gentleman with an Arab's ink-eyed allure and his favorite cheroot in his hand, a man of great expectation and opportunity, and my Sybelle, a curvaceous and full regal-bodied woman by then, and an even greater concert pianist than she could be now, her golden hair framing a woman's oval face and fuller womanish lips and eyes full of *entsagang* and secret radiance.

Could I dictate the story in this room and give them the book? This book dictated to David Talbot? Could I, as I set them free from my alchemical world, give them this book? Go forth my children, with all the wealth and guidance I could bestow, and now this book I wrote so long ago for you with David.

Yes, said my soul. Yet I turned, and ripped the black scalp of hair from my victim and stomped on it with a Rumpelstiltskin foot.

David didn't flinch. Englishmen are so polite.

'Very well,' I said. 'I'll tell you my story.'

His rooms were on the second floor, not far from where I'd paused at the top of the staircase. What a change from the barren and unheated hallways! He'd made a library for himself and with tables and chairs. A brass bed was there, dry and clean.

'These are her rooms,' he said. 'Don't you remember?'

'Dora,' I said. I breathed her scent suddenly. Why, it was all around me. But all her personal things were gone.

These were his books, they had to be. They were new spiritual explorers – Dannion Brinkley, Hilarion, Melvin Morse, Brian Weiss, Matthew Fox, the Urantia book. Add to this old texts – Cassiodorus, St. Teresa of Avila, Gregory of Tours, the Veda, Talmud, Torah, Kama Sutra – all in original tongues. He had a few obscure novels, plays, poetry.

'Yes.' He sat down at the table. 'I don't need the light. Do you want it?'

'I don't know what to tell you.'

'Ah,' he said. He took out his mechanical pen. He opened a notebook with startlingly white paper scored with fine green lines. 'You will know what to tell me.' He looked up at me.

I stood hugging myself, as it were, letting my head fall as if it could drop right off me and I would die. My hair fell long about me.

I thought of Sybelle and Benjamin, my quiet girl and exuberant boy.

'Did you like them, David, my children?' I asked.

'Yes, the first moment I saw them, when you brought them in. Everyone did. Everyone looked lovingly and respectfully at them. Such poise, such charm. I think we all dream of such confidants, faithful mortal companions of compelling grace, who aren't screaming mad. They love you, yet they are neither terrified nor entranced.'

I didn't move. I didn't speak. I shut my eyes. I heard in my heart the swift, bold march of the *Appassionata*, those rumbling, incandescent waves of music, full of throbbing and brittle metal, *Appassionata*. Only it was in my head. No golden long-limbed Sybelle.

'Light the candles that you have,' I said timidly. 'Will you do that for me? It would be sweet to have many candles, and look, Dora's lace is hanging still on the windows, fresh and clean. I am a lover of lace, that is Brussels point de gaze, or very like it, yes, I'm rather mad for it.'

'Of course, I'll light the candles,' he said.

I had my back to him. I heard the sharp delicious crack of a small wooden match. I smelt it burn, and then came the liquid fragrance of the nodding wick, the

31

curling wick, and the light rose upwards, finding the cypress boards of the stripped wooden ceiling above us. Another crack, another series of tiny sweet soft crackling sounds, and the light swelled and came down over me and fell just short of brightness along the shadowy wall.

'Why did you do it, Armand?' he said. 'Oh, the Veil has Christ on it, in some form, no doubt of it, it did seem to be the Holy Veil of Veronica, and God knows, thousands of others believed it, yes, but why in your case, why? It was blazingly beautiful, yes, I grant you that, Christ with His thorns and His blood, and His eyes gazing right at us, both of us, but why did you believe it so completely, Armand, after so long? Why did you go to Him? That's what you tried to do, didn't you?'

I shook my head. I made my words soft and pleading.

'Back up, scholar,' I said, turning around slowly. 'Mind your page. This is for you, and for Sybelle. Oh, it's for my little Benji too. But in a way, it's my symphony for Sybelle. The story begins a long time ago. Maybe I've never truly realized how long ago, until this very moment. You listen and write. Let me be the one to cry and to rant and to rail.'

I look at my hands. I think of the phrase 'not made by human hands.' I know what this means, even though every time I ever heard the phrase said with emotion it had to do with what had come from my hands.

I'd like to paint now, to pick up a brush and try it the way I did it then, in a trance, furiously, once and for only, every line and mass of color, each blending, each decision final.

Ah, I'm so disorganized, so browbeaten by what I remember.

Let me choose a place to begin.

Constantinople – newly under the Turks, by that I mean a Moslem City for less than a century when I was brought there, a slave boy, captured in the wild lands of his country for which he barely knew the proper name: the Golden Horde.

Memory had already been choked out of me, along with language, or any capacity to reason in a consistent way. I remember the squalid rooms that must have been Constantinople because other people talked, and for the first time in forever, since I'd been ripped out of what I couldn't remember, I could understand what people said.

They spoke Greek, of course, these traders who dealt in slaves for brothels in Europe. They knew no religious allegiance, which was all I knew, pitifully devoid of detail.

I was thrown down on a thick Turkey carpet, the fancified rich floor covering one saw in a palace, a display rug for high-priced goods.

My hair was wet and long; someone had brushed it enough to hurt me. All those personal things that were mine had been stripped from me and from my memory. I was naked beneath an old frayed tunic of gold cloth. It was hot and damp in the room. I was hungry, but having no hope of food, I knew this to be a pain that would spike and then, of its own, die away. The tunic must have given me a castoff glory, the shimmer of a fallen angel. It had long bell sleeves and came to my knees.

When I got to my feet, which were bare of course, I saw these men and knew what they wanted, that this was vice, and despicable, and the price of it was Hell. Curses of vanished elders echoed down on me: too pretty, too soft, too pale, eyes far too full of the Devil, ah, the devilish smile.

How intent these men were on their argument, their bargaining. How they looked at me without ever looking into my eyes.

Suddenly I laughed. Things here were being done so hastily. Those who had delivered me had left me. Those who had scrubbed me had never left the tubs. I was a bundle thrown down on the carpet.

For one moment, I had an awareness of myself as having been sharp-tongued once and cynical, and keenly aware of the nature of men in general. I laughed because these merchants thought I was a girl.

I waited, listening, catching these bits and pieces of talk.

We were in a broad room, with a low canopied ceiling, the silk of it sewn with tiny mirrors and the curlicues so loved by the Turks, and the lamps, though smoky, were scented and filled the air with a dusky hazy soot that burned my eyes.

The men in their turbans and caftans weren't

34

unfamiliar to me any more than the language. But I only caught dashes of what they said. My eyes looked for an escape. There was none. There were heavy, brooding men slouching near the entrances. A man far off at a desk used an abacus for counting. He had piles and piles of gold coins.

One of the men, a tall lean one, all cheekbones and jaw, with rotted-out teeth, came towards me and felt of my shoulders and my neck. Then he lifted up the tunic. I stood stock-still, not enraged or consciously fearful, merely paralyzed. This was the land of the Turks, and I knew what they did to boys. Only I had never seen a picture, nor heard a real story of it, or known anyone who had ever really lived in it, penetrated it and come back home.

Home. Surely I must have wanted to forget who I was. I must have. Shame must have made it mandatory. But at that moment, in the tentlike room with its flowered carpet, among the merchants and slave traders, I strained to remember as if, discovering a map in myself, I could follow it out of here and back to where I belonged.

I did recollect the grasslands, the wild lands, lands where you don't go, except for –. But that was a blank. I'd been in the grasslands, defying fate, stupidly but not unwillingly. I'd been carrying something of the utmost importance. I got off my horse, ripped this big bundle loose from the leather harness and ran with the bundle clutched against my chest.

'The trees!' he shouted, but who was he?

I knew what he had meant, however, that I had to reach the copse and put this treasure there, this splendid and magical thing that was inside the bundle, 'not made by human hands.'

I never got that far. When they grabbed hold of me, I

35

dropped the bundle and they didn't even go after it, at least not as I saw. I thought, as I was hoisted into the air: It isn't supposed to be found like that, wrapped in cloth like that. It has to be placed in the trees.

They must have raped me on the boat because I don't remember coming to Constantinople. I don't remember being hungry, cold, outraged or afraid.

Now here for the first time, I knew the particulars of rape, the stinking grease, the squabbling, the curses over the ruin of the lamb. I felt a hideous unsupportable powerlessness.

Loathsome men, men against God and against nature.

I made a roar like an animal at the turbaned merchant, and he struck me hard on the ear so that I fell to the ground. I lay still looking up at him with all the contempt I could bring into my gaze. I didn't get up, even when he kicked me. I wouldn't speak.

Thrown over his shoulder I was carried out, taken through a crowded courtyard, past wondrous stinking camels and donkeys and heaps of filth, out by the harbor where the ships waited, over the gangplank and into the ship's hold.

It was filth again, the smell of hemp, the rustling of the rats on board. I was thrown on a pallet of rough cloth. Once again, I looked for the escape and saw only the ladder by which we'd descended and above heard the voices of too many men.

It was still dark when the ship began to move. Within an hour I was so sick, I wanted simply to die. I curled up on the floor and lay as still as possible, hiding myself entirely under the soft clinging fabric of the old tunic. I slept for the longest time.

When I awoke an old man was there. He wore a different style of dress, less frightening to me than that of

36

the turbaned Turks, and his eyes were kindly. He bent near me. He spoke a new language which was uncommonly soft and sweet, but I couldn't understand him.

A voice speaking Greek told him that I was a mute, had no wits and growled like a beast.

Time to laugh again, but I was too sick.

The same Greek told the old man I hadn't been torn or wounded. I was marked at a high price.

The old man made some dismissing gestures as he shook his head and talked a song in the new speech. He laid his hands on me and gently coaxed me to my feet.

He took me through a doorway into a small chamber, draped all in red silk.

I spent the rest of the voyage in this chamber, except for one night.

On that one night – and I can't place it in terms of the journey – I awoke, and finding him asleep beside me, this old man who never touched me except to pat or console me, I went out, up the ladder, and stood for a long time looking up at the stars.

We were at anchor in a port, and a city of dark blue-black buildings with domed roofs and bell towers tumbled down the cliffs to the harbor where the torches turned beneath the ornamented arches of an arcade.

All this, the civilized shore, looked probable to me, appealing, but I had no thought that I could jump ship and get free. Men wandered beneath the archways. Beneath the arch nearest to me, a strangely garbed man in a shiny helmet, with a big broad sword dangling on his hip, stood guard against the branching fretted column, carved so marvelously to look like a tree as it supported the cloister, like the remnant of a palace into which this channel for ships had been rudely dug.

I didn't look at the shore much after this first long and

memorable glimpse. I looked up at Heaven and her court of mythical creatures fixed forever in the all powerful and inscrutable stars. Ink black was the night beyond them, and they so like jewels that old poetry came back to me, the sound even of hymns sung only by men.

As I recall it, hours passed before I was caught, beaten fiercely with a leather thong and dragged back down in the hold. I knew the beating would stop when the old man saw me. He was furious and trembling. He gathered me to him, and we bedded down again. He was too old to ask anything of me.

I didn't love him. It was clear to the witless mute that this man regarded him as something quite valuable, to be preserved for sale. But I needed him and he wiped my tears. I slept as much as I could. I was sick every time the waves were rough. Sometimes the heat alone sickened me. I didn't know real heat. The man fed me so well that sometimes I thought I was a being kept by him like a fatted calf to be sold for food.

When we reached Venice, it was late in the day. I had no hint of the beauty of Italy. I'd been locked away from it, down in this grime pit with the old keeper, and being taken up into the city I soon saw that my suspicions about the old keeper were perfectly right.

In a dark room, he and another man fell into bitter argument. Nothing could make me speak. Nothing could make me indicate that I understood anything that was happening to me. I did, however, understand. Money changed hands. The old man left without looking back.

They tried to teach me things. The soft caressing new language was all around me. Boys came, sat beside me, tried to coax me with soft kisses and embraces. They pinched the nipples on my chest and tried to touch the private parts which I'd been taught not even to look at on account of the bitter occasion of sin.

Several times I resolved to pray. But I discovered I couldn't remember the words. Even the images were indistinct. Lights had gone out forever which had guided me through all my years. Every time I drifted deep into thought, someone struck me or yanked at my hair.

They always came with ointments after they hit me. They were careful to treat the abraded skin. Once, when a man struck me on the side of the face, another shouted and grabbed his upraised hand before he could land the second blow.

I refused food and drink. They couldn't make me take it. I couldn't take it. I didn't choose to starve. I simply couldn't do anything to keep myself alive. I knew I was going home. I was going home. I would die and go home. It would be an awful painful passage. I would have cried if I'd been alone. But I was never alone. I'd have to die in front of people. I hadn't seen real daylight in forever. Even the lamps hurt my eyes because I was so much in unbroken darkness. But people were always there.

The lamp would brighten. They sat in a ring around me with grimy little faces and quick pawlike hands that wiped my hair out of my face or shook me by the shoulder. I turned my face to the wall.

A sound kept me company. This was to be the end of my life. The sound was the sound of water outside. I could hear it against the wall. I could tell when a boat passed and I could hear the wood pylons creaking, and I lay my head against the stone and felt the house sway in the water as if we were not beside it but planted in it, which of course we were.

Once I dreamed of home, but I don't remember what

39

it was like. I woke, I cried, and there came a volley of little greetings from the shadows, wheedling, sentimental voices.

I thought I wanted to be alone. I didn't. When they locked me up for days and nights in a black room without bread or water, I began to scream and pound on the walls. No one came.

After a while, I fell into a stupor. It was a violent jolt when the door was opened. I sat up, covering my eyes. The lamp was a menace. My head throbbed.

But there came a soft insinuating perfume, a mixture of the smell of sweet burning wood in snowing winter and that of crushed flowers and pungent oil.

I was touched by something hard, something made of wood or brass, only this thing moved as if it were organic. At last I opened my eyes and saw that a man held me, and these inhuman things, these things that felt so like stone or brass, were his white fingers, and he looked at me with eager, gentle blue eyes.

'Amadeo,' he said.

He was dressed all in red velvet and splendidly tall. His blond hair was parted in the middle in a saintly fashion and combed richly down to his shoulders where it broke over his cloak in lustrous curls. He had a smooth forehead without a line to it, and high straight golden eyebrows dark enough to give his face a clear, determined look. His lashes curled like dark golden threads from his eyelids. And when he smiled, his lips were flushed suddenly with a pale immediate color that made their full careful shape all the more visible.

I knew him. I spoke to him. I could have never seen such miracles in the face of anyone else.

He smiled so kindly at me. His upper lip and chin were all clean shaven. I couldn't even see the scantest hair on him, and his nose was narrow and delicate

40

though large enough to be in proportion to the other magnetic features of his face.

'Not the Christ, my child,' he said. 'But one who comes with his own salvation. Come into my arms.'

'I'm dying, Master.' What was my language? I can't say even now what it was. But he understood me.

'No, little one, you're not dying. You're coming now into my protection, and perhaps if the stars are with us, if they are kind to us, you'll never die at all.'

'But you are the Christ. I know you!'

He shook his head, and in the most common human way he lowered his eyes as he did, and he smiled. His generous lips parted, and I saw only a human's white teeth. He put his hands beneath my arms, lifted me and kissed my throat, and the shivers paralyzed me. I closed my eyes and felt his fingers on top of them, and heard him say into my ear, 'Sleep as I take you home.'

When I awoke, we were in a huge bath. No Venetian ever had such a bath as this, I can tell you that now from all the things I saw later, but what did I know of the conventions of this place? This was a palace truly; I had seen palaces.

I climbed up and out of the swaddling of velvet in which I lay – his red cloak if I'm not mistaken – and I saw a great curtained bed to my right and, beyond, the deep oval basin of the bath itself. Water poured from a shell held by angels into the basin, and steam rose from the broad surface, and in the steam my Master stood. His white chest was naked and the nipples faintly pink, and his hair, pushed back from his smooth straight forehead, looked even thicker and more beautifully blond than it had before.

He beckoned to me.

I was afraid of the water. I knelt at the edge and put my hand into it.

41

With amazing speed and grace, he reached for me and brought me down into the warm pool, pushing me until the water covered my shoulders and then tilting back my head.

Again I looked up at him. Beyond him the bright-blue ceiling was covered in startlingly vivid angels with giant white feathery wings. I had never seen such brilliant and curly angels, leaping as they did, out of all restraint and style, to flaunt their human beauty in muscled limbs and swirling garments, in flying locks. It seemed a bit of madness this, these robust and romping figures, this riot of celestial play above me to which the steam ascended, evaporating in a golden light.

I looked at my Master. His face was right before me. Kiss me again, yes, do it, that shiver, kiss –. But he was of the same ilk as those painted beings, one of them, and this some form of heathen Heaven, a pagan place of Soldiers' gods where all is wine, and fruit, and flesh. I had come to the wrong place.

He threw back his head. He gave way to ringing laughter. He lifted a handful of water again and let it spill down my chest. He opened his mouth and for a moment I saw the flash of something very wrong and dangerous, teeth such as a wolf might have. But these were gone, and only his lips sucked at my throat, then at my shoulder. Only his lips sucked at the nipple as I sought too late to cover it.

I groaned for all this. I sank against him in the warm water, and his lips went down my chest to my belly. He sucked tenderly at the skin as if he were sucking up the salt and the heat from it, and even his forehead nudging my shoulder filled me with warm thrilling sensations. I put my arm around him, and when he found the sin itself, I felt it go off as if an arrow had been shot from it, and it were a crossbow; I felt it go, this arrow, this thrust, and I cried out.

He let me lie for a while against him. He bathed me slowly. He had a soft gathered cloth with which he wiped my face. He dipped me back to wash my hair.

And then when he thought I had rested enough, we began the kisses again.

Before dawn, I woke against his pillow. I sat up and saw him as he put on his big cloak and covered his head. The room was full of boys again, but these were not the sad, emaciated tutors of the brothel. These boys were handsome, well fed, smiling and sweet, as they gathered around the bed.

They wore brightly colored tunics of effervescent colors, with fabrics carefully pleated and tight belts that gave them a girlish grace. All wore long luxuriant hair.

My Master looked at me and in a tongue I knew, I knew perfectly, he said that I was his only child, and he would come again that night, and by such time as that I would have seen a new world.

'A new world!' I cried out. 'No, don't leave me, Master. I don't want the whole world. I want you!'

'Amadeo,' he said in this private tongue of confidence, leaning over the bed, his hair dry now and beautifully brushed, his hands softened with powder. 'You have me forever. Let the boys feed you, dress you.' You belong to me, to Marius Romanus, now.

He turned to them and gave them their commands in the soft singing language.

And you would have thought from their happy faces that he had given them sweets and gold.

'Amadeo, Amadeo,' they sang as they gathered around me. They held me so that I couldn't follow him. They spoke Greek to me, fast and easily, and Greek for me was not so easy. But I understood.

43

Come with us, you are one of us, we are to be good to you, we are to be especially good to you. They dressed me up hastily in castoffs, arguing with one another about my tunic, was it good enough, and these faded stockings, well, it was only for now! Put on the slippers; here, a jacket that was too small for Riccardo. These seemed the garments of kings.

'We love you,' said Albinus, the second in command to Riccardo, and a dramatic contrast to the black-haired Riccardo, for his blond hair and pale green eyes. The other boys, I couldn't quite distinguish, but these two were easy to watch.

'Yes, we love you,' said Riccardo, pushing back his black hair and winking at me, his skin so smooth and dark compared to the others. His eyes were fiercely black. He clutched my hand and I saw his long thin fingers. Here everyone had thin fingers, fine fingers. They had fingers like mine, and mine had been unusual among my brethren. But I couldn't think of this.

An eerie possibility suggested itself to me, that I, the pale one, the one who made all the trouble, the one with the fine fingers, had been spirited away to the good land where I belonged. But that was altogether too fabulous to believe. My head ached. I saw wordless flashes of the stubby horsemen who had captured me, of the stinking hold of the ship in which I'd been brought to Constantinople, flashes of gaunt, busy men, men fussing as they had handled me there.

Dear God, why did anyone love me? What for? Marius Romanus, why do you love me?

The Master smiled as he waved from the door. The hood was up around his head, a crimson frame for his fine cheekbones and his curling lips.

My eyes filled with tears.

A white mist swirled around the Master as the door

44

closed behind him. The night was going. But the candles still burned.

We came into a large room, and I saw that it was full of paints and pots of color and brushes standing in earthen jars ready to be used. Great white squares of cloth – canvas – waited for the paint.

These boys didn't make their colors with the yoke of an egg in the time-honored manner. They mixed the bright fine ground pigments directly with the amber-colored oils. Great glossy gobs of color awaited me in little pots. I took the brush when they gave it to me. I looked at the stretched white cloth on which I was to paint.

'Not from human hands,' I said. But what did these words mean? I lifted the brush and I began to paint him, this blond-haired man who had rescued me from darkness and squalor. I threw out the hand with the brush, dipping the bristles into the jars of cream and pink and white and slapping these colors onto the curiously resilient canvas. But I couldn't make a picture. No picture came!

'Not by human hands!' I whispered. I dropped the brush. I put my hands over my face.

I searched for the words in Greek. When I said them, several of the boys nodded, but they didn't grasp the meaning. How could I explain to them the catastrophe? I looked at my fingers. What had become of –. There all recollection burnt up and I was left suddenly with Amadeo.

'I can't do it.' I stared at the canvas, at the mess of colors. 'Maybe if it was wood, not cloth, I could do it.'

What had it been that I could do? They didn't understand.

He was not the Living Lord, my Master, the blond one, the blond one with the icy blue eyes.

45

But he was my Lord. And I could not do this thing that was meant to be done.

To comfort me, to distract me, the boys took up their brushes and quickly astonished me with pictures that ran like a stream out of their quick applications of the brush.

A boy's face, cheeks, lips, eyes, yes, and reddish-golden hair in profusion. Good Lord, it was I . . . it was not a canvas but a mirror. It was this Amadeo. Riccardo took over to refine the expression, to deepen the eyes and work a sorcery on the tongue so I seemed about to speak. What was this rampant magic that made a boy appear out of nothing, most natural, at a casual angle, with knitted brows and streaks of unkempt hair over his ear?

It seemed both blasphemous and beautiful, this fluid, abandoned fleshly figure.

Riccardo spelled the letters out in Greek as he wrote them. Then he threw the brush down. He cried:

'A very different picture is what our Master has in mind.' He snatched up the drawings.

They pulled me through the house, the 'palazzo' as they called it, teaching me the word with relish.

The entire place was filled with such paintings – on its walls, its ceilings, on panels and canvases stacked against each other – towering pictures full of ruined buildings, broken columns, rampant greenery, distant mountains and an endless stream of busy people with flushed faces, their luxuriant hair and gorgeous clothing always rumpled and curling in a wind.

It was like the big platters of fruit and meats that they brought out and set before me. A mad disorder, an abundance for the sake of itself, a great drench of colors and shapes. It was like the wine, too sweet and light.

*

It was like the city below when they threw open the windows, and I saw the small black boats – gondolas, even then – in brilliant sunlight coursing through the greenish waters, when I saw the men in their sumptuous scarlet or gold cloaks hurrying along the quays.

Into our gondolas we piled, a troop of us, and suddenly we traveled in graceful darting silence among the facades, each huge house as magnificent as a Cathedral, with its narrow pointed arches, its lotus windows, its covering of gleaming white stone.

Even the older, sorrier dwellings, not too ornate but nevertheless monstrous in size, were plastered in colors, a rose so deep it seemed to come from crushed petals, a green so thick it seemed to have been mixed from the opaque water itself.

Out into the Piazza San Marco we came, amid the long fantastically regular arcades on both sides.

It seemed the very gathering place of Heaven as I stared at the hundreds milling before the distant golden domes of the church.

Golden domes. Golden domes.

Some old tale had been told to me of golden domes, and I had seen them in a darkling picture, had I not? Sacred domes, lost domes, domes in flames, a church violated, as I had been violated. Ah, ruin, ruin was gone, laid waste by the sudden eruption all around me of what was vital and whole! How had all this been born out of wintry ashes? How had I died among snows and smoking fires and come to rise here beneath this caressing sun?

Its warm sweet light bathed beggars and tradesmen; it shone on princes passing with pages to carry their ornate velvet trains behind them, on the booksellers who spread their books beneath scarlet canopies, lute players who vied for small coins.

The wares of the wide diabolical world were displayed in the shops and market stalls – glassware such as I have never beheld, including goblets of all possible colors, not to mention little figurines of glass including animals and human beings and other filmy shining trinkets. There were marvelously bright and beautifully turned beads for rosaries; magnificent laces in grand and graceful patterns, including even snowy white pictures of actual church towers and little houses with windows and doors; great feathery plumes from birds I couldn't name; other exotic species flapping and screeching in gilt cages; and the finest and most magnificently worked multicolored carpets only too reminiscent of the powerful Turks and their capital from which I'd come. Nevertheless, who resists such carpets? Forbidden by law to render human beings, Moslems rendered flowers, arabesques, labyrinthian curlicues and other such designs with bold dyes and awe-inspiring exactitude. There were oils for lamps, tapers, candles, incense, and great displays of glistering jewels of indescribable beauty and the most delicate work of the goldsmiths and silversmiths, in plate and ornamental items both newly made and old. There were shops that sold only spices. There were shops that sold medicines and cures. There were bronze statues, lion heads, lanterns and weapons. There were cloth merchants with the silks of the East, the finest woven wools dyed in miraculous tints, cotton and linen and fine specimens of embroidery, and ribbons galore.

Men and women here appeared immensely wealthy, feasting casually on fresh meat tarts in the cookshops, drinking clear red wine and eating sweet cakes full of cream.

There were booksellers offering the new printed books, of which the other apprentices told me eagerly, explaining the marvelous invention of the printing press, which had only lately made it possible for men far and wide to acquire not only books of letters and words but books of drawn pictures as well.

Venice already had dozens of small print shops and publishers where the presses were hard at work producing books in Greek as well as Latin, and in the vernacular tongue – the soft singing tongue – which the apprentices spoke amongst themselves.

They let me stop to glut my eyes on these wonders, these machines that made pages for books.

But they did have their chores, Riccardo and the others – they were to scoop up the prints and engravings of the German painters for our Master, pictures made by the new printing presses of old wonders by Memling, Van Eyck, or Hieronymus Bosch. Our Master was always in the market for them. Such drawings brought the north to the south. Our Master was a champion of such wonders. Our Master was pleased that over one hundred printing presses filled our city, that he could throw away his coarse inaccurate copies of Livy and Virgil and have now corrected printed texts.

Oh, it was such a load of information.

And no less important than the literature or paintings of the universe was the matter of my clothes. We had to get the tailors to stop everything to dress me properly according to small chalk drawings which the Master had made.

Handwritten letters of credit had to be taken to the banks. I was to have money. Everyone was to have money. I had never touched such a thing as money.

Money was pretty – Florentine gold or silver, German florins, Bohemian groschens, fancy old coins minted under the rulers of Venice who were called the Doges, exotic coins from the Constantinople of old. I was given a little sack of my own clinking clanking money. We tied our 'purses' to our belts.

One of the boys bought me a small wonder because I stared at it. It was a ticking watch. I couldn't grasp the theory of it, this tiny ticking thing, all encrusted with jewels, and not all the hands pointed at the sky would teach me. At last with a shock I realized: It was, beneath its filigree and paint, its strange glass and bejeweled frame, a tiny clock!

I closed my hand on it and felt dizzy. I had never known clocks to be anything but great venerable things in bell towers or on walls.

'I carry time now,' I whispered in Greek, looking to my friends.

'Amadeo,' said Riccardo. 'Count the hours for me.'

I wanted to say that this prodigious discovery meant something, something personal. It was a message to me from some other too hastily and perilously forgotten world. Time was not time anymore and never would be. The day was not the day, nor the night the night. I couldn't articulate it, not in Greek, nor any tongue, nor even in my feverish thoughts. I wiped the sweat from my forehead. I squinted into the brilliant sun of Italy. My eyes clapped upon the birds who flew in great flocks across the sky, like tiny pen strokes made to flap in unison. I think I whispered foolishly, 'We are in the world.'

'We are in the center of it, the greatest city of it!' Riccardo cried, urging me on into the crowds. 'We shall see it before we get locked up in the tailor's, that's for damned sure.'

But first it was time for the sweetshop, for the miracle of chocolate with sugar, for syrupy concoctions of unnameable but bright red and yellow sweets.

One of the boys showed to me his little book of the

most frightening printed pictures, men and women embraced in carnality. It was the stories of Boccaccio. Riccardo said he would read them to me, that it was in fact an excellent book to teach me Italian. And that he would teach me Dante too.

Boccaccio and Dante were Florentines, said one of the other boys, but all in all the two weren't so bad.

Our Master loved all kinds of books, I was told, you couldn't go wrong spending your money on them, he was always pleased with that. I'd come to see that the teachers who came to the house would drive me crazy with their lessons. It was the *studia humanitatis* that we must all learn, and it included history, grammar, rhetoric, philosophy and ancient authors . . . all of this so much dazzling words that only revealed its meaning to me as it was often repeated and demonstrated in the days to come.

We could not look too good for our Master either, that was another lesson I must learn. Gold and silver chains, necklaces with medallions and other such trinkets were bought for me and laid over my neck. I needed rings, jeweled rings. We had to bargain fiercely with the jewelers for these, and I came out of it wearing a real emerald from the new world, and two ruby rings carved with silver inscriptions which I couldn't read.

I couldn't get over the sight of my hand with a ring. To this very night of my life, some five hundred years after, you see, I have a weakness for jeweled rings. Only during those centuries in Paris when I was a penitent, one of Satan's discalced Children of the Night, during that long slumber only, did I give up my rings. But we'll come to that nightmare soon enough.

For now, this was Venice, I was Marius's child and romped with his other children in a manner that would be repeated for years ahead.

51

On to the tailor.

As I was measured and pinned and dressed, the boys told me stories of all those rich Venetians who came to our Master seeking to have even the smallest piece of his work. As for our Master, he, claiming that he was too wretched, sold almost nothing but occasionally did a portrait of a woman or man who struck his eye. These portraits almost always worked the person into a mythological subject – gods, goddesses, angels, saints. Names I knew and names I'd never heard of tripped off the boys' tongues. It seemed here all echoes of sacred things were swept up in a new tide.

Memory would jolt me only to release me. Saints and gods, they were one and the same? Wasn't there a code to which I should remain faithful that somehow dictated these were but artful lies? I couldn't get it clear in my head, and all around me was such happiness, yes, happiness. It seemed impossible that these simple shining faces could mask wickedness. I didn't believe it. Yet all pleasure to me was suspect. I was dazzled when I could not give in, and overcome when I did surrender, and as the days followed I surrendered with ever greater ease all the time.

This day of initiation was only one of hundreds, nay, thousands that were to follow, and I don't know when I started to understand with any preciseness what my boy companions said. That time came, however, and rather quickly. I do not remember being the naive one very long.

On this first excursion, it was magic. And high above the sky was the perfect blue of cobalt, and the breeze from the sea was fresh and moist and cool. There above were massed the scudding clouds I had seen so wondrously rendered in the paintings of the palazzo, and there came my first hint that the paintings of my Master were no lie.

Indeed when we entered, by special permission, the Doges' chapel, San Marco, I was caught by the throat by its splendor – its walls of gleaming tessellated gold. But another shock followed hard upon my finding myself virtually entombed in light and in riches. Here were stark, somber figures, figures of saints I knew.

These were no mystery to me, the almond-eyed tenants of these hammered walls, severe in their straight careful drapery, their hands infallibly folded in prayer. I knew their halos, I knew the tiny holes made in the gold to make it glitter ever more magically. I knew the judgment of these bearded patriarchs who gazed impassively on me as I stopped, dead in my tracks, unable to go on.

I slumped to the stone floor. I was sick.

I had to be taken from the church. The noise of the piazza rose over me as if I were descending to some awful denouement. I wanted to tell my friends it was inevitable, not their fault.

The boys were in a fluster. I couldn't explain it. Stunned, sweating all over and lying limp at the base of a column, I listened dully as they explained to me in Greek that this church was only part of all I had seen. Why should it frighten me so? Yes, it was old, yes, it was Byzantine, as so much in Venice was. 'Our ships have traded with Byzantium for centuries. We are a maritime empire.' I tried to grasp it.

What came clear in my pain was only that this place had not been a special judgment upon me. I had been taken from it as easily as I had been brought into it. The sweet-voiced boys with the gentle hands who surrounded me, who offered me cool wine to drink and fruit to eat that I might recover, they did not hold this place in any terrible dread.

Turning to the left of me, I glimpsed the quays, the

harbor. I ran towards it, thunderstruck by the sight of the wooden ships. They stood at anchor four and five deep, but beyond them was enacted the greatest miracle: great galleons of deep ballooning wood, their sails collecting the breeze, their graceful oars chopping the water as they moved out to sea.

Back and forth the traffic moved, the huge wooden barks dangerously close to one another, slipping in and out of the mouth of Venice, while others no less graceful and impossible at anchor disgorged abundant goods.

Leading me stumbling to the Arsenale, my companions comforted me with the sight of the ships being built by ordinary men. In days to come I would hang about at the Arsenale for hours, watching the ingenious process by which human beings made such immense barks that to my mind should rightly sink.

Now and then in snatches I saw images of icy rivers, of barges and flatboats, of coarse men reeking of animal fat and rancid leather. But these last ragged tidbits of the winter world from which I'd come faded.

Perhaps had this not been Venice, it would have been a different tale.

In all my years in Venice, I never tired of the Arsenale, of watching the ships being built. I had no problem gaining access by means of a few kind words and coins, and it was ever my delight to watch these fantastical structures being constructed of bowed ribs, bent wood and piercing masts. Of this first day, we were rushed through this yard of miracles. It was enough.

Yes, well, it was Venice, this place that must erase from my mind, at least for a while, the clotted torment of some earlier existence, some congestion of all truths I would not face.

My Master would never have been there, had it not been Venice.

Not a month later he would tell me matter-of-factly what each of the cities of Italy had to offer him, how he loved to watch Michelangelo, the great sculptor, hard at work in Florence, how he went to listen to the fine teachers in Rome.

'But Venice has an art of a thousand years,' he said as he himself lifted his brush to paint the huge panel before him. 'Venice is in itself a work of art, a metropolis of impossible domestic temples built side by side like waxen honeycombs and maintained in ever flowing nectar by a population as busy as bees. Behold our palaces, they alone are worthy of the eye.'

As time passed he would school me in the history of Venice, as did the others, dwelling on the nature of the Republic, which, though despotic in its decisions and fiercely hostile to the outsider, was nevertheless a city of 'equal' men. Florence, Milan, Rome – these cities were falling under the power of small elites or powerful families and individuals, while Venice, for all her faults, remained governed by her Senators, her powerful merchants and her Council of Ten.

On that first day, an everlasting love for Venice was born in me. It seemed singularly devoid of horrors, a warm home even for its well-dressed and clever beggars, a hive of prosperity and vehement passion as well as staggering wealth.

And in the tailor shop, was I not being made up into a prince like my new friends?

Look, had I not seen Riccardo's sword? They were all noblemen.

'Forget all that has gone before,' said Riccardo. 'Our Master is our Lord, and we are his princes, we are his royal court. You are rich now and nothing can hurt you.'

'We are not mere apprentices in the ordinary sense,'

said Albinus. 'We are to be sent to the University of Padua. You'll see. We are tutored in music and dance and manners as regularly as in science and literature. You will have time to see the boys who come back to visit, all gentlemen of means. Why, Giuliano was a prosperous lawyer, and one of the other boys was a physician in Torcello, an island city nearby.

'But all have independent means when they leave the Master,' explained Albinus. 'It's only that the Master, like all Venetians, deplores idleness. We are as well off as lazy lords from abroad who do nothing but sample our world as though it were a dish of food.'

By the end of this first sunlighted adventure, this welcome into the bosom of my Master's school and his splendid city, I was combed, trimmed and dressed in the colors he would forever choose for me, sky blue for the stockings, a darker midnight blue velvet for a short belted jacket, and a tunic of an even fairer shade of azure embroidered with tiny French fleur-de-lis in thick gold thread. A bit of burgundy there might be for trimming and fur; for when the sea breezes grew strong in winter, this paradise would be what these Italians called cold.

By nightfall, I pranced on the marble tile with the others, dancing for a while to the lutes played by the younger boys, accompanied by the fragile music of the Virginal, the first keyboard instrument I had ever seen.

When the last of twilight had died beautifully into the canal outside the narrow pointed arched windows of the palazzo, I roamed about, catching random glances of myself in the many dark mirrors that rose up from the marble tile to the very ceiling of the corridor, the salon, the alcove, or whatever beautifully appointed room I should find.

I sang new words in unison with Riccardo. The great

state of Venice was called the Serenissima. The black boats of the canals were gondolas. The winds that would come soon to make us all crazy were called the Sirocco. The most high ruler of this magical city was the Doge, our book tonight with the teacher was Cicero, the musical instrument which Riccardo gathered up and played with his plucking fingers was the lute. The great canopy of the Master's regal bed was a baldaquin trimmed each fortnight with new gold fringe.

I was ecstatic.

I had not merely a sword but a dagger.

Such trust. Of course I was lamblike to these others, and pretty much a lamb to myself. But never had anyone entrusted to me such bronze and steel weapons. Again, memory played its tricks. I knew how to throw a wooden spear, how to . . . Alas, it became a wisp of smoke, and there lay in the air around it that I'd been committed not to weapons, but to something else, something immense which exacted all I could give it. Weapons were forbidden for me.

Well, no more. No more, no more, no more. Death had swallowed me whole and thrown me forth here. In the palazzo of my Master, in a salon of brilliantly painted battle scenes, with maps upon the ceiling, with windows of thick molded glass, I drew my sword with a great singing sound and pointed it at the future. With my dagger, after examining the emeralds and rubies of its handle, I sliced an apple in two with a gasp.

The other boys laughed at me. But it was all friendly, kind.

Soon the Master would come. Look. From room to room the youngest fellows among us, little boys who had not come out with us, now moved quickly, lifting their tapers to torches and candelabra. I stood in the door, looking to yet another and another and another. Light

57

burst forth soundlessly in each of these rooms.

A tall man, very shadowy and plain, came in with a tattered book in his hand. His long thin hair and plain wool robe were black. His small eyes were cheerful, but his thin mouth was colorless and belligerently set.

The boys all groaned.

High narrow windows were closed against the cooler night air.

In the canal below, men sang as they drove their long narrow gondolas, voices seeming to ring, to splash up the wails, delicate, sparkling, then dying away.

I ate the apple to the last juicy speck of it. I had eaten more in this day of fruit, meat, bread, sweets and candy than a human being could possibly eat. I wasn't human. I was a hungry boy.

The teacher snapped his fingers, then took from his belt a long switch and cracked it against his own leg. 'Come now,' he said to the boys.

I looked up as the Master appeared.

All the boys, big and tall, babyfied and manly, ran to him and embraced him and clung to his arms as he made his inspection of the painting they had done by the long day.

The teacher waited in silence, giving the Master a humble bow.

Through the galleries we walked, the entire company, the teacher trailing behind.

The Master held out his hands, and it was a privilege to feel the touch of his cold white fingers, a privilege to catch a part of his long thick trailing red sleeves.

'Come, Amadeo, come with us.'

I wanted one thing only and it came soon enough.

They were sent off with the man who was to read Cicero. The Master's firm hands with their flashing fingernails turned me and directed me to his private

58

rooms.

It was private here, the painted wooden doors at once bolted, the burning braziers scented with incense, perfumed smoke rising from the brass lamps. It was the soft pillows of the bed, a flower garden of stenciled and embroidered silk, floral satin, rich chenille, intricately patterned brocade. He pulled the scarlet bed curtains. The light made them transparent. Red and red and red. It was his color, he told me, as blue was to be mine.

In a universal tongue he wooed me, feeding me the images:

'Your brown eyes are amber when the fire catches them,' he whispered. 'Oh, but they are lustrous and dark, two glossy mirrors in which I see myself even as they keep their secrets, these dark portals of a rich soul.'

I was too lost in the frigid blue of his own eyes, and the smooth gleaming coral of his lips.

He lay with me, kissed me, pushing his fingers carefully and smoothly through my hair, never pulling a curl of it, and brought the shivers from my scalp and from between my legs. His thumbs, so hard and cold, stroked my cheeks, my lips, my jaw so as to make the flesh quicken. Turning my head from right to left, he pressed his half formed kisses with a dainty hunger to the inner shells of my ears.

I was too young for a wet pleasure.

I wonder if it was more what women feel. I thought it couldn't end. It became an agony of rapture, being caught in his hands, unable to escape, convulsing and twisting and feeling this ecstasy again and again and again.

He taught me words in the new language afterwards, the word for the cold hard tile on the floor which was Carrara marble, the word for the curtains which was spun silk, the names of the 'fishes' and 'turtles' and the

59

'elephants' embroidered onto the pillows, the word for the lion sewn in tapestry on the heavy coverlet itself.

As I listened, rapt, to all details both large and small, he told me the provenance of the pearls sewn into my tunic, of how they had come from the oysters of the sea. Boys had dived into the depths to bring these precious round white treasures up to the surface, carrying them in their very mouths. Emeralds came from mines within the earth. Men killed for them. And diamonds, ah, look at these diamonds. He took a ring from his finger and put it on mine, his fingertips stroking my finger gently as he made sure of the fit. Diamonds are the white light of God, he said. Diamonds are pure.

God. What is God! The shock went through my body. It seemed the scene about me would wither.

He watched me as he spoke, and it seemed now and then I heard him clearly, though he had not moved his lips or made a sound.

I grew agitated. God, don't let me think of God. Be my God.

'Give me your mouth, give me your arms,' I whispered. My hunger startled and delighted him.

He laughed softly as he answered me with more fragrant and harmless kisses. His warm breath came in a soft whistling flood against my groin.

'Amadeo, Amadeo, Amadeo,' he said.

'What does this name mean, Master?' I asked. 'Why do you give it to me?' I think I heard an old self in my voice, but maybe it was only this newborn princeling gilded and wrapped in fine goods that had chosen this soft respectful but nevertheless bold voice.

'Beloved of God,' he said.

Oh, I couldn't bear to hear this. God, the inescapable God. I was troubled, panic-stricken.

He took my outstretched hand and bent my finger to

point to a tiny winged infant etched in glittering beads on a worn square cushion that lay beside us. 'Amadeo,' he said, 'beloved of the God of love.'

He found the ticking watch in the heap of my clothes at bedside. He picked it up and smiled as he looked at it. He had not seen many of these at all. Most marvelous. They were expensive enough for Kings and Queens.

'You shall have everything you want,' he said.

'Why?'

Again came his laughter in answer.

'For reddish locks such as these,' he said caressing my hair, 'for eyes of the deepest and most sympathetic brown. For skin like the fresh cream of the milk in the morning; for lips indistinguishable from the petals of a rose.'

In the small hours, he told me tales of Eros and Aphrodite; he lulled me with the fantastic sorrow of Psyche, beloved by Eros and never allowed to see him by the day's light.

I walked beside him through chilly corridors, his fingers clasping my shoulders, as he showed me the fine white marble statues of his gods and goddesses, all lovers – Daphne, her graceful limbs turned into the branches of the laurel as the god Apollo desperately sought her; Leda helpless within the grip of the mighty swan.

He guided my hands over the marble curves, the sharply chiseled and highly polished faces, the taut calves of nubile legs, the ice-cold clefts of half-opened mouths. And then to his own face he lifted my fingers. He did seem the very living and breathing statue, more marvelously made than any other, and even as he lifted me with powerful hands, a great heat came out of him, a heat of sweet breath in sighs and murmured words.

By the end of the week, I couldn't even remember one word of my Mother Tongue.

In a storm of proffered adjectives I stood in the piazza and watched spellbound as the Great Council of Venice marched along the Molo, as the High Mass was sung from the altar of San Marco, as the ships moved out on the glassy waves of the Adriatic, as the brushes dipped to gather up their colors and mix them in the earthen pots – rose madder, vermilion, carmine, cerise, cerulean, turquoise, viridian, yellow ocher, burnt umber, quinacridone, citrine, sepia, Caput Mortuum Violet – oh, too lovely – and of a thick lacquer, the name Dragon's blood.

At dancing and fencing, I excelled. My favorite partner was Riccardo, and I fast realized I was close to this elder in all skills, even surpassing Albinus, who had held that place until I came, though now he showed me no ill will.

These boys were like my brothers to me.

They took me to the home of the slender and beautiful courtesan, Bianca Solderini, a lithesome and incomparable charmer, with Botticelli-style wavy locks and almond-shaped gray eyes and a generous and kindly wit. I was the fashion in her house whenever I wanted to be, among the young women and men there who spent hours reading poetry, talking of the foreign wars, which seemed endless, and of the latest painters and who would get what commission next.

Bianca had a small, childlike voice which matched her girlish face and tiny nose. Her mouth was a mere budding rose. But she was clever, and indomitable. She turned away possessive lovers coldly; she preferred that her house be full of people at all hours. Anyone in proper dress, or carrying a sword, was admitted automatically. Almost no one but those who wanted to own her were ever turned away.

Visitors from France and Germany were common at

the home of Bianca, and all there, both from afar and from home, were curious about our Master, Marius, a man of mystery, though we had been schooled never to answer idle questions about him, and could only smile when asked if he intended to marry, if he would paint this or that portrait, if he would be home on such and such a date for this person or that to call.

Sometimes I fell asleep on the pillows of the couch at Bianca's or even on one of the beds, listening to the hushed voices of the noblemen who came there, dreaming to the music which was always of the most lulling and soothing kind.

Now and then, on the most rare occasions, the Master himself appeared there to collect me and Riccardo, always causing a minor sensation in the portego, or main salon. He would never take a chair. He stood always with his hooded cloak over his head and shoulders. But he smiled graciously to all the entreaties put to him, and did sometimes offer a tiny portrait that he had done of Bianca.

I see these now, these many *tiny* portraits that he gave her over the years, each encrusted with jewels.

'You capture my likeness so keenly from memory,' she said as she went to kiss him. I saw the reserve with which he held her aloof from his cold hard chest and face, planting kisses on her cheeks that conveyed the spell of softness and sweetness which the real touch of him would have destroyed.

I read for hours with the aid of the teacher Leonardo of Padua, my voice perfectly in time with his as I grasped the scheme of Latin, then Italian, then back to Greek. I liked Aristotle as much as Plato or Plutarch or Livy or Virgil. The truth was, I didn't much comprehend any of them. I was doing as the Master directed, letting the knowledge accumulate in my mind.

I saw no reason to talk endlessly, as Aristotle did, about things that were made. The lives of the ancients that Plutarch told with such spirit made excellent stories. I wanted to know people of the now, however. I preferred to doze on Bianca's couch rather than argue about the merits of this or that painter. Besides, I knew my Master was the best.

This world was one of spacious rooms, decorated walls, generous fragrant light and a regular parade of high fashion, to which I grew accustomed completely, never seeing much of the pain and misery of the poor of the city at all. Even the books I read reflected this new realm in which I had been so securely fixed that nothing could take me back to the world of confusion and suffering that had gone before.

I learned to play little songs on the Virginal. I learned to strum the lute and to sing in a soft voice, though I would only sing sad songs. My Master loved these songs.

We made a choir now and then, all the boys together, and presented the Master with our own compositions and sometimes our own dances as well.

In the hot afternoon, we played cards when we were supposed to be napping. Riccardo and I slipped out to gamble in taverns. We drank too much once or twice. The Master knew it and put a stop to it at once. He was particularly horrified that I'd fallen drunk into the Grand Canal, necessitating a clumsy and hysterical rescue. I could have sworn he went pale at the account, that I saw the color dance back from his whitening cheeks.

He whipped Riccardo for it. I was full of shame. Riccardo took it like a soldier without cries or comment, standing still at a large fireplace in the library, his back turned to receive the blows on his legs. Afterwards, he knelt and kissed the Master's ring. I vowed I'd never get drunk again.

I got drunk the next day, but I had the sense to stagger into Bianca's house and climb under her bed, where I could fall asleep without risk. Before midnight the Master pulled me out. I thought, Now I'll get it. But he only put me to bed, where I fell asleep before I could apologize. When I woke once it was to see him at his writing desk, writing as swiftly as he could paint, in some great book which he always managed to hide before he left the house.

When others did sleep, including Riccardo, during the worst afternoons of summer, I ventured out and hired a gondola. I lay on my back in it staring skyward, as we floated down the canal and to the more turbulent breast of the gulf. I closed my eyes as we made our way back so that I might hear the smallest cries from the quiet siesta-time buildings, the lap of the rank waters on rotting foundations, the cry of seagulls overhead. I didn't mind the gnats or the smell of the canals.

One afternoon I didn't go home for work or lessons. I wandered into a tavern to listen to musicians and singers, and another time happened upon an open drama on a trestle stage in a square before a church. No one was angry with me for my comings and goings. Nothing was reported. There were no tests of my learning or anyone else's.

Sometimes I slept all day, or until I was curious. It was an extreme pleasure to wake up and find the Master at work, either in the studio, walking up and down the scaffolding as he painted his larger canvas, or just near me, at his table in the bedroom, writing away.

There was always food everywhere, glistening bunches of grapes, and ripe melons cut open for us, and delicious fine-grained bread with the freshest oil. I ate black olives, slices of pale soft cheese and fresh leeks from the roof garden. The milk came up cool in the silver pitchers.

The Master ate nothing. All knew this. The Master was always gone by day. The Master was never spoken of without reverence. The Master could read a boy's soul. The Master knew good from evil, and he knew deceit. The boys were good boys. There was some hushed mention now and then of bad boys who had been banished from the house almost at once. But no one ever spoke even in a trivial way about the Master. No one spoke about the fact that I slept in the Master's bed.

At noon each day, we dined together formally on roasted fowl, tender lamb, thick juicy slabs of beef.

Three and four teachers came at any one time to instruct the various small groups of apprentices. Some worked while others studied.

I could wander from the Latin class to the Greek class. I could leaf through the erotic sonnets and read what I could until Riccardo came to the rescue and drew a circle of laughter around his reading, for which the teachers had to wait.

In this leniency I prospered. I learnt quickly, and could answer all the Master's casual questions, offering thoughtful questions of my own.

The Master painted four out of the seven nights a week, and usually from after midnight until his disappearance at dawn. Nothing interrupted him on these nights.

He climbed the scaffold with amazing ease, rather like a great white monkey, and, letting his scarlet cloak drop carelessly, he snatched up the brush from the boy who held it for him and painted in such a fury that the paint splattered on all of us as we watched aghast. Under his genius whole landscapes came to life within hours; gatherings of people were drawn with the greatest detail.

He hummed aloud as he worked; he announced the names of the great writers or heroes as he painted their portraits from his memory or his imagination. He drew our attention to his colors, the lines he chose, the tricks with perspective that plunged his groupings of palpable and enthusiastic subjects into real gardens, rooms, palaces, halls.

Only the fill-in work was left to the boys to do by morning – the coloring of drapery, the tinting of wings, the broad spaces of flesh to which the Master would come again to add the modeling while the oily paint was still mobile, the shining flooring of sometime palaces which after his final touches looked like real marble receding beneath the flushed chubby feet of his philosophers and saints.

The work drew us naturally, spontaneously. There were dozens of unfinished canvases and walls within the palazzo, all so lifelike they seemed portals to another world.

Gaetano, one of the youngest of us, was the most gifted. But any of the boys, except me, could match the apprentice painters of any man's workshop, even the boys of Bellini.

Sometimes there was a receiving day. Bianca was then jubilant as she would receive for the Master, and came with her servants to be lady of the house. Men and women from the finest houses in Venice came to view the Master's paintings. People were astonished at his powers. Only from listening to them on these days did I realize my Master sold almost nothing, but filled his palazzo with his own work, and that he had his own versions of most famous subjects, from the school of Aristotle to the Crucifixion of Christ. Christ. This was the curly-haired, ruddy, muscular and human-looking Christ, their Christ.

The Christ who was like Cupid or Zeus.

I didn't mind that I couldn't paint as well as Riccardo and the others, that I was half the time content to hold the pots for them, to wash the brushes, to wipe clean the mistakes that had to be corrected. I did not want to paint. I did not want to. I could feel my hands cramp at the thought of it, and there would come a sickness in my belly when I thought of it.

I preferred the conversation, the jokes, the speculation as to why our fabulous Master took no commissions, though letters came to him daily inviting him to compete for this or that mural to be painted in the Ducal Palace or in one or another of the thousand churches of the isle.

I watched the color spreading out by the hour. I breathed in the fragrance of varnishes, the pigments, the oils.

Now and then a stuporous anger overcame me, but not at my lack of skill.

Something else tormented me, something to do with the humid, tempestuous postures of the painted figures, with their glistening pink cheeks and the boiling sweep of cloudy sky behind them, or the fleecy branches of the dark trees.

It seemed madness, this, this unbridled depiction of nature. My head hurting, I walked alone and briskly along the quays until I found an old church, and a gilded altar with stiff, narrow-eyed saints, dark and drawn and rigid: the legacy of Byzantium, as I had seen it in San Marco on my first day. My soul hurt and hurt and hurt as I gazed worshipfully at these old proprieties. I cursed when my new friends found me. I knelt, stubborn, refusing to show that I knew they were there. I covered my ears to shut out the laughter of my new friends. How could they laugh in the hollow of the church where the tortured Christ bled tears like black beetles leaping from His fading hands and feet?

Now and then I fell asleep before antique altars. I had escaped my companions. I was solitary and happy on the damp cold stones. I fancied I could hear the water beneath the floor.

I took a gondola to Torcello and there sought out the great old Cathedral of Santa Maria Assunta, famous for its mosaics which some said were as splendid in the antique way as the mosaics of San Marco. I crept about under the low arches, looking at the ancient gold Iconostasis and the mosaics of the apse. High above, in the back curve of the apse there stood the great Virgin, the Theotokos, the bearer of God. Her face was austere, almost sour. A tear glistened on her left cheek. In her hands she held the infant Jesus, but also a napkin, the token of the Mater Dolorosa.

I understood these images, even as they froze my soul. My head swam and the heat of the island and the quiet Cathedral made me sick in my stomach. But I stayed there. I drifted about the Iconostasis and prayed.

I thought sure no one could find me here. Towards dusk, I became truly sick. I knew I had a fever, but I sought a corner of the church and took comfort in only the cold of the stone floor against my face and my outstretched hands. Before me, if I raised my head I could see terrifying scenes of the Last Judgment, of souls condemned to Hell. I deserve this pain, I thought.

The Master came for me. I don't remember the journey back to the palazzo. It seemed that somehow in a matter of moments he had put me in bed. The boys bathed my forehead with cool cloths. I was made to drink water. Someone said that I had 'the fever' and someone else said, 'Be quiet.'

The Master kept watch with me. I had bad dreams

which I couldn't bring with me into my waking state. Before dawn, the Master kissed me and held me close to him. I had never loved so much the chill hardness of his body as I did in this fever, wrapping my arms around him, pushing my cheek against his.

He gave me something hot and spiced to drink from a warm cup. And then he kissed me, and again came the cup. My body was filled with a healing fire.

But by the time he returned that night my fever was bad again. I did not dream so much as I wandered, half asleep, half awake, through terrible dark corridors unable to find a place that was either warm or clean. There was dirt beneath my fingernails. At one point, I saw a shovel moving, and saw the dirt, and feared the dirt would cover me, and I started to cry.

Riccardo kept watch, holding my hand, telling me it would soon be nightfall, and that the Master would surely come.

'Amadeo,' the Master said. He hoisted me up as if I were truly still a small child.

Too many questions formed in my mind. Would I die? Where was the Master taking me now? I was wrapped in velvet and furs and he carried me, but how?

We were in a church in Venice, amid new paintings of our time. The requisite candles burned. Men prayed. He turned me in his arms and told me to look up at the giant altarpiece before me.

Squinting, my eyes hurting, I obeyed him and saw the Virgin on high being crowned by her beloved Son, Christ the King.

'Look at the sweetness of her face, the natural expression to her,' the Master whispered. 'She sits there as one might sit here in the church. And the angels, look at them, the happy boys clustered around the columns beneath her. Look at the serenity and the gentleness of

70

their smiles. This is Heaven, Amadeo. This is goodness.'

My sleepy eyes moved over the high painting. 'See the Apostle who whispers so naturally to the one beside him, as men might at such a ceremony. See above, God the Father, gazing down so contentedly on all.'

I tried to form questions, to say it was not possible, this combination of the fleshly and the beatific, but I couldn't find eloquent words. The nakedness of the boy angels was enchanting and innocent, but I could not believe it. It was a lie of Venice, a lie of the West, a lie of the Devil himself.

'Amadeo,' he continued, 'there is no good that is founded in suffering and cruelty; there is no good that must root itself in the privation of little children. Amadeo, out of the love of God grows beauty everywhere. Look at these colors; these are the colors created by God.'

Secure in his arms, my feet dangling, my arms about his neck, I let the details of the immense altarpiece sink into my consciousness. I went back and forth, back and forth, over those small touches I loved.

I raised my finger to point. The lion there, just sitting so calmly at the feet of St. Mark, and look, the pages of St. Mark's book, the pages are actually in motion as he turns them. And the lion is tame and gentle as a friendly fireside dog.

'This is Heaven, Amadeo,' he said to me. 'Whatever the past has hammered into your soul, let it go.'

I smiled, and slowly, gazing up at the saints, the rows and rows of saints, I began to laugh softly and confidentially in the Master's ear.

'They're all talking, murmuring, talking amongst themselves as if they were the Venetian Senators.'

I heard his low, subdued laughter in answer. 'Oh, I think the Senators are more decorous, Amadeo. I've never seen them in such informality, but this is Heaven, as I said.'

'Ah, Master, look there. A saint holds an ikon, a beautiful ikon. Master, I have to tell you –.' I broke off. The fever rose and the sweat broke out on me. My eyes felt hot, and I couldn't see. 'Master,' I said. 'I am in the wild lands. I'm running. I have to put it in the trees.' How could he know what I meant, that I spoke of that long-ago desperate flight out of coherent recollection and through the wild grasses with the sacred bundle in my keep, the bundle that had to be unwrapped and placed in the trees. 'Look, the ikon.'

Honey filled me. It was thick and sweet. It came from a cold fount, but it didn't matter. I knew this fount. My body was like a goblet stirred so that all that was bitter dissolved in the fluids of it, dissolved in a vortex to leave only honey and a dreamy warmth.

When I opened my eyes, I was in our bed. I was cool all over. The fever was gone. I turned over and pulled myself up.

My Master sat at his desk. He was reading over what he had apparently just written. He had tied back his blond hair with a bit of cord. His face was very beautiful, unveiled as it were, with its chiseled cheekbones and smooth narrow nose. He looked at me, and his mouth worked the miracle of the ordinary smile.

'Don't chase these memories,' he said. He said it as if we'd been talking all the while that I slept. 'Don't go to the church of Torcello to find them. Don't go to the mosaics of San Marco. In time all these harmful things will come back.'

'I'm afraid to remember,' I said.

'I know,' he answered.

'How can you know?' I asked him. 'I have it in my heart. It's mine alone, this pain.' I was sorry for sounding so bold, but whatever my guilt, the boldness came more and more often.

'Do you really doubt me?' he asked.

'Your endowments are beyond measure. We all know it, and we never speak of it, and you and I never speak of it.'

'So why then don't you put your faith in me instead of things you only half recall?'

He got up from the desk and came to the bed.

'Come,' he said. 'Your fever's broken. Come with me.'

He took me into one of the many libraries of the palazzo, messy rooms in which the manuscripts lay helter-skelter, and the books in stacks. Seldom if ever did he work in these rooms. He threw his purchases there to be cataloged by the boys, taking what he needed back to the writing desk in our room.

He moved among the shelves now until he found a portfolio, a big flopping thing of old yellowed leather, frayed at the edges. His white fingers smoothed a large page of vellum. He laid it down on the oak study table for me to see.

A painting, antique.

I saw there drawn a great church of gilded domes, so beautiful, so majestic. Letters were blazoned there. I knew these letters. But I couldn't make the words come to my mind or my tongue.

'Kiev Rus,' he said. *Kiev Rus.*

An unsupportable horror came over me. Before I could stop myself, I said, 'It's ruined, burnt. There is no such place. It's not alive like Venice. It's ruined, and all is cold, and filthy and desperate. Yes, that's the very word.' I was dizzy. I felt I saw an escape from desolation, only it was cold and dark, this escape, and it led by twists and turns into a world of eternal darkness where the raw earth gave the only smell to one's hands, one's skin, one's clothes.

I pulled back and ran from the Master.

I ran the full length of the palazzo.

I ran down the stairs, and through the dark lower rooms that opened on the canal. When I came back, I found him alone in the bedroom. He was reading as always. He had his favorite book of late, *The Consolation of Philosophy* by Boethius, and he looked up from it patiently when I came in.

I stood thinking of my painful memories.

I couldn't catch them. So be it. They scurried into the nothingness rather like the leaves in the alleyways, the leaves that sometimes tumble down and down the stained green walls from the little gardens whipped in the wind up there on the rooftops.

'I don't want to,' I said again.

There was but one Living Lord. My Master.

'Some day it will all come clear to you, when you have the strength to use it,' he said. He shut his book. 'For now, let me comfort you.'

Ah, yes, I was all too ready for this.

Oh, how long the days could be without him. By nightfall, I clenched my fists as the candles were lighted.

There came nights when he didn't appear at all. The boys said he had gone on most important errands. The house must run as if he were there.

I slept in his empty bed, and no one questioned me. I searched the house for any personal trace of him. Questions plagued me. I feared he would never come back.

But he always came back.

When he came up the stairs, I flew into his embrace. He caught me, held me, kissed me and only then let me fall gently against his hard chest. My weight was nothing to him, though I seemed to grow taller and heavier every day.

I would never be anything but the seventeen-year-old boy you see now, but how could a man so slight as he heft me with such ease? I am not a waif and never have been. I am a strong child.

I liked it best – if I had to share with the others – when he read to us aloud.

Surrounding himself with candelabra, he spoke in a hushed and sympathetic voice. He read *The Divine Comedy* by Dante, the *Decameron* by Boccaccio, or in French *The Romance of the Rose* or the poems of François Villon. He spoke of the new languages we must understand as well as we understood Greek and Latin. He warned us that literature would no longer be confined to the classic works.

We sat in silence around him, on pillows, or on the naked tile. Some of us stood near him. Others rested back on their heels.

Sometimes Riccardo played the lute for us and sang those melodies he'd learned from his teacher, or even the wilder ribald tunes he'd picked up in the streets. He sang mournfully of love and made us weep over it. The Master watched him with loving eyes.

I had no jealousy. I alone shared the Master's bed.

Sometimes, he even had Riccardo sit outside the bedroom door and play for us. Obedient Riccardo never asked to come inside.

My heart raced as the curtains closed around us. The Master pulled open my tunic, sometimes even ripping it playfully, as if it were no more than a castoff thing.

I sank into the satin quilted down beneath him; I opened my legs and let my knees caress him, numbed and vibrating from the graze of his knuckles against my lips.

Once I lay half asleep. The air was rosy and golden. The place was warm. I felt his lips on mine, and his cold tongue move serpentlike into my mouth. A liquid filled my mouth, a rich and burning nectar, a potion so exquisite that I felt it roll through my body to the very tips of my outstretched fingers. I felt it descend through my torso and into the most private part of me. I burned. I burned.

'Master,' I whispered. 'What is this trick now which is sweeter than kissing?'

He laid his head down on the pillow. He turned away.

'Give it to me again, Master,' I said.

He did, but only when he chose, in droplets, and with red tears he now and then let me lick from his eyes.

I think a whole year passed before I came home one

evening, flushed from the winter air, dressed in my very finest dark blue for him, with sky blue stockings and the most expensive gold enameled slippers that I could find in all the world, a year before I came in that night and threw my book into the corner of the bedroom with a great world-weary gesture, putting my hands on my hips and glaring at him as he sat in his high thick arch-back chair looking at the coals in the brazier, putting his hands over them, watching the flames.

'Well, now,' I said cockily and with my head back, a very man of the world, a sophisticated Venetian, a prince in the Marketplace with an entire court of merchants to wait on him, a scholar who had read too much.

'Well, now,' I said. 'There's a great mystery here and you know it. It's time you told me.'

'What?' he asked obligingly enough.

'Why do you never . . . Why do you never feel anything! Why do you handle me as if I were a poppet? Why do you never . . . ?'

For the first time ever I saw his face redden; I saw his eyes gloss and narrow and then widen with reddish tears.

'Master, you frighten me,' I whispered.

'What is it you want me to feel, Amadeo?' he said.

'You're like an angel, a statue,' I said, only now I was chastened and trembling. 'Master, you play with me and I'm the toy that feels all things.' I drew nearer. I touched his shirt, sought to unlace it. 'Let me –.'

He took my hand. He took my fingers and put them to his lips, and drew my fingers inside his mouth, caressing them with his tongue. His eyes moved so that he was looking up at me.

Quite enough, said his eyes. I feel quite enough.

'I'd give you anything,' I said imploringly. I put my

hand between his legs. Oh, he was wonderfully hard. That was not uncommon, but he must let me take him further; he must trust me.

'Amadeo,' he said.

With his unaccountable strength he drew me back with him to the bed. You could hardly say he'd risen from the chair. It seemed we were there one moment and now fallen amongst our familiar pillows. I blinked. It seemed the curtains closed around us without his touching them, some trick of the breeze from the open windows. Yes, listen to the voices from the canal below. How voices sing out and up the walls in Venice, the city of palaces.

'Amadeo,' he said, his lips on my throat as they'd come a thousand times, only this time there came a sting, sharp, swift and gone. A thread stitched into my heart was jerked all of a sudden. I had become the thing between my legs, and was nothing but that. His mouth nestled against me, and again that thread snapped and again.

I dreamed. I think I saw another place. I think I saw the revelations of my sleeping hours which never stayed for me when I awoke. I think I trod a road into those bursting fantasies I knew in sleep and sleep alone.

This is what I want of you.

'And you must have it,' I said, words propelled to the near forgotten present as I floated against him, feeling him tremble, feeling him thrill to it, feeling him shudder, feeling him whip these threads from inside me, quickening my heart and making me nearly cry out, feeling him love it, and stiffen his back and let his fingers tremble and dance as he writhed against me. Drink it, drink it, drink it.

He broke loose and lay to the side.

I smiled as I lay with closed eyes. I felt my lips. I felt

the barest bit of that nectar still gathered on my lower lip, and my tongue took it up and I dreamed.

His breathing was heavy and he was somber. He shivered still, and when his hand found me it was unsteady.

'Ah,' I said smiling still, and kissing his shoulder.

'I hurt you!' he said.

'No, no, not at all, sweet Master,' I answered. 'But I hurt you! I have you, now!'

'Amadeo, you play the devil.'

'Don't you want me to, Master? Didn't you like it? You took my blood and it made you my slave!'

He laughed. 'So that's the twist you put on it, isn't it?'

'Hmmm. Love me. What does it matter?' I asked.

'Never tell the others,' he said. There was no fear or weakness or shame in it.

I turned over and drew up on my elbows and looked at him, at his quiet profile turned away from me.

'What would they do?'

'Nothing,' he answered. 'It's what they would think and feel that matters. And I have no time or place for it.' He looked at me. 'Be merciful and wise, Amadeo.'

For a long time I said nothing. I merely looked at him. Only gradually did I realize I was frightened. For one moment it seemed that fear would obliterate the warmth of the moment, the soft glory of the radiant light swelling in the curtains, of the polished planes of his ivory face, the sweetness of his smile. Then some higher graver concern overruled the fear.

'You're not my slave at all, are you?' I whispered.

'Yes,' he said, almost laughing again. 'I am, if you must know.'

'What happened, what did you do, what was it that –.'

He laid his finger on my lips.

'Do you think me like other men?' he asked.

'No,' I said, but the fear rose in the word and strangled out the wound. I tried to stop myself, but before I could I embraced him and tried to push my face into his neck. He was too hard for such things, though he cradled my head and kissed the top of it, though he gathered back my hair, and let his thumb sink into my cheek.

'Some day I want you to leave here,' he said. 'I want you to go. You'll take wealth with you and all the learning I've been able to give you. You'll take your grace with you, and all the many arts you've mastered, that you can paint, that you can play any music I ask of you – that you can do already – that you can so exquisitely dance. You'll take these accomplishments and you'll go out in search of those precious things that you want –.'

'I want nothing but you.'

'– and when you think back on this time, when in half-sleep at night you remember me as your eyes close on your pillow, these moments of ours will seem corrupt and most strange. They'll seem like sorcery and the antics of the mad, and this warm place might become the lost chamber of dark secrets and this might bring you pain.'

'I won't go.'

'Remember then that it was love,' he said. 'That this indeed was the school of love in which you healed your wounds, in which you learnt to speak again, aye, even to sing, and in which you were born out of the broken child as if he were no more than an eggshell, and you the angel, ascending out of him with widening, strengthening wings.'

'And what if I never go of my own free will? Will you pitch me from some window so that I must fly or fall? Will you bolt all shutters after me? You had better,

80

because I'll knock and knock and knock until I fall down dead. I'll have no wings that take me away from you.'

He made a study of me for the longest time. I never had such an unbroken feast on his eyes myself, and had never been let to touch his mouth with my prying fingers for such a spell.

Finally he rose up next to me and pressed me gently down. His lips, always softly pink like the inner petals of blushing white roses, turned slowly red as I watched. It was a gleaming seam of red that ran between his lips and then flowed through all the fine lines of which his lips were made, perfectly coloring them, as wine might do, only it was so brilliant, this fluid, that his lips shimmered, and when he parted them, the red burst as if it were a curled tongue.

My head was lifted. I caught it with my own mouth.

The world moved out from under me. I listed and drifted, and my eyes opened and saw nothing as he shut his mouth over mine.

'Master, I die from this!' I whispered. I tossed under him, seeking to find some firm place in this dreamy intoxicating void. My body churned and rolled with pleasure, my limbs tightening then floating, my whole body issuing from him, from his lips, through my lips, my body his very breath and his sigh.

There came the sting, there came the blade, tiny and sharp beyond measure, puncturing my soul. I twisted on it as if I'd been skewered. Oh, this could teach the gods of love what love was. This was my deliverance if I could but survive.

Blind and shaking I was wed to him. I felt his hand cover my mouth, and only then heard my cries as they were muffled away.

I wrapped my hand around his neck, pressing him against my throat all the harder, 'Do it, do it, do it, do it!'

When I awoke, it was day.

He was long gone, as was his infallible custom. I lay alone. The boys had not yet come.

I climbed out of bed and went to the high narrow window, the kind of window which is everywhere in Venice, locking out the fierce heat of summer and sealing off the cold Adriatic winds when they inevitably come.

I unbolted the thick glass panels and looked out on the walls across from my safe place as I had often done.

A common serving woman shook her cloth mop from a far balcony above. Across the canal, I watched her. Her face seemed livid and crawling, as if some tiny species of life covered her, some rampage of ants. She didn't know! I laid my hands on the sill and looked ever more keenly. It was only the life inside her, the workings of the flesh in her that made the mask of her face seem to move.

But horrid her hands seemed, knuckled and swollen, and the dust from her broom engraving every line.

I shook my head. She was too far from me for these observations.

In a faraway room, the boys talked. Time for work. Time to get up, even in the palazzo of the night Lord who never checks or prods by day. Too far away for me to hear them.

And this velvet now, this curtain made of the Master's favorite fabric, this was like fur to my touch, not velvet, I could see each tiny fiber! I dropped it. I went for the looking glass.

The house had dozens of them, great ornate mirrors, all with fancified frames and most replete with tiny cherubs. I found the tall mirror in the anteroom, the alcove behind warped yet beautifully painted doors where I kept my clothes.

82

The light of the window followed me. I saw myself. But I was not a seething corrupt mass, such as this woman had seemed. My face was baby smooth and starkly white.

'I want it!' I whispered. I knew.

'No,' he told me.

This is when he came that night. I ranted and paced and cried out to him.

He didn't give me long explanations, no sorcery or science, either of which would have been so easy for him. He told me only I was a child still, and there were things to be savored which would be lost forever.

I cried. I didn't want to work or paint or study or do anything in the world.

'It's lost its savor for a little while,' he said patiently. 'But you'd be surprised.'

'At what?'

'At how much you'll lament it when it's gone utterly, when you are perfect and unchangeable like me, and all those human mistakes can be triumphantly supplanted by a new and more stunning series of failures. Don't ask for this, not again.'

I would have died then, curled up, black and furious and too bitter for words.

But he wasn't finished.

'Amadeo,' he said, his voice thick with sorrow. 'Say nothing. You don't have to. I'll give it to you quickly enough when I think the time has come.'

At that I went to him, running, childlike, flinging myself at his neck, kissing his icy cheek a thousand times despite his mock-disdainful smile.

At last his hands became like iron. There was to be no blood play this night. I must study. I must make up the lessons I had scorned by day.

He had to see to his apprentices, to his tasks, to the

giant canvas on which he'd been working, and I did as he said.

But well before morning, I saw him change. The others had long gone to bed. I was turning the pages of the book obediently when I saw him staring, beastlike, from his chair, as if some ravener had come into him and banished all his civilized faculties and left him thus, hungry, with glazed eyes and reddening mouth, the glittering blood finding its myriad little paths over the silky margin of his lips.

He rose, a drugged thing, and came towards me with a rhythm of movements that was alien and struck the coldest terror in my heart.

His fingers flashed, closed, beckoned.

I ran to him. He lifted me in both hands, clutching my arms ever so gently, and tucked his face against my neck. From the soles of my feet up my back through my arms and my neck and scalp, I felt it.

Where he flung me I didn't know. Was it our bed or some hasty cushions he found in another closer salon? 'Give it to me,' I said sleepily, and when it came into my mouth, I was gone.

He said that I must go to the brothels, learn what it meant to couple properly – not merely in play, as we did among the boys.

Venice had many such places, very well run and devoted to pleasure in the most luxurious environment. It was firmly held that such pleasures were little more than a venial sin in the eyes of the Christ, and the young men of fashion frequented these establishments without hiding it.

I knew of a house of particularly exquisite and skilled women, where there were tall, buxom, very pale-eyed beauties from the North of Europe, some whose blond hair was almost white, deemed to be somewhat different from the shorter Italian women's which we saw every day. I don't know that difference was such a high priority with me, as I'd been somewhat dazzled by the beauty of Italian boys and women since I had come. Swan-necked Venetian girls in their fancy cushion-head dresses with abundant translucent veils were very nearly irresistible to me. But then the brothel had all kinds of women, and the name of the game was to mount as many as I could.

My Master took me to this place, paid for me, a fortune in ducats, and told the buxom enchanting mistress that he would collect me in a matter of days.

Days!

I was pale with jealousy and on fire with curiosity, as I watched him take his leave – the usual regal figure in his familiar crimson robes, climbing into the gondola and giving me his clever wink as the boat took him away.

I spent three days, as it turned out, in the house of the most voluptuous available maidens in Venice, sleeping late in the morning, comparing olive skin to blond skin and indulging myself in leisurely examinations of the nether hair of all beauties, distinguishing the more silken from the wiry and more tightly curled.

I learned little niceties of pleasure, such as how sweet it was to have one's nipples bitten (lightly, and these weren't vampires) and to have the hair under one's arms, of which I had just a little, tugged affectionately at the appropriate moments. Golden honey was painted on my nether parts only to be licked away by giggling angels.

There were other more intimate tricks, of course, including bestial acts which were strictly speaking crimes but which were in this house merely various extra accouterments to overall wholesome and tanta-lizing feasts. All was done with grace, the steamy hot perfumed baths came frequently in large deep wooden tubs, flowers floating on the surface of the rose-tinted water, and I lay back sometimes at the mercy of a bevy of soft-voiced women who cooed over me like birds in the eaves as they licked me like so many kittens and combed my hair around their fingers to make curls.

I was the little Ganymede of Zeus, an angel tumbled out of Botticelli's more ribald paintings (many of which by the way were in this brothel, having been rescued from the Bonfires of the Vanities erected in Florence by the adamant reformer Savonarola, who had urged the great Botticelli to just . . . burn up his beautiful work!), a little cherub fallen off the ceiling of a Cathedral, a Venetian prince (of which there were none in the Republic technically) delivered into their hands by his enemies to be rendered helpless with desire.

I grew hotter in desire. If one had to be human for the

rest of one's life, this was great fun, tumbling among Turkish cushions with nymphs such as most men only glimpse through magical forests in their dreams. Each soft and downy cleft was a new and exotic envelope for my romping spirit.

The wine was delicious and the food quite marvelous, including sugared and spiced dishes from the Arabs, and being altogether more extravagant and more exotic than the fare served by my Master at home.

(When I told him, he hired four new chefs.)

I wasn't awake, apparently, when my Master arrived to collect me, and I was spirited home by him, in his mysterious and infallible manner, and found myself again in my bed.

I knew I wanted only him when my eyes opened. And it seemed the fleshy repasts of the last few days had only made me more hungry, more inflamed and more eager to see if his enchanted white body would respond to the more tender tricks I'd learned. I threw myself on him when he finally came in behind the curtains, and I unloosed his shirt and sucked his nipples, discovering that for all their disturbing whiteness and coldness they were soft and obviously intimately connected in a seemingly natural way to the root of his desires.

He lay there, graceful and quiet, letting me play with him as my women teachers had played with me. When he finally gave me the blood kisses, all memories of human contact were obliterated, and I lay helpless as always in his arms. It seemed our world then was not merely one of the flesh, but of a mutual spell to which all natural laws gave way.

Towards morning on the second night, I sought him out where he was painting by himself in the studio, the scattered apprentices fallen asleep like the unfaithful Apostles in Gethsemane.

He wouldn't stop for my questions. I stood behind him and locked my arms around him and, climbing on tiptoe, I whispered my questions in his ear.

'Tell me, Master, you must, how did you gain this magic blood inside you?' I bit his earlobes and ran my hands through his hair. He wouldn't stop painting. 'Were you born into this state, am I so wrong about this as to suppose that you were transformed . . .'

'Stop it, Amadeo,' he whispered, and continued to paint. He worked furiously on the face of Aristotle, the bearded, balding elder of his great painting, *The Academy*.

'Is there ever a loneliness in you, Master, that pushes you to tell someone, anyone, to have a friend of your own mettle, to confide your heart to one who can comprehend?'

He turned, startled for once by my questions.

'And you, spoiled little angel,' he said, lowering his voice to maintain its gentleness, 'you think you can be that friend? You're an innocent! You'll be an innocent all of your days. You have the heart of an innocent. You refuse to accept truth that doesn't correspond with some deep raging faith in you which makes you ever the little monk, the acolyte—.'

I stepped backwards, as angry as I'd ever been with him. 'No, I won't be such!' I declared. 'I'm a man already in the guise of a boy, and you know it. Who else dreams of what you are, and the alchemy of your powers? I wish I could drain a cupful of your blood from you and study it as the doctors might and determine what is its makeup and how it differs from the fluid that runs through my veins! I am your pupil, yes, your student, yes, but to be that, I must be a man. When would you tolerate innocence? When we bed together, you call that innocence? I am a man.'

He burst into the most amazed laughter. It was a treat to see him so surprised.

'Tell me your secret, Sir,' I said. I put my arms around his neck and laid my head on his shoulder. 'Was there a Mother as white and strong as you were who brought you forth, the God-Bearer, from her celestial womb?'

He took my arms and moved me back away from him, so that he could kiss me, and his mouth was insistent and frightening to me for a moment. Then it moved over my throat, sucking at my flesh and causing me to become weak and, with all my heart, willing to be anything he wished.

'Of the moon and the stars, yes, I'm made, of that sovereign whiteness which is the substance of clouds and innocence alike,' he said. 'But no Mother gave birth to me, you know that's so; I was a man once, a man moving on in his years. Look –.' He lifted my face with both hands and made me study his face. 'You see here remnants of the lines of age which once marked me, here at the corners of my eyes.'

'Merely nothing, Sir,' I whispered, thinking to console him if this imperfection troubled him. He shone in his brilliance, his polished smoothness. The simplest expressions flashed in his face in luminescent heat.

Imagine a figure of ice, as perfectly made as Pygmalion's Galatea, thrown into the fire, and sizzling, and melting, and yet the features all wondrously intact still . . . well, such was my Master when human emotions infected him, as they did now.

He crushed my arms deliciously and kissed me again.

'Little man, manikin, elf,' he whispered. 'Would you be so for eternity? Haven't you lain with me often enough to know what I can and cannot enjoy?'

I won him over, captive to me, for the last hour before he was off.

But the next night he dispatched me to a more clandestine and even more luxurious house of pleasure, a house which kept for the passions of others only young boys.

It was got up in Eastern style, and I think it blended the luxuries of Egypt with those of Babylon, its small cells made up of golden latticework, and colonnettes of brass studded with lapis lazuli holding up the salmon-colored drapery of the ceilings over tasseled couches of gilt wood and damask-covered down. Incense made the air heavy, and the lights were soothingly low.

The naked boys, well fed, nubile, smooth and rounded of limb, were eager, strong, tenacious, and brought to the games their own rampant male desires.

It seemed my soul was a pendulum that swung between the hearty pleasure of conquest and the swooning surrender to stronger limbs, and stronger wills, and stronger hands that tossed me tenderly about.

Captive between two skilled and willful lovers, I was pierced and suckled, pummeled and emptied until I slept as soundly as ever I had without the Master's magic at home.

It was only the beginning.

Sometime in my drunken sleep, I woke to find myself surrounded by beings that seemed neither male nor female. Only two of them were eunuchs, cut with such skill they could raise their trusty weapons as well as any boy. The others merely shared the taste of their companions for paint. All had eyes lined in black and shaded in purple, with lashes curled and glazed to give their expressions an eerie fathomless aloofness. Their rouged lips seemed tougher than those of women and more demanding, pushing at me in their kisses as if the male element which had given them muscles and hard organs had given them as well a virility to their very mouths.

They had the smiles of angels. Gold rings decorated their nipples. Their nether hair was powdered with gold.

I made no protest when they overcame me. I feared no extreme, and even let them bind my wrists and ankles to the bed, so they could better work their craft. It was impossible to fear them. I was crucified with pleasure. Their insistent fingers would not even allow me to close my eyes. They stroked my lids, they forced me to look. They brought soft thick brushes down over my limbs. They rubbed oils into all my skin. They sucked from me, as if it were nectar, the fiery sap I gave forth, over and over, until I cried out vainly that I could give no more. A count was kept of my 'little deaths' with which to taunt me playfully, and I was turned over and cuffed and pinioned as I tumbled down into rapturous sleep.

When I awoke I knew no time or worry. The thick smoke of a pipe rose into my nostrils. I took it and sucked on it, savoring the dark familiar smell of hemp.

I stayed there for four nights.

Again, I was delivered.

This time I found myself, groggy and in dishabille, barely covered by a thin torn cream-colored silk shirt. I lay on a couch brought from the very brothel, but this was my Master's studio, and there he sat, not far away, painting my picture obviously, at a small easel from which he took his eyes only to dart glances at me.

I asked the time of day and what night it was. He didn't answer.

'And so you're angry that I enjoyed it?' I asked.

'I told you to lie still,' he said.

I lay back, cold all over, and hurt suddenly, lonely perhaps, and wanting like a child to hide in his arms.

Morning came and he left me, having said nothing

else. The painting was a gleaming masterpiece of the obscene. I was in my sleeping posture cast down on a riverbank, a fawn of sorts, over which a tall shepherd, the Master himself, in priestly robes stood watch. The woods around us were thick and richly realized with the peeling tree trunks and their clustered dusty leaves. The water of the stream seemed wet to the touch, so clever was the realism of it, and my own figure appeared guileless and lost in sleep, my mouth half-open in a natural way, my brow obviously troubled by uneasy dreams.

I threw it on the floor, in a rage, meaning to smear it.

Why had he said nothing? Why did he force me to these lessons which drove us apart? Why his anger at me for merely doing what he had told me? I wondered if the brothels had been a test of my innocence, and his admonitions to me to enjoy all of it had been lies.

I sat at his desk, picked up his pen and scribbled a message to him.

You are the Master. You should know all things. It's unsupportable to be Mastered by one who cannot do it. Make clear the way, shepherd, or lay down your staff.

The fact was, I was wrung out from the pleasure, from the drink, from the distortion of my senses, and lonely just to be with him and for his guidance and his kindness and his reassurance that I was his.

But he was gone.

I went out roaming. I spent all day in the taverns, drinking, playing cards, deliberately enticing the pretty girls who were fair game, to keep them at my side as I played the various games of chance.

Then when night came, I let myself be seduced, ho-

hum, by a drunken Englishman, a fair freckle-skinned
noble of the oldest French and English titles, of which
this one was the Earl of Harlech, who was traveling in
Italy to see the great wonders and utterly intoxicated
with its many delights, including buggery in a strange
land.

Naturally, he found me a beautiful boy. Didn't everyone? He was not at all ugly himself. Even his pale
freckles had a kind of prettiness to them, especially given
his outrageous copper hair.

Taking me back to his rooms in an overstuffed and
beautiful palazzo, he made love to me. It was not all
bad. I liked his innocence and his clumsiness. His light
round blue eyes were a marvel; he had wondrously thick
and muscular arms and a pampered but deliciously
rough-pointed orange beard.

He wrote poems to me in Latin and in French, and
recited them to me with great charm. After an hour or
two of playing the vanquishing brute, he had let on that
he wanted to be covered by me. And this I had very
much enjoyed. We played it that way after that, my
being the conquering soldier and he the victim on the
battlefield, and sometimes I whipped him lightly with a
doubled-up leather belt before I took him, which sent us
both into a tidy froth.

From time to time, he implored me to confess who I
really was and where he might afterwards find me,
which of course I wouldn't.

I stayed there for three nights with him, talking about
the mysterious islands of England with him, and reading
Italian poetry aloud to him, and even sometimes playing
the mandolin for him and singing any number of the
soft love songs I knew.

He taught me a great deal of rank gutter-tramp
English, and wanted to take me home. He had to regain

his wits, he said; he had to return to his duties, his estates, his hateful wicked adulterous Scottish wife whose father was an assassin, and his innocent little child whose paternity he was most certain of, due to its orange curly hair so like his own.

He would keep me in London in a splendid house he had there, a present from His Majesty King Henry VII. He could not now live without me, the Harlechs to a man had to have what they must have, and there was nothing for me to do but yield to him. If I was the son of a formidable nobleman I should confess it, and this obstacle would be dealt with. Did I hate my Father, perchance? His was a scoundrel. All the Harlechs were scoundrels and had been since the days of Edward the Confessor. We would sneak out of Venice this very night.

'You don't know Venice, and you don't know her noblemen,' I said kindly. 'Think on all this. You'll be cut to pieces for giving it a try.'

I now perceived that he was fairly young. Since all older men seemed old to me, I had not thought about it before. He couldn't have been more than twenty-five. He was also mad.

He leapt on the bed, his bushy copper hair flying, and pulled his dagger, a formidable Italian stiletto, and stared down into my upturned face.

'I'll kill for you,' he said confidentially and proudly, in the Venetian dialect. Then he drove the dagger into the pillow and the feathers flew out of it. 'I'll kill you if I have to.' The feathers went up into his face.

'And then you'll have what?' I asked.

There was a creaking behind him. I felt certain someone was at the window, beyond the bolted wooden shutters, even though we were three stories above the Grand Canal. I told him so. He believed me.

'I come from a family of murderous beasts,' I lied. 'They'll follow you to the ends of the Earth if you think of taking me out of here; they'll dismantle your castles stone by stone, chop you in half and cut out your tongue and your private parts, wrap them in velvet and send them to your King. Now calm down.'

'Oh, you bright, saucy little demon,' he said, 'you look like an angel and hold forth like a tavern knave in that sweet crooning mannish voice.'

'That's me,' I said gaily.

I got up, dressed hastily, warning him not to kill me just yet, as I would return as soon as I possibly could, longing to be nowhere but with him, and kissing him hastily, I made for the door.

He hovered in the bed, his dagger still tightly clutched in his hand, the feathers having settled on his carrot-colored head and on his shoulders and on his beard. He looked truly dangerous.

I'd lost count of the nights of my absence.

I could find no churches open. I wanted no company.

It was dark and cold. The curfew had come down. Of course the Venetian winter seemed mild to me after the snowy lands of the north, where I'd been born, but it was nevertheless an oppressive and damp winter, and though cleansing breezes purified the city, it was inhospitable and unnaturally quiet. The illimitable sky vanished in thick mists. The very stones gave forth the chill as if they were blocks of ice.

On a water stairs, I sat, not caring that it was brutally wet, and I burst into tears. What had I learned from all this?

I felt very sophisticated on account of this education. But I had no warmth from it, no lasting warmth, and it seemed my loneliness was worse than guilt, worse than the feeling of being damned.

95

Indeed it seemed to replace that old feeling. I feared it, being utterly alone. As I sat there looking up at the tiny margin of black Heaven, at the few stars that drifted over the roofs of the houses, I sensed how utterly terrible it would be to lose both my Master and my guilt simultaneously, to be cast out where nothing bothered to love me or damn me, to be lost and tumbling through the world with only those humans for companions, those boys and those girls, the English lord with his dagger, even my beloved Bianca.

It was to her house that I went. I climbed under her bed, as I'd done in the past, and wouldn't come out.

She was entertaining a whole flock of Englishmen, but not, fortunately, my copper-haired lover, who was no doubt still stumbling around in the feathers, and I thought, Well, if my charming Lord Harlech shows up, he won't risk shame before his countrymen in making a fool out of himself. She came in, looking most lovely in her violet silk gown with a fortune of radiant pearls around her neck. She knelt down and put her head near mine.

'Amadeo, what's the matter with you?'

I had never asked for her favors. To my knowledge no one did such a thing. But in my particular adolescent frenzy, nothing seemed more appropriate than that I should ravage her.

I scrambled out from under the bed and went to the doors and shut them, so the noise of her guests would leave us alone.

When I turned around she knelt on the floor, looking at me, her golden eyebrows knotted and her peach-soft lips open in a vague wondering expression that I found enchanting. I wanted to smash her with my passion, but not all that hard, of course, assuming all the while that she'd come back together again afterwards as if a beautiful vase, broken into pieces, could pull itself together again from all the tiniest shards and particles and be restored to its glory with an even finer glaze.

I pulled her up by the arms and threw her down on her bed. It was quite an affair, this marvelous coffered thing in which she slept alone, as far as all men knew. It had great gilded swans at its head, and columns rising to a framed canopy of painted dancing nymphs. Its curtains were spun gold and transparent. It had no winter aspect to it, like my Master's red velvet bed.

I bent down and kissed her, maddened by her sharp, pretty eyes which stared coolly at me as I did it. I held her wrists and then, swinging her left wrist over with her right, entrapped both her hands in one so that I was free to rip open her fine dress. I ripped it carefully so that all the little pearl buttons flew off the side of it, and her girdle was opened and underneath was her fine whale-bone and lace. This I broke open as if it were a tight shell.

Her breasts were small and sweet, far too delicate and youngish for the brothel where voluptuousness had been the order of the day. I meant to pillage them never-theless. I crooned against her, humming a bit of a song to her, and then I heard her sigh. I swooped down, still clutching her wrists firmly, and I sucked hard at her nipples in quick order and then drew back. I slapped her breasts playfully, from left to right until they turned pink.

Her face was flushed and she had her little golden frown still, the wrinkles almost incongruous in her smooth white forehead.

Her eyes were like two opals, and though she blinked slowly, near sleepily, she didn't flinch.

I finished my work on her fragile clothes. I ripped open the ties of her skirt and pushed it down away from her and found her splendidly and daintily naked as I had supposed she would be. I really had no idea what was beneath the skirts of a respectable woman in the way of obstacles. There was nothing except the small golden nest of her pubic hair, all feathery beneath her very slightly rounded little belly, and a dampness gleaming on her inner thighs.

I knew at once she favored me. She was hardly helpless. And the sight of the glittering down on her legs drove me mad. I plunged into her, amazed at her smallness and the way that she cringed, for she was not very well used, and it hurt her just a little.

I worked her hard, delighting to see her blush. My own weight I held up above her with my right arm, because I wouldn't let go of her wrists. She tossed and turned, and her blond tresses worked themselves out of her pearl and ribbon coif, and she became moist all over and pink and gleaming, like the inner curve of a great shell.

At last I couldn't contain myself any longer, and it seemed when I would give up the timing, she gave herself up to the final sigh. I spent with it, and we rocked together, as she closed her eyes, turned blood red as if she were dying and tossed her head in a final frenzy before going limp.

I rolled over and covered my face with both my arms, as if I were about to be slapped.

I heard her little laughter, and she did slap me suddenly, hard on my arms. It was nothing. I made as if I were weeping with shame.

'Look what you've done to my beautiful gown, you dreadful little satyr, you secret conquistador! You vile precocious child!'

I felt her weight leave the bed. I heard her dressing. She sang to herself.

'What's your Master going to think of this, Amadeo?' she asked.

I removed my arms and looked to find her voice. She dressed behind her painted paneled screen, a gift from Paris, if I recalled, given her by one of her favorite French poets. She appeared quickly, clothed as splendidly as before in a dress of pale spring green, embroidered with the flowers of the field. She seemed a very garden of delight with these tiny yellow and pink blooms so carefully made in rich thread over her new bodice and her long taffeta skirts.

'Well, tell me, what is the great Master going to say when he finds out his little lover is a veritable god of the wood?'

'Lover?' I was astonished.

She was very gentle in her manner. She sat down and began to comb out her tousled hair. She wore no paint and her face was unmarred by our games, and her hair came down around in a glorious hood of rippling gold. Her forehead was smooth and high.

'Botticelli made you,' I whispered. I often said this to her, because she was so like his beauties. Indeed everyone thought so, and they would bring her small copies of this famous Florentine's paintings from time to time.

I thought on it, I thought on Venice and this world in which I lived. I thought on her, a courtesan, receiving those chaste yet lascivious paintings as if she were a saint.

Some echo came to me of old words that I had been told long ago, when I knelt in the presence of old and burnished beauty, and thought myself at the pinnacle, that I must take up my brush and I must paint only 'what represented the world of God.'

There was no tumult in me, only a great mixing of

currents, as I watched her braid her hair again, stringing the fine ropes of pearls in with it, and the pale green ribbons, the ribbons themselves sewn with the same pretty little flowers that decorated her gown. Her breasts were blushing, half-covered beneath the press of her bodice. I wanted to rip it open again.

'Pretty Bianca, what makes you say this, that I'm his lover?'

'Everyone knows it,' she whispered. 'You are his favorite. Do you think you've made him angry?'

'Oh, if only I could,' I said. I sat up. 'You don't know my Master. Nothing makes him lift his hand to me. Nothing makes him even raise his voice. He sent me forth to learn all things, to know what men can know.'

She smiled and nodded. 'So you came and hid under the bed.'

'I was sad.'

'I'm sure,' she said. 'Well, sleep now, and when I come back, if you're still here, I'll keep you warm. But need I tell you, my rambunctious one, that you will never utter one careless word of what happened here? Are you so young that I have to tell you this?' She bent down to kiss me.

'No, my pearl, my beauty, you needn't tell me. I won't even tell *him*.'

She stood and gathered up her broken pearls and wrinkled ribbons, the remnants of the rape. She smoothed the bed. She looked as lovely as a human swan, a match for the gilded swans of her boatlike bed.

'Your Master will know,' she said. 'He's a great magician.'

'Are you afraid of him? I mean in general, Bianca, I don't mean on account of me?'

'No,' she said. 'Why should I fear him? Everyone knows not to anger him or offend him or break his solitude or question him, but it's not fear. Why do you cry, Amadeo, what's wrong?'

'I don't know, Bianca.'

'I'll tell you then,' she said. 'He has become the world to you as only such a great being can. And you are out of it now and longing to return to it. A man such as that becomes all things to you, and his wise voice becomes the law by which everything is measured. All that lies beyond has no value because he doesn't see it, and he doesn't declare that it is valuable. And so you have no choice but to leave the wastes that lie outside his light and return to it. You must go home.'

She went out, closing the doors. I slept, refusing to go home.

The next morning, I breakfasted with her, and spent all day with her. Our intimacy had given me a radiant sense of her. No matter how much she talked of my Master, I had eyes only for her just now, in these quarters of hers which were perfumed with her and full of all her private and special things.

I will never forget Bianca. Never.

I told her, as one can do with a courtesan, all about the brothels to which I'd been. Perhaps I remember them in such detail because I told her. I told her with delicate words, of course. But I told her. I told her how my Master wanted me to learn everything and had taken me to these splendid academies himself.

'Well, that's fine, but you can't linger here, Amadeo. He's taken you to places where you'll have the pleasure of much company. He may not want you to remain in the company of one.'

I didn't want to go. But when nightfall came, and the house filled with her English and French poets, and the music started, and the dancing, I didn't want to share her with all the admiring world.

For a while I watched her, confusingly conscious that I had had her in her secret chamber as none of these, her admirers, had or might have, but it gave me no solace.

I wanted something from my Master, something final and conclusive and obliterating, and maddened by this desire, suddenly fully aware of it, I got drunk in a tavern, drunk enough to be nervy and nasty, and I went blundering home.

I felt bold and defiant and very independent for having stayed away from my Master and all his mysteries for so long.

He was painting furiously when I returned. He was high on the scaffold, and I figured he was attending to the faces of his Greek philosophers, working the alchemy by which vivid countenances came out of his brush, as though uncovered rather than applied.

He wore a bedraggled gray tunic that hung down to his feet. He didn't turn to look at me when I came in. Every brazier in the house it seemed had been crammed into the room to give him the light he wanted.

The boys were frightened at the speed with which he covered the canvas.

I soon realized, as I staggered into the studio, that he wasn't painting on his Greek Academy.

He was painting a picture of me. I knelt in this picture, a boy of our time, with my familiar long locks and a quiet suit of clothing as if I had taken leave of the high-toned world, and seemingly innocent, my hands clasped in prayer. Around me were gathered angels, gentle-faced and glorious as they always appeared, only these had been graced with black wings.

Black wings. Great black feathery wings. Hideous they seemed, the more I looked upon this canvas. Hideous, and he had almost completed it. The auburn-haired boy seemed real as he looked unchallengingly to Heaven, and the angels appeared avid yet sad.

But nothing therein was as monstrous as the spectacle of my Master painting this, of his hand and brush whipping across the picture, realizing sky, clouds, broken pediment, angel wing, sunlight.

The boys clung to one another, certain of his madness or his sorcery. Which was it? Why did he so carelessly reveal himself to those whose minds had been at peace?

Why did he flaunt our secret, that he was no more a man than the winged creatures he painted! Why had he the Lord lost his patience in such a manner as this?

Suddenly in a rage, he threw a pot of paint at the far corner of the room. A splatter of dark green disfigured the wall. He cursed and cried in a language none of us knew.

He hurled the pots down, and the paint spilt in great shiny splashes from the wooden scaffold. He sent the brushes flying like arrows.

'Get out of here, go to your beds, I don't want to see you, innocents. Go. Go.'

The apprentices ran from him. Riccardo reached out to gather to him the smaller boys. All hurried out the door.

High up on the scaffold, he sat down, his legs dangling, and merely looked at me as I stood beneath him, as if he didn't know who I was.

'Come down, Master,' I said.

His hair was disheveled and matted here and there with paint. He showed no surprise that I was there, no start at the sound of my voice. He had known I was there. He knew all such things. He could hear words spoken in other rooms. He knew the thoughts of those around him. He was pumped full of magic, and when I drank from that magic, I reeled.

103

'Let me comb your hair out for you,' I said. I was insolent, I knew it.

His tunic was stained and filthy. He'd wiped his brush on it over and over again.

One of his sandals fell with a clatter to the marble. I picked it up.

'Master, come down. Whatever I said to worry you, I won't say it again.'

He wouldn't answer me.

Suddenly all my rage came up in me, my loneliness to have been separated from him for days on end, obeying his injunctions, and now to come home and find him staring at me wild and unconfiding. I would not tolerate his staring off, ignoring me as if I weren't there. He must admit that I was the cause of his anger. He must speak.

I wanted suddenly to cry.

His face became anguished. I couldn't watch this; I couldn't think that he felt pain as I did, as the other boys did. I was in wild revolt.

'You frighten everyone selfishly, Lord and Master!' I declared.

Without regarding me, he vanished in a great flurry, and I heard his footsteps rushing through the empty rooms.

I knew he had moved with a speed men couldn't master. I hurried after him, only to hear the bedroom doors slammed shut against me, to hear the lock slid closed before I reached out to grab the latch.

'Master, let me in,' I cried. 'I went only because you told me to.' I turned around and around. It was quite impossible to break these doors. I pounded on them with my fists and kicked them. 'Master, you sent me to the brothels. You sent me on damnable errands.'

After a long time, I sat down at the foot of the door,

my back against it, and wept and wailed. I made a riotous amount of noise. He waited until I stopped.

'Go to sleep, Amadeo,' he said. 'My rages have nothing to do with you.'

Impossible. A lie! I was infuriated and insulted, and hurt and cold! This whole house was damnably cold.

'Then let your peace and calm have to do with me, Sir!' I said. 'Open the damned door.'

'Go to bed with the others,' he said quietly. 'You belong with the others, Amadeo. They are your loved ones. They are your kind. Don't seek the company of monsters.'

'Ah, is that what you are, Sir?' I asked contemptuously and crossly. 'You that can paint like Bellini or Mantegna, who can read all words and speak all tongues, who has love without end and patience to match it, a monster! Is that it? A monster spreads the roof over our head and feeds us our daily supper from the kitchens of the gods! Oh, indeed, a monster.'

He didn't answer.

I was further enraged. I went down to the lower floor. I took a great battle-ax from the wall. It was one of many weapons on display in the house which I'd scarcely ever noticed. Well, it was time for it, I thought. I've had enough of this coldness. I can't stand it. I can't stand it.

I went upstairs and heaved the battle-ax at the door. Of course it went through the brittle wood, shattering the painted panel, cracking through the old lacquer and the pretty yellow and red roses. I pulled it back and smashed it into the door again.

This time the lock was broken. I kicked the shattered frame with my foot and it fell back.

In utter amazement he sat in his large dark oak chair looking at me, his hands clutching the two lion's head arms. Behind him loomed the massive bed with its rich red baldaquin trimmed in gold.

'How dare you!' he said.

He stood before me in an instant, took the ax and hurled it with ease so that it crashed into the stone wall opposite. Then he picked me up and threw me towards the bed. The entire bed shivered, baldaquin and draperies as well. No man could have made me span that distance. But he had done it. With arms and legs flying, I landed on the pillows.

'Despicable monster!' I said. I turned over, steadied myself and drew up on my left side, glaring at him, one knee crooked.

He stood with his back to me. He had been about to close the inner doors of the apartment, which had been open before and therefore were not broken. But he stopped. He turned. A playful expression came over him.

'Oh, what a vile temper we have for such an angelic countenance,' he said mildly.

'If I'm an angel,' I said, drawing back from the edge of the bed, 'paint me with black wings.'

'You dare knock down my door.' He folded his arms. 'Need I tell you why I will not tolerate such from you, or from anyone?'

He stood gazing at me with raised eyebrows.

'You torture me,' I said.

'Oh, indeed, how and since when?'

I wanted to bawl. I wanted to say, 'I love only you.'

Instead I said, 'I detest you.'

He couldn't help but laugh. He lowered his head, his fingers curled under his chin, as he stared at me.

Then he extended his hand and snapped his fingers.

I heard a rustling from the rooms beyond. I sat up petrified with amazement.

I saw the long switch of the teacher come slithering along the floor as if a wind had sent it hither, and then it twisted and turned and rose and dropped into his waiting hand.

Behind him, the inner doors slammed shut and the bolt slipped into place with a loud metallic clatter.

I drew back in the bed.

'It's going to be a pleasure to whip you,' he said, smiling sweetly, his eyes almost innocent. 'You may chalk it up as another human experience, rather like cavorting with your English lord.'

'Do it. I hate you,' I said. 'I'm a man and you deny it.'

He looked superior and gentle but not amused.

He came towards me, and grabbed at my head, and threw me face down on the bed.

'Demon!' I said.

'Master,' he replied calmly.

I felt the nudge of his knee in the small of my back and then down came the switch across my thighs. Of course I wasn't wearing anything but the thin stockings that fashion decreed, so I might as well have been naked.

I cried out in pain and then shut my mouth tight. When the next few blows came, walloping my legs, I swallowed all noise, furious to hear myself make a careless impossible groan.

Again and again, he brought the switch down, whipping my thighs and then my lower legs as well. Enraged, I struggled to get up, pushing vainly on the covers with the heels of my hands. I couldn't move. I was pinioned by his knee, and he whacked away without the slightest deterrent.

Suddenly as rebellious as I'd ever been, I decided to play games with this. I'd be damned if I'd lie there crying, and the tears were coming up in my eyes. I closed my eyes shut, gritted my teeth and decided that each blow was the divine color red and that I liked, and that the hot crashing pain I felt was red, and that the warmth swelling up in my leg after was golden and sweet.

'Oh, that's lovely!' I said.

'You make a fool's bargain, little boy!' he said.

He whipped me harder and faster. I couldn't keep my pretty visions. It hurt, it bloody hurt.

'I'm not a boy!' I cried.

I felt a wetness on my leg. I knew I was bleeding.

'Master, you mean to disfigure me?'

'There's nothing worse than for a fallen saint to be a horrid devil!'

More blows. I knew I was bleeding from more than one place. I would surely be bruised all over. I wouldn't be able to walk.

'I don't know what you mean! Stop!'

To my astonishment, he did. I curled my arm up under my face and I sobbed. I sobbed for a long moment, and my legs burned as if the switch were still hitting them. It seemed the blows were being laid on over and over, but they weren't. I kept hoping, Let this pain die away to something warm again, something tingling and nice, the way it felt the first couple of times. That would be all right, but this is terrible. I hate it!

Suddenly I felt him cover me. I felt the sweet tickling of his hair on my legs. I felt his fingers as he grabbed the torn cloth of the stockings and ripped it, tearing it off both my legs very quickly, leaving them bare. He reached up under my tunic and tore loose the remnants of the hose.

The pain throbbed, grew worse, then a little better. The air was cool on my bruises. When his fingers touched them, I felt such terrible pleasure that all I could do was moan.

'You going to break down my door again?'

'Never,' I whispered.

'You going to defy me in any way in particular?'

'Never in any way ever.'

'Further words?'

'I love you.'

'I'm sure.'

'But I do,' I said sniffling.

The stroking of his fingers on my hurt flesh was insupportably delicious. I didn't dare raise my head. I pressed my cheek against the scratchy embroidered coverlet, against the great picture of the lion stitched into it, and I sucked in my breath and let my tears flow. I felt calm all over; this pleasure robbed me of any control of my limbs.

I closed my eyes, and there came his lips on my leg. He kissed one of the bruises. I thought I would die. I would go to Heaven, that is, some other higher more delicious Heaven even than this Venetian Heaven. Beneath me, my groin was alive with thankful and desperate and isolated strength.

The burning blood flowed over the bruise. The slightly rough stroke of his tongue touched it, lapped at it, pressed it, and the inevitable tingling made a fire in my closed eyes, a blazing fire across a mythical horizon in the darkness of my blind mind.

To the next bruise he went, and there came the trickles of the blood and the lap of his tongue, and the hideous pain departed and there was nothing but a throbbing sweetness. And as he went to the next, I thought, I cannot bear this, I will simply die.

He moved fast, from bruise to bruise, depositing his magical kiss and the stroke of his tongue, and I quivered all over and moaned.

'Some punishment!' I suddenly said with a gasp.

It was a dreadful thing to say! Instantly, I regretted it, the sassiness of it.

But his hand had already come down with a fierce slap on my backside.

'I didn't mean it,' I said. 'I mean, I didn't mean it to sound so ungrateful. I mean, I'm sorry I said it!' But there was another slap as hot as the first.

'Master, have pity on me. I'm mixed up!' I cried.

His hand lay on me, on the warm surface that he had slapped, and I thought, Oh, now he's going to beat me till I'm unconscious.

But his fingers only gently clasped the skin, which was not broken, only warm as the first welts from the switch had been.

I felt his lips again on the calf of my left leg, and the blood, and his tongue. The pleasure moved all through me, and helpless, I let the air escape my lips in a rosary of sighs.

'Master, Master, Master, I love you.'

'Yes, well, that's not so unusual,' he whispered. He didn't stop his kissing. He lapped at the blood. I writhed under the weight of his hand on my backside. 'But the question is, Amadeo, why do I love you? Why? Why did I have to go into that stinking brothel and look upon you? I am strong by nature . . . whatever my nature . . .'

He greedily kissed a large bruise on my thigh. I could feel his sucking at it, and then the tongue lapping it, eating the blood, and then his blood coming down into it. The pleasure sent shock after shock through me. I saw nothing, though I thought that my eyes were now open. I struggled to make certain that my eyes were open, but nothing came visible, only a golden haze.

'I love you, I do love you,' he said. 'And why? Quick-witted, yes, beautiful, yes, and inside you, the burnt-up relics of a saint!'

'Master, I don't know what you're saying to me. I was never a saint, never, I don't claim to be a saint. I'm a wretched disrespectful and ungrateful being. Oh, I adore you. It's so delicious to be helpless and at your mercy.'

'Stop mocking me.'

'But I don't,' I said. 'I want to speak, the truth, I want to be a fool for the truth, a fool for –. I want to be a fool for you.'

'No, I don't guess you do mean to mock me. You mean it. You don't realize the absurdity of it.'

He had finished his progress. My legs had lost any shape they possessed in my mist-filled mind. I could only lie there, my whole body vibrating from his kisses. He laid his head on my hips, against the warm place that he had smacked with his hand, and I felt his fingers come up under me and touch the most private part of me.

My organ hardened in his fingers, hardened with the infusion of his searing blood, but all the more with the young male in me who had so often mingled pleasure with pain at his will.

Harder and harder I grew, and bucked and pumped beneath his head and shoulders as he lay on my backside, as he held tight to the organ, and then into his slippery fingers I gave forth in violent unsurpassed spasms a great gush.

I rose on my elbow and looked back at him. He was sitting up, staring at the pearly white semen that clung to his fingers.

'Good God, is that what you wanted?' I asked. 'To see the viscous whiteness in your hand?'

He looked at me with anguish. Oh, such anguish.

'Doesn't it mean?' I asked, 'that the time has come?'

The misery in his eyes was too much for me to question him anymore.

Drowsy and blind, I felt him turn me over and rip off my tunic and jacket. I felt him lift me and then came the sting of his assault into my neck. A fierce pain gathered itself around my heart, slackening just when I feared it, and then I sank down beside him into the perfumed cleft of the bed; and against his chest, warm under covers that he pulled up over us, I slept.

It was still thick and heavy night when I opened my eyes. I had learnt with him to feel the coming of morning. And morning was not yet really near.

I looked around for him. I saw him at the foot of the bed. He was dressed in his finest red velvet. He wore a jacket with slashed sleeves and a heavy tunic with a high collar. This cloak of red velvet was trimmed in ermine.

His hair was thoroughly brushed and very slightly oiled so that it gave off its most civilized and artful shimmer, swept back from his clean straight hairline and turning in mannered curls on his shoulders. He looked sad.

'Master, what is it?'

'I have to go for a few nights. No, it's not out of anger at you, Amadeo. It's one of those journeys I have to make. I'm long overdue for it.'

'No, Master, not now, please. I'm sorry, I beg you, not now! What I—.

'Child. I go to see Those Who Must Be Kept. I have no choice in this.'

For a moment I said nothing. I tried to understand the denotation of the words he'd spoken. His voice had dropped, and he had said the words halfheartedly.

'What is that, Master?' I asked.

'Some night perhaps I'll take you with me. I'll ask permission . . .' His voice trailed off.

'For what, Master? When have you ever needed anyone's permission for anything?'

112

I had meant this to be simple and candid, but I knew now it had an impertinent sound.

'It's all right, Amadeo,' he said. 'I ask permission now and then from my Elders, that's all. Who else?' He looked weary. He sat beside me and leaned down next to me and kissed my lips.

'Elders, Sir? You mean Those Who Must Be Kept – these are creatures like you?'

'You be kind to Riccardo and the others. They worship you,' he said. 'They wept for you the whole time you were away. They didn't quite believe me when I told them you were coming home. Then Riccardo spied you with your English lord and was terrified I'd break you in little pieces, yet afraid the Englishman would kill you. He has quite the reputation, your English lord, slamming down his knife on the board in any tavern he chooses. Do you have to consort with common murderers? You have a nonpareil here when it comes to those who take life. When you went to Bianca, they didn't dare to tell me, but made fancy pictures in their minds so I couldn't read their thoughts. How docile they are with my powers.'

'They love you, my Lord,' I said. 'Thank God that you forgive me for the places I went. I'll do whatever you wish.'

'Good night then.' He rose to go.

'Master, how many nights?'

'Three at most,' he said over his shoulder. He made for the door, a tall gallant figure in his cloak.

'Master.'

'Yes.'

'I'll be very good, a saint,' I said. 'But if I'm not will you whip me again, please?'

The moment I saw the anger in his face I regretted this. What made me say such things!

113

'Don't tell me you didn't mean it!' he said, reading my mind and hearing the words before I could get them out.

'No. It's just I hate it when you go. I thought maybe if I taunted you, you wouldn't.'

'Well, I will. And don't taunt me. As a matter of policy, don't taunt me.'

He was out the door before he changed his mind and returned. He came towards the bed. I expected the worst. He was going to slap me and then not be around to kiss the bruise.

But he didn't.

'Amadeo, while I'm gone, *think on it*,' he said.

I was sobered, looking at him. His very manner made me reflect before I uttered a word.

'On everything, Sir?' I asked.

'Yes,' he said. Then he came again to kiss me. 'Will you be this forever?' he asked. 'This man, this young man, that you are now?'

'Yes, Master! Forever, and with you!' I wanted to tell him that there was nothing I couldn't do that a man could do, but this seemed most unwise, and also it would not seem true to him.

He laid his hand fondly on my head, pushing my hair back.

'For two years, I've watched you grow,' he said. 'You've reached your full height, but you're small, and your face is a baby's face, and for all your good health, you're slight and not the robust man yet that you are surely meant to be.'

I was too enthralled to interrupt him. When he paused, I waited.

He sighed. He looked off as if he couldn't find words. 'When you were gone, your English lord drew his dagger on you, but you weren't afraid. Do you remember? It wasn't two days ago.'

'Yes, Sir, it was stupid.'

'You could easily have died then,' he said with a raise of his eyebrow. 'Easily.'

'Sir, please open up these mysteries to me,' I said. 'Tell me how you came to your powers. Entrust these secrets to me. Lord, make it so that I can be with you forever. I don't care anything for my own judgment of such things. I yield to yours.'

'Ah, yes, you yield if I fulfill your request.'

'Well, Sir, that is a form of yielding, to give myself up to you, your will and your power, and yes, I would have it and be like you. Is that what you promise, Master, is that what you hint at, that you can make me like you? You can fill me with this blood of yours that makes a slave out of me, and it will be accomplished? It seems at times I know this, Master, that you can do it, and yet I wonder if I know it only because you know it, and you are lonely to do it to me.'

'Ah!' He put his hands to his face, as though I had displeased him totally.

I was at a loss.

'Master, if I offended, hit me, beat me, do anything to me but don't turn away. Don't cover your eyes that would look on me, Master, because I can't live without your gaze. Explain it to me. Master, take away what divides us; if it be only ignorance then take away that.'

'Oh, I will, I will,' he said. 'You are so clever and deceiving, Amadeo. You would be the fool for God all right, as you were told a long time ago that a saint should be.'

'You lose me, Sir. I am no saint, and a fool, yes, because I conjecture it's a form of wisdom and I want it because you prize wisdom.'

'I mean that you appear simple, and out of your simplicity comes a clever grasp. I am lonely. Oh, yes, I

115

am lonely, and lonely to tell my woes if nothing else. But who would burden one so young as you with my woes? Amadeo, what age do you think I am? Gauge my age with your simplicity.'

'You have none, Sir. You neither eat nor drink, nor change with time. You need no water to wash you clean. You are smooth and resistant to all things of nature. Master, we all know this. You are a clean and fine and whole thing.'

He shook his head. I was distressing him when I wanted just the opposite.

'I have done it already,' he whispered.

'What, my Lord, what have you done?'

'Oh, brought you to me, Amadeo, for now——.' He stopped. He frowned, and his face was so soft and wondering that it made me ache. 'Ah, but these are just self-serving delusions. I could take you, with a heap of gold, and plant you down in a distant city where——.'

'Master, kill me. Kill me before you do this, or make sure your city is beyond the compass of the known world, because I will journey back! I will spend the last ducat of your heap of gold to journey here and beat on your doors.'

He looked wretched, more a man than I'd ever seen him, in pain and trembling as he looked off, deep into the endless dark divide that separated us.

I clung to his shoulder and kissed him. There was a stronger, more virile intimacy due to my crude act of hours ago.

'No, no time for such comforts,' he said. 'I have to be gone. Duty calls me. Ancient things call to me, things which have been my burden for so very long. I am so weary!'

'Don't go tonight. When the morning comes, take me with you, Master, take me to where you conceal yourself from the sun. It is from the sun that you must hide, isn't it, Master, you who paint blue skies and the light of Phoebus more brilliantly than those who see it, you never see it—.'

'Stop,' he begged me, pressing his fingers about my hand. 'Stop your kisses and your reason, and do as I say.'

He took a deep breath, and for the first time in all my life with him, I saw him take a handkerchief from his coat and pat the moisture on his own forehead and his lips. The cloth was faintly red. He looked at it.

'I want to show you something before I go,' he said. 'Dress yourself, quickly. Here, I'll help you.'

I was fully dressed for the cold winter night in less than a few minutes. He put a black cape over my shoulders, and gave me gloves trimmed in miniver, and put a black velvet cap on my head. The shoes he chose were black leather boots, which he never wanted me to wear before. To him the ankles of the boys were beautiful, and he did not favor boots, though he did not mind if we wore them by day when he could not see.

He was so troubled, so distressed, and all his face, despite its blanched cleanliness, was so infused with it, that I couldn't keep from embracing him and kissing him, just to make his lips part, just to feel his mouth locking onto mine.

I closed my eyes. I felt his hand cover up my face and cover my eyelids.

There was a great noise around me, as of the flapping of the wooden doors, and the flying about of the broken fragments of that door I'd shattered, and of draperies billowed and snapped.

The cold air of outside surrounded me. He set me down, blind, and I knew my feet were on the quay. I could hear the water of the canal near me, lapping, lapping, as the winter wind stirred it and drove the sea

117

into the city, and I could hear a wooden boat knocking persistently against a dock.

He let slip his fingers, and I opened my eyes.

We were far from the palazzo. I was abashed to see us at such a distance, though I was not really surprised. He could do wonders, and so he let me know this now. We were in back alleyways. We stood on a small landing by a narrow canal. I had never ventured into this mean district where workmen lived.

I saw only the back porches of houses, and their ironclad windows, and a general squalor and blindness, and a rankness as refuse floated on the water of the dipping, splashing winter-blown canal.

He turned and drew me with him away from the water's edge, and for a moment I couldn't see. His white hand flashed out. I beheld one finger pointed and then I beheld a man sleeping in a long rotted gondola that had been drawn up out of the water and set on workmen's blocks. The man stirred and threw back his covering. I saw his hulking fussing shape as he grumbled and cursed at us that we dared to disturb his sleep.

I reached for my dagger. I saw the flash of his blade. The white hand of the Master, glowing like quartz, seemed only to touch the man's wrist and send the weapon flying and rolling on the stones. Befuddled and enraged, the man charged my Master in a great clumsy bid to knock my Master off his feet.

My Master caught him easily, as if he were no more than a great swaddling of evil-smelling wool. I saw my Master's face. His mouth opened. There came two tiny sharp teeth, like daggers unto themselves, as he bit down into the man's throat. I heard the man cry out, but only for an instant, and then his stinking body went still.

Astonished and enthralled, I watched as my Master closed his smooth eyes, his golden eyelashes seeming silvery in the dimness, and I heard a low wet sound, barely audible but horribly suggestive of the flow of something, and that something had to be the man's blood. My Master pressed himself ever more closely to his victim, his plainly visible white fingers coaxing the life fluid from the dying body, as he gave off a long sweet savoring sigh. He drank. He drank, and there was no mistaking it. He even twisted his head a little as if to bring the last draught all the more quickly, and at this the man's form, now seemingly frail and plastic, shuddered all over, as if the man had gone into a final convulsion, and then was still.

The Master drew himself up and ran his tongue over his lips. There was not a drop of blood to be seen. But the blood was visible. It was visible inside my Master. His face took on a florid gleam. He turned and looked at me, and I could make out the vivid flush of his cheeks, the ruddy glister of his lips.

'This is where it comes from, Amadeo,' he said. He shoved the corpse towards me, the filthy clothes brushed all against me, and as the heavy head fell back in death, he pushed it even closer so that I had to look down at the doomed man's coarse and lifeless face. He was young, he was bearded, he was not beautiful, and he was pale and he was dead.

A seam of white showed beneath each limp and expressionless eyelid. A greasy spittle hung from his decaying yellowed teeth, his breathless and colorless mouth.

I was speechless. Fear, loathing, these things had no part in it. I was simply amazed. If I thought, I thought it was wondrous.

In a sudden fit of seeming anger, my Master hurled the man's body to his left and out into the water where it fell with a dull splashing and bubbling sound.

He snatched me up, and I saw the windows falling past me. I almost screamed as we rose above the roofs. His hands clamped over my mouth. He moved so swiftly it was as if something propelled him or thrust him upwards.

We spun round or so it must have been, and when I opened my eyes we stood in a familiar room. Long golden curtains settled around us. It was warm here. In the shadows I saw the glinting outline of a golden swan.

It was Bianca's room, her private sanctuary, her very own room.

'Master!' I said in fear and revulsion, that we should come like this, into her chamber, without so much as a word.

From the closed doors a tiny seam of light laid itself out upon her parqueted floor and its thick Persian carpet. It laid itself upon the deep-carved feathers of her swan bed.

Then came her footsteps hastily, emerging from an airy cloud of voices, so that she might investigate alone the noise she heard.

The cold wind swept into the room from the open window as she opened her doors. Against the draught she slammed them shut, such a fearless creature, and she reached out with unerring accuracy and raised the wick of her nearby lamp. The flame rose and I saw her staring at my Master, though she had seen me as well, for sure.

She was herself, as I had left her a world of hours ago, in gold velvet and silk tissue, her braid coiled about the back of her head to weigh down her voluminous tresses which fell in their rippled splendor over her shoulders and down her back.

Her small face was quick with questioning and alarm.

'Marius,' she said. 'How now, my Lord, do you come here like this, into my private room? How now, you come by the window, and with Amadeo? What is this, jealousy of me?'

'No, only I would have a confession,' my Master said. His very voice trembled. He held me tight by my hand as if I were a mere child as he approached her, his long finger flying out to accuse her . . . 'Tell him, my darling angel, tell him what lies behind your fabulous face.'

'I don't know what you mean, Marius. But you anger me. And I order you out of my house. Amadeo, what do you say to this abuse?'

'I don't know, Bianca,' I murmured. I was totally in fear. Never had I heard my Master's voice tremble, and never had I heard anyone address him so familiarly by name.

'Get out of my house, Marius. Go now. I speak to the honorable man in you.'

'Ah, and how then did your friend Marcellus go, the Florentine, the one you were told to lure here with your clever words, the one whose drink you laced with enough poison to kill twenty men?'

My damsel's face grew brittle but never really hard. She seemed a porcelain princess as she appraised my angry, trembling Master.

'What is this to you, my Lord?' she asked. 'Have you become the Grand Council or the Council of Ten? Take me up before the courts on charges, if you will, you stealthy sorcerer! Prove your words.'

There was a great high-strung dignity to her. She craned her neck and raised her chin.

'Murderess,' my Master said. 'I see it now within the solitary cell of your mind, a dozen confessions, a dozen cruel and importunate acts, a dozen crimes –.'

'No, you cannot judge me! A magician you might

121

be, but you are no angel, Marius. Not you with your boys.'

He dragged her forward, and once again I saw his mouth open. I saw his deadly teeth.

'No, Master, no!' I ripped loose of his slack neglected hand and flew at him with my fists, crashing my body between hers and his and pounding on him with all my might. 'You can't do it, Master. I don't care what she's done. You seek these reasons for what. Call her importunate? Her! And what is it with you?'

She fell backwards against her bed and struggled up onto it, her legs bent. She drew back into the shadows.

'You are the Fiend from Hell himself,' she whispered. 'You are a monster, and I have seen it. Amadeo, he'll never let me live.'

'Let her live, my Lord, or I die with her!' I said. 'She's no more than a lesson here, and I will not see her die.'

My Master was wretched. He was dazed. He pushed me away from him, steadying me so that I didn't fall. He moved towards the bed, but not in pursuit of her. He sat down beside her. She recoiled ever deeper against the headboard, her hand reaching out vainly for the sheer gold drapery as if it could save her.

She was wan and small, and her fierce blue eyes remained fixed and wide.

'We are killers together, Bianca,' he whispered to her. He reached out.

I rushed forward, but only to be stopped casually by his right hand, and with his left he smoothed her few tiny loose curls back from her forehead. He rested his hand on her as if he were a priest giving a blessing.

'Of rude necessity, Sir, all of it,' she said. 'What choice after all did I have?' How brave she was, how strong like fine silver suffused with steel. 'Once given the commissions, what am I to do, for I know what is to be done and

122

for whom? How clever they were. It was a brew which took days to kill its victim far from my warm rooms.'

'Call your oppressor here, child, and poison him, instead of those he points out.'

'Yes, that ought to do it,' I said hastily. 'Kill the man who put you up to it.'

She seemed in truth to think on this and then to smile. 'And what of his guards, his kinsmen? They would strangle me for the grand betrayal.'

'I'll kill him for you, sweet,' said Marius. 'And for that, you'll owe me no high crimes, only your gentle forgetfulness of the appetite you have seen tonight in me.'

For the first time, her courage seemed to waver. Her eyes filled with clear pretty tears. A tiny weariness showed itself in her. She hung her head for a moment. 'You know who he is, you know where he lodges, you know that he is in Venice now.'

'He's a dead man, my beautiful lady,' my Master said.

I slipped my arm around his neck. I kissed his forehead. He kept his eyes on her.

'Come, then, cherub,' he said to me while he still looked at her. 'We'll go to rid the world of this Florentine, this banker, who uses Bianca to dispatch those who have given him accounts in secret.'

This intelligence amazed Bianca, but once again she made a soft, knowing smile. How graceful she was, how devoid of pride and bitterness. How these horrors were cast aside.

My Master held me fast to him with his right arm. He reached inside his jacket with his left and took out of it a large beautiful pear-shaped pearl. It seemed a priceless thing. He gave it to Bianca, who took it only with hesitation, watching it drop into her lazy, open hand.

'Let me kiss you, darling princess,' he said.

To my astonishment, she allowed it, and he covered her now with feathery kisses, and I watched her pretty golden eyebrows pucker, and I saw her eyes become dazzled, and her body go limp. She lay back on her pillows and then fell into a fast sleep.

We withdrew. I thought I heard the shutters close behind us. The night was wet and dark. My head was pressed to my Master's shoulder. I couldn't have looked up or moved if I wanted to.

'Thank you, my beloved Lord, that you didn't kill her,' I whispered.

'She is more than a practical woman,' he said. 'She is unbroken still. She has the innocence and cunning of a duchess or a queen.'

'But where do we go now?'

'We are there, Amadeo. We are on the roof. Look about you. Do you hear the din below?'

It was tambourines and drums and flutes playing.

'Ah, so, they will die at their banquet,' my Master said thoughtfully. He stood at the edge of the roof, holding to the stone railing. The wind blew his cloak back, and he turned his eyes up to the stars.

'I want to see it all,' I said.

He shut his eyes as if I'd struck him a blow.

'Don't think me cold, Sir,' I said. 'Don't think me tired and used to things brutal and cruel. I am only the fool, Sir, the fool for God. We don't question, if memory serves me right. We laugh and we accept and we turn all life into joy.'

'Come down with me, then. There are a crowd of them, these crafty Florentines. Oh, but I am so hungry. I have starved myself for a night such as this.'

Perhaps mortals feel this way when they hunt the big beasts of the forest and of the jungle.

For me, as we went down the stairs from the ceiling into the banquet room of this new and highly decorated palazzo, I felt a rabid excitement. Men were going to die. Men would be murdered. Men who were bad, men who had wronged the beautiful Bianca, were going to be killed without risk to my all-powerful Master, and without risk to anyone whom I knew or loved.

An army of mercenaries could not have felt less compassion for these individuals. The Venetians in attacking the Turks perhaps had more feeling for their enemy than I.

I was spellbound; the scent of blood was already in me insofar as it was symbolic. I wanted to see blood flow. I didn't like Florentines anyway, and I certainly didn't understand bankers, and I most definitely wanted swift vengeance, not only for those who had bent Bianca to their will but on those who had put her in the path of my Master's thirst.

So be it.

We entered a spacious and impressive banquet hall where a party of some seven men was gorging itself on a splendid supper of roast pork. Flemish tapestries, all very new and with splendid hunting scenes of lords and ladies with their horses and hounds, were hung from great iron rods all through the room, covering even the windows and falling heavily to the very floor.

The floor itself was a fine inlay of multicolored

marble, fashioned in pictures of peacocks, complete with jewels in their great fanlike tails.

The table was very broad, and three men sat behind the table all on one side, virtually slobbering over heaps of gold plates littered with the sticky bones of fish and fowl, and the roasted pig himself, poor swollen creature, whose head remained, ignominiously grasping the inevitable apple as though it were the ultimate expression of his final wish.

The other three men – all young and somewhat pretty and most athletic, by the look of their beautifully muscled legs – were busy dancing in an artful circle, hands meeting in the center, as a small gathering of boys played the instruments whose pounding march we had heard on the roof.

All appeared somewhat greasy and stained from the feast. But not a member of the company lacked long thick fashionable hair, and ornate, heavily worked silk tunics and hose. There was no fire for heat, and indeed none of these men needed any such, and all were tricked out in velvet jackets with trimmings of powdered ermine or miniver or silver fox.

The wine was being slopped from the pitcher into the goblets by one who seemed quite unable to manage such a gesture. And the three who danced, though they had a courtly design to enact, were also roughhousing and shoving one another in some sort of deliberate mockery of the dance steps that all knew.

I saw at once that the servants had been dismissed. Several goblets had spilled. Tiny gnats, despite the winter, had congregated over the shiny half-eaten carcasses and the heaps of moist fruit.

A golden haze hung over the room which was the smoke from the tobacco of the men which they smoked in a variety of different pipes. The background of the tapestries was invariably a dark blue, and this gave the whole scene a warmth against which the rich varicolored clothes of the boy musicians and the dinner guests shone brilliantly.

Indeed, as we entered the smoky warmth of the room, I felt intoxicated by the atmosphere, and when my Master bid me sit down at one end of the table, I did so out of weakness, though I shrank from touching even the top of the table, let alone the edge of the various plates.

The red-faced, bawling merrymakers took no notice of us. The thumping din of the musicians was sufficient to render us invisible, because it overpowered the senses. But the men were far too drunk to have seen us in perfect silence. Indeed, my Master, after planting a kiss on my cheek, went to the very center of the table, to a space left there, presumably by one of those cavorting to the music, and he stepped over the padded bench and sat down.

Only then did the two men on either side of him, who had been shouting at one another adamantly about some point or other, take notice of this resplendent scarlet-clad guest.

My Master had let the hood of his cape fall, and his hair was wondrously shaped in its prodigious length. He looked the Christ again at the Last Supper with his lean nose and mild full mouth, and the blond hair parted so cleanly in the middle, and the whole mass of it alive from the damp of the night.

He looked from one to the other of these guests, and to my astonishment as I looked down the table at him, he plunged into their conversation, discussing with them the atrocities visited upon those Venetians left in Constantinople when the twenty-one-year-old Turk, Sultan Mehmet II, had conquered the city.

It seemed there was some argument as to how the Turks actually breached the sacred capital, and one man was saying that had not the Venetian ships sailed away from Constantinople, deserting her before the final days, the city might have been saved.

No chance at all, said the other, a robust red-haired man with seemingly golden eyes. What a beauty! If this was the rogue who misled Bianca, I could see why. Between red beard and mustache, his lips were a lush Cupid's bow, and his jaw had the strength of Michelangelo's superhuman marble figure.

'For forty-eight days, the cannons of the Turk had bombarded the walls of the city,' he declared to his consort, 'and eventually they broke through. What could be expected? Have you ever seen such guns?'

The other man, a very pretty dark-haired olive-skinned fellow with rounded cheeks very close to his small nose and large velvet black eyes, became furious and said that the Venetians had acted like cowards, and that their supported fleet could have stopped even the cannons if they had ever come. With his fist he rattled the plate in front of him. 'Constantinople was abandoned!' he declared. 'Venice and Genoa did not help her. The greatest empire on Earth was allowed on that horrible day to collapse.'

'Not so,' said my Master somewhat quietly, raising his eyebrows and tilting his head slightly to one side. His eyes swept slowly from one man to the other. 'There were in fact many brave Venetians who came to the rescue of Constantinople. I think, and with reason, that even if the entire Venetian fleet had come, the Turks would have continued. It was the dream of the young Sultan Mehmet II to have Constantinople and he would never have stopped.'

Oh, this was most interesting. I was ready for such a

lesson in history. I had to hear and see this more clearly, so I jumped up and went round the table, pulling up a light cross-legged chair with a comfortable red leather sling seat, so that I might have a good vantage point on all of them. I put it at an angle so that I might better see the dancers, who even in their clumsiness made quite a picture, if only because of their long ornate sleeves flapping about and the slap of their jeweled slippers on the tile floor.

The red-haired one at table, tossing back his long richly curling mane, was most encouraged by my Master, and gave him a wild adoring look.

'Yes, yes, here is a man who knows what happened, and you lie, you fool,' he said to the other man. 'And you know the Genoese fought bravely, right to the end. Three ships were sent by the Pope; they broke through the blockade of the harbor, slipping right by the Sultan's evil castle of Rumeli Hisar. It was Giovanni Longo, and can you imagine the bravery?'

'Frankly, no!' said the black-haired one, leaning forward in front of my Master as if my Master were a statue.

'It was brave,' said my Master casually. 'Why do you say nonsense you don't believe? You know what had happened to the Venetian ships caught by the Sultan, come now.'

'Yes, speak up on that. Would you have gone into that harbor?' demanded the red-haired Florentine. 'You know what they did to the Venetian ships they caught six months before? They beheaded every man on board.'

'Except the man in charge!' cried out a dancer who had turned to join the conversation, but went on so as not to lose his step. 'They impaled him on a stake. This was Antonio Rizzo, one of the finest men there ever was.' He went on dancing with an offhand contemptuous gesture over his shoulder. Then he slipped as he pivoted and almost fell. His dancing companions caught him.

The black-haired man at the table shook his head.

'If it had been a full Venetian fleet –,' cried the black-haired man. 'But you Florentines and you Venetians are all the same, treacherous, hedging your bets.'

My Master laughed as he watched the man.

'Don't you laugh at me,' declared the black-haired man. 'You're a Venetian; I've seen you a thousand times, you and that boy!'

He gestured to me. I looked at my Master. My Master only smiled. Then I heard him whisper distinctly to me, so that it struck my ear as if he were next to me rather than so many feet away. 'Testimony of the dead, Amadeo.'

The black-haired man picked up his goblet, slopped some wine down his throat and spilt as much down his pointed beard. 'A whole city of conniving bastards!' he declared. 'Good for one thing, and that's borrowing money at high interest when they spend everything they've got on fancy clothes.'

'You should talk,' said the red-haired one. 'You look like a goddamned peacock. I ought to cut off your tail. Let's get back to Constantinople since you're so damned sure it could have been saved!'

'You are a damned Venetian yourself now.'

'I'm a banker; I'm a man of responsibility,' said the redhead. 'I admire those who do well by me.' He picked up his own goblet, but instead of drinking the wine, he threw it in the face of the black-haired man.

My Master did not bother to lean back, so undoubtedly some of the wine spilled on him. He looked from one to the other of the ruddy sweating faces on either side of him.

130

'Giovanni Longo, one of the bravest Genoese ever to captain a ship, stayed in that city during the entire siege,' cried the red-haired man. 'That's courage. I'll put money on a man like that.'

'I don't know why,' cried the dancer again, the same one as before. He broke from the circle long enough to declare, 'He lost the battle, and besides, your Father had plenty enough sense not to bank on any of them.'

'Don't you dare!' said the red-haired man. 'Here's to Giovanni Longo and the Genoese who fought with him.' He grabbed the pitcher, all but knocking it over, showered wine on his goblet and the table, then took a deep gulp. 'And here's to my Father. May God have mercy on his immortal soul. Father, I have slain your enemies, and I'll slay those who make of ignorance a pastime.'

He turned, jammed his elbow into my Master's clothes and said, 'That boy of yours is a beauty. Don't be hasty. Think this over. How much?'

My Master burst out laughing more sweetly and naturally than I'd ever heard him laugh.

'Offer me something, something I might want,' said my Master as he looked at me, with a secretive, glittering shift of his eyes.

It seemed every man in the room was taking my measure, and understand, these were not lovers of boys; these were merely Italians of their time, who, fathering children as was required of them and debauching women any chance they got, nevertheless appreciated a plump and juicy young man, the way that men now might appreciate a slice of golden toast heaped with sour cream and the finest blackest caviar.

I couldn't help but smile. Kill them, I thought, slaughter them. I felt fetching and even beautiful. Come on, somebody, tell me I make you think of Mercury

131

chasing away the clouds in Botticelli's *Primavera*, but the red-haired man, fixing me with an impish playful glance, said:

'Ah, he is Verrocchio's *David*, the very model for the bronze statue. Don't try to tell me he is not. And immortal, ah, yes, I can see it, immortal. He shall never die.' Again he lifted his goblet. Then he felt of the breast of his tunic, and pulled up out of the powdered ermine trim of his jacket a rich gold medallion with a table diamond of immense size. He ripped the chain right off his neck and extended this proudly to my Master, who watched it spin on the dangle in front of him as if it were an orb with which he was to be spellbound.

'For all of us,' said the black-haired man, turning and looking hard at me. There was laughter from the others. The dancers cried, 'Yes, and for me,' 'Unless I go second with him, nothing' and 'Here, to go first, even before you.'

This last was said to the red-haired man, but the jewel the dancer tossed at my Master, a carbuncle ring of some glittering purple stone, I didn't know.

'A sapphire,' said my Master in a whisper, with a teasing looking to me. 'Amadeo, you approve?'

The third dancer, a blond-haired man, somewhat shorter than anyone present and with a small hump on his left shoulder, broke free of the circle and came towards me. He took off all his rings, as if shearing himself of gloves, and tossed them all clattering at my feet.

'Smile sweetly on me, young god,' he said, though he panted from the dance and the velvet collar was drenched. He wobbled on his feet and almost turned over but managed to make fun of it, twirling heavily back into his dance.

The music thumped on and on, as if the dancers

132

thought it meet to drown out the very drunkenness of their Masters.

'Does anybody care about the siege of Constantinople?' asked my Master.

'Tell me what became of Giovanni Longo,' I asked in a small voice. All eyes were on me.

'It's the siege of . . . Amadeo, was it? . . . Yes, Amadeo, that I have in mind!' cried the blond-haired dancer.

'By and by, Sir,' I said. 'But teach me some history.'

'You little imp,' said the black-haired man. 'You don't even pick up his rings.'

'My fingers are covered with rings,' I said politely, which was true.

The red-haired man immediately went back into the battle. 'Giovanni Longo stayed for forty days of bombardment. He fought all night when the Turk breached the walls. Nothing frightened him. He was carried to safety only because he was shot.'

'And the guns, Sir?' I asked. 'Were they so very big?'

'And I suppose you were there!' cried the black-haired man to the redhead, before the redhead could answer me.

'My Father was there!' said the redhead man. 'And lived to tell it. He was with the last ship that slipped out of the harbor with the Venetians, and before you speak, Sir, mind you, you don't speak ill of my Father or those Venetians. They carried the citizenry to safety, Sir, the battle was lost . . .'

'They deserted, you mean,' said the black-haired man.

'I mean slipped out carrying the helpless refugees after the Turks had won. You call my Father a coward? You know no more about manners than you know about war. You're too stupid to fight with, and too drunk.'

'Amen,' said my Master.

'Tell him,' said the red-haired man to my Master. 'You, Marius De Romanus, you tell him.' He took another slobbering gulp. 'Tell him about the massacre, what happened. Tell him how Giovanni Longo fought on the walls until he was hit in the chest. Listen, you crackbrained fool!' he shouted at his friend. 'Nobody knows more about all of it than Marius De Romanus. Sorcerers are clever, so says my whore, and here is to Bianca Solderini.' He drained his glass.

'Your whore, Sir?' I demanded. 'You say that of such a woman and here in the presence of drunken disrespectful men?'

They paid no mind to me, not the red-haired man, who was again draining his goblet, or the others.

The blond-haired dancer staggered over to me. 'They're too drunk to remember you, beautiful boy,' he said. 'But not I.'

'Sir, you stumble at your dance,' I said. 'Don't stumble in your rounds with me.'

'You miserable little whelp,' said the man, and fell towards me, losing his balance. I darted out of the chair to the right. He slipped over the chair and fell to the floor.

There was uproarious laughter from the others. The two remaining dancers gave up their patterned steps.

'Giovanni Longo was brave,' my Master said calmly, surveying everything and then returning his cool glance to the red-haired man. 'They were all brave. But nothing could save Byzantium. Her hour had come. Time had run out for the Emperors and chimney sweeps. And in the holocaust that followed, so much was irretrievably lost. Libraries by the hundreds were burnt. So many sacred texts with all their imponderable mysteries went up in smoke.'

134

I backed away from the drunk attacker, who rolled over on the floor.

'You lousy little lapdog!' the sprawling man shouted at me. 'Give me your hand, I tell you.'

'Ah, but Sir,' I said, 'I think you want more than that.'

'And I'll have it!' he said, but he only skidded and fell back down again with a miserable groan.

One of the other men at table – handsome but older, with long thick wavy gray hair and a beautifully lined face, a man who had been gorging himself in silence on a greasy joint of mutton – looked up at me over the joint and at the fallen, twisting man who struggled to get to his feet.

'Hmmm. So Goliath falls, little David,' he said, smiling up at me. 'Mind your tongue, little David, we are not all stupid giants, and your stones are not for throwing just yet.'

I smiled back at him. 'Your jest is as clumsy as your friend, Sir. As for my stones, as you put it, they'll stay right where they are in their pouch and wait for you to stumble in the way of your friend.'

'Did you say the books, Sir,' asked the red-haired man of Marius, completely oblivious to this little exchange. 'The books were burnt in the fall of the greatest city in the world?'

'Yes, he cares about books, this fellow,' said the black-haired man. 'Sir, you better look to your little boy. He's a goner, the dance has changed. Tell him not to mock his elders.'

The two dancers came towards me, both as drunk as the man who had fallen. They made to caress me, simultaneously becoming with great odoriferous and heavy breathing a beast with four arms.

'You smile at our friend rolling around on the

ground?' one of them asked, sticking his knee between my legs.

I backed up, barely escaping the rude blow. 'Seemed the kindest thing I could do,' I answered. 'Being that my worship was the cause of his fall. Don't plunge into such devotions, yourself, Sirs. I haven't the slightest inclination to answer your prayers.'

My Master had risen.

'I tire of this,' he said in a cold, clear voice that echoed through the tapestries off the walls. It had a chilling sound to it.

All looked at him, even the struggling man on the floor.

'Indeed!' said the black-haired man, looking up. 'Marius De Romanus, is it? I've heard of you. I don't fear you.'

'How merciful for you,' said my Master in a whisper with a smile. He placed his hand on the man's head and the man whipped himself back and away, almost falling off the bench, but now he was most definitely afraid.

The dancers took their measure of my Master, no doubt trying to gauge whether he would be easy to overwhelm.

One of them turned on me again. 'Prayers, Hell!' he said.

'Sir, mind my Master. You weary him, and in weariness he is a perfect crank.' I snatched back my arm as he meant to take it.

I backed away even further, into the very midst of the boy musicians so that the music rose about me like a protective cloud.

I could see panic in their faces, yet they played all the faster, ignoring the sweat on their brows.

'Sweet, sweet, gentlemen,' I said. 'I like it. But play a requiem, if you will.'

They gave me desperate glances but no other regard. The drum beat on and the pipe made its snaky melody and the room throbbed with the strumming of the lutes.

The blond-haired man on the floor screamed for help, as he absolutely couldn't get up, and the two dancers went to his aid, though one shot his watchful darts at me.

My Master looked down at the black-haired challenger and then pulled him straight up from the bench with one hand and went to kiss his neck. The man hung in my Master's grip. He froze like a small tender mammal in the teeth of a great beast, and I almost heard the great draught of blood run out of him as my Master's hair shivered and fell down to cover the fatal repast.

Quickly, he let the man drop. Only the red-haired fellow observed all this. And he seemed in his intoxication not to know what to make of it. Indeed he raised one eye, wondering, and drank again from his filthy sloppy cup. He licked the fingers of his right hand, one by one, as if he were a cat, as my Master dropped his black-haired companion facedown on the table, indeed, right into a plate of fruit.

'Drunken idiot,' said the red-haired man. 'No one fights for valor, or honor, or decency.'

'Not many in any event,' said my Master looking down at him.

'They broke the world in half, those Turks,' said the red-haired man, still staring at the dead one, who surely stared stupidly at him from the smashed plate. I couldn't see the dead man's face, but it excited me tremendously that he was dead.

'Come now, gentlemen,' said my Master, 'and you, Sir, come here, you who gave my child so many rings.'

'Is he your son, Sir?' cried the blond humpback, who

was finally on his feet. He pushed his friends away from him. He turned and went to the summons. 'I'll father him better than you ever did.'

My Master appeared suddenly and without a sound on our side of the table. His garments settled at once, as if he had only taken a step. The red-haired man did not even seem to see it.

'Skanderbeg, the great Skanderbeg, I raise a toast to him,' said the red-haired man, to himself apparently. 'He's been dead too long, and give me but five Skanderbegs and I'd raise a new Crusade to take back our city from the Turks.'

'Indeed, who wouldn't with five Skanderbegs,' said the elderly man further down the table, the one nibbling and tearing at the joint. He wiped his mouth with his naked wrist. 'But there is no general like unto Skanderbeg, and there never was, save the man himself. What's the matter with Ludovico? You fool!' He stood up.

My Master had put his arm around the blond one, who pushed at him, quite dismayed that my Master was immovable. Now as the two dancers offered my Master pushes and shoves to free their companion, my Master again planted his fatal kiss. He lifted the chin of the blond one and went right for the big artery in the neck. He swung the man around and appeared to draw up the blood from him in one great draught. In a flash, he closed the man's eyes with two white fingers and let the body slip to the floor.

'It is your time to die, good Sirs,' he said to the dancers who now backed away from him.

One of them pulled his sword.

'Don't be so stupid!' shouted his companion. 'You're drunk. You'll never—.'

'No, you won't,' said my Master with a little sigh. His lips were more pink than I had ever seen them, and the blood he'd drunk paraded in his cheeks. Even his eyes had a greater gloss, and a greater gleam.

He closed his very hand over the man's sword and with the press of his thumb snapped the metal, so that the man held only a fragment in his hand.

'How dare you!' cried the man.

'How did you is more to the point!' sang out the red-haired man at the table. 'Cracked in half, is it? What kind of steel is that?'

The joint nibbler laughed very loud and threw back his head. He tore more meat from the bone.

My Master reached out and plucked from time and space the wielder of the broken sword, and now to bare the vein, broke the man's neck with a loud snap.

It seemed the other three had heard it – the one who ate the joint, the wary dancer and the man with the red hair.

It was the last of the dancers whom my Master embraced next. He caught the man's face in his hands as if it were love, and drank again, gasping the man's throat so that I saw the blood just for an instant, a veritable deluge of it, which my Master then covered with his mouth and his bent head.

I could see the blood pump into my Master's hand. I couldn't wait for him to raise his head, and this he did very soon, sooner even than he had left his last victim, and he looked at me dreamily and his countenance was all afire. He looked as human as any man in the room, even crazed with his special drink, as they were with their common wine.

His vagrant blond curls were plastered to his forehead by the sweat that rose in him, and I saw it was a fine sheen of blood.

The music abruptly stopped.

It was not the mayhem but the sight of my Master

139

which had stopped it, as he let this last victim slip, a loose sack of bones, to the floor.

'Requiem,' I said again. 'Their ghosts will thank you, kind Gentlemen.'

'Either that,' said Marius to the musicians as he drew close, 'or fly the room.'

'I say fly the room,' whispered the lute player. At once they all turned and made for the doors. They pulled and pulled upon the latch in their haste, cursing and shouting.

My Master backed up and gathered the jeweled rings from around the chair where I'd been seated before.

'My boys, you go without payment,' he said.

In their helpless whining fear, they turned and beheld the rings being tossed to them, and stupidly and eagerly and full of shame, they each caught a single treasure as my Master aimed it.

Then the doors flew open and cracked against the walls.

Out they went, all but scraping the doorframe, and the doors then shut.

'That's clever!' remarked the man with the joint which he laid aside at last, as all the meat was gone. 'How you'd do it, Marius De Romanus? I hear tell you're a powerful magician. Don't know why the Great Council doesn't call you up on charges of witchcraft. Must be all the money you have, no?'

I stared at my Master. Never had I seen him so lovely as now when he was flushed with this new blood. I wanted to touch him. I wanted to go into his arms. His eyes were drunken and soft as he looked at me.

But he broke off his seductive stare and went back to the table, and around it properly, and stood beside the man who had feasted on the joint.

The gray-haired man looked up at him and then

140

glanced at his red-haired companion. 'Don't be a fool, Martino,' he said to the redhead. 'It's probably perfectly legal to be a witch in the Veneto as long as a man pays his tax. Put your money in Martino's bank, Marius De Romanus.'

'Ah, but I do,' said Marius De Romanus, my Master, 'and it earns me quite a good return.'

He sat down again between the dead man and the red-haired man, who seemed quite delighted and exhilarated to have him return.

'Martino,' said my Master. 'Let's talk some more of the fall of Empires. Your Father, why was he with the Genoese?'

The red-haired man, now quite aflame with the whole discussion, declared with pride that his Father had been the representative of the family bank in Constantinople, and that he had died afterwards due to the wounds he'd suffered on that last and awful day.

'He saw it,' said the red-haired man, 'he saw the women and children slaughtered. He saw the priests torn from the altars of Santa Sofia. He knows the secret.'

'The secret!' scoffed the elderly man. He moved down the table and, with a big swipe of his left arm, shoved the dead man off over the bench so that he fell back on the floor.

'Good God, you heartless bastard,' said the red-haired man. 'Did you hear his skull crack? Don't treat my guest in that manner, not if you want to live.'

I came closer to the table.

'Yes, do come on, pretty one,' said the redhead. 'Sit down.' He turned on me his blazing golden eyes. 'Sit here, opposite me. Good God, look at Francisco there. I swear I heard his skull crack.'

'He's dead,' said Marius softly. 'It's all right for the

141

moment, don't worry on it.' His face was all the more bright from the blood he'd drunk. Indeed the color was even now, and radiant overall, and his hair seemed all the fairer against his blushing skin. A tiny spider's web of veins lived within each of his eyes, not detracting one jot from their awesome lustrous beauty.

'Oh, all right, fine, they're dead,' said the redhead, with a shrug. 'Yes, I was telling you, and you damned well better mark my words because I know. The priests, the priests picked up the sacred chalice and the Sacred Host and they went into a hiding place in Santa Sofia. My Father saw this with his own eyes. I know the secret.'

'Eyes, eyes, eyes,' said the elderly man. 'Your Father must have been a peacock to have had so many eyes!'

'Shut up or I'll slit your throat,' said the red-haired man. 'Look what you did to Francisco, knocking him over like that..Good God!' He made the Sign of the Cross rather lazily. 'There's blood coming from the back of his head.'

My Master turned and, leaning down, swept up five fingerfuls of this blood. He turned to me slowly and then to the redhead. He sucked the blood off one finger. 'Dead,' he said with a little smile. 'But it's plenty warm and thick.' He smiled slowly.

The red-haired man was as fascinated as a child at a puppet show.

My Master extended his bloody fingers, palm up, and made a smile as if to say, 'You want to taste it?'

The red-haired man grabbed Marius's wrist and licked the blood off his forefinger and thumb. 'Hmmm, very good,' he said. 'All my companions are of the best blood.'

'You're telling me,' said my Master. I couldn't rip my eyes off him, off his changing face. It seemed now his

142

cheeks did darken, or maybe it was only their curve as he smiled. His lips were rosy.

'And I'm not finished, Amadeo,' he whispered. 'I've only begun.'

'He's not bad hurt!' insisted the elderly man. He studied the victim on the floor. He was worried. Had he killed him? 'It's just a mere cut on the back of his head, that's all. Isn't it?'

'Yes, a tiny cut,' said Marius. 'What's this secret, my dear friend?' He had his back to the gray-haired man, speaking to the redhead with much more interest as he had been all along.

'Yes, please,' I said. 'What's the secret, Sir?' I asked. 'Is that the secret, that the priests ran?'

'No, child, don't be dense!' said the red-haired man looking across the table at me. He was powerfully beautiful. Had Bianca loved him? She never said.

'The secret, the secret,' he said. 'If you don't believe in this secret, then you'll believe nothing, nothing sacred or otherwise.'

He lifted his goblet. It was empty. I picked up the pitcher and filled it with the dark lovely-smelling red wine. I considered taking a taste of it, then a revulsion filled me.

'Nonsense,' whispered my Master. 'Drink to their passing. Go ahead. There's a clean goblet.'

'Oh, yes, forgive me,' said the redhead. 'I haven't even offered you a cup. Good God, to think I threw a mere table diamond on the board for you, when I would have your love.' He picked up the goblet, a rich fancy thing of inlaid silver with tiny stones. I saw now that all the goblets were a set, all carved with tiny delicate figures and set with these same bright little stones. He set down this goblet for me with a clonk. He took the pitcher from me and filled the goblet and then thrust it at me.

143

I thought I would become so sick I'd vomit on the floor. I looked up at him, at his near sweet face and his pretty blazing red hair. He gave a boyish smile, showing small but perfect white teeth, very pearly, and he seemed to dote on me and to drift, not uttering a word.

'Take it, drink,' said my Master. 'Yours is a dangerous road, Amadeo, drink for knowledge and drink for strength.'

'You don't mock me now, Sir, do you?' I asked, staring at the red-haired man though I spoke to Marius.

'I love you, Sir, as I always have,' said my Master, 'but you do see something in what I say, for I'm coarsened by human blood. It's always the fact. Only in starvation do I find an ethereal purity.'

'Ah, and you turn me from penance at every juncture,' I said, 'towards the senses, towards pleasure.'

The red-haired man and I had locked eyes. Yet I heard Marius answer me.

'It's a penance to kill, Amadeo, that's the rub. It's a penance to slay for nothing, nothing, not "honor, not valor, not decency," as our friend says here.'

'Yes!' said 'our friend,' who turned to Marius and then back to me. 'Drink!' He thrust the goblet at me.

'And when it's all done, Amadeo, gather up these goblets for me and bring them home so I might have a trophy of my failure and my defeat, for they will be one and the same, and a lesson for you as well. Seldom is it all so rich and clear as it is to me now.'

The red-haired man leaned forward, deep into the flirt, and put the goblet right against my lip. 'Little David, you'll grow up to be the King, remember? Oh, I would worship you now, tender-cheeked little man that you are, and beg for one psalm from your harp, just one, were it given with your own will.'

My Master whispered low, 'Can you grant a man's dying request?'

'I think he is dead!' said the gray-haired man with obnoxious loudness. 'Look, Martino, I think I did kill him; his head's bleeding like a damned tomato. Look!'

'Oh, shut up about him!' said Martino, the redhead, without taking his eyes off mine. 'Do grant a dying man's request, little David,' he went on. 'We are all dying, and I for you, and that you die with me, just a little, Sir, in my arms? Let us make a little game of it. It will amuse you, Marius De Romanus. You'll see I ride him and stroke him with one artful rhythm, and you'll behold a sculpture of flesh that becomes a fountain, as what I pump into him comes forth from him in my hand.'

He cupped his hand as if he had my organ already in it. He kept his eyes on me. Then in a low whisper, he said, 'I'm too soft to make my sculpture. Let me drink it from you. Have mercy on the parched.'

I snatched the goblet out of his wavering hand and drank down the wine. My body tightened. I thought the wine would come back up and spew. I made it go down. I looked at my Master.

'This is ugly, I hate it.'

'Oh, nonsense,' he said, barely moving his lips. 'There's beauty all around!'

'Damned if he isn't dead,' said the gray-haired man. He kicked the body of Francisco on the floor. 'Martino, I'm out of here.'

'Stay, Sir,' said Marius. 'I would kiss you good night.' He clapped his hand over the gray-haired man's wrist and lunged at his throat, but what did it look like to the red-haired one, who gave it only a bleary glance before he continued his worship? He filled my goblet again.

A moan came from the gray-haired man, or was it from Marius?

145

I was petrified. When he turned from his victim, I would see even more blood teeming in him, and I would have given all the world to see him white again, my marble god, my graven Father in our private bed.

The red-haired man rose before me as he leant over the table and put his wet lips on mine. 'I die for you, boy!' he said.

'No, you die for nothing,' said Marius.

'Master, not him, please!' I cried.

I fell back, nearly losing my balance on the bench. My Master's arm had come between us, and his hand covered the red-haired man's shoulder.

'What's the secret, Sir?' I cried frantically, 'the secret of Santa Sofia, the one we must believe?'

The red-haired man was utterly befuddled. He knew he was drunk. He knew things around him didn't make sense. But he thought it was because he was drunk. He looked at Marius's arm across his chest, and he even turned and looked at the fingers clutching his shoulder. Then he looked at Marius and so did I.

Marius was human, utterly human. There was no trace of the impermeable and indestructible god left. His eyes and his face simmered in the blood. He was flushed as a man from running, and his lips were bloody, and when he licked them now, his tongue was ruby red. He smiled at Martino, the last of them, the only one left alive.

Martino pulled his gaze away from Marius and looked at me. At once he softened and lost his alarm. He spoke with reverence.

'In the midst of the siege, as the Turks stormed the church, some of the priests left the altar of Santa Sofia,' he said. 'They took with them the chalice and the Blessed Sacrament, our Lord's Body and Blood. They are hidden this very day in the secret chambers of Santa

146

Sofia, and on the very moment that we take back the city, on the very moment when we take back the great church of Santa Sofia, when we drive the Turks out of our capital, those priests, those very priests will return. They'll come out of their hiding place and go up the steps of the altar, and they will resume the Mass at the very point where they were forced to stop.'

'Ah,' I said, sighing and marveling at it. 'Master,' I said softly. 'That's a good enough secret to save a man's life, isn't it?'

'No,' said Marius. 'I know the story, and he made our Bianca a whore.'

The red-haired man strained to follow our words, to fathom the depth of our exchange.

'A whore? Bianca? A murderer ten times over, Sir, but not a whore. Nothing so simple as a whore.' He studied Marius as though he thought this heated passionately florid man was beautiful, indeed. And well he was.

'Ah, but you taught her the art of murder,' said Marius almost tenderly, his fingers massaging the man's shoulder, while with his left arm he reached around Martino's back, until his left hand might lock on the man's shoulder with his right. He bent his forehead to touch Martino's temple.

'Hmmm,' Martino shook himself all over. 'I've drunk too much. I never taught her any such thing.'

'Ah, but you did, you taught her, and to kill for such paltry sums.'

'Master, what is it to us?'

'My son forgets himself,' said Marius, still looking at Martino. 'He forgets that I am bound to kill you on behalf of our sweet lady, whom you so finagled into your dark, sticky plots.'

'She rendered me a service,' said Martino. 'Let me have the boy!'

'Beg pardon?'

'You mean to kill me, so do it. But let me have the boy. A kiss, Sir, that's all I ask. A kiss, that is the world. I'm too drunk for anything else!'

'Please, Master, I can't endure this,' I said.

'Then, how will you endure eternity my child? Don't you know that's what I mean to give you? What power under God is there that can break me?' He threw a fierce angry glance at me, but it seemed more artifice than true emotion.

'I've learnt my lessons,' I said. 'I only hate to see him die.'

'Ah, yes, then you have learnt. Martino, kiss my child if he'll allow it, and mark you, be gentle when you do.'

It was I who leant across the table now and planted my kiss on the man's cheek. He turned and caught my mouth with his, hungry, sour with wine, but enticingly, electrically hot.

The tears sprang to my eyes. I opened my mouth to him and let his tongue come into me. And with my eyes shut, I felt it quiver, and his lips become tight, as if they had been turned to hard metal clamped to me and unable to close.

My Master had him, had his throat, and the kiss was frozen, and I, weeping, put out my hand blindly to find the very place in his neck where my Master's evil teeth had driven in. I felt my Master's silky lips, I felt the hard teeth beneath them, I felt the tender neck.

I opened my eyes and pulled myself away. My doomed Martino sighed and moaned and closed his lips, and sat back in my Master's grip with his eyes half-mast.

He turned his head slowly towards my Master. In a small raw drunken voice, he spoke. 'For Bianca . . .'

'For Bianca,' I said. I sobbed, muffling it with my hand.

My Master drew up. With his left hand, he smoothed back Martino's damp and tangled hair. 'For Bianca,' he said into his ear.

'Never . . . never should have let her live,' came the last sighing words from Martino. His head fell forward over my Master's right arm.

My Master kissed the back of his head, and let him slip down onto the table.

'Charming to the last,' said he. 'Just a real poet to the bottom of your soul.'

I stood up, pushing the bench away behind me, and I moved out into the center of the room. I cried and cried, and couldn't muffle it with my hand. I dug into my jacket for a handkerchief, and just as I went to wipe my tears, I stumbled backwards over the dead humpbacked man and almost fell. I cried out, a terrible weak and ignominious cry.

I moved back away from him and away from the bodies of his companions until I felt behind me the heavy, scratchy tapestry, and smelled its dust and threads.

'Ah, so this was what you wanted of me,' I sobbed. I veritably sobbed. 'That I should hate it, that I should weep for them, fight for them, beg for them.'

He sat at the table still, Christ of the Last Supper, with his neatly parted hair, his shining face, his ruddy hands folded one on top of the other, looking with his hot and swimming eyes at me.

'Weep for one of them, at least one!' he said. His voice grew wrathful. 'Is that too much to ask? That one death be regretted among so many?' He rose from the table. He seemed to quake with his rage.

I pushed the handkerchief over my face, sobbing into it.

'For a nameless beggar in a makeshift boat for a bed

149

we have no tears, do we, and would not our pretty Bianca suffer because we've played the young Adonis in her bed! And of some of those, we weep for none but that one, the very most evil without question, because he flatters us, is it not so?'

'I knew him,' I whispered. 'I mean, in this short time I knew him, and . . .'

'And you would have them run from you, anonymous as foxes in the brush!' He pointed to the tapestries blazoned with the Courtly Hunt. 'Behold with a man's eyes what I show you.'

There was a sudden darkening of the room, a flutter of all the many candles. I gasped, but it was only he, come to stand right in front of me and look down at me, a feverish, blushing being whose very heat I could feel as if every pore of him gave forth warm breath.

'Master,' I cried, swallowing my sobs. 'Are you happy with what you've taught me or not? Are you happy with what I've learnt or not! Don't you play with me over this! I'm not your puppet, Sir, no, never that! What would you have me be, then? Why this anger?' I shuddered all over, the tears veritably flooding from my eyes. 'I would be strong for you, but I . . . I knew him.'

'Why? Because he kissed you?' He leant down and picked up my hair in his left hand. He yanked me towards him.

'Marius, for the love of God!'

He kissed me. He kissed me as Martino had, and his mouth was as human and as hot. He slipped his tongue into mine, and I felt not blood but manly passion. His finger burnt against my cheek.

I broke away. He let me break away. 'Oh, come back to me, my cold white one, my god,' I whispered. I lay my face on his chest. I could hear his heart. I could hear it beating. I had never before heard it, never heard a pulse within the stone chapel of his body. 'Come back to me, most dispassionate teacher. I don't know what you want.'

'Oh, my darling,' he sighed. 'Oh, my love.' And there came the old demon shower of his kisses, not the mock of a passionate man, but his affection, petal soft, so many tributes laid upon my face and hair. 'Oh, my beautiful Amadeo, oh, my child,' he said.

'Love me, love me, love me,' I whispered. 'Love me and take me into it with you. I am yours.'

In stillness, he held me. I drowsed on his shoulders.

A little breeze came, but it did not move the heavy tapestries in which the French lords and ladies drifted in their eternal and leafy green forest among hounds that would forever bay and birds that would always sing.

Finally, he released me and he stepped back.

He walked away from me, his shoulders hunched, his head down.

Then with a lazy gesture he beckoned for me to come, and yet he moved out of the room too fast.

I ran after him, down the stone stairs to the street. The doors were open when I got there. The cold wind washed away my tears. It washed away the evil heat of the room. I ran and ran along the stone quays, over the bridges, and after him towards the square.

I didn't catch him until I reached the Molo, and there he was walking, a tall man in a red hood and cape, past San Marco and towards the harbor. I ran after him. The wind from the sea was icy and very strong. It blasted me, and I felt doubly cleansed.

'Don't leave me, Master,' I called out. My words were swallowed up, but he heard.

He came to a stop, as if it really were my doing. He turned and waited for me to catch up with him, and then he picked up my outstretched hand.

'Master, hear my lesson,' I said. 'Judge my work.' I caught my breath in haste and went on. 'I saw you drink from those who were evil, convicted in your heart of some gross crime. I saw you feast as it is your nature; I saw you take the blood with which you must live. And all about you lies this evil world, this wilderness of men no better than beasts who will yield up a blood as sweet and rich for you as innocent blood. I see it. That's what you meant for me to see, and it's done.'

His face was impassive. He merely studied me. It seemed the burning fever in him was already dying away. The distant torches along the arcades shone on his face, and it was whitening and as ever hard. The ships creaked in the harbor. There came distant murmurs and cries from those, perhaps, who cannot or never sleep.

I glanced up at the sky, fearful I would see the fatal light. He'd be gone.

'If I drink such as that, Master, the blood of the wicked and those whom I overpower, will I become like you?'

He shook his head. 'Many a man has drunk another's blood, Amadeo,' he said in a low but calm voice. His reason had come back to him, his manners, his seeming soul. 'Would you be with me, and be my pupil and my love?'

'Yes, Master, always and forever, or for so long as nature gives to you and me.'

'Oh, it isn't fanciful the words I spoke. We are immortal. And only one enemy can destroy us – it's the fire that burns in that torch there, or in the rising sun. Sweet to think on it, that when we are at last weary of all this world there is the rising sun.'

'I am yours, Master.' I hugged him close and tried to vanquish him with kisses. He endured them, and even smiled, but he didn't move.

But when I broke off, and made a fist of my right hand as if to hit him, which I could never have done, to my amazement he began to yield.

He turned and took me in his powerful and ever careful embrace.

'Amadeo, I can't go on without you,' he said. His voice was desperate and small. 'I meant to show you evil, not sport. I meant to show you the wicked price of my immortality. And that I did. But in so doing, I saw it myself, and my eyes are dazzled and I am hurt and tired.'

He laid his head against my head, and he held tight to me.

'Do what you will to me, Sir,' I said. 'Make me suffer and long for it, if that's what you want. I am your fool. I am yours.'

He released me and kissed me formally.

'Four nights, my child,' he said. He moved away. He kissed his fingers and planted that last kiss on my lips, and then he was gone. 'I go now to an ancient duty. Four nights. Till then.'

I stood alone in the earliest chill of the morning. I stood alone beneath a paling sky. I knew better than to look for him.

In the greatest dejection, I walked back through the alleys, cutting across little bridges to wander into the depth of the waking city, for what I didn't know.

I was half-surprised when I realized I had returned to the house of the murdered men. I was surprised when I saw their doorway still open, as if a servant would at any moment appear.

No one appeared.

Slowly the sky above ripened to a pale white and then to a faint blue. Mist crawled along the top of the canal. I went over the small bridge to the doorway, and again went up the stairs.

A powdery light came in from the loosely slatted windows. I found the banquet room where the candles still burnt. The smell of tobacco and wax and of pungent food was close and hanging in the air.

I walked inside, and I inspected the dead men, who lay as we had left them, disheveled, and now slightly yellowed and waxen and a prey to the gnats and the flies.

There was no sound but the humming of the flies.

The spilt wine had dried on the table in pools. The corpses were clean of all the rampant marks of death.

I was sick again, sick to trembling, and I took a deep breath that I shouldn't retch. Then I realized why I had come.

Men in those days wore short cloaks on their jackets, sometimes affixed, as you probably know. I needed one of these, and took it, ripping it loose from the humpback man, who lay almost on his face. It was a flaring coat of canary yellow with white fox for its border and a lining of heavy silk. I tied knots in it and made a thick deep sack of it, and then I went up and down the table, gathering up the goblets, dashing out the contents first, and then putting them in my sack.

Soon my sack was red with drops of wine and grease from where I'd rested it on the board.

I stood when finished, making certain that no goblet had escaped. I had them all. I studied the dead men – my sleeping red-haired Martino, his face on the bare marble in a puddle of the slopped wine, and Francisco, from whose head did leak a small bit of darkened blood.

The flies buzzed and droned over this blood as they did over the grease pooled around the remnants of the roasted pig. A battalion of little black beetles had come, most common in Venice, for they are carried by the water, and it made its way over the table, towards Martino's face.

A quiet warming light came in through the open doorway. The morning had come.

With one sweeping glance that imprinted on my mind the details of this scene for all time, I went out and home.

The boys were awake and busy when I arrived. An old carpenter was already there, fixing the door which I had shattered with the ax.

I gave to the maid my bulky sack of clanking cups, and she, sleepy and having just arrived, took it without a remark.

I felt a tightening inside me, a sickening, a sudden feeling that I would burst. My body seemed too small, too imperfect an enclosure for all I knew and felt. My head throbbed. I wanted to lie down, but before that I had to see Riccardo. I had to find him and the older boys.

I had to.

I went walking through the house until I came to them, all gathered for a lesson with the young lawyer who came from Padua only once or twice a month to begin our instructions in the law. Riccardo saw me in the door and motioned for me to be quiet. The teacher was speaking.

I had nothing to say. I only leant against the door and looked at my friends. I loved them. Yes, I did love them. I would die for them! I knew it, and with a terrible relief I began to cry.

Riccardo saw me turn away, and slipping out, he came to me.

'What is it, Amadeo?' he asked.

I was too delirious with my own torment. I saw again the slaughtered dinner party. I turned to Riccardo and wound him in my arms, so comforted by his warmth and his human softness compared to the Master, and then I told him that I would die for him, die for any of

155

them, die for the Master too.

'But why, what is this, why vow this to me now?' he asked.

I couldn't tell him about the slaughter. I couldn't tell him of the coldness in me that had watched the men die.

I went off into my Master's bedchamber, and I lay down and tried to sleep.

In late afternoon, when I woke to find the doors had been closed, I climbed out of the bed and went to the Master's desk. To my astonishment I saw his book was there, the book that was always hidden when out of his sight.

Of course I could not turn a page of it, but it was open, and there lay a page covered in writing, in Latin, and though it seemed a strange Latin, and hard for me, there was no mistaking the final words:

How can so much beauty hide such a bruised and steely heart, and why must I love him, why must I lean in my weariness upon his irresistible yet indomitable strength? Is he not the wizened funereal spirit of a dead man in a child's clothes?

I felt a strange prickling over my scalp and over my arms.

Is this what I was? A bruised and steely heart! The wizened funereal spirit of a dead man in a child's clothes? Oh, but I couldn't deny it; I couldn't say it wasn't true. And yet how hurtful, how positively cruel it seemed. No, not cruel, merely merciless and accurate, and what right had I to expect anything else?

I started to cry.

I lay down in our bed, as was my custom, and plumped the softest pillows to make a nest for my crooked left arm and my head.

Four nights. How should I endure it? What did he want of me? That I go forth to all the things I knew and loved and take my leave of them as a mortal boy. That is what he would instruct. And that I should do.

Only a few hours were allowed to me by fate.

I was awakened by Riccardo, who shoved a sealed note in my face.

'Who's sent this?' I asked sleepily. I sat up, and I pushed my thumb beneath the folded paper and broke the wax seal.

'Read it and you tell me. Four men came to deliver it, a company of four. Must be some damned important thing.'

'Yes,' I said unfolding it, 'and to make you look so fearful too.'

He stood there with his arms folded.

I read:

Dearest darling one,

Stay indoors. Do not on any account leave the house and bar any who seek to enter. Your wicked English lord, the Earl of Harlech, has discovered your identity through the most unscrupulous nosing about, and in his madness vows to take you back with him to England or leave you in fragments at your Master's door. Confess all to your Master. Only his strength can save you. And do send me something in writing, lest I too lose my wits over you, and over the tales of horror which are cried out this morning in every canal and piazza for every ear.

Your devoted Bianca

'Well, damn it,' I said folding up the letter. 'Four

157

nights Marius will be gone, and now this. Am I to hide for these crucial four nights under this roof?'

'You had better,' said Riccardo.

'Then you know the story.'

'Bianca told me. The Englishman, having traced you there and heard tell of you being there all the time, would have torn her lodgings to pieces if her guests had not stopped him en masse.'

'And why didn't they kill him, for the love of God,' I said disgustedly.

He looked most worried and sympathetic.

'I think they count on our Master to do it,' he said, 'as it is you that the man wants. How can you be certain the Master means to stay away for four nights? When has he ever said such things? He comes, he goes, he warns no one.'

'Hmmm, don't argue with me,' I answered patiently. 'Riccardo, he isn't coming home for four nights, and I will not stay cooped up in this house, and not while Lord Harlech stirs up dirt.'

'You'd better stay here!' Riccardo answered. 'Amadeo, this Englishman is famous with his sword. He practices with a fencing master. He's the terror of the taverns. You knew that when you picked up with him, Amadeo. Think on what you do! He's famous for everything bad and nothing good.'

'So then come with me. You need only distract him and I'll take him.'

'No, you're good with your sword, true enough, but you can't take a man who's been practicing with the blade since before you were born.'

I lay back down on the pillow. What should I do? I was on fire to go out into the world, on fire to gaze at things with my great sense of the drama and significance of my last days among the living, and now this! And the

158

man who had been worth a few nights' riotous rough-house pleasure was no doubt advertising far and wide his discontent.

It was bitter, but it seemed I had to stay at home. There was nothing to do. I wanted very much to kill this man, kill him with my own dagger and sword, and even thought I had a good chance of it, but what was this petty adventure to what lay before me when my Master returned?

The fact was, I had already left the world of regular things, the world of regular scores to be settled, and could not be drawn now into a foolish blunder that might be my forfeit of the strange destiny towards which I moved.

'All right, and Bianca is safe from this man?' I asked Riccardo.

'Quite safe. She has more admirers than can fit in the door of her house, and she's marshaled all against this man and for you. Now write her something of gratitude and common sense, and swear to me as well that you'll remain indoors.'

I got up and went to the Master's writing desk. I picked up the pen.

I was stopped by an awful clatter, and then a series of piercing irritating cries. They echoed through the stone rooms of the house. I heard people running. Riccardo leapt to attention and put his hand on the hilt of his sword.

I gathered up my own weapons, unsheathing my light rapier and my dagger, both.

'Good Lord Jesus, the man can't be in the house.'

A horrid scream drowned out the others.

The smallest of us all, Giuseppe, appeared in the door, his face a luminous white, and his eyes big and round.

'What the hell's the matter?' Riccardo demanded, catching hold of him.

'He's been stabbed. Look, he's bleeding!' I said.

'Amadeo, Amadeo!' It rang loudly from the stone stairwell. It was the Englishman's voice.

The boy doubled over in his pain. The wound was in the pit of his stomach, utterly cruel.

Riccardo was beside himself.

'Shut the doors!' he shouted.

'How can I,' I cried, 'when the other boys may blunder right into his path?'

I ran out and into the big salon and into the portego, the great room of the house.

Another boy, Jacope, lay crumpled on the floor, pushing at it with his knees. I saw the blood running on the stones.

'Oh, this is beyond all fairness; this is a slaughter of innocents!' I shouted. 'Lord Harlech, show yourself. You're about to die.'

I heard Riccardo cry out behind me. The little boy was obviously dead.

I ran towards the stairs. 'Lord Harlech, I'm here!' I called out. 'Come out, you brutish coward, you slayer of children! I have a millstone ready for your neck!'

Riccardo spun me around. 'There, Amadeo,' he whispered. 'I'm with you.' His blade sang out as he drew it. He was much better than me with the sword, but this battle was mine.

The man was at the far end of the portego. I had hoped he would be staggering drunk, but no such luck. I saw in a moment that any dream he might have had of taking me away by force was now gone; he had slain two boys, and he knew his lust had led him to a final stand. This was hardly an enemy crippled by love.

'Jesus in Heaven, help us!' whispered Riccardo.

'Lord Harlech,' I cried. 'You dare make a shambles of my Master's house!' I stepped aside from Riccardo to give us both room, as I motioned Riccardo to come forward, away from the head of the steps. I felt the weight of the rapier. Not heavy enough. I wished to God I had practiced with it more.

The Englishman came towards me, a taller man than I had ever noted, with a great reach to his arm that would be a powerful advantage, his cape flapping, his feet sheathed in heavy boots, his rapier raised and his long Italian dagger ready in the other hand. At least he didn't have a true and heavy sword.

Dwarfed by the great room, he was nevertheless big of stature and had a head of roaring British copper hair. His blue eyes were stewed in blood, but he was steady in his walk and in his murderous gaze. His face was wet with bitter tears.

'Amadeo,' he called out over the vast room as he came on. 'You cut my heart out of my chest while I lived and breathed, and you took it with you! We shall be together this night in Hell.'

The high long portego of our house, the entrance hall, was a perfectly wonderful place to die. There was nothing in it to mar its gorgeous mosaic floors with their circles of colored marble stones, and their festive pattern of winding flowers and tiny wild birds.

We had the entire field upon which to fight, with not a chair in the way to stop us from killing each other.

I advanced on the Englishman before I had time to really admit that I wasn't very good with the sword yet, had never shown an instinct for it, and I had no inkling of just what my Master would have me do just now, that is, what he would advise if he were here.

. I made several bold thrusts at Lord Harlech, which he parried so easily that I should have lost heart. But just when I thought I'd catch my breath and maybe even run, he swept in with his dagger and slashed my left arm. The cut stung me and infuriated me.

I went after him again, this time managing with considerable luck to get him across the throat. It was just a scratch, but it bled furiously down his tunic, and he was as angry as I was to be cut.

'You horrid damnable little devil,' he said. 'You made me adore you so you could draw and quarter me at your pleasure. You promised me you'd come back!'

In fact, he kept up this sort of verbal barrage the entire time we fought. He seemed to need it, rather like a goading battle drum and fife.

'Come on, you despicable little angel, I'll tear your wings off!' he said.

He drove me back with a fast volley of thrusts. I stumbled, lost my balance and fell but managed to scramble up again, using the low position to stab dangerously close to his scrotum as I did so, which gave him a start. I ran at him, knowing now there was nothing to be gained by drawing this out.

He dodged my blade, laughed at me and caught me with the dagger, this time on the face.

'Pig!' I growled before I could stop myself. I hadn't known I was so completely vain. My face, no less. He'd cut it. My face. I felt the blood gushing as it does from face wounds, and I rushed at him again, this time forgetting all the rules of the encounter and thrashing the air with my sword in a fierce crazy series of circles. Then as he parried frantically left and right, I ducked and caught him with the dagger in the belly and ripped upward, stopped by the thick gold-encrusted leather of his belt.

I backed up as he sought to slaughter me with both his weapons, and then he dropped them and grabbed, as men do, for the belching wound.

He fell down on his knees.

'Finish him!' shouted Riccardo. He stood back, a man of honor already. 'Finish him now, Amadeo, or I do it. Think what he's done under this roof.'

I lifted my sword.

The man suddenly grabbed up his own with his bloody hand and flashed it at me, even as he groaned and winced with his pain. He rose up and ran at me in one gesture. I jumped back. He fell to his knees. He was sick and shivering. He dropped the sword, feeling again for his wounded belly. He didn't die, but he couldn't fight on.

'Oh, God,' said Riccardo. He clutched his dagger. But he obviously couldn't bring himself to hack away at the unarmed man.

The Englishman went over on his side. He drew his knees up. He grimaced and he laid his head down on the stone, his face formal as he took a deep breath. He fought terrible pain and the certainty that he would die.

Riccardo stepped forward and laid the tip of his sword on Lord Harlech's cheek.

'He's dying, let him die,' I said. But the man continued to breathe.

I wanted to kill him, I really wanted to, but it was impossible to kill someone who lay there so placid and so brave.

His eyes took on a wise, poetical expression. 'And so it ends here,' he said in a small voice that perhaps Riccardo didn't even hear.

'Yes, it ends,' I said. 'End it nobly.'

'Amadeo, he slew the two children!' said Riccardo.

'Pick up your dagger, Lord Harlech!' I said. I kicked the weapon at him. I pushed it right at his hand. 'Pick it up, Lord Harlech,' I said. The blood was running down my face and down my neck, tickling and sticky. I couldn't stand it. I wanted more to wipe my own wounds than to bother with him.

He turned over on his back. The blood came out of his mouth and out of his gut. His face was wet and shiny, and his breathing became very labored. He seemed young again, young as he had when he threatened me, an overgrown boy with a big mop of flaming curls.

'Think about me when you begin to sweat, Amadeo,' he said, his voice still small, and now hoarse. 'Think about me when you realize that your life, too, is finished.'

'Run him through,' said Riccardo in a whisper. 'He could take two days to die with that wound.'

'And you won't have two days,' said Lord Harlech from the floor, panting, 'with the poisoned cuts I gave you. Feel it in your eyes? Your eyes burn, don't they Amadeo? The poison goes into the blood, and it strikes the eyes first. Are you dizzy?'

'You bastard,' said Riccardo. He stabbed the man with his rapier right through his tunic, once, twice, then three times. Lord Harlech grimaced. His eyelids fluttered, and out of his mouth came a final gout of blood. He was dead.

'Poison?' I whispered. 'Poison on the blade?' Instinctively, I felt my arm where he had cut me. My face, however, bore the deeper wound. 'Don't touch his sword or dagger. Poison!'

'He was lying, come, let me wash you,' said Riccardo. 'There's no time to waste.'

He tried to pull me from the room.

'What are we going to do with him, Riccardo! What can we do! We're here alone without the Master. There are three dead in this house, maybe more.'

As I spoke I heard steps at both ends of the great room. The little boys were coming out of their hiding places, and I saw one of the teachers with them, who had apparently been keeping them out of the way.

I had mixed feelings on this score. But these were all children, and the teacher an unarmed man, a helpless scholar. The older boys had all gone out, as was the custom in the morning. Or so I thought.

'Come on, we have to get them all to a decent place,' I said. 'Don't touch the weapons.' I signaled for the little ones to come. 'We'll carry him to the best bedchamber, come on. And the boys as well.'

As the little ones struggled to obey, some of them began to cry.

'You, give us a hand!' I said to the teacher. 'Watch out for the poisoned weapons.' He stared at me wildly. 'I mean it. It's poison.'

'Amadeo, you're bleeding all over!' he cried shrilly in a panic. 'What poisoned weapons? Dear God save us all!'

'Oh, stop it!' I said. But I could stand this situation no longer, and as Riccardo took charge of the moving of the bodies, I rushed into my Master's bedroom to attend to my wounds.

I dumped the whole pitcherful of water into the basin in my haste, and grabbed up a napkin with which to catch the blood that was flowing down my neck and into my shirt. Sticky, sticky mess, I cursed. My head swam, and I almost fell. Grabbing the edge of the table, I told myself not to be Lord Harlech's fool. Riccardo had been right. Lord Harlech had made up that lie about the poison! Poison the blade, indeed!

But as I told myself this story, I looked down and saw for the first time a scratch, apparently made by his rapier on the back of my right hand. My hand was swelling as if this were an insect's venomous work.

I felt my arm and my face. The wounds there were swelling, great welts forming behind the cuts. Again, there came the dizziness. The sweat dripped off me right into the basin, which was now full of red water that looked like wine.

'Oh, my God, the Devil's done this to me,' I said. I turned and the entire room began to tilt and then to float. I rocked on my feet.

Someone caught me. I didn't even see who it was. I tried to say Riccardo's name, but my tongue was thick in my mouth.

Sounds and colors mingled in a hot, pulsing blur. Then with astonishing clarity I saw the embroidered baldaquin of the Master's bed, over my head. Riccardo stood over me.

He spoke to me rapidly and somewhat desperately,

but I couldn't make out what he said. Indeed, it seemed he spoke a foreign tongue, a pretty one, very melodious and sweet, but I couldn't understand a word of it.

'I'm hot,' I said. 'I'm burning, I'm so hot that I can't bear it. I have to have water. Put me in the Master's bath.'

He didn't seem to have heard me at all. On and on he went with his obvious pleading. I felt his hand on my forehead and it burned me, positively burned me. I begged him not to touch me, but this he didn't hear, and neither did I! I wasn't even speaking. I wanted to speak, but my tongue was too heavy and too big. *You'll get the poison*, I wanted to cry. I could not.

I closed my eyes. Mercifully I drifted. I saw a great sparkling sea, the waters off the island of the Lido, crenelated and beautiful beneath the noonday sun. I floated on this sea, perhaps in a small bark, or maybe just on my back. I couldn't feel the water itself, but there seemed nothing between me and its gentle tossing waves that were big and slow and easy and carried me up and then down. Far off, a great city gleamed on the shore. At first I thought it was Torcello, or even Venice, and that I had been turned around somehow and was floating towards the land. Then I saw it was much bigger than Venice, with great piercing reflective towers, as if it had been made entirely of brilliant glass. Oh, it was so lovely.

'Am I going there?' I asked.

The waves seemed then to fold over me, not with a suffocating wetness, but merely a quiet blanket of heavy light. I opened my eyes. I saw the red of the taffeta baldaquin above. I saw the golden fringe sewn on the velvet bed curtains, and then I saw Bianca Solderini there above me. She had a cloth in her hand.

'There wasn't enough poison on those blades to kill

you,' she said. 'It's merely made you sick. Now, listen to me, Amadeo, you must take each breath with quiet force and resolve to fight this sickness and to get well. You must ask the very air itself to make you strong, and be confident of it, that's it, you must breathe deeply and slowly, yes, exactly, and you must realize that this poison is being sweated out of you, and you must not believe in this poison, and you must not fear.'

'The Master will know,' said Riccardo. He looked drawn and miserable, and his lips quivered. His eyes were flooded with his tears. Oh, ominous sign, certainly. 'The Master will know somehow. He knows all things. The Master will break his journey and come home.'

'Wash his face,' said Bianca calmly. 'Wash his face and be quiet.' How brave she was.

I moved my tongue but I couldn't form words. I wanted to say that they must tell me when the sun sank, for then and only then might the Master come. There was surely a chance. Then and only then. He might appear.

I turned my head to the side, away from them. The cloth was burning me.

'Softly, quietly,' said Bianca. 'Take in the air, yes, and do not be afraid.'

A long time passed as I lay there, hovering just below perfect consciousness, and thankful that their voices were not sharp, and their touch was not so terrible, but the sweating was awful, and I despaired utterly of being cool.

I tossed and tried to get up once, only to feel terribly sick, sick unto vomiting. With a great relief I realized they had laid me back down.

'Hold on to my hands,' said Bianca, and I felt her fingers grasping mine, so small and too hot, hot like everything else, hot like Hell, I thought, but I was too

168

sick to think of Hell, too sick to think of anything but vomiting up my insides into a basin, and getting to somewhere cool. Oh, just open the windows, open them on the winter; I don't care, open them!

It seemed quite a nuisance that I might die, and nothing more. Feeling better was of far greater importance, and nothing troubled me as to my soul or any world to come.

Then abruptly all things changed.

I felt myself rise upwards, as if someone had yanked me by my head out of the bed and sought to pull me up through the red cloth baldaquin and through the ceiling of the room. Indeed, I looked down, and to my utter amazement I saw myself lying on the bed. I saw myself as if there were no baldaquin above my body to block the view.

I looked far more beautiful than I ever imagined myself to be. Understand, it was utterly dispassionate. I did not feel an exultation in my own beauty. I only thought, What a beautiful young boy. How gifted he has been by God. Look at his long delicate hands, how they lie beside him, and look at the deep russet of his hair. And that was me all the time, and I didn't know it or think of it, or think what effect it had on those who saw me as I moved through life. I didn't believe their blandishments. I had only scorn for their passion. Indeed, even the Master had seemed before to be a weak and deluded being for ever desiring me. But I understood now why people had somewhat taken leave of their senses. The boy there, dying on the bed, the boy who was the cause of weeping all around in this large chamber, the boy seemed the very embodiment of purity and the very embodiment of youth on the verge of life.

What did not make sense to me was the commotion in the room. Why did everyone weep? I saw a priest in

169

the doorway, a priest I knew from the nearby church, and I could see that the boys argued with him and feared to let him near me as I lay on the bed, lest I be afraid. It all seemed a pointless imbroglio. Riccardo should not wring his hands. Bianca should not work so hard, with her damp cloth and her soft but obviously desperate words.

Oh, poor child, I thought. You might have had a little more compassion for everyone if you had known how beautiful you were, and you might have thought yourself a little bit stronger and more able to gain something for yourself. As it was, you played sly games on those around you, because you did not have faith in your own self or even know what you were.

It seemed very clear, the error in all this. But I was leaving this place! The same draught that had pulled me up out of the pretty young body that lay on the bed was pulling me upwards into a tunnel of fierce, noisy wind.

The wind swirled around me, enclosing me completely and tightly in this tunnel, yet I could see in it other beings who looked on even as they were caught in it and moved by the incessant fury of this wind. I saw eyes looking on me; I saw mouths open as if in distress. I was pulled higher and higher through this tunnel. I didn't feel fear, but I felt a fatality. I could not help myself.

That was your error when you were that boy down there, I found myself thinking. But this is indeed hopeless. And just as I concluded, so I came to the end of this tunnel; it dissolved. I stood on the shore of that lovely sparkling sea.

I wasn't wet from the waves, but I knew them, and I said out loud, 'Oh, I'm here, I've come to the shore! Look, there are the towers of glass.'

As I looked up, I saw that the city was far away, over

a series of deep green hills, and that a path led to it, and that flowers bloomed richly and gorgeously on either side of the path. I had never seen such flowers, never seen such shapes and petal formations, and never never beheld such colors in all my life. There were no names in the artistic canon for these colors. I couldn't call them by the few weak inadequate labels which I knew.

Oh, would the painters of Venice ever be astonished at these colors, I thought, and to think how they would transform our work, how they would set ablaze our paintings if only they could be discovered in some source that might be ground into pigment and blended with our oils. But what a pointless thing to do. No more painting was needed. All the glory that could be accomplished by color was here in this world revealed. I saw it in the flowers; I saw it in the variegated grass. I saw it in the boundless sky that rose up and over me and behind the distant blinding city, and it too flashed and glowed with this great harmony of colors, blending and twinkling and shimmering as if the towers of this city were made of a miraculous thriving energy rather than a dead or earthly matter or mass.

A great gratitude flowed out of me; my whole being gave itself up to this gratitude. 'Lord, I see now,' I said aloud. 'I see and I understand.' It did at that moment seem very clear to me, the implications of this varied and ever increasing beauty, this pulsing, radiant world. It was so very pregnant with meaning that all things were answered, all things were utterly resolved. I whispered the word 'Yes' over and over. I nodded, I think, and then it seemed quite absurd to bother to say anything in words at all.

A great force emanated from the beauty. It surrounded me as if it were air or breeze or water, but it was none of these. It was far more rarefied and pervasive, and though it held me with a formidable strength it was nevertheless invisible and without pressure or palpable form. The force was love. Oh, yes, I thought, it is love, it is complete love, and in its completeness it makes all that I have ever known meaningful, for every disappointment, every hurt, every misstep, every embrace, every kiss was but a foreshadowing of this sublime acceptance and goodness, for the bad steps had told me what I lacked, and the good things, the embraces, had shown me a glimpse of what love could be.

All my life this love made meaningful, sparing nothing, and as I marveled at this, accepting it completely and without urgency or questioning, a miraculous process began. All my life came to me in the form of all those I had ever known.

I saw my life from the very first moments and up until the moment that had brought me here. It was not a terribly remarkable life; it contained no great secret or twist or pregnant matter that changed my heart. On the contrary, it was but a natural and common string of myriad tiny events, and these events involved all the other souls whom I had ever touched; I saw now the hurts I'd inflicted, and the words of mine which had brought solace, and I saw the result of the most casual and unimportant things I had done. I saw the banquet hall of the Florentines, and again in the midst of them, I saw the blundering loneliness with which they stumbled into death. I saw the isolation and the sadness of their souls as they had fought to stay alive.

What I could not see was my Master's face. I could not see who he was. I could not see into his soul. I could not see what my love meant to him, or what his love meant for me. But this was of no importance. In fact, I only realized it afterwards when I tried to recount the entire event. What mattered now was only that I understood what it meant to cherish others and to cherish life itself. I realized what it had meant when I painted pictures, not the ruby-red bleeding and vibrant pictures of Venice, but old pictures in the antique Byzantine style, which had once flowed so artlessly and perfectly from my brush. I knew then I had painted wondrous things, and I saw the effects of what I had painted . . . and it seemed then a great crowd of information inundated me. Indeed, there was such a wealth of it, and it was so easy to comprehend, that I felt a great light joy.

The knowledge was like the love and like the beauty; indeed, I realized with a great triumphant happiness that they were all – the knowledge, the love, and the beauty – they were all one.

'Oh, yes, how could one not see it. It's so simple!' I thought.

If I had had a body with eyes, I would have wept, but it would have been a sweet weeping. As it was, my soul was victorious over all small and enervating things. I stood still, and the knowledge, the facts, as it were, the hundreds upon hundreds of small details which were like transparent droplets of magical fluid passing through me and into me, filling me and vanishing to make way for more of this great shower of truth – all this seemed suddenly to fade.

There beyond stood the glass city, and beyond it a blue sky, blue as a sky at midday, only one which was now filled with every known star.

I started out for the city. Indeed, I started with such impetuosity and such conviction that it took three people to hold me back.

I stopped. I was quite amazed. But I knew these men. These were priests, old priests of my homeland, who

173

had died long before I had even come to my calling, all of which was quite clear to me, and I knew their names and how they had died. They were in fact the saints of my city, and of the great house of catacombs where I had lived.

'Why do you hold me?' I asked. 'Where's my Father? He's here now, is he not?' No sooner had I asked this than I saw my Father. He looked exactly as he had always looked. He was a big, shaggy man, dressed in leather for hunting, with a full grizzled beard and thick long auburn hair the same color as my own. His cheeks were rosy from the cold wind, and his lower lip, visible between his thick mustache and his gray-streaked beard, was moist and pink as I remembered. His eyes were the same bright china blue. He waved at me. He gave his usual, casual, hearty wave, and he smiled. He looked just like he was going off into the grasslands, in spite of everyone's advice, and everyone's caution to hunt, with no fear at all of the Mongols or the Tatars swooping down on him. After all, he had his great bow with him, the bow only he could string, as if he were a mythical hero of the great grassy fields, and he had his own sharpened arrows, and his big broadsword with which he could hack off a man's head with one blow.

'Father, why are they holding me?' I asked.

He looked blank. His smile simply faded and his face lost all expression, and then to my sadness, to my terrible shocking sadness, he faded in his entirety and he wasn't there.

The priests beside me, the men with their long gray beards and their black robes, spoke to me in soft sympathetic whispers and they said, 'Andrei, it's not time for you to come.'

I was deeply distressed, deeply. Indeed, I was so sad that I could form no words of protest. Indeed, I under-

174

stood that no protest I might make mattered, and then one of the priests took my hand.

'No, this is always the way with you,' he said. 'Ask.'

He didn't move his lips when he spoke, but it wasn't necessary. I heard him very clearly, and I knew that he meant no personal malice to me. He was incapable of such a thing.

'Why, then,' I asked, 'can't I stay? Why can't you let me stay when I want to, and when I've come this far?'

'Think on all you've seen. You know the answer.'

And I had to admit that in an instant I did know the answer. It was complex and yet profoundly simple, and it had to do with all the knowledge I had gained.

'You can't take this back with you,' said the priest. 'You'll forget all the particular things you learned here. But remember the overall lesson, that your love for others, and their love for you, that the increase of love in life itself around you, is what matters.'

It seemed a marvelous and comprehensive thing! It seemed no simple small cliché. It seemed so immense, so subtle, yet so total that all mortal difficulties would collapse in the face of its truth.

I was at once returned to my body. I was at once the auburn-haired boy dying in the bed. I felt a tingling in my hands and feet. I twisted, and a wretched pain flamed down my back. I was all afire, sweating and writhing as before, only now my lips were badly cracked and my tongue was cut and blistered against my teeth.

'Water,' I said, 'please, water.'

A soft sobbing came from those around me. It was mingled with laughter and expressions of awe.

I was alive, and they had thought me dead. I opened my eyes, and I looked at Bianca.

'I won't die now,' I said.

'What is it, Amadeo?' she asked. She bent down and put her ear to my lips.

'It isn't time,' I said.

They brought me cool white wine. It was mixed with honey and lemon. I sat up and I drank gulp after gulp of it. 'It's not enough,' I said softly, weakly, but I was falling asleep.

I went down into the pillows, and I felt Bianca's cloth wipe my forehead and my eyes. What a sweet mercy it was, and how very grand to give that small comfort, which was all the world to me. All the world. All the world.

I had forgotten what I had seen on the other side! My eyes snapped open. Recover it, I thought desperately. But I remembered the priest, vividly as though I had just talked to him in another room. He had said I couldn't remember. And there was so much more to it, infinitely more, such things as only my Master might understand.

I closed my eyes. I slept. Dreams couldn't come to me. I was too ill, too feverish, but in my own way, stretched thin upon a consciousness of the moist hot bed and the sluggish air beneath the baldaquin, upon the blurred words of the boys and Bianca's sweet insistence, I did sleep. The hours ticked. I knew them, and gradually some comfort came to me in that I got used to the sweat that smothered my skin, and the thirst that hurt my throat, and I lay without protest, drifting, waiting for my Master to come.

I have so many things to tell you, I thought. You will know about the glass city! I must explain that I was once . . . but I couldn't quite remember. A painter, yes, but what sort of painter, and how, and my name? Andrei? When had I been so called?

Slowly over my consciousness of the sickbed and the humid room there dropped the dark veil of Heaven. Spread out in all directions were the sentinel stars, splendid as they shone above the glinting towers of the glass city, and in this half-sleep, now aided by the most tranquil and blissful of illusions, the stars sang to me.

Each from its fixed position in constellation and in void gave forth a precious glimmering sound, as if great chords were struck inside each flaming orb and by means of its brilliant gyrations broadcast through all the universal world.

Such sounds I had never heard with my earthly ears. But no disclaimer can approximate this airy and translucent music, this harmony and symphony of celebration.

Oh, Lord, if Thou wert music, this then would be Thy voice, and no discord could ever prevail against Thee. Thou wouldst cleanse the ordinary world of every troubling noise with this, the fullest expression of Thy most intricate and wondrous design, and all triviality would fade away, overwhelmed by this resounding perfection.

This was my prayer, my heartfelt prayer, coming in an ancient tongue, most intimate and effortless as I lay slumbering.

Stay with me, beauteous stars, I begged, and let me never seek to fathom this fusion of light and sound, but only give myself to it utterly and unquestionably.

The stars grew large and infinite in their cold majestic light, and slowly all the night was gone and there remained one great glorious and sourceless illumination.

I smiled. I felt my smile with blind fingers on my lips, and as the light grew brighter still and ever closer, as though it were an ocean of itself, I felt a great saving coolness over all my limbs.

'Don't fade, don't go away, don't leave me.' My own whisper was a woeful small thing. I pressed my throbbing head into the pillow.

But it had spent its time, this grand and overriding light, and now must fade and let the common blink of candles move against my half-closed eyes, and I must see the burnished gloom around my bed, and simple things, such as a rosary laid across my right hand with ruby beads and golden cross, and there a prayer book open to my left, its pages gently folding in a small stir of breeze that moved as well the smooth taffeta in ripples overhead in its wood frame.

How lovely it all did seem, these plain and ordinary things that made up this silent and elastic moment. Where had they gone, my lovely swan-necked nurse and my weeping comrades? Had night worn them down to where they slept, so that I might cherish these quiet moments of unobserved wakefulness? My mind was gently crowded with a thousand lively recollections.

I opened my eyes. All were gone, save one who sat beside me on the bed, looking down at me with eyes both dreamy and remote and coldly blue, far paler than a summer sky and filled with a near faceted light as they fixed so idly and indifferently upon me.

My Master here, with hands folded in his lap, a seeming stranger viewing all as if it could not touch his chiseled grandeur. The smileless expression set upon his face seemed made there forever.

'Merciless!' I whispered.

'No, oh, no,' he said. His lips did not move. 'But tell me once again the whole tale. Describe this glassy city.'

'Ah, yes, we've talked of it, have we not, of those priests who said I must come back, and those old paintings, so antique, which I thought so very beautiful. Not made by human hands, you see, but by the power invested in me, which passed through me, and I had only to take up the brush and there the Virgin and the Saints were mine to discover.'

'Don't cast those old forms away,' he said, and once again his lips showed no sign of the voice I heard so distinctly, a voice that pierced my very ears as any human voice might do, with his tone, his very timbre. 'For forms change, and reason now is but tomorrow's superstition, and in that old restraint there lay a great sublime intent, an indefatigable purity. But tell me once again about the glassy city.'

I sighed. 'You've seen the molten glass, as I have,' I said, 'when taken from the furnace, a glowing blob of horrifying heat upon a spear of iron, a thing that melts and drips so that the artist's wand may pull and stretch it, or fill it full of breath to form the perfect rounded vessel. Well, it was as if that glass came up out of the moist Mother Earth herself, a molten torrent spewing to the clouds, and out of these great liquid jets were born the crowded towers of the glassy city – not imitating any form built by men, but perfect as the heated force of Earth had naturally ordained, in colors unimaginable. Who lived in such a place? How far away it seemed, yet utterly attainable. But one short walk over hills sweet with willowing green grass and leafy fluttering flowers of the same fantastical hues and tints, a quiet thunderous and impossible apparition.'

I looked at him, because I had been looking off and back into my vision.

'Tell me what these things mean,' I asked. 'Where is this place, and why was I allowed to see it?'

He gave a sad sigh and looked away himself and now back at me, his face as aloof and unbending as before, only now I saw the thick blood in it, that once again, as it had been the night before, was pumped full of human heat from human veins, which had no doubt been his late repast this same evening.

'Won't you even smile now as you say farewell?' I asked. 'If this bitter coldness now is all you feel, and you would let me die of this rampant fever? I'm sick unto death, you know it. You know the nausea that I feel, you know the hurt inside my head, you know the ache in all my joints and how these cuts burn in my skin with their indisputable poison. Why are you so very far away, yet here, come home, to sit beside me and feel nothing?'

'I feel the love I've always felt when I look at you,' he said, 'my child, my son, my sweet enduring one. I feel it. It's walled up inside where it should stay, perhaps, and let you die, for yes, you will, and then perhaps your priests will take you, for how can they not when there is no returning?'

'Ah, but what if there are many lands? What if on the second fall, I find myself on yet another shore, and sulfur rises from the boiling earth and not the beauty first revealed to me? I hurt. These tears are scalding. So much is lost. I can't remember. It seems I say those same words so much. I can't remember!'

I reached out. He didn't move. My hand grew heavy and dropped on the forgotten prayer book. I felt the stiff vellum pages beneath my fingers.

'What's killed your love? Was it the things I did? That I brought the man here who slew my brothers? Or that I died and saw such wonders? Answer me.'

'I love you still. I will all my nights and all my slumbering days, forever. Your face is as a jewel given me, which I can never forget, though I may foolishly lose it. Its glister will torture me forever. Amadeo, think on these things again, open your mind as if it were a shell, and let me see the pearl of all they taught you.'

'Can you, Master? Can you understand how love and love alone could mean so very much, and all the world be made of it? The very blades of grass, the leaves of trees, the fingers of this hand that reaches for you? Love, Master. Love. And who will believe such simple and immense things when there are dexterous and labyrinthian creeds and philosophies of manmade and ever seductive complexity? Love. I heard the sound of it. I saw it. Were these the delusions of a feverish mind, a mind afraid of death?'

'Perhaps,' he said, his face still feelingless and motionless. His eyes were narrow, prisoners of their own shrinking from what they saw. 'Ah, yes,' he said. 'You die and I let you, and I think there might be for you but one shore, and there you'll find again your priests, your city.'

'It's not my time,' I said. 'I know it. And such a statement cannot be undone by a mere handful of hours. Smash the ticking clock. They meant, by a soul's incarnate life, it wasn't time. Some destiny carved in my infant hand will not be so soon fulfilled or easily defeated.'

'I can tip the odds, my child,' he said. This time his lips moved. The pale sweet coral brightened in his face, and his eyes grew wide and unguarded, the old self I knew and cherished. 'I can so easily take the last strength left in you.' He leant over me. I saw the tiny variegations in the pupils of his eyes, the bright deep-pointed stars behind the darkening irises. His lips, so wondrously decorated with all the tiny lines of human lips, were rosy as if a human kiss resided there. 'I can so easily take one last fatal drink of your child's blood, one last quaff of all the freshness I so love, and in my arms I'll hold a corpse so rich in beauty that all who see it will weep, and that corpse will tell me nothing. You are gone, that much I'll know, and no more.'

'Do you say these things to torture me? Master, if I cannot go there, I want to be with you!'

His lip worked in plain desperation. He seemed a man, and only that, the red blood of fatigue and sadness hovering on the borders of his eyes. His hand, out now to touch my hair, was trembling.

I caught it as if it were the high waving branch of a tree above me. I gathered his fingers to my lips like so many leaves and kissed them. Turning my head I laid them on my wounded cheek. I felt the throb of the venomous cut beneath them. But more keenly still, I felt a strong tremor within them.

I blinked my eyes. 'How many died tonight to feed you?' I whispered. 'And how can this be, and love be the very thing the world is made of? You are too beautiful to be overlooked. I'm lost. I cannot understand it. But could I, if I were to live from this moment on, a simple mortal boy, could I forget it?'

'You cannot live, Amadeo,' he said sadly. 'You cannot live!' His voice broke. 'The poison's traveled in you too deep, too far and wide, and little draughts of my blood cannot overtake it.' His face was filled with anguish. 'Child, I can't save you. Close your eyes. Take my farewell kiss. There is no friendship between me and those on the far shore, but they must take what dies so naturally.'

'Master, no! Master, I cannot try it alone. Master,

they sent me back, and you are here, and were bound to be, and how could they not have known it?'

'Amadeo, they didn't care. The guardians of the dead are powerfully indifferent. They speak of love, but not of centuries of blundering ignorance. What stars are these that sing so beautifully when all the world is languishing in dissonance? I would you would force their hand, Amadeo.' His voice all but broke in his pain. 'Amadeo, what right have they to charge me with your fortune?'

I laughed a weak sad little laugh.

My fever shook me. A great wave of sickness overcame me. If I moved or spoke I would suffer a dread dry nausea that would shake me to no advantage. I'd rather die than feel this.

'Master, I knew you would give it some powerful analysis,' I said. I tried not to make a bitter or sarcastic smile, but to seek the simple truth. My breath was now so hard for me. It seemed I could leave off breathing with no hardship at all. All Bianca's stern encouragements came back to me. 'Master,' I said, 'there is no horror in this world that is without final redemption.'

'Yes, but for some,' he pressed, 'what is the price of such salvation? Amadeo, how dare they requisition me to their obscure designs! I pray they were illusions. Don't speak anymore about their marvelous light. Don't think on it.'

'No, Sir? And for whose comfort do I sweep my mind so clean? Who is dying here!'

He shook his head.

'Go ahead, wring the blood tears from your eyes,' I said. 'And for what death do you hope yourself, Sir, for you told me that it wasn't impossible for even you to die? Explain to me, that is, if there's time left before all the light I shall ever know winks out on me, and the Earth devours the incarnate jewel that you found wanting!'

183

'Never wanting,' he whispered.

'Come now, where will you go, Sir? More comfort, please. How many minutes do I have?'

'I don't know,' he whispered. He turned away from me and bowed his head. I had never seen him so forlorn.

'Let me see your hand,' I said weakly. 'There are closeted witches who in the shadows of the taverns of Venice have taught me how to read the lines in it. I'll tell you when you are like to die. Give it to me.' I could scarcely see. A haze had come down over all things. But I meant my words.

'You come too late,' he replied. 'There are no lines left.' He held up his palm for me to see. 'Time has erased what men call fate. I have none.'

'I am sorry that you come at all,' I said. I turned away from him. I turned away against the clean cool linen of the pillow. 'Would you leave me now, my beloved teacher? I would rather the company of a priest, and my old nurse if you haven't sent her home. I have loved you with my whole heart, but I don't want to die in your superior company.'

Through a haze I saw the shape of him as he grew nearer to me. I felt his hands cup my face and turn it towards him. I saw the glimmer of his blue eyes, wintry flames, indistinct yet burning fiercely.

'Very well, beautiful one. This is the moment. Would you come with me, and be like me?' His voice was rich and soothing, though it was full of pain.

'Yes, always and forever yours.'

'Forever to thrive in secret on the blood of the evildoer, as I thrive, and to abide with these secrets until the end of the world, if need be.'

'I shall. I want it.'

'To learn from me all the lessons I can give.'

'Yes, all of them.'

He picked me up from the bed. I tumbled against him, my head spinning and the pain in it so sharp, I cried out softly.

'Only a little while, my love, my young and tender love,' he said in my ear.

I was lowered into the warm water of the bath, my clothes softly stripped away, my head laid back against the tiled edge ever so carefully. I let my arms float in the water. I felt it lap around my shoulders.

He broke up handfuls of water to bathe me. He bathed first my face and then all of me. His hard satiny fingertips moved over my face.

'Not a vagrant hair yet of your beard, and yet you have the nether endowments of a man, and must now rise above the pleasures you have so loved.'

'I do, I will,' I whispered. A terrible burning lashed my cheek. The cut was spread wide. I struggled to touch it. But he held my hand. It was only his blood fallen into the festering wound. And as the flesh tingled and burnt I felt it closing. He did the same with the scratch on my arm, and then with the small scratch on the back of my hand. With my eyes closed, I surrendered to the eerie paralyzing pleasure of it.

His hand touched me again, running smoothly down my chest, past my private parts, examining first one leg and then the other, searching out the smallest break or flaw in the skin, perhaps. Again the rich throbbing chills of pleasure overcame me.

I felt myself lifted from the water, warmly wrapped, and then there came that shock of moving air that meant he carried me, that he moved more swiftly than any spying eye could see. I felt the marble floor before my bare feet, and in my fever, this jolting cold was very good to me.

We stood in the studio. We had our backs to the painting on which he'd worked only nights ago, and faced another masterly canvas of immense size, on which beneath a brilliant sun and cobalt sky a great copse of trees surrounded two rushing windblown figures.

The woman was Daphne, her upstretched arms changing into the branches of the laurel, already thick with leaves, her feet grown into roots that sought the deep brown earth beneath her. And behind her, the desperate and beautiful god Apollo, a champion of golden hair and finely muscled limbs, come too late to stop her frantic magical escape from his threatening arms, her fatal metamorphosis.

'See the indifferent clouds above,' my Master whispered in my ear. He pointed to the great streaks of sun he had painted with more skill than the men who daily beheld them.

He spoke words I confided to Lestat so long ago when I told him my story, words that he salvaged so mercifully from the few images of these times which I was able to give him.

I hear Marius's voice when I repeat these words, the last I was ever to hear as a mortal child:

'This is the only sun that you will ever see again. But a millennium of nights will be yours to see light as no mortal has ever seen it, to snatch from the distant stars, as if you were Prometheus, an endless illumination by which to understand all things.'

And I, who had beheld a far more wondrous celestial light in that realm from which I'd been turned away, longed only for him to eclipse it now forever.

The Master's private salons: a string of rooms in which he had covered the walls with flawless copies of the works of those mortal painters he so admired – Giotto, Fra Angelico, Bellini.

We stood in the room of Benozzo Gozzoli's great work, from the Medici Chapel in Florence: *The Procession of the Magi.*

In the middle of the century, Gozzoli had created this vision, wrapping it around three walls of that small sacred chamber.

But my Master, with his supernatural memory and skill, had spread out the great work, rendering the whole flat from end to end on one great side of this immense and broad gallery.

Perfect as Gozzoli's original it loomed, with its hordes of beautifully dressed young Florentines, each pale face a study in thoughtful innocence, astride a cavalry of gorgeous horses following the exquisite figure of the young Lorenzo de' Medici himself, a youth with soft curling brownish-blond hair to his shoulders, and a carnal blush in his white cheeks. With a tranquil expression he appeared to gaze indifferently at the viewer of the painting as he sat, regal in his fur-trimmed gold jacket with its long slashed sleeves, on a beautifully caparisoned white horse. No detail of the painting was unworthy of another. Even the horse's bridle and fittings were of beautifully worked gold and velvet, a match for the tight sleeves of Lorenzo's tunic and his red velvet knee-high boots.

But the enchantment of the painting arose most powerfully from the faces of the youths, as well as the few old men who made up the immense crowded procession, all with small quiet mouths and eyes drifting to the sides as if a forward glance would have broken the spell. On and on they came past castles and mountains, winding their way to Bethlehem.

To illuminate this masterpiece, dozens of silver branching candelabra had been lighted up and down both sides of the room. The thick white candles of the purest beeswax gave off a luxurious illumination. High above a glorious wilderness of painted clouds surrounded an oval of floating saints who touched each other's outstretched hands as they looked down benevolently and contentedly upon us.

No furniture covered the rosy Carrara marble tiles of the highly polished floor. A wandering border pattern of green leafy vine marked off in great squares these tiles, but the floor was otherwise plain and deeply lustrous, and silken smooth to bare feet.

I found myself staring with the fascination of a feverish brain into this hall of glorious surfaces. *The Procession of the Magi*, rising as it did to fill the entire wall to the right of me, seemed to give off a soft plethora of real sounds . . . the muted crunch of the hoofs of the horses, the shuffling steps of those who walked beside them, the rustling of the red-flowered shrubbery beyond them and even the distant cries of the hunters who, with their lean hounds, streaked along the mountain paths beyond.

My Master stood in the very center of the hall. He had taken off his familiar red velvet. He wore only an open robe of gold tissue, with long bell sleeves down to his wrists, his hem just skirting his bare white feet.

His hair seemed to make for him a halo of yellow

brilliance, hanging softly to his shoulders.

I wore a gown of the same sheerness and simplicity.

'Come, Amadeo,' he said.

I was weak, thirsting for water, barely able to stand. He knew this however, and no excuse seemed appropriate. I took my faltering steps one after another until I reached his outstretched arms.

His hands slid about the back of my head.

He bent his lips. A sense of dreadful awesome finality swept over me.

'You will die now to be with me in life eternal,' he whispered in my ear. 'Never for a moment must you really fear. I will hold your heart safe in my hands.'

His teeth cut into me, deeply, cruelly with the precision of twin daggers, and I heard my heart thud in my ears. My very bowels contracted, and my stomach was knotted in pain. Yet a savage pleasure swept through all my veins, a pleasure which coursed towards the wounds in my neck. I could feel my blood rush towards my Master, towards his thirst and my inevitable death.

Even my hands were transfixed with vibrant sensation. Indeed, I seemed suddenly to be but a puppet map of circuitry, all of it aglow, as with a low, obvious and deliberate sound, my Master drank my life's blood. The sound of his heart, slow, steady, a deep reverberating pounding, filled my ears.

The pain in my intestines was alchemized to a soft sheer rapture; my body lost all weight, all knowledge of itself in space. The throb of his heart was within me. My hands felt the long satin locks of his hair, but I did not hold to them. I floated, supported only by the insistent heartbeat and thrilling current of all my swiftly flowing blood.

'I die now,' I whispered. This ecstasy could not endure.

Abruptly the world died.

I stood alone on the desolate and windy shore of the sea.

It was the land to which I'd journeyed before, but how different it was now, devoid of its shining sun and abundant flowers. The priests were there, but their robes were dusty and dark and reeked of the earth. I knew these priests, I knew them well. I knew their names. I knew their narrow bearded faces, their thin greasy hair and the black felt hats that they wore. I knew the dirt in their fingernails, and I knew the hungry hollow of their sunken gleaming eyes.

They beckoned for me to come.

Ah, yes, back to where I belonged. We climbed higher and higher until we stood on the bluff of the glass city, and it lay to the far left of us, and how forlorn and empty it was.

All the molten energy which had lighted its multitudinous and translucent towers was now dead and gone, turned off at the source. Nothing remained of the blazing colors except a deep dull residue of tints beneath the featureless span of hopeless gray sky. Oh, sad, sad, to see the glass city without its magic fire.

A chorus of sounds rose from it, a tinkling, as of glass dully striking glass. There was no music in it. There was only a bleary luminous despair.

'Walk on, Andrei,' said one of the priests to me. His soiled hand with its thin bits of caked mud touched me and pulled at me, hurting my fingers. I looked down to see that my fingers were thin and luridly white. My knuckles shone as though the flesh had already been stripped away, but it had not.

All my skin merely cleaved to me, hungry and loose as their skin.

Before us came the water of the river, filled with ice

190

sloughs and great tangles of blackened driftwood, covering the flatlands with a murky lake. We had to walk through it, and its coldness hurt us. Yet on we went, the four of us, the three priest guides and me. Above loomed the once golden domes of Kiev. It was our Santa Sofia, standing still after the horrid massacres and conflagrations of the Mongols who had laid waste our city and all her riches and all her wicked and worldly women and men.

'Come, Andrei.'

I knew this doorway. It was to the Monastery of the Caves. Only candles illuminated these catacombs, and the smell of the earth overpowered all, even the stench of dried sweat on soiled and diseased flesh.

In my hands, I held the rough wooden handle of a small shovel. I dug into the heap of earth. I opened up the soft wall of rubble, until my eyes fell on a man not dead but dreaming as the dirt covered his face.

'Still alive, Brother?' I whispered, to this soul buried up to his neck.

'Still alive, Brother Andrei, give me only what will sustain me,' said the cracked lips. The white eyelids were never lifted. 'Give me only that much, so that our Lord and Savior, Christ Himself, will choose the time that I am to come home.'

'Oh, Brother, how courageous you are,' I said. I put a jug of water to his lips. The mud streaked them as he drank. His head rested back in soft rubble.

'And you, child,' he said with labored breaths, turning ever so slightly from the proffered jug, 'when will you have the strength to choose your earthen cell among us, your grave, and wait for Christ to come?'

'Soon, I pray, Brother,' I answered. I stepped back. I lifted the shovel.

I dug into the next cell, and soon a dreadful

unmistakable stench assailed me. The priest beside me stayed my hand.

'Our Good Brother Joseph is finally with the Lord,' he said. 'That's it, uncover his face so that we may see for ourselves that he died at peace.'

The stench grew thicker. Only dead human beings reek this strongly. It's the smell of desolate graves and carts coming from those districts where the plague is at its worst. I feared I would be sick. But I continued to dig, until at last we uncovered the dead man's head. Bald, a skull encased in shrunken skin.

Prayers rose from the brothers behind me. 'Close it up, Andrei.'

'When will you have the courage, Brother? Only God can tell you when—.'

'The courage to what!' I know this booming voice, this big-shouldered man who barrels his way down the catacomb. No mistaking his auburn hair and beard, his leather jerkin and his weapons hung on his leather belt.

'This is what you do with my son, the ikon painter!'

He grabbed me by the shoulder, as he'd done a thousand times, with the same huge paw of a hand that had beaten me senseless.

'Let go of me, please, you impossible and ignorant ox,' I whispered. 'We're in the house of God.'

He dragged me so that I fell on my knees. My robe was tearing, black cloth ripping.

'Father, stop it and go away,' I said.

'Deep in these pits to bury a boy who can paint with the skill of the angels!'

'Brother Ivan, stop your shouting. It's for God to decide what each of us will do.'

The priests ran behind me. I was dragged into the workroom. Ikons in rows hung from the ceiling, covering all of the far wall. My Father flung me down in the chair at the large heavy table. He lifted the iron candlestick with its fluttering, protesting candle to light all the tapers around.

The illumination made a fire on his huge beard. Long gray hairs sprung from his thick eyebrows, combed upwards, diabolical.

'You behave like the village idiot, Father,' I whispered. 'It's a wonder I'm not a slobbering idiot beggar myself.'

'Shut up, Andrei. Nobody's taught you any manners here, that's clear enough. You need me to beat you.'

He slammed his fist into the side of my head. My ear went numb.

'I thought I'd beaten you enough before I brought you here, but not so,' he said. He smacked me again.

'Desecration!' cried the priest, looming above me. 'The boy's consecrated to God.'

'Consecrated to a pack of lunatics,' said my Father. He took a packet out of his coat. 'Your eggs, Brothers!' he said with contempt. He lay back the soft leather and removed an egg. 'Paint, Andrei. Paint to remind these lunatics that you have the gift from God Himself.'

'And God Himself it is who paints the picture,' cried the priest, the eldest of them, whose sticky gray hair was so soiled in time with oil that it was near black. He pushed his way between my chair and my Father.

My Father set down all but one egg. Leaning over a small earthen bowl on the table, he broke the shell of the egg, carefully gathering the yoke in one side, and letting all the rest spill into his leather cloth. 'There, there, pure yoke, Andrei.' He sighed, and then threw the broken shell on the floor.

He picked up the small pitcher and poured the water into the yoke.

'You mix it, mix your colors and work. Remind these—.'

'He works when God calls him to work,' declared the Elder, 'and when God calls him to bury himself within the Earth, to live the life of the reclusive, the hermit, then will he do that.'

'Like Hell,' said my Father. 'Prince Michael himself has asked for an Ikon of the Virgin. Andrei, paint! Paint three for me that I may give the Prince the ikon for which he asks, and take the others to the distant castle of his cousin, Prince Feodor, as he has asked.'

'That castle's destroyed, Father,' I said contemptuously. 'Feodor and all his men were massacred by the wild tribes. You'll find nothing out there in the wild lands, nothing but stones. Father, you know this as well as I do. We've ridden plenty far enough to see for ourselves.'

'We'll go if the Prince wants us to go,' said my Father, 'and we'll leave the ikon in the branches of the nearest tree to where his brother died.'

'Vanity and madness,' said the Elder. Other priests came into the room. There was much shouting.

'Speak clearly to me and stop the poetry!' cried my Father. 'Let my boy paint. Andrei, mix your colors. Say your prayers, but begin.'

'Father, you humiliate me. I despise you. I'm ashamed that I'm your son. I'm not your son. I won't be your son. Shut your filthy mouth or I'll paint nothing.'

'Ah, that's my sweet boy, with the honey rolling off his tongue, and the bees that left it there left their sting too.'

Again, he struck me. This time I became dizzy, but I refused to lift my hands to my head. My ear throbbed.

'Proud of yourself, Ivan the Idiot!' I said. 'How can I paint when I can't see or even sit in the chair?'

The priests shouted. They argued amongst one another.

194

I tried to focus on the small row of earthen jars ready for the yoke and the water. Finally I began to mix the yoke and the water. Best to work and shut them all out. I could hear my Father laugh with satisfaction.

'Now, show them, show them what they mean to wall up alive in a lot of mud.'

'For the love of God,' said the Elder.

'For the love of stupid idiots,' said my Father. 'It isn't enough to have a great painter. You have to have a saint.'

'You do not know what your son is. It was God who guided you to bring him here.'

'It was money,' said my Father. Gasps rose from the priests.

'Don't lie to them,' I said under my breath. 'You know damned good and well it was pride.'

'Yes, pride,' said my Father, 'that my son could paint the Face of Christ or His Blessed Mother like a Master! And you, to whom I commit this genius, are too ignorant to see it.'

I began to grind the pigments I needed, the soft brownish-red powder, and then to mix it over and over with the yoke and water until every tiny fragment of pigment was broken up and the paint was smooth and perfectly thin and clear. On to the yellow, and then to the red.

They fought over me. My Father lifted his fist to the Elder, but I didn't bother to look up. He wouldn't dare. He kicked my leg in his desperation, sending a cramp through my muscle, but I said nothing. I went on mixing the paint.

One of the priests had come round to my left, and he slipped a clean whitewashed panel of wood in front of me, primed and ready for the holy image.

At last I was ready. I bowed my head. I made the

Sign of the Cross in our way, touching my right shoulder first, not my left.

'Dear God, give me the power, give me the vision, give my hands the tutelage which only your love can give!' At once I had the brush with no consciousness of having picked it up, and the brush began to race, tracing out the oval of the Virgin's face, and then the sloping lines of her shoulders and then the outline of her folded hands.

Now when their gasps came, they were tributes to the painting. My Father laughed in gloating satisfaction.

'Ah, my Andrei, my sharp-tongued, sarcastic, nasty ungrateful little genius of God.'

'Thank you, Father,' I whispered bitingly, right from the middle of my trancelike concentration, as I myself watched the work of the brush in awe. There her hair, cleaving close to the scalp and parted in the middle. I needed no instrument to make the outline of her halo perfectly round.

The priests held the clean brushes for me. One held a clean rag in his hands. I snatched up a brush for the red color which I then mixed with white paste, until it was the appropriate color of flesh.

'Isn't that a miracle!'

'That's just the point,' said the Elder between clenched teeth. 'It's a miracle, Brother Ivan, and he will do what God wills.'

'He won't wall himself up in here, damn you, not as long as I'm alive. He's coming with me into the wild lands.'

I burst out laughing. 'Father,' I said sneering at him. 'My place is here.'

'He's the best shot in the family, and he's coming with me into the wild lands,' said my Father to the others, who had flown into a flurry of protests and negations all around.

196

'Why do you give Our Blessed Mother that tear in her eye, Brother Andrei?'

'It's God who gives her the tear,' said one of the others.

'It is the Mother of All Sorrows. Ah, see the beautiful folds of her cloak.'

'Ah, look, the Christ child!' said my Father, and even his face was reverent. 'Ah, poor little baby God, soon to be crucified and die!' His voice was for once subdued and almost tender. 'Ah, Andrei, what a gift. Oh, but look, look at the child's eyes and his little hand, at the flesh of his thumb, his little hand.'

'Even you are touched with the light of Christ,' said the Elder. 'Even such a stupid violent man as you, Brother Ivan.'

The priests pressed in close around me in a circle. My Father held out a palmful of small twinkling jewels. 'For the halos, Andrei. Work fast, Prince Michael has ordained that we go.'

'Madness, I tell you!' All voices were set to babbling at once. My Father turned and raised his fist.

I looked up, reached for a fresh, clean panel of wood. My forehead was wet with sweat. I worked on and on.

I had done three ikons.

I felt such happiness, such pure happiness. It was sweet to be so warm in it, so aware of it, and I knew, though I said nothing, that my Father had made it possible, my Father, so cheerful and ruddy-cheeked and overpowering with his big shoulders and his glistening face, this man I was supposed to hate.

The Sorrowful Mother with her Child, and the napkin for her tears, and the Christ Himself. Weary, bleary-eyed, I sat back. The place was intolerably cold. Oh, if there were only a little fire. And my hand, my left hand was cramped from the cold. Only my right hand was all right because of the pace at which I had done my work. I wanted to suck the fingers of my left hand, but this would not do, not here at this moment, when all gathered to coo over the ikons.

'Masterly. The Work of God.'

An awful sense of time came over me, that I had traveled far from this moment, far from this the Monastery of the Caves to which I had vowed my life, far from the priests who were my brethren, far from my cursing, stupid Father, who was in spite of his ignorance so very proud.

Tears flowed from his eyes. 'My son,' he said. He clutched my shoulder proudly. He was beautiful in his own way, such a fine strong man, afraid of nothing, a prince himself when among his horses and his dogs and his followers, of which I, his son, had been one.

'Let me alone, you thick-skulled oaf,' I said. I smiled up at him to further outrage him. He laughed. He was too happy, too proud, to be provoked.

'Look what my son has done.' His voice had a telltale thickness to it. He was going to cry. And he wasn't even drunk.

'Not by human hands,' said the priest.

'No, naturally not!' boomed my Father's scornful voice. 'Just by my son Andrei's hands, that's all.'

A silken voice said in my ear, 'Would you place the jewels into the halos yourself, Brother Andrei, or shall I perform this task?'

Behold, it was done, the paste applied, the stones set, five in the Ikon of Christ. The brush was in my hand again to stroke the brown hair of the Lord God, which was parted in the middle and brought back behind His ears, with only part of it to show on either side of His neck. The stylus appeared in my hand to thicken and darken the black letters on the open book which Christ

198

held in His left hand. The Lord God stared, serious and severe, from the panel, His mouth red and straight beneath the horns of His brown mustache.

'Come now, the Prince is here, the Prince has come.'

Outside the entrance of the Monastery, the snow fell in cruel gusts. The priests helped me with my leather vest, my jacket of shearling. They buckled my belt. It was good to smell this leather again, to breathe the fresh cold air. My Father had my sword. It was heavy, old, taken from his long-ago fighting against the Teutonic Knights in lands far to the east, the jewels long ago chipped out of its handle, but a fine, fine battle sword.

Through the snowy mist a figure appeared, on horseback. It was Prince Michael himself, in his fur hat and fur-lined cape and gloves, the great Lord who ruled Kiev for our Roman Catholic conquerors, whose faith we would not accept but who let us keep to our own. He was decked out in foreign velvet and gold, a fancy figure fit for royal Lithuanian courts, of which we heard fantastical tales. How did he endure Kiev, the ruined city?

The horse reared up on its hind legs. My Father ran to catch the reins, and threaten the animal as he threatened me.

The ikon for Prince Feodor was wrapped thickly in wool for me to carry.

I placed my hand on the hilt of my sword.

'Ah, you will not take him on this Godless mission,' cried the Elder. 'Prince Michael, Your Excellency, our mighty ruler, tell this Godless man that he cannot take our Andrei.'

I saw the face of the Prince through the snow, square and strong, with gray eyebrows and beard and huge hard blue eyes. 'Let him go, Father,' he cried out to the priest. 'The boy has hunted with Ivan since he was four years old. Never has anyone provided such bounty for my table, and for yours, Father. Let him go.'

The horse danced backwards. My Father pulled down on the reins. Prince Michael blew the snow from off his lips.

Our horses were led to the fore, my Father's powerful stallion with the gracefully curved neck and the shorter gelding which had been mine before I had come to the Monastery of the Caves.

'I'll be back, Father,' I said to the Elder. 'Give me your blessing. What can I do against my gentle, sweet-tempered and infinitely pious Father when Prince Michael himself commands?'

'Oh, shut your lousy little mouth,' said my Father. 'You think I want to listen to this all the way to the Castle of Prince Feodor?'

'You'll hear it all the way to Hell!' declared the Elder. 'You take my finest novice to his death.'

'Novice, novice to a hole in the dirt! You take the hands that have painted these marvels –.'

'God painted them,' I said in a biting whisper, 'and you know it, Father. Will you please stop making a display of your Godlessness and belligerence.'

I was on the back of my horse. The ikon was strapped in wool to my chest.

'I don't believe my brother Feodor is dead!' the Prince said, trying to control his mount, to bring it in line with that of my Father. 'Perhaps these travelers saw some other ruin, some old—.'

'Nothing survives in the grasslands now,' pleaded the Elder. 'Prince, don't take Andrei. Don't take him.'

The priest ran alongside of my horse. 'Andrei, you will find nothing; you will find only the wild blowing grass and the trees. Put the ikon in the branches of a tree. Place it for the will of God, so that when it is found by the Tatars they will know His Divine power. Place it there for the pagans. And come home.'

The snow came down so fierce and thick I couldn't see his face.

I looked up at the stripped and barren domes of our Cathedral, that remnant of Byzantine glory left to us by Mongol invaders, who now exacted their greedy tribute through our Catholic Prince. How bleak and desolate was this, my homeland. I closed my eyes and longed for the mud cubicle of the cave, for the smell of the earth close around me, for the dreams of God and His Goodness which would come to me, once I was half-entombed.

Come back to me, Amadeo. Come back. Do not let your heart stop!

I spun around. 'Who calls to me?' The thick white veil of the snow broke to reveal the distant glass city, black and glimmering as if heated by hellish fires. Smoke rose to feed the ominous clouds of the darkening sky. I rode towards the glass city.

'Andrei!' This was my Father's voice behind me.

Come back to me, Amadeo. Don't let your heart stop!

The ikon fell from my left arm as I struggled to bridle my mount. The wool had come undone. On and on we rode. The ikon fell downhill beside us, turning over and over, corner bouncing upon corner, as it tumbled, the swaddling of wool falling loose. I saw the shimmering face of Christ.

Strong arms caught me, pulled me upwards as if from a whirlwind. 'Let me go!' I protested. I looked back. Against the frozen earth lay the ikon, and the staring, questioning eyes of the Christ.

Firm fingers pressed my face on either side. I blinked and opened my eyes. The room was filled with warmth and light. There loomed the familiar face of my Master

201

right above me, his blue eyes shot with blood. 'Drink, Amadeo,' he said. 'Drink from me.'

My head fell forward against his throat. The blood fount had started; it bubbled out of his vein, flowing thickly down onto the neck of his golden tissue robe. I closed my mouth over it. I lapped at it.

I let out a cry as the blood inflamed me.

'Draw it from me, Amadeo. Draw it hard!'

My mouth filled with blood. My lips closed against his silky white flesh so that not a drop would be lost. Deeply I swallowed. In a dim flash I saw my Father riding through the grasslands, a powerful leather-clad figure, his sword tied firmly to his belt, his leg crooked, his cracked and worn brown boot firmly in the stirrup. He turned to the left, rising and falling gracefully and perfectly with the huge strides of his white horse.

'All right, leave me, you coward, you impudent and miserable boy! Leave me!' He looked before him. 'I prayed for it, Andrei, I prayed they wouldn't get you for their filthy catacombs, their dark earthen cells. Well, so my prayer is answered! Go with God, Andrei. Go with God. Go with God!'

My Master's face was rapt and beautiful, a white flame against the wavering golden light of countless candles. He stood over me.

I lay on the floor. My body sang with the blood. I climbed to my feet, my head swimming. 'Master.'

At the far end of the room he stood, his bare feet composed on the glowing rose-colored floor, his arms outstretched. 'Come to me, Amadeo, walk towards me, come to me, to take the rest.'

I struggled to obey him. The room raged with colors around me. I saw the Procession of the searching Magi. 'Oh, that it's so vivid, so utterly alive!'

'Come to me, Amadeo.'

'I'm too weak, Master, I'm fainting, I'm dying in this glorious light.'

I took one step after another, though it seemed impossible. I placed one foot before the other, drawing ever closer to him. I stumbled.

'On your hands and knees, then, come. Come to me.'

I clung to his robe. I had to climb this great height if I wanted it. I reached up and took hold of the crook of his right arm. I lifted myself, feeling the gold cloth against me. I straightened my legs until I stood. Once again, I embraced him; once again I found the fount. I drank, and drank, and drank.

In a gilded gush the blood went down into my bowels. It went through my legs and my arms. I was a Titan. I crushed him under me. 'Give it to me,' I whispered. 'Give it to me.' The blood hovered on my lips and then flooded down my throat.

It was as if his cold marble hands had seized my heart. I could hear it struggling, beating, the valves opening and closing, the wet sound of his blood invading it, the swoosh and flap of the valves as they welcomed it, utilizing it, my heart growing ever larger and more powerful, my veins becoming like so many invincible metallic conduits of this most potent fluid.

I lay on the floor. He stood above me, and his hands were open to me. 'Get up, Amadeo. Come, come up, into my arms. Take it.'

I cried. I sobbed. My tears were red, and my hand was stained with red. 'Help me, Master.'

'I do help you. Come, seek it out for yourself.'

I was on my feet with this new strength, as if all human limitations had been loosened, as if they were bonds of rope or chain and had fallen away. I sprang at him, pulling back his robe, the better to find the wound.

'Make a new wound, Amadeo.'

I bit into the flesh, puncturing it, and the blood squirted over my lips. I clapped my mouth against it. 'Flow into me.'

My eyes closed. I saw the wild lands, the grass blowing, the sky blue. My Father rode on and on with the small band behind him. Was I one of them?

'I prayed you'd escape!' he called out to me, laughing, 'and so you have. Damn you, Andrei. Damn you and your sharp tongue and your magical painter's hands. Damn you, you foul-mouthed whelp, damn you.' He laughed and laughed, and rode on, the grass bending and falling for him.

'Father, look!' I struggled to shout. I wanted him to see the stony ruins of the castle. But my mouth was full of blood. They had been right. Prince Feodor's fortress was destroyed, and he himself long gone. My Father's horse reared up suddenly as it came to the first heap of vine-covered stones.

With a shock, I felt the marble floor beneath me, so wondrously warm. I lay with both hands against it. I lifted myself. The swarming rosy pattern was so dense, so deep, so wondrous, it was like water frozen to make the finest stone. I could have looked into its depths forever.

'Rise up, Amadeo, once more.'

Oh, it was easy to make this climb, to reach for his arm and then his shoulder. I broke the flesh of his neck. I drank. The blood washed through me, once again revealing my entire form with a shock against the blackness of my mind. I saw the boy's body that was mine, of arms and legs, as with this form I breathed in the warmth and light around me, as if all of me had become one great multipored organ for seeing, for hearing, for breathing. I breathed with millions of minute and strong tiny mouths.

The blood filled me so that I could take no more.

I stood before my Master. In his face I saw but the hint of weariness, but the smallest pain in his eyes. I saw for the first time the true lines of his old humanity in his face, the soft inevitable crinkles at the corners of his serenely folded eyes.

The drapery of his robe glistened, the light traveling on it as the cloth moved with his small gesture. He pointed. He pointed to the painting of *The Procession of the Magi*.

'Your soul and your physical body are now locked together forever,' he said. 'And through your vampiric senses, the sense of sight, and of touch, and of smell, and of taste, you'll know all the world. Not from turning away from it to the dark cells of the Earth, but through opening your arms to endless glory will you perceive the absolute splendor of God's creation and the miracles wrought, in His Divine Indulgence, by the hands of men.'

The silk-clad multitudes of *The Procession of the Magi* appeared to move. Once more I heard the horses' hooves on the soft earth, and the shuffle of booted feet. Once more I thought I saw the distant hounds leap on the mountainside. I saw the masses of flowered shrubbery wobble with the press of the gilded procession against them; I saw petals fly from the flowers. Marvelous animals frolicked in the thick wood. I saw the proud Prince Lorenzo, astride his mount, turn his youthful head, just as my Father had done, and look at me. On and on went the world beyond him, the world with its white rocky cliffs, its hunters on their brown steeds and its leaping prancing dogs.

'It's gone forever, Master,' I said, and how rounded and resonant was my voice, responding to all that I beheld.

'What is that, my child?'

'Russia, the world of the wild lands, the world of those dark terrible cells within the moist Mother Earth.'

I turned around and around. Smoke rose from the wilderness of burning candles. Wax crawled and dripped over the chased silver that held them, dripping even to the spotless and shimmering floor. The floor was as the sea, so transparent suddenly, so silken, and high above the painted clouds in illimitable sweetest blue. It seemed a mist emanated from these clouds, a warm summer mist made up of mingling land and sea.

Once again, I looked at the painting. I moved towards it and threw out my hands against it, and stared upwards at the white castles atop the hills, at the delicate groomed trees, at the fierce sublime wilderness that waited so patiently for the sluggish journey of my crystal-clear gaze.

'So much!' I whispered. No words could describe the deep colors of brown and gold in the beard of the exotic magus, or the shadows at play in the painted head of the white horse, or in the face of the balding man who led him, or the grace of the arch-necked camels or the crush of rich flowers beneath soundless feet.

'I see it with all of me,' I sighed. I closed my eyes and lay against it, recalling perfectly all aspects as the dome of my mind became this room itself, and the wall was there colored and painted by me. 'I see it without any omission. I see it,' I whispered.

I felt my Master's arms around my chest. I felt his kiss on my hair.

'Can you see again the glassy city?' he asked.

'I can make it!' I cried. I let my head roll back against his chest. I opened my eyes, and drew out of the riot of painting before me the very colors I wanted, and made this metropolis of bubbling, leaping glass rise in my imagination, until its towers pierced the sky. 'It's there, do you see it?'

In a torrent of tumbling, laughing words I described it, the glittering green and yellow and blue spires that sparkled and wavered in the Heavenly light. 'Do you see it?' I cried out.

'No. But you do,' said my Master. 'And that is more than enough.'

In the dim chamber, we dressed in the black morn.

Nothing was difficult, nothing had its old weight and resistance. It seemed I only needed to run my fingers up the doublet to have it buttoned.

We hurried down the steps, which seemed to disappear beneath my feet, and out into the night.

To climb the slimy walls of a palazzo was nothing, to anchor my feet over and over in the chinks of the stone, to poise on a tuft of fern and vine as I reached for the bars of a window and finally pulled open the grate, it was nothing, and how easily I let the heavy metal grid drop into the glistening green water below. How sweet to see it sink, to see the water splash around the descending weight, to see the glimmer of the torches in the water.

'I fall into it.'

'Come.'

Inside the chamber, the man rose from his desk. Against the cold, he had wrapped his neck in wool. His dark blue robe was banded in pearly gold. Rich man, banker. Friend of the Florentine, not mourning his loss over these many pages of vellum, smelling of black ink but calculating the inevitable gains, all partners murdered by the blade and by poison, it seemed, in a private banquet room.

Did he guess now that we had done it, the red-cloaked man and the auburn-haired boy who came

207

through his high fourth-story window in this frozen winter night?

I caught him as if he were the love of my young life, and unwound the wool from around the artery where I would feed.

He begged me to stop, to name my price. How still my Master looked, watching only me, as the man begged and I ignored him, merely feeling for this large pulsing, irresistible vein.

'Your life, Sir, I must have it,' I whispered. 'The blood of thieves is strong, isn't it, Sir?'

'Oh, child,' he cried, all resolve shattering, 'does God send His justice in such an unlikely form?'

It was sharp, pungent and strangely rank this human blood, spiked with the wine he'd drunk and the herbs of the foods he'd eaten, and almost purple in the light of his lamps as it flowed over my fingers before I could lap them with my tongue.

At the first draught I felt his heart stop.

'Ease up, Amadeo,' whispered my Master.

I let go and the heart recovered.

'That's it, feed on it slowly, slowly, letting the heart pump the blood to you, yes, yes, and gently with your fingers that he not suffer unduly, for he suffers the worst fate he can know and that is to know that he dies.'

We walked along the narrow quay together. No need anymore to keep my balance, though my gaze was lost in the depths of the singing, lapping water, gaining its movement through its many stonewalled connections from the faraway sea. I wanted to feel the wet green moss on the stones.

We stood in a small piazza, deserted, before the angled doors of a high stone church. They were bolted now. All windows were blinded, all doors locked. Curfew. Quiet.

'Once more, lovely one, for the strength it will give you,' said my Master, and his lethal fangs pierced me, as his hands held me captive.

'Would you trick me? Would you kill me?' I whispered, as I felt myself again helpless, no preternatural effort that I could summon strong enough to escape his grasp.

The blood was pulled out of me in a tidal wave that left my arms dangling and shaking, my feet dancing as if I were a hanged man. I struggled to remain conscious. I pushed against him. But the flow continued, out of me, out of all my fibers and into him.

'Now, once again, Amadeo, take it back from me.'

He dealt one fine blow to my chest. I almost toppled off my feet. I was so weak, I fell forward, only at the last grasping for his cloak. I pulled myself up and locked my left arm around his neck. He stepped back, straightening, making it hard for me. But I was too determined, too challenged and too determined to make a mockery of his lessons.

'Very well, sweet Master,' I said as I tore at his skin once again. 'I have you, and will have every drop of you, Sir, unless you are quick, most quick.' Only then did I realize! I too had tiny fangs!

He started to laugh softly, and it heightened my pleasure, that this which I fed upon should laugh beneath these new fangs.

With all my might I sought to tug his heart out of his chest. I heard him cry out and then laugh in amazement. I drew and drew on his blood, swallowing with a hoarse disgraceful sound.

'Come on, let me hear you cry out again!' I whispered, sucking the blood greedily, widening the gash with my teeth, my sharpened, lengthened teeth, these fang teeth that were now mine and made for this slaughter. 'Come on, beg for mercy, Sir!'

His laughter was sweet.

I took his blood swallow after swallow, glad and proud at his helpless laughing, at the fact that he had fallen down on his knees in the square and that I had him still, and he must now raise his arm to push me away.

'I can't drink anymore!' I declared. I lay back on the stones.

The frozen sky was black and studded with the white blazing stars. I stared at it, deliciously aware of the stone beneath me, of the hardness under my back and my head. No care now about the soil, the damp, the threat of disease. No care now whether the crawling things of the night came near. No care now what men might think who peeped from their windows. No care now for the lateness of the hour. Look at me, stars. Look at me, as I look at you.

Silent and glistering, these tiny eyes of Heaven.

I began to die. A withering pain commenced in my stomach, then moved to my bowels.

'Now, all that's left of a mortal boy will leave you,' my Master said. 'Don't be afraid.'

'No more music?' I whispered. I rolled over and put my arms around my Master, who lay beside me, his head resting on his elbow. He gathered me to him.

'Shall I sing to you a lullaby?' he said softly

I moved away from him. Foul fluid had begun to flow from me. I felt an instinctive shame, but this quite slowly vanished. He picked me up, easily as always, and pushed my face into his neck. The wind rushed around us.

Then I felt the cold water of the Adriatic, and I found myself tumbling on the unmistakable swell of the sea. The sea was salty and delicious and held no menace. I turned over and over, and finding myself alone, tried to get my bearings. I was far out, near to the island of the Lido. I looked back to the main island, and I could see through the great congregation of ships at anchor the blazing torches of the Palazzo Ducale, with a vision that was awesomely clear.

The mingled voices of the dark port rose, as if I were secretly swimming amongst the ships, though I was not.

What a remarkable power, to hear these voices, to be able to hone in on one particular voice and hear its early-morning mumblings, and then to pitch my hearing to yet another and let other words sink in.

I floated under the sky for a while, until all the pain was gone from me. I felt cleansed, and I didn't want to be alone. I turned over and effortlessly swam towards the harbor, moving under the surface of the water when I neared the ships.

What astonished me now was that I could see beneath the water! There was enough life for my vampiric eyes to see the huge anchors lodged in the mushy bottom of the lagoon, and to see the curved bottoms of the galleys. It was an entire underwater universe. I wanted to explore it further, but I heard my Master's voice – not a telepathic voice, as we would call it now, but his audible voice – calling me very softly to return to the piazza where he waited for me.

I peeled off my rank clothes and climbed out of the water naked, hurrying to him in the cold darkness, delighted that the chill itself meant little. When I saw him I spread out my arms and smiled.

He held a fur cloak in his arms, which he opened now to receive me, rubbing my hair dry with it and winding it around me.

'You feel your new freedom. Your bare feet are not hurt by the deep cold of the stones. If you're cut, your resilient skin will heal instantly, and no small crawling creature of the dark will produce revulsion in you. They can't hurt you. Disease can't hurt you.' He covered me with kisses. 'The most pestilential blood will only feed you, as your preternatural body cleanses it and absorbs it. You are a powerful creature, and deep in here? In your chest, which I touch now with my hand, there is your heart, your human heart.'

'Is it really so, Master?' I asked. I was exhilarated, I was playful. 'Why so human still?'

'Amadeo, have you found me inhuman? Have you found me cruel?'

My hair had shaken off the water, drying almost instantly. We walked now, arm in arm, the heavy fur cloak covering me, out of the square.

When I didn't answer, he stopped and embraced me again and began his hungry kisses.

'You love me,' I said, 'as I am now, even more than before.'

'Oh, yes,' he said. He hugged me roughly and kissed my throat all over, and my shoulders, and began to kiss my chest. 'I can't hurt you now, I can't snuff out your life with an accidental embrace. You're mine, of my flesh and of my blood.'

He stopped. He was crying. He didn't want me to see. He turned away when I tried to catch his face with my impertinent hands.

'Master, I love you,' I said.

'Pay attention,' he said brushing me off, obviously impatient with his tears. He pointed to the sky. 'You'll always know when morning's coming, if you pay attention. Do you feel it? Do you hear the birds? There are in all parts of the world those birds who sing right before dawn.'

A thought came to me, dark and horrid, that one of the things I had missed in the deep Monastery of the

Caves under Kiev was the sound of birds. Out in the wild grasses, hunting with my Father, riding from copse to copse of trees, I had loved the song of the birds. We had never been too long in the miserable riverside hovels of Kiev without those forbidden journeys into the wild lands from which so many didn't return.

But that was gone. I had all of sweet Italy around me, the sweet Serenissima. I had my Master, and the great voluptuous magic of this transformation.

'For this I rode into the wild lands,' I whispered. 'For this he took me out of the Monastery on that last day.'

My Master looked at me sadly. 'I hope so,' he said. 'What I know of your past, I learnt from your mind when it was open to me, but it's closed now, closed because I've made you a vampire, the same as I am, and we can never know each other's minds. We're too close, the blood we share makes a deafening roar in our ears when we try to talk in silence to one another, and so I let go forever of those awful images of that underground Monastery which flashed so brilliantly in your thoughts, but always with agony, always with near despair.'

'Yes, despair, and all that is gone like the pages of a book torn loose and thrown into the wind. Just like that, gone.'

He hurried me along. We were not going home. It was another way through the back alleys.

'We go now to our cradle,' he said, 'which is our crypt, our bed which is our grave.'

We entered an old dilapidated palazzo, tenanted only with a few sleeping poor. I didn't like it. I had been brought up by him on luxury. But we soon entered a cellar, a seeming impossibility in rank and watery Venice, but a cellar it was, indeed. We made our way down stone stairs, past thick bronze doors, which men alone could not open, until in the inky blackness we had found the final room.

'Here's a trick,' my Master whispered, 'which some night you yourself will be strong enough to work.'

I heard a riot of crackling and a small blast, and a great flaring torch blazed in his hand. He had lighted it with no more than his mind.

'With each decade you'll grow stronger, and then with each century, and you will discover many times in your long life that your powers have made a magical leap. Test them carefully, and protect what you discover. Use cleverly all that you discover. Never shun any power, for that's as foolish as a man shunning his strength.'

I nodded, staring spellbound at the flames. I had never seen such colors in simple fire before, and I felt no aversion to it, though I knew that it was the one thing that could destroy me. He had said so, had he not?

He made a gesture. I should regard the room.

What a splendid chamber it was. It was paved in gold! Even its ceiling was of gold. Two stone sarcophagi stood in the middle of it, each graced with a carved figure in the old style, that is, severe and more solemn than natural; and as I drew closer, I saw that these figures were helmeted knights, in long tunics, with heavy broadswords carved close to their flanks, their gloved hands clasped in prayer, their eyes closed in eternal sleep. Each had been gilded, and plated with silver, and set with countless tiny gems. The belts of the knights were set with amethyst. Sapphires adorned the necks of their tunics. Topaz gleamed in the scabbards of their swords.

'Is this not a fortune to tempt a thief?' I asked. 'Lying as it does here beneath this ruined house?'

He laughed outright.

'You're teaching me to be cautious already?' he asked, smiling. 'What back talk! No thief can gain access here. You didn't measure your own strength when you opened the doors. Look at the bolt I've closed behind us, since you are so concerned. Now see if you can lift the lid of that coffin. Go ahead. See if your strength meets your nerve.'

'I didn't mean it to be back talk,' I protested. 'Thank God you're smiling.' I lifted the lid and then moved the lower part of it to one side. It was nothing to me, yet I knew this was heavy stone. 'Ah, I see,' I said meekly. I gave him a radiant and innocent smile. The inside was cushioned in damask of royal purple.

'Get into this crib, my child,' he said. 'Don't be afraid as you wait for the rise of the sun. When it comes you'll sleep soundly enough.'

'Can I not sleep with you?'

'No, here in this bed which I have long ago prepared for you, this is where you belong. I have my own narrow place there next to you, which is not big enough for two. But you are mine now, mine, Amadeo. Vouchsafe me one last bevy of kisses, ah, sweet, yes, sweet –.'

'Master, don't let me ever make you angry. Don't let me ever—.'

'No, Amadeo, be my challenger, be my questioner, be my bold and ungrateful pupil.' He looked faintly sad. He pushed me gently. He gestured to the coffin. The purple satin damask shimmered.

'And so I lie in it,' I whispered, 'so young.'

I saw the shadow of pain in his face after I'd said this. I regretted it. I wanted to say something to undo it, but he gestured that I must go on.

Oh, how cold this was, cushions be damned, and how hard. I moved the lid into place above me and lay still, listening, listening to the sound of the torch snuffed, and

215

to the grinding of stone on stone as he opened his own grave.

I heard his voice:

'Good night, my young love, my child love, my son,' he said.

I let my body go limp. How delicious was this simple relaxation. How new were all things.

Far away in the land of my birth, the monks chanted in the Monastery of the Caves.

Sleepily, I reflected on all I'd remembered. I had gone home to Kiev. I had made of my memories a tableau to teach me all that I might know. And in the last moments of nighttime consciousness, I said farewell to them forever, farewell to their beliefs and their restraints.

I envisaged *The Procession of the Magi* splendidly glowing on the Master's wall, the procession which would be mine to study when the sun set again. It seemed to me in my wild and passionate soul, in my newborn vampiric heart, that the Magi had come not only for Christ's birth but for my rebirth as well.

If I had thought my transformation into a vampire meant the end of my tutelage or apprenticeship to Marius, I was quite wrong. I wasn't immediately set free to wallow in the joys of my new powers.

The night after my metamorphosis, my education began in earnest. I was to be prepared now not for a temporal life but for eternity.

My Master gave me to know that he had been created a vampire almost fifteen hundred years ago, and that there were members of our kind all over the world. Secretive, suspicious and often miserably lonely, the wanderers of the night, as my Master called them, were often ill prepared for immortality and made nothing of their existence but a string of dreary disasters until despair consumed them and they immolated themselves through some ghastly bonfire, or by going into the light of the sun.

As for the very old, those who like my Master had managed to withstand the passage of empires and epochs, they were for the most part misanthropes, seeking for themselves cities in which they could reign supreme among mortals, driving off fledglings who attempted to share their territory, even if it meant destroying creatures of their own kind.

Venice was the undisputed territory of my Master, his hunting preserve, and his own private arena in which he could preside over the games which he had chosen as significant for him in this time of life.

'There is nothing that will not pass,' he said, 'except

you yourself. You must listen to what I say because my lessons are first and foremost lessons in survival; the garnishes will come later on.'

The primary lesson was that we slay only 'the evil-doer.' This had once been, in the foggiest centuries of ancient time, a solemn commission to blood drinkers, and indeed there had been a dim religion surrounding us in antique pagan days in which the vampires had been worshiped as bringers of justice to those who had done wrong.

'We shall never again let such superstition surround us and the mystery of our powers. We are not infallible. We have no commission from God. We wander the Earth like the giant felines of the great jungles, and have no more claim upon those we kill than any creature that seeks to live.

'But it is an infallible principle that the slaying of the innocent will drive you mad. Believe me when I tell you that for your peace of mind you must feed on the evil, you must learn to love them in all their filth and degeneracy, and you must thrive on the visions of their evil that will inevitably fill your heart and soul during the kill.

'Kill the innocent and you will sooner or later come to guilt, and with it you will come to impotence and finally despair. You may think you are too ruthless and too cold for such. You may feel superior to human beings and excuse your predatory excesses on the ground that you do but seek the necessary blood for your own life. But it won't work in the long run.

'In the long run, you will come to know that you are more human than monster, all that is noble in you derives from your humanity, and your enhanced nature can only lead you to value humans all the more. You'll come to pity those you slay, even the most unredeemable, and you will come to love humans so desperately that there will be nights when hunger will seem far preferable to you than the blood repast.'

I accepted this wholeheartedly, and quickly plunged with my Master into the dark underbelly of Venice, the wild world of taverns and vice which I had never, as the mysterious velvet-clad 'apprentice' of Marius De Romanus, really seen before. Of course I knew drinking places, I knew fashionable courtesans such as our beloved Bianca, but I really didn't know the thieves and murderers of Venice, and it was on these that I fed.

Very soon, I understood what my Master meant when he said that I must develop a taste for evil and maintain it. The visions from my victims became stronger for me with every kill. I began to see brilliant colors when I killed. In fact, I could sometimes see these colors dancing around my victims before I ever even closed in. Some men seem to walk in red-tinged shadows, and others to emanate a fiery orange light. The anger of my meanest and most tenacious victims was often a brilliant yellow which blinded me, searing me, as it were, both when I first attacked and while I drank the victim dry of all blood.

I was at the onset a dreadfully violent and impulsive killer. Having been set down by Marius in a nest of assassins, I went to work with a clumsy fury, drawing out my prey from the tavern or the flophouse, cornering him on the quay and then tearing open his throat as if I were a wild dog. I drank greedily often rupturing the victim's heart. Once the heart is gone, once the man is dead, there is nothing to pump the blood into you. And so it is not so good.

But my Master, for all his lofty speeches on the virtues of humans, and his adamant insistence on our own responsibilities, nevertheless taught me to kill with finesse.

'Take it slowly,' he said. We walked along the narrow banks of the canals where such existed. We traveled by gondola listening with our preternatural ears for conversation that seemed meant for us. 'And half the time, you needn't enter a house in order to draw out a victim. Stand outside of it, read the man's thoughts, throw him some silent bait. If you read his thoughts, it is almost a certainty that he can receive your message. You can lure without words. You can exert an irresistible pull. When he comes out to you, then take him.

'And there is never any need for him to suffer, or for blood actually to be spilt. Embrace your victim, love him if you will. Fondle him slowly and sink your teeth with caution. Then feast as slowly as you can. This way his heart will see you through.

'As for the visions, and these colors you speak of, seek to learn from them. Let the victim in his dying tell you what he can about life itself. If images of his long life trip before you, observe them, or rather savor them. Yes, savor them. Devour them slowly as you do his blood. As for the colors, let them pervade you. Let the entire experience inundate you. That is, be both active and utterly passive. Make love to your victim. And listen always for the actual moment when the heart ceases to beat. You will feel an undeniably orgiastic sensation at this moment, but it can be overlooked.

'Dispose of the body after, or make certain that you have licked away all sign of the puncture wounds in the victim's throat. Just a little bit of your blood on the tip of your tongue will accomplish this. In Venice dead bodies are common. You need not take such pains. But when we hunt in the outlying villages, then often you may have to bury the remains.'

I was eager for all these lessons. That we hunted together was a magnificent pleasure. I came to realize quickly enough that Marius had been clumsy in the murders he had committed for me to witness before I'd been transformed. I knew then, as perhaps I've made plain in this story, that he wanted me to feel pity for these victims; he wanted me to experience horror. He wanted me to see death as an abomination. But due to my youth, my devotion to him and the violence done me in my short mortal life, I had not responded as he hoped.

Whatever the case, he was now a much more skilled killer. We often took the same victim, together, I drinking from the throat of our captive, while he fed from the man's wrist. Sometimes he delighted in holding the victim tightly for me while I drank all of the blood.

Being new, I was thirsty every night. I could have lived for three or more without killing, yes, and sometimes I did, but by the fifth night of denying myself – this was put to the test – I was too weak to rise from the sarcophagus. So what this meant was that, when and if I were ever on my own, I must kill at least every fourth night.

My first few months were an orgy. Each kill seemed more thrilling, more paralyzingly delicious than the one which had gone before. The mere sight of a bared throat could bring about in me such a state of arousal that I became like an animal, incapable of language or restraint. When I opened my eyes in the cold stony darkness, I envisioned human flesh. I could feel it in my naked hands and I wanted it, and the night could have no other events for me until I had laid my powerful hands on that one which would be the sacrifice to my need.

For long moments after the kill, sweet throbbing sensations passed through me as the warm fragrant blood found all the corners of my body, as it pumped its magnificent heat into my face.

This, and this alone, was enough to absorb me utterly, young as I was.

But Marius had no intention of letting me wallow in blood, the hasty young predator, with no other thought but to glut himself night after night.

'You must really begin to learn history and philosophy and the law in earnest,' he told me. 'You are not destined for the University of Padua now. You are destined to endure.'

So after our stealthy missions were completed, and we returned to the warmth of the palazzo, he forced me to my books. He wanted some distance between me and Riccardo and the others anyway, lest they become suspicious of the change that had occurred.

In fact, he told me they 'knew' about the change whether they realized it or not. Their bodies knew that I was no longer human, though it might take their minds some time to accept the fact.

'Show them only courtesy and love, only complete indulgence, but keep your distance,' Marius told me. 'By the time they realize the unthinkable is the fact, you will have assured them that you are no enemy to them, that you are indeed Amadeo still, whom they love, and that though you have been changed, you yourself have not changed towards them.'

I understood this. At once I felt a greater love for Riccardo. I felt it for all of the boys.

'But Master,' I asked, 'don't you ever become impatient with them, that they think more slowly, that they are so clumsy? I love them, yes, but surely you see them in a more pejorative light even than I do.'

'Amadeo,' he said softly, 'they are all going to die.' His face was charged with grief.

I felt it immediately and totally, which was always the way with feelings now. They came on in a torrent and taught their lessons at once.

They are all going to die. Yes, and I am immortal.

After that, I could only be patient with them, and indeed, I indulged myself in the manner in which I looked at them and studied them, never letting them know it, but glorying in all the details of them as if they were exotic because . . . they were going to die.

There is too much to describe, too much. I can't find a way to put down all that became clear to me in the first few months alone. And there was nothing made known to me in that time which was not deepened afterwards.

I saw process everywhere I looked; I smelled corruption, but I also beheld the mystery of growth, the magic of things blossoming and ripening, and in fact all process, whether towards maturity or towards the grave, delighted and enthralled me, except, that is, the disintegration of the human mind.

My study of government and law was more of a challenge. Though reading was accomplished with infinitely greater speed and near instantaneous comprehension of syntax, I had to force myself to be interested in such things as the history of Roman Law from ancient times, and the great code of the Emperor Justinian, called the *Corpus Juris Civilis*, which my Master thought to be one of the finest codes of law ever written.

'The world is only getting better,' Marius instructed me. 'With each century, civilization becomes more enamored of justice, ordinary men make greater strides towards sharing the wealth which was once the booty of the powerful, and art benefits by every increase in freedom, becoming ever more imaginative, ever more inventive and ever more beautiful.'

I could understand this only theoretically. I had no faith or interest in law. In fact, I had a total contempt in the abstract for my Master's ideas. What I mean is, I didn't have contempt for him, but I had an underlying contempt for law and for legal institutions and governmental institutions that was so total that I did not even understand it myself.

My Master said that he understood it.

'You were born in a dark savage land,' he said. 'I wish I could take you back two hundred years in time to the years before Batu, the son of Genghis Khan, sacked the magnificent city of Kiev Rus, to the time when indeed the domes of its Santa Sofia were golden, and its people full of ingenuity and hope.'

'I heard ad nauseam of that old glory,' I said quietly, not wanting to anger him. 'I was stuffed with tales of the olden times when I was a boy. In the miserable wooden house in which we lived, only yards from the frozen river, I listened to that rot as I shivered by the fire. Rats lived in our house. There was nothing beautiful in it but the ikons, and my Father's songs. There was nothing but depravity there, and we speak now, as you know, of an immense land. You cannot know how big Russia is unless you have been there, unless you have traveled as I did with my Father into the bitter-cold northern forests to Moscow, or to Novgorod, or east to Cracow.' I broke off. 'I don't want to think of those times or that place,' I said. 'In Italy one cannot dream of enduring such a place.'

'Amadeo, the evolution of law, of government, is different in each land and with each people. I chose Venice, as I told you long ago, because it is a great Republic, and because its people are firmly connected to the Mother Earth by the simple fact that they are all merchants and engaged in trade. I love the city of Florence because its great family, the Medici, are bankers, not idle titled aristocrats who scorn all effort in the name of what they believe has been given them by

God. The great cities of Italy are made by men who work, men who create, men who do, and on account of this, there is a greater compassion to all systems, and infinitely greater opportunity for men and women in all walks of life.'

I was discouraged by all this talk. What did it matter?

'Amadeo, the world now is yours,' my Master said. 'You must look at the larger movements of history. The state of the world will begin in time to oppress you, and you will find, as all immortals do, that you cannot simply shut your heart on it, especially not you.'

'Why so?' I asked a little crossly. 'I think I can shut my eyes. What do I care if a man is a banker or a merchant? What do I care whether I live in a city which builds its own merchant fleet? I can look forever on the paintings in this palazzo, Master. I have not yet begun to see all the details in *The Procession of the Magi*, and there are so many others. And what of all the paintings in this city?'

He shook his head. 'The study of painting will lead you to the study of man, and the study of man will lead you to lament or celebrate the state of the world of men.'

I didn't believe it, but I was not allowed to change the curriculum. I studied as I was told.

Now, my Master had many gifts which I did not possess, but which he told me I would develop in time. He could make fire with his mind, but only if conditions were optimum – that is, he could ignite a torch already prepared with pitch. He could scale a building effortlessly with only a few quick handholds on its window-sills, propelling himself upwards with graceful darting motions, and he could swim to any depth of the sea.

Of course his vampiric vision and his hearing were far more acute and powerful than my own, and while voices intruded upon me, he knew how to emphatically shut them out. I had to learn this, and indeed I worked at it desperately, for there were times when all Venice seemed nothing but a cacophony of voices and prayers.

But the one great power he possessed which I did not possess was that he could take to the air and cover immense distances with great speed. This had been demonstrated to me many times, but almost always, when he had lifted me and carried me, he had made me cover my face, or he had forced my head down so that I couldn't see where we went and how.

Why he was so reticent about it, I couldn't understand. Finally, one night when he refused to transport us as if by magic to the Island of the Lido so that we could watch one of the nighttime ceremonies of fireworks and torch-lit ships on the water, I pressed the question.

'It's a frightening power,' he said coolly. 'It's frightening to be unanchored from the Earth. In the early stages, it is not without its blunders and disasters. As one acquires skill, rising smoothly into the highest atmosphere, it becomes chilling not only to the body but to the soul. It seems not preternatural, but supernatural.' I could see he suffered over this. He shook his head. 'It is the one talent which seems genuinely inhuman. I cannot learn from humans how best to use it. With every other talent, humans are my teacher. The human heart is my school. Not so with this. I become the magician; I become the witch or the warlock. It's seductive, and one could become its slave.'

'But how so?' I asked him.

He was at a loss. He didn't even want to talk about it. Finally he became just a little impatient.

'Sometimes, Amadeo, you grill me with your questions. You ask if I owe you this tutelage. Believe me, I do not.'

'Master you made me, and you insist on my obedience. Why would I read Abelard's *History of My*

Calamities and the writings of Duns Scotus of Oxford University if you didn't make me do it?' I stopped. I remembered my Father and how I never stopped throwing acidic words at him, fast answers and slurs.

I became discouraged. 'Master,' I said. 'Just explain it to me.'

He made a gesture as if to say 'Oh, so simple, eh?'

'All right,' he went on. 'It's this way. I can go very high in the air, and I can move very fast. I cannot often penetrate the clouds. They're frequently above me. But I can travel so fast that the world itself becomes a blur. I find myself in strange lands when I descend. And I tell you, for all its magic, this is a deeply jarring and disturbing thing. I am lost sometimes, dizzy, unsure of my goals or my will to live, after I make use of this power. Transitions come too quickly; that's it, perhaps. I never spoke of this to anyone, and now I speak to you, and you're a boy, and you can't begin to understand.'

I didn't.

But within a very short time, it was his wish that we undertake a longer journey than any we'd made before. It was only a matter of hours, but to my utter astonishment, we traveled between sundown and early evening to the far city of Florence itself.

There, set down in a wholly different world than that of the Veneto, walking quietly amongst an entirely different breed of Italian, into churches and palaces of a different style, I understood for the first time what he meant.

Understand, I'd seen Florence before, traveling as Marius's mortal apprentice, with a group of the others. But my brief glimpse was nothing to what I saw as a vampire. I had the measuring instruments now of a minor god.

But it was night. The city lay under the usual curfew.

And the stones of Florence seemed darker, more drab, suggestive of a fortress, the streets narrow and gloomy, as they were not brightened by luminescent ribbons of water as were our own. The palaces of Florence lacked the extravagant Moorish ornament of Venice's showplaces, the high-gloss fantastical stone facades. They enclosed their splendor, as is more common to Italian cities. Yet the city was rich, dense and full of delights for the eye.

It was after all Florence – the capital of the man called Lorenzo the Magnificent, the compelling figure who dominated Marius's copy of the great mural which I had seen on the night of my dark rebirth, a man who had died only a few years before.

We found the city unlawfully busy, though it was quite dark, with groups of men and women lingering about in the hard paved streets, and a sinister quality of restlessness hung about the Piazza della Signoria, which was one of the most important of all the many squares of the town.

An execution had taken place that day, hardly an uncommon occurrence in Florence, or Venice for that matter. It had been a burning. I smelled wood and charred flesh though all the evidence had been cleared before night.

I had a natural distaste for such things, which not everyone has, by the way, and I edged towards the scene cautiously, not wishing with these heightened senses to be jarred by some horrible remnant of cruelty.

Marius had always cautioned us as boys not to 'enjoy' these spectacles, but to place ourselves mentally in the position of the victim if we were to learn the maximum from what we saw.

As you know from history, the crowds at executions were often merciless and unruly, taunting the victim sometimes, I think, out of fear. We, the boys of Marius, had always found it terribly difficult to cast our mental lot with the man being hanged or burnt. In sum, he'd taken all the fun out of it for us.

Of course, as these rituals happened almost always by day, Marius himself had never been present.

Now, as we moved into the great Piazza della Signoria, I could see that he was displeased by the thin ash that still hung in the air, and the vile smells.

I also noticed that we slipped past others easily, two dark-draped swiftly moving figures. Our feet scarce made a sound. It was the vampiric gift that we could move so stealthily, shifting quickly out of sudden and occasional mortal observation with an instinctive grace.

'It's as though we're invisible,' I said to Marius, 'as if nothing can hurt us, because we don't really belong here and will soon take our leave.' I looked up at the grim battlements that fronted on the Square.

'Yes, but we are not invisible, remember it,' he whispered.

'But who died here today? People are full of torment and fear. Listen. There is satisfaction, and there is weeping.'

He didn't answer.

I grew uneasy.

'What is it? It can't be any common thing,' I said. 'The city is too vigilant and unquiet.'

'It's their great reformer, Savonarola,' Marius said. 'He died on this day, hanged, and then burnt here. Thank God, he was already dead before the flames rose.'

'You wish mercy for Savonarola?' I asked. I was puzzled. This man, a great reformer in the eyes of some perhaps, had always been damned by all I knew. He had condemned all pleasures of the senses, denying any validity to the very school in which my Master thought all things were to be learnt.

'I wish mercy for any man,' said Marius. He beckoned for me to follow, and we moved towards the nearby street.

We headed away from the grisly place.

'Even this one, who persuaded Botticelli to heap his own paintings on the Bonfires of the Vanities?' I asked. 'How many times have you pointed to the details of your own copies of Botticelli's work to show me some graceful beauty you wanted me to never forget?'

'Are you going to argue with me until the end of the world!' said Marius. 'I'm pleased that my blood has given you new strength in every aspect, but must you question every word that falls from my lips?' He threw me a furious glance, letting the light of nearby torches fully illuminate his half-mocking smile. 'There are some students who believe in this method, and that greater truths rise out of the continued strife between teacher and pupil. But not me! I believe you need to let my lessons settle in quiet at least for the space of five minutes in your mind before you begin your counterattack.'

'You try to be angry with me but you can't.'

'Oh, what a muddle!' he said as if he were cursing. He walked fast ahead of me.

The small Florentine street was dreary, like a passageway in a great house rather than a city street. I longed for the breezes of Venice, or rather, my body did, out of habit. I was quite fascinated to be here.

'Don't be so provoked,' I said. 'Why did they turn on Savonarola?'

'Give men enough time and they'll turn on anyone. He claimed to have been a prophet, divinely inspired by God, and that these were the Last Days, and this is the oldest most tiresome Christian complaint in the world, believe you me. The Last Days! Christianity is a religion based on the notion that we are living in the Last Days!

It's a religion fueled by the ability of men to forget all the blunders of the past, and get dressed once more for the Last Days.'

I smiled, but bitterly. I wanted to articulate a strong presentiment, that we were always in the Last Days, and it was inscribed in our hearts, because we were mortals, when quite suddenly and totally I realized that I was no longer mortal, except insofar as the world itself was mortal.

And it seemed I understood more viscerally than ever the atmosphere of purposeful gloom which had over-hung my childhood in far-off Kiev. I saw again the muddy catacombs, and the half-buried monks who had cheered me on to become one of them.

I shook it off, and now how bright Florence seemed as we came into the broad torch-lighted Piazza del Duomo – before the great Cathedral of Santa Maria del Fiore.

'Ah, my pupil does listen now and then,' Marius was saying to me in an ironic voice. Yes, I am more than glad that Savonarola is no more. But to rejoice at the end of something is not to approve the endless parade of cruelty that is human history. I wish it were otherwise. Public sacrifice becomes grotesque in every respect. It dulls the senses of the populace. In this city, above all others, it's a spectacle. The Florentines enjoy it, as we do our Regattas and Processions. So Savonarola is dead. Well, if any mortal man asked for it, it was Savonarola, predicting as he did the end of the world, damning princes from his pulpit, leading great painters to immolate their works. The hell with him.'

'Master, look, the Baptistery, let's go, let's look at the doors. The piazza's almost empty. Come on. It's our chance to look at the bronzes.' I tugged on his sleeve.

He followed me, and he stopped his muttering, but he was not himself.

231

What I wanted so to see is work that you can see in Florence now, and in fact, almost every treasure of this city and of Venice which I've described here you can see now. You have only to go there. The panels in the door which were done by Lorenzo Ghiberti were my delight, but there was also older work done by Andrea Pisano, portraying the life of St. John the Baptist, and this, I didn't intend to overlook.

So keen was the vampiric vision that as I studied these various detailed bronze pictures, I could hardly keep from sighing with pleasure.

This moment is so clear. I think that I believed, then, that nothing ever could hurt me or make me sad again, that I had discovered the balm of salvation in the vampiric blood, and the strange thing is, that as I dictate this story now, I think the same thing once more.

Though unhappy now, and possibly forever, I believe again in the paramount importance of the flesh. My mind wanders to the words of D. H. Lawrence, the twentieth-century writer, who in his writings on Italy, recalled Blake's image of the 'Tyger, Tyger, burning bright/In the forests of the night.' Lawrence's words are:

> This is the supremacy of the flesh, which devours all, and becomes transfigured into a magnificent brindled flame, a burning bush indeed.
>
> This is one way of transfiguration into the eternal flame, the transfiguration through ecstasy in the flesh.

But I have done a risky thing here for a storyteller. I have left my plot, as I'm sure The Vampire Lestat (who is more skilled perhaps than I am, and so in love with the image of William Blake's tiger in the night, and who has, whether he cares to admit it or not, used the tiger in his work in the very same way) would point out to me, and I must speedily return to this moment in the Piazza del Duomo, where I left myself of long ago standing, side by side with Marius, looking at the burnished genius of Ghiberti, as he sings in bronze of Sybils and saints.

We took our time with these things. Marius said softly that next to Venice, Florence was the city of his choice, for here so much had magnificently flowered.

'But I can't be without the sea, not even here,' he confided. 'And as you see all around you, this city hugs her treasures close with shadowy vigilance, whereas in Venice, the very facades of our palaces are offered up in gleaming stone beneath the moon to Almighty God.'

'Master, do we serve Him?' I pressed. 'I know you condemn the monks who brought me up, you condemn the ravings of Savonarola, but do you mean to guide me by another route back to the Very Same God?'

'That's just it, Amadeo, I do,' said Marius, 'and I don't mean as the pagan I am to admit it so easily, lest its complexity be misunderstood. But I do. I find God in the blood. I find God in the flesh. I find it no accident that the mysterious Christ should reside forever for His followers in the Flesh and Blood within the Bread of the Transubtantiation.'

I was so moved by these words! It seemed the very sun I had forever forsworn had come again to brighten the night.

We slipped into the side door of the darkened Cathedral called the Duomo. I stood gazing over the long vista of its stone floor, towards the altar.

Was it possible that I could have the Christ in a new way? Perhaps I had not after all renounced Him forever. I tried to speak these troubled thoughts to my Master. Christ . . . in a new way. I couldn't explain it, and said finally:

'I stumble with my words.'

'Amadeo, we all stumble, and so do all those who enter history. The concept of a Great Being stumbles down the centuries; His words and those principles attributed to Him do tumble after Him; and so the Christ is snatched up in His wandering by the preaching puritan on one side, the muddy starving hermit on the other, the gilded Lorenzo de' Medici here who would celebrate his Lord in gold and paint and mosaic stone.'

'But is Christ the Living Lord?' I whispered.

No answer.

My soul hit a pitch of agony. Marius took my hand, and said that we go now, stealthily to the Monastery of San Marco.

'This is the sacred house that gave up Savonarola,' he said. 'We'll slip into it unbeknownst to its pious inhabitants.'

We again traveled as if by magic. I felt only the Master's strong arms, and did not even see the frame of the doors as we exited and made our way to this other place.

I knew he meant to show me the work of the artist called Fra Angelico, long dead, who had labored all his life in this very Monastery, a painter monk, as I perhaps had been destined to be, far away in the lightless Monastery of the Caves.

Within seconds, we set down soundlessly on the moist grass of the square cloister of San Marco, the serene garden enclosed by Michelozzo's loggias, secure within its walls.

At once I heard many prayers reach my inner vampiric hearing, desperate agitated prayers of the brothers who had been loyal or sympathetic to Savonarola. I put my hands to my head as if this foolish

234

human gesture could signal to the Divine that I had had more than I could bear.

My Master broke the current of thought reception with his soothing voice.

'Come,' he said, grasping my hand. 'We'll slip into the cells one by one. There is enough light for you to see the works of this monk.'

'You mean that Fra Angelico painted the very cells where monks go to sleep?' I had thought his works would be in the chapel, and in the other public or communal rooms.

'That's why I want you to see this,' said my Master. He led me up a stairs and into a wide stone corridor He made the first door spring open, and gently we moved inside, fleet and silent, not disturbing the monk who lay curled on his hard bed, his head sweating against the pillow.

'Don't look at his face,' said my Master gently. 'If you do you'll see the troubled dreams he suffers. I want you to look at the wall. What do you see, now, look!'

I understood at once. This art of Fra Giovanni, called Angelico in honor of his sublime talent, was a strange mixture of the sensuous art of our time with the pious and forswearing art of the past.

I gazed on the bright, elegant rendering of the arrest of Christ in the Garden of Gethsemane. The slender flattened figures resembled very much the elongated and elastic images of the Russian ikon, and yet the faces were softened and plastic with genuine and touching emotion. It seemed a kindness infused all beings here, not merely Our Lord Himself, condemned to be betrayed by one of His own, but the Apostles, who looked on, and even the unfortunate soldier, in his tunic of mail, who reached out to take the Lord away, and the soldiers watched.

235

I was transfixed by this unmistakable kindness, this seeming innocence that infected everyone, this sublime compassion on the part of the artist for all players in this tragic drama which had prefaced the salvation of the world.

Into another cell I was taken immediately. Once again the door gave way at Marius's command, and the sleeping occupant of the cell never knew that we were there.

This painting showed again the Garden of Agony, and Christ, before the arrest, alone among His sleeping Apostles, left to beg His Heavenly Father for strength. Once again I saw the comparison to the old styles in which I, as a Russian boy, had felt so sure. The folds in the cloth, the use of arches, the halo for each head, the discipline of the whole – all was connected to the past, and yet there shone again the new Italian warmth, the undeniable Italian love of the humanity of all included, even Our Lord Himself.

We went from cell to cell. Backwards and forwards through the Life of Christ we traveled, visiting the scene of the First Holy Communion, in which, so touchingly, Christ gave out the bread containing His Body and Blood as if it were the Host at Mass, and then the Sermon on the Mount, in which the smooth pleated rocks around Our Lord and His listeners seemed made of cloth as surely as his graceful gown.

When we came to the Crucifixion, in which Our Lord gave over to St. John His Blessed Mother, I was heart-struck by the anguish in the Lord's face. How thoughtful in her distress was the face of the Virgin, and how resigned was the saint beside her, with his soft fair Florentine face, so like that of a thousand other painted figures in this city, barely fringed with a light brown beard.

Just when I thought I understood my Master's lessons

perfectly, we happened upon another painting, and I would feel yet a stronger connection with the long-ago treasures of my boyhood and the quiet incandescent splendor of the Dominican monk who had graced these walls. Finally we left this clean, lovely place of tears and whispered prayers.

We went out into the night and back to Venice, traveling in cold and noisy darkness, and arriving at home in time to sit a while in the warm light of the sumptuous bedchamber and talk.

'Do you see?' Marius pressed me. He was at his desk with his pen in hand. He dipped it and wrote even as he talked, turning back the large vellum page of his diary. 'In far off Kiev, the cells were the earth itself, moist and pure, but dark and omnivorous, the mouth that eats all life finally, that would bring to ruin all art.'

I shivered. I sat rubbing the backs of my arms, looking at him.

'But there in Florence, what did this subtle teacher Fra Angelico bequeath to his brothers? Magnificent pictures to put them in mind of the Suffering of Our Lord?'

He wrote several lines before he resumed.

'Fra Angelico never scorned to delight your eye, to fill your vision with all the colors God has given you the power to see, for you were given by him two eyes, Amadeo, and not to be . . . not to be shut up in the dark earth.'

I reflected for a long time. To know these things theoretically had been one thing. To have passed through the hushed and sleeping rooms of the Monastery, to have seen my Master's principles there emblazoned by a monk himself – this was something else.

'It is a glorious time, this,' Marius said softly. 'That which was good among the ancients is now redis- covered, and given a new form. You ask me, is Christ

237

the Lord? I say, Amadeo, that He can be, for He never taught anything Himself but love, or so His Apostles, whether they know it or not, have led us to believe . . .'

I waited on him, as I knew he wasn't finished. The room was so sweetly warm and clean and bright. I have near my heart forever a picture of him at this moment, the tall fair-haired Marius, his red cloak thrown back to free his arm for the pen he held, his face smooth and reflecting, his blue eyes looking, beyond that time and any other in which he had lived, for the truth. The heavy book was propped on a low portable lectern for him, to give it a comfortable angle. The little ink pot was set inside a richly embellished silver holder. And the heavy candelabra behind him, with its eight thick melting candles, was made up of numberless engraved cherubs half-embedded in the deeply worked silver, with wings struggling, perhaps, to fly loose, and tiny round-cheeked faces turned this way and that with large contented eyes beneath loose serpentine curls.

It seemed an audience of little angels to watch and listen as Marius spoke, so many, many tiny faces peering indifferently forth from the silver, quite immune to the falling rivulets of pure, melted wax.

'I cannot live without this beauty,' I said suddenly, though I had meant to wait. 'I cannot endure without it. Oh, God, you have shown me Hell and it lies behind me, surely in the land where I was born.'

He heard my little prayer, my little confession, my desperate plea.

'If Christ is the Lord,' he said, returning to his point, returning us both to the lesson, 'if Christ is the Lord, then what a beautiful miracle it is, this Christian mystery—.' His eyes filmed with tears. 'That the Lord Himself should come to Earth and clothe Himself in flesh the better to know us and to comprehend us. Oh, what God, ever made in the image of Man by His fancy, was ever better than one who would become Flesh? Yes, I would say to you, yes, your Christ, their Christ, the Christ even of the Monks of Kiev, He is the Lord! Only mark forever the lies they tell in His Name, and the deeds they do. For Savonarola called on His Name when he praised a foreign enemy bearing down on Florence, and those who burnt Savonarola as a false prophet, they too, as they lit the faggots beneath his dangling body, they too called on Christ the Lord.'

I was overcome with tears.

He sat in silence, respecting me perhaps, or only collecting his thoughts. Then he dipped his pen again and wrote for a long time, much faster than men do, but deftly and gracefully, and never marking out a word.

At last, he set down the pen. He looked at me and he smiled.

'I set out to show you things, and it's never as I plan. I wanted you tonight to see the dangers in this power of flight, that we can too easily transport ourselves to other places, and that this feeling of slipping in and out so easily is a deception of which we must beware. But look, how differently it has all gone.'

I didn't answer him.

'I wanted you,' he said, 'to be a little afraid.'

'Master,' I said, wiping my nose with the back of my hand, 'count on me to be properly frightened when the time comes. I'll have this power, I know it. I can feel it now. And for now, I think it's splendid, and because of it, this power, one dark thought falls over my heart.'

'What is that?' he asked in the kindest way. 'You know, I think your angelic face is no more fit for sad things than those faces painted by Fra Angelico. What's this shadow I see? What is this dark thought?'

'Take me back there, Master,' I said. I trembled, yet I

239

said it. 'Let us use your power to cover miles and miles of Europe. Let us go north. Take me back to see that cruel land that has become a Purgatorio in my imagination. Take me back to Kiev.'

He was slow in giving his answer.

The morning was coming. He gathered up his cloak and robe, rose from the chair and took me with him up the stairs to the roof.

We could see the distant already paling waters of the Adriatic, twinkling under the moon and stars, beyond the familiar forest of the masts of the ships. Tiny lights flickered on the distant islands. The wind was mild and full of salt and sea freshness, and a particular deliciousness that comes only when one has lost all fear of the sea.

'Yours is a brave request, Amadeo. If you really wish it, tomorrow night we'll begin the journey.'

'Have you ever traveled so far before?'

'In miles, in space, yes, many times,' he said. 'But in another's quest for understanding? No, never so very far.'

He embraced me and took me to the palazzo where our tomb lay hidden. I was cold all over by the time we reached the soiled stone stairway, where so many of the poor slept. We picked our way among them, until we reached the entrance to the cellar.

'Light the torch for me, Sir,' I said. 'I am shivering. I want to see the gold around us, if I may.'

'There, you have it,' he said. We stood in our crypt with the two ornate sarcophagi before us. I lay my hand on the lid of the one which was mine, and quite suddenly there came over me another presentiment, that all I loved would endure for a very brief time.

Marius must have seen this hesitation. He passed his right hand through the very fire of the torch, and touched his warmed fingers to my cheek. Then he kissed me where this warmth hovered, and his kiss was warm.

It took us four nights to reach Kiev.

Only in the early hours before dawn did we hunt.

We made our graves in actual burial places, the dungeon vaults of old neglected castles and in the sepulchers beneath forlorn and ruined churches where the profane were wont now to stash their livestock and their hay.

There are tales I could tell of this journey, of those brave fortresses we roamed near morning, of those wild mountain villages where we found the evildoer in his rude den.

Naturally, Marius saw lessons in all this, teaching me how easy it was to find hiding places and approving the speed with which I moved through the dense forest, and had no fear of the scattered primitive settlements which we visited on account of my thirst. He praised me that I didn't shrink from the dark dusty nests of bones in which we lay down by day, reminding me that these burial places, having already been pillaged, were the least likely for men to trouble even in the light of the sun.

Our fancy Venetian clothes were soon streaked with dirt, but we were provided with thick fur-lined cloaks for the journey, and these covered all. Even in this Marius saw a lesson, that we must remember what fragile and meaningless protection our garments provide. Mortal men forget how to wear their garments lightly and that they are a mere covering for the body and no more. Vampires must never forget it, for we are far less dependent upon our raiment than men.

By the last morning before our arrival in Kiev, I knew the rocky northern woods only too well. The dread winter of the north was all around us. We had come upon one of the most intriguing of all my memories: the presence of snow.

'It no longer hurts me to hold it,' I said, gathering the soft delicious cold snow in my hands and pressing it to my face. 'It no longer chills me to see it, and indeed how beautiful it is, covering the poorest of towns and hovels with its blanket. Master, look, look how it throws back the light even of the weakest stars.'

We were on the edge of the land that men call the Golden Horde – the southern steppes of Russia, which for two hundred years, since the conquest of Genghis Khan, had been too dangerous for the farmer, and often the death of the army or the knight.

Kiev Rus had once included this fertile and beautiful prairie, stretching far to the East, almost to Europe, as well as south of the city of Kiev where I had been born.

'The final stretch will be nothing,' my Master told me. 'We make it tomorrow night so that you will be rested and fresh when you catch the first sight of home.'

As we stood on a rocky crag looking out at the wild grass, flowing in the winter wind beneath us, for the first time in the nights since I'd become a vampire, I felt a terrible longing for the sun. I wanted to see this land by the light of the sun. I didn't dare confess it to my Master. After all, how many blessings can a being want?

On the final night, I awoke just after sunset. We had found a hiding place beneath the floor of a church in a village where no one lived now at all. The horrid Mongol hordes, which had destroyed my homeland over and over again, had long ago burnt this town to nothing, or so Marius had told me, and this church did not even possess a roof. There had been no one left here to pull the stones of the floor away for profit or building, and so we had gone down a forgotten stairway to lie with monks buried here some thousand years ago.

Rising from the grave, I saw high above a rectangle of sky where my Master had removed a marble paving block, an inscribed tombstone no doubt, for me to make my ascent. I propelled myself upwards. That is, I bent my knees and, using all my strength, shot upwards, as if I could fly, and passed through this opening to land on my feet.

Marius, who invariably rose before me, was sitting nearby. He immediately gave out the expected appreciative laugh.

'Have you been saving that little trick for such a moment?' he said.

I was dazed by the snow, as I looked around me. How afraid I was, merely looking at the frozen pines that had everywhere sprung up on the ruins of the village. I could scarce speak.

'No,' I managed to say. 'I didn't know I could do it. I don't know how high I can leap, or how much strength I have. You're pleased, however?'

'Yes, why shouldn't I be? I want you to be so strong that no one can ever hurt you.'

'And who would, Master? We travel the world, but who even knows when we go and when we come?'

'There are others, Amadeo. And there are others here. I can hear them if I want to, but there is a good reason for not hearing them.'

I understood. 'You open your mind to hear them, and they know you are there?'

'Yes, clever one. Are you ready now to go home?'

I closed my eyes. I made the Sign of the Cross in our old way, touching the right shoulder before the left. I thought of my Father. We were in the wild fields and he stood high in his stirrups with his giant bow, the bow only he could bend, like unto the mythical Ulysses, shooting arrow after arrow at the raiders who thundered down on us, riding as if he were one of the Turks or Tatars himself, so great was his skill. Arrow after arrow, drawn out with a swift snap from the pouch on his back, went into the bow and was shot across the high blowing grass even as his horse galloped at full speed. His red beard was blowing in the fierce wind, and the sky was so blue, so richly blue that –.

I broke off this prayer and almost lost my balance. My Master held me.

'Pray, you'll be finished with all this very quickly,' he said.

'Give me your kisses,' I said, 'give me your love, give me your arms as you always have, I need them. Give me your guidance. But give me your arms, yes. Let me rest my head against you. I need you, yes. Yes, I want it to be quick and done, and all its lessons in here, in my mind, to be taken back home.'

He smiled. 'Home is Venice now? You've made the decision so soon?'

'Yes, I know it even at this moment. What lies beyond is the birth land, and that's not always home. Shall we go?'

Gathering me in his arms, he took to the air. I shut my eyes, even forfeiting my last glimpse of the motionless stars. I seemed to sleep against him, dreamlessly and fearlessly.

Then he set me down on my feet.

At once I knew this great dark hill, and the leafless oak forest with its frozen black trunks and skeletal branches. I could see the gleaming strip of the Dnieper River far below. My heart scudded inside me. I looked about for the bleak towers of the high city, the city we called Vladimir's City, which was old Kiev.

Piles of rubble which had once been city walls were only yards from where I stood.

I led the way, easily climbing over them and wandering among the ruined churches, churches which had been of legendary splendor when Batu Khan had burnt the city in the year 1240.

I had grown up among this jungle of ancient churches and broken monasteries, often hurrying to hear Mass in our Cathedral of Santa Sofia, one of the few monuments which the Mongols had spared. In its day, it had been a spectacle of golden domes, dominating all those of the other churches, and was rumored to be more grand than its namesake in faraway Constantinople, being larger and packed with treasures.

What I had known was a stately remnant, a wounded shell.

I didn't want to enter the church now. It was enough to see it from the outside, because I knew now, from my happy years in Venice, just what the glory of this church had once been. I understood from the splendid Byzantine mosaics and paintings of San Marco, and from the old Byzantine church on the Venetian island of Torcello what glory had once been here for all to see. When I thought of the lively crowds of Venice, her students, scholars, lawyers, merchants, I could paint a dense vitality on this bleak and wasted scene.

The snow was deep and thick, and few Russians were out in it this frigid early evening. So we had it to ourselves, walking through it with ease, not having to pick our way as mortals would.

We came to a long stretch of ruined battlement, a shapeless guardrail now beneath the snow, and standing there, I looked down on the lower city, the city we called

Podil, the only real city of Kiev that remained, the city where in a rough timber and clay house only a few yards from the river, I had grown up. I looked down on deep-pitched roofs, their thatch covered in cleansing snow, their chimneys smoking, and on narrow crooked snow-filled streets. A great grid of such houses and other buildings had long ago formed against the river and managed to survive fire after fire and even the worst Tatar raids.

It was a town made up of traders and merchants and craftsmen, all bound to the river and the treasures she brought from the Orient, and the money some would pay for the goods she took south into the European world.

My Father, the indomitable hunter, had traded bear skins which he himself had brought back singlehanded from the interior of the great forest which spread towards the north. Fox, martin, beaver, sheep, all these skins he had dealt in, so great was his strength and luck, that no man or woman of our household ever sold their handiwork or wanted for food. If we starved, and we had starved, it was because the winter ate the food, and the meat was gone, and there was nothing for my Father's gold to buy.

I caught the stench of Podil as I stood on the battlements of Vladimir's City. I caught the stench of rotting fish, and livestock, of soiled flesh, and river mud.

I pulled my fur cloak around me, blowing the snow off the fur when it came up to my lips, and I looked back up at the dark domes of the Cathedral against the sky.

'Let's walk on, let's go past the castle of the Voievoda,' I said. 'You see that wooden building, you would never call it a palace or a castle in fair Italy. That is a castle here.'

Marius nodded. He made a little soothing gesture. I

246

owed him no explanation of this alien place from which I'd come.

The Voievoda was our ruler, and in my time it had been Prince Michael of Lithuania. I didn't know who it would be now.

I surprised myself that I used the proper word for him. In my deathly dream vision, I had no consciousness of language, and the strange word for ruler, 'voievoda,' had never passed my lips. But I had seen him clearly then in his round black fur hat, his dark thick velvet tunic and his felt boots.

I led the way.

We approached the squat building, which seemed more a fortress than anything else, built as it was out of such enormous logs. Its walls had a graceful slope as they ascended; its many towers had four-tiered roofs. I could see its central roof, a great five-sided wooden dome of sorts, in stark outline against the starry sky. Torches blazed at its huge doorways and along the outer walls of its enclosures. All its windows were sealed against the winter and the night.

Time was when I thought it was the grandest building yet standing in Christendom.

It was no task at all to dazzle the guards with a few swift soft words and darting movements, to pass them and to enter the castle itself.

We found our way in by means of a rear storage room, and quietly made our way to a vantage point where we could spy upon the small crowd of fur-trimmed nobles or lords who clustered in the Great Room, beneath the bare beams of a wooden ceiling around the roaring fire.

On a great sprawling mass of brilliant Turkey rugs they sat, in huge Russian chairs whose geometrical carvings were no mystery to my eye. They drank from gold goblets, the wine being provided by two leather-clad serving boys, and their long belted robes were the colors of blue and red and gold as bright as the many designs in the rugs.

European tapestries covered the rudely stuccoed walls. Same old scenes of the hunt in the never-ending woodlands of France or England or Tuscany. On a long board set with blazing candles sat a simple meal of joints and fowl.

So cold was the room that these lords wore their Russian fur hats.

How exotic it had looked to me in boyhood when I'd been brought with my Father to stand before Prince Michael, who was eternally grateful for my Father's feats of bravery in bringing down delicious game in the wild fields, or delivering bundles of valuables to the allies of Prince Michael in the Lithuanian forts to the west.

But these were Europeans. I had never respected them.

My Father had taught me too well that they were but lackeys of the Khan, paying for the right to rule us.

'No one goes up against those thieves,' my Father had said. 'So let them sing their songs of honor and valor. It means nothing. You listen to the songs that I sing.'

And my Father could sing some songs.

For all his stamina in the saddle, for all his dexterity with the bow and arrow, and his blunt brute force with the broadsword, he had the ability with his long fingers to pluck out music on the strings of an old harp and sing with cleverness the narrative songs of the ancient times when Kiev had been a great capital, her churches rivaling those of Byzantium, her riches the wonder of all the world.

Within a moment, I was ready to go. I took one last memorial glance at these men, huddled as they were over their golden wine cups, their big fur-trimmed boots resting on fancy Turkish foot rests, their shoulders hunkered, their shadows crowding the walls. And then, without their ever having known we were there, we slipped away.

It was time now to go to the other hilltop city, the Pechersk, under which lay the many catacombs of the Monastery of the Caves.

I trembled at the mere thought of it. It seemed the mouth of the Monastery would swallow me and I should burrow through the moist Mother Earth, forever seeking the light of the stars, never to find my way out.

But I went there, trudging through the mud and snow, and again with a vampire's silky ease, I gained access, this time leading the way, snapping the locks silently with my superior strength and lifting the doors as I opened them so no weight would fall upon their creaky hinges, and dashing swiftly across rooms so that mortal eyes perceived no more than cold shadows, if they perceived anything at all.

The air was warm and motionless here, a blessing, but memory told me it had not been so terribly warm for a mortal boy. In the Scriptorium, by the smoky light of cheap oil, several brothers were bent over their slanted desks, working on their copying, as if the printing press were of no concern to them, and surely it was not.

I could see the texts on which they worked and I knew them – the Paterikon of the Kievan Caves Monastery, with its marvelous tales of the Monastery's founders and its many colorful saints.

In this room, laboring over that text, I had learned fully to read and write. I crept now along the wall until my eyes could fall on the page which one monk copied, his left hand steadying the crumbling model from which he worked.

I knew this part of the Paterikon by heart. It was the Tale of Isaac. Demons had fooled Isaac; they had come to him as beautiful angels, and even pretending to be Christ Himself. When Isaac had fallen for their tricks, they had danced with glee and taunted him. But after much meditation and penance, Isaac stood up to these demons.

The monk had just dipped his pen and he wrote now the words with which Isaac spoke:

> When you deceived me in the form of Jesus Christ and the angels, you were unworthy of that rank. But now you appear in your true colors—

I looked away. I didn't read the rest. Cleaving there so well to the wall I might have gone on unseen forever. Slowly I looked at the other pages which the monk had copied, which were being left to dry. I found an earlier passage which I'd never forgotten, describing Isaac as he lay, withdrawn from all the world, motionless, and without food for two years:

> For Isaac was weakened in mind and body and could not turn over on his side, stand up, or sit down; he just lay there on one side, and often worms collected under his thighs from his excrement and urine.

The demons had driven Isaac to this, with their deception. Such temptations, such visions, such confusion and such penance I myself had hoped to experience for the rest of my life when I entered here as a child.

I listened to the pen scratch on the paper. I withdrew, unseen, as if I'd never come.

I looked back at my scholarly brethren.

All were emaciated, dressed in cheap black wool, reeking of old sweat and dirt, and their heads were all but shaved. Their long beards were thin and uncombed.

I thought I knew one of them, had loved him somewhat even, but this seemed remote and not worth considering anymore.

To Marius, who stood beside me as faithfully as a shadow, I confided that I could not have endured it, but we both knew this was a lie. In all likelihood I would have endured it, and I would have died without ever knowing any other world.

I moved into the first of the long tunnels where the monks were buried, and, closing my eyes and cleaving to the mud wall, I listened for the dreams and prayers of those who lay entombed alive for the love of God.

It was nothing but what I could imagine, and exactly as I recalled. I heard the familiar, no longer mysterious words whispered in the Church Slavonic. I saw the prescribed images. I felt the sputtering flame of true devotion and true mysticism, kindled from the weak fire of lives of utter denial.

I stood with my head bowed. I let my temple rest against the mud. I wished to find the boy, so pure of soul, who had opened these cells to bring the hermits just enough food and drink to keep them alive. But I couldn't find the boy. I couldn't. And I felt only a raging pity for him that he had ever suffered here, thin and miserable, and desperate, and ignorant, oh, so terribly ignorant, having but one sensuous joy in life and that was to see the colors of the ikon catch fire.

I gasped. I turned my head and fell stupidly into Marius's arms.

'Don't cry, Amadeo,' he said tenderly in my ear.

He brushed my hair from my eyes, and with his soft

251

thumb he even wiped away my tears.

'Tell it all farewell now, son,' he said.

I nodded.

In a twinkling we stood outside. I didn't speak to him. He followed me. I headed down the slope towards the waterfront city.

The smell of the river grew stronger, the stench of humans grew stronger, and finally I came to the house that I knew had been my own. What madness this seemed suddenly! What was I seeking? To measure all this by new standards? To confirm for myself that as a mortal child I had never had the slightest chance?

Dear God, there was no justification for what I was, an impious blood drinker, feeding off the luxurious stews of the wicked Venetian world, I knew it. Was this all a vain exercise in self-justification? No, something else pulled me towards the long rectangular house, like so many others, its thick clay walls divided by rough timbers, its four-tiered roof dripping with icicles, this large and crude house that was my home.

As soon as we reached it, I crept around the sides. The slush of the snow had here turned to water, and indeed, the water of the river leaked down the street and into everywhere as it had when I was a child. The water leaked into my fine-stitched Venetian boots. But it could not paralyze my feet as it had once done, because I drew my strength now from gods unknown here, and creatures for whom these filthy peasants, of which I had been one, had no name.

I lay my head against the rough wall, just as I had done in the Monastery, cleaving to the mortar as if the solidity would protect me and transmit to me all that I wanted to know. I could see through a tiny hole in the broken clumps of clay that were forever crumbling, and I beheld in the familiar blaze of candles, and the

252

brighter light of lamps, a family gathered around the warmth of the large brick stove.

I knew them all, these people, though some of their names were gone from my mind. I knew that they were kindred, and I knew the atmosphere that they shared.

But I had to see beyond this little gathering. I had to know if these people were well. I had to know if after that fateful day, when I'd been kidnapped, and my Father no doubt murdered in the wild lands, they had managed to go on with their usual vigor. I had to know, perhaps, what they prayed when they thought of Andrei, the boy with the gift to make ikons so perfectly, ikons not made by human hands.

I heard the harp inside, I heard singing. The voice was that of one of my uncles, one so young he might have been my brother. His name was Borys, and he had since early childhood been good with singing, memorizing easily the old dumys, or sagas, of the knights and heroes, and it was one of them, very rhythmical and tragic, which he was singing now. The harp was small and old, my Father's harp, and Borys strummed the strings in time with his phrases as he all but spoke the story of a lusty and fatal battle for ancient and great Kiev.

I heard the familiar cadences that had been passed down by our people from singer to singer for hundreds of years. I put my fingers up and broke loose a bit of mortar. I saw through the tiny opening the Ikon corner – directly opposite the family gathering around the shimmering fire in the open stove.

Ah, what a spectacle! Amid dozens of little candle stubs and earthen lamps full of burning fat, there stood propped some twenty or more ikons, some very old and darkened in their gold frames, and some radiant, as though only yesterday they'd come alive through the power of God. There were painted eggs stuffed amongst the pictures, eggs beautifully decorated and colored with patterns I could well recall, though even with my vampire eyes I was too far away to see them now. Many times I had watched the women decorating these sacred eggs for Easter, applying the hot melting wax to them with their wooden pens to mark the ribbons or the stars or the crosses or the lines which meant the ram's horns, or the symbol which meant the butterfly or the stork. Once the wax had been applied, the egg would be dipped in cold dye of amazingly deep color. It had seemed there was an endless variety, and endless possibility for meaning, in these simple patterns and signs.

These fragile and beautiful eggs were kept for curing the sick, or for protection against the storm. I had hidden such eggs in an orchard for good luck with the coming harvest. I had placed one once over the door of the house in which my sister went to live as a young bride.

There was a beautiful story about these decorated eggs, that as long as the custom was followed, as long as such eggs existed, then the world would be safe from the monster of Evil who wanted always to come and devour all that was.

It was sweet to see these eggs placed there in the proud corner of the Ikons, as always, among the Holy Faces. That I had forgotten this custom seemed a shame and a warning of tragedy to come.

But the Holy Faces caught me suddenly and I forgot all else. I saw the Face of Christ blazing in the firelight, my brilliant scowling Christ, as I had so often painted Him. I had done so many of these pictures, and yet how like the one lost that day in the high grasses of the wild lands was this very one!

But that was impossible. How could anyone have recovered the ikon I had dropped when the raiders took me prisoner? No, it must surely be another, for as I said, I had done so many before my parents had ever gotten up the courage to take me to the monks. Why, all through this town were my ikons. My Father had even brought them to Prince Michael as proud gifts, and it was the Prince who had said that the monks must see my skill.

How stern Our Lord looked now compared to the recollection of the tender musing Christs of Fra Angelico or the noble sorrowful Lord of Bellini. And yet He was warm with my love! He was the Christ in our style, the old style, loving in severe lines, loving in somber color, loving in the manner of my land. And He was warm with the love that I believed He gave to me!

A sickness rose up in me. I felt my Master's hands on my shoulders. He didn't pull me back as I feared. He merely held me and put his cheek against my hair.

I was about to go. It was enough, was it now? But the music broke off. A woman there, my Mother, was she? No, younger, my sister Anya, grown into a woman, talked wearily of how my Father could sing again if somehow they could hide all the liquor from him and make him come back to himself.

My Uncle Borys sneered. Ivan was hopeless, said Borys. Ivan would never see another sober night or day, and would soon die. Ivan was poisoned with liquor, both with the fine spirits he got from the traders by selling off what he stole from this very house, and from the peasant brew he got from those he battered and bullied, still being the terror of the town.

I bristled all over. Ivan, my Father, alive? Ivan, alive to die again in such dishonor? Ivan not slain in the wild fields?

But in their thick skulls, the thoughts of him and the words of him stopped together. My uncle sang another song, a dancing song. No one would dance in this house, where all were tired from their labor, and the women half-blind as they continued to mend the clothes that lay piled in their laps. But the music cheered them and one of them, a boy younger than I had been when I died, yes, my little brother, whispered a soft prayer for my Father, that my Father would not freeze to death tonight, as he had almost done so many times, falling down drunk as he did in the snow.

'Please bring him home,' came the little boy's whisper.

Then behind me, I heard Marius say, seeking to put it in order and to calm me:

'Yes, it seems it is true, beyond doubt. Your Father is alive.'

Before he could caution me, I went around and opened the door. It was a fierce thing to do, a reckless thing to do, and I ought to have asked Marius's permission, but I was, as I've told you, an unruly pupil. I had to do this.

The wind gusted through the house. The huddled figures shivered and pushed their thick furs up around their shoulders. The fire deep in the mouth of the brick stove flared beautifully.

I knew that I should remove my hat, which in this case was my hood, and that I should face the Ikon corner and cross myself, but I couldn't do this.

In fact, to conceal myself, I pulled my hood up over my head as I shut the door. I stood alone against it. I held the fur cloak up against my mouth, so that nothing was visible of my face except my eyes, and perhaps a shock of reddish hair.

'Why has the drink gotten Ivan?' I whispered, the old Russian tongue coming back to me. 'Ivan was the strongest man in this city. Where is he now?'

They were wary and angry at my intrusion. The fire in the stove crackled and danced from its feast of fresh air. The Ikon corner seemed a group of perfect radiant flames unto itself, with its brilliant images and random candles, another fire of a different and eternal sort. The Face of Christ was clear to me in the fluttering light, the eyes seeming to fix me as I stood against the door.

My uncle rose and shoved the harp into the arms of a younger boy I didn't know. I saw in the shadows the children sitting up in their heavily draped beds. I saw their shining eyes looking at me in the dark. The others in the firelight clumped together and faced me.

I saw my Mother, wizened and sad as if centuries had passed since I left her, a veritable crone in the corner, clinging to the rug that covered her lap. I studied her, trying to fathom the cause of her decay. Toothless, decrepit, her knuckles big and chafed and shiny from work, perhaps she was merely a woman being worked too rapidly towards her grave.

A great collection of thoughts and words struck me, as if I were being pelted with blows. Angel, devil, night visitor, terror from the dark, what are you? I saw hands raised, hastily making the Sign of the Cross. But the thoughts came clear in answer to my query.

Who does not know that Ivan the Hunter had become Ivan the Penitent, Ivan the Drunkard, Ivan the Mad, on account of the day in the wild lands when he couldn't stop the Tatars from kidnapping his beloved son, Andrei?

I shut my eyes. It was worse than death what had happened to him! And I had never so much as wondered, never so much as dared to think of him alive, or cared enough to hope that he was, or thought what his fate might be had he lived? All over Venice were the shops in which I might have penned a letter to him, a letter that the great Venetian traders could have carried to some port where it might have been delivered over the famous post roads of the Khan.

I knew all this. Selfish little Andrei knew all this, the details that might have sealed the past for him neatly so that he could have forgotten it. I might have written:

Family, I live and am happy, though I can never come home. Take this money I send to you for my brothers and sisters and my Mother—.

But then I hadn't really ever known. The past had been misery and chaos.

Whenever the most trivial picture had become vivid, then torment had reigned.

My uncle stood before me. He was as big as my Father, and was well dressed in a belted leather tunic and felt boots. He looked down at me calmly but severely.

'Who are you that comes into our house in this manner?' he asked. 'What is this Prince that stands before us? You carry a message for us? Then speak, and we will forgive you that you broke the lock on our door.'

I drew in my breath. I had no more questions. I knew that I could find Ivan the Drunkard. That he was in the tavern with the fishermen and the fur traders, for that was the only enclosed place he'd ever loved other than his home.

With my left hand, I reached over and found the purse that I always carried, tied, as it should be, to my belt. I ripped it loose, and I handed it to this man. He merely looked at it. Then he drew himself up, offended, and he stepped back.

He seemed then to become part of a deliberate picture with the house. I saw the house. I saw the hand-

258

carved furniture, the pride of the family which had done it, the hand-carved wooden crosses and candlesticks which held the many candles. I saw the painted symbols decorating the wood frames of the windows, and the shelves on which fine homemade pots, kettles and bowls were displayed.

I saw them all in their pride, then, the entire family, the women with the embroidery, as well as those with mending, and I remembered with a lulling comfort the stability and the warmth of their daily life.

Yet it was sad, oh, woefully sad, compared to the world I knew!

I stepped forward and I held out the purse again to him, and I said in a muffled voice, still veiling my face:

'I beg you to take this as a kindness to me and that I might save my soul. It's from your nephew, Andrei. He is far, far away in the land to which the slave traders took him, and he will never come home. But he is well and must share some of what he has with his family. He bids me to tell him which of you lives and which of you is dead. If I do not give you this money, and if you don't take it, I will be damned to Hell.'

There came no response from them verbally. But I had what I wanted from their minds. I had all of it. Yes, Ivan was alive, and now I, this strange man, was saying that Andrei lived too. Ivan mourned for a son who not only lived but prospered. Life is a tragedy, one way or another. What is certain is that you die.

'I beg you,' I said.

My uncle took the proffered purse but with misgivings. It was full of gold ducats, which would buy anywhere.

I let my cloak drop and I pulled off my left glove, and then the rings that covered every finger of my left hand. Opal, onyx, amethyst, topaz, turquoise. I moved past

259

the man and the boys, to the far side of the fire, and laid these respectfully in the lap of the old woman who had been my Mother as she looked up.

I could see that, in a moment, she would know who I was. I covered my face again, but with my left hand, I took my dagger from my belt. It was only a short Misericorde, that little dagger which a warrior takes into battle to dispatch his victims if they are too far gone for salvation and yet not dead. It was a decorative thing, an ornament more than a weapon, and its gold-plated scabbard was thickly lined with perfect pearls.

'For you,' I said. 'For Andrei's Mother, who always loved her necklace of river pearls. Take this for Andrei's soul.' I laid the dagger at my Mother's feet.

And then I made a deep, deep bow with my head almost touching the floor, and I went out, without looking back, closing the door behind me, and hovering near, to hear them as they jumped up and crowded about to see the rings and the dagger, and some to see to the lock.

For a moment, I was weak with emotion. But nothing was going to stop me from what I meant to do. I didn't turn to Marius, because it would have been craven to ask his support in this, or assent to it. I went on down the muddy snowy street, through the sludge, towards the tavern nearest to the river, where I thought my Father might be.

I had rarely entered this place as a child, and then only to summon my Father home. I had no real memory of it, except as a place where foreign people drank and cursed.

It was a long building, made of the same rude unfinished logs as my house, with the same mud for mortar, and the same inevitable seams and cracks to let in the dreadful cold. Its roof was very high, with some six tiers to shed the weight of the snow, and its eaves too dripped with icicles, as had those of my house.

It marveled me that men could live like this, that the cold itself did not push them to make something more permanent and more sheltering, but it had always been the way of this place, it seemed to me, of the poor and the sick and overburdened and the hungry, that the brutal winter took too much from them, and that the short spring and summer gave them too little, and that resignation became their greatest virtue in the end.

But I might have been wrong then about all of it, and I might be wrong now. What is important is this – it was a place of hopelessness, and though it was not ugly, for wood and mud and snow and sadness are not ugly, it was a place without beauty except for the ikons, and perhaps for the distant outline of the graceful domes of Santa Sofia, high on the hill, against the star-studded sky. And that was not enough.

When I entered the tavern, I counted some twenty men at a glance, all of them drinking and talking to one another with a conviviality that surprised me, given the Spartan nature of this place, which was no more than a shelter against the night which kept them safely ranged round the big fire. There were no ikons here to comfort them. But some of them were singing, and there was the inevitable harp player strumming his little stringed instrument, and another blowing on a small pipe.

There were many tables, some covered with linen, and others bare at which these fellows gathered, and some of the men were foreigners, as I had recalled. Three were Italian, I heard this instantly, and figured them to be Genoese. There were more foreigners indeed than I had expected. But these were men drawn by the trade of the river, and perhaps Kiev did not do so poorly just now.

There were plenty of kegs of beer and wine behind the counter, where the bartender sold his stock by the cup. I saw too many bottles of Italian wine, quite expensive no doubt, and crates of Spanish sack.

Lest I attract notice, I moved forward and far off to the left, into the depth of the shadows, where perhaps a European traveler clad in rich fur might not be noticed, for, after all, fine fur was one thing they did indeed seem to have.

These people were much too drunk to care who I was. The bartender tried to get excited about the idea of a new customer, but then went back to snoozing on the palm of his upturned hand. The music continued, another one of the dumy, and this one much less cheerful than the one my uncle had been singing at home, because I think the musician was very tired.

I saw my Father.

He lay on his back, full length, on a broad crude greasy bench, dressed in his leather jerkin and with his biggest heaviest fur cloak folded neatly over him, as though the others had done the honors with it after he had passed out. This was bearskin, his cloak, which marked him as a pretty rich man.

He snored in his drunken sleep, and the fumes of the drink rose from him, and he didn't stir when I knelt right beside him and looked down into his face.

His cheeks though thinner were still rosy, but there were hollows beneath the bones, and there were streaks of gray, most prominent in his mustache and long beard. It seemed to me that some of the hair of his temples was gone, and that his fine smooth brow was steeper, but this may have been an illusion. The flesh all around his eyes was tender-looking and dark. His hands, clutched together beneath the cloak, were not visible to me, but I could see that he was still strong, of powerful build, and his love of drink had not destroyed him yet.

I had a disturbing sense of his vitality suddenly; I could smell the blood of him and the life of him, as though of a possible victim stumbling across my path. I put all this away from my mind and stared at him, loving him and thinking only that I was so glad that he was alive! He had come out of the wild grasses. He had escaped that party of raiders, who had seemed then the very heralds of death itself.

I pulled up a stool so that I might sit quietly beside my Father, studying his face.

I had not put on my left glove.

I laid my cold hand now on his forehead, lightly, not wanting to take liberties, and slowly he opened his eyes. They were murky yet still beautifully bright, despite the broken blood vessels and the wetness, and he looked at me softly and wordlessly for a while, as if he had no cause to move, as if I were a vision near to his dreams.

I felt the hood fall back from my head and I did nothing to stop it. I couldn't see what he saw, but I knew what it was – his son, with a cleanshaven face, such as his son had had when this man knew him, and long loose auburn hair in snow-dusted waves.

Beyond, their bodies mere bulky outlines against the huge blaze of the fire, the others sang or talked. And the wine flowed.

Nothing came between me and this moment, between me and this man who had tried hard to bring down the Tatars, who had sent one arrow after another sailing at his enemies, even as their arrows rained down upon him in vain.

'They never wounded you,' I whispered. 'I love you and only now do I know how strong you were.' Was my voice even audible?

263

He blinked as he looked at me, and then I saw his tongue roll out along his lips. His lips were bright, like coral, shining through the heavy red fringe of mustache and beard.

'They wounded me,' he said in a low voice, small but not weak. 'They got me, twice they got me, in the shoulder and in the arm. But they didn't kill me, and they didn't let go of Andrei. I fell off my horse. I got up. They never got me in the legs. I ran after them. I ran and ran and I kept shooting. I had a cursed arrow sticking right out of my right shoulder here.'

His hand appeared from beneath the fur and he placed it up on the dark curve of his right shoulder.

'I kept shooting. I didn't even feel it. I saw them ride away. They took him. I don't even know if he was alive. I don't know. Would they have bothered to take him if they had shot him? There were arrows everywhere. The sky rained arrows! There must have been fifty of them. They killed every other man! I told the others, You have to keep shooting, don't stop even for an instant, don't cower, shoot and shoot and shoot, and when you have no more arrows, bring up your sword and go for them, ride straight into them, get down, get down close to your horse's head and ride into them. Well, maybe they did. I don't know.'

He lowered his lids. He glanced around. He wanted to get up, and then he looked at me.

'Give me something to drink. Buy me something decent. The man has Spanish sack. Get me some of that, a bottle of sack. Hell, in the old days, I laid in wait for the traders out there in the river, and I never had to buy anything from any man. Get me a bottle of sack. I can see you're rich.'

'Do you know who I am?' I asked.

He looked at me in plain confusion. This hadn't even

occurred to him, this question.

'You come from the castle. You speak with the accent of the Lithuanians. I don't care who you are. Buy me some wine.'

'With the accent of the Lithuanians?' I asked softly. 'What a dreadful thing. I think it's the accent of a Venetian, and I'm ashamed.'

'Venetian? Well, don't be. God knows they tried to save Constantinople, they tried. Everything's gone to Hell. The world will end in flame. Get me some sack before it ends, all right?'

I stood up. Did I have some more money? I was puzzling over it when the dark silent figure of my Master loomed over me and he handed me the bottle of Spanish sack, uncorked and ready for my Father to drink.

I sighed. The smell of it meant nothing to me now, but I knew that it was fine good stuff, and besides it was what he wanted.

He had meantime sat up on the bench, staring straight at the bottle as it hung from my hand. He reached out for it, and took it and drank it as thirstily as I drink blood.

'Take a good look at me,' I said.

'It's too dark in here, idiot,' he said. 'How can I take a good look at anything? Hmmm, but this is good. Thank you.'

Suddenly, he paused with the bottle just beneath his lips. It was a strange thing the way in which he paused. It was as if he were in the forest, and he'd just sensed a bear coming up on him, or some other lethal beast. He froze, as it were, with the bottle in hand, and only his eyes moved as he looked up at me.

'Andrei,' he whispered.

'I'm alive, Father,' I said gently. 'They didn't kill me.

265

They took me for booty and sold me for profit. And I was taken by ship south and north again and up to the city of Venice, and that is where I live now.'

His eyes were calm. Indeed, a beautiful serenity settled over him. He was far too drunk for his reason to revolt or for cheap surprise to delight him. On the contrary, the truth stole in and over him in a wave, subduing him, and he understood all of its ramifications, that I had not suffered, that I was rich, I was well.

'I was lost, Sir,' I said in the same gentle whisper, which surely was only audible to him. 'I was lost, yes, but found by another, a kindly man, and was restored, and have never suffered since. I've journeyed a long time to tell you this, Father. I never knew you were alive. I never dreamed. I mean, I thought you'd died that day when all the world died for me. And now I'm come here to tell you that you must never, never grieve for me.'

'Andrei,' he whispered, but there was no change in his face. There was only the sedate wonder. He sat still, both hands on the bottle which he had lowered to his lap, his huge shoulders very straight, and his flowing red and gray hair as long as I'd ever seen it, melting into the fur of his cloak.

He was a beautiful, beautiful man. I needed a monster's eyes to know it. I needed a demon's vision to see the strength in his eyes coupled with the power in his giant frame. Only the bloodshot eyes gave him away in his weakness.

'Forget me now, Father,' I said. 'Forget me, as if the monks had sent me away. But remember this, on account of you, I shall never be buried in the muddy graves of the Monastery. No, other things may befall me. But that, I won't suffer. Because of you, that you wouldn't have it, that you came that day and demanded I ride out with you, that I be your son.'

I turned to go. He shot forward, clasping the bottle by the neck in his left hand and clamping his powerful right hand over my wrist. He pulled me down to him, as if I were a mere mortal, with his old strength and he pressed his lips against my bowed head.

Oh, God, don't let him know! Don't let him sense any change in me! I was desperate. I closed my eyes.

But I was young, and not so hard and cold as my Master, no, not even by half or a half of that half. And he felt only the softness of my hair, and perhaps a cold icy softness, redolent of winter, to my skin.

'Andrei, my angel child, my gifted and golden son!'

I turned around and clasped him firmly with my left arm. I kissed him all over his head in a way I would never, never have done as a child. I held him to my heart.

'Father, don't drink anymore,' I said in his ear. 'Get up and be the hunter again. Be what you are, Father.'

'Andrei, no one will ever believe me.'

'And who are they to say that to you if you are yourself again, man?' I asked.

We looked into each other's eyes. I kept my lips sealed that he should never, never see the sharp teeth in my mouth that the vampiric blood had given me, the tiny evil vampire's teeth as a man as keen as himself, the natural hunter, might very definitely see.

But he was looking for no such disqualification here. He wanted only love, and love we gave one another.

'I have to go, I have no choice,' I said, 'I stole this time to come to you. Father, tell my Mother that it was I who came to the house earlier, and that it was I who gave her the rings and gave your brother the purse.'

I drew back. I sat down on the bench beside him, for he had placed his feet on the floor. I pulled off my right glove and I looked at the seven or eight rings I wore, all of them made of gold or silver and rich with jewels, and then I slipped them off one by one, over his loud groan of protest, and I deposited the handful of them into his hand. How soft and hot was his hand, how flushed and alive.

'You take them because I have a world of them. And I will write to you and send you more, more so that you will never need to do anything but what you want to do – ride and hunt, and tell the tales of old times by the fire. Buy a fine harp with this, buy books if you will for the little ones, buy what you will.'

'I don't want this; I want you, my son.'

'Yes, and I want you, my Father, but this little power is all we may have.'

I took his head in both my hands, displaying my strength, perhaps unwisely, but making him stay still while I gave him my kisses, and then with one long warm embrace, I rose to go.

I was out of the room so fast, he couldn't have seen anything but the door swinging shut.

The snow was coming down. I saw my Master several yards away, and I went to meet him and together we started up the hill. I didn't want for my Father to come out. I wanted to get away as fast as I could.

I was about to ask that we take to vampire speed and get clear of Kiev when I saw that a figure was hurrying towards us. It was a small woman, her long heavy furs trailing in the wet snow. She had something bright in her arms.

I stood fixed, my Master waiting on me. It was my Mother who had come to see me. It was my Mother who was making her way to the tavern, and in her arms, facing me, was an ikon of the scowling Christ, the one I looked at so long through the chink in the wall of the house.

I drew in my breath. She lifted the ikon by either side and she presented it to me.

'Andrei,' she whispered.

'Mother,' I said. 'Keep it for the little ones, please.' I embraced her and kissed her. How much older, how miserably older she seemed. But childbearing had done that to her, pulling the strength out of her, if only for babies to be buried in small plots in the ground. I thought of how many babies she had lost during my youth, and how many were still counted before I was born. She had called them her angels, her little babies, not big enough to live.

'Keep it,' I said to her. 'Keep it for the family here.'

'All right, Andrei,' she said. She looked at me with pale, suffering eyes. I could see that she was dying. I understood suddenly that it wasn't mere age that worked on her, nor the hardship of children. She was diseased from within, and would soon truly die. I felt such a terror, looking at her, such a terror for the whole mortal world. It was just a tiresome, common and inevitable disease.

'Goodbye, darling angel,' I said.

'And goodbye to you, my darling angel,' she answered. 'My heart and soul are happy that you are a proud Prince. But show me, do you make the Sign of the Cross in the right way?'

How desperate she sounded. She meant these words. She meant simply, Had I gotten all this apparent wealth by converting to the church of the West? That is what she meant.

'Mother, you put a simple test to me.' I made the Sign of the Cross for her, in our way, the Eastern Way, from right shoulder to left, and I smiled.

She nodded. Then she took something carefully from inside her heavy wool shift coat and she gave it to me, only releasing it when I had made a cradle for it with my hand. It was a dark ruby-red painted Easter egg.

Such a perfect and exquisitely decorated egg. It was banded with long lengthwise ribbons of yellow, and in a center created by them was painted a perfect rose or eight-pointed star.

I looked down at it and then I nodded to her.

I took out a handkerchief of fine Flemish linen and wrapped the egg in this, padding it over and over, and I slipped the little burden faithfully into the folds of my tunic beneath my jacket and cloak.

I bent over and kissed her again on her soft dry cheek. 'Mother,' I said, 'the joy of All Sorrows, that is what you are to me!'

'My sweet Andrei,' she answered. 'Go with God if you must go.'

She looked at the ikon. She wanted me to see it. She turned the ikon around so that I could look at the gleaming golden Face of God, as waxen and fine as the day I'd painted it for her. Only I hadn't painted it for her. No, it was the very ikon which I had taken that day on our march into the wild lands.

Oh, what a marvel, that my Father had brought it back with him, all the way from the scene of such loss. And yet why not? Why not would such a man as he have done such a thing?

The snow fell onto the painted ikon. It fell on the stern Face of Our Savior, which had come ablaze under my racing brush as if by magic, a face which with its stern and smooth lips and slightly furrowed brow meant love. Christ, my Lord, could look even more stern peering out from the mosaics of San Marco. Christ, my Lord, could look as stern in many an old painting. But Christ, my Lord, in any manner and in any style, was full of unstinting love.

270

The snow came in flurries and seemed to melt when it touched His Face.

I feared for it, this fragile panel of wood, and this glistering lacquered image, meant to shine for all time. But she thought of this too, and she quickly shielded the ikon from the wetness of the melting snow with her cloak.

I never saw it again.

But is there anyone who needs now to ask me what an ikon means to me? Is there anyone who needs now to know why, when I saw the Face of Christ before me on the Veil of Veronica, when Dora held it high, this Veil, brought back from Jerusalem and the hour of Christ's passion, by Lestat himself, through Hell and into the world, that I fell down on my knees, and cried, 'It is the Lord'?

The journey from Kiev seemed a journey forwards in time, towards the place where I truly belonged.

All of Venice, upon my return, seemed to share the shimmer of the gold-plated chamber in which I made my grave. In a daze, I spent my nights roaming, with or without Marius, drinking up the fresh air of the Adriatic and perusing the splendid houses and government palaces to which I'd grown accustomed over the last few years.

Evening church services drew me like honey draws flies. I drank up the music of the choirs, the chanting of the priests and above all the joyous sensual attitude of the worshipers, as if all this would be a healing balm to those parts of me that were skinned and raw from my return to the Monastery of the Caves.

But in my heart of hearts I reserved a tenacious and heated flame of reverence for the Russian monks of the Monastery of the Caves. Having glimpsed a few words of the sainted Brother Isaac, I walked in the living memory of his teachings – Brother Isaac, who had been a Fool for God, and a hermit, and a seer of spirits, the victim of the Devil and then his Conqueror in the name of Christ.

I had a religious soul, there was no doubt of it, and I had been given two great modes of religious thought, and now in surrendering to a war between these modes, I made war on myself, for though I had no intention of giving up the luxuries and glories of Venice, the ever shining beauty of Fra Angelico's lessons and the stunning and gilded accomplishments of all those who followed him, making Beauty for Christ, I secretly beatified the loser in my battle, the blessed Isaac, whom I imagined, in my childish mind, to have taken the true path to the Lord.

Marius knew of my struggle, he knew of the hold which Kiev had upon me, and he knew of the crucial importance of all this to me. He understood better than anyone I've ever known that each being wars with his own angels and devils, each being succumbs to an essential set of values, a theme, as it were, which is inseparable from living a proper life.

For us, life was the vampiric life. But it was in every sense life, and sensuous life, and fleshly life. I could not escape into it from the compulsions and obsessions I'd felt as a mortal boy. On the contrary, they were now magnified.

Within the month after my return, I knew I had set the tone for my approach to the world around me. I should wallow in the luscious beauty of Italian painting and music and architecture, yes, but I would do it with the fervor of a Russian saint. I would turn all sensuous experiences to goodness and purity. I would learn, I would increase understanding, I would increase in compassion for the mortals around me, and I would never cease to put a pressure upon my soul to be that which I believed was good.

Good was above all kind; it was to be gentle. It was to waste nothing. It was to paint, to read, to study, to listen, even to pray, though to whom I prayed I wasn't sure, and it was to take every opportunity to be generous to those mortals whom I did not kill.

As for those I killed, they were to be dispatched mercifully, and I was to become the absolute master of mercy, never causing pain and confusion, indeed snaring my victims as much as I could by spells induced by my soft voice or the depths of my eyes offered for soulful looks, or by some other power I seemed to possess and seemed able to develop, a power to thrust my mind into that of the poor helpless mortal and to assist him in the manufacture of his own comforting images so that the death became the flicker of a flame in a rapture, and then silence most sweet.

I also concentrated on enjoying the blood, on moving deeper, beneath the turbulent necessity of my own thirst, to taste this vital fluid of which I robbed my victim, and to feel most fully that which it carried with it to ultimate doom, the destiny of a mortal soul.

My lessons with Marius were broken off for a while. But at last he came to me gently and told me it was time to study again in earnest, that there were things that we must do.

'I make my own study,' I said. 'You know it well enough. You know I haven't been idle in my wanderings, and you know my mind is as hungry as my body. You know it. So leave me alone.'

'That's all well and good, little Master,' he said to me kindly, 'but you must come back into the school I keep for you. I have things which you must know.'

For five nights I put him off. Then, as I was dozing on his bed sometime after midnight, having spent the earlier evening in the Piazza San Marco at a great festival, listening to musicians and watching the jugglers, I was startled to feel his switch come crashing down on the back of my legs.

'Wake up, child,' he said.

I turned over and looked up. I was startled. He stood, holding the long switch, with his arms folded. He wore a long belted tunic of purple velvet and his hair was tied back at the base of his neck.

I turned away from him. I figured he was being dramatic and that he would go away. The switch came crashing down again and this time there followed a volley of blows.

I felt the blows in a way I'd never felt them when mortal. I was stronger, more resistant to them, but for a split second each blow broke through my preternatural guard and caused a tiny exquisite explosion of pain.

I was furious. I tried to climb up off the bed, and probably would have struck him, so angry was I to be treated in this manner. But he placed his knee on my back and whipped me over and over with the switch, until I cried out.

Then he stood up and dragged me up by the collar. I was shaking with rage and with confusion.

'Want some more?' he asked.

'I don't know,' I said, throwing off his arm, which he allowed with a little smile. 'Perhaps so! One minute my heart is of the greatest concern to you, and the next I'm a schoolboy. Is that it?'

'You've had enough time to grieve and to weep,' he said, 'and to reevaluate all you've been given. Now it's back to work. Go to the desk and prepare to write. Or I'll whip you some more.'

I flew into a tirade. 'I'm not going to be treated this way; there's absolutely no necessity for this. What should I write? I've written volumes in my soul. You think you can force me into the dreary little mold of an obedient pupil, you think this is appropriate to the cataclysmic thoughts that I have to ponder, you think—.'

He smacked me across the face. I was dizzy. As my eyes cleared, I looked into his.

'I want your attention again. I want you to come out of your meditation. Go to the desk and write for me a summary of what your journey to Russia meant to you, and what you see now here that you could not see before. Make it concise, use your finest smiles and metaphors and write it cleanly and quickly for me.'

'Such crude tactics,' I muttered. But my body was throbbing from the blows. It was altogether different from the pain of a mortal body, but it was bad, and I hated it.

I sat down at the desk. I was going to write something really churlish such as 'I've learned that I'm the slave of a tyrant.' But when I looked up and saw him standing there with the switch in his hand, I changed my mind.

He knew it was the perfect moment to come to me and kiss me. And he did this, and I realized I had lifted my face for his kiss before he bent his head. This didn't stop him.

I felt the overwhelming happiness of giving in to him. I put my arm up and around his shoulders.

He let me go after a long sweet moment, and then I did write out many sentences, pretty much describing what I've explained above. I wrote about the battle in me between the fleshly and the ascetic; I wrote of my Russian soul as seeking after the highest level of exaltation. In the painting of the ikon I had found it, but the ikon had satisfied the need for the sensual because the ikon was beautiful. And as I wrote, I realized for the first time that the old Russian style, the antique Byzantine style, embodied a struggle in itself between the sensual and the ascetic, the figures suppressed, flattened, disciplined, in the very midst of rich color, the whole giving forth pure delight to the eyes while representing denial.

While I wrote, my Master went away. I was aware of it, but it didn't matter. I was deep into my writing, and gradually I slipped out of my analysis of things, and began to tell an old tale.

In the old days, when the Russians didn't know Jesus Christ, the great Prince Vladimir of Kiev – and in those days Kiev was a magnificent city – sent his emissaries to study the three religions of the Lord: the Moslem religion, which these men found to be frantic and foul-smelling; the religion of Papal Rome, in which these men did not find any glory; and finally the Christianity of Byzantium. In the city of Constantinople, the Russians were led to see the magnificent churches in which the Greek Catholics worshiped their God, and they found these buildings so beautiful that they didn't know whether they were in Heaven or still on Earth. Never had the Russians seen anything so splendid; they were certain then that God dwelt among men in the religion of Constantinople, and so it was this Christianity which Russia embraced. It was beauty therefore that gave birth to our Russian Church.

In Kiev once men could find what Vladimir sought to recreate, but now that Kiev is a ruin and the Turks have taken Santa Sofia of Constantinople, one must come to Venice to see the great Theotokos, the Virgin who is the God-Bearer, and her Son when He becomes the Pantokrator, the Divine Creator of All. In Venice, I have found in sparkling gold mosaics and in the muscular images of a new age the very miracle which brought the Light of Christ Our Lord to the land where I was born, the Light of Christ Our Lord which burns still in the lamps of the Monastery of the Caves.

I put down the pen. I pushed the page aside, and I laid my head down on my arms and cried softly to myself in the quiet of the shadowy bedroom. I didn't care if I was beaten, kicked or ignored.

Finally, Marius came for me to take me to our crypt, and I realize now, centuries later, as I look back, that his forcing me to write on this night caused me to remember always the lessons of those times.

The next night, after he'd read what I had written, he was contrite about having hit me, and he said that it was difficult for him to treat me as anything but a child, but that I was not a child. Rather I was some spirit like unto a child – naive and maniacal in my pursuit of certain themes. He had never expected to love me so much.

I wanted to be aloof and distant, on account of the whipping, but I couldn't be. I marveled that his touch, his kisses, his embraces meant more to me than they had when I was human.

I wish I could slip away now from the happy picture of Marius and me in Venice and take up this tale in New York City; in modern times. I want to go to the moment in the room in New York City when Dora held up Veronica's Veil, the relic brought back by Lestat from his journey into the Inferno, for then I would have a tale told in two perfect halves – of the child I had been and of the worshiper I became, and of the creature I am now.

But I cannot fool myself so easily. I know that what happened to Marius and to me in the months that followed my journey to Russia is part and parcel of my life.

There is nothing to do but cross The Bridge of Sighs in my life, the long dark bridge spanning centuries of my tortured existence which connects me to modern times. That my time in this passage has been described so well already by Lestat doesn't mean that I can escape without adding my own words, and above all my own acknowledgment of the Fool for God that I was to be for three hundred years.

I wish I had escaped this fate. I wish that Marius had escaped what happened to us. It is plain now that he survived our separation with far greater insight and strength than I survived it. But then he was already centuries old and a wise being, and I was still a child.

Our last months in Venice were unmarred by any premonition of what was to come. Vigorously, he taught me the essential lessons.

One of the most important of these was how to pass for human in the midst of human beings. In all the time

279

since my transformation, I had not kept good company with the other apprentices, and I had avoided altogether my beloved Bianca, to whom I owed a vast debt of gratitude not merely for past friendship but for nursing me when I was so ill.

Now, I had to face Bianca, or so Marius decreed. I was the one who had to write a polite letter to her explaining that on account of my illness I had not been able to come to her before.

Then, one evening early, after a brief hunt in which I drank the blood of two victims, we set out to visit her, laden with gifts for her, and found her surrounded by her English and Italian friends.

Marius had dressed for the occasion in smart dark blue velvet, with a cloak of the same color for once, which was unusual for him, and he had urged me to dress in sky blue, his favorite color for me. I carried the wine figs and sweet tarts in a basket for her.

We found her door open as always, and we entered unobtrusively, but she saw us at once.

The moment I saw her I felt a heartbreaking desire for a certain kind of intimacy, that is, I wanted to tell her everything that had happened! Of course this was forbidden, and that I could love her without confiding in her – this was something that Marius insisted I learn.

She got up and came to me, and put her arms around me, accepting the usual ardent kisses. I realized at once why Marius had insisted on two victims for this evening. I was warm and flushed with blood.

Bianca felt nothing that frightened her. She slipped her silken arms around my neck. She was radiant in a dress of yellow silk tissue and dark-green velvet, the underdress of yellow, powdered with embroidered roses, and her white breasts were barely covered as only a courtesan would have them.

280

When I began to kiss her, careful to conceal my tiny fanged teeth from her, I felt no hunger because the blood of my victims had been more than enough. I kissed her with love and love only, my mind quickly plunging into heated erotic memories, my body surely demonstrating the urgency that it had had with her in the past. I wanted to touch her all over, as a blind man might touch a sculpture, the better to see each curve of her with his hands.

'Oh, you're not only well, you're splendid,' Bianca said. 'You and Marius, come in, come, let's go into the next room.' She made a careless gesture to her guests, who were all busy anyway, talking, arguing, playing cards in small groups. She drew us with her into her more intimate parlor adjacent to the bedroom, a room cluttered with frightfully expensive damask chairs and couches, and told me to sit down.

I remembered the candles, that I must never get too close to them, but must use the shadows so no mortal would have an optimum opportunity to study my changed and more perfect skin.

This wasn't so hard as, in spite of her love of light and her penchant for luxury, she had the candelabra scattered for the mood.

The lack of light would also make the sparkle of my eyes less noticeable; I knew this too. And the more I spoke, the more animated I became, the more human I would appear.

Stillness was dangerous for us when we were among mortals, Marius had taught me, for in stillness we appear flawless and unearthly and finally even faintly horrible to mortals, who sense that we are not what we seem.

I followed all these rules. But I was overcome with anxiety that I could never tell her what had been done to me. I started to talk. I explained that the illness had abated entirely, but that Marius, wiser by far than any physician, had ordered solitude and rest. When I had not been in bed, I had been alone, struggling to regain my strength.

'Make it as near to the truth as you can, the better to make it a lie,' Marius had taught. Now I followed these words.

'Oh, but I thought I'd lost you,' she said. 'When you sent word, Marius, that he was recovering, I didn't at first believe you. I thought you meant to soften the inevitable truth.'

How lovely she was, a perfect flower. Her blond hair was parted in the middle, and a thick lock on either side was wound with pearls and bound back with a clasp encrusted with them. The rest of her hair fell down à la Botticelli, in rivulets of shining yellow over her shoulders.

'You had cured him as completely as any human being could,' Marius told her. 'My task was to give him some old remedies of which only I know. And then to let the remedies do their work.' He spoke simply, but to me he seemed sad.

A terrible sadness gripped me. I couldn't tell her what I was, or how different she seemed now, how richly opaque with human blood she seemed compared to us, and how her voice had taken on for me a new timbre that was purely human, and which gently nudged my senses if she but said one word.

'Well, you are both here, and you must both come often,' she said. 'Don't ever let such a separation occur again. Marius, I would have come to you, but Riccardo told me you wanted peace and quiet. I would have nursed Amadeo in any state.'

'I know you would have, my darling,' Marius said. 'But as I said, it was solitude he needed, and your beauty is an intoxicant, and your words a stimulus more intense perhaps than you realize.' It had no tone of flattery but sounded like a sincere confession.

She shook her head a little sadly. 'I've discovered that Venice is not my home unless you're here.' She looked cautiously towards the front parlor, and then she lapsed into a low voice. 'Marius, you freed me from those who had a hold on me.'

'That was simple enough,' he said. 'It was a pleasure, in fact. How rank those men were, cousins of yours, if I'm not mistaken, and eager to use you and your great reputation for beauty in their twisted financial affairs.'

She blushed, and I lifted my hand to beg him to go easy with what he said. I knew now that during the slaughter of the Florentine banquet chamber, he had read from the victims' minds all kinds of things which were unknown to me.

'Cousins? Perhaps,' she said. 'I have conveniently forgotten that. That they were a terror to those whom they lured into expensive loans and dangerous opportunities, that I can say without a doubt. Marius, the strangest things have happened, things upon which I never counted.'

I loved the look of seriousness on her delicate features. She seemed too beautiful to have a brain.

'I find myself richer,' she said, 'as I can keep the larger portion of my own income, and others – this is the strange part – others, in gratitude that our banker and our extortionist is gone, have lavished on me countless gifts of gold and jewels, yes, even this necklace, look, and you know these are all sea pearls and matched in size, and this is a veritable rope of them, see, and all this is given me, though I have averred a hundred times that I never had the deed done.'

'But what of blame?' I asked. 'What of the danger of a public accusation?'

283

'They have no defenders or mourners,' she said quickly. She planted another little bouquet of kisses on my cheek. 'And earlier today, my friends among the Great Council were here as always, to read a few new poems to me and settle in quiet where they could know peace from clients and the endless demands of their families. No, I don't think anyone is going to accuse me of anything, and as everyone knows, on the night of the murders, I was here in company with that awful Englishman, Amadeo, the very one who tried to kill you, who has of course . . .'

'Yes, what?' I asked.

Marius narrowed his eyes as he looked at me. He made a light gesture of tapping the side of his head with his gloved finger. Read her mind, he meant. But I couldn't think of such a thing. Her face was too pretty.

'The Englishman,' she said, 'who has disappeared. I suspect he's drowned somewhere, that, staggering drunk about the town, he fell into one of the canals or, worse yet, into the lagoon.'

Of course my Master had told me that he had taken care of all our difficulties on account of the Englishman, but I had never asked in what particular way.

'So they think you hired killers to dispatch the Florentines?' Marius asked her.

'Seems so,' she said. 'And there are even those who think that I had the Englishman dispatched as well. I've become a rather powerful woman, Marius.'

Both of them laughed, his laugh the deep but metallic laugh of a preternatural being, and her laugh higher yet thicker with the sound of her human blood.

I wanted to go into her mind. I tried but cast away the idea at once. I was inhibited, just as I was with Riccardo and the boys closest to me. In fact, it seemed such a terrible invasion of the privacy of the person that I used

284

this power only in hunting to find those who were evil and whom I might kill.

'Amadeo, you blush, what is it?' Bianca asked. 'Your cheeks are scarlet. Let me kiss them. Oh, you are hot as if the fever has come back.'

'Look into his eyes, angel,' said Marius. 'They are clear.'

'You're right,' she said, peering into my eyes with such a sweet frank curiosity that she became irresistible to me.

I pushed back the yellow cloth of her underdress and the heavy velvet of her dark-green sleeveless overgarment and kissed her bare shoulder.

'Yes, you're well,' she cooed into my ear, her lips moist against it.

I was blushing still as I drew back.

I looked at her, and I went into her mind; it seemed I had loosened the gold clasp beneath her breasts and parted her voluminous dark-green velvet skirts. I stared at the well between her half-exposed breasts. Blood or no blood, I could remember hot passion for her, and I felt it now in a strange overall manner, not localized in the forgotten organ as it had been before. I wanted to take her breasts in my hands and suckle them slowly, arousing her, making her moist and fragrant for me and making her head fall back. Yes, I blushed. A dim sweet swoon came over me.

I want you, I want you now, you and Marius both in my bed, together, a man and a boy, a god and a cherub. This is what her mind was saying to me, and she was remembering me. I saw myself as if in a smoky mirror, a boy naked except for a full-sleeved open shirt, seated on the pillows beside her, displaying the half-erect organ, ever ready to be completely aroused by her tender lips or her long graceful white hands.

I banished all this. I focused my gaze only on her beautiful tapering eyes. She studied me, not suspiciously but in fascination. Her lips were not rouged in any vulgar manner but deeply pink by nature, and her long lashes, darkened and curled only with a clear pomade, looked like the points of stars around her radiant eyes.

I want you, I want you now. These were her thoughts. They struck my ears. I bowed my head and put my hands up.

'Angel darling,' she said. 'Both of you!' she whispered to Marius. She took my hands. 'Come in with me.'

I was certain he would put a stop to it. He had cautioned me to avoid close scrutiny. But he only rose from his chair and moved towards her bedchamber, pushing back the two painted doors.

From the distant parlors came the steady sound of conversation and laughter. Singing had been added. Someone played the Virginal. All this went on.

We slipped into her bed. I was shaking all over. I saw that my Master had adorned himself in a thick tunic and beautiful dark blue doublet which I'd hardly noticed before. He wore soft sleek dark blue gloves over his hands, gloves which perfectly cleaved to his fingers, and his legs were covered by thick soft cashmere stockings all the way to his beautiful pointed shoes. He has covered all the hardness, I thought.

Having settled against the headboard of the bed, he had no compunction about helping Bianca to sit directly next to him. I looked across from him as I took my place beside her. As she turned to me, putting her hands on my face and kissing me eagerly again, I saw him perform a small act which I hadn't seen before.

Lifting her hair, he appeared to kiss her on the back of the neck. This she neither felt nor acknowledged. When he drew back, however, his lips were bloody. And lifting the finger of his gloved hand, he smoothed this blood, her blood, but a few droplets of it from a shallow scratch, undoubtedly, all over his face. It appeared to me as a living sheen, and to her it would look very different.

It quickened the pores in his skin, which had become all but invisible, and it deepened a few lines around his eyes and his mouth which otherwise were lost. It gave him a more human look, overall, and served as a barrier to her gaze, which was now so close.

'I have my two, as I always dreamed,' she said softly.

Marius came round in front of her, tucking his arm behind her and began to kiss her as greedily as I had ever done. I was astonished for a moment, and jealous, but then her free hand found me and pulled me down close to her, and she turned from Marius, dazed with desire, and kissed me as well.

Marius reached over and brought me close to her, so that I was against her soft curves, feeling all the warmth rising from her voluptuous thighs.

He lay on top of her, but lightly, not letting his weight hurt her, and with his right hand he drew up her skirt and moved his fingers between her legs.

It was so bold. I lay against her shoulder, looking at the swell of her breasts, and beyond that the tiny, down-covered mound of her sex which he clasped in his entire hand.

She was past all decorum. He laid kisses on her neck and on her breasts as he embraced her lower down with his fingers, and she began to writhe with undisguised longing, her mouth open, her eyelids fluttering, her body suddenly moist all over and fragrant with this new heat.

That was the miracle, I realized, that a human could be brought to this higher temperature, and thereby give forth all of her sweet scents and even a strong invisible shimmer of emotions; it was rather like stoking a fire until it became a blaze.

The blood of my victims teemed in my face as I kissed her. It seemed to become living blood again, heated by my passion, and yet my passion had no demonic focus. I pressed my open mouth to the skin of her throat, covering the place where the artery showed like a blue river moving down from her head. But I didn't want to hurt her. I felt no need to hurt her. Indeed, I felt only pleasure as I embraced her, as I slipped my arm between her and Marius, so that I could cradle her tightly as he continued to toy with her, his fingers lifting and falling on the tender little mound of her sex.

'You tease me, Marius,' she whispered, her head tossing. The pillow was damp beneath her and drenched with the perfume of her hair. I kissed her lips. They locked to my mouth. To keep her tongue from discovering my vampiric teeth, I drove my tongue into her. Her nether mouth couldn't have been sweeter, tighter, more moist.

'Ah, then this, my sweet,' said Marius tenderly, his fingers sliding inside her.

She lifted her hips, as though the fingers were lifting her as she would have them do.

'Oh, Heaven help me,' she whispered, and then came the fullness of her passion, her face darkening with blood, and the rosy fire spreading down her breasts. I pushed back the cloth and saw the redness consume her bosom, her nipples standing rigid in tiny raisinlike points.

I closed my eyes and lay beside her. I let myself feel the passion rock her, and then the heat was lessened in her, and she seemed to become sleepy. She turned her head away. Her face was still. Her eyelids were beautifully molded over her closed eyes. She sighed and her pretty lips parted in a natural way.

Marius brushed her hair back from her face, smoothing the tiny unruly ringlets that were caught in the moisture, and then he kissed her forehead.

'Sleep now, knowing you're safe,' he said to her. 'I'll take care of you forever. You saved Amadeo,' he whispered. 'You kept him alive until I could come.'

Dreamily she turned to look up at him, her eyes glossy and slow.

'Am I not beautiful enough for you to love me for that alone?' she asked.

I realized suddenly that what she said was bitter, and that she was bestowing a confidence on him. I could feel her thoughts!

'I love you whether or not you dress in gold or wear pearls, whether or not you speak wittily and quickly, whether or not you make a well-lighted and elegant place in which I can rest, I love you for the heart here inside you, which came to Amadeo when you knew there was danger that those who knew or loved the Englishman might hurt you, I love you for courage and for what you know of being alone.'

Her eyes widened for a moment. 'For what I know of being alone? Oh, I know very well what it means to be utterly alone.'

'Yes, brave one, and now you know I love you,' he whispered. 'You always knew that Amadeo loved you.'

'Yes, I do love you,' I whispered, lying next to her, holding her.

'Well, now you know I love you as well.'

She studied him as best she could in her languor. 'There are so many questions on the tip of my tongue,' she said.

'They don't matter,' Marius said. He kissed her and I think he let his teeth touch her tongue. 'I take all your questions and I cast them away. Sleep now, virginal

289

heart,' he said. 'Love whom you will, quite safe in the love we feel for you.'

It was the signal to withdraw.

As I stood at the foot of the bed, he placed the embroidered covers over her, careful to fold the fine Flemish linen sheet over the edge of the rougher white wool blanket, and then he kissed her again, but she was like a little girl, soft and safe, and fast asleep.

Outside, as we stood on the edge of the canal, he lifted his gloved hand to his nostrils, and he savored the fragrance of her on it.

'You've learnt much today, haven't you? You cannot tell her anything of who you are. But do you see now how close you might come?'

'Yes,' I said. 'But only if I want nothing in return.'

'Nothing?' he asked. He looked at me reprovingly. 'She gave you loyalty, affection, intimacy; what more could you want in return?'

'Nothing now,' I said. 'You've taught me well. But what I had before was her understanding, that she was a mirror in which I could study my reflection and thereby judge my own growth. She can't be that mirror now, can she?'

'Yes, in many ways she can. Show her by gestures and simple words what you are. You needn't tell her tales of blood drinkers that would only drive her mad. She can comfort you marvelously well without ever knowing what hurts you. And you, you must remember that to tell her everything would be to destroy her. Imagine it.'

I was silent for a long moment.

'Something's occurred to you,' he said. 'You have that solemn look. Speak.'

'Can she be made into what we—.'

'Amadeo, you bring me to another lesson. The answer is no.'

'But she'll grow old and die, and—.'

'Of course she will, as she is meant to do. Amadeo, how many of us can there be? And on what grounds would we bring her over to us? And would we want her as our companion forever? Would we want her as our pupil? Would we want to hear her cries if the magic blood were to drive her mad? It is not for any soul, this blood, Amadeo. It demands a great strength and a great preparation, all of which I found in you. But I do not see it in her.'

I nodded. I knew what he meant. I didn't have to think over all that had befallen me, or even think back to the rude cradle of Russia where I'd been nursed. He was right.

'You will want to share this power with them all,' he said. 'Learn that you cannot. Learn that with each one you make there comes a terrible obligation, and a terrible danger. Children rise against their parents, and with each blood drinker made by you you make a child that will live forever in love for you or hate. Yes, hate.'

'You needn't say any more,' I whispered. 'I know. I understand.'

We went home together, to the brightly lighted rooms of the palazzo.

I knew then what he wanted of me, that I mingle with my old friends among the boys, that I show kindness in particular to Riccardo, who blamed himself, I soon realized, for the death of those few undefended ones whom the Englishman had murdered on that fateful day.

'Pretend, and grow strong with each pretense,' he whispered in my ear. 'Rather, draw close and be loving and love, without the luxury of complete honesty. For love can bridge all.'

In the following months, I learned more than I can ever recount here. I studied vigorously, and paid attention even to the government of the city, which I thought basically as tiresome as any government, and read voraciously the great Christian scholars, completing my time with Abelard, Duns Scotus and other thinkers whom Marius prized.

Marius also found for me a heap of Russian literature so that for the first time I could study in writing what I had only known from the songs of my uncles and my Father in the past. At first I deemed this too painful for a serious inquiry, but Marius laid down the law and wisely. The inherent value of the subject matter soon absorbed my painful recollections and a greater knowledge and understanding was the result.

All of these documents were in Church Slavonic, the written language of my childhood, and I soon fell into reading this with extraordinary ease. *The Lay of Igor's Campaigns* delighted me, but I also loved the writings, translated from the Greek, of St. John Chrysostom. I also reveled in the fantastical tales of King Solomon and of the Descent of the Virgin into Hell, works which were not part of the approved New Testament but which were very evocative of the Russian soul. I read also our great chronicle, *The Tale of Bygone Years*. I read also *Orison on the Downfall of Russia* and the *Tale of the Destruction of Riasan*.

This exercise, the reading of my native stories, helped me to put them in perspective alongside the other learning which I acquired. In sum, it lifted them from the realm of personal dreams.

Gradually, I saw the wisdom of this. I made my reports to Marius with more enthusiasm. I asked for more of the manuscripts in Church Slavonic, and I soon had for reading the *Narrative of the Pious Prince Dovmont and His Courage* and *The Heroic Deeds of Mercurius of Smolensk*. Finally, I came to regard the works in Church Slavonic to be a pure pleasure, and I kept them for the hours after official study when I might pour over the old tales and even make up from them my own mournful songs.

I sang these sometimes to the other apprentices when they went to sleep. They thought the language very exotic, and sometimes the pure music and my sad inflection could make them cry.

Riccardo and I, meantime, became close friends again. He never asked why I was now a creature of night like the Master. I never sounded the depths of his mind. Of course I would do it if I had to for my safety and for Marius's safety, but I used my vampiric wits to gloss him in another way, and I always found him devoted, unquestioning and loyal.

Once I asked Marius what Riccardo thought of us.

'Riccardo owes me too great a debt to question anything I do,' Marius answered, but without any haughtiness or pride.

'Then he is far better bred than I am, isn't he? For I owe you the same debt and I question everything you say.'

'You're a smart, devil-tongued little imp, yes,' Marius conceded with a small smile. 'Riccardo was won in a card game from his drunken Father by a beastly merchant who worked him night and day. Riccardo detested his Father, which you never have. Riccardo was eight years old when I bought him for the price of a gold necklace. He'd seen the worst of men whom children don't move to natural pity. You saw what men will do with the flesh of children for pleasure. It's not as bad. Riccardo, unable to believe that a tender little one could move anyone to compassion, believed in nothing until I wrapped him in safety and filled him with learning, and told him in terms on which he could count that he was my prince.

'But to answer you more in the way you ask the question, Riccardo thinks that I am a magician, and that with you I've chosen to share my spells. He knows that you were on death's door when I bestowed on you my secrets, and that I do not tease him or the others with this honor, but regard it rather as something of dire consequence. He doesn't seek after our knowledge. And will defend us with his life.'

I accepted this. I didn't have the need in me to confide in Riccardo as I had with Bianca.

'I feel the need to protect him,' I said to my Master. 'Pray he should never have to protect me.'

'So I feel also,' said Marius. 'I feel this for them all. God granted your Englishman a great mercy that he was not alive when I came home to find my little ones slain by him. I don't know what I would have done. That he had injured you was bad enough. That he had laid out two child sacrifices at my door to his pride and bitterness, this was even more despicable. You had made love to him, and you could fight him. But they were innocents who stood in his path.'

I nodded. 'What did happen to his remains?' I asked.

'Such a simple thing,' he said with a shrug. 'Why do you want to know? I can be superstitious too. I broke him into fragments and scattered those fragments to the wind. If the old tales are true that his shade will pine for the restoration of his body, then his soul wanders the winds.'

'Master, what will become of our shades if our bodies are destroyed?'

'God only knows, Amadeo. I despair of knowing. I have lived too long to think of destroying myself. My fate is perhaps the same fate of the whole physical world. That we could have come from nothing and return to nothing, this is entirely possible. But let us enjoy our illusions of immortality, as mortals enjoy theirs.'

Good enough.

My Master was absent from the palazzo twice, when he went on those mysterious journeys which he wouldn't explain to me any more now than he had before.

I hated these absences, but I knew that they were tests of my new powers. I had to rule within the house gently and unobtrusively, and I had to hunt on my own and make some account, upon Marius's return, of what I had done with my leisure time.

After the second journey, he came home weary and uncommonly sad. He said, as he had said once before, that 'Those Who Must Be Kept' seemed to be at peace.

'I hate it what these creatures are!' I said.

'No, never say such a thing to me, Amadeo!' he burst out. In a flash I'd seen him more angry and uncomposed than ever in our lives. I'm not sure I'd ever seen him really angry in our lives.

He approached me and I shrank back, actually afraid. But by the time he struck me, hard across the face, he'd recovered himself, and it was just the usual brain-jarring blow.

I accepted it, and then threw him one exasperated searing glance. 'You act like a child,' I said, 'a child playing Master, and so I must master my feelings and put up with this.'

Of course it took all my reserves to say this, especially when my head was swimming, and I made my face such an obdurate mask of contempt that suddenly he burst out laughing.

I started to laugh too.

'But really, Marius,' I said, feeling very cheeky, 'what are these creatures you speak of?' I made my wisdom nice and reverent. My question was, after all, sincere. 'You come home miserable, Sir. You know you do. So what are they, and why must they be kept?'

'Amadeo, don't ask me anymore. Sometimes just before morning, when my fears are at their worst, I imagine that we have enemies among the blood drinkers, and they're close.'

'Others? As strong as you?'

'No, those who have come in past years are never as strong as me, and that is why they're gone.'

I was enthralled. He had hinted at this before, that he kept our territory clean of others, but he wouldn't elaborate, and now he seemed softened up with unhappiness and willing to talk.

'But I imagine that there are others, and that they'll come to disturb our peace. They won't have a good reason. They never do. They'll want to hunt the Veneto, or they will have formed some willful little battalion, and they'll try to destroy us out of sheer sport. I imagine . . . but the point is, my child – and you are my child, smart one! – I don't tell you any more about the ancient mysteries than you need to know. That way, no one can pick your apprentice mind for its deepest secrets, either with your cooperation or without your knowledge, or against your will.'

'If we have a history worth knowing, Sir, then you

should tell me. What ancient mysteries? You wall me up with books on human history. You've made me learn Greek, and even this miserable Egyptian script which no one else knows, and you question me all the time on the fate of ancient Rome and ancient Athens, and the battles of every Crusade ever sent from our shores to the Holy Land. But what of us?'

'Always here,' he said, 'I told you. Ancient as mankind itself. Always here, and always a few, and always warring and best when alone and needing the love only of one other or two at most. That's the history, plain and simple. I will expect you to write it out for me in all five languages you now know.'

He sat down on the bed, disgruntled, letting his muddy boot dig into the satin. He fell back on the pillows. He was really raw and strange and seemingly young.

'Marius, come on now,' I coaxed. I was at the desk. 'What ancient mysteries? What are Those Who Must Be Kept?'

'Go dig into our dungeons, child,' he said, lacing his voice with sarcasm. 'Find the statues there I have from so-called pagan days. You'll find things as useful as Those Who Must Be Kept. Leave me alone. I'll tell you some night, but for now, I give you what counts. In my absence you were supposed to study. Tell me now what you learnt.'

He had in fact demanded that I learn all of Aristotle, not from the manuscripts which were common currency in the piazza, but from an old text of his own which he said was purer Greek. I'd read it all.

'Aristotle,' I said. 'And St. Thomas Aquinas. Ah, well, great systems give comfort, and when we feel ourselves slipping into despair, we should devise great schemes of the nothing around us, and then we will not slip but hang on a scaffold of our making, as meaningless as nothing, but too detailed to be so easily dismissed.'

'Well done,' he said with an eloquent sigh. 'Maybe some night in the far distant future, you'll take a more hopeful approach, but as you seem as animated and full of happiness as you can be, why should I complain?'

'We must come from somewhere,' I said, pushing the other point.

He was too crestfallen to answer.

Finally, he rallied, climbing up off the pillows and coming towards me. 'Let's go out. Let's find Bianca, and dress her up as a man for a while. Bring your finest. She needs to be freed of those rooms for a spell.'

'Sir, this may come as a rude shock to you, but Bianca, like many women, already has that habit. In the guise of a boy, she slips out all the time to make the rounds of the city.'

'Yes, but not in our company,' he said. 'We shall show her the worst places!' He made a dramatic comical face. 'Come on.'·

I was excited.

As soon as we told the little plan to her, she was excited too.

We came bursting in with an armful of fine clothes, and she immediately slipped away with us to get dressed.

'What have you brought me? Oh, I'm to be Amadeo tonight, splendid,' she said. She shut the doors on her company, who as usual carried on without her, several men singing around the Virginal and others arguing heatedly over their dice.

She stripped off her clothes and stepped out of them, naked as Venus from the sea. We both dressed her in blue leggings and tunic and doublet. I pulled her belt tight, and Marius caught her hair up in a soft velvet hat.

'You're the prettiest boy in the Veneto,' he said stepping back. 'Something tells me I'll have to protect you with our life.'

'Are you really going to take me to the worst haunts? I want to see dangerous places!' She threw up her arms. 'Give me my stiletto. You don't expect me to go unarmed.'

'I have all the proper weapons for you,' Marius said. He had brought a sword with a beautiful diamond-studded diagonal belt which he clasped at her hip. 'Try to draw this. It's no dancing rapier. It's a war sword. Come on.'

She took the handle with both hands and brought it forth in a wide sure sweep. 'I wish I had an enemy,' she cried out, 'who was ready to die.'

I looked at Marius. He looked at me. No, she couldn't be one of us.

'That would be too selfish,' he whispered in my ear.

I couldn't help but wonder, if I had not been dying after my fight with the Englishman, if the sweating sickness had not taken me over, would he have ever made me a vampire?

The three of us hurried down the stone steps to the quay. There was our canopied gondola waiting. Marius gave the address.

'Are you sure you want to go there, Master?' asked the gondolier, shocked because he knew the district where the worst of the foreign seamen congregated and drank and fought.

'Most sure of it,' he said.

As we moved off in the black waters, I put my arm around tender Bianca. Leaning back on the cushions, I felt invulnerable, immortal, certain that nothing would ever defeat me or Marius, and in our care Bianca would always be safe.

How very wrong I was.

Nine months perhaps we had together after our trip to Kiev. Nine or maybe ten, I cannot mark the climax by any exterior event. Let me say only, before I proceed to bloody disaster, that Bianca was always with us in those last months. When we were not spying upon the carousers, we were in our house, where Marius painted her portraits, devising her as this or that goddess, as the Biblical Judith with the head of the Florentine for her Holofernes, or as the Virgin Mary staring rapt at a tiny Christ child, as perfectly rendered by Marius as any image he ever made.

Those pictures – perhaps some of them endure to this very day.

One night, when all slept except for the three of us, Bianca, about to give up on a couch as Marius painted, sighed and said, 'I like your company too much. I don't ever want to go home.'

Would that she had loved us less. Would that she had not been there on the fatal evening in 1499, just before the turn of the century, when the High Renaissance was in its glory, ever to be celebrated by artists and historians, would that she had been safe when our world went up in flames.

300

14

If you've read *The Vampire Lestat* you know what happened, for I showed it all to Lestat in visions two hundred years ago. Lestat set down in writing the images I made known to him, the pain I shared with him. And though I now propose to relive these horrors, to flesh out the tale in my own words, there are points where I cannot improve on his words, and may from time to time freely call them up.

It began suddenly. I awoke to find that Marius had lifted back the gilded cover of the sarcophagus. A torch blazed behind him on the wall.

· 'Hurry, Amadeo, they're here. They mean to burn our house.'

'Who, Master? And why?'

He snatched me from the shining coffin box, and I rushed after him up the decaying stairs to the first floor of the ruined dwelling.

He wore his red cape and hood, and he moved so fast it took all my power to keep up with him.

'Is it Those Who Must Be Kept?' I asked. He slung his arm around me, and off we went to the rooftop of our own palazzo.

'No, child, it's a pack of foolish blood drinkers, bent on destroying all the work I've done. Bianca is there, at their mercy, and the boys too.'

We entered by the roof doors and went down the marble steps. Smoke rose from the lower floors.

'Master, the boys, they're screaming!' I shouted.

Bianca came running to the foot of the stairs far below.

'Marius! Marius, they are demons. Use your magic!' she cried out, her hair streaming from the couch, her garments undone. 'Marius!' Her wail echoed up the three floors of the palazzo.

'Dear God, the rooms are everywhere on fire!' I cried out. 'We must have water to put this out. Master, the paintings!'

Marius dropped down over the railing and appeared, suddenly below, at her side. As I ran to join him, I saw a crowd of black-robed figures close in on him, and to my horror, try to set his clothes afire with the torches they brandished, as they gave forth horrid shrieks and hissed curses from beneath their hoods.

From everywhere these demons came. The cries of the mortal apprentices were terrible.

Marius knocked his assailants away, turning his arm in a great arc, the torches rolling on the marble floor. He closed his cloak about Bianca.

'They mean to kill us!' she screamed. 'They mean to burn us, Marius, they've slaughtered the boys, and others they've taken prisoner!'

Suddenly more of the black figures came running before the first attackers could climb to their feet. I saw what they were. All had the same white faces and hands as we had; all possessed the magic blood.

They were creatures such as we!

Again, Marius was attacked, only to fling off all of them. The tapestries of the great hall were ignited. Dark odoriferous smoke belched forth from the adjacent rooms. Smoke filled the stairwell above. An infernal flickering light suddenly made the place as bright as day.

I pitched myself into battle with the demons, finding them amazingly weak. And picking up one of their torches I rushed at them, driving them back, away from me, just as the Master did.

'Blasphemer, heretic!' came a hiss from one. 'Demon idolator, pagan!' cursed another. They came on, and I fought them again, setting their robes afire so that they screamed and fled to the safety of the waters of the canal.

But there were too many of them. More poured into the hall even as we fought.

Suddenly, to my horror, Marius shoved Bianca away from him towards the open front doors of the palazzo.

'Run, darling, run. Get clear of the house.'

Savagely he fought those who would follow her, running after her, to bring them down one by one as they tried to stop her, until I saw her vanish through the open doors.

There was no time to make certain she had reached safety. More of them had closed in on me. The flaming tapestries fell from their rods. Statues were overturned and smashed on the marble. I was nearly dragged down by two of the little demons who clutched at my left arm, until I drove my torch into the face of one, and set the other completely alight.

'To the roof, Amadeo, come!' Marius shouted.

'Master, the paintings, the paintings in the storage rooms!' I cried.

'Forget the paintings. It's too late. Boys, run from here, get out now, save yourselves from the fire.'

Knocking the attackers back, he shot up the stairwell and called down to me from the uppermost railing. 'Come, Amadeo, fight them off, believe in your strength, child, fight.'

Reaching the second floor, I was everywhere surrounded, and no sooner did I set one ablaze than another was on me, and not seeking to burn me they grabbed my arms and my legs. All my limbs were caught by them, until finally the torch was wrenched from my hand.

'Master, leave me, get away!' I called. I turned, kicking and writhing, and looked up to see him high above, and again surrounded, and this time a hundred torches were plunged into his ballooning red cloak, a hundred fiery brands were beating against his golden hair and his furious white face. It was as a swarm of blazing insects, and so by such numbers and such tactics the swarm rendered him first motionless; and then, with a great loud gust, his entire body went up in flames.

'Marius!' I screamed and screamed, unable to take my eyes off him, warring still with my captors, jerking loose my legs only to have them caught again by cold, hurting fingers, shoving with my arms, only to be pinioned once more. 'Marius!' This cry came out of me with all my worst anguish and terror.

It seemed that nothing I had ever feared could be so unspeakable, so unendurable as the sight of him, high above, at the stone banister, completely engulfed in flame. His long slender form became a black outline but for one second, and it seemed I saw his profile, head thrown back, as his hair exploded and his fingers were like black spiders clawing up out of the fire for air.

'Marius!' I cried. All comfort, all goodness, all hope was burning in this black figure which my eyes would not let go, even as it dwindled, and lost all perceptible form.

Marius! My will died.

What remained was a remnant of it, and the remnant, as if commanded by a secondary soul made up of magic blood and power, fought mindlessly on.

A net was thrown over me, a net of steel mesh so heavy and so fine that I could see nothing suddenly, only feel myself bound up in it, rolled over and over in it, by enemy hands. I was being carried out of the house. I could hear screams all around me. I could hear the running feet of those who carried me, and when the wind howled past us, I knew we had come to the shore.

Down into the bowels of a ship I was carried, my ears still full of mortal wails. The apprentices had been taken prisoner with me. I was thrown down among them, their soft frantic bodies heaped on me and beside me, and I, tightly bound in the net, could not even speak to utter words of comfort, and had no words to give them besides.

I felt the oars rise and fall, heard the inevitable splash in the water, and the great wooden galley shivered and moved out towards the open sea. It gained speed as if there were no night to fight its passage, and on and on plowed the oarsmen with a force and strength that mortal men could not have commanded, driving the ship south.

'Blasphemer,' came a whisper near my ear.

The boys sobbed and prayed.

'Stop your impious prayers,' said a cold preternatural voice, 'you servants of the pagan Marius. You will die for your Master's sins, all of you.'

I heard a sinister laughter, rumbling like low thunder over the moist soft sounds of their anguish and suffering. I heard a long, dry cruel laugh.

I closed my eyes, I went deep deep inside myself. I lay in the dirt of the Monastery of the Caves, a wraith of myself, tumbled back into safest and most terrible memories.

'Dear God,' I whispered without moving my lips, 'save them, and I swear to You I shall bury myself alive among the monks forever, I shall give up all pleasures, I shall do nothing hour by hour but praise Your Holy Name. Lord, God, deliver me. Lord, God——.' But as the madness of panic took over, as I lost all sense of time and place, I called out for Marius. 'Marius, for the love of God, Marius!'

Someone struck me. A leather-clad foot struck my head. Another struck my ribs, and yet another crushed my hand. All around me were these wicked feet, kicking me and bruising me. I went soft. I saw the shocks of the blows as so many colors, and I thought to myself bitterly, ah, what beautiful colors, yes, colors. Then came the increased wails of my brothers. They too must suffer this, and what mental refuge did they have, these fragile young students, each so well loved and so well taught and groomed for the great world, to find themselves now at the mercy of these demons whose purpose was unknown to me, whose purpose lay beyond anything of which I could conceive.

'Why do this to us?' I whispered.

'To punish you!' came a gentle whisper. 'To punish you for all your vain and blasphemous deeds, for the worldly and Godless life you've lived. What is Hell to this, young one?'

Ah, so the executioners of the mortal world said a thousand times when they led heretics to the stake. 'What are the fires of Hell to this brief suffering?' Oh, such self-serving and arrogant lies.

'Do you think so?' came the whisper. 'Lay a caution on your thoughts, young one, for there are those who can pick your mind barren of all its thoughts. There may be no Hell for you, child, but there will be suffering eternal. Your nights of luxury and lasciviousness are over. The truth awaits you now.'

Once again, I retreated into my deepest mental hiding place. I had no body anymore. I lay in the Monastery, in the earth, unfeeling of my body. I put my mind at work on the tone of the voices near me, such sweet and pitiable voices. I picked out the boys by name and slowly made a count of them. Over half our little company, our splendid cherubic company, was in this abominable prison.

I did not hear Riccardo. But then, when our captors had finished their abuse for a while, I did hear Riccardo.

He intoned a litany in Latin, in a raw and desperate whisper. 'Blessed be God.' The others were quick to answer. 'Blessed be His Holy Name.' And so on it went, the prayers, the voice gradually becoming weak in the silence until Riccardo alone prayed.

I did not give the responses.

Yet on he went, now that his charges mercifully slept, praying to comfort himself, or perhaps merely for the glory of God. He moved from the litany into the *Pater Noster*, and from then into the comforting age-old words of the *Ave* which he said over and over, as if making a rosary, all alone, as he lay imprisoned in the bottom of the ship.

I spoke no words to him. I did not even let him know that I was there. I couldn't save him. I couldn't comfort him. I couldn't even explain this terrible fate which had befallen us. I couldn't above all reveal what I had seen: the Master perishing, the great one gone into the simple and eternal agony of fire.

I had slipped into a shock near to despair. I let my mind recover the sight of Marius burning, Marius a living torch, turning and twisting in the fire, his fine fingers reaching heavenward like spiders in the orange flame. Marius was dead; Marius was burned. There had been too many of them for Marius. I knew what he would have said if he had come to me a comforting specter. 'There were simply too many of them, Amadeo, too many. I couldn't stop them, though I tried.'

I slipped into tormented dreams. The ship bore on through the night, carrying me away from Venice, away from the ruin of all that I believed in, all that I held dear.

I awoke to the sounds of singing and to the smell of the earth, but it was not Russian earth.

We were no longer at sea. We were imprisoned on land.

Still bound in the net, I listened to hollow preternatural voices chanting with a villainous gusto the awful hymn, *Dies Irae*, or Day of Wrath.

A low drum carried on the zesty rhythm as if it were a song for dancing rather than a terrible lament of the Final Days. On and on went the Latin words speaking of the day when all the world would be turned to ashes, when the great trumpets of the Lord would blast to signal the opening of all graves. Death itself and nature would both shudder. All souls would be brought together, no soul able anymore to hide anything from the Lord. Out of His book, every sin would be read aloud. Vengeance would fall upon everyone. Who was there to defend us, but the Judge Himself, Our Majestic Lord? Our only hope was the pity of Our God, the God who had suffered the Cross for us, who would not let His sacrifice be in vain.

Yes, beautiful old words, but they issued from an evil mouth, the mouth of one who did not even know their meaning, who tapped at his eager drum as if ready for a feast.

A night had passed. We were entombed and now being released from our prison, as the dreaded little voice sang on to its spirited little drum.

I heard the whispers of the older boys, seeking to give the young ones comfort, and the steady voice of Riccardo assuring all of them that surely they would soon discover what these creatures wanted, and perhaps be allowed to go free.

Only I heard the rustling, impish laughter everywhere. Only I knew how many preternatural monsters

308

lurked about us, as we were brought into a light of a monstrous fire.

The net was torn from me. I rolled over, clutching at the grass. I looked up and saw that we were in a great clearing beneath high and indifferent bright stars. It was the summery air, and great towering green trees surrounded us. But the blast of the raging bonfire distorted everything. The boys, chained together, their clothes torn, their faces scratched and streaked with blood, cried out frantically when they saw me, yet I was snatched away from them and held, a bevy of little hooded demons fastened to both my hands.

'I can't help you!' I cried. It was selfish and terrible. It came from my pride. It made only panic among them.

I saw Riccardo, as badly beaten as the rest, turn from right to left, trying to quiet them, his hands bound before him, his doublet almost torn off his back.

He turned his glance to me, and then together we looked around us at the great wreath of dark-dressed figures that enclosed us. Could he see the whiteness of their faces and hands? Did he, on an instinctive level, know what they were?

'Be quick if you mean to kill us!' he called out. 'We've done nothing. We don't know who you are or why you've taken us. We are innocent, to a one.'

I was touched by his bravery, and I pulled my thoughts together. I must stop shrinking in horror from my last memory of the Master, but imagine him living, and think what he would tell me to do.

We were outnumbered, that was obvious, and I could now detect smiles on the faces of the hooded figures, who though they draped their eyes in shadow, revealed their long twisted mouths.

'Where is the leader here?' I demanded, raising my voice above the level of human power. 'Surely you see these boys are nothing but mortals! Your argument must be with me!'

The long string of surrounding black-robed figures caved in to whispering and murmuring amongst themselves at this. Those clustered about the band of enchained boys tightened their ranks. And as others whom I could scarce see threw more and more wood and pitch onto the great fire, it seemed the enemy prepared for action.

Two couples placed themselves before the apprentices who seemed not in their wailing and crying to realize what this meant.

I realized it at once.

'No, you must speak with me, reason with me!' I shouted, straining against those who held me. To my horror, they only laughed.

Suddenly drums began again, some one-hundredfold louder than before, as if an entire circle of drummers surrounded us and the hissing, spitting fire.

They took up that steady beat of the *Dies Irae* hymn, and suddenly the wreath of figures all to a one straightened and locked hands. They began to sing the words in Latin of the terrible day of woe. Each figure began to rock playfully, lifting knees in playful march as a hundred voices spit out the words to the obvious rhythm of a dance. It made an ugly mockery of the piteous words.

The drums were joined by the shrill squeal of pipes, and the repeated slam of tambourines, and suddenly the entire wreath of dancers, still hand in hand, was moving, bodies swaying side to side from the waist up, heads bobbing, mouths grinning. 'Dee-eees -a- - ray, dee-ees- eee- raw!' they sang.

I panicked. But I couldn't shake loose of my captors. I screamed.

The first pair of robed beings before the boys had broken out the first of them who was to suffer and tossed his struggling body high in the air. The second pair of figures caught it, and, with great preternatural thrusts, hurled the helpless child in an arc into the great fire.

With piteous shrieks, the boy fell into the flames and vanished, and the other apprentices, now certain of their fate, went wild with crying and sobbing and screaming, but to no avail.

One after another, boys were disentangled from the others and hurled into the flames.

I thrashed back and forth, kicking at the ground and at my opponents. Once I broke one arm loose only to have it imprisoned by three other figures with hard pinching fingers. I sobbed:

'Don't do this, they're innocent. Don't kill them. Don't.'

No matter how loud I cried out I could hear the dying cries of the boys who burned, *Amadeo, save us*, whether there were words to the final terror or no. Finally all the living took up this chant. '*Amadeo, save us!*' but their band was not halved and soon only a fourth remained, squirming and struggling, as they were finally heaved up to the unspeakable death.

The drums played on, with the mocking chink, chink, chink of the tambourines and the whining melody of the horns. The voices made a fearful chorus, each syllable sharpened with venom as the hymn was sung out.

'So much for your cohorts!' hissed the figure nearest me. 'So you sob for them, do you? When you should have made a meal of them each and every one for the love of God!'

'The love of God!' I cried. 'How dare you speak of the love of God! You slaughter children!' I managed to turn and kick at him, wounding him far worse than he expected, but as ever, three more guards took his place.

Finally in the lurid blast of the fire, only three white-faced children were left, the very youngest of our household, and none of them made a sound. It was eerie their silence, their little faces wet and quivering, as they were given up, their eyes dull and unbelieving, into the flames.

I called their names. At the top of my lungs, I called out: 'In Heaven, my brothers, in Heaven, you go into the arms of God!'

But how could their mortal ears hear over the deafening song of the chanters.

Suddenly, I realized Riccardo had not been among them. Riccardo had either escaped or been spared, or been saved for something worse. I knotted my brows in a tight frown to help me lock these thoughts in my mind, lest these preternatural beasts remember Riccardo.

But I was yanked from my thoughts and dragged towards the pyre.

'Now you, brave one, little Ganymede of the blasphemers, you, you willful, brazen cherub.'

'No!' I dug in my heels. It was unthinkable. I couldn't die like this; I couldn't go into the flames. Frantically I reasoned with myself, 'But you have just seen your brothers die, why not you?' and yet I couldn't accept this as possible, no, not me, I was immortal, no!

'Yes, you, and fire will make a roast of you as it has of them. Do you smell their flesh roasting? Do you smell their burnt bones?'

I was thrown high in the air, high enough by their powerful hands to feel the very breeze catch hold of my hair, and then to peer down into the fire, as its annihilating blast struck my face, my chest, my outstretched arms.

Down, down, down into the heat I went, sprawled out, in the thunder of crackling wood and dancing orange flames. *So I die!* I thought if I thought anything, but I think that all I knew was panic, and surrender, surrender to what would be unspeakable pain.

Hands clutched me, burning wood tumbled and roared beneath me. I was being dragged off the fire. I was being dragged across the ground. Feet stomped on my burning clothes. My burning tunic was ripped off me. I gasped for air. I felt pain all over my body, the dread pain of burnt flesh, and I deliberately rolled my eyes up into my head to seek oblivion. *Come, Master, come if there is a paradise for us, come to me.* I pictured him, burnt, a black skeleton, but he put out his arms to receive me.

A figure stood over me. I lay on the moist Mother Earth, thank God, the smoke still rising from my scorched hands and face and my hair. The figure was big-shouldered, tall, black-haired.

He lifted two strong thick-knuckled white hands and drew his hood back off his head, revealing a huge mass of shining black hair. His eyes were large with pearly whites and pupils of jet, and his eyebrows, though very thick, were beautifully arched and curved over his eyes. He was a vampire, as were the others, but he was one of unique beauty and immense presence, looking down at me as though he were more interested in me than himself, though he expected to be the center of all eyes.

A tiny shiver of thanks passed through me, that he seemed by virtue of these eyes and his smooth Cupid's bow mouth to be possessed of the semblance of human reason.

'Will you serve God?' he asked. His voice was cultured and gentle, and his eyes held no mockery. 'Answer me, Will you serve God, for if you will not, you

313

will be thrown back into the fire.'

I felt pain in all my frame. No thought came to me except that the words he spoke were impossible, they made no sense, and I could therefore make no response.

At once, his vicious helpers lifted me again, laughing, and chanting in time with the loud singing of the hymn which had never ceased, 'Into the fire, into the fire!'

'No!' the leader cried out. 'I see in him the pure love of our Savior.' He lifted his hand. The others released their grip, though they held me suspended, my legs and arms spread out, in the air.

'You are good?' I whispered desperately to the figure. 'How can this be?' I wept.

He drew nearer. He leant over me. What beauty he possessed! His thick mouth was the perfect Cupid's bow, as I have said, but only now did I see its rich dark color, natural to it, and the even shadow of beard, shaven away for the last time in mortal life no doubt, that covered all his lower face, giving it the strong mask of a man. His high broad forehead seemed made of pure white bone only by comparison, with full rounded temples and a peaked hairline, from which his dark curls fell back gracefully to make a striking frame for his face.

But it was the eyes, yes, as always with me, the eyes that held me, the large oval and shimmering eyes.

'Child,' he whispered. 'Would I suffer such horrors if it were not for God?'

I wept all the more.

I was no longer afraid. I didn't care that I was in pain. The pain was red and golden as the flames had been and ran through me as if it were fluid, but though I felt it, it didn't hurt me, and I didn't care.

Without protest, I was carried, my eyes closed, into a passage, where the shuffling feet of those who carried me made a soft, crumbling echo against low ceiling and walls.

Let loose to roll over on the ground, I turned my face to it, sad that I lay on a nest of old rags because I couldn't feel the moist Mother Earth when I needed her, and then this too was of no import whatsoever, and I laid my cheek on the soiled linen and drifted, as if I had put there to sleep.

My scalded skin was a part from me, and not a part of me. And I let a long sigh come out of me, knowing, though I didn't form words in my mind, that all my poor boys were safely dead. The fire could not have tortured them for long, no. Its heat was too great, and surely their souls had fled Heavenward like nightingales that had drifted into the smoky blast.

My boys were of the Earth no more and no one could do them harm. All the fine things which Marius had done for them, the teachers, the skills they'd been taught, the lessons they'd learned, their dancing, their laughter, their singing, the works they had painted – all of this was gone, and the souls went Heavenward on soft white wings.

Would I have followed? Would God have received the soul of a blood drinker into his golden cloudy Heaven? Would I have left the awful sound of these demons chanting Latin for the realm of angels' song?

Why did those near me allow these thoughts in me, for surely they read them from my mind. I could feel the presence of the leader, the black-eyed one, the powerful one. Perhaps I was here with him alone. If he could make sense of this, if he could lend it meaning and thereby contain its monstrousness, then he would be some saint of God. I saw soiled and starving monks in caves.

I rolled over on my back, luxuriating in the splashy red and yellow pain that bathed me, and I opened my eyes.

A mellow and comforting voice spoke to me, directly to me:

'Your Master's vain works are all burnt; nothing but ashes remain now of his paintings. God forgive him, that he used his sublime powers not in the service of God but in the service of the World, the Flesh and the Devil, yes, I say the Devil, though the Devil is our standard bearer, for the Evil One is proud of us and satisfied with our pain; but Marius served the Devil with no regard to the wishes of God, and the mercies granted us by God, that rather than burn in the flames of Hell, we rule in the shadows of the Earth.'

'Ah,' I whispered. 'I see your twisted philosophy.'

There came no admonition.

Gradually, though I had rather hear only the voice, my eyes began to focus. There were human skulls, bleached and covered with dust, pressed in the domed earth over my head. Skulls pressed into the earth with mortar so that they formed the entire ceiling, like clean white shells from the sea. Shells for the brain, I thought, for what is left of them, as they protrude from the mortared soil behind them, but the dome that covers the brain and the round black holes where once the jellied eyes were poised, acute as dancers, ever vigilant to report the splendors of the world to the carapaced mind.

All skulls, a dome of skulls, and where the dome came down to meet the walls, a lacing of thigh bones all around it, and below that the random bones of the mortal form, making no pattern, any more than random stones do when they are similarly pressed in mortar to make a wall.

All bones, this place, and lighted with candles. Yes, I smelled the candles, purest beeswax, as for the rich.

'No,' said the voice, thoughtfully, 'rather for the church, for this is God's church, though the Devil is our Superior General, the founding saint of our Order, so why not beeswax? Leave it to you, a vain and a worldly Venetian, to think it luxury, to confuse it with the wealth in which you wallowed rather like the pig in his slops.'

I laughed softly. 'Give me more of your generous and idiotic logic,' I said. 'Be the Aquinas of the Devil. Speak on.'

'Don't mock me,' he said imploringly and sincerely. 'I saved you from the fire.'

'I would be dead now if you had not.'

'You want to burn?'

'No, not to suffer so, no, I can't bear the thought of it, that I or anyone should suffer so. But to die, yes.'

'And what do you think will be your destination if you do die? Are the fires of Hell not fifty times as hot as the fires we lighted for you and your friends? You are Hell's child; you were from the first moment that the blasphemer Marius infused you with our blood. No one can reverse this judgment. You are kept alive by blood that is cursed and unnatural and pleasing to Satan, and pleasing to God only because He must have Satan to show forth His goodness, and to give mankind a choice to be good or bad.'

I laughed again, but as respectfully as I could. 'There are so many of you,' I said. I turned my head. The numerous candles blinded me, but it wasn't unpleasant. It was as if a different species of flame danced on the

317

wicks, than the species that had consumed my brothers.

'Were they your brothers, these spoilt and pampered mortals?' he asked. His voice was unwavering.

'Do you believe all the rot you're talking to me?' I asked, imitating his tone.

He laughed now, and it was a decently, churchly laugh as though we were whispering together about the absurdity of a sermon. But the Blessed Sacrament was not here as it would be in a consecrated church, so why whisper?

'Dear one,' he said. 'It would be so simple to torture you, to turn your arrogant little mind inside out, and make you nothing but an instrument for raucous screams. It would be nothing to wall you up so that your screams would not be too loud for us, but merely a pleasing accompaniment to our nightly meditation. But I have no taste for such things. That is why I serve the Devil so well; I have never come to like cruelty or evil. I despise them, and would that I could look upon a Crucifix, I would do so and weep as I did when I was a mortal man.'

I let my eyes close, forsaking all the dancing flames that besprinkled the gloom. I sent my strongest most stealthy power into his mind, but came upon a locked door.

'Yes, that is my image for shutting you out. Painfully literal for such an educated infidel. But then your dedication to Christ the Lord was nourished among the literal and the naive, was it not? But here, someone comes with a gift for you which will greatly hasten our agreement.

'Agreement, Sir, and what agreement will that be?' I asked.

I too heard the other. A strong and terrible odor penetrated my nostrils. I did not move or open my eyes.

I heard the other one laughing in that low rumbling fashion so perfected by the others who had sung the *Dies Irae* with such lewd polish. The smell was noxious, the smell was that of human flesh burnt or something thereof. I hated it. I began to turn my head and tried to stop myself. Sound and pain I could endure, but not this terrible, terrible odor.

'A gift for you, Amadeo,' said the other.

I looked up. I stared into the eyes of a vampire formed like a young man with whitish-blond hair and the long lean frame of a Norseman. He held up a great urn with both hands. And then he turned it.

'Ah, no, stop!' I threw up my hands. I knew what it was. But it was too late.

The ashes came down in a torrent on me. I choked and cried, and turned over. I couldn't get them out of my eyes and my mouth.

'The ashes of your brothers, Amadeo,' said the Norse vampire. He gave way to a wild peal of laughter.

Helpless, lying on my face, my hands up to the sides of my face, I shook myself all over, feeling the hot weight of the ashes. At last I turned over and over, and then sprang up to my knees, and to my feet. I backed into the wall. A great iron rack of candles went over, the little flames arcing in my blurred vision, the tapers themselves thudding in the mud. I heard the clatter of bones. I flung my arms up in front of my face.

'What's happened to our pretty composure?' asked the Norse vampire. 'We are a weeping cherub, aren't we? That is what your Master called you, cherub, no? Here!' He pulled at my arm, and with the other hand tried to smear the ashes on me.

'You damnable fiend!' I cried. I went mad with fury and indignation. I grabbed his head with both my hands, and using all my strength turned it around on his

319

neck, snapping all the bones, and then I kicked him hard with my right foot. He sank down on his knees, moaning, living still with his broken neck, but not in one piece would he live, I vowed, and kicking at him with the full weight of my right foot, I tore his head from him, the skin ripping and snapping, and the blood pouring out of the gaping trunk, I yanked the head free.

'Ah, look at you now, Sir!' I said, staring down into his frantic eyes. The pupils still danced. 'Oh, die, will you, for your own sake.' I buried my left fingers tight in his hair, and turning this way and that, I found a candle with my right hand, ripped it from the iron nail that held it and jammed it into his eye sockets one after the other, until he saw no more.

'Ah, then it can be done this way as well,' I said looking up and blinking in the dazzle of the candles.

Slowly, I made out his figure. His thick curly black hair was free and tangled, and he sat at an angle, black robes flowing down around his stool, facing slightly away from me, but regarding me so that I could trace the lineaments of his face easily in the light. A noble and beautiful face, with the curling lips as strong as the huge eyes.

'I never liked him,' he said softly, raising his eyebrows, 'though I must say, you do impress me, and I did not expect to see him gone so soon.'

I shuddered. A horrible coldness seized me, a soulless ugly anger, routing sorrow, routing madness, routing hope.

I hated the head I held and wanted to drop it, but the thing still lived. The bleeding sockets quivered, and the tongue darted from side to side out of the mouth. 'Oh, this is a revolting thing!' I cried.

'He always said such unusual things,' said the black-haired one. 'He was a pagan, you see. That you never were. I mean he believed in the gods of the north forest, and in Thor ever circling the world with his hammer . . .'

'Are you going to talk forever?' I asked. 'I must burn this thing even after this, mustn't I?' I asked.

He threw me the most charming innocent smile.

'You are a fool to be in this place,' I whispered. My hands shook uncontrollably.

Not waiting for a response, I turned and snatched up another candle, having so thoroughly snuffed the other, and set fire to the dead being's hair. The stench sickened me. I made a sound like a boy crying.

I dropped the flaming head into the robed and headless body. I threw the candle down into the flames, so that the wax might feed it. Gathering up the other candles I had knocked down, I fed them to the fire and stepped back as a great heat rose from the dead one.

The head appeared to roll about in the flames, more than was likely, so I grabbed up the iron candelabra I had knocked over, and using this like a rake, I plunged it into the burning mass to flatten and crush what lay beneath the fire.

At the very last his outstretched hands curled, fingers digging into the palms. Ah, to have life in this state, I thought wearily, and with the rake I knocked the arms against the torso. The fire reeked of rags and human blood, blood he'd drunk no doubt, but there was no other human scent to it, and with despair I saw that I had made a fire of him right in the middle of the ashes of my friends.

Well, it seemed appropriate. 'You are revenged in one of them,' I said with a defeated sigh. I threw down the crude candleholder rake. I left him there. The room was large. I walked dejectedly, my feet bare from the fire having burned off my felt slippers, to another broad

321

place among iron candelabra, where the moist good earth was black and seemingly clean, and there I lay down again, as I had before, not caring that the black-haired one had a very good view of me there, as I was more in front of him than even before.

'Do you know that Northern worship?' he asked, as if nothing dreadful had happened. 'Oh, that Thor is forever circling with his hammer, and the circle grows smaller and smaller, and beyond lies chaos, and we are here, doomed within the dwindling circle of warmth. Have you ever heard it? He was a pagan, made by renegade magicians who used him to murder their enemies. I am glad to be rid of him, but why do you cry?'

I didn't answer. This was beyond all hope, this horrid domed chamber of skulls, the myriad candles illuminating only remnants of death, and this being, this beautiful powerfully built black-haired being ruling amid all this horror and feeling nothing on the death of one who had served him, who was now a pile of smoldering stinking bones.

I imagined I was home. I was safe within my Master's bedchamber. We sat together. He read from a Latin text. It did not matter what the words were. All around us were the accouterments of civilization, sweet and pretty things, and the fabrics of the room had all been worked by human hands.

'Vain things,' said the black-haired one. 'Vain and foolish, but you'll come to see it. You are stronger than I reckoned. But then he was centuries old, your Maker, nobody even tells of a time when there wasn't Marius, the lone wolf, who abides no one in his territory, Marius, the destroyer of the young.'

'I never knew him to destroy any but those who were evil,' I said in a whisper.

322

'We are evil, aren't we? All of us are evil. So he destroyed us without compunction. He thought he was safe from us. He turned his back on us! He considered us not worthy of his attentions, and look, how he has lavished all his strength on a boy. But I must say you are a most beautiful boy.'

There was a noise, an evil rustling, not unfamiliar. I smelled rats.

'Oh, yes, my children, the rats,' he said. 'They come to me. Do you want to see? Turn over and look up at me, if you will? Think no more on St. Francis, with his birds and squirrels and the wolf at his side. Think on Santino, with his rats.'

I did look. I drew in my breath. I sat up in the dirt and stared at him. A great gray rat sat on his shoulder, its tiny whiskered snout just kissing his ear, its tail curling behind his head. Another rat had come to sit sedately, as if spellbound, in his lap. There were others gathered at his feet.

Seeming loath to move lest they startle, he carefully dipped his right hand into a bowl of dried bread crumbs. I caught the scent only now, mingled with that of the rats. He offered a handful of crumbs to the rat on his shoulder, who ate from it gratefully and with strange delicacy, and then he dropped some of the bread in his lap, where three rats came to feast at once.

'Do you think I love such things?' he said. He looked intently at me, his eyes widening with the emphasis on his words. His black hair was a dense tangled veil on his shoulders, his forehead very smooth and shining white in the candlelight.

'Do you think I love to live here in the bowels of the world,' he asked sadly, 'under the great city of Rome, where the earth seeps waste from the foul throng above, and have these, the vermin, as my familiars? Do you think I was never flesh and blood, or that, having undergone this change for the sake of Almighty God and His Divine Plan, I don't long for the life you lived with your greedy Master? Have I not eyes to see the brilliant colors which your Master spread over his canvases? Do I not like the sounds of ungodly music?' He gave a soft agonizing sigh.

'What has God made or ever suffered to be made that is distasteful in itself?' he continued. 'Sin is not repulsive in itself; how absurd to think so. No one comes to love pain. We can only hope to endure it.'

'Why all this?' I asked. I was sick unto vomiting, but I held it back. I breathed as deeply as I could to let all the smells of this horror chamber flood my lungs and cease to torment me.

I sat back, crossing my legs so that I could study him. I wiped the ashes out of my eye. 'Why? Your themes are entirely familiar, but what is this realm of vampires in black monkly robes?'

'We are the Defenders of Truth,' he said sincerely.

'Oh, who is not the defender of truth, for the love of Heaven,' I said bitterly. 'Look, the blood of your brother in Christ is stuck all over my hands! And you sit, the freakish blood-stuffed replicant of a human being staring on all this as if it were so much chitchat among the candles!'

'Ah, but you have a fiery tongue for one with such a sweet face,' he said in cool wonder. 'So pliant you seem with your soft brown eyes and dark autumnal red hair, but you are clever.'

'Clever? You burnt my Master! You destroyed him. You burnt up his children! I am your prisoner here, am I not? What for? And you talk of the Lord Jesus Christ to me? You? You? Answer me, what is this morass of filth and fancy, molded out of clay and blessed candles!'

He laughed. His eyes crinkled at the edges, and his face was cheerful and sweet. His hair, for all its filth and tangles, kept its preternatural luster. How fine he would have been if freed from the dictates of this nightmare.

'Amadeo,' he said. 'We are the Children of Darkness,' he explained patiently. 'We vampires are made to be the scourge of man, as is pestilence. We are part of the trials and tribulations of this world; we drink blood, and we kill for the glory of God who would test his human creatures.'

'Don't speak horrors.' I put my hands over my ears. I cringed.

'Oh, but you know it's true,' he insisted without raising his voice. 'You know it as you see me in my robes and you look about my chamber. I am restrained for The Living Lord as were the monks of old before they learned to paint their walls with erotic paintings.'

'You talk madness, and I don't know why you do it.' I would not remember the Monastery of the Caves!

'I do it because I have found my purpose here and the purpose of God, and there is nothing Higher. Would you be damned and alone, and selfish and without purpose? Would you turn your back on a design so magnificent that not one tiny child is forgotten! Did you think you could live forever without the splendor of that great scheme, struggling to deny the handiwork of God in every beautiful thing which you coveted and made your own?'

I fell silent. Don't think on the old Russian saints. Wisely, he did not press. On the contrary, very softly, without the devilish lilt, he began to sing the Latin hymn . . .

Dies irae, dies illa
Solvet saeclum in favilla
Teste David cum Sibylla
Quantus tremor est futurus . . .

That day of wrath, that day will turn the earth to ashes.
As both David and Sybelle have foretold
How great a tremor there will be . . .

'And on that Day, that Final Day, we shall have duties for Him, we His Dark Angels shall take the Evil souls down into the inferno as is His Divine Will.'

I looked up at him again. 'And then the final plea of this hymn, that He have mercy on us, was His Passion not for us?'

I sang it softly in Latin:

Recordare, Jesu pie,
Quod sum causa tuae viae . . .

Remember, merciful Jesus,
That I was the cause of your way . . .

I pressed on, scarcely having the spirit for it, to fully acknowledge the horror. 'What monk was there in the Monastery of my childhood who didn't hope one day to be with God? What do you say to me now, that we, the Children of Darkness, serve Him with *no hope of ever being with Him?*'

He looked broken suddenly.

'Pray there is some secret that we don't know,' he whispered. He looked off as if he were in fact praying. 'How can He not love Satan when Satan has done so well? How can He not love us? I don't understand, but I am what I am, which is this, and you are the same.' He looked at me, eyebrows rising gently again to under-score his wonder. 'And we must serve Him. Otherwise we are lost.'

He slipped from the stool and came down towards me, settling on the floor opposite me, cross-legged, and putting his long arm out to place his hand on my shoulder.

'Splendid being,' I said, 'and to think God made you as he made the boys you destroyed tonight, the perfect bodies you rendered to the fire.'

He was in deep distress. 'Amadeo, take another name and come with us, be with us. We need you. And what will you do alone?'

'Tell me why you killed my Master.'

He let go of me and let his hand fall in the lap made by his black robe stretched across his knees.

'It's forbidden to us to use our talents to dazzle mortals. It is forbidden us to trick them with our skills. It is forbidden us to seek the solace of their company. It is forbidden us to walk in the places of light.'

Nothing in this surprised me.

'We are monks as pure at heart as those of Cluny,' he said. 'We make our Monasteries strict and holy, and we hunt and we kill to perfect the Garden of Our Lord as a Vale of Tears.' He paused, and then making his voice all the more soft and wondering, he continued. 'We are as the bees that sting, and the rats that steal the grain; we are as the Black Death come to take young or old, beautiful or ugly, that men and women shall tremble at the power of God.'

He looked at me, imploring me for understanding.

'Cathedrals rise from dust,' he said, 'to show man wonder. And in the stones men carve the Danse Macabre to show that life is brief. We carry scythes in the army of the robed skeleton who is carved on a thousand doorways, a thousand walls. We are the followers of Death, whose cruel visage is drawn in a million tiny prayer books which the rich and the poor alike hold in their hands.' His eyes were huge and dreamy. He looked about us at the grim domed cell in which we sat. I could see the candles in the black pupils of his eyes. His eyes closed for a moment, and then opened, clearer, more bright.

'Your Master knew these things,' he said regretfully. 'He knew. But he was of a pagan time, obdurate and angry, and refusing ever the grace of God. In you, he saw God's grace, because your soul is pure. You are young and tender and open like the moonflower to take the light of the night. You hate us now, but you will come to see.'

'I don't know that I will ever see anything again,' I said. 'I'm cold and small and have no understanding now of feeling, of longing, even of hate. I don't hate you, when I should. I'm empty. I want to die.'

'But it's God's will when you die, Amadeo,' he said. 'Not your own.' He stared hard at me, and I knew I couldn't hide from him any longer my recollection – the monks of Kiev, starving slowly in their earthen cells, saying they must take sustenance for it was God's will when they should die.

I tried to hide these things, I drew these tiny pictures to myself and locked them up. I thought of nothing. One word came to my tongue: horror. And then the thought that before this time I had been a fool.

Another came into the room. It was a female vampire. She entered through a wooden door, letting it close carefully behind her as a good nun might do, in order that no unnecessary noise be made. She came up to him and stood behind him.

Her full gray hair was tangled and filthy, as was his,

and it too had formed a shapely veil of beauteous weight and density behind her shoulders. Her clothes were antique rags. She wore the low hip belt of women of olden times adorning a shapely dress that revealed her small waist and gently flaring hips, the courtly costume one sees graven on the stone figures of rich sarcophagi. Her eyes, like his, were huge as if to summon every precious particle of light in gloom. Her mouth was strong and full, and the fine bones of her cheeks and jaw shone well for the thin layer of silvery dust that covered her. Her neck and bosom were almost bare.

'Will he be one of us?' she asked. Her voice was so lovely, so comforting, that I felt I'd been touched by it. 'I have prayed for him. I have heard him weeping inside though he makes no sound.'

I looked away from her, bound to be disgusted by her, my enemy, who had slain those I loved.

'Yes,' said Santino, the dark-haired one. 'He'll be one of us, and he can be a leader. He has such strength. He slew Alfredo there, you see? Oh, it was wonderful to behold how he did it, with such rage and with such a baby's scowl on his face.'

She looked beyond me, at the ruin of what that vampire had been, and I didn't know myself what was left. I didn't turn to look at it.

A deep bitter sorrow softened her expression. How beautiful she must have been in life; how beautiful still if the dust were taken away from her.

Her eyes shot to me suddenly, accusingly, and then became mild.

'Vain thoughts, my child,' she said. 'I don't live for looking glasses, as your Master did. I need no velvet or silks to serve my Lord. Ah, Santino, such a newborn thing he is, look at him.' She spoke of me. 'In centuries gone by I might have penned verses in honor of such

329

beauty, that it should come to us to grace God's sooted fold, a lily in the dark he is, a fairy's child planted by moonlight in a milkmaid's cradle to thrall the world with his girlish gaze and manly whisper.'

Her flattery enraged me, but I could not bear in this Hell to lose the sheer beauty of her voice, its deep sweetness. I didn't care what she said. And as I looked at her white face in which many a vein had become a ridge in stone, I knew she was far too old for my impetuous violence. Yet kill, yes, yank head from body, yes, and stab with candles, yes. I thought of these things with clenched teeth, and him, how I would dispatch him for he was not so old, not nearly by half with his olive skin, but these compulsions died like weeds sprung from my mind stung by a northern wind, the deep frozen wind of my will dying inside of me.

Ah, but they were beautiful.

'You will not renounce all beauty,' she said kindly, having drunk up my thoughts perhaps, despite all my devices for concealing them. 'You will see another variant of beauty – a harsh and variegated beauty – when you take life and see that marvelous corporeal design become a blazing web as you do suck it dry, and dying thoughts do fall on you like wailing veils to dim your eyes and make you but the school of those poor souls you hasten to glory or perdition – yes, beauty. You will see beauty in the stars that can forever be your comfort. And in the earth, yes, the earth itself, you will find a thousand shades of darkness. This will be your beauty. You do but forswear the brash colors of mankind and the defiant light of the rich and the vain.'

'I forswear nothing,' I said.

She smiled, her face filling with a warm and irresistible warmth, her huge long mat of white hair curling here and there in the ardent flicker of the candles.

She looked to Santino. 'How well he understands the things we say,' she said. 'And yet he seems the naughty boy who mocks all things in ignorance.'

'He knows, he knows,' the other answered with surprising bitterness. He fed his rats. He looked at her and me. He seemed to muse and even to hum the old Gregorian chant again.

I heard others in the dark. And far away the drums still beat, but that was unendurable. I looked to the ceiling of this place, the blinded mouthless skulls that looked on all with limitless patience.

I looked at them, the seated figure of Santino brooding or lost in thought, and behind him and above him, her statuesque form in its ragged raiment, her gray hair parted in the middle, her face ornamented by the dust.

'Those Who Must Be Kept, child, who were they?' she asked suddenly.

Santino raised his right hand and made a weary gesture.

'Allesandra, of that he does not know. Be sure of it. Marius was too clever to tell him. And what of it, this old legend we've chased for countless years? Those Who Must Be Kept. If They are such that They must be kept, then They are no more, for Marius is no more to keep Them.'

A tremor ran through me, a terror that I would break into uncontrollable weeping, that I should let them see this, no, an abomination. Marius no more . . .

Santino hastened to go on, as if in fear for me.

'God willed it. God has willed that all edifices should crumble, all texts be stolen or burnt, all eyewitnesses to mystery be destroyed. Think on it, Allesandra. Think. Time has plowed under all those words written in the hand of Matthew, Mark, Luke and John and Paul.

Where is there one parchment scroll left which bears the signature of Aristotle? And Plato, would that we had one scrap he threw into the fire when feverishly working—?'

'What are those things to us, Santino?' she asked reprovingly, but her hand touched his head as she looked down. She smoothed his hair as though she were his Mother.

'I meant to say that it is the way of God,' Santino said, 'the way of His creation. Even what is writ in stone is washed away by time, and cities lie beneath the fire and ash of roaring mountains. I meant to say the Earth eats all, and now it's taken him, this legend, this Marius, this one so much older than any we ever knew by name, and with him go his precious secrets. So be it.'

I locked my hands together to stop their trembling. I said nothing.

'There was a town in which I lived,' he went on, murmuring. He held a fat black rat now in his arms, stroking its fur as if it were the prettiest of cats, and it with its tiny eye seemed unable to move, its tail a great curved scythe turned downward. 'A lovely town it was, with high thick walls, and such a Fair each year; words can't describe where all the merchants showed their wares and all the villages both far and near sent young and old to buy, to sell, to dance, to feast . . . it seemed a perfect place! And yet the plague took it. The plague came, respecting no gate or wall or tower, invisible to the Lord's men, and to the Father in the field and the Mother in her kitchen garden. The plague took all, all it seemed except the most wicked. In my house they walled me up, with bloating corpses of my brothers and sisters. It was a vampire found me out, for foraging there he found no other blood to drink but mine. And there had been so many!'

332

'Do we not give up our mortal history for the love of God?' Allesandra asked but most carefully. Her hand worked on his hair and brushed it back from his forehead.

His eyes were huge with thought and memory, yet as he spoke again he looked at me, perhaps not even seeing me.

'There are no walls there now. It's gone to trees and blowing grass and piles of rubble. And in castles far away one finds the stones which once made up our lord's keep, our finest hard-paved street, our proudest houses. It is the very nature of this world that all things are devoured and time is a mouth as bloody as any other.'

A silence fell. I could not stop my shivering. My body quaked. A moan broke from my lips. I looked from right to left and bowed my head, my hands tight to my neck to stop from screaming.

When I looked up again, I spoke.

'I won't serve you!' I whispered. 'I see your game. I know your scriptures, your piety, your love of resignation! You're spiders with your dark and intricate webs, no more than that, and breed for blood is all you know, all you know round which to weave your tiresome snares, as wretched as the birds that make their nests in filth on marble casements. So spin your lies. I hate you. I will not serve you!'

How lovingly they both looked at me.

'Oh, poor child,' Allesandra said with a sigh. 'You have only just begun to suffer. Why must it be for pride's sake and not for God?'

'I curse you!'

Santino snapped his fingers. It was such a small gesture. But out of the shadows, through doorways like secretive dumb mouths in the mud walls, there came his servants, hooded, robed, as before. They gathered me up, securing my limbs, but I didn't struggle.

They dragged me to a cell of iron bars and earthen walls. And when I sought to dig my way out of it, my clawing fingers came upon iron-bound stone, and I could dig no more.

I lay down. I wept. I wept for my Master. I didn't care if anyone heard or mocked. I didn't care. I knew only loss and in that loss the very size of my love, and in knowing the size of love could somehow feel its splendor. I cried and cried. I turned and groveled in the earth. I clutched at it, and tore at it, and then lay still with only silent tears flowing.

Allesandra stood with her hands on the bars. 'Poor child,' she whispered. 'I will be with you, always with you. You have only to call my name.'

'And why is that? Why?' I called out, my voice echoing off the stony walls. 'Answer me.'

'In the very depths of Hell,' she said, 'do not demons love one another?'

An hour passed. The night was old.

I thirsted.

I burned with it. She knew it. I curled up on the floor, my head bowed, sitting back on my heels. I would die before I would drink blood again. But it was all that I could see, all that I could think of, all that I could want. Blood.

After the first night, I thought I would die of this thirst.

After the second, I thought I would perish screaming.

After the third, I only dreamed of it in weeping and in desperation, licking at my own blood tears on my fingertips.

After six nights of this when I could bear the thirst no longer, they brought a struggling victim to me.

Down the long black passage I smelled the blood. I smelled it before I saw their torchlight.

A great stinking muscular youth who was dragged towards my cell, who kicked at them and cursed them, growling and drooling like a madman, screaming at the very sight of the torch with which they bullied him, forcing him towards me.

I climbed to my feet, too weak almost for this effort, and I fell on him, fell on his succulent hot flesh and tore open his throat, laughing and weeping as I did it, as my mouth was choked with blood.

Roaring and stammering, he fell beneath me. The blood bubbled up out of the artery over lips and my thin fingers. How like bones they looked, my fingers. I drank and drank and drank until I could contain no more, and all the pain was gone from me, and all the despair was gone in the pure satisfaction of hunger, the pure greedy hateful selfish devouring of the blessed blood.

To this gluttonous, mindless, mannerless feast they left me.

Then falling aside, I felt my vision clear again in the dark. The walls around me sparkled once more with tiny bits of ore like a starry firmament. I looked and saw that the victim I had taken was Riccardo, my beloved Riccardo, my brilliant and goodhearted Riccardo – naked, wretchedly soiled, a fattened prisoner, kept all this while in some stinking earthen cell just for this.

I screamed.

I beat at the bars and bashed my head against them. My white-faced warders rushed to the bars and then backed away in fear and peered at me across the dark corridor. I fell down on my knees crying.

I grabbed up the corpse. 'Riccardo, drink!' I bit into my tongue and spit the blood on his greasy staring face. 'Riccardo!' But he was dead and empty, and they had

335

gone, leaving him there to rot in this place with me, to rot beside me.

I began to sing *'Dies irae, dies illa'* and to laugh as I sang it.

Three nights later, screaming and cursing, I tore the reeking corpse of Riccardo limb from limb so I could hurl the pieces out of the cell. I could not endure it! I flung the bloated trunk at the bars again and again and fell down, sobbing, unable to drive my fist or foot into it to break its bulk. I crawled into the farthest corner to get away from it.

Allesandra came. 'Child, what can I say to comfort you?' A bodiless whisper in the darkness.

But there was another figure there, Santino. Turning I saw by some errant light which only a vampire's eyes could gather that he put his finger to his lip and he shook his head, gently correcting her. 'He must be alone now,' Santino said.

'Blood!' I screamed. I flew at the bars, my arm stretched out so that both were affrighted and rushed away from me.

At the end of seven more nights, when I was starved to the point where even the scent of the blood didn't rouse me, they laid the victim – a small boy child of the streets crying for pity – directly in my arms.

'Oh, don't be afraid, don't,' I whispered, sinking my teeth quickly into his neck. 'Hmmmmm, trust in me,' I whispered, savoring the blood, drinking it slowly, trying not to laugh with delight, my blood tears of relief falling down on his little face. 'Oh, dream, dream sweet and pretty things. There are saints who will come; do you see them?'

Afterwards I lay back, satiated, and picking from the muddy ceiling over my head those infinitesimal stars of hard bright stone or flinty iron that lay embedded in

336

the earth. I let my head roll to the side, away from the corpse of the poor child which I had arranged carefully, as for the shroud, against the wall behind me.

I saw a figure in my cell, a small figure. I saw its gauzy outline against the wall as it stood gazing at me. Another child? I rose up, aghast. No scent came from it. I turned and stared at the corpse. It lay as before. Yet there, against the far wall, was the very boy himself, small and wan and lost, looking at me.

'How is this?' I whispered.

But the wretched little thing couldn't speak. It could only stare. It was clothed in the very same white shift that its corpse wore, and its eyes were large and colorless and soft with musing.

A distant sound came into my hearing. It was of a shuffling step in the long catacomb that led to my little prison. This was no vampire's step. I drew up, my nostrils flaring ever so slightly as I tried to catch the scent of this being. Nothing changed in the damp musty air. Only the scent of death was the aroma of my cell, of the poor broken little body.

I fixed my eyes on the tenacious little spirit.

'Why do you linger here?' I asked it desperately in a whisper. 'Why can I see you?'

It moved its little mouth as if it meant to speak, but it only shook its head ever so slightly, piteously eloquent of its confusion.

The steps came on. And once again I struggled to catch the scent. But there was nothing, not even the dusty reek of a vampire's robes, only this, the approach of this shuffling sound. And finally there came to the bars the tall shadowy figure of a haggard woman.

I knew that she was dead. I knew. I knew she was as dead as the little one who hovered by the wall.

337

'Speak to me, please, oh, please, I beg you, I pray you, speak to me!' I cried out.

But neither phantom could look away from the other. The child with a quick soft tread hurried into the woman's arms, and she, turning, with her babe restored, began to fade even as her feet once again made the dry scraping sound on the hard mud floor which had first announced her.

'Look at me!' I begged in a low voice. 'Just one glance.'

She paused. There was almost nothing left of her. But she turned her head and the dim light of her eye fixed on me. Then soundlessly, totally, she vanished.

I lay back, and flung out my arm in careless despair and felt the child's corpse, still faintly warm beside me.

I did not always see their ghosts.

I did not seek to master the means of doing so.

They were no friends to me – it was a new curse – these spirits that would now and then collect about the scene of my bloody destruction. I saw no hope in their faces when they did pass through those moments of my wretchedness when the blood was warmest in me. No bright light of hope surrounded them. Was it starvation that had brought about this power?

I told no one about them. In that damned cell, that cursed place where my soul was broken week after week without so much as the comfort of an enclosing coffin, I feared them and then grew to hate them.

Only the great future would reveal to me that other vampires, in the main, never see them. Was it a mercy? I didn't know. But I get ahead of myself.

Let me return to that intolerable time, that crucible.

Some twenty weeks were passed in this misery.

I didn't even believe anymore that the bright and fantastical world of Venice had ever existed. And I knew my Master was dead. I knew it. I knew that all I loved was dead.

I was dead. Sometimes I dreamt I was home in Kiev in the Monastery of the Caves, a saint. Then I awoke to anguish.

When Santino and the gray-haired Allesandra came to me, they were gentle as ever, and Santino shed tears to see me as I was, and said:

'Come to me, come now, come study with me in earnest, come. Not even those as wretched as we should suffer as you suffer. Come to me.'

I entrusted myself to his arms, I opened my lips to his, I bowed my head to press my face to his chest, and as I listened to his beating heart, I breathed deep, as if the very air had been denied me until that moment.

Allesandra laid her cool, soft hands so gently on me.

'Poor orphan child,' she said. 'Wandering child, oh, such a long road you've traveled to come to us.'

And what a wonder it was that all they had done to me should seem but a thing we shared, a common and inevitable catastrophe.

Santino's cell.

I lay on the floor in the arms of Allesandra, who rocked me and stroked my hair.

'I want you to hunt with us tonight,' said Santino. 'You come with us, with Allesandra and with me. We won't let the others torment you. You are hungry. You are so very hungry, are you not?'

And so my tenure with the Children of Darkness began.

Night after night I did hunt in silence with my new companions, my new loved ones, my new Master and my new Mistress, and then I was ready to begin my new apprenticeship in earnest, and Santino, my teacher, with Allesandra to help him now and then, made me his own pupil, a great honor in the Coven, or so the others were quick to tell me when they had the chance.

I learnt what Lestat has already written from what I revealed to him, the great laws.

One, that we were formed in Covens throughout the world, and each Coven would have its leader, and I was destined to be such a one, like unto the Superior of a convent, and that all matters of authority would be in my hands. I and I alone should determine when a new vampire should be made to join us; I and I alone would see to it that the transformation was made in the proper way.

Two, the Dark Gift, for that is what we called it, must never be given to those who were not beautiful, for the enslaving of the beautiful with the Dark Blood was more pleasing to a just God.

Three, that never should an ancient vampire make the new fledgling, for our powers increase with time and the power of the old ones is too great for the young. Witness the tragedy of myself, made by the last of the known Children of the Millennia, the great and terrible Marius. I had the strength of a demon in the body of a child.

Four, that no one among us can destroy another among us, save the Coven leader, who must at any time be prepared to destroy the disobedient of his flock. That all vagabond vampires, belonging to no Coven, must be destroyed by that leader on sight.

Five, no vampire must ever reveal his identity or his magical strengths to a mortal and thereafter be let to live. No vampire must ever write any words that reveal these secrets. Indeed no vampire's name was ever to be known in the mortal world, and any evidence of our existence which ever escaped into that realm must at all costs be eradicated, along with those who allowed such a terrible violation of God's will.

There were other things. There were rituals, there were incantations, there was a folklore of sorts.

'We do not enter churches, for God should strike us dead if we do,' declared Santino. 'We do not look upon the crucifix, and its mere presence on a chain about the neck of a victim is sufficient to save that mortal's life. We turn our eyes and fingers from the medals of the Virgin. We cower before the images of the saints.

'But we strike with a holy fire those who go unprotected. We feast when and where we will and with cruelty, and upon the innocent and upon those most blessed with beauty and riches. But we make no boast to the world of what we do, nor boast to one another.

'The great castles and courtrooms of the world are shut to us, for we must never, never, meddle in the destiny which Christ Our Lord had ordained for those made in His Image, any more than do the vermin, or the blazing fire, or the Black Death.

'We are a curse of the shadows; we are a secret. We are eternal.

'And when our work is done for Him, we gather without the comfort of riches or luxuries, in those places blessed by us underground for our slumber, and there with only fire and candles for light, we come together to say the prayers and sing the songs and dance, yes, dance about the fire, thereby to strengthen our will, thereby to share with our sisters and brothers our strength.'

Six long months passed during which I studied these things, during which I ventured forth into the back alleys of Rome to hunt with the others, to gorge myself upon the abandoned of fate who fell so easily into my hands.

No more did I search the mind for a crime that

justified my predatory feasting. No more did I practice the fine art of drinking without pain to the victim, no more did I shield the wretched mortal from the horror of my face, my desperate hands, my fangs.

One night, I awoke to find myself surrounded by my brothers. The gray-haired woman helped me from my coffin of lead and told me that I should come with them.

Out under the stars we went together. The bonfire had been built high, as it had been on the night my mortal brothers had died.

The air was cool and full of the scent of spring flowers. I could hear the nightingale singing. And far off the whisperings and murmurings of the great crowded city of Rome. I turned my eyes towards the city. I saw her seven hills covered over with soft flickering lights. I saw the clouds above, tinged with gold, as they bore down on these scattered and beautiful beacons, as if the darkness of the sky were full with child.

I saw the circle had formed around the fire. Two and three deep were the Children of Darkness. Santino, in a costly new robe of black velvet, ah, such a violation of our strict rubrics, came forward to kiss me on either cheek.

'We are sending you far away, to the north of Europe,' he said, 'to the city of Paris, where the Coven leader has gone, as we all go sooner or later, into the fire. His children wait for you. They have heard tales of you, of your gentleness and your piety and your beauty. You will be their leader and their saint.'

My brothers one by one came to kiss me. My sisters, who were few in number, planted their kisses on my cheeks as well.

I said nothing. I stood quiet, listening still for the song of the birds in the nearby pines, my eyes drifting now and then to the lowering Heavens and wondering if the rain would come, the rain which I could smell, so clean and pure, the only cleansing water allowed to me now, the sweet Roman rain, gentle and warm.

'Do you take the solemn vow to lead the Coven in the Ways of Darkness as Satan would have it and his Lord and Creator, God, would have it?'

'I do.'

'Do you vow to obey all orders sent to you from the Roman Coven?'

'I do . . .'

Words and words and words.

Wood was heaped on the fire. The drums had begun. The solemn tones.

I began to cry.

Then came the soft arms of Allesandra, the soft mass of her gray hair against my neck.

'I will go with you north, my child,' she said.

I was overwhelmed with gratitude. I threw my arms around her, I held her hard cold body close to me, and I shook with sobs.

'Yes, dear, dear little one,' she said. 'I will stay with you. I am old and I will stay with you until it is time for me to go to God's Justice, as we all must.'

'Then we dance in jubilation!' cried Santino. 'Satan and Christ, brothers in the House of the Lord, we give you this perfected soul!'

He threw up his arms.

Allesandra stepped back from me, her eyes bright with tears. I could think of nothing but only my gratitude that she would be with me, that I would not make this awful terrible journey alone. With me, Allesandra, with me. Oh, Fool for Satan and the God Who made him!

She stood beside Santino, tall as he was, majestic as she too threw up her arms and swung her hair from side to side.

'Let the dancing begin!' she cried.

The drums became a thunder, the horns wailed, and the thump of the tambourines filled my ears.

A long low cry rose from the huge thick circle of vampires, and all at once, locking hands, they began to dance.

I was pulled back into the chain they made about the raging bonfire. I was jerked from left to right as the figures turned this way, then that, then broke free and leapt spinning into the air.

I felt the wind on the back of my neck as I turned, as I leapt. I reached out with perfect accuracy to receive the hands on either side of me, then to sway to the right and to the left again.

Above, the silent clouds thickened, curled and sailed across the darkling sky. The rain came, its soft roar lost in the cries of the mad dancing figures, in the crackle of fire and the torrent of drums.

I heard it. I turned and leapt high into the air and received it, the silvery rain floating down to me like the blessing of the dark Heavens, the baptismal waters of the damned.

The music surged. A barbarous rhythm broke loose everywhere, the orderly chain of dancers forgotten. In rain and in the unquenchable blaze of the giant fire, the vampires threw out their arms, howling, writhing, their limbs constricting so that they stomped with backs bent, heels pounded into the earth, and then sprang free, arms outstretched, mouths open, hips churning as they whirled and leapt, and caught in raucous open-throated volume the hymn came again, *Dies irae, dies illa*. Oh, yes, oh, yes, day of woe, oh, day of fire!

Afterwards, when the rain came down solemnly and steadily, when the bonfire was no more but a black wreckage, when they all had gone off to hunt, when only a few milled the dark ground of the Sabbat, chanting their prayers in anguished delirium, I lay still, the rain washing me, as I put my face against the ground.

It seemed the monks were there from the old Monastery in Kiev. They laughed at me but gently. They said, 'Andrei, what made you think you could escape? Didn't you know that God had called you?'

'Get away from me, you are not here, and I am nowhere; I am lost in the dark wastes of a winter without end.'

I tried to picture Him, His Holy Face. But there was only Allesandra, come to help me to my feet. Allesandra, who promised to tell me of dark times, long before Santino was made, when she had been given the Dark Gift in the forests of France to which we now would be going together.

'Oh Lord, Lord hear my prayer,' I whispered. If I could but see the Holy Face.

But we were forbidden such things. We could never, never look upon His Image! Until the end of the world, we would work without that comfort. Hell is the absence of God.

What can I say in defense of myself now?

What can I say?

Others have told the tale, how for centuries I was the stalwart leader of the Paris Coven, how I lived out those years in ignorance and shadow, obeying old laws until there was no more any Santino or Roman Coven to send them to me, how in rags and quiet despair, I clung to the Old Faith and the Old Ways as others went into the fire to destroy themselves, or simply wandered away.

What can I say in defense of the convert and the saint that I became?

For three hundred years I was the vagabond angel child of Satan, I was his baby-faced killer, his lieutenant, his fool. Allesandra was always with me. When others perished or deserted, there was Allesandra who kept the faith. But it was my sin, it was my journey, it was my terrible folly, and I alone must carry the burden of it for as long as I exist.

That last morning in Rome, before I was to leave for the north, it was decided that my name must be changed.

Amadeo, containing the very word for God, was most unseemly for a Child of Darkness, especially one meant to lead the Paris Coven.

From various choices given me, Allesandra chose the name Armand.

So I became Armand.

PART II

The BRIDGE of SIGHS

I refuse to discuss the past another moment. I don't like it. I don't care about it. How can I tell you about something that doesn't interest me? Is it supposed to interest you?

The problem is that too much has been written about my past already. But what if you haven't read those books? What if you haven't wallowed in The Vampire Lestat's florid descriptions of me and my alleged delusions and errors?

All right, all right. A little bit more, but only to bring me to New York, to the moment when I saw Veronica's Veil, so that you don't have to go back and read his books, so that my book will be enough.

All right. We must continue to cross this Bridge of Sighs.

For three hundred years, I was faithful to the Old Ways of Santino, even after Santino himself had disappeared. Understand, this vampire was by no means dead. He turned up in the modern era, quite healthy, strong, silent and without apology for the credos he had stuffed down my throat in the year 1500 before I was sent north to Paris.

I was mad during those times. Lead the Coven I did, and of its ceremonies, his fanciful dark litanies and bloody baptisms, I became the architect and the master. My physical strength increased with each year, as is the case with all vampires, and drinking greedily from my victims, for it was the only pleasure of which I could dream, I fed my vampiric powers.

Spells I could make around those I killed, and choosing the beautiful, the promising, the most audacious and splendid for my feast, I nevertheless conveyed upon them fantastical visions to blunt their fear or suffering.

I was mad. Denied the places of light, the comfort of entering the smallest church, bent on perfection in the Dark Ways, I wandered as a dusty wraith through the blackest alleyways of Paris, turning her noblest poetry and music into a din by the wax of piety and bigotry by which I stopped my ears, blind to the soaring majesty of her cathedrals or palaces.

The Coven took all my love, with chatter in the dark of how we might best be Satan's saints, or whether a beautiful and bold poisoner should be offered our demonic pact and made one of us.

But sometimes I went from an acceptable madness to a state of which I alone knew the dangers. In my earthen cell in the secret catacombs beneath the great Paris Cemetery of Les Innocents where we made our lair, I dreamt night after night of one strange and meaningless thing: What had become of that fine little treasure my mortal Mother had given me? What had become of that strange artifact of Podil which she'd taken from the Ikon corner and put in my hands, that painted egg, that crimson painted egg with the star so beautifully painted on it? Now, where could it be? What had become of it? Had I not left it, wrapped thickly in fur in a golden coffin in which I'd once lodged, ah, had all that really ever taken place, that life I thought I recalled from a city of brilliant white-tiled palaces and glittering canals and a great sweet gray sea full of swift and graceful ships, plying their long oars in perfect unison as if they were living things, those ships, those beautifully painted ships, so often decked with flowers, and with the whitest sails, oh, that could not have been real, and to think, a golden chamber with a golden coffin in it, and this special treasure, this fragile and lovely thing, this painted egg, this brittle and perfect egg, whose painted covering locked inside to utter perfection a moist, mysterious concoction of living fluids – oh, what strange imaginings. But what had happened to it! Who had found it!

Somebody had.

Either that or it was still there, hidden far below a palazzo in that floating city, hidden in a waterproof dungeon built deep into the oozing earth beneath the waters of the lagoon. No, never. Not so, not there. Don't think of it. Don't think of profane hands getting that thing. And you know, you lying treacherous little soul, you never, never went back to any such place as the low city with the icy water in its streets, where your Father, a thing of myth and nonsense to be sure, drank wine from your hands and forgave you that you had gone to become a dark and strong winged bird, a bird of the night soaring higher even than the domes of Vladimir's City, as if someone had broken that egg, that meticulously and wondrously painted egg which your Mother so cherished as she gave it you, broken that egg with a vicious thumb, cracked right into it, and out of that rotten fluid, that stinking fluid, you had been born, the night bird, flying high over the smoking chimneys of Podil, over the domes of Vladimir's Town, higher and farther and farther away over the wild lands and over the world and into this dark wood, this deep and dark and endless forest from which you will never escape, this cold and comfortless wilderness of the hungry wolf and the chomping rat and the crawling worm and the screaming victim.

Allesandra would come. 'Wake, Armand. Wake. You

351

dream the sad dreams, the dreams that precede madness, you cannot leave me, my child, you cannot, I fear death more than I fear this and will not be alone, you cannot go into the fire, you cannot go and leave me here.'

No. I couldn't. I did not have the passion for such a step. I did not have the hope for anything, even though no word of the Roman Coven had come in decades.

But there came an end to my long centuries of Satan's service.

Clad in red velvet it came, the very covering my old Master had so loved, the dream king, Marius. It came swaggering and camping through the lighted streets of Paris as though God had made it.

But it was a vampire child, the same as I, son of the seventeen hundreds, as they reckoned the time to be then, a blazing, brash, bumbling, laughing and teasing blood drinker in the guise of a young man, come to stomp out whatever sacred fire yet burnt in the cleft scar tissue of my soul and scatter the ashes.

It was The Vampire Lestat. It wasn't his fault. Had one of us been able to strike him down one night, break him apart with his own fancy sword and set him ablaze, we might have had a few more decades of our wretched delusions.

But nobody could. He was too damned strong for us.

Created by a powerful and ancient renegade, a legendary vampire by the name of Magnus, this Lestat, aged twenty in mortal years, an errant and penniless country aristocrat from the wild lands of Auvergne, who had thrown over custom and respectability and any hope of court ambitions, of which he had none anyway since he couldn't even read or write, and was too insulting to wait on any King or Queen, who became a wild blond-haired celebrity of the boulevard gutter theatricals, a lover of men and women, a laughing happy-go-lucky blindly ambitious self-loving genius of sorts, this Lestat, this blue-eyed and infinitely confident Lestat, was orphaned on the very night of his creation by the ancient monster who made him, bequeathed to him a fortune in a secret room in a crumbling medieval tower, and then went into the eternal comfort of the ever devouring flames.

This Lestat, knowing nothing of Old Covens and Old Ways, of soot covered gangsters who thrived under cemeteries and believed they had a right to brand him a heretic, a maverick and a bastard of the Dark Blood, went strutting about fashionable Paris, isolated and tormented by his supernatural endowments yet glorying in his new powers, dancing at the Tuileries with the most magnificently clad women, reveling in the joys of the ballet and the high court theater and roaming not only in the Places of Light, as we called them, but meandering mournfully in Notre Dame de Paris itself, right before the High Altar, without the lightning of God striking him where he stood.

He destroyed us. He destroyed me.

Allesandra, mad by then as most of the old ones were in those times, had one merry argument with him after I dutifully arrested him and dragged him to our underground Court to stand trial, and then she too went into the flames, leaving me with the obvious absurdity: that Our Ways were finished, our superstitions obviously laughable, our dusty black robes ludicrous, our penance and self-denial pointless, our beliefs that we served God and the Devil self-serving, naive and stupid, our organization as preposterous in the gay atheistic Parisian world of the Age of Reason as it might have seemed to my beloved Venetian Marius centuries before.

Lestat was the smasher, the laughing one, the pirate who, worshiping nothing and no one, soon left Europe to find his own safe and agreeable territory in the colony of New Orleans in the New World.

He had no comforting philosophy for me, the baby-faced deacon who had come forth out of the darkest prison, shorn of all belief, to put on the fashionable clothes of the age and walk once again on its high streets as I had done over three hundred years ago in Venice.

And my followers, those few whom I could not overpower and bitterly consign to the flames, how helplessly they blundered in their new freedom – free to pick the gold from the pockets of their victims and don their silks and their white-powdered wigs, and sit in marvelous astonishment before the glories of the painted stage, the lustrous harmony of a hundred violins, the antics of versifying actors.

What was to be our fate, as with dazzled eyes we made our way through crowded early evening boulevards, fancy mansions and grandly decorated ballrooms?

In satin-lined boudoirs we fed, and against the damask cushions of gilded carriages. We bought fine coffins for ourselves, full of fancy carvings and padded velvet, and were closeted for the night in gilded mahogany-paneled cellars.

What would have become of us, scattered, my children fearful of me, and I uncertain of when the fopperies and frenzy of the French City of Light might drive them to rash or hideously destructive antics?

It was Lestat who gave me the key, Lestat who gave me the place where I could lodge my crazed and pounding heart, where I could bring my followers together for some semblance of newfangled sanity.

Before leaving me stranded in the waste of my old

ways, he bequeathed to me the very boulevard theater in which he had once been the young swain of the Commedia dell'Arte. All its human players were gone. Nothing remained but the elegant and inviting husk, with its stage of gaily painted backdrops and gilded proscenium arch, its velvet curtains and empty benches just waiting for a clamoring audience again. In it we found our safest refuge, so eager to hide behind the mask of greasepaint and glamour that flawlessly disguised our polished white skin and fantastical grace and dexterity.

Actors we became, a regular company of immortals bound together to perform cheerfully decadent pantomimes for mortal audiences who never suspected that we white-faced mummers were more monstrous than any monster we ever presented in our little farces or tragedies.

The Théâtre des Vampires was born.

And worthless shell that I was, dressed up like a human with less claim to that title than ever in all my years of failure, I became its mentor.

It was the least I could do for my orphans of the Old Faith, giddy and happy as they were in a gaudy and Godless world on the verge of political revolution.

Why I governed this palladian theater so long, why I remained year after long year with this Coven of sorts, I know not except that I needed it, needed it as surely as I'd ever needed Marius and our household in Venice, or Allesandra and the Coven beneath the Paris Cemetery of Les Innocents. I needed a place to turn my steps before sunrise where I knew others of my kind were safely at rest.

And I can say truthfully that my vampire followers needed me.

They needed to believe in my leadership, and when

worst came to worst I did not fail them, exercising some restraint upon those careless immortals who now and then endangered us by public displays of supernatural power or extreme cruelty, and by managing with the arithmetical skill of an idiot savant our business affairs with the world.

Taxes, tickets, handbills, heating fuel, foot lamps, the fostering of ferocious fabulists, I managed it all.

And now and then, I took exquisite pride and pleasure in it.

With the seasons we grew, as did our audiences, crude benches giving way to velvet seats, and penny pantomimes to more poetical productions.

Many a night as I took my place alone in my velvet-curtained box, a gentleman of obvious means in the narrow trousers of the age, with fitted waistcoat of printed silk and close-cut coat of bright wool, my hair combed back beneath a black ribbon or finally trimmed above my high stiff white collar, I thought upon those lost centuries of rancid ritual and demonic dreams as one might think back on a long painful illness in a lightless room amid bitter medicines and pointless incantations. It could not have been real, all that, the ragged plague of predatory paupers that we were, singing of Satan in the rimy gloom.

And all the lives I'd lived, and worlds I'd known, seemed even less substantial.

What lurked beneath my fancy frills, behind my quiet unquestioning eyes? Who was I? Had I no remembrance of a warmer flame than that which gave its silvery glow to my faint smile at those who asked it of me? I remembered no one who had ever lived and breathed within my quietly moving form. A crucifix with painted blood, a saccharine Virgin on a prayer book page or made of pastel-painted bisque, what were

356

these things but vulgar remnants of a coarse, unfathomable time when powers now dismissed had hovered in the chalice of gold, or blazed most fearfully inside a face above a glowing altar.

I knew nothing of such things. The crosses snatched from virgin necks were melted down to make my golden rings. And rosaries cast aside with other paste as thieving fingers, mine, tore off a victim's diamond buttons.

I developed in those eight decades of the Théâtre des Vampires – we weathered the Revolution with amazing resiliency, the public clamoring to our seemingly frivolous and morbid entertainments – and maintained, long after the theatre was gone, into the late twentieth century a silent, concealed nature, letting my childlike face deceive my adversaries, my would-be enemies (I rarely took them seriously) and my vampire slaves.

I was the worst of leaders, that is, the indifferent cold leader who strikes fear in the hearts of everyone but bothers to love no one, and I maintained the Théâtre des Vampires, as we called it well into the 1870s, when Lestat's child Louis came wandering into it, seeking the answers which his cocky insolent maker had never given him to the age-old questions: Where do we vampires come from? Who made us and for what?

Ah, but before I discourse on the coming of the famous and irresistible vampire Louis, and his small exquisite paramour, the vampire Claudia, let me relate one tiny incident that happened to me in the earlier years of the nineteenth century.

It may mean nothing; or perhaps it is the betrayal of another's secret existence. I don't know. I relate it only because it touches fancifully, if not certainly, upon one who has played a dramatic role in my tale.

I cannot mark the year of this little event. Let me say

only that Chopin's lovely, dreamy piano music was well revered in Paris, that the novels of George Sand were the rage, and that women had already given up the slender lascivious gowns of the Empire to wear the huge heavy-skirted, small-waisted taffeta dresses in which they appear so often in old shining daguerreotypes.

The theatre was booming as one would say in modern parlance, and I, the manager, having grown tired of its performances, was wandering alone one night in the wooded land just beyond the glow of Paris, not far from a country house full of merry voices and blazing chandeliers.

It was there that I came upon another vampire.

I knew her immediately by her silence, lack of scent and the near divine grace with which she made her way through the wild brush, managing a full flowing cape and abundant skirt with small pale hands, her goal the nearby brilliantly lighted and beckoning windows.

She realized my presence almost as quickly as I sensed hers; quite alarming to me at my age and with my powers. She froze without turning her head.

Though the vicious vampire players of the theatre maintained their right to do away with mavericks or intruders among the Undead, I, the leader, after my years as deluded saint, did not give a damn for such things.

I meant the creature no harm, and, carelessly, I tossed out in a soft casual voice, speaking in French, a warning.

'Ravaged territory, my dear. No game unbespoken here. Make for a safer city before sunup.'

No human ear could have heard this.

The creature made no reply, her taffeta hood drooping as she had obviously bowed her head. Then, turning, she revealed herself to me in the long shafts of

358

golden light falling from the multipaned glass windows beyond her.

I knew this creature. I knew her face. I knew it.

And in a dreadful second – a fateful second – I perceived that she might not know me, not with my hair nightly clipped short for these times, not in these sombre trousers and dull coat, not in this tragic moment when I posed as a man, so utterly transformed from the lushly adorned child she'd known, she couldn't.

Why didn't I cry out? Bianca!

But I couldn't grasp it, couldn't believe in it, couldn't rouse my dulled heart to triumph in what my eyes told me to be true, that the exquisite oval face surrounded by its golden hair and taffeta hood was hers, most definitely, framed exactly as it might have been in those days, and it was she, she whose face had been etched into my fevered soul before and after any Dark Gift had ever been given me.

Bianca.

She was gone! For less than a second I saw her wide wary eyes, full of vampiric alarm, more urgent and menacing than any human could ever evince, and then the figure was vanished, disappeared from the wood, gone from the environs, gone from all the large rambling gardens that I searched, sluggishly, shaking my head, mumbling to myself, saying, No, couldn't be, no, of course, not. No.

I never saw her again.

I do not know at this very moment whether or not this creature was Bianca. But I believe in my soul now, now as I dictate this tale, I believe in a soul that is healed and no stranger to hope, that it was Bianca! I can picture her too perfectly as she turned on me in the wooded garden, and in that picture lies one last detail which confirms it for me – because on that night outside

359

of Paris, she had in her blond hair pearls interwoven. Oh, how Bianca had loved pearls, and how she had loved to weave them in her hair. And I had seen them in the light of the country house, beneath the shadow of her hood, ropes of tiny pearls wound in her blond hair, and within that frame was the Florentine beauty I could never forget – as delicate in vampiric whiteness as it had been when filled with Fra Filippo Lippi's colors.

It did not hurt me then. It did not shake me. I was too pale of soul, too numbed, too used to seeing all things as figments in a series of unconnected dreams. Very likely, I could not allow myself to believe such a thing.

Only now do I pray it was she, my Bianca, and that someone, and you can guess very well who that might be, someone might tell me whether or not it was my darling courtesan.

Did some member of the hateful murderous Roman Coven, chasing her out into the Venetian night, fall under her spell so that he deserted his Dark Ways, and made her his lover forever? Or did my Master, surviving the horrid fire, as we know he did, seek her out for sustaining blood and bring her over into immortality to assist him in his recovery?

I cannot bring myself to ask Marius this question. Perhaps you will. And perhaps I prefer to hope that it was she, and not to hear denials that render it less likely.

I had to tell you this. I had to tell you. I think it was Bianca.

Let me return now to the Paris of the 1870s – some decades after – to the moment when the young New World vampire, Louis, came through my door, seeking so sadly the answers to the terrible questions of why we are here, and for what purpose.

How sad for Louis that he should put those questions to me. How sad for me.

Who could have scoffed more coldly than I at the whole idea of a redemptive framework for the creatures of the night who, once having been human, could never be absolved of fratricide, their feasting on human blood? I had known the dazzling, clever humanism of the Renaissance, the dark recrudescence of asceticism in the Roman Coven and the bleak cynicism of the Romantic era.

What did I have to tell this sweet-faced vampire, Louis, this all too human creation of the stronger and brasher Lestat, except that in the world Louis would find enough beauty to sustain him, and that in his soul he must find the courage to exist, if indeed it was his choice to go on living, without looking to images of God or the Devil to give him an artificial or short-lived peace.

I never imparted to Louis my own bitter history; I confessed to him the awful anguishing secret, however, that as of the year 1870, having existed for some four hundred years among the Undead, I knew of no blood drinker older than myself.

The very avowal brought me a crushing sense of loneliness, and when I looked into Louis's tortured face, when I followed his slim, delicate figure as it picked its way through the clutter and nineteenth-century Paris, I knew that this black-clad dark-haired gentleman, so lean, so finely sculpted, so sensitive in all his lineaments, was the alluring embodiment of the misery I felt.

He mourned the loss of grace of one human lifetime. I mourned the loss of the grace of centuries. Amenable to the styles of the age which had shaped him – given him his flaring black frock coat, and fine waistcoat of white silk, his high priestly-looking collar and frills of immaculate linen – I fell in love with him hopelessly, and leaving the Théâtre des Vampires in ruins (he burnt it to the ground in a rage for a very good reason), I wandered the world with him until very late in this modern age.

Time eventually destroyed our love for one another. Time withered our gentle intimacy. Time devoured whatever conversation or pleasures we once agreeably shared.

One other horrible inescapable and unforgettable ingredient went into our destruction. Ah, I don't want to speak of it, but who among us is going to let me be silent on the matter of Claudia, the child vampire whom I am accused for all time by all of having destroyed?

Claudia. Who among us today for whom I dictate this narrative, who among the modern audience who reads these tales as palatable fiction does not have in mind a vibrant picture of her, the golden-curled child vampire made by Louis and Lestat one wicked and foolish night in New Orleans, the child vampire whose mind and soul became as immense as that of an immortal woman while her body remained that of a precious all too perfect painted bisque French bébé doll?

For the record, she was slain by my Coven of mad demon actors and actresses, for, when she surfaced at the Théâtre des Vampires with Louis as her mournful, guilt-ridden protector and lover, it became all too clear to too many that she had tried to murder her principal Maker, The Vampire Lestat. It was a crime punishable by death, the murdering of one's creator or the attempt at it, but she herself stood among the condemned the moment she became known to the Paris Coven, for she was a forbidden thing, a child immortal, too small, too fragile for all her charm and cunning to survive on her own. Ah, poor blasphemous and beauteous creature. Her soft monotone voice, issuing from diminutive and ever kissable lips, will haunt me forever.

362

But I did not bring about her execution. She died more horribly than anyone has ever imagined, and I have not the strength now to tell the tale. Let me say only that before she was shoved out into a bricklined air well to await the death sentence of the god Phoebus, I tried to grant her fondest wish, that she should have the body of a woman, a fit shape for the tragic dimension of her soul.

Well, in my clumsy alchemy, slicing heads from bodies and stumbling to transplant one to another, I failed. Some night when I am drunk on the blood of many victims, and more accustomed than I am now to confession, I will recount it, my crude and sinister operations, conducted with a sorcerer's willfulness and a boy's blundering, and describe in grim and grotesque detail the writhing jerking catastrophe that rose from beneath my scalpel and my surgical needle and thread.

Let me say here, she was herself again, hideously wounded, a botched reassemblage of the angelic child she'd been before my attempts, when she was locked out in the brutal morning to meet her death with a clear mind. The fire of Heaven destroyed the awful unhealed evidence of my Satanic surgery as it turned her to a monument in ash. No evidence remained of her last hours within the torture chamber of my makeshift laboratory. No one need ever have known what I say now.

For many a year, she haunted me. I could not strike from my mind the faltering image of her girlish head and tumbling curls fixed awkwardly with gross black stitching to the flailing, faltering and falling body of a female vampire whose discarded head I'd thrown into the fire.

Ah, what a grand disaster was that, the child-headed monster woman unable to speak, dancing in a frenetic circle, the blood gurgling from her shuddering mouth, her eyes rolling, arms flapping like the broken bones of invisible wings.

It was a truth I vowed to conceal forever from Louis de Pointe du Lac and all whoever questioned me. Better let them think that I had condemned her without trying to effect her escape, both from the vampires of the theatre and from the wretched dilemma of her small, enticing, flat-chested and silken-skinned angelic form.

She was not fit for deliverance after the failure of my butchery; she was as a prisoner subjected to the cruelty of the rack who can only smile bitterly and dreamily as she is led, torn and miserable, to the final horror of the stake. She was as a hopeless patient, in the reeking antiseptic death cubicle of a modern hospital, freed at last from the hands of youthful and overzealous doctors, to give up the ghost on a white pillow alone.

Enough. I won't relive it.

I will not.

I never loved her. I didn't know how.

I carried out my schemes in chilling detachment and with fiendish pragmatism. Being condemned and therefore being nothing and no one, she was a perfect specimen for my whim. That was the horror of it, the secret horror which eclipsed any faith I might have pleaded later in the high-blown courage of my experiments. And so the secret remained with me, with Armand, who had witnessed centuries of unspeakable and refined cruelties, a story unfit for the tender ears of a desperate Louis, who could never have borne such descriptions of her degradation or suffering, and who did not truly, in his soul, survive her death, cruel as it was.

As for the others, my stupid cynical flock, who listened so lasciviously at my door to the screaming, who maybe guessed the extent of my failed wizardry, those vampires died by Louis's hand.

Indeed the entire theatre paid for his grief and his rage, and justly so perhaps.

I can make no judgment.

I did not love those decadent and cynical French mummers. Those I had loved, and those who I could love, were, save for Louis de Pointe du Lac, utterly beyond my grasp.

I must have Louis, that was my injunction. I knew no other. So I did not interfere when Louis incinerated the Coven and the infamous theatre, striking, at the risk of his own life, with flame and scythe at the very hour of dawn.

Why did he come away with me afterwards?

Why did he not abhor the one whom he blamed for Claudia's death? 'You were their leader; you could have stopped them.' He did say those words to me.

Why did we wander for so many years together, drifting like elegant phantoms in our lace and velvet cerements into the garish electric lights and electronic noise of the modern age?

He remained with me because he had to do it. It was the only way that he could go on existing, and for death he has never had the courage, and never will.

And so he endured after the loss of Claudia, just as I had endured through the dungeon centuries, and through the years of tawdry boulevard spectacle, but in time he did learn to be alone.

Louis, my companion, dried up of his own free will, rather like a beautiful rose skillfully dehydrated in sand so that it retains its proportions, nay, even its fragrance and even its tint. For all the blood he drank, he himself became dry, heartless, a stranger to himself and to me.

Understanding all too well the limits of my warped

spirit, he forgot me long before he dismissed me, but I too had learnt from him.

For a short time, in awe of the world and confused by it, I too went on alone – perhaps for the first time really and truly alone.

But how long can any of us endure without another? For me at my darkest hours there had been the ancient nun of the Old Ways, Allesandra, or at least the babble of those who thought I was a little saint.

Why in this final decade of the twentieth century do we seek each other out if only for occasional words and exchanges of concern? Why are we here gathered in this old and dusty convent of so many brick-walled empty rooms to weep for The Vampire Lestat? Why have the very ancient among us come here to witness the evidence of his most recent and terrifying defeat?

We can't stand it, to be alone. We cannot bear it, any more than the monks of old could bear it, men who though they had renounced all else for Christ's sake, nevertheless came together in congregations to be with one another, even as they enforced upon themselves the harsh rules of single solitary cells and unbroken silence. They couldn't bear to be alone.

We are too much men and women; we are yet formed in the image of the Creator, and what can we say of Him with any certainty except that He, whoever He may be – Christ, Yahweh, Allah – He made us, did He not, because even He in His Infinite Perfection could not bear to be alone.

In time I conceived another love naturally, a love for a mortal boy Daniel, to whom Louis had poured out his story, published under the absurd title *Interview with the Vampire*, whom I later made into a vampire for the same reasons that Marius had made me so long ago: the boy, who had been my faithful mortal companion, and only

366

sometimes an intolerable nuisance, was about to die.

That is no mystery unto itself, the making of Daniel. Loneliness will always inevitably press us to such things. But I was a firm believer that those we make ourselves will always despise us for it. I cannot claim that I have never despised Marius, both for making me and never returning to me to assure me that he had survived the horrible fire created by the Roman Coven. I had sought Louis rather than create others. And having created Daniel I saw at last my fear realized within a short time.

Daniel, though alive and wandering, though civil and gentle, can no more stand my company than I can stand his. Equipped with my powerful blood, he can contend with any who should be foolish enough to interrupt his plans for an evening, a month or a year, but he cannot contend with my continuous company, and I cannot contend with his.

I turned Daniel from a morbid romantic into a true killer; I made real in his natural blood cells the horror that he so fancied he understood in mine. I pushed his face into the flesh of the first young innocent he had to slaughter for his inevitable thirst, and thereby fell off the pedestal on which he'd placed me in his demented, overimaginative, feverishly poetical and ever exuberant mortal mind.

But I had others around me when I lost Daniel, or rather when gaining Daniel as a fledgling, I lost him as a mortal lover and gradually began to let him go.

I had others because I had again, for reasons that I cannot explain to myself or anyone, made yet another Coven – another successor to the Paris Coven of Les Innocents, and the Théâtre des Vampires, and this was a swank, modern hiding place for the most ancient, the most learned, the most enduring of our kind. It was a honeycomb of luxurious chambers hidden in that most concealing of edifices – a modern resort hotel and shopping palace on an island off the coast of Miami, Florida, an island on which the lights never went out and the music never ceased to play, an island where men and women came by the thousands in small boats from the mainland to browse the expensive boutiques, or to make love in opulent, decadent, magnificent and always fashionable hotel suites and rooms.

'The Night Island,' that was my creation, with its own copter pad and marina, its secret illegal gambling casinos, its mirror-lined gymnasiums and overheated swimming pools, its crystal fountains, its silver escalators, its emporium of dazzling consumables, its bars, taverns, lounges and theaters where I myself, decked out in smart velvet jackets, tight denim pants and heavy black glasses, hair clipped each night (for it grows back to its Renaissance length each day), could roam in peace and anonymity, swimming in the soft caressing murmurs of the mortals around me, searching out when thirst prompted it that one individual who truly wanted me, that one individual who for reasons of health or poverty or sanity or insanity wanted to be taken into the tentative and never overpowering arms of death and sucked free of all blood and all life.

I didn't go hungry. I dropped my victims in the deep warm clean waters of the Caribbean. I opened my doors to any of the Undead who would wipe their boots before entering. It was like the old days of Venice, with Bianca's palazzo open to all ladies and gentlemen, indeed, to all artists, poets, dreamers and schemers who dared to present themselves, had come again.

Well, they had not come again.

It took no bunch of black-robed tramps to disperse the Coven of The Night Island. Indeed those who were couched there for a short while simply wandered off on their own. Vampires do not really want the company of other vampires. They want the love of other immortals, yes, always, and they need it, and they need the deep bonds of loyalty which inevitably grow amongst those who refuse to become enemies. But they don't want the company.

And my splendid glass-walled drawing rooms on The Night Island were soon empty, and I myself had long before that started to wander for weeks, even months on my own.

It is there still, The Night Island. It is there, and now and then I do go back, and I find there some lone immortal who has checked in, as we say in the modern age, to see how it goes with the rest of us, or with some other who might be visiting as well. The great enterprise I sold for a mortal fortune – but I maintain my ownership of the four-story villa (a private club: name, Il Villagio), with its deep secret underground crypts to which all of our kind are welcome to come.

All of our kind.

There are not so many. But let me tell you now who they were. Let me tell you now who has survived the centuries, who has resurfaced after hundreds of years of mysterious absence, who has come forward to be counted in the unwritten census of the modern Living Dead.

There is Lestat, first and foremost, the author of four books of his life and his adventures comprising everything you could ever possibly want to know about him and some of us. Lestat, ever the maverick and the laughing trickster. Six feet tall, a young man of twenty when made, with huge warm blue eyes and thick flashy blond hair, square of jaw, with a generous beautifully shaped mouth and skin darkened by a sojourn in the sun which would have killed a weaker vampire, a ladies' man, an Oscar Wildean fantasy, the glass of fashion, the most bold and disregarding dusty vagabond on occasion, loner, wanderer, heartbreaker and wise guy, dubbed the 'Brat Prince' by my old Master – yes, imagine it, my Marius, yes, my Marius, who did indeed survive the torches of the Roman Coven – dubbed by Marius the 'Brat Prince,' though in whose Court and by whose Divine Right and whose Royal Blood I should like to know. Lestat, stuffed with the blood of the most ancient of our kind, indeed the very blood of the Eve of our species, some five to seven thousand years the survivor of her Eden, a perfect horror who, emerging from the deceptive poetical title of Queen Akasha of Those Who Must Be Kept, almost destroyed the world.

Lestat, not a bad friend to have, and one for whom I would lay down my immortal life, one for whose love and companionship I have ofttimes begged, one whom I find maddening and fascinating and intolerably annoying, one without whom I cannot exist.

So much for him.

Louis de Pointe du Lac, already described above but always fun to envisage: slender, slightly less tall than Lestat, his maker, black of hair, gaunt and white of skin, with amazingly long and delicate fingers, and feet that do not make a sound. Louis, whose green eyes are soulful, the very mirror of patient misery, soft-voiced, very human, weak, having lived only two hundred years, unable to read minds, or to levitate, or to spellbind others except inadvertently, which can be hilarious, an immortal with whom mortals fall in love. Louis, an indiscriminate killer, because he cannot satisfy his thirst without killing, though he is too weak to risk the death of the victim in his arms, and because he has no pride or vanity which would lead him to a hierarchy of intended victims, and therefore takes those who cross his path, regardless of age, physical endowments, or blessings bestowed by nature or fate. Louis, a deadly and romantic vampire, the kind of night creature who hovers in the deep shadows at the Opera House to listen to Mozart's Queen of the Night give forth her piercing and irresistible song.

Louis, who has never vanished, who has always been known to others, who is easy to track and easy to abandon, Louis who will not make others after his tragic blunders with vampiric children, Louis who is past questing for God, for the Devil, for Truth or even for love.

Sweet, dusty Louis, reading Keats by the light of one candle. Louis standing in the rain on a slick deserted downtown street watching through the store window the brilliant young actor Leonardo DiCaprio as Shakespeare's Romeo kissing his tender and lovely Juliet (Claire Danes) on a television screen.

Gabrielle. She's around now. She was around on The Night Island. Everyone hates her. She is Lestat's Mother, and abandons him for centuries, and somehow doesn't manage to heed Lestat's periodic and inevitable frantic cries for help, which though she could not receive them, being his fledgling, could certainly learn of them from other vampiric minds which are on fire with the news round the world when Lestat is in trouble. Gabrielle, she looks just like him, except she's a woman, totally a woman, that is, sharper of feature, small-waisted, big-breasted, sweet-eyed in the most unnerving and dishonest fashion, gorgeous in a black ball gown with her hair free, more often dusty, genderless, sheathed in supple leather or belted khaki, a steady walker, and a vampire so cunning and cold that she has forgotten what it ever meant to be human or in pain. Indeed, I think she forgot overnight, if she ever knew it.

371

She was in mortal life one of those creatures who always wondered what the others were carrying on about. Gabrielle, low-voiced, unintentionally vicious, glacial, forbidding, ungiving, a wanderer through snowy forests of the far north, a slayer of giant white bears and white tigers, an indifferent legend to untamed tribes, something more akin to a prehistoric reptile than a human. Beautiful, naturally, blond hair in a braid down her back, almost regal in a chocolate-colored leather safari jacket and a small droopy brimmed rain hat, a stalker, a quick killer, a pitiless and seemingly thoughtful but eternally secretive thing. Gabrielle, virtually useless to anyone but herself. Some night she'll say something to someone, I suppose.

Pandora, child of two millennia, consort to my own beloved Marius a thousand years before I was ever born. A goddess, made of bleeding marble, a powerful beauty out of the deepest and most ancient soul of Roman Italy, fierce with the moral fiber of the old Senatorial class of the greatest Empire the Western world has ever known. I don't know her. Her oval face shimmers beneath a mantle of rippling brown hair. She seems too beautiful to hurt anyone. She is tender-voiced, with innocent, imploring eyes, her flawless face instantly vulnerable and warm with empathy, a mystery. I don't know how Marius could ever have left her. In a short shift of filmy silk, with a snake bracelet on her bare arm, she is too ravishing for mortal males and the envy of females. In her longer concealing gowns, she moves as a wraith through the rooms around her as if they are not real to her, and she, the ghost of a dancer, seeks for some perfect setting that she alone can find. Her powers certainly rival those of Marius. She has drunk from the Eden fount, that is, the blood of Queen Akasha. She can kindle crisp dry objects into fire with the power of her mind, levitate and vanish in the dark sky, slay the young blood drinkers if they menace her, and yet she seems harmless, forever feminine though indifferent to gender, a wan and plaintive woman whom I want to close in my arms.

Santino, the old saint of Rome. He has wandered into the disasters of the modern era with all his beauty unblemished, still the big-shouldered, strong-chested one, olive skin paler now with the workings of the fierce magical blood, huge head of black curling hair often clipped each night at sunset for the sake of anonymity perhaps, unvain, perfectly dressed in black. He says nothing to anyone. He looks at me silently as if we never talked together of theology and mysticism, as if he never broke my happiness, burnt my youth to cinders, drove my Maker into century-long convalescence, divided me from all comfort. Perhaps he fancies us as fellow victims of a powerful intellectual morality, an infatuation with the concept of purpose, two lost ones, veterans of the same war.

At times he looks shrewd and even hateful. He knows plenty. He doesn't underestimate the powers of the ancient ones, who, eschewing the social invisibility of centuries past, now walk among us with perfect ease. When he looks at me, his black eyes are unflinching and passive. The shadow of his beard, fixed forever into the tiny cut-off dark hairs embedded in his skin, is beautiful as it always was. He is all in all conventionally virile, crisp white shirt open at the throat to show the portion of the thick curly black hair that covers his chest, a similar enticing black fleece covering the visible flesh of his arms at the wrists. He favors sleek but sturdy black coats lapeled in leather or fur, low-slung black cars that move at two hundred miles an hour, a golden cigarette lighter reeking of combustible fluid, which he lights over and over again just to peer into the flame. Where he actually lives, and when he will surface, nobody knows.

Santino. I know no more about him than that. We keep a gentlemanly distance from one another. I suspect his own suffering has been terrible; I do not seek to break the shiny black fashionable carapace of his demeanor to discover some raw bloody tragedy beneath it. To know Santino, there is always time.

Now let me describe for the most virginal of readers my Master, Marius, as he is now. So much time and experience divide us now that it is like a glacier between us, and we stare at each other across the glowing whiteness of that impassable waste, able only to speak in lulled and polite voices, so mannerly, the young creature I appear to be, too sweet-faced for casual belief, and he, ever the worldly sophisticate, the scholar of the moment, the philosopher of the century, ethicist of the millennium, historian for all time.

He walks tall as he always did, imperial still in his subdued twentieth-century fashion, carving his coats out of old velvet that they may give some faint clue of the magnificence that was once his nightly dress. On occasions now he clips the long flowing yellow hair which he wore so proudly in old Venice. He is ever quick of wit and tongue and eager for reasonable solutions, possessed of infinite patience and unquenchable curiosity and a refusal to give up on the fate of himself, or of us, or of this world. No knowledge can defeat him; tempered by fire and time, he is too strong for the horrors of technology or the spells of science. Neither microscopes nor computers shake his faith in the infinite, though his once solemn charges – Those Who Must Be Kept, who held such promise of redemptive meaning – have long been toppled from their archaic thrones.

I fear him. I don't know why. Perhaps I fear him because I could love him again, and loving him, I would come to need him, and needing him, I would come to learn from him, and learning from him, I would be again his faithful pupil in all things, only to discover that his patience for me is no substitute for the passion which long ago blazed in his eyes.

I need that passion! I need it. But enough of him. Two thousand years he had survived, slipping in and out of the very mainstream of human life without compunction, a great practitioner of the art of being human, carrying with him forever the grace and quiet dignity of the Augustan Age of seemingly invincible Rome, in which he was born.

There are others who are not here now with me, though they have been on The Night Island, and I will see them again. There are the ancient twins, Mekare and Maharet, custodians of the primal blood fount from which our life flows, the roots of the vine, so to speak, upon which we so stubbornly and beautifully bloom. They are our Queens of the Damned.

Then there is Jesse Reeves, a twentieth-century fledgling made by Maharet, the very eldest and therefore a dazzling monster, unknown to me, but greatly admired. Bringing with her into the world of the Undead an incomparable education in history, the paranormal, philosophy and languages, she is the unknown. Will the fire consume her, as it has so many others who, weary of life, cannot accept immortality? Or will her twentieth-century wit give her some radical and indestructible armor for the inconceivable changes that we now know must lie ahead?

Ah, there are others. There are wanderers. I can hear their voices from time to time in the night. There are those far away who know nothing of our traditions and

375

have styled us, in hostility to our writings and in amusement at our antics, 'The Coven of the Articulate,' strange 'unregistered' beings of various ages, strengths, attitudes, who sometimes seeing on a paperback rack a copy of *The Vampire Lestat* tear it loose and grind the small book to powder within their powerful and scornful hands.

They may lend their wisdom or their wit to our unfolding chronicle in some unpredictable future. Who knows?

For now, there is but one more player who must be described before my tale can be advanced.

That one is you, David Talbot, whom I scarcely know, you, who write with furious speed all the words that come slowly tumbling from me as I watch you, mesmerized on some level by the mere fact that these sentiments so long allowed to burn inside of me are now recorded on the seemingly eternal page.

What are you, David Talbot – over seven decades old in mortal education, a scholar, a deep and loving soul? How can one tell? That which you were in life, wise in years, strengthened by routine calamity and deepened by the full four seasons of a man's span upon the Earth, was transported with all memory and learning intact into the splendid body of a younger man. And then that body, a precious chalice for the Grail of your very self, who knew so well the value of both elements, was then assaulted by your closest of friends, the loving monster, the vampire who would have you as his fellow traveler in eternity whether or not you gave him leave, our beloved Lestat.

I cannot imagine such a rape. I stand too far from all humanity, never having been a full man. In your face I see the vigor and beauty of the dark golden-skinned Anglo-Hindi whose body you enjoy, and in your eyes the calm and dangerously well-tempered soul of the old man.

Your hair is black and soft and handily trimmed below your ears. You dress with high vanity submitted to a staunch British sense of style. You look at me as though your curiosity will put me off guard, when nothing of the sort is true.

Hurt me and I'll destroy you. I don't care how strong you are, or what blood Lestat gave you. I know more than you do. Because I show you my pain, I do not of necessity love you. I do this for myself and for others, for the very idea of others, for any who would know, and for my mortals, those two I've gathered to me so recently, those two precious ones who have become the ticking clock of my capacity to go on.

Symphony for Sybelle. That might as well be the name of this confession. And having done my best for Sybelle, I do my best for you as well.

Is this not enough of the past? Is this not enough prologue to the moment in New York when I saw Christ's Face in the Veil? There begins the final chapter of my life of late. There is nothing more to it. You have all the rest, and what must needs come now is but the brief harrowing account of what has brought me here.

Be my friend, David. I didn't mean to say such terrible things to you. My heart aches. I need you just to tell me that I may rush on. Help me with your experience. Isn't this enough? May I go on? I want to hear Sybelle's music. I want to talk of beloved rescuers. I can't measure the proportions of this story. I only know I am ready . . . I have reached the far side of the Bridge of Sighs.

Ah, but it's my decision, yes, and you wait to write what I will say.

Well, let me go now to the Veil.

Let me go now to the Face of Christ, as if I were walking uphill in the long-ago snowy winter in Podil, beneath the broken towers of Vladimir's City, to seek within the Monastery of the Caves the paint and the wood on which to see it take form before me: His Face. Christ, yes, the Redeemer, the Living Lord once more.

PART III

APPASSIONATA

I didn't want to go to him. It was winter, and I was contented in London, haunting the theatres to see the plays of Shakespeare, and reading the plays and the sonnets the whole night long. I had no other thoughts just now but Shakespeare. Lestat had given him to me. And when I'd had a bellyful of despair, I'd opened the books and begun to read.

But Lestat was calling. Lestat was, or so he claimed, afraid.

I had to go. The last time he'd been in trouble, I hadn't been free to rush to his rescue. There is a story to that, but nothing as important as this one which I tell now.

Now I knew that my hard-won peace of mind might be shattered by the mere contact with him, but he wanted me to come, so I went.

I found him first in New York, though he didn't know it and he couldn't have led me into a worse snowstorm if he'd tried. He slew a mortal that night, a victim with whom he'd fallen in love, as was his custom of late – to pick these celebrities of high crimes and horrid murders – and to stalk them before the night of the feast.

So what did he want of me, I wondered. You were there, David. You could help him. Or so it seemed. Being his fledgling you hadn't heard his call directly, but he'd reached you somehow, and the two of you, such proper gentlemen, came together to discuss in low, sophisticated whispers Lestat's latest fears.

When next I caught up with him he was in New

Orleans. And he put it to me plain and simple. You were there. The Devil had come to him in the guise of a man. The Devil could change shapes, being at one moment horrific and ghastly with webbed wings and hoofed feet; and then next, the Devil could be an ordinary man. Lestat was wild with these stories. The Devil had offered him a dreadful proposition, that he, Lestat, become the Devil's helper in the service of God.

Do you remember how calmly I responded to his story, his questions, his pleading for our advice? Oh, I told him firmly it was madness to follow this spirit, to believe that any discarnate thing was bound to tell him the truth.

But only now do you know the wounds he opened with this strange and marvelous fable. So the Devil would make him a hellish helper and thereby a servant of God? I might have laughed outright, or wept, throwing it in his face that I had once believed myself a saint of evil, shivering in rags as I stalked my victims in the Parisian winter, all for the honor and glory of God.

But he knew all this. There was no need to wound him further, to shift from him the limelight of his own tale, which Lestat, being the bright star, must always have.

Under moss-hung oaks we talked in civilized voices. You and I begged him to be cautious. Naturally, he ignored all we said.

It was all mixed up with the entrancing mortal Dora, who was living then in this very building, this old brick convent, the daughter of the man Lestat had stalked and slain.

When he bound us to look out for her, I was angry, but only mildly so. I have fallen in love with mortals. I have those tales to tell. I am in love now with Sybelle and Benjamin, whom I call my children, and I had been a secret troubadour to other mortals in the dim past.

All right, he was in love with Dora, he'd laid his head on a mortal breast, he wanted the womb blood of her that would be no loss to her, he was smitten, crazed, goaded by the ghost of her Father and courted by the Prince of Evil Himself.

And she, what shall I say of her? That she possessed the power of a Rasputin behind the face of a nunnery postulant, when in fact she is a practiced theologian and not a mystic, a ranting raving leader, not a visionary, whose ecclesiastical ambitions would have dwarfed those of Saints Peter and Paul put together, and that of course, she is like any flower Lestat ever gathered from the Savage Garden of this world: a most fine and fetching little creature, a glorious specimen of God's Creation – with raven hair, a pouty mouth, cheeks of porcelain and the dashing limbs of a nymph.

Of course I knew the very moment that he left this world. I felt it. I was in New York already, very near to him and aware that you were there as well. Neither of us meant to let him out of our sight if at all possible. Then came the moment when he vanished in the blizzard, when he was sucked out of the earthly atmosphere as if he'd never been there.

Being his fledgling you couldn't hear the perfect silence that descended when he vanished. You couldn't know how completely he'd been withdrawn from all things minuscule yet material which had once echoed with the beating of his heart.

I knew, and I think it was to distract us both that I proposed we go to the wounded mortal who must have been shattered by her Father's death at the hands of a blond-haired handsome blood-swilling monster who'd made her his confidant and a friend.

It was not difficult to help her in the short event-filled

nights that followed, when horror was heaped upon horror, her Father's murder discovered, his sordid life at once made by media magic the madcap conversation of the wide world.

It seems a century ago, not merely so short a time, that we moved south to these rooms, her father's legacy of crucifixes and statues, of ikons which I handled so coolly as if I'd never loved such treasures at all.

It seems a century ago that I dressed decently for her, finding in some fashionable Fifth Avenue shop a shapely coat of old red velvet, a poet's shirt, as they call it now, of starched cotton and ample flopping lace, and to set this off, pegged-leg trousers of black wool and shiny boots that buckled at the ankle, all this the better to accompany her to identify her Father's severed head under the leeching fluorescent lights of some immense and overcrowded morgue.

One good thing about this final decade of the twentieth century is that a man of any age can wear his hair at any length.

It seems a century ago that I combed out mine, full and curly and clean for once, just for her.

It seems a century ago we stood so staunchly beside her, indeed even held her, this long-necked, short-haired, spellbinding witchlet, in our very arms as she wept over the death of her Father and pelted us with feverish and maniacally intelligent and dispassionate questions about our sinister nature, as if a great crash course in the anatomy of the vampire could somehow close the cycle of horror threatening her wholesomeness and her sanity and somehow bring her wicked conscienceless Father back.

No, it wasn't the return of Roger, actually, that she prayed for; she believed too totally in the omniscience and mercy of God. Besides, seeing a man's severed head is a bit of a shock, even if the head is frozen, and a dog had chomped on Roger a bit before he'd been discovered, and what with the strict 'no touch' rules of modern forensics, he was – for me even – quite a sight. (I remember the coroner's assistant saying soulfully to me that I was awfully young to have to see such a thing. She thought I was Dora's little brother. What a sweet woman she was. Perhaps it's worth it to make a foray into the official mortal world once in a while in order to be called 'a real trouper' instead of a Botticelli angel, which has become my tag line among the Undead.)

It was the return of Lestat Dora dreamed of. What else would ever allow her to break free of our enchantment but some final blessing from the crowned prince himself?

I stood at the dark glass windows of the high-rise apartment, looking out over the deep snows of Fifth Avenue, waiting and praying with her, wishing the great Earth were not so empty of my old enemy and thinking in my foolish heart that in time this mystery of his disappearance would be resolved, as were all miracles, with sadness and small losses, with no more than little revelations that would leave me as I had always been left since that long-ago night in Venice when my Master and I were divided forever, simply a little more clever at pretending that I was still alive.

I didn't fear for Lestat, not really. I had no hopes for his adventure, except that he would appear sooner or later and tell us some fantastical yarn. It would be regular Lestat talk, for nobody aggrandizes as he does his preposterous adventures. This is not to say that he hasn't switched bodies with a human. I know that he has. This is not to say that he didn't wake our fearsome goddess Mother, Akasha; I know that he did. This is not to say that he didn't smash my old superstitious Coven to bits and pieces in the garish years before the French Revolution. I've already told you so.

But it's the way he describes things that happen to him that maddens me, the way that he connects one incident to another as though all these random and grisly occurrences were in fact links in some significant chain. They are not. They are capers. And he knows it. But he must make a gutter theatrical out of stubbing his toe.

The James Bond of the Vampires, the Sam Spade of his own pages! A rock singer wailing on a mortal stage for all of two hours and, on the strength of that, retiring with a slew of recordings that feed him filthy lucre still from human agencies to this very night.

He has a knack for making tragedy of tribulation, and forgiving himself for anything and everything in every confessional paragraph he pens.

I can't fault him, really. I cannot help but hate it that he lies now in a coma on the floor of his chapel here, staring into a self-contained silence, despite the fledglings that circle him – for precisely the same reason as I did, to see for themselves if the blood of Christ has transformed him somehow and he does not represent some magnificent manifestation of the miracle of the Transubstantiation. But I'll come to that soon enough.

I've ranted myself into a little corner. I know why I resent him so, and find it so soothing to hammer at his reputation, to beat upon his immensity with both my fists.

He has taught me too much. He has brought me to this very moment, here, where I stand dictating to you my past with a coherence and calm that would have been impossible before I came to his assistance with his precious Memnoch the Devil and his vulnerable little Dora.

386

Two hundred years ago he stripped me of illusions, lies, excuses, and thrust me on the Paris pavements naked to find my way back to a glory in the starlight that I had once known and too painfully lost.

But as we waited finally in the handsome high-rise apartment above St. Patrick's Cathedral, I had no idea how much more he could strip from me, and I hate him only because I cannot imagine my soul without him now, and, owing him all that I am and know, I can do nothing to make him wake from his frigid sleep.

But let me take things one at a time. What good is it to go back down now to the chapel here and lay my hands on him again and beg him to listen to me, when he lies as though all sense has truly left him and will never return.

I can't accept this. I won't. I've lost all patience; I've lost the numbness that was my consolation. I find this moment intolerable—.

But I have to tell you things.

I have to tell you what happened when I saw the Veil, and when the sun struck me and, more wretchedly for me, what I saw when finally I reached Lestat and drew so close to him that I could drink his blood.

Yes, stay on course. I know now why he makes the chain. It isn't pride, is it? It's the necessity. The tale can't be told without one link being connected to the other, and we poor orphans of ticking time know no other means of measure but those of sequence. Dropped into the snowy blackness, into a world worse than a void, I reached for a chain, did I not? Oh, God, what I would have given in that awful descent to grasp the firmness of a metal chain!

He came back so suddenly – to you and Dora and me.

It was the third morning, and not long enough before

dawn. I heard the doors slam far below us in the glass tower, and then that sound, that sound which gains in eerie volume each year, the beating of his heart.

Who was first to rise from the table? I was still with fear. He came too fast, and there were those wild fragrances whirling about him, of woodland and raw earth. He crashed through all barriers as if he were pursued by those who'd stolen him away, and yet there was no one behind him. He came alone into the apartment, slamming the door in his wake and then standing before us, more horrible than I could ever have imagined, more ruined than I had ever seen him in any of his former little defeats.

With absolute love Dora ran to him, and in a desperate need that was all too human he clutched at her so fiercely that I thought he would destroy her.

'You're safe now, darling,' she cried, struggling so as to make him understand.

But we had only to look at him to know it wasn't finished, though we murmured the same hollow words in the face of what we beheld.

He had come from the maelstrom. One shoe was left to him, the other foot bare, his coat torn, his hair wild and snagged with thorns and dried leaves and bits of errant flowers.

In his arms, to his chest he clutched a flat bundle of folded cloth as if it carried the whole fate of the world embroidered on it.

But the worst, the very worst horror of all, was that one eye had been torn from his beautiful face, and the socket of vampiric lids puckered and shuddered, seeking to close, refusing to acknowledge this horrid disfigurement to the body rendered perfect for all time when he'd been made immortal.

I wanted to take him in my arms. I wanted to comfort him, to tell him wherever he'd gone and whatever had taken place, he was now safe again with us, but nothing could quiet him.

A deep exhaustion saved us all from the inevitable tale. We had to seek our dark corners away from the prying sun, we had to wait until the following night when he would come out to us and tell us what had happened.

Still clutching the bundle, refusing all help, he closeted himself up with his wound. I had no choice but to leave him.

As I sank down that morning into my own resting place, secure in clean modern darkness, I cried and cried like a child on account of the sight of him. Oh, why had I come to his aid? Why must I see him brought low like this when it had taken so many painful decades to cement my love for him forever?

Once before, a hundred years ago, he'd come stumbling into the Théâtre des Vampires on the trail of his renegade fledglings, sweet gentle Louis and the doomed child, and I hadn't pitied him then, his skin scored with scars from Claudia's foolish and clumsy attempt to kill him.

Loved him then, yes, I had, but this had been a bodily disaster which his evil blood would heal, and I knew from our old lore that in the healing he would gain even greater strength than serene time itself would have given him.

But what I'd seen now was a devastation of the soul in his anguished face, and the vision of the one blue eye, shining so vividly in his streaked and wretched face, had been unbearable.

I don't remember that we spoke, David. I remember only that the morning hastened us away, and if you cried too, I never heard you, I never thought to listen. As for the bundle he had carried in his arms, what could it have possibly been? I do not even think I thought of it.

The next night:

He came quietly into the parlor of the apartment as the darkness clambered down, starry for a few precious moments before the dreary descent of snow. He was washed and dressed, his torn and bleeding foot no doubt healed. He wore new shoes.

But nothing could lessen the grotesque picture of his torn face where the cuts of a claw or fingernails surrounded the gaping, puckering lids. Quietly he sat down.

He looked at me, and a faint charming smile brightened his face. 'Don't fear for me, little devil Armand,' he said. 'Fear for all of us. I am nothing now. I am nothing.'

390

In a low voice I whispered to him my plan. 'Let me go down into the streets, let me steal from some mortal, some evil being who has wasted every physical gift that God ever gave, an eye for you! Let me put it here in the empty socket. Your blood will rush into it and make it see. You know. You saw this miracle once with the ancient one, Maharet, indeed, with a pair of mortal eyes swimming in her special blood, eyes that could see! I'll do it. It won't take me but a moment, and then I'll have the eye in my hand and be the doctor myself and place it here. Please.'

He only shook his head. He kissed me quickly on the cheek.

'Why do you love me after all I've done to you?' he asked. There was no denying the beauty of his smooth poreless sun-darkened skin, and even as the dark slit of the empty socket seemed to peer at me with some secret power to relay its vision to his heart. He was handsome and radiant, a darkish ruddy glow coming from his face as though he'd seen some powerful mystery.

'Yes, but I have,' he said, and now began to cry. 'I have, and I must tell you everything. Believe me, as you believe what you saw last night, the wildflowers clinging still to my hair, the cuts – look, my hands, they heal but not fast enough – believe me.'

You intervened then, David. 'Tell us, Lestat. We would have waited here forever for you. Tell us. Where did this demon Memnoch take you?' How comforting and reasonable your voice sounded, just as it does now. I think you were made for this, for reasoning, and given to us, if I may speculate, to force us to see our catastrophes in the new light of modern conscience. But we can talk of those things for many nights hereafter.

Let me return to the scene, the three of us gathered in the black-lacquered Chinese chairs around the thick

391

glass table, and Dora coming in, at once struck by the presence of him, of which her mortal senses hadn't given her a clue, a pretty picture with her short gleaming knavish black hair, cut high to show the fragile nape of her swanlike neck, her long supple body clad in a loose ungirdled gown of purple red tissue that folded itself about her small breasts and slender thighs exquisitely. Ah, what an angel of the Lord, this, I thought musing, this heiress of the druglord Father's severed head. She teaches doctrines with every step that would make the pagan gods of lust canonize her with glee.

About her pale sweet throat she wore a crucifix so tiny it seemed a gilded gnat suspended from a weightless chain of minuscule links woven by fairies. What are such holy objects now, tumbling on milky bosoms with such ease, but trinkets of the marketplace? My thoughts were merciless, but I was but an indifferent cataloger of her beauty. Her swelling breasts, their shadowy cleft quite visible against the simple stitching of her dark low-cut dress, told more of God and Divinity.

But her greatest adornment in these moments was the tearful and eager love for him, her lack of fear of his mutilated face, the grace of her white arms as she enclosed him again, so sure of herself and so grateful for the gentle yielding of his body in towards her. I was so thankful that she loved him.

'So the Prince of Lies had a tale to tell, did he?' she asked. She could not kill the quaver in her voice. 'So he's taken you to his Hell and sent you back?' She took Lestat's face in her hands and turned it towards her. 'Then tell us what it was, this Hell, tell us why we must be afraid. Tell us why you are afraid, but I think it's something far worse than fear that I see now in you.'

He nodded his head to say that it was. He pushed

back the Chinese chair, and wringing his hands he began to pace, the inevitable prelude to his tale telling.

'Listen to all I say, before you judge,' he declared, fixing us now, the three who crowded about the table, an anxious little audience willing to do whatever he asked of us. His eyes lingered on you, David, you, the English scholar in your manly tweed, who in spite of love abundantly clear beheld him with a critical eye, ready to evaluate his words with a wisdom natural to you.

He began to talk. Hour by hour he talked. Hour by hour the words streamed out of him, heated and rushing and sometimes tumbling over one another so that he had to stop and catch his breath, but he never really paused, as he poured it out over the long night, this tale of his adventure.

Yes, Memnoch the Devil had taken him to Hell, but it was a Hell of Memnoch's devising, a Purgatorial place in which the souls of all who had ever lived were welcome to come of their own accord from the whirlwind of death which had inherited them. And in that Purgatorial Hell, confronted with all the deeds they'd ever done, they learnt the most hideous lesson of all, the endless consequences of every action ever committed by them. Murderer and Mother alike, vagrant children slaughtered in seeming innocence and soldiers bathed in blood from battlefields, all were admitted to this awful place of smoke and sulfurous fire, but only to see the gaping wounds in others made by their wrathful or unwitting hands, to plumb the depths of other souls and hearts which they had injured!

All horror was an illusion in this place, but the worst horror of all was the person of God Incarnate, who had allowed this Final School for those who would be worthy to enter His Paradise. And this too Lestat had seen, the Heaven glimpsed a million times by saints and deathbed victims, of ever blooming trees and flowers eternally sweet and endless crystal towers of happy, happy beings, shorn of all flesh and one at last with countless choirs of singing angels.

It was an old tale. It was too old. It had been told too many times, this tale – of Heaven with her open gates, and God Our Maker sending forth His endless light to those who climbed the mythic stairs to join the celestial court forever.

How many mortals waking from a near death sleep have struggled to describe these same wonders!

How many saints have claimed to have glimpsed this indescribable and eternal Eden?

And how cleverly this Devil Memnoch had laid out his case to plead for mortal compassion for his sin, that he and he alone had opposed a merciless and indifferent God, to beg that Deity to look down with compassionate eyes on a fleshly race of beings who had by means of their own selfless love managed to engender souls worthy of His interest?

This, then, was the fall of Lucifer like the Star of Morning from the sky – an angel begging for the Sons and Daughters of Men that they had now the countenances and hearts of angels.

'Give them Paradise, Lord, give it to them when they have learnt in my school how to love all that you have created.'

Oh, a book has been filled with this adventure. *Memnoch the Devil* cannot be condensed here in these few unjust paragraphs.

But this was the sum of what fell on my ears as I sat in this chilly New York room, gazing now and then past Lestat's frantic, pacing figure at the white sky of ever falling snow, shutting out beneath his roaring narrative the rumble of the city far below, and struggling with the awful fear in myself that I must at the climax of his tale disappoint him. That I must remind him that he had done no more than shape the mystic journey of a thousand saints in a new and palatable fashion.

So it is a school that replaces those rings of eternal fire which the poet Dante described in such degree as to sicken the reader, and even the tender Fra Angelico felt compelled to paint, where naked mortals bathed in flame were meant to suffer for eternity.

A school, a place of hope, a promise of redemption great enough perhaps to welcome even us, the Children of the Night, who counted murders among their sins as numerous as those of ancient Huns or Mongols.

Oh, this was very sweet, this picture of the life hereafter, the horrors of the natural world laid off upon a wise but distant God, and the Devil's folly rendered with such keen intelligence.

Would that it were true, would that all the poems and paintings of the world were but a mirror of such hopeful splendor.

It might have saddened me; it might have broken me down to where I hung my head and couldn't look at him.

But a single incident from his tale, one which to him had been a passing encounter, loomed large for me beyond all the rest and locked itself to my thoughts, so that as he went on and on, I couldn't banish this from my mind: that he, Lestat, had drunk the very blood of Christ on the road to Calvary. That he, Lestat, had spoken to this God Incarnate, who by His own will had walked towards this horrible Death on Golgotha. That he, Lestat, a fearful and trembling witness had been made to stand in the narrow dusty streets of ancient Jerusalem to see Our Lord pass, and that this Lord, Our

Living Lord, had, with the crossbeam of the crucifix strapped to His shoulders, offered His throat to Lestat, the chosen pupil.

Ah, such fancy, this madness, such fancy. I had not expected to be so hurt by anything in this tale. I had not expected this to make a burning in my chest, a tightness in my throat from which no words could escape. I had not wanted this. The only salvation of my wounded heart was to think how quaint and foolish it was that such a tableau – Jerusalem, the dusty street, the angry crowds, the bleeding God, now scourged and limping beneath His wooden weight – should include a legend old and sweet of a woman with a Veil outstretched to wipe the bloody Face of Christ in comfort, and thereby to receive for all time His Image.

It does not take a scholar, David, to know such saints were made by other saints in centuries to come as actors and actresses chosen for a Passion Play in a country village. Veronica! Veronica, whose very name means True Ikon.

And our hero, our Lestat, our Prometheus, with that Veil given him by the very hand of God, had fled this great and ghastly realm of Heaven and Hell and the Stations of the Cross, crying No! and I will not! and come back, breathless, running like a madman through the snows of New York, seeking only to be with us, turning his back on all of it.

My head swam. There was a war inside of me. I couldn't look at him.

On and on he went, going over it, talking again of the sapphiric Heavens and the angels' song, arguing with himself and with you and with Dora, and the conversation seemed like so much shattered glass. I couldn't bear it.

The Blood of Christ inside him? The Blood of Christ

passing his lips, his unclean lips, his Undead lips, the Blood of Christ making of him a monstrous Ciborium? The Blood of Christ?

'Let me drink!' I cried out suddenly. 'Lestat, let me drink, from you, let me drink your blood that has His blood inside it!' I couldn't believe my own earnestness, my own wild desperation. 'Lestat, let me drink. Let me look for the blood with my tongue and my heart. Let me drink, please; you can't deny me that one moment of intimacy. And if it was Christ . . . if it was . . .' I couldn't finish it.

'Oh, mad and foolish child,' he said. 'All you'll know if you sink your teeth into me is what we learn from the visions we see with all our victims. You'll learn what I think I saw. You'll learn what I think was made known to me. You'll learn that my blood runs in my veins, which you know now. You'll learn that I believe it was Christ, but no more than that.'

He shook his head in disappointment as he glared at me.

'No, I'll know,' I said. I rose from the table, my hands quivering. 'Lestat, give me this one embrace and I'll never ask another thing of you for all eternity. Let me put my lips to your throat, Lestat, let me test the tale, let me do it!'

'You break my heart, you little fool,' he said with tears welling. 'You always did.'

'Don't judge me!' I cried.

He went on, speaking to me alone, from his mind as much as with his voice. I couldn't tell if anyone else there could even hear him. But I heard him. I would not forget a single word.

'And what if it was the Blood of God, Armand,' he asked, 'and not part and parcel of some titanic lie, what would you find in me? Go out to the early morning

Mass and snatch your victims from those just come from the Communion Rail! What a pretty game that would be, Armand, to feed forever only on Holy Communicants! You can have your Blood of Christ from any one of them. I tell you, I do not believe these spirits, God, Memnoch, these liars; I tell you, I refuse! I wouldn't stay, I fled their damned school, I lost my eye as I battled them, they snatched it from me, wicked angels clawing at me when I ran away from them! You want the Blood of Christ, then go down now in the dark church to the fisherman's Mass and knock the sleepy priest aside from the Altar, if you will, and grab the Chalice from his consecrated hands. Go ahead, do it!

'Blood of Christ!' he continued, his face one great eye fixing me in its merciless beam. 'If it was ever in me, this sacred blood, then my body has dissolved it and burnt it up like candle wax devours the wick. You know this. What's left of Christ in the belly of His faithful when they leave the church?'

'No,' I said. 'No, but we are not humans!' I whispered, seeking somehow in softness to drown out his angry vehemence. 'Lestat, I'll know! It was His blood, not transubstantiated bread and wine! His blood, Lestat, and I'll know if it's inside of you. Oh, let me drink, I beg you. Let me drink so I can forget every damned thing you've told us, let me drink!'

I could scarcely keep myself from laying hands on him, from forcing him to my will, never mind his legendary strength, his gruesome temper. I'd lay hold of him and make him submit. I'd take the blood –.

But these thoughts were foolish and vain. His whole tale was foolish and vain, and yet I turned around, and in a fury I spit the words at him:

'Why didn't you accept? Why didn't you go with Memnoch if he could have taken you from this awful living Hell we share, why didn't you?'

'They let you escape,' you said to him, David. You broke in, quieting me with a small pleading gesture of your left hand.

But I had no patience for analysis or inevitable interpretation. I couldn't get the image out of my mind, Our Bloody Lord, Our Lord with the crossbeam bound to His shoulders, and she, Veronica, this sweet figment with the Veil in her hands. Oh, how is it such a fantasy could get its hook so deep?

'Back away from me, all of you,' he cried. 'I have the Veil. I told you. Christ gave it to me. Veronica gave it to me. I took it with me out of Memnoch's Hell, when all his imps tried to take it from me.'

I scarcely heard. Veil, the actual Veil, what trick is this? My head ached. The fisherman's Mass. If there was such a thing in St. Patrick's below, I wanted to go there. I was weary of this glass-walled tower room, cut off from the taste of the wind and the wild refreshing wetness of the snow.

Why did Lestat back up against the wall? What did he take out of his coat? The Veil! Some gaudy trick to seal this whole masterpiece of mayhem?

I looked up, my eyes roaming over the snowy night beyond the glass and only slowly finding their mark: the opened cloth which he held up in his hands, his own head bowed, the cloth revealed as reverently as it might have been by Veronica.

'My Lord!' I whispered. All the world was gone in curls of weightless sound and light. I saw Him there. 'My Lord.' I saw His Face, not painted, printed or otherwise daintily tricked into the tiny fibers of the fine white cloth, but blazing with a flame that would not consume the vehicle that bore the heat of it. My Lord, my Lord the Man, my Lord, my Christ, the Man with black and sharpened crown of thorns, and long twisted brown hair so fearfully clotted with blood, and great wondering dark eyes that stared straight at me, the sweet and vivid portals of the Soul of God, so radiant their immeasurable love that all poetry dies before it, and a soft and silken mouth of unquestioning and unjudging simplicity, open to take a silent and agonizing breath at the very moment the Veil had come to soothe this hideous suffering.

I wept. I clamped my hand to my mouth, but I couldn't stop my words.

'Oh, Christ, my tragic Christ!' I whispered. 'Not made by human hands!' I cried out. 'Not made by human hands!' How wretched my words, how feeble, how filled with sorrow. 'This Man's Face, this Face of God and Man. He bleeds. For the love of Almighty God, look at it!'

But not a sound had come from me. I couldn't move. I couldn't breathe. I'd fallen down on my knees in my shock and in my helplessness. I never wanted to take my eyes from it. I never wanted anything anymore again ever. I wanted only to look at it. I wanted only to look at Him, and I saw Him, and I saw back, back over the centuries, back to His Face in the light of the earthen lamp burning in the house in Podil, His Face gazing at me from the panel between my quivering fingers amid the candles of the Scriptorium of the Monastery of the Caves, His Face as I had never seen it on those glorious walls of Venice or Florence where I had for so long and so desperately sought it.

His Face, His manly Face infused with the Divine, my tragic Lord gazing at me from my Mother's arms in the frozen sludge of the long-ago street of Podil, my loving Lord in bloody Majesty.

I didn't care what Dora said.

I didn't care that she screamed His Holy Name. I didn't care. I knew.

.And as she declared her faith, as she snatched the Veil from Lestat's very hands and ran with it out of this apartment, I followed, moving after her and after the Veil – though in the sanctuary of my heart I never moved.

I never stirred.

A great stillness had overtaken my mind, and my limbs no longer mattered.

It did not matter that Lestat fought with her, and cautioned her that she must not believe this thing, and that the three of us stood on the steps of the Cathedral and that the snow fell like some splendid blessing from the invisible and fathomless Heavens.

It did not matter that the sun was soon to rise, a fiery silver ball beyond the canopy of melting clouds.

I could die now.

I had seen Him, and all the rest – the words of Memnoch and his fanciful God, the pleas of Lestat that we come away, that we hide ourselves before the morning devoured us all – it did not matter.

I could die now.

'Not made by human hands,' I whispered.

A crowd gathered around us at the doors. The warm air came out of the church in a deep delicious gust. It didn't matter.

'The Veil, the Veil,' they cried. They saw! They saw His Face.

Lestat's desperate imploring cries were dying away.

The morning came down in its thunderous white-hot light, rolling over roofs and curdling the night in a thousand glassy walls and slowly unleashing its monstrous glory.

'Bear witness,' I said. I held up my open arms to the

401

blinding light, this molten silvery death. 'This sinner dies for Him! This sinner goes to Him.'

Cast me into Hell, Oh Lord, if that is Your will. You have given me Heaven. You have shown me Your Face. And Your Face was human.

I shot upwards. The pain I felt was total, scalding away all will or power to choose momentum. An explosion inside me sent me skyward, right into the pearly snowy light which had come in a sudden flood, as it always does, from a threatening eye one moment, sending its endless rays over the cityscape, to a tidal wave of weightless molten illumination, rolling over all things great and small.

Higher and higher I went, spinning as if the force of the interior explosion would not stop its intensity, and in my horror I saw that my clothes had been burnt away, and a smoke veered off my limbs into the whirling wind.

I caught one full glimpse of my limbs, my naked outstretched arms and splayed legs, silhouetted against the obliterating light. My flesh was burnt black already, shiny, sealed to the sinews of my body, collapsed to the intricate tangle of muscles which encased my bones.

The pain reached the zenith of what I could bear, but how can I explain that it didn't matter to me; I was on the way to my own death, and this seemingly endless torture was nothing, nothing. I could endure all things, even the burning in the eyes, the knowledge that they would soon melt or explode in this furnace of sunlight, and that all that I was would pass out of flesh.

Abruptly the scene changed. The roar of the wind was gone, my eyes were quiet and focused, and all around there arose a great familiar chorus of hymns. I stood at an altar, and as I looked up I beheld a church before me thronged with people, its painted columns rising like so many ornate tree trunks out of the wilderness of singing mouths and wondering eyes. Everywhere, to right and to left, I saw this immense and endless congregation. The church had no walls to bind it, and even the rising domes, decorated in the purest and most glittering gold with the hammered saints and angels, gave way to the great ever thinning and never ending blue sky.

Incense filled my nostrils. Around me, the tiny golden bells rang in unison, and with one riff of delicate melody tumbling fast upon another. The smoke burnt my eyes but so sweetly, as the fragrance of the incense filled my nostrils and made my eyes water, and my vision become one with all I tasted and touched and heard.

I threw out my arms, and I saw long golden-trimmed white sleeves covering them, falling back from wrists which were covered with the soft fleecy down of a man's natural hair. These were my hands, yes, but my hands years past the mortal point where life had been fixed in me. They were the hands of a man.

Out of my mouth there came a song, echoing loudly and singly over the congregation, and then their voices rose in answer, and once again I intoned my conviction, the conviction that had overcome me to the marrow of my bones:

'Christ is come. The Incarnation is begun in all things and in all men and women, and will go on forever!' It seemed a song of such perfection that the tears flowed from me, and as I bowed my head and clasped my hands I looked down to see the bread and the wine in front of me, the rounded loaf waiting to be blessed and broken and the wine in the golden chalice there to be transformed.

'This is the Body of Christ, and this is Blood shed for us now and before and forever, and in every moment of which we are alive!' I sang out. I laid my hands on the loaf and lifted it, and a great stream of light poured forth out of it, and the congregation gave forth their sweetest loudest hymn of praise.

In my hands I held the chalice. I held it high as the bells pealed from the towers, towers and towers that crowded near the towers of this grand church, stretching for miles in all directions, the whole world having becoming this great and glorious wilderness of churches, and here beside me the little golden bells chimed.

Once again came the gusts of incense. Setting down the chalice I looked at the sea of faces stretching before me. I turned my head from left to right, and then I looked Heavenward at the disappearing mosaics which became one with the rising, roiling white clouds.

I saw gold domes beneath Heaven.

I saw the endless rooftops of Podil.

I knew it was Vladimir's City in all its glory, and that I stood in the great sanctuary of Santa Sofia, all screens having been taken away that would have divided me from the people, and all those other churches which had been but ruins in my long-ago dim childhood were now restored to magnificence, and the golden domes of Kiev drank the light of the sun and gave it back with the power of a million planets basking eternal in the fire of a million stars.

'My Lord, my God!' I cried out. I looked down at the embroidered splendor of my vestments, the green satin and its threads of pure metallic gold.

On either side of me stood my brothers in Christ, bearded, eyes glowing as they assisted me, as they sang the hymns which I sang, as our voices mingled, pressing on from anthem to anthem in notes that I could almost see rising before me to the airy firmament above.

405

'Give it to them! Give it to them because they are hungry,' I cried. I broke the loaf of bread in my hands. I broke it into halves, and then into quarters, and tore these hastily into small morsels which crowded the shining golden plate.

En masse, the congregation mounted the steps, tender pink little hands reaching for the morsels, which I gave out as fast as I could, morsel after morsel, not a crumb spilling, the bread divided among dozens, and then scores, and then hundreds, as they pressed forward, the newcomers barely allowing those who had been fed to make their way back.

On and on they came. But the hymns did not cease. Voices, muted at the altar, silenced as the bread was devoured, soon burst forth loud and jubilant again.

The bread was eternal.

I tore its soft thick crust again and again and put it into the outstretched palms, the gracefully cupped fingers.

'Take it, take the Body of Christ!' I said.

Dark wavering shadowy forms rose around me, rising up out of the gleaming gold and silver floor. They were trunks of trees, and their limbs arched upward and then down towards me, and leaves and berries fell from these branches, down onto the altar, onto the golden plate and onto the sacred bread now in a great mass of fragments.

'Gather them up!' I cried. I picked up the soft green leaves and the fragrant acorns and I gave these too to the eager hands. I looked down and I saw grain pouring through my fingers, grain which I offered to opened lips, grain which I poured into open mouths.

The air was thick with the soundless falling of the green leaves, so much so that the soft brilliant shade of green tinted all around it, broken suddenly everywhere by the flight of tiny birds. A million sparrows flushed Heavenward. A million finches soared, the brilliant sun flitting on their tiny outstretched wings.

'Forever, ongoing, always in every cell and every atom,' I prayed. 'The Incarnation,' I said. 'And the Lord has dwelt among us.' My words rang out again as if a roof covered us, a roof that could echo my song, though our roof was now the roofless sky alone.

The crowd pressed in. They surrounded the altar. My brothers had slipped away, thousands of hands tugging gently at their vestments, pulling them back from the table of God. All around me there pressed these hungry ones who took the bread as I gave it, who took the grain, who took the acorns by the handful, who took even the tender green leaves.

There stood my Mother beside me, my beautiful and sad-faced Mother, a fine embroidered headdress gracing her thick gray hair, with her wrinkled little eyes fastened on me, and in her trembling hands, her dried and fearful fingers, she held the most splendid of offerings, the painted eggs! Red and blue, and yellow and golden, and decorated with bands of diamonds and chains of the flowers of the field, the eggs shimmered in their lacquered splendor as if they were giant polished jewels.

And there in the very center of her offering, this offering which she held up with shivering wrinkled arms, there lay the very egg which she had once so long ago entrusted to me, the light, raw egg so gorgeously decorated in brilliant ruby red with the star of gold in the very center of the framed oval, this precious egg which had surely been her finest creation, the finest achievement of her hours with the burning wax and boiling dye.

It wasn't lost. It had never been lost. It was there. But

something was happening. I could hear it. Even under the great swelling song of the multitudes I could hear it, the tiny sound inside the egg, the tiny fluttering sound, the tiny cry.

'Mother,' I said. I took it. I held it in both hands and brought my thumbs down against the brittle shell.

'No, my son!' she cried. She wailed. 'No, no, my son, no!'

But it was too late. The lacquered shell was smashed beneath my thumbs and out of its fragments had risen a bird, a beautiful and full-grown bird, a bird of snow-white wings and tiny yellow beak and brilliant black eyes like bits of jet.

A long full sigh came out of me.

Out of the egg, it rose, unfolding its perfectly feathered white wings, its tiny beak open in a sudden shrill cry. Up it flew, this bird, freed of the broken red shell, up and up, over the heads of the congregation, and up through the soft swirling rain of the green leaves and fluttering sparrows, up through the glorious clamour of the pealing bells, it flew.

The bells of the towers rang out so loud that they shook the swirling leaves in the atmosphere, so loud that the soaring columns quivered, that the crowd rocked and sang all the more heartily as if to be in perfect unison with the great resounding golden-throated peals.

The bird was gone. The bird was free.

'Christ is born,' I whispered. 'Christ is risen. Christ is in Heaven and on Earth. Christ is with us.'

But no one could hear my voice, my private voice, and what did it matter, for all the world sung the same song?

A hand clutched me. Rudely, meanly, it tore at my white sleeve. I turned. I drew in my breath to scream and froze in terror.

A man, come out of nowhere, stood beside me, so close that our faces almost touched. He glared down at me. I knew his red hair and beard, his fierce and impious blue eyes. I knew he was my Father, but he was not my Father but some horrific and powerful presence infused into my Father's visage, and there, planted beside me, a colossus beside me, glaring down at me, mocking me by his power and his height.

He reached out and slammed the back of his hand against the golden chalice. It wobbled and fell, the consecrated wine staining the morsels of bread, staining the altar cloth of woven gold.

'But you can't!' I cried. 'Look what you've done!' Could nobody hear me over the singing? Could no one hear me above the peal of the bells?

I was alone.

I stood in a modern room. I stood beneath a white plaster ceiling. I stood in a domestic room.

I was myself, a smallish man figure with my old tousled shoulder-length curls and the purple-red coat of velvet and the ruff of layered white lace. I leant against the wall. Stunned and still, I leant there, knowing only that every particle of this place, every particle of me, was as solid and real as it had been a split second before.

The carpet beneath my feet was as real as the leaves which had fallen like snowflakes throughout the immense Cathedral of Santa Sofia, and my hands, my hairless boyish hands, were as real as the hands of the priest I'd been a moment before, who had broken the bread.

A terrible sob rose in my throat, a terrible cry that I myself could not bear to hear. My breath would stop if I didn't release it, and this body, damned or sacred, mortal or immortal, pure or corrupt, would surely burst.

But a music comforted me. A music slowly articulated

itself, clean and fine, and wholly unlike the great seamless and magnificent chorus which I had only just heard.

Out of the silence there leapt these perfectly formed and discrete notes, this multitude of cascading sounds that seemed to speak with crispness and directness, as if in beautiful defiance of the inundation of sound which I had so loved.

Oh, to think that ten fingers alone could draw these sounds from a wooden instrument in which the hammers, with a dogged rigid motion, would strike upon a bronze harp of tautly stretched strings.

I knew it, I knew this song, I knew the piano Sonata, and had loved it in passing, and now its fury paralyzed me. *Appassionata*. Up and down the notes rang in gorgeous throbbing arpeggios, thundering downward to rumble in a staccato drumming, only to rise and race again. On and on went the sprightly melody, eloquent, celebratory and utterly human, demanding to be felt as well as heard, demanding to be followed in every intricate twist and turn.

Appassionata.

In the furious torrent of notes, I heard the resounding echo of the wood of the piano; I heard the vibration of its giant taut bronze harp. I heard the sizzling throb of its multitudinous strings. Oh, yes, on, and on, and on, and on, and on, louder, harder, ever pure and ever perfect, ringing out and wrung back as if a note could be a whip. How can human hands make this enchantment, how can they pound out of these ivory keys this deluge, this thrashing, thundering beauty?

It stopped. So great was my agony I could only shut my eyes and moan, moan for the loss of those racing crystalline notes, moan for the loss of this pristine sharpness, this wordless sound that had nevertheless spoken to me, begged me to bear witness, begged me to share and understand another's intense and utterly demanding furor.

A scream jolted me. I opened my eyes. The room around me was large and jammed with rich and random contents, framed paintings to the ceiling, flowered carpets running rampant beneath the curly legs of modern chairs and tables, and there the piano, the great piano out of which had come this sound, shining in the very middle of this mayhem, with its long strip of grinning white keys, such a triumph of the heart, the soul, the mind.

Before me on the floor a boy knelt praying, an Arab boy of glossy close-cropped curls and a small perfectly fitted djellaba, that is, a cotton desert robe. His eyes were shut, his round little face pointed upwards, though he didn't see me, his black eyebrows knit and his lips moving frantically, the words tumbling in Arabic:

'Oh, come some demon, some angel and stop him, oh, come something out of the darkness I care not what, something of power and vengeance, I care not what, come, come out of the light and out of the will of the gods who won't stand to see the oppression of the wicked. Stop him before he kills my Sybelle. Stop him, this is Benjamin, son of Abdulla, who calls upon you, take my soul in forfeit, take my life, but come, come, that which is stronger than me and save my Sybelle.'

'Silence!' I shouted. I was out of breath. My face was wet. My lips were shuddering uncontrollably. 'What do you want, tell me?'

He looked at me. He saw me. His round little Byzantine face might have come wonder-struck from the church wall, but he was here and real and he saw me and I was what he wanted to see.

'Look, you angel!' he shouted, his youthful voice

411

sharpened with its Arab accent. 'Can't you see with your big beautiful eyes!'

I saw.

The whole reality of it came down at once. She, the young woman, Sybelle, was fighting to cling to the piano, not to be snatched off the bench, her hands out struggling to reach the keys, her mouth shut, and a terrible groan pushing up against her sealed lips, her yellow hair flying about her shoulders. And the man who shook her, who pulled at her, who screamed at her, suddenly dealing her one fine blow with his fist that sent her over backwards, falling off the piano bench so that a scream escaped from her and she fell over herself, an ungainly tangle of limbs on the carpeted floor.

'*Appassionata, Appassionata,*' he growled at her, a bear of a creature in his megalomaniacal temper. 'I won't listen to it, I will not, I will not, you will not do this to me, to my life. It's my life!' He roared like a bull. 'I won't let you go on!'

The boy leapt up and grabbed me. He clutched at my wrists and when I shook him off, staring at him in bafflement, he clutched my velvet cuffs.

'Stop him, angel. Stop him, devil! He cannot beat her anymore. He will kill her. Stop him, devil, stop him, she is good!'

She crawled to her knees, her hair a shredded veil concealing her face. A great smear of dried blood covered the side of her narrow waist, a stain sunk deep into the flowered fabric.

Incensed, I watched as the man withdrew. Tall, his head shaven, his eyes bulging, he put his hands to his ears, and he cursed her: 'Mad stupid bitch, mad mad selfish bitch. Do I have no life? Do I have no justice? Do I have no dreams?'

But she had flung her hands on the keys again. She

was racing right into the Second Movement of the *Appassionata* as though she had never been interrupted. Her hands beat on the keys. One furious volley of notes after another rose, as if written for no other purpose than to answer him, to defy him, as if to cry out, I will not stop, I will not stop—.

I saw what was to happen. He turned around and glared at her, but it was only to let the rage rise to its full power, his eyes wide, his mouth twisted in anguish. A lethal smile formed on his lips.

Back and forth she rocked on the piano bench, her hair flying, her face lifted, her mind having no need to see the keys she struck, to plot the course of her hands that raced from right to left, that never lost control of the torrent.

Out of her sealed lips there came a low humming, a grinding humming right in tune with the melodies that gushed from the keys. She arched her back and lowered her head, her hair falling down on the backs of her racing hands. On she went, on into thunder, on into certainty, on into refusal, on into defiance, on into affirmation, yes, yes, yes, yes, yes.

The man made his move for her.

The frantic boy, leaving me in desperation, darted to come between them, and the man slammed him aside with such fury that the boy was knocked flat and sprawling on the floor.

But before the man's hands could reach her shoulders, before he could so much as touch her – and she went now into the First Movement again, ah, ah aaaah! the *Appassionata* all over again in all its power – I had hold of him, and spun him round to face me.

'Kill her, will you?' I whispered. 'Well, we shall see.'

'Yes!' he cried out, face sweating, protuberant eyes glistening. 'Kill her! She's vexed me to utter madness, that's what she's done, and she'll die!' Too incensed even to question my presence, he tried to push me aside, his sights fixed already once again on her. 'Damn you, Sybelle, stop that music, stop it!'

Her melody and chords were in the mode of thunder again. Flinging her hair from side to side, she charged onward.

I forced him backwards, my left hand catching his shoulder, my right pushing his chin up out of my way as I nuzzled in against his throat, tore it open and let the blood come into my mouth. It was scalding and rich and full of his hatred, full of bitterness, full of his blasted dreams and vengeful fancies.

Oh, the heat of it. I took it in in deep draughts, seeing it all, how he had loved her, nourished her, she his talented sister, he the clever, vicious-tongued and tone-deaf brother, guiding her towards the pinnacle of his precious and refined universe, until a common tragedy had broken her ascent and left her mad, turning from him, from memory, from ambition, locked forever in mourning for the victims of that tragedy, their loving and applauding parents, struck down on a winding road through a dark and distant valley in the very nights before her greatest triumph, her debut as full-fledged genius of the piano for all the wide world.

I saw their car rattling and plummeting through the darkness. I heard the brother in the back seat chattering, his sister beside him fast asleep. I saw the car strike the other car. I saw the stars above in cruel and silent witness. I saw the bruised and lifeless bodies. I saw her stunned face as she stood unharmed, her clothes torn, by the side of the road. I heard him cry out in horror. I heard him curse in disbelief. I saw the broken glass. Broken glass everywhere glittering beautifully in the light of headlamps. I saw her eyes, her pale blue eyes. I saw her heart close.

My victim was dead. He slipped out of my grasp.

He was as lifeless as his parents had been in that hot desert place.

He was dead and crumpled and could never hurt her again, could never pull her long yellow hair, or beat her, or stop her as she played.

The room was sweetly still except for her playing. She had come again to the Third Movement, and she swayed gently with its quieter beginning, its polite and measured steps.

The boy danced for joy. In his fine little djellaba, his feet bare, his round head covered with thick black curls, he was the Arab angel leaping into the air, dancing, crying out, 'He's dead, he's dead, he's dead.' He clapped his hands, he rubbed them together, he clapped them again, he flung them up. 'He's dead, he's dead, he's dead, he'll never hurt her, he'll never vex her, he's double-vexed forever, he's dead, he's dead.'

But she didn't hear him. On she played, making her way through these slumberish low notes, humming softly and then parting her lips to make a monosyllabic song.

I was full with his blood. I felt it washing through me. I loved it, I loved every drop of it. I regained my breath from the effort of having so quickly consumed it, and then I walked slowly, quietly as I could, as if she could hear when she could not, and stood at the end of the piano looking at her.

What a small tender face she had, so girlish with deep-set, huge and pale blue eyes. But look at the bruises on her face. Look at the blood-red scratches on her cheek. Look at the field of tiny red bleeding pinpoint wounds on her temple where a shock of her hair had been ripped right out by the roots.

She didn't care. The greenish-black bruises on her bare arms meant nothing to her. She played on.

How delicate her neck was, even with the blackish swelling imprint of his fingers, and how graceful her small bony shoulders, barely holding up the sleeves of her thin flowered cotton dress. Her strong ashen eyebrows came together in the sweetest frown of concentration as she gazed before her at nothing but her lilting, peaking music, her long clean fingers alone envincing her titanic and indomitable strength.

She let her gaze drift to me, and she smiled as if she had seen something that momentarily pleased her; she bowed her head once, twice, three times in rapid time with the music, but as though she were nodding to me.

'Sybelle,' I whispered. I put my fingers to my lips and kissed them and blew the kiss to her, as her fingers marched on.

But then her vision misted, and she was off again, the Movement demanding speed from her, her head jerked back with the effort of her assault on the keys. And the Sonata sprang once again into its most triumphant life.

Something more powerful than the light of the sun engulfed me. It was a power so total that it utterly surrounded me and sucked me up out of the room, out of the world, out of the sound of her playing, out of my senses.

'Noooo, don't take me now!' I screamed. But an immense and empty blackness swallowed the sound.

I was flying, weightless, with my burnt black limbs outstretched, and in a Hell of excruciating pain. This cannot be my body, I sobbed, seeing the black flesh sealed to my muscles like leather, seeing every tendon of my arms, my fingernails bent and blackened like bits of burnt horn. No, not my body, I cried, Oh, Mother help me, help me! Benjamin, help me . . .

I began to fall. Oh, there was no one who could help me now but one Being.

416

'God, give me the courage,' I cried. 'God if it's begun, give me the courage, God, I can't give up my reason, God, let me know where I am, God, let me understand what is happening, God, where is the church, God, where is the bread and the wine, God, where is she, God help me, help me.'

Down and down I fell, past spires of glass, past grids of blind windows. Past rooftops and pointed towers. I fell through the harsh and wild wailing of the wind. I fell through the stinging torrent of snow. I fell and I fell. I fell past the window where the unmistakable figure of Benjamin stood with his tiny hand on the drape, his black eyes fixed on me for one split second, his mouth open, tiny Arab angel. I fell down and down, the skin shriveling and tightening on my legs so that I couldn't bend them, tightening on my face so that I couldn't open my mouth, and with an agonizing explosion of raw pain, I struck hard-packed snow.

My eyes were open and fire flooded them.

The sun had fully risen.

'I shall die now. I shall die!' I whispered. 'And in this last moment of burning paralysis, when all the world is gone and there is nothing left, I hear her music! I hear her playing the final notes of the *Appassionata*! I hear her. I hear her tumultuous song.'

I didn't die. Not by any means.

I awoke to hear her playing, but she and her piano were very far away. In the first few hours after twilight, when the pain was at its worst, I used the sound of her music, used the search for it, to keep myself from screaming in madness because nothing could make the pain stop.

Deeply encased in snow, I couldn't move and couldn't see, save what my mind could see if I chose to use it, and wishing to die, I used nothing. I only listened to her playing the *Appassionata*, and sometimes I sang along with her in my dreams.

All the first night and the second, I listened to her, that is, when she was disposed to play. She would stop for hours, to sleep perhaps. I couldn't know. Then she would begin again and I'd begin with her.

I followed her Three Movements until I knew them, as she must know them, by heart. I knew the variations she worked into her music; I knew how no two musical phrases she played were ever the same.

I listened to Benjamin calling for me, I heard his crisp little voice, speaking very rapidly and very much in New York style, saying, 'Angel, you've not done with us, what are we to do with him? Angel, come back. Angel, I'll give you cigarettes. Angel, I have plenty of good cigarettes. Come back. Angel, that's just a joke. I know you can get your own cigarettes. But this is really vexing, you leaving this dead body, Angel. Come back.'

There were hours when I heard nothing of either of

them. My mind hadn't the strength to reach out telepathically to them, just to see them, one through the eyes of the other. No. That kind of strength was gone.

I lay in mute stillness, burnt as much by all that I'd seen and felt as by any sunlight, hurt and empty inside, and dead of mind and heart, save for my love for them. It was easy enough, wasn't it, in blackest misery to love two pretty strangers, a mad girl and a mischievous streetwise boy who cared for her? There was no history to it, my killing her brother. Bravo, and finished. There was five hundred years of history to the pain of everything else.

There were hours when only the city talked to me, the great clattering, rolling, rustling city of New York, with its traffic forever clanking, even in the thickest snow, with its layers upon layers of voices and lives rising up to the plateau on which I lay, and then beyond it, vastly beyond it in towers such as the world before this time has never beheld.

I knew things but I didn't know what to make of them. I knew that the snow covering me was growing ever deeper, and ever harder, and I didn't understand how such a thing as ice could keep away from me the rays of the sun.

Surely, I must die, I thought. If not this coming day, then the next. I thought of Lestat holding up the Veil. I thought of His Face. But the zeal had left me. All hope had left me.

I will die, I thought. Morning by morning, I will die.

But I didn't.

In the city far below, I heard others of my kind. I didn't really try to hear them, and so it was not their thoughts that came to me, but now and then their words. Lestat and David were there, Lestat and David thought that I was dead. Lestat and David mourned for me. But far worse horrors plagued Lestat because Dora and the world had taken the Veil, and the city was now crowded with believers. The Cathedral could scarce control the multitudes.

Other immortals came, the young, the feeble and sometimes, most horribly, the very ancient, wanting to view this miracle, slipping into the nighttime Church among the mortal worshipers and looking with crazed eyes on the veil.

Sometimes they spoke of poor Armand or brave Armand or St. Armand, who in his devotion to the Crucified Christ had immolated himself at this very Church door!

Sometimes they did the same. And just before the sun was to rise again, I'd have to hear them, hear their last desperate prayers as they waited for the lethal light. Did they fare better than I? Did they find their refuge in the arms of God? Or were they screaming in agony, agony such as I felt, unendurably burnt and unable to break away from it, or were they lost as I was, remnants in alleyways or on distant roofs? No, they came and they went, whatever their fate.

How pale it all was, how far away. I felt so sad for Lestat that he had bothered to weep for me, but I was to die here. I was to die sooner or later. Whatever I had seen in that moment when I'd risen into the sun didn't matter. I was to die. That was all there was.

Piercing the snowy night, electronic voices spoke of the miracle, that Christ's Face upon a Veil of linen had cured the sick and left its imprint on other cloths pressed to it. Then came an argument of clergymen and skeptics, a perfect din.

I followed the sense of nothing. I suffered. I burned. I couldn't open my eyes, and when I tried, my eyelashes scratched my eyes and the agony was too much to bear. In darkness, I waited for her.

420

Sooner or later, without fail, there came her magnificent music, with all its new and wondrous variations, and nothing mattered to me then, not the mystery of where I was, or what I might have seen, or what it was that Lestat and David meant to do.

It was not until the seventh night perhaps that my senses were fully restored to me, and the full horror of my state was understood.

Lestat was gone. So was David. The Church had been shut up. From the murmurings of mortals I soon realized that the Veil had been taken away.

I could hear the minds of all the city, a din that was unsupportable. I shut myself off from it, fearing the vagrant immortal who'd home in on me if he caught but one spark from my telepathic mind. I couldn't endure the thought of some attempted rescue by immortal strangers. I couldn't endure the thought of their faces, their questions, their possible concern or merciless indifference. I hid myself from them, coiled up in my cracked and tightened flesh. Yet I heard them, as I heard the mortal voices around them, speaking of miracles and redemption and the love of Christ.

Besides, I had enough to think about to figure my present predicament and how it had come to be.

I was lying on a roof. That is where my fall had left me, but not under the open sky, as I might have hoped or supposed. On the contrary, my body had tumbled down a slope of metal sheeting, to lodge beneath a torn and rusted overhang, where it had been repeatedly buried in the wind-stirred snow.

How had I gotten here? I could only suppose.

By my own will, and with the first explosion of my blood in the light of the morning sun, I had been driven upwards, as high perhaps as I could go. For centuries I'd known how to climb to airy heights and how to move

421

there, but I'd never pushed it to a conceivable limit, but with my zeal for death, I had strained with all my available strength to move Heavenward. My fall had been from the greatest height.

The building beneath me was empty, abandoned, dangerous, without heat or light.

Not a sound issued from its hollow metal stairwells or its battered, crumbling rooms. Indeed the wind played the structure now and then as if it were a great pipe organ, and when Sybelle was not at her piano it was to this music I listened, shutting out the rich cacophony of the city above, beyond and below.

Now and then mortals crept inside the lower floors of the building. I felt a sudden wrenching hope. Would one be fool enough to wander to this rooftop where I might lay hands on him and drink the blood I needed merely to crawl free of the overhang which protected me and thereby give myself unsheltered to the sun? As I lay now, the sun could scarce reach me. Only a dull white light scorched me through the snowy shroud in which I was wound, and with the lengthening of each night this newly inflicted pain would mellow into the rest.

But nobody ever came up here.

Death would be slow, very slow. It might have to wait until the warm weather came and the snow melted.

And so each morning, as I longed for death, I came to accept that I would wake, more burnt perhaps than ever, but all the more concealed by the winter blizzard, as I had been concealed all along, from the hundreds of lighted windows that looked down upon this roof from above.

When it was deadly quiet, when Sybelle slept and Benji had ceased praying to me and talking to me at the window, the worst happened. I thought, in a cold listless broken way, of those strange things that had befallen me when I'd been tumbling through space, because I could think of nothing else.

How utterly real it had been, the altar of Santa Sofia and the bread I'd broken in my hands. I'd known things, so many things, things which I couldn't recall any longer or put into words, things which I could not articulate here in this narrative even as I sought to relive the tale.

Real. Tangible. I had felt the altar cloth and seen the wine spill, and before that the bird rise out of the egg. I could hear the sound of the cracking of the shell. I could hear my Mother's voice. And all the rest.

But my mind didn't want these things anymore. It didn't want them. The zeal had proved fragile. It was gone, gone like the nights with my Master in Venice, gone like the years of wandering with Louis, gone like the festive months on The Night Island, gone like those long shameful centuries with the Children of Darkness when I had been a fool, such a pure fool.

I could think of the Veil, I could think of Heaven, I could think of my standing at the Altar and working the miracle with the Body of Christ in my hands. Yes, I could think of all of it. But the totality had been too terrible, and I was not dead, and there was no Memnoch pleading with me to become his helper, and no Christ with arms outstretched against the backdrop of God's unending light.

It was sweeter by far to think of Sybelle, to remember that her room of rich red and blue Turkey carpets and darkly varnished overblown paintings had been every bit as real as Santa Sofia of Kiev, to think of her oval white face when she'd turned to glance at me, to think of the sudden brightness of her moist, quick eyes.

One evening, as my eyes actually opened, as the lids

truly drew back over the orbs of my eyes so that I could see through the white cake of ice above me, I realized I was healing.

I tried to flex my arms. I could raise them ever so slightly, and the encasing ice shattered; what an extraordinary electric sound.

The sun simply couldn't reach me here, or not enough to work against the preternatural fury of the powerful blood my body contained. Ah, God, to think of it, five hundred years of growing ever stronger and stronger, and born from the blood of Marius in the first place, a monster from the start who never knew his own strength.

It seemed for a moment that my rage and despair could grow no greater. It seemed the fiery pain in all my body could be no worse.

Then Sybelle started to play. She began to play the *Appassionata*, and nothing else mattered.

It wouldn't matter again until her music had stopped. The night was warmer than usual; the snow had melted slightly. There seemed no immortals anywhere near. I knew that the Veil had been spirited away to the Vatican in Rome. No cause now, was there, for immortals to come here?

Poor Dora. The nightly news said that her prize had been taken from her. Rome must examine this Veil. Her tales of strange blond-haired angels were the stuff of tabloids, and she herself was no longer here.

In a moment of daring, I fastened my heart upon Sybelle's music, and with an aching straining head, sent out my telepathic vision as if it were a fleshly part of me, a tongue requiring stamina, to see through Benjamin's eyes, the room where they were both lodged.

In a lovely golden haze, I saw it, saw the walls covered with the heavy framed paintings, saw my beautiful one herself, in a fleecy white gown with worn slippers, her fingers hard at work. How grand the sweep of the music. And Benjamin, the little worrier, frowning, puffing on a black cigarette, with hands folded behind his back, pacing in his bare feet and shaking his head as he mumbled to himself.

'Angel, I have told you to come back!'

I smiled. The creases in my cheeks hurt as if someone had made them with the point of a sharp knife. I shut my telepathic eye. I let myself slumber in the rushing crescendos of the piano. Besides, Benjamin had sensed something; his mind, unwarped by Western sophistication, had picked up some glimmer of my prying. Enough.

Then another vision came to me, very sharp, very special and unusual, something that would not be ignored. I turned my head again and made the ice crackle. I held my eyes open. I could see a blur of lighted towers high above.

Some immortal down there in the city was thinking of me, someone far away, many blocks from the closed-up Cathedral. In fact, I sensed in an instant the distant presence of two powerful vampires, vampires I knew, and vampires who knew of my death and lamented it bitterly as they went about some important task.

Now there was a risk to this. Try to see them and they might catch much more than the glimmer of me which Benjamin had been so quick to catch. But the city was empty of blood drinkers save for them, for all I could figure, and I had to know what it was that caused them to move with such deliberation and such stealth.

An hour passed perhaps. Sybelle was silent. They, the powerful vampires, were still at their work. I decided to chance it.

I drew in close with my disincarnate vision, and

quickly realized that I could see one through the eyes of the other, but that it did not work for me the other way around.

The reason was plain. I sharpened my sight. I was looking through the eyes of Santino, my old Roman Coven Master, Santino, and the other whom I saw was Marius, my Maker, whose mind was locked to me for all time.

It was a vast official building in which they made their careful progress, both dressed as gentlemen of the moment in trim dark blue clothes, even to starched white collars and thin silk ties. Both had trimmed their hair in deference to corporate fashion. But this was no corporation in which they prowled, clearly putting into harmless thrall any mortal who tried to disturb them. It was a medical building. And I soon guessed what their errand must be.

It was the forensics laboratory of the city through which they wandered. And though they had taken their time in gathering up documents for their heavy briefcases, they were quick now with agitation as they pulled from refrigerated compartments the remains of those vampires who, following my example, had turned themselves over to the mercy of the sun.

Of course, they were confiscating what the world now had on us. They were scooping up the remains. Into simple glistening plastic sacks they put the residue, out of coffinlike drawers and off shining steel trays. Whole bones, ashes, teeth, ah, yes, even teeth, they swept into their little sacks. And now from a series of filing cabinets they withdrew the plastic-wrapped samples of clothing that remained.

My heart quickened. I stirred in the ice and the ice spoke back to me again. Oh, heart be still. Let me see. It was my lace, my very lace, the thick Venetian Rose

Point, burnt at the edges, and with it a few shredded rags of purple-red velvet! Yes, my pitiful clothes which they took from the labeled compartment of the filing drawer and slipped into their bags.

Marius stopped. I turned my head and my mind elsewhere. Do not see me. See me and come here, and I swear to God I will . . . I will what? I have no strength even to move. I have no strength to escape. Oh, Sybelle, please, play for me, I have to escape this.

But then, remembering that he was my Master, remembering that he could trace me only through the weaker more muddled mind of his companion, Santino, I felt my heart go quiet.

From the bank of recent memory, I took her music, I framed it with numbers and figures and dates, all the little detritus I had brought with me over the centuries to her: that Beethoven had written her sweet masterpiece, that it was Sonata No. 23 in F Minor, Opus 57. Think on that. Think on Beethoven. Think on a make-believe night in cold Vienna, make-believe for I knew nothing really about it, think on him writing music with a noisy scratchy quill, which he himself perhaps could not hear. Think on him being paid in pittances. And think with a smile, yes, a painful cutting smile that makes your face bleed, of how they brought him piano after piano, so powerful was he, so demanding, so fiercely did he bang away.

And she, pretty Sybelle, what a fine daughter to him she was, her powerful fingers striking the keys with terrifying power that would surely have delighted him had he ever seen in the distant future, amid all his frenzied students and worshipers, just this particular maniacal girl.

It was warmer tonight. The ice was melting. There was no denying it. I pressed my lips together and again

427

lifted my right hand. A cavity existed now in which I could move my right fingers.

But I couldn't forget about them, the unlikely pair, the one who'd made me and the one who'd tried to destroy him, Marius and Santino. I had to check back. Cautiously I sent out my weak and tentative beam of probing thought. And in an instant, I'd fixed them.

They stood before an incinerator in the bowels of the building and heaved into a fiery mouth all the evidence which they had brought together, sack after sack curling and crackling in the flames.

How odd. Didn't they themselves want to look at these fragments under microscopes? But then surely others of our kind had done this, and why look at the bones and teeth of those who have been baked in Hell when you can carve pale white tissue from your own hand, and place this on the glass slide while your hand heals itself miraculously, as I was healing even now?

I lingered on the vision. I saw the hazy basement round about them. I saw the low beams above their heads. Gathering all my power into my projected gaze, I saw Santino's face, so troubled, soft, the very one who had shattered the only youth I might have ever had. I saw my old Master gazing almost wistfully at the flames. 'We're finished,' Marius said in his quiet, commanding voice, speaking Italian perfectly to the other. 'I cannot think of another thing that we should do.'

'Break apart the Vatican, and steal the veil from them,' answered Santino. 'What right have they to claim such a thing?'

I could only see Marius's reaction, his sudden shock and then his polite and poised smile. 'Why?' he asked, as if he held no secrets. 'What's the Veil to us, my friend? You think it will bring him back to his senses? Forgive me, Santino, but you are so very young.'

428

His senses, bring him back to his senses. This had to mean Lestat. There was no other possible meaning. I pushed my luck. I scanned Santino's mind for all he knew, and found myself recoiling in horror, but holding fast to what I saw.

Lestat, my Lestat – for he was never theirs, was he? – my Lestat was crazed and railing as the result of his awful saga, and held prisoner by the very oldest of our kind on the final decree that if he did not cease to disturb the peace, which meant of course our secrecy, he would be destroyed, as only the oldest could accomplish, and no one could plead for him on any account.

No, that could not happen! I writhed and twisted. The pain sent its shocks through me, red and violet and pulsing with orange light. I hadn't seen such colors since I'd fallen. My mind was coming back, and coming back for what? Lestat to be destroyed! Lestat imprisoned, as I had once been centuries ago under Rome in Santino's catacombs. Oh, God, this is worse than the sun's fire, this is worse than seeing that bastard brother strike the little plum-cheeked face of Sybelle and knock her away from her piano, this is murderous rage I feel.

But the smaller damage was done. 'Come, we have to get out of here,' said Santino. 'There's something wrong, something I sense that I can't explain. It's as if someone is right near us yet not near us; it's as if someone as powerful as myself has heard my footfall over miles and miles.'

Marius looked kindly, curious, unalarmed. 'New York is ours tonight,' he said simply. And then with faint fear he looked into the mouth of the furnace one last time. 'Unless something of spirit, so tenacious of life, clung still to his lace and to the velvet he wore.'

I closed my eyes. Oh, God, let me close my mind. Let me shut it up tight.

His voice went on, piercing the little shell of my consciousness where I had so softened it.

'But I have never believed such things,' he said. 'We're like the Eucharist itself, in some measure, don't you think? Being Body and Blood of a mysterious god only so long as we hold to the chosen form. What's strands of reddish hair and scorched and tattered lace? He's gone.'

'I don't understand you,' Santino confessed gently. 'But if you think I never loved him, you are very very wrong.'

'Let's go then,' Marius said. 'Our work's done. Every trace of every one is now obliterated. But promise me in your old Roman Catholic soul, you won't go seeking the Veil. A million pairs of eyes have looked on it, Santino, and nothing's changed. The world is the world, and children die in every quadrant under Heaven, hungry and alone.'

I could risk no more.

I veered away, searching the night like a high beam, casting about for the mortals who might see them leave the building in which they'd done their all-important work, but their retreat was too secret, too swift for that.

I felt them go. I felt the sudden absence of their breath, their pulse, and knew the winds had taken them away.

At last when another hour had ticked, I let my eye roam the same old rooms where they had wandered.

All was quiet with those poor muddled technicians and guards whom white-faced specters from another realm had gently spellbound as they went about their gruesome task.

By morning, the theft and all the missing work would be discovered, and Dora's miracle would suffer yet another dreary insult, receding ever more swiftly out of current time.

430

I was sore; I wept a dry, hoarse weeping, unable even to muster tears.

I think that once in the glimmering ice I saw my hand, a grotesque claw, more like a thing flayed than burnt, and shiny black as I had remembered it or seen it.

Then a mystery began to prey upon me. How could I have killed the evil brother of my poor love? How could it have been anything but an illusion, that swift horrible justice, when I had been rising and falling beneath the weight of the morning sun?

And if that had not happened, if I had not sucked dry that awful vengeful brother, then they too were a dream, my Sybelle and my little Bedouin. Oh, please, was that the final horror?

The night struck its worst hour. Dim clocks chimed in painted plastered rooms. Wheels churned the crunching snow. Again, I raised my hand. There came the inevitable crack and snap. Tumbling all around me was the broken ice like so much shattered glass!

I looked above on pure and sparkling stars. How lovely this, these guardian glassy spires with all their fast and golden squares of light cut in ranks run straight across and sharply down to score the airy blackness of the winter night, and here now comes the tyrant wind, whistling through crystalline canyons down across this small neglected bed where one forgotten demon lies, gazing with the larcenous vision of a great soul at the city's emboldened lights on clouds above. Oh, little stars, how much I've hated you, and envied you that in the ghastly void you can with such determination plot your dogged course.

But I hated nothing now. My pain was as a purgative for all unworthy things. I watched the sky cloud over, glisten, become a diamond for a still and gorgeous moment, and then again the white soft limitless haze took up the golden glow of city lamps and sent in answer the softest lightest fall of snow.

It touched my face. It touched my outstretched hand. It touched me all over as it melted in its tiny magical flakes.

'And now the sun will come,' I whispered, as if some guardian angel held me close, 'and even here beneath this twisted little awning of tin, it will find me through this broken canopy and take my soul to further depths of pain.'

A voice cried out in protest. A voice begged that it not be so. My own, I thought, of course, why not this self-deception? I am mad to think that I can bear the burning that I've suffered and that I could willingly endure it once again.

But it wasn't my voice. It was Benjamin, Benjamin at his prayers. Flinging out my disembodied eyes, I saw him. He knelt in the room as she lay sleeping like a ripe and succulent peach amid her soft tangled bedcovers. 'Oh, angel, Dybbuk, help us. Dybbuk, you came once. So come again. You vex me that you don't come!'

How many hours is it till sunrise, little man? I whispered this to his little seashell ear, as if I didn't know.

'Dybbuk,' he cried out. 'It's you, you speak to me. Sybelle, wake up, Sybelle.'

Ah, but think before you wake her. It's a horrid errand. I'm not the resplendent being you saw who sucked your enemy dry of blood and doted on her beauty and your joy. It's a monster you come to collect if you mean to pay your debt to me, an insult to your innocent eyes. But be assured, little man, that I'll be yours forever if you do me this kindness, if you come to me, if you succor me, if you help me, because my will is leaving me, and I'm alone, and I would be restored now and cannot help myself and my years mean nothing now, and I'm afraid.

432

He scrambled to his feet. He stood staring at the distant window, the window through which I had seen him in a dream glimpse me with his mortal eyes, but through which he could not possibly see me now, as I lay on a roof far far below the fine apartment which he shared with my angel. He squared his little shoulders, and now with black eyebrows in their perfect serious frown he was the very image off the Byzantine wall, a cherub smaller than myself.

'Name it, Dybbuk, I come for you!' he declared, and made his mighty little right hand into a fist. 'Where are you, Dybbuk, what do you fear that we cannot conquer together! Sybelle, wake up, Sybelle! Our Divine Dybbuk has come back and he needs us!'

They were coming for me. It was the building beside their own, a derelict heap. Benjamin knew it. In a few faint telepathic whispers I'd begged him to bring a hammer and a pick to break up the ice such as remained and to have big soft blankets with which to wrap me.

I knew I weighed nothing. Painfully twisting my arms, I broke up more of the transparent covering. I felt with my clawlike hand that my hair had come back, thick and red-brown as ever. I held up a lock to the light, and then my arm could stand the scalding pain no more and I let it drop, unable to close or move my dried and twisted fingers.

I had to throw a spell, at least when they first came. They could not see the thing that I was, this black leathery monster. No mortal could bear the sight of this, no matter what words came from my lips. I had to shield myself somehow.

And having no mirror, how could I know how I looked or what I must do precisely? I had to dream, dream of the old Venetian days when I had been a beauty well known to myself from the tailor's glass, and project that vision right into their minds even if it took all the strength I possessed; yes, that, and I must give them some instructions.

I lay still, gazing up into the soft warm snowfall of tiny flakes, so unlike the terrible blizzards that had come earlier. I didn't dare to use my wits to track their progress.

Suddenly I heard the loud crash of breaking glass. A door slammed far below. I heard their uneven steps rushing up the metal stairs, clambering over the landings.

My heart beat hard, and with each little convulsion, the pain was pumped through me, as if my blood itself were scalding me.

Suddenly, the steel door on the roof was flung back. I heard them rushing towards me. In the faint dreamy light of the high towers all around, I saw their two small figures, she the fairy woman, and he the child of no more than twelve years perhaps, hurrying towards me.

Sybelle! Oh, she came out on the roof without a coat, hair streaming, the terrible pity of it, and Benjamin no better in his thin linen djellaba. But they had a big velvet comforter to cover me, and I had to make a vision.

Give me the boy I was, give the finest green satin and ruff upon ruff of fancy lace, give me stockings and braided boots, and let my hair be clean and shining.

Slowly I opened my eyes, looking from one to the other of their small pale and rapt faces. Like two vagrants of the night they stood in the drifting snow.

'Oh, but Dybbuk, you had us so very worried,' said Benjamin, in his wildly excited voice, 'and look at you, you are beautiful.'

'No, don't think it's what you see, Benjamin,' I said. 'Hurry with your tools, chop at the ice, and lay the cover over me.'

It was Sybelle who took up the wooden-handled iron hammer and with both hands slammed it down, fracturing the soft top layer of ice immediately. Benjamin chopped at it all with the pick as if he had become a small machine, thrusting to left and to right over and over, sending the shards flying.

The wind caught Sybelle's hair and whipped around into her eyes. The snow clung to her eyelids.

I held the image, a helpless satin-clad child, with soft pinkish hands upturned and unable to help them.

'Don't cry, Dybbuk,' declared Benjamin, grabbing a giant thin slab of ice with both hands. 'We'll get you out, don't cry, you're ours now. We have you.'

He threw aside the shining jagged broken sheets, and then he himself appeared to freeze, more solid than any ice, staring at me, his mouth a perfect O of amazement.

'Dybbuk, you are changing colors!' he cried. He reached to touch my illusory face.

'Don't do it, Benji,' said Sybelle.

It was the first time I'd heard her voice, and now I saw the deliberate brave calm of her blanched face, the wind making her eyes tear, though she herself remained staunch. She picked the ice from my hair.

A terrible chill came over me, quelling the heat, yes, but sending the tears down my face. Were they blood? 'Don't look at me,' I said. 'Benji, Sybelle, look away. Just put the cover into my hands.'

Her tender eyes squinted as she stared, disobediently, steadily, one hand up to close the collar of her flimsy cotton bed gown against the wind, the other poised above me.

'What's happened to you since you came to us?' she asked in the kindest voice. 'Who's done this to you?'

I swallowed hard, and made the vision come again. I pushed it up from all my pores, as if my body were one agency of breath.

'No, don't do it anymore,' said Sybelle. 'It weakens you and you suffer terribly.'

'I can heal, my sweet,' I said, 'I promise I can. I won't be like this always, not even soon. Only take me off this roof. Take me out of this cold, and take me where the sun can't get to me again. It's the sun that did this. Only the sun. Take me, please. I can't walk. I can't crawl. I'm a night thing. Hide me in the darkness.'

'Enough, don't say any more,' cried Benji.

I opened my eyes to see a huge wave of brilliant blue settle over me as though a summer sky had come down to be my wrapping. I felt the soft pile of the velvet, and even this was pain, pain on the blazing skin, but it was pain that could be borne because their ministering hands were on me, and for this, for their touch, for their love, I would have endured anything.

I felt myself lifted. I knew that I was light, and yet how dreadful it was to be so helpless, as they wrapped me.

'Am I not light enough to carry?' I asked. My head had fallen back, and I could see the snow again, and I fancied that when I sharpened my gaze I could see the stars too, high above, biding their time beyond the haze of one tiny planet.

'Don't be afraid,' whispered Sybelle, her lips close to the covers.

The smell of their blood was suddenly rich and thick as honey.

Both of them had me, hoisted in their arms, and they ran together over the roof. I was free of the hurtful snow and ice, almost free forever. I couldn't let myself think about their blood. I couldn't let this ravenous burnt body have its way. That was unthinkable.

Down through the metal stairwell we went, making turn after turn, their feet strumming the brittle steel treads, my body shocked and throbbing with agony. I could see the ceiling above, and then the smell of their blood, mingling together, overpowered me, and I shut my eyes and clenched my burnt fingers, hearing the leathery flesh crack as I did so. I dug my nails into my palms.

I heard Sybelle at my ear. 'We have you, we're holding you tight, we won't let you go. It isn't far. Oh, God, but look at you, look what the sun's done to you.'

437

'Don't look!' said Benji crossly. 'Just hurry! Do you think such a powerful Dybbuk doesn't know what you think? Be wise, hurry up.'

They had come to the lower floor and to the broken window. I felt the arms of Sybelle lift me beneath my head and beneath my crooked knees, and I heard Benji's voice from beyond, no longer echoing on enclosing walls.

'That's it, now give him to me, I can hold him!' How furious and excited he sounded, but she had come through the window with me, I could tell this much, though my clever Dybbuk's mind was utterly spent, and I knew nothing, nothing but pain and the blood and the pain again and the blood and that they were running through a long dark alleyway from which I could see nothing of Heaven.

But how sweet it was. The rocking motion, the swinging of my burnt legs and the soft touch of her soothing fingers through the blanket, all this was wickedly wondrous. It wasn't pain anymore, it was merely sensation. The cover fell over my face.

On they hurried, feet crunching in the snow, Benji sliding once with a loud cry, and Sybelle grabbing hold of him. He caught his breath.

What labor it was for them in this cold. They must get out of it.

We entered the hotel in which they lived. The pungent warm air rushed out to take hold of us even as the doors were pulled open and before they fell shut, the hallway echoing with the sharp steps of Sybelle's little shoes and the quick shuffle of Benji's sandals.

With a sudden burst of agony through my legs and back, I felt myself doubled, knees brought up and head tipped towards them, as we crowded into the elevator. I bit down on the scream in my throat. Nothing could matter less. The elevator, smelling of old motors and tried and true oil, began its swaying jerking progress upwards.

'We're home, Dybbuk,' whispered Benji with his hot breath on my cheek, his little hand grasping for me through the cover and pushing painfully against my scalp. 'We are safe now, we have captured you and we have you.'

Click of locks, feet on hardwood floors, the scent of incense and candles, of a woman's rich perfume, of rich polish for fine things, of old canvases with cracked oil paint, of fresh and overpoweringly sweet white lilies.

My body was laid down gently into the bed of down, the blanket loosened so that I sank into layers of silk and velvet, the pillows seeming to melt beneath me.

It was the very disheveled nest in which I'd glimpsed her with my mind's eye, golden and sleeping in her white gown, and she had given it over to such a horror.

'Don't pull away the cover,' I said. I knew that my little friend wanted so to do it.

Undaunted, he gently pulled it away. I struggled with my one recovering hand to catch it, to bring it back, but I couldn't do any more than flex my burnt fingers.

They stood beside the bed, gazing down at me. The light swirled around them, mingled with warmth, these two fragile figures, the gaunt porcelain girl, the bruises gone from her milk-white skin, and the little Arab boy, the Bedouin boy, for I realized now that that is what he truly was. Fearlessly they stared at what must be unspeakable to behold for human eyes.

'You are so shiny!' said Benji. 'Does it hurt you?'

'What can we do!' said Sybelle, so muted, as if her very voice might injure me. Her hands covered her lips. The unruly wisps of her full straight pale hair moved in the light, and her arms were blue from the cold outside, and she could not help but shiver. Poor spare being, so delicate. Her nightdress was crumpled, thin white cotton, stitched with flowerets and trimmed with thin sturdy lace, a thing for a virgin. Her eyes brimmed with sympathy.

'Know my soul, my angel,' I said. 'I'm an evil thing. God wouldn't take me. And the Devil wouldn't either. I went into the sun so they could have my soul. It was a loving thing, without fear of Hellfire or pain. But this Earth, this very Earth has been my purgatorial prison. I don't know how I came to you before. I don't know what power it was that gave me those brief seconds to stand here in your room and come between you and death that was looming like a shadow over you.'

'Oh, no,' she whispered fearfully, her eyes glistering in the dim lights of the room. 'He would never have killed me.'

'Oh, yes, he would!' I said, and Benjamin said the very same exact words in concert with me.

'He was drunk and he didn't care what he did,' said Benji in instant rage, 'and his hands were big and clumsy and mean, and he didn't care what he did, and after the last time he hit you, you lay still like the dead in this very bed for two hours without moving! Do you think a Dybbuk kills your own brother for nothing?'

'I think he's telling you the truth, my pretty girl,' I said. It was so hard to talk. With each word I had to lift my chest. In crazy desperation, suddenly I wanted a mirror. I tossed and turned on the bed, and went rigid with pain.

The two were thrown into a panic.

'Don't move, Dybbuk, don't!' Benji pleaded. 'Sybelle, the silk, all the silk scarves, get them out, wind them around him.'

'No!' I whispered. 'Put the cover up over me. If you

440

must see my face, then leave it bare, but cover the rest of me. Or . . .'

'Or what, Dybbuk, tell me?'

'Lift me so that I can see myself and how I look. Stand me before a long mirror.'

They fell silent in perplexity. Sybelle's long yellow hair lay flaxen and flat down over her large breasts. Benji chewed at his little lip.

All the room swam with colors. Behold the blue silk sealed to the plaster of the walls, the heaps of richly embellished pillows all around me, look at the golden fringe, and there beyond, the wobbling baubles of the chandelier, filled with the glistering colors of the spectrum. I fancied I heard the tinkling song of the glass as these baubles touched. It seemed in my feeble deranged mind that I had never seen such simple splendor, that I had forgotten in all my years just how shining and exquisite the world was.

I closed my eyes, taking with me to my heart an image of the room. I breathed in, fighting the scent of their blood, the sweet clean fragrance of the lilies. 'Would you let me see those flowers?' I whispered. Were my lips charred? Could they see my fang teeth, and were they yellowed from the fire? I floated on the silks beneath me. I floated and it seemed that I could dream now, safe, truly safe. The lilies were close. I reached up again. I felt the petals against my hand, and the tears came down my face. Were they pure blood? Pray not, but I heard Benji's frank little gasp, and Sybelle making her soft sound to hush him.

'I was a boy of seventeen, I think, when it happened,' I said. 'It was hundreds of years ago. I was too young, really. My Master, he was a loving one; he didn't believe we were evil things. He thought we could feed off the badlings. If I hadn't been dying, it wouldn't have been

441

done so soon. He wanted me to know things, to be ready.'

I opened my eyes. They were spellbound! They saw again the boy I'd been. I had done it without intention.

'Oh, so handsome,' said Benji. 'So fine, Dybbuk.'

'Little man,' I said with a sigh, feeling the fragile illusion about me crumble to air, 'call me by my name from now on; it's not Dybbuk. I think you picked up that one from the Hebrews of Palestine.'

He laughed. He didn't flinch as I faded back into my horrid self.

'Then tell me your name,' he said.

I did.

'Armand,' said Sybelle. 'Tell us, what can we do? If not silk scarves, ointments then, aloe, yes, aloe will heal your burns.

I laughed but only in a small soft way, meant to be purely kindly.

'My aloe is blood, child. I need an evil man, a man who deserves to die. Now, how will I find him?'

'What will this blood do?' asked Benji. He sat right down beside me, leaning over me as though I were the most fascinating specimen. 'You know, Armand, you are black as pitch, you are made out of black leather, you are like those people they fish from the bogs in Europe, all shiny with all of you sealed inside. I could take a lesson in muscles from looking at you.'

'Benji, stop,' said Sybelle, struggling with her disapproval and her alarm. 'We have to think how to get an evil man.'

'You serious?' he said, looking up and across the bed at her. She stood with her hands clasped as if in prayer. 'Sybelle, that's nothing. It's how to get rid of him afterwards that's so hard.' He looked at me. 'Do you know what we did with her brother?'

She put her hands over her ears and bowed her head. How many times had I done that very thing myself when it seemed a stream of words and images would utterly destroy me.

'You are so glossy, Armand,' said Benji. 'But I can get you an evil man, like that, it's nothing. You want an evil man? Let's make a plan.' He bent down over me, as though trying to peer into my brain. I realized suddenly that he was looking at my fangs.

'Benji,' I said, 'don't come any closer. Sybelle, take him away.'

'But what did I do?'

'Nothing,' she said. She dropped her voice, and said desperately, 'He's hungry.'

'Lift the covers off again, will you do that?' I asked. 'Lift them off and look at me and let me look into your eyes, and let that be my mirror. I want to see how very bad it is.'

'Hmmm, Armand,' said Benji. 'I think you are crazy mad or something.'

Sybelle bent down and with her two careful hands peeled the cover back and down, exposing the length of my body.

I went into her mind.

It was worse than I had ever imagined.

The glossy horror of a bog corpse, as Benji had said, was perfectly true, save for the horror of the full head of red-brown hair and huge, lidless bright brown eyes, and the white teeth arrayed perfectly below and above lips that had shriveled to nothing. Down the tightly drawn wrinkled black leather of the face were heavy red streaks of blood that had been my tears.

I whipped my head to the side and deep into the downy pillow. I felt the covers come up over me.

'This cannot go on for you, even if it could go on for

me,' I said. 'It's not what I would have you see another moment, for the longer you live with this, the more like you are to live with anything. No. It cannot continue.'

'Anything,' Sybelle said. She crouched down beside me. 'Is my hand cool if I lay it on your forehead? Is it gentle if I touch your hair?'

I looked at her from one narrow-slitted eye.

Her long thin neck was part of her shivering and emaciated loveliness. Her breasts were voluptuous and high. Beyond her in the lovely warm glow of the room, I saw the piano. I thought of these long gentle fingers touching the keys. I could hear in my head the throb of the *Appassionata*.

There came a loud flick, a crackle, a snap, and then the rich fragrance of fine tobacco.

Benji strode back and forth beyond her, with his black cigarette on his lip.

'I have a plan,' he declared, effortlessly holding forth with the cigarette firmly grasped between his half-open lips. 'I go down to the streets. I meet a bad, bad guy in no time. I tell him I'm alone here in this apartment, up here in the hotel, with a man who is drunk and drooling and crazy and we have all this cocaine to sell and I don't know what to do and I need help with it.'

I started to laugh in spite of the pain.

The little Bedouin shrugged his shoulders and held up his palms, puffing away on the black cigarette, the smoke curling about him like a magical cloud.

'What you think? It will work. Look, I'm a good judge of character. Now, you, Sybelle, you get out of the way, and let me lead this miserable sack of filth, this bad guy whom I lure into my trap, right to the very bed, and pitch him down on his face, like this, I trip him with my foot, like this, and he falls, boink, right into your arms, Armand, what do you think of it?'

'And if it goes wrong?' I asked.

'Then my beautiful Sybelle cracks him over the head with her hammer.'

'I have a better thought,' I said, 'though God knows that what you've just devised is unsurpassingly brilliant. You tell him of course that the cocaine is under the coverlet in neat little plastic sacks all stretched out, but if he doesn't take this bait and come here to see for himself, then let our beautiful Sybelle simply throw back the cover, and when he sees what truly lies in this bed, he'll be out of here with no thought to harm anyone!'

'That's it!' Sybelle cried. She clapped her hands together. Her pale luminous eyes were wide.

'That's perfect,' Benji agreed.

'But mark, don't carry a copper penny into the streets with you. If only we had but a little bit of the evil white powder with which to bait the beast.'

'But we do,' said Sybelle. 'We have just that, a little bit which we took from my brother's pockets.' She looked down at me thoughtfully, not seeing me but running the plan through the tight coils of her soft and yielding mind. 'We took everything out so that when we left him to be found, they'd find nothing with him. There are so many who are left that way in New York. Of course it was an unspeakable chore to drag him.'

'But we have that evil white powder, yes!' said Benji, clasping her shoulder suddenly and then bolting out of my sight to return within the instant with a small flat white cigarette case.

'Put it here, where I can smell what's inside,' I said. I could see that neither of them knew for certain.

Benji snapped open the lid of the thin silver box. There, nestled in a small plastic bag, folded with impeccable neatness, was the powder with the very exact smell that I wanted it to have. I needn't put it to my tongue,

445

on which sugar would have tasted just as alien.

'That's fine. Only empty out half of that at once down a drain, so that there's just a little left, and leave the silver case here, lest you run into some fool who'll kill you for it.'

Sybelle shivered with obvious fear. 'Benji, I'll go with you.'

'No, that would be most unwise,' I said. 'He can get away from anyone much faster without you.'

'Oh, so right you are!' said Benji, taking the last drag from his cigarette and then crushing it out in a big glass ashtray beside the bed, where a dozen other little white butts were curled waiting for it. 'And how many times do I tell her that when I go out for cigarettes in the middle of the night? Does she listen?'

He was off without waiting for an answer. I heard the rush of water from the tap. He was washing away half the cocaine. I let my eyes roam the room, veering away from the soft blood-filled guardian angel.

'There are people innately good,' I said, 'who want to help others. You are one of them, Sybelle. I won't rest as long as you live. I'll be at your side. I'll be there always to guard you and to repay you.'

She smiled.

I was astonished.

Her lean face, with its well-shaped pale lips, broke into the freshest and most robust smile, as if neglect and pain had never gnawed at her.

'You'll be a guardian angel to me, Armand?' she asked.

'Always.'

'I'm off,' Benji declared. With a crackle and snap, he lit another cigarette. His lungs must have been charcoal sacks. 'I'm going out into the night. But what if this son of a bitch is sick or dirty or—.'

'Means nothing to me. Blood's blood. Just bring him here. Don't try this fancy tripping with your foot. Wait till you have him right here beside the bed, and as he reaches to lift the cover, you, Sybelle, pull it back, and you, Benji, push on him with all your might, so the side of the bed trips his shins, and he'll fall into my arms. And after that, I'll have him.'

He headed for the door.

'Wait,' I whispered. What was I thinking of in my greed? I looked up at her mute smiling face, and then at him, the little engine puffing away on the black cigarette, with nothing on for the fierce winter outside but the damned djellaba.

'No, it has to be done,' said Sybelle with wide eyes. 'And Benji will choose a very bad man, won't you, Benji? An evil man who wants to rob and kill you.'

'I know where to go,' said Benji with a little twisted smile. 'Just play your cards when I come back, both of you. Cover him up, Sybelle. Don't look at the clock. Don't worry about me!'

Off he went with the slam of the door, the big heavy lock slipping shut behind him automatically.

So it was coming. Blood, thick red blood. It was coming. It was coming, and it would be hot and delicious, and there would be a manful of it, and it was coming, it was coming within seconds.

I closed my eyes, and opening them, I let the room take shape again with its sky-blue draperies on every window, hanging down in rich folds to the floor, and the carpet a great writhing oval of cabbage roses. And she, this stalk of a girl staring at me and smiling her simple sweet smile, as if the crime of the night would be nothing to her.

She came down on her knees next to me, perilously close, and again she touched my hair with delicate hand.

447

Her soft unfettered breasts touched my arm. I read her thoughts as if I read her palm, pushing back through layer after layer of her conscious, seeing the dark winding road again whipping and turning through the Jordan Valley, and the parents driving too fast for the pitch dark and the hairpin curves and the Arab drivers who came on plunging at even greater speed so that each meeting of headlamps became a grueling contest.

'To eat the fish from the Sea of Galilee,' she said, her eyes drifting away from me. 'I wanted it. It was my idea we go there. We had one more day in the Holy Land, and they said it's a long drive from Jerusalem to Nazareth, and I said, 'But He walked on the water.' It was to me always the strangest tale. You know it?'

'I do,' I said.

'That He was walking right on the water, as if He'd forgotten the Apostles were there or that anyone might see Him, and they from the boat, said, 'Lord!' and He was startled. Such a strange miracle, as if it was all . . . accidental. I was the one who wanted to go. I was the one who wanted to eat the fresh fish right out of the sea, the same water that Peter and the others had fished. It was my doing. Oh, I don't say it was my fault that they died. It was my doing. And we were all headed home for my big night at Carnegie Hall, and the record company was set up to record it, live. I'd made a recording before, you know. It had done much better than anyone ever expected. But that night . . . this night that never happened, that is, I was going to play the *Appassionata*. It was all that mattered to me. The other sonatas I love, the *Moonlight*, the *Pathétique*, but really for me . . . it was the *Appassionata*. My Father and Mother were so proud. But my brother, he was the one who always fought, always got me the time, the space, the good piano, the teachers I needed. He was the one who made them see, but then of course, he didn't have any life at all, and all of us saw what was coming. We'd talk about it round the table at night, that he had to get a life of his own, it was no good his working for me, but then he'd say that I would need him for years to come, I couldn't even imagine. He'd manage the recordings and the performances and the repertoire, and the fees we asked. The agents couldn't be trusted. I had no idea, he said, of how high I'd rise.'

She paused, cocking her head to one side, her face earnest yet still simple.

'It wasn't a decision I made, you understand,' she said. 'I just wouldn't do anything else. They were dead. I just wouldn't go out. I just wouldn't answer the phone. I just wouldn't play anything else. I just wouldn't listen to what he said. I just wouldn't plan. I just wouldn't eat. I just wouldn't change my clothes. I just played the *Appassionata*.'

'I understand,' I said softly

'He brought Benji back with us to take care of me. I always wondered how. I think Benji was bought, you know, bought with cold cash?'

'I know.'

'I think that's what happened. He couldn't leave me alone, he said, not even at the King David, that was the hotel—.'

'Yes.'

'—because he said I'd stand in the window without my clothes, or I wouldn't let the maid come in, and I'd play the piano in the middle of the night and he couldn't sleep. So he got Benji. I love Benji.'

'I know.'

'I'd always do what Benji said. He never dared to hit Benji. Only towards the end he started to really hurt me. Before that it was slaps, you know, and kicks. Or he'd pull my hair. He'd grab me by the hair, all my hair in one hand, and he'd throw me down on the floor. He did that often. But he didn't dare to hit Benji. He knew if he hit Benji I'd scream and scream. But then sometimes, when Benji would try to make him stop—. But I'm not so sure about that because I would be so dizzy. My head would ache.'

'I understand,' I said. Of course, he had hit Benji.

She mused, quietly, her eyes large still, and so bright without tears or puckering.

'We're alike, you and I,' she whispered, looking down at me. Her hand lay close to my cheek, and she very lightly pressed the soft upper part of her forefinger against me.

'Alike?' I asked. 'What in the world can you be thinking of?'

'Monsters,' she said. 'Children.'

I smiled. But she didn't smile. She looked dreamy.

'I was so glad when you came,' she said. 'I knew he was dead. I knew when you stood at the end of the piano and you looked at me. I knew when you stood there listening to me. I was so happy that there was someone who could kill him.'

'Do this for me,' I said.

'What?' she asked. 'Armand, I'll do anything.'

'Go to the piano now. Play it for me. Play the *Appassionata*.'

'But the plan,' she asked in a small wondering voice. 'The evil man, he's coming.'

'Leave this to Benji and me. Don't turn around to look. Just play the *Appassionata*.'

'No, please,' she asked gently.

'But why not?' I said. 'Why must you put yourself through such an ordeal?'

'You don't understand,' she said with the widest eyes. 'I want to see it!'

Benji had just returned below. The distant sound of his voice, quite inaudible to Sybelle, instantly drove back the pain from all the surfaces of my limbs.

'That's what I mean, you see,' he was talking away, 'it's all underneath the dead body, and we don't wanna lift it, the dead body, and you being a cop, you know, you being Drug Enforcement, they said you would know how to take care of it . . .'

I started to laugh. He had really done himself proud. I looked again at Sybelle, who was staring at me with a quiet resolute expression, one of profound intelligence and reflection.

'Push this cover up over my face,' I said, 'and move away, far away. He's bringing us a regular prince of rogues. Hurry.'

She snapped into action. I could smell the blood of this victim already, though he was still in the ascending elevator, talking to Benji in low guarded terms.

'And all this you just happen to have in this apartment, you and she, and there's nobody else in on this?'

Oh, he was a beauty. I heard the murderer in his voice.

'I told you everything,' Benji said in the most natural of little voices. 'You just help with this, you know, I can't have the police coming in here!' Whisper. 'This is a fine hotel. How did I know this guy was going to die here! We don't use this stuff, you take the stuff, just get the body out of here. Now let me tell you—.'

The elevator opened to our floor.

'—this body is pretty messed up, so don't go all slobbering on me when you see it.'

'Slobbering on you,' growled the victim under his breath. Their shoes made soft hastening sounds on the carpet.

Benji fumbled with his keys, pretending to be mixed up.

'Sybelle,' he called out in warning. 'Sybelle, open the door.'

'Don't do it,' I said in a low voice.

'Of course not,' came her velvety answer.

The barrels of the big lock turned.

'And this guy just happens to come up here and die on you with all this stuff.'

'Well, not exactly,' said Benji, 'but you made a bargain with me, no, I expect you to stick to it.'

'Look, you little guttersnipe, I didn't make any bargain with you.'

'Okay, then maybe I call the regular police then. I know you. Everybody in the bar knows you, who you are, you're always around. What are you going to do, big shot? Kill me?'

The door closed behind them. The smell of the man's blood flooded the apartment. He was besotted with brandy and had the poison cocaine in his veins as well, but none of this would make a particle of difference to my cleansing thirst. I could scarce contain myself. I felt my limbs tighten and try to flex beneath the coverlet.

'Well, isn't she the perfect princess,' he said, his eyes obviously having fallen on Sybelle. Sybelle made no answer.

'Never mind her, you look there, under the covers. Sybelle, you come here by me. Come on, Sybelle.'

'Under there? You're telling me the body's under

there, and the cocaine is under the body?'

'How many times I have to tell you?' asked Benji, no doubt with his characteristic shrug. 'Look, what part don't you understand, I'd like to know. You don't want this cocaine? I give it away. I'll be very popular in your favorite bar. Come on, Sybelle, this man says he will help, then he won't help, talk, talk, talk, typical government sleaze.'

'Who are you calling a sleaze, kid?' demanded the man with mock gentleness, the fragrance of the brandy thickening. 'That's some big vocabulary you have for such a little body. How old are you, kid? How the Hell did you get into this country? You go around in that nightgown all the time?'

'Yeah, sure, just call me Lawrence of Arabia,' said Benji. 'Sybelle, come over here.'

I didn't want her to come. I wanted her as far away from this as possible. She didn't move, and I was very glad of it.

'I like my clothes,' Benji chattered on. Puff of sweet cigarette smoke. 'I should dress like kids in this place, I suppose, in blue jeans? As if. My people dressed like this when Mohammed was in the desert.'

'Nothing like progress,' said the man with a deep throaty laugh.

He approached the bed with quick crisp steps. The scent of blood was so rich I could feel the pores of my burnt skin opening for it.

I used the tiniest part of my strength to form a telepathic picture of him through their eyes – a tall brown-eyed man, sallow white skin, gaunt cheeks, receding brown hair, in a handmade Italian suit of shining black silk with flashing diamond cufflinks on his rich linen. He was antsy, fingers working at his sides, almost unable to stand still, his brain a riot of dizzy

453

humor, cynicism and crazed curiosity. His eyes were greedy and playful. The ruthlessness underscored all, and there seemed in him a strong streak of genuine drug-nourished insanity. He wore his murders as proudly as he wore his princely suit and the shiny brown boots on his feet.

Sybelle came near the bed, the sharp sweet scent of her pure flesh mingling with the heavier richer scent of the man. But it was his blood I savored, his blood that brought the juices up into my parched mouth. I could barely keep from making a sigh beneath the covers. I felt my limbs about to dance right out of their painful paralysis.

The villain was sizing up the place, glancing left and right through open doors, listening for other voices, debating whether he should search this fancy over-stuffed and rambling hotel apartment before he did anything else. His fingers would not be still. In a flash of wordless thought, I caught the quick realization that he'd snorted the cocaine Benji had brought, and he wanted more immediately.

'My, but you are a beautiful young lady,' he said to Sybelle.

'Do you want me to lift the cover?' she asked.

I could smell the small handgun that was jammed in his high black leather boot, and the other gun, very fancy and modern, a distinctly different collection of metallic scents, in the holster under his arm. I could smell cash on him too, that unmistakable stale smell of filthy paper money.

'Come on, you chicken, buster?' asked Benji. 'You want me to pull back the cover? Say when. You're gonna be real surprised, believe me!'

'There's no body under there,' he said with a sneer. 'Why don't we sit down and have a little talk? This isn't

454

really your place, is it? I think you children need a little paternal guidance.'

'The body's all burnt up,' said Benji. 'Don't get sick now.'

'Burnt up!' said the man.

It was Sybelle's long hand that suddenly whipped the coverlet back. The cool air skidded across my skin. I stared up at the man who drew back, a half-strangled growl caught in his throat.

'For the love of God!'

My body sprang up, drawn by the plump fountain of blood like a hideous puppet on a score of whipping strings. I flailed against him, then anchored my burnt fingernails hard into his neck and wrapped the other arm around him in an agonizing embrace, my tongue flashing at the blood that spilled from the claw marks as I drew in and, ignoring the blazing pain in my face, opened my mouth wide and sank my fangs.

Now I had him.

His height, his strength, his powerful shoulders, his huge hands clamping to my hurt flesh, none of this could help him. I had him. I drew up the first thick swallow of blood and thought I would swoon. But my body wasn't about to allow it. My body had locked to him as if I were a thing of voracious tentacles.

At once, his crazed and luminous thoughts drew me down into a glitzy swirl of New York images, of careless cruelty and grotesque horror, of rampant drug-driven energy and sinister hilarity. I let the images flood me. I couldn't go for the quick death. I had to have every drop of blood inside him, and for that the heart must pump and pump; the heart must not give up.

If I had ever tasted blood this strong, this sweet and salty, I had no memory of it; there was no way in which memory could record such deliciousness, the absolute rapture of thirst slaked, of hunger cured, of loneliness dissolved in this hot and intimate embrace, in which the sound of my own seething, straining breath would have horrified me if I had cared about it.

Such a noise I made, such a dreadful feasting noise. My fingers massaged his thick muscles, my nostrils were pressed into his pampered soap-scented skin.

'Hmmm, love you, wouldn't hurt you for the world, you feel it, it's sweet, isn't it?' I whispered to him over the shallows of gorgeous blood. 'Hmmm, yes, so sweet, better than the finest brandy, hmmm . . .'

In his shock and disbelief, he suddenly let go utterly, surrendering to the delirium that I stoked with each word. I ripped at his neck, widening the wound, rupturing the artery more fully. The blood gushed anew.

An exquisite shiver ran down my back; it ran down the backs of my arms, and down my buttocks and legs. It was pain and pleasure commingled as the hot and lively blood forced itself into the microfibers of my shriveled flesh, as it plumped the muscles beneath the roasted skin, as it sank into the very marrow of my bones. More, I had to have more.

'Stay alive, you don't want to die, no, stay alive,' I crooned, rubbing my fingers up through his hair, feeling that they were fingers now, not the pterodactyl digits they'd been moments before. Oh, they were hot; it was the fire all over again, it was the fire blazing in my scorched limbs, this time death had to come, I couldn't bear this any longer, but a pinnacle had been reached, and now it was past and a great soothing ache rushed through me.

My face was pumped and teeming, my mouth full again and again, and my throat now swallowing without effort.

'Ah, yes, alive, you're so strong, so wonderfully

strong . . .' I whispered. 'Hmmm, no, don't go . . . not yet, it's not time.'

His knees buckled. He sank slowly to the carpet, and I with him, pulling him gently over with me against the side of the bed, and then letting him fall beside me, so that we lay like lovers entangled. There was more, much more, more than ever I could have drunk in my regular state, more than ever I could have wanted.

Even on those rare occasions when I was a fledgling and greedy and new, and had taken two or three victims a night, I had never drunk so deeply from any one of them. I was now into the dark tasty dregs, pulling out the very vessels themselves in sweet clots that dissolved on my tongue.

'Oh, you are so precious, yes, yes.'

But his heart could take no more. It was slowing to a lethal irretrievable pace. I closed my teeth on the skin of his face and ripped it open over his forehead, lapping at the rich tangle of bleeding vessels that covered his skull. There was so much blood here, so much blood behind the tissues of the face. I sucked up the fibers, and then spit them out bloodless and white, watching them drop to the floor like so much slop.

I wanted the heart and the brain. I had seen the ancients take it. I knew how. I'd seen the Roman Pandora once reach right into the chest.

I went for it. Astonished to see my hand fully formed though dark brown in color, I made my fingers rigid like a deadly spade and drove it into him, tearing linen and cracking breastbone, and then reaching his soft entrails until I had the heart and held it as I'd seen Pandora hold it. I drank from it. Oh, it had plenty of blood. This was magnificent. I sucked it to pulp and then let it fall.

I lay as still as he, at his side, my right hand on the back of his neck, my head bowed against his chest, my breath coming in heavy sighs. The blood danced in me. I felt my arms and legs jerking. Spasms ran through me, so that the sight of his white dead carcass blinkered in my gaze. The room flashed on and off.

'Oh, what a sweet brother,' I whispered. 'Sweet, sweet brother.' I rolled on my back. I could hear the roar of his blood in my very ears, feel it moving over my scalp, feel it tingling in my cheeks and in the palms of my hands. Oh, good, too good, too lusciously good.

'Bad guy, hmmm?' It was Benji's voice, far away in the world of the living.

Far away in another realm where pianos ought to be played, and little boys should dance, they stood, the two like painted cutout figures against the swimming light of the room, merely gazing at me, he the little desert rogue with his fancy black cigarette, puffing away and smacking his lips and raising his eyebrows, and she merely floating it seemed, resolute and thoughtful as before, unshocked, untouched perhaps.

I sat up and pulled up my knees. I rose to my feet, with only a quick handhold on the side of the bed to steady myself. I stood naked looking at her.

Her eyes were filled with a deep rich gray light, and she smiled as she looked at me.

'Oh, magnificent,' she whispered.

'Magnificent?' I said. I lifted my hands and pushed my hair back off my face. 'Show me to the glass. Hurry. I'm thirsting. I'm thirsting again already.'

It had begun, this was no lie. In a stupor of shock I stared into the mirror. I had seen such ruined specimens as this before, but each of us is ruined in our own way, and I, for alchemical reasons I couldn't proclaim, was a dark brown creature, the very perfect color of chocolate, with remarkably white opal eyes set with reddish-brown pupils. The nipples of my chest were black as raisins.

My cheeks were painfully gaunt, my ribs perfectly defined beneath my shiny skin, and the veins, the veins that were so full of sizzling action, stood like ropes along my arms and the calves of my legs. My hair, of course, had never seemed so lustrous, so full, so much a thing of youth and natural beneficence.

I opened my mouth. I ached with thirst. All the awakened flesh sang with thirst or cursed me with it. It was as if a thousand crushed and muted cells were now chanting for blood.

'I have to have more. I have to. Stay away from me.' I hurried past Benji, who all but danced at my side.

'What do you want, what can I do? I'll get another one.'

'No, I'll get him for myself.' I fell on the victim and slipped loose his silk tie. I quickly undid the buttons of his shirt.

Benji fell at once to unbuckling his belt. Sybelle, on her knees, tugged at his boots.

'The gun, beware of the gun,' I said in alarm. 'Sybelle, back away from him.'

'I see the gun,' she said reprovingly. She laid it aside carefully, as if it were a freshly caught fish and might flop from her hands. She peeled off his socks. 'Armand, these clothes,' she said, 'they're too big.'

'Benji, you have shoes?' I asked. 'My feet are small.'

I stood up and hastily put on the shirt, fastening the buttons with a speed that dazzled them.

'Don't watch me, get the shoes,' I said. I pulled on the trousers, zipped them up, and with Sybelle's quick fingers to help, buckled the flapping leather belt. I pulled it as tight as I could. This would do.

She crouched before me, her dress a huge flowered circle of prettiness around her, as she rolled the pant legs over my brown bare feet.

I had slipped my hands through his fancy linked shirt cuffs without ever disturbing them.

Benji threw down the black dress shoes, fine Bally pumps, never even worn by him, divine little wretch. Sybelle held one sock for my foot. Benji gathered up the other.

When I put on the coat it was done. The sweet tingling in my veins had stopped. It was pain again, it was beginning to roar, as if I were threaded with fire, and the witch with the needle pulled on the thread, hard, to make me quiver.

'A towel, my dears, something old, common. No, don't, not in this day and age, don't think of it.'

Full of loathing I gazed down at his livid flesh. He lay staring dully at the ceiling, the soft tiny hair in his nostrils very black against his drained and awful skin, his teeth yellow above his colorless lip. The hair on his chest was a matted swarm in the sweat of his death, and against the giant gaping slit lay the pulp that had been his heart, ah, this was the evil evidence which must be shut from the eyes of the world on general principles.

I reached down and slipped the ruins of his heart back into the cavity of his chest. I spit upon the wound and rubbed it with my fingers.

Benji gasped. 'Look at it heal, Sybelle,' he cried.

'Just barely,' I said. 'He's too cold, too empty.' I looked about. There lay the man's wallet, papers, a bag in leather, lots of green bills in a fancy silver clip. I gathered all this up. I stuffed the folded money in one pocket, and all else in the other. What else did he have? Cigarette, a deadly switchblade knife, and the guns, ah, yes, the guns.

Into my coat pockets I put these items.

Swallowing my nausea, I reached down and scooped him up, horrid flaccid white man in his pitiable silk shorts and fancy gold wristwatch. My old strength was indeed coming back. He was heavy, but I could easily heave him over my shoulder.

'What will you do, where will you go?' Sybelle cried. 'Armand, you can't leave us.'

'You'll come back!' said Benji. 'Here, gimme that watch, don't throw away that man's watch.'

'Sshhh, Benji,' Sybelle whispered. 'You know damned good and well I've bought you the finest watches. Don't touch him. Armand, what can we do now to help you?' She drew close to me. 'Look!' she said pointing to the dangling arm of the corpse which hung just below my right elbow. 'He has manicured nails. How amazing.'

'Oh, yeah, he always took very good care of himself,' said Benji. 'You know the watch is worth five thousand dollars.'

'Hush up about the watch,' she said. 'We don't want his things.' She looked at me again. 'Armand, even now you're still changing. Your face, it's getting fuller.'

'Yes, and it hurts,' I said. 'Wait for me. Prepare a dark room for me. I'll come back as soon as I've fed. I have to feed now, feed and feed to heal the scars that are left. Open the door for me.'

'Let me see if there's anyone out there,' said Benji with a quick dutiful rush to the door.

I went out into the hallway, easily carrying the poor corpse, its white arms hanging down, swinging and banging against me just a little.

What a sight I was in these big clothes. I must have looked like a mad poetical schoolboy who had raided the thrift stores for the finest threads and was off now in fancy new shoes to search out the rock bands.

'There isn't anyone out here, my little friend,' I said. 'It's three of the clock and the hotel's asleep. And if reason serves me right, that's the door of the fire stairs there, at the very end of the hall, correct? There isn't anyone in the fire stairs either.'

'Oh, clever Armand, you delight me!' he said. He narrowed his little black eyes. He jumped up and down soundlessly on the hallway carpet. 'Give me the watch!' he whispered.

'No,' I said. 'She's right. She's rich, and so am I, and so are you. Don't be a beggar.'

'Armand, we'll wait for you,' said Sybelle in the doorframe. 'Benji, come inside immediately.'

'Oh, listen to her now, how she wakes up! How she talks! "Benji, come inside," she says. Hey, sweetheart, don't you have something to do just now, like perhaps play the piano?'

She gave a tiny burst of laughter in spite of herself. I smiled. What a strange pair they were. They did not believe their own eyes. But that was typical enough in this century. I wondered when they would start to see, and having seen, start screaming.

'Goodbye, sweet loves,' I said. 'Be ready for me.'

'Armand, you will come back.' Her eyes were full of tears. 'You promise me.'

I was stunned. 'Sybelle,' I said. 'What is it that women want so often to hear and wait so long to hear it? I love you.'

I left them, racing down the stairs, hefting him to the other shoulder when the weight on the one side became too hurtful. The pain passed over me in waves. The shock of the outside cold air was scalding.

'Feed,' I whispered. And what was I to do with him? He was far too naked to carry down Fifth Avenue.

I slipped off his watch because it was the only identification on him left, and almost vomiting with revulsion from my closeness to these fetid remains, I dragged him by one hand after me very fast through the

462

back alley, and then across a small street, and down another sidewalk.

I ran into the face of the icy wind, not stopping to observe those few hulking shapes that hobbled by in the wet darkness, or to take stock of the one car that crept along on the shining wet asphalt.

Within seconds I had covered two blocks, and finding a likely alleyway, with a high gate to keep out the beggars of the night, I quickly mounted the bars and flung his carcass to the very far end of it. Down into the melting snow he fell. I was rid of him.

Now I had to have blood. There was no time for the old game, the game of drawing out those who wanted to die, those who truly craved my embrace, those in love already with the far country of death of which they knew nothing.

I had to shuffle and stumble along, the mark, in my floppy silk jacket and rolled pants, long hair veiling my face, poor dazzled kid, perfect for your knife, your gun, your fist.

It didn't take long.

The first was a drunken, sauntering wretch who plied me with questions before he revealed the flashing blade and went to sink it into me. I pushed him up against the side of the building, and fed like a glutton.

The next was a common desperate youth, full of festering sores, who had killed twice before for the heroin he needed as badly as I needed the doomed blood inside him.

I drank more slowly.

The thickest worst scars of my body yielded with much defense, itching, throbbing and only slowly melting away. But the thirst, the thirst would not stop. My bowels churned as if devouring themselves. My eyes pulsed with pain.

But the cold wet city, so full of rankling hollow noise, grew ever brighter before me. I could hear voices many blocks away, and small electronic speakers in high buildings. I could see beyond the breaking clouds the true and numberless stars.

I was almost myself again.

So who will come to me now, I thought, in this barren desolate hour before dawn, when the snow is melting in the warmer air, and neon lights have all died out, and the wet newspaper blows like leaves through a stripped and frozen forest?

I took all the precious articles which had belonged to my first victim, and dropped them here and there into deep hollow public trash cans.

One last killer, yes, please, fate, do give me this, while there's time, and indeed he came, blasted fool, out of a car as behind him the driver waited, the motor idling.

'What's taking you so damn long?' said the driver at last.

'Nothing,' I said, dropping his friend. I leaned in to look at him. He was as vicious and stupid as his companion. He threw up his hand, but helplessly and too late. I pushed him over on the leather seat and drank now for rank pleasure, pure sweet crazed pleasure.

I walked slowly through the night, my arms out, my eyes directed Heavenward.

From the scattered black grates of the gleaming street there gushed the pure white steam of heated places below. Trash in shiny plastic sacks made a fantastical modern and glittering display on the curbs of the slate-gray sidewalks.

Tiny tender trees, with little year-round leaves like short pen strokes of bright green in the night, bent their stemlike trunks with the whining wind. Everywhere the high clean glass doors of granite-faced buildings contained the radiant splendor of rich lobbies. Shop windows displayed their sparkling diamonds, lustrous furs and smartly cut coats and gowns on grandly coiffed and faceless pewter mannequins.

The Cathedral was a lightless, soundless place of frost-rimmed turrets and ancient pointed arches, the pavement clean where I had stood on the morning when the sun caught me.

Lingering there, I closed my eyes, trying perhaps to recall the wonder and the zeal, the courage and the glorious expectation.

There came instead, clear and shining through the dark air, the pristine notes of the *Appassionata*. Roiling, rumbling, racing on, the crashing music came to call me home. I followed it.

The clock in the hotel foyer was striking six. The winter dark would break up in moments like the very ice that had once imprisoned me. The long polished desk was deserted in the muted lights.

In a wall mirror of dim glass framed in rococo gold, I saw myself, paled and waxen, and unblemished. Oh, what fun the sun and ice had had with me in turns, the fury of the one quick-frozen by the merciless grip of the other. Not a scar remained of where the skin had burnt to muscle. A sealed and solid thing with seamless agony within, I was, all of a piece, restored, with sparkling clear white fingernails, and curling lashes round my clear brown eyes, and clothes a wretched heap of stained, misfitted finery on the old familiar rugged cherub.

Never before had I been thankful to see my own too youthful face, too hairless chin, too soft and delicate hands. But I could have thanked the gods of old for wings at this moment.

Above, the music carried on, so grand, so legible of tragedy and lust and dauntless spirit. I loved it so. Who in the whole wide world could ever play that same Sonata as she did, each phrase as fresh as songs sung all their livelong life by birds who know but one such set of patterns.

I looked about. It was a fine, expensive place, of old wainscoting and a few deep chairs, and door keys ranged up a wall in tiny dark-stained wooden boxes.

A great vase of flowers, the infallible trademark of the vintage New York hotel, stood boldly and magnificently in the middle of the space, atop a round black marble table. I skirted the bouquet, snapping off one big pink lily with a deep red throat and petals curling to yellow at the outside, and then I went silently up the fire stairs to find my children.

She did not stop her playing when Benji let me in.

'You're looking really good, Angel,' he said.

On and on she went, her head moving unaffectedly and perfectly with the rhythm of the Sonata.

He led me through a chain of finely decorated plastered chambers. Mine was too sumptuous by far, I whispered, seeing the tapestry spread and pillows of old gracious threadbare gold. I needed only perfect darkness.

'But this is the least we have,' he said with a little shrug.

He had changed to a fresh white linen robe lined with a fine blue stripe, a kind I'd often seen in Arab lands. He wore white socks with his brown sandals. He puffed his little Turkish cigarette, and squinted up at me through the smoke.

'You brought me back the watch, didn't you!' He nodded his head, all sarcasm and amusement.

'No,' I said. I reached into my pocket. 'But you may

have the money. Tell me, since your little mind is such a locket and I have no key, did anyone see you bring that badge-carrying, gun-toting villain up here?'

'I see him all the time,' he said with a little weary wave of his hand.

'We left the bar separately. I killed two birds with one stone. I'm very smart.'

'How so?' I asked. I put the lily in his little hand.

'Sybelle's brother bought from him. That cop was the only guy ever missed him.' He gave a little laugh. He tucked the lily in the thick curls above his left ear, then pulled it down and twirled its tiny ciborium in his fingers. 'Clever, no? Now nobody asks where he is.'

'Oh, indeed, two birds with one stone, you're quite right,' I said. 'Though I'm sure there's a great deal more to it.'

'But you'll help us now, won't you?'

' I will indeed. I'm very rich, I told you. I'll patch things up. I have an instinct for it. I owned a great playhouse in a faraway city, and after that an island of fancy shops, and other such things. I am a monster in many realms, it seems. You'll never, ever have to fear again.'

'You're truly beauty full, you know,' he said raising one eyebrow and then giving me a quick wink. He drew on his tasty-looking little cigarette and then offered it to me. His left hand kept the lily safe.

'Can't. Only drink blood,' I said. 'A regular vampire out of the book in the main. Need deep darkness in the light of day, which is coming very soon. You mustn't touch this door.'

'Ha!' he laughed with impish delight. 'That's what I told her!' He rolled his eyes and glanced in the direction of the living room. 'I said we had to steal a coffin for you right away, but she said, no, you'd think of that.'

'How right she was. The room will do, but I like coffins well enough. I really do.'

'And can you make us vampires too?'

'Oh, never. Absolutely not. You're pure of heart and too alive, and I don't have such a power. It's never done. It can't be.'

Again, he shrugged. 'Then who made you?' he asked.

'I was born out of a black egg,' I said. 'We all are.'

He gave a scoffing laugh.

'Well, you've seen all the rest,' I said. 'Why not believe the best part of it?'

He only smiled and puffed his smoke, and looked at me most knavishly.

The piano sang on in crashing cascades, the rapid notes melting as fast as they were born, so like the last thin snowflakes of the winter, vanishing before they strike the pavements.

'May I kiss her before I go to sleep?' I asked.

He cocked his head, and shrugged. 'If she doesn't like it, she'll never stop playing long enough to say so.'

I went back into the parlor. How clear it all was, the grand design of sumptuous French landscapes with their golden clouds and cobalt skies, the Chinese vases on their stands, the massed velvet tumbling from the high bronze rods of the narrow old windows. I saw it all of a piece, including the bed where I had lain, now heaped with fresh down-filled coverlets and pillowed with embroidered antique faces.

And she, the center diamond of it all, in long white flannel, flounced at wrists and hem with rich old Irish lace, playing her long lacquered grand with agile unerring fingers, her hair a broad smooth yellow glow about her shoulders.

I kissed her scented locks, and then her tender throat, and caught her girlish smile and gleaming glance as she played on, her head tilting back to brush my coat front.

Down around her neck, I slipped my arms. She leant her gentle weight against me. With crossed arms, I clasped her waist. I felt her shoulders moving against my snug embrace with her darting fingers.

I dared in whisper-soft tones with sealed lips to hum the song, and she hummed with me.

'*Appassionata*,' I whispered in her ear. I was crying. I didn't want to touch her with blood. She was too clean, too pretty. I turned my head.

She pitched forward. Her hands pounded into the stormy finish.

A silence fell, abrupt, and crystalline as the music before it.

She turned and threw her arms around me, and held me tight and said the words I'd never heard a mortal speak in all my long immortal life:

'Armand, I love you.'

Need I say they are the perfect companions?

Neither of them cared about the murders. I could not for the life of me understand it. They cared about other things such as world peace, the poor suffering homeless in the waning winter cold of New York, the price of medicines for the sick, and how dreadful it was that Israel and Palestine were forever in battle with each other. But they did not care one whit about the horrors they'd beheld with their own eyes. They did not care that I killed every night for blood, that I lived off it and nothing else, and that I was a creature wed by my very nature to human destruction.

They did not care one whit about the dead brother (his name was Fox, by the way, and the last name of my beautiful child is best left unmentioned).

In fact if this text ever sees the light of the real world, you're bound to change both her first name and that of Benjamin.

However, that's not my concern now. I can't think of the fate of these pages, except that they are very much for her, as I mentioned to you before, and if I'm allowed to title them I think it will be *Symphony for Sybelle*.

Not, please understand, that I love Benji no less. It's only that I haven't the same overwhelming protective feeling for him. I know that Benji will live out a great and adventurous life, no matter what should befall me or Sybelle, or even the times. It's in his flexible and enduring Bedouin nature. He is a true child of the tents and the blowing sands, though in his case, the house was a dismal cinder block hovel on the outskirts of Jerusalem where he induced tourists to pose for overpriced pictures with him and a filthy snarling camel.

He'd been flat out kidnapped by Fox under the felonious terms of a long-term lease of bondage for which Fox paid Benji's father five thousand dollars. A fabricated emigration passport was thrown into the bargain. He'd been the genius of the tribe, without doubt, had mixed feelings about going home and had learnt in the New York streets to steal, smoke and curse, in that order. Though he swore up and down he couldn't read, it turned out that he could, and began to do so obsessively just as soon as I started throwing books at him.

In fact, he could read English, Hebrew and Arabic, having read all three in the newspapers of his homeland since before he could remember.

He loved taking care of Sybelle. He saw to it that she ate, drank milk, bathed and changed her clothes when none of these routine tasks interested her. He prided himself on the fact that he could by his wits obtain for her whatever she needed, no matter what happened to her.

He was the front man for her with the hotel, tipping the maids, making normal talk at the front desk, which included remarkably finespun lies about the whereabouts of the dead Fox, who had become in Benji's never ending saga a fabulous world traveler and amateur photographer; he handled the piano tuner, who was called as often as once a week because the piano stood by the window, exposed to sun and cold, and also because Sybelle did indeed pound it with the fury that would indeed have impressed the great Beethoven. He spoke on the phone to the bank, all of whose personnel thought he was his older brother,

David, pronounced Dahveed, and then made the requisite calls at the teller's window for cash as little Benjamin.

I was convinced within nights of talking with him that I could give him as fine an education as Marius had ever given me, and that he would end up having his choice of universities, professions or amateur pursuits of mind-engaging substance. I didn't overplay my hand. But before the week was out I was dreaming of boarding schools for him from which he might emerge a gold-buttoned blue blazer-wearing American East Coast social conquistador.

I love him enough to tear limb from limb anyone who so much as lays a finger on him.

But between me and Sybelle there lies a sympathy which sometimes eludes mortals and immortals for the space of their entire lives. I know Sybelle. I know her. I knew her when I first heard her play, and I know her now, and I wouldn't be here with you if she were not under the protection of Marius. I will during the space of Sybelle's life never be parted from her, and there is nothing she can ever ask of me that I shall not give.

I will endure unspeakable anguish when Sybelle inevitably dies. But that has to be borne. I have no choice now in the matter. I am not the creature I was when I laid eyes on Veronica's Veil, when I stepped into the sun.

I am someone else, and that someone else has fallen deeply and completely in love with Sybelle and Benjamin and I cannot go back on it.

Of course I am keenly conscious that I thrive in this love; being happier than I have ever been in my entire immortal existence, I have gained great strength from having these two as my companions. The situation is too nearly perfect to be anything but utterly accidental.

Sybelle is not insane. She is nowhere near it, and I

fancy that I understand her perfectly. Sybelle is obsessed with one thing, and that is playing the piano. From the first time she laid her hands on the keys she has wanted nothing else. And her 'career,' as so generously planned for her by her proud parents and by the burningly ambitious Fox, never meant much of anything to her.

Had she been poor and struggling perhaps recognition would have been indispensable to her love affair with the piano, as it would have given her the requisite escape from life's dreary domestic traps and routines. But she was never poor. And she is truly, in the very root of her soul, indifferent as to whether people hear her play her music or not.

She needs only to hear it herself, and to know that she is not disturbing other people.

In the old hotel, mostly full of rooms rented by the day, with only a handful of tenants rich enough to be lodged there year by year, as was Sybelle's family, she can play forever without disturbing anyone.

And after her parents' tragic death, after she lost the only two witnesses who had been intimate to her development, she simply could not cooperate with Fox's plans for her career any further.

Well, all this I understood, almost from the beginning. I understood it in her incessant repetition of the Sonata No. 23, and I think if you were to hear it, you would understand it too. I want you to hear it.

Understand, it will not at all faze Sybelle if other people do gather to listen to her. It won't bother her one whit if she's recorded. If other people enjoy her playing and tell her so, she's delighted. But it's a simple thing with her. 'Ah, so you too love it,' she thinks. 'Isn't it beautiful?' This is what she said to me with her eyes and her smiles the very first time I ever approached her.

And I suppose before I go any further – and I do have

473

more to put down about my children – I should address this question: How did I approach her? How did I come to be in her apartment on that fateful morning, when Dora stood in the Cathedral crying to the crowds about the miraculous Veil, and I, the blood in my veins having combusted, was in fact rocketing skyward?

I don't know. I have rather tiresome supernatural explanations that read like tomes by members of the Society for the Study of Psychic Phenomena, or the scripts for Mulder and Scully on the television show called *The X-Files*. Or like a secret file on the case in the archives of the order of psychic detectives called the Talamasca.

Bluntly, I see it this way. I have most-powerful abilities to cast spells, to dislocate my vision, and to transmit my image over distances, and to affect matter both at close range and matter which is out of sight. I must somehow, in this morning journey towards the clouds, have used this power. It might have been drawn from me in a moment of harrowing pain when I was for all purposes deranged and completely unaware of what was happening to me. It might have been a last desperate hysterical refusal to accept the possibility of death, or of the horrible predicament, so close to death, in which I found myself.

That is, having fallen on the roof, burnt and in unspeakable torment, I might have sought a desperate mental escape, projecting my image and my strength into Sybelle's apartment long enough to kill her brother. It certainly is possible for spirits to exert enough pressure on matter to change it. So perhaps that is exactly what I did – project myself in spirit form and lay hands upon the substance that was Fox, and kill him.

But I don't really believe all this. I'll tell you why.

First off, though Sybelle and Benjamin are no

experts, for all their savvy and seeming detachment, on the subject of death and its subsequent forensic analysis, they both insisted that Fox's body was bloodless when they got rid of it. The puncture wounds were apparent on his neck. In sum, they believe to this very hour that I was there, in substantial form, and that I did indeed drink Fox's blood.

Now that a projected image cannot do, at least not insofar as I know it. No, it cannot devour the blood of an entire circulatory system and then dissolve itself, returning to the cicatricula of the mind from which it came. No, that is not possible.

Of course, Sybelle and Benji could be wrong. What do they know about blood and bodies? But the fact is, they let Fox lie there, quite dead for some two days, or so they said, while they waited for the return of the Dybbuk or Angel whom they were sure would help them. Now in that time, the blood of a human body sinks down to the very lowest part of the carcass, and such a change would have been visible to these children. They noted no such thing.

Ah, it makes my brain ache! The fact is, I don't know how I got to their apartment, or why. I don't know how it happened. And I do know, as I have already said, that as regards the entire experience – everything I saw and felt in the great restored Cathedral at Kiev, an impossible place – was as real as what I knew in Sybelle's apartment.

There is one other small point, and though it is small it is crucial. After I had slain Fox, Benji did see my burnt body falling from the sky. He did see me, just as I saw him, from the window.

There is one very terrible possibility. It is this. I was going to die that morning. It was going to happen. My ascent was driven by immense will and an immense love of God of which I have no doubt as I dictate these words now.

But perhaps at the crucial moment, my courage failed me. My body failed me. And seeking some refuge from the sun, some way to thwart my martyrdom, I struck upon the predicament of Sybelle and her brother, and feeling her great need of me, I commenced to fall towards the shelter of the roof on which the snow and ice quickly covered me. My visit to Sybelle could have been, according to this interpretation, only a passing illusion, a powerful projection of self, as I've said, a wish fulfillment of the need of this random and vulnerable girl about to be fatally beaten by her brother.

As for Fox, I killed him, without doubt. But he died from fear, from failure of the heart, perhaps, from the pressure of my illusory hands on his fragile throat, from the power of telekinesis or suggestion.

But as I stated before, I don't believe this.

I was there in the Cathedral in Kiev. I broke the egg with my thumbs. I saw the bird fly free.

I know my Mother stood at my side, and I know that my Father knocked over the chalice. I know because I know there is no part of me that could have imagined such a thing. And I know too because the colors I saw then and the music I heard were not made up of anything I had ever experienced.

Now, there is simply no other dream I have ever had about which I can say this. When I said the Mass in Vladimir's City, I was in a realm made up of ingredients which my imagination simply does not have at its disposal.

I don't want to say any more about it. It's too hurtful and awful to try to analyze it. I didn't will it, not with my conscious heart, and I had no conscious power over it. It simply happened.

476

I would, if I could, forget it entirely. I am so extraordinarily happy with Sybelle and Benji that surely I want to forget it all for the space of their lifetimes. I want only to be with them, as I have been since the night I described to you.

As you realize, I took my time in coming here. Having returned to the ranks of the dangerous Undead, it was very easy for me to discern from the roaming minds of other vampires that Lestat was safe in his prison here, and indeed was dictating to you the entire story of what had happened to him with God Incarnate and with Memnoch the Devil.

It was very easy for me to discern, without revealing my own presence, that an entire world of vampires mourned for me with greater anguish and tears than I could ever have predicted.

So, being confident of Lestat's safety, being baffled yet relieved by the mysterious fact that his stolen eye had been returned to him, I was at leisure to stay with Sybelle and Benji and I did so.

With Benji and Sybelle I rejoined the world in a way which I had not done since my fledgling, my one and only fledgling, Daniel Molloy, had left me. My love for Daniel had never been entirely honest, and always viciously possessive, and quite entangled with my own hatred of the world at large, and my confusion in the face of the baffling modern times which had begun to open up to me when I emerged in the late years of the Eighteenth Century from the catacombs beneath Paris.

Daniel himself had no use for the world, and had come to me hungering for our Dark Blood, his brain swimming with macabre, grotesque tales which Louis de Pointe du Lac had told him. Heaping every luxury upon him, I only sickened him with mortal sweets so that finally he turned away from the riches I offered, becoming a vagabond. Mad, roaming the streets in rags, he shut out the world almost to the point of death, and I, weak, muddled, tormented by his beauty, and lusting for the living man and not the vampire he might become, only brought him over to us through the working of the Dark Trick because he would have died otherwise.

I was no Marius to him afterwards. It was too exactly as I supposed: he loathed me in his heart for having initiated him into Living Death, for having made him in one night both an immortal and a regular killer.

As a mortal man, he had no real idea of the price we pay for what we are, and he did not want to learn the truth; he fled from it, in reckless dreams and spiteful wandering.

And so it was as I feared. Making him to be my mate, I made a minion who saw me all the more clearly as a monster.

There was never any innocence for us, there was never any springtime. There was never any chance, no matter how beautiful the twilight gardens in which we wandered. Our souls were out of tune, our desires crossed and our resentments too common and too well watered for the final flowering.

It's different now.

For two months I remained in New York with Sybelle and Benji, living as I've never lived before, not since those long-ago nights with Marius in Venice.

Sybelle is rich, as I think I've told you, but only in a tedious struggling sort of way, with an income that pays for her exorbitant apartment and daily room service meals, with a margin for fine clothes, tickets to the symphony and an occasional spending spree.

I am fabulously rich. So the first thing I did, with pleasure, was lavish upon Sybelle and Benjamin all the riches I had once lavished upon Daniel Molloy to much greater effect.

They loved it.

Sybelle, when she was not playing the piano, had no objections whatsoever to wandering to the picture shows with Benji and me, or to the symphony and the opera. She loved the ballet, and loved to take Benjamin to the finest restaurants, where he became a regular marvel to the waiters with his crisp enthusiastic little voice and his lilting way of rattling off the names of dishes, French or Italian, and ordering vintage wines which they poured for him, unquestioningly, despite all the good-intentioned laws that prohibit the serving of such strong spirits to children.

I loved all this too, of course, and was delighted to discover that Sybelle also took a sporadic and playful interest in dressing me, in choosing jackets, shirts and such from racks with a quick point of her finger, and in picking out for me from velvet trays all kinds of jeweled rings, cufflinks, neck chains and tiny crucifixes of rubies and gold, solid-gold clips for money and that sort of thing.

It was I who had played this masterly game with Daniel Molloy. Sybelle plays it with me in her own dreamy way, as I take care of the tiresome cash register details.

I in turn have the supreme pleasure of carrying Benji about like a doll and getting him to wear all the Western finery I purchase, at least now and then, for an hour or two.

We make a striking trio, the three of us dining at Lutèce or Sparks (of course I don't dine) – Benji in his immaculate little desert robe, or got up in a finely fitted little suit with narrow lapels, white buttondown shirt and flash of tie; me in my highly acceptable antique velvet and chokers of old crumbling lace; and Sybelle in the lovely dresses that spill endlessly out of her closet, confections her Mother and Fox once bought for her, close cut around her large breasts and small waist and always flaring magically about her long legs, hem high enough to reveal the splendid curve of her calf and its tautness when she slips her dark-stockinged feet into dagger-heeled slippers. Benji's close-cropped cap of curls is always the Byzantine halo for his dark enigmatic little face, her flowing waves are free, and my hair is the Renaissance mop again of long unruly curls that used to be my secret vanity.

My deepest pleasure with Benji is education. Right off, we started having powerful conversations about history and the world, and found ourselves stretched out on the carpet of the apartment, poring over maps, as we discussed the entire progress of East and West and the inevitable influences upon human history of climate, culture and geography. Benji gabbles away all during television broadcasts of the news, calling each anchor-person intimately by his or her first name, slamming his fist in anger at the actions of world leaders and wailing loudly over the deaths of great princesses and humanitarians. Benji can watch the news, talk steadily, eat popcorn, smoke a cigarette and sing intermittently with Sybelle's playing, always on key – all more or less simultaneously.

If I fall to staring at the rain as if I've seen a ghost, it's Benji who beats on my arm and cries, 'What shall we do, Armand? We have three splendid movies to see tonight. I'm vexed, I tell you, vexed, because if we go to any of these, we'll miss Pavarotti at the Met and I'll go pastywhite with sickness.'

Many times the two of us dress Sybelle, who looks at us as if she doesn't know what we're doing. We always sit talking with her when she bathes, because if we don't she's likely to go to sleep in the bathtub, or simply stay in there for hours, sponging the water over her beautiful breasts.

Sometimes the only words she says all night are things like, 'Benji, tie your shoes,' or 'Armand, he's stolen the silverware. Make him put it back,' or with sudden astonishment, 'It's warm, isn't it?'

I have never told anyone my life story as I've told it to you here and now, but in conversation with Benji I have caught myself telling him many things which Marius told me – about human nature, and the history of the law, about painting and even about music.

It was in these conversations, more than in anything else, that I came to realize in the last two months that I was a changed being.

Some stifling dark terror is gone from me. I do not see history as a panorama of disasters, as once I think I did; and often I find myself remembering Marius's generous and beautifully optimistic predictions – that the world is ever improving; that war, for all the strife we see around us, has nevertheless gone out of fashion with those in power, and will soon pass from the arenas of the Third World as it has passed from the arenas of the West; and we will truly feed the hungry and shelter the homeless and take care of those who need love.

With Sybelle, education and discussion are not the substance of our love. With Sybelle it is intimacy. I don't care if she never says anything. I don't go inside her mind. She doesn't want anybody to do that.

As completely as she accepts me and my nature, I accept her and her obsession with the *Appassionata*. Hour after hour, night after night, I listen to Sybelle play, and with each fresh start I hear the minute changes of intensity and expression which pour forth in her playing. Gradually, on account of this, I have become the only listener of whom Sybelle has ever been conscious.

Gradually, I have become part of Sybelle's music. I am there with her and the phrases and movements of the *Appassionata*. I am there and I am one who has never asked anything of Sybelle except that she do what she wants to do, and what she can do so perfectly.

That's all Sybelle ever has to do for me – is what she will.

If or when she wants to rise in 'fortune and men's eyes,' I'll clear the way for her. If or when she wants to be alone, she will not see or hear me. If or when she wants anything, I will get it for her.

And if or when she loves a mortal man or mortal woman, I'll do what she wants me to do. I can live in the shadows. Doting on her, I can live forever in gloom because there is no gloom when I am near her.

Sybelle often goes with me when I hunt. Sybelle likes to see me feed and kill. I don't think I have ever allowed a mortal to do that. She tries to help me dispose of the remains or confuse the evidence of the cause of death, but I'm very strong and swift and capable at this, so she is mostly the witness.

I try to avoid taking Benji on these escapades because he becomes wildly and childishly excited, and it does him no good. To Sybelle it simply does nothing.

There are other things I could tell you – how we handled the details of her brother's disappearance, how I transferred immense sums of money into her name and set up the appropriate and unbreakable trust funds for Benji, how I bought for her a substantial interest in the hotel in which she lives, and have put into her apartment, which is very huge for a hotel apartment, several other fine pianos which she enjoys, and how I have set aside for myself a safe distance from the apartment a lair with a coffin which is unfindable, unbreachable and indestructible, and to which I go on occasion, though I am more accustomed to sleeping in the little chamber they first gave to me, in which velvet curtains have been fitted tightly over the one window to the airwell.

But the hell with all that.

You know what I want you to know.

What remains for us but to bring it to the moment, to sunset on this night when I came here, entering the very den of the vampires with my brother and with my sister, one on either side to see Lestat at last.

This is all a little too simple, isn't it? I mean by that, my transformation from the zealous child who stood on the porch of the Cathedral to the happy monster making up his mind one spring night in New York City that it was time to journey south and look in on his old friend.

You know why I came here.

Let me begin at the start of this evening. You were there in the chapel when I arrived.

You greeted me with undisguised good will, so pleased to see I was alive and unharmed. Louis almost wept.

Those others, those raggedy young ones who were clustered about, two boys, I believe, and a girl, I don't know who they were, and still don't, only that later they drifted off.

I was horrified to see him undefended, lying on the floor, and his mother, Gabrielle, far off in the corner merely staring at him, coldly, the way she stares at everything and everyone as though she never knew a human feeling for what it was.

I was horrified that the young tramps were about, and felt instantly protective of Sybelle and Benji. I had no fear of their seeing the classics among us, the legends, the warriors – you, beloved Louis, even Gabrielle, and certainly not Pandora or Marius, who were all there.

But I hadn't wanted my children to look on common trash infused with our blood, and I wondered, arrogantly and vainly perhaps, as I always do at such moments, how these roguish sophomoric slob vampires ever came to be. Who made them and why and when?

At such times, the fierce old Child of Darkness wakes in me, the Coven Master beneath the Paris Cemetery who decreed when and how the Dark Blood should be given and, above all, to whom. But that old habit of authority is fraudulent and just a nuisance at best.

I hated these hangers-on because they were there looking at Lestat as though he were a Carnival Curiosity, and I wouldn't have it. I felt a sudden temper, an urge to destroy.

But there are no rules among us now that authorize such rash actions. And who was I to make a mutiny here under your roof? I didn't know you lived here then, no, but you certainly had custody of the Master of the Place, and you allowed it, the ruffians, and the three or four more of them that came shortly after and dared to circle him, none of them, I noticed, getting any too close.

Of course everyone was most curious about Sybelle and Benjamin. I told them quietly to stay directly beside me and not to stray. Sybelle couldn't get it out of her mind that the piano was so near at hand, and it would have a whole new sound for her Sonata. As for Benji, he was striding along like a little Samurai, checking out monsters all around, with his eyes like saucers though his mouth was very puckered up and stern and proud.

The chapel struck me as beautiful. How could it not? The plaster walls are white and pure, and the ceiling is gently coved, as in the oldest churches, and there is a deep coved shell where once the altar stood, which makes a well for sound, so that one footfall there echoes softly throughout the entire place.

The stained glass I'd seen brilliantly lighted from the street. Unfigured, it was nevertheless lovely with its vivid colors of blue and red and yellow, and its simple serpentine designs. I liked the old black lettering of the mortals long gone in whose memory each window had been erected. I liked the old plaster statues scattered about, which I had helped you to clear from the New York apartment and send south.

I had not looked at them much; I had shielded myself from their glass eyes as if they were basilisks. But I certainly looked at them now.

There was sweet suffering St. Rita in her black habit and white wimple, with the fearful awful sore in her forehead like a third eye. There was lovely, smiling Thérèse of Lisieux, the Little Flower of Jesus with His Crucifix and the bouquet of pink roses in her arms.

There was St. Teresa of Avila, carved out of wood and finely painted, with her eyes turned upwards, the mystic, and the feather quill in her hand that marked her as a Doctor of the Church.

There was St. Louis of France with his royal crown; St. Francis, of course, in humble brown monk's robes, with his gathering of tamed animals; and some others whose names I'm ashamed to say I didn't know.

What struck me more perhaps even than these scattered statues, standing like so many guardians of an old and sacred history, were the pictures on the wall that marked Christ's road to Calvary: the Stations of the Cross. Someone had put them all in the proper order, maybe even before our coming into the world of this place.

I divined that they were painted in oil on copper, and they had a Renaissance style to them, imitative certainly, but one which I find normal and which I love.

Immediately, the fear that had been hovering inside me during all my happy weeks in New York came to the fore. No, it was not fear so much as it was dread.

My Lord, I whispered. I turned and looked up at the Face of Christ on the high Crucifix above Lestat's head.

This was an excruciating moment. I think the image on Veronica's Veil overlaid what I saw there in the carved wood. I know it did. I was back in New York, and Dora was holding up the cloth for us to see.

I saw His dark beautifully shadowed eyes perfectly fixed on the cloth, as though part of it but not in any way absorbed by it, and the dark streaks of His eyebrows and, above His steady unchallenging gaze, the tricklets of blood from His thorns. I saw His lips partway open as if He had volumes to speak.

With a shock, I realized that from far off by the altar steps Gabrielle had fixed her glacial gray eyes on me, and I locked up my mind and digested the key. I wouldn't have her touch me or my thoughts. And I felt a bristling hostility for all those gathered in the room.

Louis came then. He was so happy that I had not perished. Louis had something to say. He knew I was concerned and he was anxious about the presence of the others. He looked his usual ascetic self, got up in tired black clothes of beautiful cut but impossible dustiness and a shirt so thin and worn that it seemed an elfin web of threads rather than true lace and cloth.

'We let them in because if we don't, they circle like jackals, and wolves, and won't go away. As it is, they come, they see and they leave here. You know what they want.'

I nodded. I didn't have the courage to admit to him that I wanted exactly the same thing. I had never stopped thinking about it, not really, not for one moment, beneath the grand rhythm of all that had befallen me since I'd spoken to him on that last night of my old life.

I wanted his blood. I wanted to drink it. Calmly, I let Louis know.

'He'll destroy you,' Louis whispered. He was flushed

suddenly with terror. He looked questioningly at gentle silent Sybelle, who held fast to my hand, and Benjamin, who was studying him with enthusiastic bright eyes. 'Armand, you can't chance it. One of them got too close. He smashed the creature. The motion was quick, automatic. But it has an arm like living stone and he blasted the creature to fragments there on the floor. Don't go near him, don't try it.'

'And the elders, the strong ones, have they never tried?'

Pandora spoke then. She had been watching us all the while, playing in the shadows. I'd forgotten how very beautiful she was in a downplayed and very basic way.

Her long rich brown hair was combed back, a shadow behind her slender neck, and she looked glossy and pretty because she had smoothed into her face a fine dark oil to make herself more passably human. Her eyes were bold and flaming. She put her hand on me with a woman's liberty. She too was happy to see me alive.

'You know what Lestat is,' she said pleadingly. 'Armand, he's a furnace of power and no one knows what he might do.'

'But have you never thought of it, Pandora? Has it never even entered your mind, to drink the blood from his throat and search for the vision of Christ when you drank it? What if inside him there is the infallible proof that he drank the blood of God?'

'But Armand,' she said. 'Christ was never my god.'

It was so simple, so shocking, so final.

She sighed, but only out of concern for me. She smiled. 'I wouldn't know your Christ if He were inside Lestat,' she said gently.

'You don't understand,' I said. 'Something happened, something happened to him when we went with this spirit called Memnoch, and he came back with that Veil. I saw it. I saw the . . . power in it.'

'You saw the illusion,' said Louis kindly.

'No, I saw the power,' I answered. Then in a moment I totally doubted myself. The long corridors of history wound back and away from me, and I saw myself plunged into darkness, carrying a single candle, searching for the ikons I had painted. And the pity of it, the triviality, the sheer hopelessness of it crushed my soul.

I realized I had frightened Sybelle and Benji. They had their eyes fastened on me. They had never seen me as I was now.

I closed my arms around them both and pulled them towards me. I had hunted before I'd come to them tonight, to be at my strongest, and I knew my skin was pleasingly warm. I kissed Sybelle on her pale pink lips, and then kissed Benji's head.

'Armand, you vex me, truly you do,' said Benji. 'You never told me that you believed in this Veil.'

'And you, little man,' I said in a hushed voice, not wishing to make a spectacle of us to the others. 'Did you ever go into the Cathedral and look at it when it was on display there?'

'Yes, and I say to you what this great lady said.' He shrugged, of course. 'He was never my god.'

'Look at them, prowling,' said Louis softly. He was emaciated and shivering a little. He had neglected his own hunger to be here on guard. 'I should throw them out now, Pandora,' he said in a voice that couldn't have threatened the most timid soul.

'Let them see what they came for,' she said coolly under her breath. 'They may not have so long to enjoy their satisfaction. They make the world harder for us, and disgrace us, and do nothing for anything living or dead.'

489

I thought it a lovely threat. I hoped she would clean out the lot of them, but I knew of course that many a Child of the Millennia thought the very same thing about those such as me. And what an impertinent creature I was to bring, without anyone's permission, my children to see my friend who lay on the floor.

'These two are safe with us,' Pandora said, obviously reading my fretting mind. 'You realize they are glad to see you, young and old,' she said making a small gesture to include the entire room. 'There are some who don't want to step out from the shadows, but they know of you. They didn't want for you to be gone.'

'No, no one wanted it,' said Louis rather emotionally. 'And like a dream, you've come back. We all had inklings of it, wild whispers that you'd been seen in New York, as handsome and vigorous as you ever were. But I had to lay eyes on you to believe it.'

I nodded in thanks for these kind words. But I was thinking of the Veil. I looked up at the wooden Christ on the tree again, and then down at the slumbering figure of Lestat.

It was then that Marius came. He was trembling. 'Unburnt, whole,' he whispered. 'My son.'

He had that wretched neglected old gray cloak over his shoulders, but I didn't notice then. He embraced me at once, which forced my girl and my boy to step away. They didn't go far, however. I think they were reassured when they saw me put my arms around him and kiss him several times on the face and mouth, as we had always done so many years ago. He was so splendid, so softly full of love.

'I'll keep these mortals safe if you're determined to try,' he said. He had read the whole script from my heart. He knew I was bound to do it. 'What can I say to prevent you?' he asked.

I only shook my head. Haste and anticipation wouldn't let me do anything else. I gave Benji and Sybelle to his care.

I went over to Lestat and I walked up in front of him, that is, on the left side of him as he lay there to my right. I knelt down quickly, surprised at how cold the marble was, forgetting, I suppose, how very damp it is here in New Orleans and how stealthy the chills can be.

I knelt with my hands before me on the floor and I looked at him. He was placid, still, both blue eyes equally clear as if one had never been torn from his face. He stared through me, as we say, and on and on, and out of a mind that seemed as empty as a dead chrysalis.

His hair was mussed and full of dust. Not even his cold, hateful Mother had combed it, I supposed, and it infuriated me, but then in a frosty flash of emotion, she said hissingly:

'He will not let anyone touch him, Armand.' Her distant voice echoed deeply in the hollow of the chapel. 'If you try it, you will soon find out for yourself.'

I looked up at her. She had her knees drawn up in a careless clasp of her arms, and her back against the wall. She wore her usual thick and frayed khaki, the narrow pants and the British safari coat for which she was more or less famous, stained from the wild outdoors, her blond hair as yellow and bright as his, braided and lying down her back.

She got up suddenly, angrily, and she came towards me letting her plain leather boots echo sharply and disrespectfully on the floor.

'What makes you think the spirits he saw were gods?' she demanded. 'What makes you think the pranks of any of those lofty beings who play with us are any more than capers, and we no more than beasts, from the lowest to the very highest that walk the Earth?' She stood a few feet from him. She folded her arms. 'He tempted something or something. That entity could not resist him. And what was the sum of it? Tell me. You ought to know.'

'I don't,' I said in a soft voice. 'I wish you would leave me alone.'

'Oh, do you, well, let me tell you what was the sum of it. A young woman, Dora by name, a leader of souls as they call it, who preached for the good that comes of tending to the weak who need it, was thrown off course! That was the sum of it – her preachings, grounded in charity and sung to a new tune so that people could hear them, were obliterated by the bloody face of a bloody god.'

My eyes filled with tears. I hated that she saw it so clearly, but I couldn't answer her and I couldn't shut her up. I rose to my feet.

'Back to the cathedrals they flocked,' she said scornfully, 'the lot of them, and back to an archaic and ludicrous and utterly useless theology which it seems that you have plainly forgot.'

'I know it well enough,' I said softly. 'You make me miserable. What do I do to you? I kneel beside him, that's all.'

'Oh, but you mean to do more, and your tears offend me,' she said.

I heard someone behind me speak out to her. I thought perhaps it was Pandora, but I was unsure. In a sudden evanescent flash I was aware of all those who made a recreation of my misery, but then I didn't care.

'What do you expect, Armand?' she asked me cunningly and mercilessly. Her narrow oval face was so like his and yet so not. He had never been so divorced from feeling, never so abstract in his anger as she was now. 'You think you'll see what he saw, or that the

Blood of Christ will still be there for you to savor on your tongue? Shall I quote the catechism for you?'

'No need, Gabrielle,' I said again in a meek voice. My tears were blinding me.

'The bread and wine are the Body and Blood as long as they remain that species, Armand; but when it's bread and wine no more then no more is it Body and Blood. So what do you think of the Blood of Christ in him, that it has somehow retained its magical power, despite the engine of his heart that devours the blood of mortals as if it were mere air that he breathed?'

I didn't answer. I thought quietly in my soul. *It was not the bread and the wine; it was His Blood, His Sacred Blood and He gave it on the road to Calvary, and to this being who lies here.*

I swallowed hard on my grief and my fury that she had made me commit myself in these terms. I wanted to look back for my poor Sybelle and Benji, for I knew by their scent they were still in the room. Why didn't Marius take them away! Oh, but it was plain enough. Marius wanted to see what I meant to do.

'Don't tell me,' Gabrielle said slurringly, 'that it's a matter of faith.' She sneered and shook her head. 'You come like doubting Thomas to thrust your bloody fangs in the very wound.'

'Oh, stop, please, I beg you,' I whispered. I put up my hands. 'Let me try, and let him hurt me, and then be satisfied, and turn away.'

I only meant it as I said it, and I felt no power in it, only meekness and unutterable sadness.

But it struck her hard, and for the first time her face became absolutely and totally sorrowful, and she too had moist and reddening eyes, and her lips even pressed together as she looked at me.

'Poor lost child, Armand,' she said. 'I am so sorry for you. I was so glad that you had survived the sun.'

493

'Then that means I can forgive you, Gabrielle,' I said, 'for all the cruel things you've said to me.'

She raised her eyebrows thoughtfully, and then slowly nodded in silent assent. Then putting up her hands, she backed away without a sound and took up her old station, sitting on the altar step, her head leaning back against the Communion rail. She brought up her knees as before, and she merely looked at me, her face in shadow.

I waited. She was still and quiet, and not a sound came from the occupants scattered about the chapel. I could hear the steady beat of Sybelle's heart and the anxious breath of Benji, but they were many yards away.

I looked down on Lestat, who was unchanged, his hair fallen as before, a little over his left eye. His right arm was out, and his fingers curling upwards, and there came from him not the slightest movement, not even a breath from his lungs or a sigh from his pores.

I knelt down beside him again. I reached out, and without flinching or hesitating, I brushed his hair back from his face.

I could feel the shock in the room. I heard the sighs, the gasps from the others. But Lestat himself didn't stir.

Slowly, I brushed his hair more tenderly, and I saw to my own mute shock one of my tears fall right onto his face.

It was red yet watery and transparent and it appeared to vanish as it moved down the curve of his cheekbone and into the natural hollow below.

I slipped down closer, turning on my side, facing him, my hand still on his hair. I stretched my legs out behind me, and alongside of him, and I lay there, letting my face rest right on his outstretched arm.

Again there came the shocked gasps and sighs, and I tried to keep my heart absolutely pure of pride and pure of anything but love.

It was not differentiated or defined, this love, but only love, the love I could feel perhaps for one I killed or one I succored, or one whom I passed in the street, or for one whom I knew and valued as much as him.

All the burden of his sorrows seemed unimaginable to me, and in my mind a notion of it expanded to include the tragedy of all of us, those who kill to live, and thrive on death even as the very Earth decrees it, and are cursed with consciousness to know it, and know by what inches all things that feed us slowly anguish and at last are no more. Sorrow. Sorrow so much greater than guilt, and so much more ready for accounting, sorrow too great for the wide world.

I climbed up. I rested my weight on my elbow, and I sent my right fingers slipping gently across his neck. Slowly I pressed my lips to his whitened silky skin and breathed in the old unmistakable taste and scent of him, something sweet and undefinable and utterly personal, something made up of all his physical gifts and those given him afterwards, and I pressed my sharp eyeteeth through his skin to taste his blood.

There was no chapel then for me, or outraged sighs or reverential cries. I heard nothing, and yet knew what was all around. I knew it as if the substantial place was but a phantasm, for what was real was his blood.

It was as thick as honey, deep and strong of taste, a syrup for the very angels.

I groaned aloud drinking it, feeling the searing heat of it, so unlike to any human blood. With each slow beat of his powerful heart there came another small surge of it, until my mouth was filled and my throat swallowed without my bidding, and the sound of his heart grew louder, ever louder, and a reddish shimmer filled my vision, and I saw through this shimmer a great swirling dust.

495

A wretched dreary din rose slowly out of nothingness, commingled with an acid sand that stung my eyes. It was a desert place, all right, and old and full of rank and common things, of sweat and filth and death. The din was voices crying out, and echoing up the close and grimy walls. Voices crowded upon voices, taunts and jeers and cries of horror, and gruff riffs of foul indifferent gossip rushing over the most poignant and terrible cries of outrage and alarm.

Against sweating bodies I was pressed, struggling, the slanting sun burning on my outstretched arm. I understood the babble all around me, the ancient tongue hollered and wailed in my ears as I fought to get ever closer to the source of all the wet and ugly commotion that swamped me and tried to hold me back.

It seemed they'd crush the very life out of me, these ragged, rough-skinned men and veiled women in their coarse homespun, thrusting elbows at me and stepping on my feet. I couldn't see what lay before me. I flung my arms out, deafened by the cries and the wicked boiling laughter, and suddenly, as if by decree, the crowd parted, and I beheld the lurid masterpiece itself.

He stood in His torn and bloody white robe, this very Figure whose Face I'd seen imprinted into the fibers of the Veil. Arms bound up with thick uneven iron chains to the heavy and monstrous crossbeam of His crucifix, He hunched beneath it, hair pouring down on either side of His bruised and lacerated face. The blood from the thorns flowed into His open and unflinching eyes.

He looked at me, quite startled, even faintly amazed. He stared with wide and open gaze as if the multitude didn't surround Him, and a whip did not crack over His very back and then His bowed head. He stared past the tangle of his clotted hair and from beneath His raw and bleeding lids.

'Lord!' I cried.

I must have reached out for Him, for those were my hands, my smallish and white hands that I saw! I saw them struggling to reach His Face.

'Lord!' I cried again.

And back He stared at me, unmoving, eyes meeting my eyes, hands dangling from the iron chains and mouth dripping with blood.

Suddenly a fierce and terrible blow struck me. It pitched me forward. His Face filled all my sight. Before my eyes it was the very measure of all that I could possibly see – His soiled and broken skin, the wetted, darkened tangle of His eyelashes, the great bright orbs of His dark-pupiled eyes.

Closer and closer it came, the blood flowing down and into His thick eyebrows, and dripping down His gaunt cheeks. His mouth opened. A sound came out of Him. It was a sigh at first and then a dull rising breath that grew louder and louder as His Face became even larger, losing its very lineaments, and became the sum of all its swimming colors, the sound now a positive and deafening roar.

In terror, I cried out. I was thrust back. Yet even as I saw His familiar Figure and the ancient frame of His Face with its Thorny Crown, the Face grew ever larger and larger and utterly indistinct and seemed again to bear down on me, and then suddenly to suffocate all my face with its immense and total weight.

I screamed. I was helpless, weightless, unable to draw breath.

I screamed as I've never in all my miserable years screamed, the scream so loud that it shut out the roar that filled my ears, but the vision pressed on, a great driving inescapable mass that had been His Face.

'Oh, Lord!' I screamed with all the power of my

burning lungs. The very wind rushed in my ears.

Something struck the back of my head so hard that it cracked my skull. I heard the crack. I felt the wet splash of blood.

I opened my eyes. I was staring forward. I was far across the chapel, sprawled against the plaster wall, my legs out in front of me, my arms dangling, my head on fire with the pain of the great concussion where I had struck the wall.

Lestat had never moved. I knew he hadn't.

No one had to tell me. It was not he who threw me back.

I tumbled over onto my face, pulling my arm up under my head. I knew there were feet gathered all around me, that Louis was near, and that even Gabrielle had come, and I knew too that Marius was taking Sybelle and Benjamin away.

I could hear in the ringing silence only Benjamin's small sharp mortal voice. 'But what happened to him. What happened? The blond one didn't hit him. I saw it. It didn't happen. He didn't—.'

My face hidden, my face soaked with tears, I covered my head with my trembling hands, my bitter smile unseen, though my sobs were heard.

I cried and cried for a long time, and then gradually, as I knew it would, my scalp began to heal. The evil blood mounted to the surface of my skin and, tingling there, did its evil ministrations, sewing up the flesh like a little laser beam from Hell.

Someone gave me a napkin. It had the faint scent of Louis on it, but I couldn't be sure. It was a long long time, perhaps even so long as an hour before I finally clasped it and wiped all the blood off my face.

It was another hour, an hour of quiet and of people respectfully slipping away, before I turned over and rose and sat back against the wall. My head no longer hurt, the wound was gone, the blood that had dried there would soon flake away.

I stared at him for a long and quiet time.

I was cold and solitary and raw. Nothing anyone murmured penetrated my hearing. I did not note the gestures or the movements around me.

In the sanctum of my mind I went over, mostly slowly, exactly, what I had seen, what I had heard – all that I've told you here.

I rose finally. I went back to him and I looked down at him.

Gabrielle said something to me. It was harsh and mean. I didn't actually hear it. I heard only the sound of it, the cadence, that is, as if her old French, so familiar to me, was a language I didn't know.

I knelt down and I kissed his hair.

He didn't move. He didn't change. I wasn't the slightest bit afraid that he would, or hopeful that he would either. I kissed him one more time on the side of his face, and then I got up, and I wiped my hands on the napkin which I still had, and I went out.

I think I stood in a torpor for a long while, and then something came back to me, something Dora had said a long long time ago, about a child having died in the attic, about a little ghost and about old clothes.

Grasping that, clutching it tight, I managed to propel myself towards the stairs.

It was there that I met you a short time afterwards. Now you know, for better or worse, what I did or didn't see.

And so my symphony is finished. Let me write my name to it. When you're finished with your copying, I will give my transcript to Sybelle. And Benji too perhaps. And you may do with the rest what you will.

This is no Epilogue. It is the last chapter to a tale I thought was finished. I write it in my own hand. It will be brief, for I have no drama left me and must manipulate with the utmost care the bare bones of the tale.

Perhaps in some later time the proper words will come to me to deepen my depiction of what happened, but for now to record is all that I can do.

I did not leave the convent after I inscribed my name to the copy which David had so faithfully written out. It was too late.

The night had spent itself in language, and I had to retire to one of the secret brick chambers of the place which David showed me, a place where Lestat had once been imprisoned, and there sprawled on the floor in perfect darkness, overexcited by all that I'd told David, and, more completely exhausted than I'd ever been, I went into immediate sleep with the rise of the sun.

At twilight, I rose, straightened out my clothes and returned to the chapel. I knelt down and gave Lestat a kiss of unreserved affection, just as I had the night before. I took no notice of anyone and did not even know who was there.

Taking Marius at his word, I walked away from the convent, in a wash of early evening violet light, my eyes drifting trustingly over the flowers, and I listened for the chords of Sybelle's Sonata to lead me to the proper house.

Within seconds I heard the music, the distant but

rapid phrases of the *Allegro assai,* or the First Movement, of Sybelle's familiar song.

It was played with an unusual ringing preciseness, indeed, a new languid cadence which gave it a powerful and ruby-red authority which I immediately loved.

So I hadn't scared my little girl out of her mind. She was well and prospering and perhaps falling in love with the drowsy humid loveliness of New Orleans as so many of us have.

I sped at once to the location, and found myself standing, only a little mussed by the wind, in front of a huge three-story redbrick house in Metairie, a countrified suburb of New Orleans which is actually very close to the city, with a feel that can be miraculously remote.

The giant oaks which Marius described were all around this new American mansion, and, as he had promised, all his French doors of shining clean panes were open to the early breeze.

The grass was long and soft beneath my shoes, and a splendid light, so very precious to Marius, poured forth from every window as did the music of the *Appassionata* now, which was just moving with exceptional grace into the Second Movement, *Andante con motto,* which promises to be a tame segment of the work but quickly works itself into the same madness as all the rest.

I stopped in my tracks to listen to it. I had never heard the notes quite as limpid and translucent, quite as flashing and exquisitely distinct. I tried for sheer pleasure to divine the differences between this performance and so many I'd heard in the past. They were all different, magical and profoundly affecting, but this was passing spectacular, helped in slight measure by the immense body of what I knew to be a concert grand.

For a moment, a misery swept over me, a terrible, gripping memory of what I'd seen when I drank Lestat's blood the night before. I let myself relive it, as we say so innocently, and then with a positive blush of pleasant shock, I realized that I didn't have to tell anyone about it, that it was all dictated to David and that when he gave me my copies, I could entrust them to whomever I loved, who would ever want to know what I'd seen.

As for myself, I wouldn't try to figure it out. I couldn't. The feeling was too strong that whom I had seen on the road to Calvary, whether He was real or a figment of my own guilty heart, had not wanted me to see Him and had monstrously turned me away. Indeed the feeling of rejection was so total that I could scarce believe that I had managed to describe it to David.

I had to get the thoughts out of my mind. I banished all reverberations of this experience and let myself fall into Sybelle's music again, merely standing under the oaks, with the eternal river breeze, which can reach you anywhere in this place, cooling me and soothing me and making me feel that the Earth itself was filled with irrepressible beauty, even for someone such as I.

The music of the Third Movement built to its most brilliant climax, and I thought my heart would break.

It was only then, as the final bars were played out, that I realized something which should have been obvious to me from the start.

It wasn't Sybelle playing this music. It couldn't be. I knew every nuance of Sybelle's interpretations. I knew her modes of expression; I knew the tonal qualities that her particular touch invariably produced. Though her interpretations were infinitely spontaneous, nevertheless I knew her music, as one knows the writing of another or the style of a painter's work. This wasn't Sybelle.

And then the real truth dawned on me. It was Sybelle, but Sybelle was no longer Sybelle.

For a second I couldn't believe it. My heart stopped in my chest.

Then I walked into the house, a steady furious walk that would have stopped for nothing but to find the truth of what I believed.

In an instant I saw it with my own eyes. In a splendid room, they were gathered together, the beautiful lithe figure of Pandora in a gown of brown silk, girdled at the waist in the old Grecian style, Marius in a light velvet smoking jacket over silk trousers, and my children, my beautiful children, radiant Benji in his white gown, dancing barefoot and wildly around the room with his fingers flung out as if to grasp the air in them, and Sybelle, my gorgeous Sybelle, with her arms bare too in a dress of deep rose silk, at the piano, her long hair swept back over her shoulders, just striding into the First Movement again.

All of them vampires, every one.

I clenched my teeth hard, and covered my mouth lest my roars wake the world. I roared and roared into my collapsed hands.

I cried out the single defiant syllable No, No, No, over and over again. I could say nothing else, scream nothing else, do nothing else.

I cried and cried.

I bit down so hard with my teeth that my jaw ached, and my hands shuddered like wings of a bird that wouldn't let me shut up my mouth tight enough, and once again the tears streamed out of my eyes as thickly as they had when I kissed Lestat.

No, No, No, No!

Then suddenly I flung out my hands, coiling them into fists, and the roar would have got loose, it would have burst from me like a raging stream, but Marius took hold of me with great force and flung me against

503

his chest and buried my face against himself.

I struggled to get free. I kicked at him with all of my strength, and I beat at him with my fists.

'How could you do it!' I roared.

His hands enclosed my head in a hopeless trap, and his lips kept covering me with kisses I hated and detested and fought off with desperate flinging gestures.

'How could you? How dare you? How could you?'

At last I gained enough leverage to smash his face with blow after blow.

But what good did it do me? How weak and meaningless were my fists against his strength. How helpless and foolish and small were my gestures, and he stood there, bearing it all, his face unspeakably sad, and his own eyes dry yet full of caring.

'How could you do it, how could you do it!' I demanded. I would not cease.

But suddenly Sybelle rose from the piano, and with her arms out ran to me. And Benji, who had been watching all the while, rushed to me also, and they imprisoned me gently in their tender arms.

'Oh, Armand, don't be angry, don't be, don't be sad,' Sybelle cried softly against my ear. 'Oh, my magnificent Armand, don't be sad, don't be. Don't be cross. We're with you forever.'

'Armand, we are with you! He did the magic,' cried Benji. 'We didn't have to be born from black eggs, you Dybbuk, to tell us such a tale! Armand, we will never die now, we will never be sick, and never hurt and never afraid again.' He jumped up and down with glee and spun in another mirthful circle, astonished and laughing at his new vigor, that he could leap so high and with such grace. 'Armand, we are so happy.'

'Oh, yes, please,' cried Sybelle softly in her deeper gentler voice. 'I love you so much, Armand, I love you

504

so very very much. We had to do it. We had to. We had to do it, to always and forever be with you.'

My fingers hovered about her, wanting to comfort her, and then, as she ground her forehead desperately into my neck, hugging me tight around the chest, I couldn't not touch her, couldn't not embrace her, couldn't not assure her.

'Armand, I love you, I adore you, Armand, I live only for you, and now with you always,' she said.

I nodded, I tried to speak. She kissed my tears. She began to kiss them rapidly and desperately. 'Stop it, stop crying, don't cry,' she kept saying in her urgent low whisper. 'Armand, we love you.'

'Armand, we are so happy!' cried Benji. 'Look, Armand, look! We can dance together now to her music. We can do everything together. Armand, we have hunted already.' He dashed up to me and bent his knees, poised to spring with excitement as if to emphasize his point. Then he sighed and flung out his arms to me again, 'Ah, poor Armand, you are all wrong, all filled with wrong dreams. Armand, don't you see?'

'I love you,' I whispered in a tiny voice into Sybelle's ear. I whispered it again, and then my resistance broke completely, and I crushed her gently to me and with rampant fingers felt her silky white skin and the zinging fineness of her shining hair.

Still holding her to me, I whispered, 'Don't tremble, I love you, I love you.'

I clasped Benji to me with my left hand. 'And you, scamp, you can tell me all of it in time. Just let me hold you now. Let me hold you.'

I was shivering. I was the one shivering. They enclosed me again with all their tenderness, seeking to keep me warm.

Finally, patting them both, taking my leave of them

with kisses, I shrank away and fell down exhausted into a large old velvet chair.

My head throbbed and I felt my tears coming again, but with all my force I swallowed my tears for their sake. I had no choice.

Sybelle had gone back to the piano, and striking the keys she began the Sonata again. This time she sang out the notes in a beautiful low monosyllabic soprano, and Benji began dancing again, whirling, and prancing, and stomping with his bare feet, in lovely keeping with Sybelle's time.

I sat forward with my head in my hands. I wanted my hair to come down and hide me from all eyes, but for all its thickness it was only a head of hair.

I felt a hand on my shoulder and I stiffened, but I could not say a word, lest I'd start crying again and cursing with all my might. I was silent.

'I don't expect you to understand,' he said under his breath.

I sat up. He was beside me, seated on the arm of the chair. He looked down at me.

I made my face pleasant, all smiles even, and my voice so velvet and placid that no one could have thought I was talking to him of anything but love.

'How could you do it? Why did you do it? Do you hate me so much? Don't lie to me. Don't tell me stupid things that you know I will never, never believe. Don't lie to me for Pandora's sake or their sake. I'll care for them and love them forever. But don't lie. You did it for vengeance, didn't you, Master, you did it for hate?'

'How could I?' he asked in the same voice, expressive of pure love, and it seemed the very genuine voice of love talking to me from his sincere and pleading face. 'If ever I did anything for love, I have done this for it. I did it for love and for you. I did it for all the wrongs done you, and the loneliness you've suffered, and the horrors that the world put upon you when you were too young and too untried to know how to fight them and then too vanquished to wage a battle with a full heart. I did it for you.'

'Oh, you lie, you lie in your heart,' I said, 'if not with your tongue. You did it for spite, and you have just revealed it all too plainly to me. You did it for spite because I wasn't the fledgling you wanted to make of me. I wasn't the clever rebel who could stand up to Santino and his band of monsters, and I was the one, after all those centuries, that disappointed you yet again and horribly because I went into the sun after I saw the Veil. That's why you did it. You did it for vengeance and you did it for bitterness and you did it for disappointment, and the crowning horror is you don't know it yourself. You couldn't bear it that my heart swelled to burst when I saw His Face on the Veil. You couldn't bear it that this child you plucked from the Venetian brothel, and nursed with your own blood, this child you taught from your own books and with your hands, cried out to Him when he saw His Face on the Veil.'

'No, that is so very very far from the truth it breaks my heart.' He shook his head. And tearless and white as he was, his face was a perfect picture of sorrow as though it was a painting he had done with his own hands. 'I did it because they love you as no one has ever loved you, and they are free and have within their generous hearts a deep cunning which doesn't shrink from you and all that you are. I did it because they were forged in the same furnace as myself, the two of them, keen to reason and strong to endure. I did it because madness had not defeated her, and poverty and ignorance had not defeated him. I did it because they were your chosen ones, utterly perfect, and I knew that you would not do it, and they would come to hate you for this, hate you, as you once hated me for withholding it, and you would lose them to alienation and death before you would give in.

'They are yours now. Nothing separates you. And it's my blood, ancient and powerful, that's filled them to the brim with power so that they can be your worthy companions and not the pale shadow of your soul which Louis always was.

'There is no barrier of Master and Fledgling between you, and you can learn the secrets of their hearts as they learn the secrets of yours.'

I wanted to believe it.

I wanted to believe it so badly that I got up and left him, and making the gentlest smile at my Benjamin and kissing her silkily in passing, I withdrew to the garden and stood alone beneath and between a pair of massive oaks.

Their thunderous roots rose up out of the ground, forming hillocks of hard dark blistering wood. I rested my feet in this rocky place and my head against the nearer of the two trees.

The branches came down and made a veil for me, as I had wanted the hair of my own head to do. I felt shielded and safe in the shadows. I was quiet in my heart, but my heart was broken and my mind was shattered, and I had only to look through the open doorway into the brilliant glory of the light at my two white vampire angels for me to start crying again.

Marius stood for a long time in a distant door. He didn't look at me. And when I looked to Pandora, I saw her coiled up as if to defend herself from some terrible pain – possibly only our quarrel – in another large old velvet chair.

Finally Marius drew himself up and came towards me, and I think it took a force of will for him to do it. He seemed suddenly just a little angry and even proud.

I didn't give a damn.

He stood before me but he said nothing, and it seemed he was there to face whatever I had yet to say.

'Why didn't you let them have their lives!' I said. 'You, of all people, whatever you felt for me and my follies, why didn't you let them have what nature gave them? Why did you interfere?'

He didn't answer, but I didn't allow for it. Softening my tone so as not to alarm them, I went on.

'In my darkest times,' I said, 'it was always your words that upheld me. Oh, I don't mean during those centuries when I was in bondage to a warped creed and morbid delusion. I mean long afterwards, after I had come out of the cellar, at Lestat's challenge, and I read what Lestat wrote of you, and then heard you for myself. It was you, Master, who let me see what little I could of the marvelous bright world unfolding around me in ways I couldn't have imagined in the land or time in which I was born.'

I couldn't contain myself. I stopped for breath and to listen to her music, and realizing how lovely it was, how plaintive and expressive and newly mysterious, I almost cried again. But I couldn't allow such to happen. I had a great deal more to say, or so I thought.

'Master, it was you who said we were moving in a world where the old religions of superstition and violence were dying away. It was you who said we lived in a time when evil no longer aspired to any necessary place. Remember it, Master, you told Lestat that there was no creed or code that could justify our existence, for men knew now what was real evil, and real evil was hunger, and want, and ignorance and war, and cold.

509

You said those things, Master, far more elegantly and fully than I could ever say them, but it was on this great rational basis that you argued, you, with the worst of us, for the sanctity and the precious glory of this natural and human world. It was you who championed the human soul, saying it had grown in depth and feeling, that men no longer lived for the glamour of war but knew the finer things which had once been the forte only of the richest, and could now be had by all. It was you who said that a new illumination, one of reason and ethics and genuine compassion, had come again, after dark centuries of bloody religion, to give forth not only its light but its warmth.'

'Stop, Armand, don't say any more,' he said. He was gentle but very stern. 'I remember those words. I remember all of them. But I don't believe those things anymore.'

I was stunned. I was stunned by the awesome simplicity of this disavowal. It was sweeping beyond my imagination, and yet I knew him well enough to know that he meant every word. He looked at me steadily.

'I believed it once, yes. But you see, it was not a belief based on reason and on observation of mankind as I told myself it was. It was never that, and I came to realize it and when I did, when I saw it for what it was – a blind desperate irrational prejudice – I felt it suddenly and completely collapse.

'Armand, I said those things because I had to hold them to be true. They were their own creed, the creed of the rational, the creed of the atheistic, the creed of the logical, the creed of the sophisticated Roman Senator who must turn a blind eye to the nauseating realities of the world around him, because if he were to admit what he saw in the wretchedness of his brothers and sisters, he would go mad.'

510

He drew in his breath and continued, turning his back to the bright room as if to shield the fledglings from the heat of his words, as surely as I wanted him to do it.

'I know history, I read it as others read their Bibles, and I will not be satisfied until I have unearthed all stories that are written and knowable, and cracked the codes of all cultures that have left me any tantalizing evidence that I might pry loose from earth or stone or papyrus or clay.

'But I was wrong in my optimism, I was ignorant, as ignorant as I accused others of being, and refusing to see the very horrors that surrounded me, all the worse in this century, this reasonable century, than ever before in the world.

'Look back, child, if you care to, if you would argue the point. Look back to golden Kiev, which you knew only in songs after the raging Mongols had burnt its Cathedrals and slaughtered its population like so much cattle, as they did all through the Kiev Rus for two hundred years. Look back to the chronicles of all Europe and see the wars waged everywhere, in the Holy Land, in the forests of France or Germany, up and down the fertile soil of England, yes, blessed England, and in every Asian corner of the globe.

'Oh, why did I deceive myself for so long? Did I not see those Russian grasslands, those burnt cities. Why, all of Europe might have fallen to Ghenghis Khan. Think of the great English Cathedrals torn down to rubble by the arrogant King Henry.

'Think of the books of the Mayas heaved into the flames by Spanish priests. Incas, Aztecs, Olmec – peoples of all nations ground to oblivion—.

'It's horrors, horrors upon horrors, and it always was, and I can pretend no longer. When I see millions gassed to death for the whims of an Austrian madman, when I

511

see whole African tribes massacred till the rivers are stuffed with their bloated bodies, when I see rank starvation claim whole countries in an age of gluttonous plenty, I can believe all these platitudes no more.

'I don't know what single event it was that destroyed my self-deception. I don't know what horror it was that ripped the mask from my lies. Was it the millions who starved in the Ukraine, imprisoned in it by their own dictator, or the thousands after who died from the nuclear poisoning spewing into the skies over the grasslands, unprotected by the same governing powers who had starved them before? Was it the monasteries of noble Nepal, citadels of meditation and grace that had stood for thousands of years, older even than myself and all my philosophy, destroyed by an army of greedy grasping militarists who waged war without quarter upon monks in their saffron robes, and priceless books which they heaved into the fire, and ancient bells which they melted down no more to call the gentle to prayer? And this, this within two decades of this very hour, while the nations of the West danced in their discos and swilled their liquor, lamenting in casual tones for the poor sad fate of the distant Dalai Lama, and turning the television dial.

'I don't know what it was. Perhaps it was all the millions – Chinese, Japanese, Cambodian, Hebrew, Ukrainian, Polish, Russian, Kurdish, oh, God, the litany goes on without end. I have no faith, I have no optimism, I have no firm conviction in the ways of reason or ethics. I have no reproof for you as you stand on the Cathedral steps with your arms out to your all-knowing and all-perfect God.

'I know nothing, because I know too much, and understand not nearly enough and never will. But this you taught me as much as any other I've ever known, that love is necessary, as much as rain to the flowers and the trees, and food to the hungry child, and blood to the starving thirsting predators and scavengers that we are. Love we need, and love can make us forget and forgive all savagery, as perhaps nothing else can.

'And so I took them out of their fabulous promising modern world with its diseased and desperate masses. I took them out and gave them the only might I possess, and I did it for you. I gave them time, time perhaps to find an answer which those mortals living now may never know.

'That was it, all of it. And I knew you would cry, and I knew you would suffer, but I knew you would have them and love them when it was finished, and I knew that you needed them desperately. So there you are . . . joined now with the serpent and the lion and the wolf, and far superior to the worst of men who have proved themselves in this time to be colossal monsters, and free to feed with care upon a world of evil that can swallow every bit of pruning they care to do.'

A silence fell between us.

I thought for a long while, rather than plunge into my words.

Sybelle had stopped her playing, and I knew that she was concerned for me and needed me, I could feel it, feel the strong thrust of her vampire soul. I would have to go to her and soon.

But I took my time to say a few more words:

'You should have trusted them, Master, you should have let them have their chance. Whatever you thought of the world, you should have let them have their time with it. It was their world and their time.'

He shook his head as though he was disappointed in me, and a little weary, and as he had resolved all these matters long ago in his mind, perhaps before I had even appeared last night, he seemed willing to let it all go.

'Armand, you are my child forever,' he said with great dignity. 'All that is magical and divine in me is bounded by the human and always was.'

'You should have let them have their hour. No love of me should have written their death warrant, or their admission to our strange and inexplicable world. We may be no worse than humans in your estimation, but you could have kept your counsel. You could have let them alone.'

It was enough.

Besides, David had appeared. He had a copy already of the transcript we'd labored on, but this was not his concern. He approached us slowly, announcing his presence obviously to give us the chance to become silent, which we did.

I turned to him unable to restrain myself. 'Did you know this was to happen? Did you know when it did?'

'No, I did not,' he said solemnly.

'Thank you,' I said.

'They need you, your young ones,' David said. 'Marius may be the Maker but they are utterly yours.'

'I know,' I said. 'I'm going. I'll do what I'm bound to do.'

Marius put his hand out and touched my shoulder. I realized suddenly that he was truly on the verge of losing his self-control.

When he spoke his voice was tremulous and lustrous with feeling. He hated the storm inside himself and he was overcome by my sorrow. I knew this plainly enough. It gave me no satisfaction at all.

'You despise me now, and perhaps you're right. I knew you would weep, but in a very profound way, I misjudged you. I didn't realize something about you. Perhaps I never have.'

'What's that, Master,' I said with acidic drama.

'You loved them selflessly,' he whispered. 'For all their strange faults, and wild evil, they were not compromised for you. You loved them perhaps more respectfully than I . . . than I ever loved you.'

He seemed so amazed.

I could only nod. I wasn't so sure he was right. My need for them had never been tested, but I didn't want to tell him so.

'Armand,' he said. 'You know you can stay here as long as you like.'

'Good, because I just might,' I said. 'They love it, and I'm weary. So thank you very much for that.'

'But one thing more,' he went on, 'and I mean this with all my heart.'

'What is it, Master?' I said.

David stood by, and I was happy for that, for it seemed to act as a certain curb upon my tears.

'I honestly don't know the answer to this, and I ask you in humility,' Marius said. 'When you saw the Veil, what was it you really saw? Oh, I don't mean was it Christ, or was it God, or was it a miracle. What I mean is this. There was the face of a being, drenched in blood, who had given birth to a religion guilty of more wars and more cruelty than any creed the world has ever known. Don't be angry with me, please, just explain to me. What was it you saw? Was it only a magnificent reminder of the ikons you once painted? Or was it truly something drenched in love and not in blood? Tell me. If it was love and not blood, I would honestly like to know.'

'You ask an old and simple question,' I said, 'and from where I stand you don't really know a thing. You wonder how He could have been my Lord, given this world as you describe it, and knowing what you know of

515

the Gospels and the Testaments printed in His name. You wonder how I could have believed all that because you don't believe it, isn't that so?'

He nodded. 'Yes, I do wonder. Because I know you. And I know that faith is something which you simply do not have.'

I was startled. But instantly I knew he was right.

I smiled. I felt a sort of tragic thrilling happiness suddenly.

'Well, I see what you mean,' I said. 'And I'll tell you my answer. I saw Christ. A kind of bloody light. A personality, a human, a presence that I felt I knew. And He wasn't the Lord God Father Almighty and He wasn't the maker of the universe and the whole world. And He wasn't the Savior or the Redeemer for sins inscribed on my soul before I was born. He wasn't the Second Person of the Holy Trinity, and He wasn't the Theologian expounding from the Holy Mount. He wasn't those things for me. Maybe for others, but not for me.'

'But who was He, then, Armand?' David asked. 'I have your story, full of marvels and suffering, yet I don't know. What *was* the concept of the *Lord* when you spoke the word?'

'*Lord*,' I repeated it. 'It doesn't mean what you think. It's spoken with too much intimacy and too much warmth. It's like a secret and sacred name. Lord.' I paused, and then continued:

'He is the Lord, yes, but only because He is the symbol of something infinitely more accessible, something infinitely more meaningful than a ruler or king or lord can ever be.'

Again, I hesitated, wanting to find the right words since they were so sincere.

'He was . . . *my brother*,' I said. 'Yes. That is what He

was, my brother, and the symbol of all brothers, and that is why He was the Lord, and that is why His core is simply love. You scorn it. You look askance at what I say. But you don't grasp the complexity of what He was. It's easy to feel, perhaps, but not so easy to really see. He was another man like me. And maybe for many of us, millions upon millions, that's all He's ever been! We're all somebody's sons and daughters and He was somebody's son. He was human, whether He was God or not, and He was suffering and He was doing it for things He thought were purely and universally good. And that meant that His blood might as well have been my blood too. Why, it had to be. And maybe that is the very source of His magnificence for thinkers such as me. You said I had no faith. I don't. Not in titles or in legends or in hierarchies made by other beings like ourselves. He didn't make a hierarchy, not really. He was *the very thing.* I saw in Him magnificence for simple reasons. There was flesh and blood to what He was! And it could be bread and wine to feed the whole Earth. You don't get it. You can't. Too many lies about Him swim in your ken. I saw Him before I heard so much about Him. I saw Him when I looked at the ikons in my house, and when I painted Him long before I even knew all His names. I can't get Him out of my head. I never have. I never will.'

I had no more to say.

They were very amazed but not particularly respecting, pondering the words in all the wrong ways, perhaps, I couldn't absolutely know. It didn't matter what they felt anyway. It wasn't really so good that they had asked me or that I had tried so hard to tell them my truth. I saw the old ikon in my mind, the one my Mother had brought to me in the snow. *Incarnation.* Impossible to explain in their philosophy. I wondered.

Perhaps the horror of my own life was that, no matter what I did or where I went, I always understood. *Incarnation*. A kind of bloody light.

I wanted to be left alone by them now.

Sybelle was waiting, which was of far greater importance, and I went to take her in my arms.

For many hours we talked together, Sybelle and Benji and me, and finally Pandora, who was very distraught but would say nothing of it, came to talk casually and gaily with us too. Marius joined us and also David.

We were gathered in a circle on the grass under the stars. For the young ones, I put on the bravest of faces and we spoke of beautiful things, and places we would wander, and wonders which Marius and Pandora had seen, and we argued now and then amiably about trivial things.

About two hours before dawn, we had broken up, with Sybelle sitting by herself deep in the garden, looking at one flower after another with great care. Benji had discovered that he could read at preternatural speed and was tearing through the library, which was very impressive indeed.

David, seated at Marius's desk, corrected his misspellings and abbreviations in the typescript, painstakingly correcting the copy he had made for me in haste.

Marius and I sat very close together against the same oak tree, my shoulder against his. We didn't talk. We were watching things, and listening perhaps to the same songs of the night.

I wanted Sybelle to play again. I had never known her to go so long without playing, and I wanted badly to hear her play the Sonata again.

It was Marius who first heard an unusual sound, and stiffened with alarm, only to give it up and rest back beside me again.

'What was it?' I asked.

'Only a little noise. I couldn't . . . I couldn't read it,' he said. He rested his shoulder against me as he had before.

Almost immediately I saw David look up from his work. And then Pandora appeared, walking slowly but warily towards one of the lighted doors.

Now I heard the sound. And so did Sybelle, for she too looked in the direction of the garden gate. Even Benji had finally deigned to notice it, and he dropped his book in mid-sentence and came marching with a very stern little scowl to the door to take stock of this new situation and get it firmly under control.

At first I thought my eyes had deceived me, but very quickly I realized the identity of the figure who appeared as the gate opened and closed quietly behind his stiff and ungainly arm.

He limped as he approached, or seemed rather the victim of a weariness and a loss of practice at the simple act of walking as he came into the light that fell on the grass before our feet.

I was astonished. No one knew his intentions. No one moved.

It was Lestat, and he was tattered and dusty as he had been on the chapel floor. No thoughts emanated from his mind as far as I could figure, and his eyes looked vague and full of exhausting wonder. He stood before us, merely staring, and then as I rose to my feet, scrambled in fact, to embrace him; he came near to me, and whispered in my ear.

His voice was faltering and weak from lack of use, and he spoke very softly, his breath just touching my flesh.

'Sybelle,' he said.

'Yes, Lestat, what is it, what about her, tell me,' I

519

said. I held his hands as firmly and lovingly as I could.

'Sybelle,' he said again. 'Do you think she would play the Sonata for me if you asked her? The *Appassionata*?'

I drew back and looked into his vague drifting blue eyes.

'Oh, yes,' I said, near breathless with excitement, with overflowing feeling. 'Lestat, I'm sure she would. Sybelle!'

She had already turned. She watched him in amazement as he made his way slowly across the lawn and into the house. Pandora stepped back for him, and we all watched in respectful silence as he sat down near the piano, his back to the front right leg of it, and his knees brought up and his head resting wearily on his folded arms. He closed his eyes.

'Sybelle,' I asked, 'would you play it for him? The *Appassionata*, again, if you would.'

And of course, she did.

THE END

8:12 a.m.
January 6, 1998
Little Christmas